Three Complete Mrs. Pollifax Mysteries

Dorothy Gilman

Three Complete Mrs. Pollifax Mysteries

A Palm for Mrs. Pollifax

Mrs. Pollifax on Safari

Mrs. Pollifax on the China Station

8578

BARNES
&NOBLE
B O O K S
NEW YORK

This edition published by Barnes & Noble, Inc.,
by arrangement with Doubleday and Company, Inc.

1994 Barnes and Noble Books

ISBN 1-55619-470-9

Book design by Stephen Morse

Printed and bound in the United States of America

M 9 8 7 6 5 4 3 2

Contents

A Palm for
Mrs. Pollifax

Palm: a leaf of the palm as a symbol
of victory or rejoicing.

Chapter One

It was morning and Mrs. Pollifax was seated on the floor of her living room, legs crossed beneath her as she tried to sustain the lotus position. She had been practising Yoga for a number of months now. She could almost touch her forehead to her knee, she could roll over backward into a ball, and once—propped up by Miss Hartshorne—she had stood dizzyingly on her head. But she could not manage the lotus position for more than a minute and she had begun to despair of becoming a Contemplative.

"I'm too cushiony, I can't fold," she sighed, and rued the more than sixty years in which she had sat on chairs, couches, stools, and pillows but never on the floor. At the moment this mattered a great deal to her but the moment passed. It was, after all, a delightful and sunny day, there was work to do and at noon a meeting of the Save-Our-Environment Committee. As she climbed to her feet she heard Miss Hartshorne calling her name from the hall, and a moment later her neighbor in 4-C reinforced the summons with a loud knock on the door.

Mrs. Pollifax padded across the room in her leotards. It was only 9:15 but the middle of the day for Miss Hartshorne, who took brisk walks at six, and Miss Hartshorne's energy could be devitalizing. Mrs. Pollifax braced herself.

But her neighbor was not disposed to linger this morning. "I was just leaving the building," she cried breathlessly, "when a

special delivery came for you, Emily, and knowing you probably aren't even *dressed* yet"—here her voice wavered between
disapproval and tolerance of a friend's eccentricities—"I took
the liberty of signing for it."

"Kindness itself," said Mrs. Pollifax cheerfully. "Going
shopping?"

"Oh dear no," said Miss Hartshorne, shocked. "It's Tuesday." And presenting Mrs. Pollifax with the letter she hurried
away.

"Tuesday," repeated Mrs. Pollifax blankly, but having no
idea what that meant she turned her attention to the letter. It
was postmarked Baltimore, Maryland, and she wondered who
on earth she knew in Baltimore who would send a letter both
airmail and special delivery. It implied a distinct note of urgency. Baltimore . . . urgency . . . At once Mrs. Pollifax
found herself recalling certain small, secret trips she had made
in the past for a gentleman named Carstairs, and the cover
address in Baltimore that she had twice been given. She felt a
catch of excitement. Closing the door she slid a finger under
the flap of the envelope and drew out a sheet of paper emblazoned with the letterhead of one William H. Carstairs, Attorney-at-Law, The Legal Building, Baltimore, Maryland.

"Attorney-at-law indeed!" she sniffed, and sat down.
"What on earth—!" The letter appeared to be a carbon copy of
the original but the address to which it had been sent was
carefully deleted. Across the bottom of the page, in red pencil,
Carstairs's assistant had scribbled, *We need you, what are you
doing on Thursday?*

Mrs. Pollifax began to read the letter:

Dear M. Royan, it began. *In reply to our telephone conversation of this morning I am enclosing the suggested deposit of
five hundred dollars for the convalescence of my mother-in-
law, Mrs. Emily Pollifax . . .*

"Mother-in-law!" said Mrs. Pollifax in a startled voice.
"Convalescence?"

*. . . at your Hotel-Clinic Montbrison. It is of the utmost
urgency that she be given rest and treatment . . .*

The telephone began to ring and Mrs. Pollifax edged toward
it, her eyes on the letter. Plucking the receiver from its cradle

she said, "Yes, yes, I'm here," in an absent voice . . . *and I shall persuade her to place herself entirely in your hands. I am delighted to hear . . .*

"Mrs. Pollifax?"

"Speaking, yes." . . . *that room 113 will be reserved for her with its private bath and view of the lake . . .*

"Mr. Carstairs's office calling, will you hold, please?"

"Oh, gladly," she cried in relief and put down the letter, thoroughly alert now, her heart beating rapidly because both letter and telephone call meant that her life was about to accelerate again, adjust to that fine edge of danger which—like eating fish riddled with small bones—exacted the most scrupulous awareness in order to survive.

The next voice on the phone belonged, not to Carstairs, but to Bishop, his assistant. "He's already left for the airport," Bishop told her. "He's hoping you can meet him in New York at twelve o'clock noon at the Hotel Taft. If you can't manage this I'm to intercept him at the airport, but since it takes so damn long to get to the airport these days—"

"It's that important?" breathed Mrs. Pollifax.

Bishop sighed. "Isn't it always?"

"I have this letter, it just arrived and I was reading it."

"Damn, it should have arrived yesterday," said Bishop. "I insisted Carstairs give you some advance notice this time. Well, hang onto it, that's clue number one for you. I haven't asked how you are yet, Mrs. Pollifax, but I will as soon as I hear whether you can possibly get to New York this morning."

"Yes, I can. Let me think," she said. "It's just 9:45 here—"

"Here, too," put in Bishop helpfully.

"And there's a train at—I can be there by noon, yes," she said. *"If I hurry."*

"Then I won't ask how you are," Bishop said frankly. "You're to go directly to room 321 at the Taft, have you got that? Don't stop at the desk to ask, we'd rather you didn't. I hope to hell your telephone isn't tapped."

Mrs. Pollifax said in a shocked voice, "Why ever should it be?"

"God knows. Have you joined anything lately?"

"Only the Save-Our-Environment Committee."

"Bad," he said gloomily. "Room 321," he repeated and hung up.

"Well," thought Mrs. Pollifax, "I daresay whatever Mr. Carstairs has in mind helps save the environment, too. Loosely speaking," she added, and hurried into the bedroom to exchange leotards for a suit. "Wrinkled," she noted crossly as she glimpsed herself in the mirror, and sighed over the multiplying hobbies—environment, karate, Garden Club, Yoga, a little spying now and then—that left her so little time for grooming. She solved the immediate problem by jamming her newest hat over her flyaway white hair, telephoned for a taxi and several minutes later was descending by elevator to the front door of the Hemlock Arms.

At 11:58 Mrs. Pollifax stepped out of the elevator at the third floor of the Hotel Taft and walked down a carpeted hall. The door of room 321 stood wide open, and for just the briefest of moments Mrs. Pollifax entertained thoughts of skulduggery, of Carstairs lying inside in a pool of blood, perhaps, and then a white-jacketed waiter backed into view; behind him stood Carstairs, tall, leaner than ever and very much alive.

"Hello there," he said, glancing up, and after tipping the waiter he shook hands warmly with her. "I ordered coffee and sandwiches—it *is* good of you to hurry. Come inside so we can talk."

"You've grown sideburns!"

"One must move with the times," he said modestly, closing the door behind them. He turned and studied her with equal frankness. "You look splendid. As a matter of fact much too healthy for what we want. White powder," he mused. "A cane perhaps?" He shook his head over her hat. "Wild. Sit down and have some coffee."

Mrs. Pollifax sat down and he wheeled the cart toward her, pouring coffee for them both.

"Bishop says you received a copy of the letter?"

"This morning," she acknowledged. "Something about becoming your mother-in-law and convalescing from some nameless disease but no hint as to where the letter or I would be going."

"Exactly," he said. "The sandwiches, by the way, are bacon, lettuce, and tomato." He seated himself nearby, coffee cup in one hand. "That letter was supposed to have reached you yesterday, damn it. Because *if* you can do this job for us you'll have to leave day after tomorrow, on Thursday."

"If?" she inquired with a lift of an eyebrow.

"Yes." He hesitated. "We need you but I have to warn you this assignment is different from the others. It's not a courier job."

Mrs. Pollifax put down her sandwich and looked at him. "I'm being promoted!"

He laughed. "Promoted to new hazards is more like it. Mrs. Pollifax, I have to ask if you're still open to these insane games of Russian roulette or if your sentiments on that score have changed."

"You mean the dangers," she said, nodding. "But of course it isn't at all like Russian roulette," she added earnestly. "Not at all. I always enjoy myself so much—quite selfishly, I can assure you—and meet the most astonishing people. In any case it's difficult to look ahead, isn't it? I can only look back to previous trips, in which there were a number of risks—"

"To put it mildly," agreed Carstairs.

"—but they never seemed excessive at the time, or less than worthwhile. No, my sentiments haven't changed, Mr. Carstairs."

"Thank God," he murmured, and then with a snap of his fingers, "I forgot Bishop!" Jumping to his feet he hurried to the telephone and Mrs. Pollifax saw that during their conversation the receiver had been removed from its cradle and propped against the lamp. Picking up the receiver Carstairs said, "You heard, Bishop? Call Schoenbeck in Geneva and set things in motion. Have him deliver my letter within the hour and remind him to double-check those postal markings." He hung up. "Now you know where you're going. Switzerland."

She brightened. "Oh, how nice! I did hope I wasn't going behind the iron curtain again. After being expelled from Bulgaria—"

He grinned. "Well, it's not every member of the New Brunswick Garden Club who can be expelled from Bulgaria, is it?

Ushered to the airport and told to get out and stay out, forcibly and irrevocably. Let's see what you can do with Switzerland. I want to place you in the Hotel-Clinic Montbrison as a patient, but while you're there under medical observation, so to speak, you will in turn please observe the Clinic."

"Is it a clinic *or* a hotel?" asked Mrs. Pollifax, puzzled.

"We're not accustomed to the combination in America," he admitted, "but European habits differ. Montbrison is a medical clinic to which the wealthy of the world repair for treatment, to rest, convalesce, lose weight, that sort of thing. The hotel concept makes it all palatable and exceedingly pleasant and I'm told the food is superb. It has a considerable reputation internationally, drawing people from the Middle East as well as Europe."

"But you're not sending me there to rest," she said tactfully.

Carstairs shook his head. "No indeed." Returning to his chair he sank into its depths to ponder her over steepled fingers. "We're in trouble, Mrs. Pollifax," he said at last bluntly. "I can't tell you all the facts, it's classified information and since it now involves Interpol it's not my story to tell. To wrap it up in one sentence, however, there have lately been two small, very alarming thefts of plutonium, the first one here in America, the more recent in England."

"Plutonium!" echoed Mrs. Pollifax. "But that's used in—"

"Exactly. The stolen pounds add up to a dangerous amount when put together—almost enough, in fact, to make a small atom bomb. Plutonium is man-made, you know, it's processed in a nuclear reactor. This has kept it a toy of the moneyed countries and completely inaccessible to any underdeveloped countries—or was," he added savagely. "The two thefts took place within the same month and with uncanny efficiency. We think they're related. We've no idea who's behind them but we've reason to believe that one of the shipments was sent by mail to the Hotel-Clinic Montbrison."

"Can something like that be sent through the *mail?*" said Mrs. Pollifax incredulously.

"Oh yes. To make that one small atom bomb, for instance, you need only eleven pounds of plutonium. Which is what terrifies us," he added pointedly. "So far nine pounds are missing, and if you've managed a package of that weight you know it's relatively light, you could carry it easily in a suitcase. Damnable business, as you can see." He moved to a leather case on the table and drew out a slide projector. Wheeling the table to the center of the room he said, "Mind turning off the switch just behind you?"

With the room in twilight he turned on the projector and a square of white light appeared on the opposite wall. A moment later it was occupied by a close-up of a small wooden crate. "This is how we think the shipment looked," said Carstairs, "or so we've deduced from the information we have. Black letters stenciled on each side of the box saying *MEDI-CAL—HANDLE WITH CARE.* On the top, stenciled in red the words *MEDICAL SUPPLIES—FRAGILE.*"

"That's not the actual box?"

Carstairs shook his head. "A reconstruction from a description given us, but how accurate it is we don't know. It's believed to have been shipped *Airmail-Special Delivery-Special Handling.* It would have been delivered to the Clinic—unless it was intercepted on the way—nine days ago."

"Would it still be there?" asked Mrs. Pollifax in surprise.

"We can't be sure. Interpol put one of their men into the Clinic as a waiter, with the co-operation of the Swiss police. This man—his name is Marcel, by the way, and he's still there —found no traces on the premises. After his search produced nothing the British sent one of their Intelligence people in as a patient, a man named Fraser." He hesitated and then said quietly, "Unfortunately Fraser had an accident, Mrs. Pollifax. There's no possible way of describing it without sounding ridiculous but two days ago Fraser fell off the mountain near the Clinic. He was dead when they brought him out of the ravine."

"Oh dear," said Mrs. Pollifax. "Under the circumstances it sounds more suspicious than ridiculous, don't you think?"

He nodded grimly. "We thought so, yes. We'd nearly crossed the Clinic off our list when that happened but Fraser's death made it a whole new ball game." He frowned. "I should add that we've not been completely frank with the people at the Clinic."

"Oh?"

"They've been told it's hard drugs that we're investigating, and that some kind of surveillance would be set up. They asked only that we be discreet, which is quite understandable, but we've not taken them into our confidence about Fraser or Marcel. We won't about your presence, either." He added dryly: "After all, it could be someone closely connected with the Clinic who's using the place for illegal activities."

"So they don't know."

"They don't know, and now Fraser's dead. It could have been a freak accident or he could have stumbled onto something. In that case—" He tactfully refrained from completing the sentence and said instead, "You have me to blame, Mrs. Pollifax, for recommending you and volunteering your services. The Swiss are co-operating in every way they can. Interpol is, of course, heavily involved, as well as the American government—and therefore my department—and the English have a stake in this, too."

The compliment was unspoken but obvious; Mrs. Pollifax leaned forward and said doubtfully, "But do you really think that I—?"

He threw up his hands. "I can think of at least ten agents of mine who are well-trained, experienced and Gung Ho, and I'm sure the English can, too." He frowned. "But aside from your record, which is startling, I have a feeling that this situation needs something more than training and experience. It needs a rare kind of intuitiveness, a talent for sniffing out what others miss. You're rather good with people and you simply don't act or react like a professional agent." He added abruptly: "What we are looking for—aside from stolen plutonium, Mrs. Pollifax —is evil in its purest form."

"Evil," she mused. "That's an old-fashioned word."

"Positively Biblical," he agreed, "but you have to remember that stolen plutonium is not quite the same as stolen money, Mrs. Pollifax. The uses to which illicit plutonium can be put are very limited but one of its uses is hideous to contemplate."

"Hideous," she said, nodding.

He leaned over his slides again. "I think you'd better see what was inside that crate. It's quite unlikely you'll discover any of these items sitting about on someone's desk as a paperweight but one never knows. Here we are—exhibit number one."

Mrs. Pollifax studied the innocent-looking object projected on the wall. *"That's* plutonium?"

"Yes, shaped into a metal button weighing about two kilograms. Not very prepossessing, is it?" He switched to another slide. "Each button was then individually packed into a plastic bag—there's your plastic bag—and then," he added, changing slides, "the bag was placed in a can filled with inert gas, which in turn was placed inside this odd-looking contraption they call a birdcage, probably because—"

"Because it looks like a birdcage," finished Mrs. Pollifax.

"Yes. Five pounds of plutonium were in the crate stolen from England. If you come across any of these items, don't touch. If you have to touch, use surgeon's gloves." He shook his head. *"If* you find anything. *If* it's there. *If* more should be sent. If, if, if." He sighed and returned to the projector. "Now I want to show you a diagram of the Hotel-Clinic Montbrison before we conclude this. You recall it's room 113 that's been reserved for you."

"Any special reason?"

"Oh, yes. From the balcony of room 113 you'll have a marvelous view of Lake Geneva. You will also be able to see from your balcony, on your left, a narrow, very primitive dirt road, incredibly steep, that winds and circles up the next mountain. From any other floor it's screened by the trees." He flicked on a new slide, a larger diagram that showed the terrain surrounding the Clinic. Standing up he pointed to a small X. "There's your road, off on this mountain here. Every night at ten o'clock—it's quite dark by then—there'll be a car parked at a point on the road that you can see from your room. You'll signal from your balcony with a flashlight. That will be your contact with the outside world."

She frowned. "Won't anyone else see me signaling?"

He shook his head. "Room 113 is quite high. Actually it's

on the third floor because the Clinic's built into the mountainside. The massage and treatment rooms are on the ground level, the reception and dining rooms are on the next level, and the patients' rooms begin above that. As soon as you've signaled each evening the car will turn on its lights—you'll be able to see that—and proceed down the hill. You'll flash your light twice if all's well but if you've something urgent to report you'll blink your light four times."

"And what will happen then?" she asked with interest.

"Then you can expect an incoming phone call within the half hour. Since it will come through the Clinic's switchboard we'll work out some kind of simple code for you, based on your health." He unplugged the projector and carried it back to its case. "Other than this," he said, "your job will be to mingle with the guests, do as much judicious exploring of the building as possible, watch, eavesdrop, listen, and don't admire any sunrises at the edge of a one-hundred-foot drop."

"I won't," she promised.

"We've booked you for a flight to Geneva on Thursday—the day after tomorrow. The letter confirming your arrival at the Clinic will be received by them today, and tomorrow I'll cable them the hour of your arrival and ask that you be met at the airport by a limousine, as befits the mother-in-law of a noted Baltimore lawyer," he added with a grin.

"And what am I recovering from?" asked Mrs. Pollifax.

"If you've nothing more exotic in mind, how about a stubborn case of good old Hong Kong flu?"

"All right," she agreed, "but what equally concerns me if I'm leaving so soon is what I tell people when I announce I shall be away. People like my son in Chicago, my daughter in Arizona. The Garden Club. My neighbor Miss Hartshorne, the Art Association—"

"Go on," said Carstairs, looking fascinated.

"—the Hospital Auxiliary, the Save-Our-Environment Committee and"—she paused to frown at the expression on his face—"my karate instructor."

"I waited for the last with bated breath," Carstairs said. "It still carries impact."

"My karate strikes do, too," she told him modestly. "But

what is my New Brunswick—" She searched for the proper word. "Cover."

"Ah yes. Well, at short notice the easiest is the best, I think. I suggest you visit an old friend named Adelaide Carstairs living in Baltimore. If any calls come through for Adelaide they'll be diverted to my office." He grinned. "I'll leave it up to you to embroider on Adelaide, I'm sure you can come up with something dramatic."

He glanced at his watch. "Good Lord, one o'clock! Have I covered everything? Damned nuisance not having Bishop with me, I'll have to spend the next hour making arrangements for your departure."

"On Thursday," she reminded him.

"Right, at 6 p.m. but I want you at Kennedy International by four o'clock. You'll be paged over the loudspeaker system and given another briefing, as well as your tickets and the code that we'll establish for you. I'd rather not have you paged under your own name. Can you suggest one?"

"Jones, Johnson, Smith," she said quickly.

"We'll make it Johnson. Mrs. Virgil Johnson." Rising he held out his hand to her. "Well, Mrs. Pollifax," he said with a rueful smile, "here we go again."

"Yes," she said, rising and shaking his hand.

"Bon voyage. Finish your bacon, tomato, and lettuce and leave the key at the desk downstairs." At the door he stopped with one hand on the knob. "And damn it, don't disappoint me by getting your head bashed in."

She was really quite touched by the emotion in his voice. She returned to her sandwich wondering whether Adelaide Carstairs should be an elderly aunt who had broken her hip—rather dull, that; a niece who had eloped with a scoundrel, or a friend who had just been swindled and desperately needed comfort and advice.

She would have been swindled, decided Mrs. Pollifax, by a tall man with a scar over his left eyebrow. He might have a slight limp, too—that always aroused maternal feelings—but he would definitely be very distinguished and have impeccable credentials.

*   *   *

In the end Mrs. Pollifax sadly dispensed with her distinguished swindler and turned Adelaide Carstairs into a plain old school friend, recently widowed.

I'm sure you remember my speaking of her, Mrs. Pollifax wrote her daughter in Arizona that evening. Of course Jane would not remember her, but since children paid very little attention to their parents' friends Jane would probably reply that of course she recalled Adelaide Carstairs. *I'll just go down for a week or two and cheer her up,* she added, giving the Baltimore address in case of emergency, but after sealing the letter Mrs. Pollifax sat and stared at her desk blotter without seeing it for a few minutes. She was thinking of her grandchildren and the vocabulary that had been devised for the world into which they'd been born, words that were as familiar as cat and dog to them: megaton and isotope, military-industrial complex, nuclear capability, ABM, MIRV, arms race, defoliants, and at the end of that list DNA, the genetic material that one reckless person could distort forever with a small bomb containing eleven pounds of plutonium.

Madness, she thought with a shudder.

The next morning, feeling more cheerful, she walked downtown to do a little shopping, but with no intention of buying either a dowdy hat or a cane; she had in mind a dinner dress. For a long time Mrs. Pollifax had nursed a secret longing to buy something more contemporary than offered by the third floor matrons' department. She headed for the Psychedelic Den and spent a very interesting hour chatting with a young clerk in mini-dress and boots who labored under the impression that Mrs. Pollifax was going to a masquerade party. "Which, in a way, is quite true," she thought.

What she brought home was a long purple robe and an assortment of prayer beads. The robe made her look rather like a fortune-teller or the high priestess of a religious cult but it was a satisfying change. It was also drip-dry, she reminded herself virtuously.

Next it was important to explain her departure to Miss Hartshorne, and this required tact. "She's feeling lonely," Mrs.

Pollifax told her neighbor over a cup of tea. "Period of adjustment, you know." By this time Adelaide had taken on shape and substance and she was finding it difficult to remember that Adelaide did not exist. "She and her husband were very close," she added.

Miss Hartshorne's mouth tightened. "I think I've been your friend long enough to say what I think of this, Emily, and I don't think much of it at all. You leave New Brunswick only when a sick daughter-in-law or a friend sends out an S.O.S. and I must say these calls for help have been increasing lately. You let people take advantage of you."

"Grace, I'm quite happy to—"

"I've tried for years to persuade you to do some traveling with me but no, you simply won't travel at all. What you lead, Emily, is an unhealthily dull life."

"Yes," said Mrs. Pollifax meekly.

"You know that ever since my retirement I've taken one Cook's tour a year—religiously—and if I may say so, Emily, it's what keeps me young. You never go anywhere interesting, you never meet new people, now do you?"

"Well," began Mrs. Pollifax, taking a deep breath, but Miss Hartshorne was not waiting for a reply.

"It's no vacation at all, cheering up an old friend, and don't think I haven't noticed how tired you are when you return from these little trips. Your essential problem, Emily, is that you have no sense of adventure."

"None at all," said Mrs. Pollifax, beaming at her friend, "but won't you have another cup of tea, anyway, Grace?"

Chapter Two

"Y our attention, please . . . your attention, please . . ."
Mrs. Pollifax glanced up from her thoughts, which
had been occupied by the people hurrying past her
intent on carrying babies, cameras, back-packs, luggage, attaché cases, odd packages, and nameless hopes. She had been
thinking that her own plans were small and tentative: she
hoped to find several pounds of plutonium.

". . . will Mrs. Virgil Johnson go to the Information Desk
. . . Mrs. Virgil Johnson . . ."

Obligingly Mrs. Pollifax picked up her suitcase and carried
it across the aisle to the Information Desk. Almost at once a
man detached himself from the crowd and hurried toward her
carrying a suitcase in one hand and a bouquet of flowers in the
other. She peered at him in astonishment. *"Bishop?"*

He leaned over and kissed her lightly on the cheek. "In the
flesh, isn't it amazing?" He thrust the flowers into her hand.
"Beware the Greeks bearing gifts. How are you? I'm delighted
to see you."

"And I you," she said, beaming at him. "It never occurred
to me they'd send—that is—"

"Ssh, Mrs. Johnson," he said conspiratorially, and picked up
her suitcase. "Follow me." He led her around the corner to a
door marked PRIVATE. PERSONNEL ONLY. Opening the door he
ushered her in and locked the door behind them. "We're being

loaned this office for ten minutes. Displaced Personnel is—are?—having a coffee break."

"Are, surely?" she suggested, frowning.

He shook his head. "Is, I think. Oh, grammar be damned, they're gone anyway." He placed his suitcase on the desk. "You realize you're giving me a disastrous time of it by taking on this job, don't you? Carstairs can't make up his mind whether he's sending you up a blind alley or into a lion's den. Today it's a lion's den and he's in a dither."

"Oh, but he appeared *quite* calm about it all when I saw him," she told him. "Really, everything sounds very simple."

"It does?" Bishop looked startled.

"Yes, and it will be such a pleasant change for me, staying in one place."

"I see." He sounded amused. "Well, then, let's get on with it, shall we?" He opened his suitcase. "My bag of tricks," he explained. "I have here for you one flashlight of unparalleled quality." He handed it to her. "Plus a supply of spare batteries in case the quality is not unparalled—we can't risk a communications breakdown."

"Flashlight and batteries," repeated Mrs. Pollifax, opening her own suitcase and tucking both inside.

"One code in a sealed envelope that also contains rather a lot of money in Swiss francs. The code you will kindly memorize en route and then very thoroughly destroy. One pack of matches with which to destroy said code—"

"You think of everything," she told him admiringly.

"Of course," he said blithely. "And—oh, you are going to have a fun time!—one Geiger counter."

"Geiger counter!" She was startled. "Carstairs didn't mention a Geiger counter."

"Actually a scintillator counter," he amended, pulling out a handsome leather box. "He left it for me to mention because when he saw you we were still working out how to conceal it. You simply can't go poking about for radioactive stuff without some help, can you? Take a look at this." He opened the box.

"Jewels!" she gasped. "Are they real?" She was staring at a flannel-lined tray in which nested an emerald pendant, an enormous diamond pin and two necklaces glittering with rubies.

"I'm sorry to tell you they're absolutely fake," he said. "But damn expensive fakes, and aren't they gorgeous? They're just in case no one recognizes this as a jewelry case—"

"I didn't," admitted Mrs. Pollifax.

"—and they say to themselves, 'let's see if this is a geiger counter,' and they open it to find—presto, jewelry." He bent over the box. "See this tiny gold button on the hinge? Give it a good push and you'll have released the lock and can pull out the tray." He removed it and displayed a machine inside, a dial and two knobs set into a smooth metallic surface. He turned one of the knobs and they listened to a faint humming sound. "That's normal," he said. "Proves it's working and all that, and you're ready to pan for gold. The needle on the dial zooms, of course, when it sniffs out anything interesting. Check it out while I find your tickets, will you?"

Mrs. Pollifax closed, opened and closed the interior of the case. "It works," she said.

"Good—now I'll take it away from you."

"Take it away!"

"It'll be delivered to you on the plane when they hand out the duty-free cigarettes and perfume that people have ordered. There's a rigorous search of every passenger boarding the plane and we'd rather not risk the wrong chap hauling you away for explanations."

"I see."

"I'm glad you do. And here are your tickets." He tapped a list with one finger as he studied it. "Tickets, jewel case, flashlight, batteries—"

"And violets," she reminded him. "Very handsome of you, too. I adore violets."

He glanced in amusement at her hat, which looked like a bathing cap overgrown with violets and pansies. "So I see. Is that thing called a cloche?"

"Bishop, you surprise me!"

"It's mutual. Oh yes—one more item here," he said. "The waiter Marcel." He brought a small photograph from his wallet and showed her a dark-haired, high cheekboned, gloomy face. "About five feet five. Broad-shouldered. There'll be a number of waiters and you'll want to know which one is Marcel. But avoid him, let him be the one to find you."

"Right," said Mrs. Pollifax efficiently, took a last glance and nodded.

"And that's about it," he concluded sadly. "So I daresay you'd better leave before too long a line forms at the check-in counter." He unlocked the door and opened it and then he closed the door again and said sternly, "You *will* take care? Not go around making citizens' arrests and that sort of thing? Just try to find the you-know-what and be well-behaved?"

"I shall feel I've behaved very well if I find the you-know-what," she told him.

He sighed. "Yes but I want to point out very strongly to you that any international crook who takes on this sort of game is tough and mercenary. Not your common ordinary garden type. Strictly jungle."

Mrs. Pollifax put down her suitcase and looked at him. "What's wrong, Bishop?"

"It's that obvious?" He scowled. "Hang it all, Carstairs didn't want you shaken up but I frankly think you ought to know."

"Know what?"

"The autopsy report on Fraser came in this noon, just before I left. The chap was dead before he fell down the mountainside."

"Before he fell," she repeated automatically.

"Yes. The actual blow that killed him couldn't possibly have come from any of the rocks he—uh—his body hit on the way down."

"I see," she said quietly. "You mean he was very definitely murdered."

"Yes."

She nodded. "Thank you for mentioning it, Bishop, I'll keep it in mind. You'll let me go now?"

"Reluctantly," he said, opening the door. "Very, very reluctantly."

Chapter Three

The code, when Mrs. Pollifax opened it in the plane's lavatory, struck her as being really very funny. It read like Dick-and-Jane.

All is quiet—I AM GETTING RESTED.

I am worried—I HAVE A COUGH.

I feel I may be in danger—I BELIEVE I AM RUNNING A TEMPERATURE.

Below these simple sentences had been appended the following code names:

Marcel—COUSIN MATTHEW

Plutonium—UNCLE BILL

Police—PETER

Carstairs—ADELAIDE

After several trips to the lavatory she burned the code in an ashtray and returned to watch a Western film on the ingeniously placed moving picture screen. She had never before crossed the Atlantic and watched a film at the same time, and she was not sure that she approved of it. She enjoyed it but that, she felt, was not quite the same as approving of it. She wondered, for instance, how Columbus or Magellan would react if they could see them all sitting in comfortable chairs watching a movie in the sky as they crossed the ocean insulated from wind, tides, storm and distance, and without any decent sense of awe. One ought, she felt, to suffer just a little. Not much but a little.

As to Bishop's parting words she preferred not to think about them for the moment. He and Carstairs had each of them been right: it was kinder for her to know the worst, yet the news did have its jarring effect. Obviously Fraser's death meant there was something worth murdering for at Montbrison.

Long before the film ended the sky beyond her window had turned silver and she watched horizon-long bands of orange and pink dissolve into sunshine. It was only midnight in New York but they had crossed a time zone to meet Europe's dawn. Mrs. Pollifax made a last trip to the lavatory and then sat quietly attempting to enter her new role.

"I'm a mother-in-law recovering from the flu," she repeated to herself, and tried out an appropriate small cough . . . but a cough, codewise, meant that she was worried and was not to be confused with a flu cough. Her son-in-law was named Carstairs and he lived in Baltimore. There would be a limousine waiting for her, a delightful thought, and she would be whisked off to the Clinic—about an eighty-minute drive, Carstairs had said—and there she must look suitably tired.

Mrs. Pollifax coughed again, very delicately, and practised looking tired.

The driver of the limousine spoke almost no English. He drove silently and skillfully, and Mrs. Pollifax's attempts to compliment him on the weather lapsed. She stared out of the window at the countryside instead, at gentler mountains than she remembered seeing in the north, at red-tiled roofs and brief glimpses of a pale and shining Lake Geneva. They passed terraces of vineyards, villages just waking up—it was, after all, barely eight o'clock in the morning—and after an hour of driving they began to climb.

Mrs. Pollifax leaned forward eagerly. They were negotiating breathtakingly abrupt turns on a road that zigzagged high above the town and the lake; looking down she could see only the roofs of chalets, cottages and villas, and the tops of trees. Slowing somewhat they entered a village laid out at a 70-

degree angle on the slopes of the mountain. Shops edged the
slanting street, among them a cafe with umbrellas blossoming
over rows of bright tables. The car turned down a narrow
paved road, they passed a stone church clinging to the mountainside, a chalet, a few gardens and then entered a green-
shaded wood with a ravine far below them on the right. Ahead
Mrs. Pollifax saw a discreet sign: PRIVATE, it read. HOTEL-CLINIC
MONTBRISON.

The driver cleared his throat and pointed. Mrs. Pollifax saw
the rear of a large, rambling building almost suffocated by
trees and shrubbery. They entered between two laurel bushes,
drove down a steep narrow drive past a greenhouse, and arrived at the main door of the Clinic.

The sun had not yet reached the back of the building and
the shadows were deep. At the entrance a stocky young man
in a green apron was sweeping the steps with a broom while a
small boy of ten or eleven sat on the top stair and watched
him. Both looked up curiously at the limousine.

Mrs. Pollifax stepped out of the car. While the driver
opened up the trunk to remove her suitcase she stood on the
asphalt and glanced through the open door into the reception
hall—it looked singularly gloomy with its dark paneling and
rugs—and then the boy jumped up and called out shrilly, *"Bon
jour, madame!"* This was followed by a torrent of words in
French.

Mrs. Pollifax smiled and shook her head. "I'm sorry, I speak
only English."

"But madame, I speak English, too," he told her, jumping
up and down. "Why have you come? Are you to be a patient
here? Are you English? Have you arrived by air? Why are you
in that limousine? Will you stay long? Have you brought a
nurse?"

A man in a black uniform appeared on the step, said something quieting to the boy in French and smiled at Mrs. Pollifax. "I am the head concierge, madame. Welcome to the
Clinic. You are Madame Pollifax?"

She nodded.

"This way." He gave brisk orders to the man in the green
apron, who dropped his broom and picked up Mrs. Pollifax's

suitcase. "Please, you will come in and register, the secretary has not yet arrived in the office. It is very early, you see. Emil will show you to your room. You will wish breakfast, of course, it will be sent up to you at once."

He ushered her inside to the reception desk and held out paper and pen. Behind the desk she saw a switchboard, a wall of pigeonholes for mail and beyond that a pair of glass doors through which could be seen an empty office. She signed the register and handed over her passport.

"Yes, this I shall keep, it will be returned to you within the hour," he said. He appeared refreshingly business-like, a little harassed and eminently likable. "May you enjoy your visit here, madame."

As she moved slowly upward in the elevator she looked down and saw the boy standing just inside the door staring after her. His brief excitement had collapsed; his eyes were huge and filled with a haunting sadness. She was glad when the ascent cut her off from his view.

Air and light was her first impression. As soon as Emil left, Mrs. Pollifax put down her jewelry case and crossed the room to open the door to her balcony. "Oh, *lovely*," she whispered, moving to the railing. At this level she looked across the tops of high trees stirring in a light breeze. Beyond, and almost straight down, a toy steamer on the lake was disappearing between the treetops; it left behind it a V of tiny crepe paper wrinkles. Lake Geneva occupied the view almost to the horizon, like a pale blue, upside-down sky touched with glitter. A wash of insistent gray along the shores hinted at mountains still obscured by haze. Quiet morning sounds rose to her balcony: a tide-like rise and fall of traffic far away, birds calling, a muffled toot from the steamer, a church bell, all muted by distance and height.

She looked down in search of the garden, and had to stand on tiptoe to see over the wide jut of gallery that ran from her balcony to the next and continued along the floor to the end of the building. The broad ledge cut off much of the view below but she could see thick, well-kept grass, a circle of bright flowers, a graveled path overhung with pink roses, and a gazebo. The hush was incredible.

She turned and looked for her road and found it off to her left, just where Carstairs had said it would be, a narrow scar on the next hillside, unpaved and climbing at a precipitous angle. A flock of swallows interrupted her gaze. They dove in among the trees, almost encircling one tall Lombardy poplar, but they were the only sign of motion at Montbrison. Nothing seemed to move here, not even time.

I could be happy here, she thought, and found that she had to wrench her attention back to the reasons behind her arrival. Remembering, her glance fell to the ledge beyond the railing and she found herself studying it with interest. It was nearly four feet wide and neatly graveled. "Like a path three floors above the garden," she mused, and wondered if the other guests on her floor realized how accessible their rooms were. She thought it presented delightful possibilities for retreat or reconnaissance.

A knock on the door of her room distracted her. Reluctantly she left the balcony and walked inside, calling, "Come in."

A waiter in a white jacket entered, tray in hand. With a flourish he placed it on the tray table in the corner and wheeled the table to the center of the room. "Madame wishes it here, or on the balcony?"

"I think I'd fall asleep if I breakfasted on the balcony," she told him, and they exchanged a long and interested glance. He was a short and stocky young man, quite swarthy, with bright blue eyes and black hair parted in the center like a Victorian bartender. In Bishop's photograph he'd looked gloomy. He still looked gloomy but it was the sourness of a comedian who could fire off a string of ribald witticisms without a muscle quivering in his face. Marcel was something of a clown, she thought.

"I'll sit here," she said, and promptly sat down.

He wheeled the table beside her, "Madame has been sent the European *petit déjeuner*—very small," he explained with a rueful shrug. "If Madame wishes more she may dial the room service and a waiter will bring whatever she desires. I may pour your coffee, madame?" Before she could protest he leaned

over and said in a low voice, "There is one particular counter-
feit among the guests, madame, name of Robin Burke-Jones,
usually in the garden afternoons, following three o'clock. We
are most curious: none of his credentials check out, all data he
gave upon registering is false."

"Thank you," said Mrs. Pollifax, smiling at him and nodding. "I think I have everything I need now."

"*Mon Dieu*, one hopes!" he said, returning to his humorous
role. "If not—" He shrugged. "If not, the menu for service is on
the desk. *Jambon ou lard, oeuf plat, oeuf poache sur toaste*—"
His eyes were positively dancing at her. "My name is Marcel,
madame. *Bon appetit!*" he said with a bow, and walked out.

My confederate, she thought, and was grateful to him for
giving her something specific to do because a night without
sleep had left her feeling jaded and just a little disoriented. She
realized that she was also ravenous, and began to spread mar-
malade on her croissants. Over coffee she gazed around the
room, which was cool, pale, and high-ceilinged, all white with
small touches of blue and a deep red Oriental rug on the floor.
Tonight, she decided, she would begin her explorations with
the Geiger counter, and as her glance fell upon the bed, heaped
high with pillows, she conceded that a brief morning nap
would not be decadent.

Moving to the bed she saw that Marcel had left the door
ajar, and that it was slowly opening wider. "Who's there?" she
called out, and when no one answered she walked to the door.

"*Bon jour, madame,*" said the small boy she had seen at the
entrance. He looked even smaller standing there, and more
forlorn, his arms slack at his side. He lifted huge dark eyes to
her face. "Would you be my friend, madame?" He pronounced
the word *m'domm*.

She stared down at him in astonishment. "Are you a patient here?" she asked. He was very brown, very thin and wiry
and leggy, with jet-black hair. In the small-boned dark face his
eyes looked enormous. She had thought him the gardener's
son.

He shook his head. "Grandmama is a patient and I am here
to be with her. Have you grandchildren, madame?"

"Yes, three," she told him.

From somewhere down the hall a voice called, "Hafez? Hafez!"

The boy turned with a sigh. "Here, Serafina," he called.

A sallow-faced woman in black joined him in the framework of the door, took his hand, bent over him and admonished him in a language new to Mrs. Pollifax.

Hafez pushed out his underlip. "But this is my friend—one *must* have friends!" he cried, and there were tears in his eyes.

The woman pulled him away without so much as a glance at Mrs. Pollifax, who took a few steps into the hall to peer after them. Down at the far end of the hall, near the solarium, a man in a wheelchair sat watching the boy and the woman approach. Seeing Mrs. Pollifax he pushed his way back into the room behind him. Hafez and the woman went into the room opposite, two doors closed at once and there was silence.

A curious child, thought Mrs. Pollifax, the sound of his voice lingering in her ear.

She walked to the bed, lay down and fell asleep.

Twice she was awakened by knocks on the door, the first by a young woman in white who said she was a nurse but would return, the second time by a woman in white who said she was a dietician and would return. The third knock brought the secretary of the Clinic, a pigeon-breasted woman profuse with apologies at not having welcomed Mrs. Pollifax earlier. Seeing that it was eleven o'clock Mrs. Pollifax abandoned the idea of further sleep and got up. Lunch, said the secretary, was from noon to one o'clock, and dinner from six to eight. Mrs. Pollifax would be examined by a doctor tomorrow morning.

"Doctor? I'm only tired," pointed out Mrs. Pollifax.

"Ah, but it is the prerequisite, a how you say, a must? Everyone is examined, it is the rule of the Clinic. I understand also that you have not been weighed by the nurse yet, nor given menu instruction to the dietician." She shook her head reproachfully. "But you were tired?"

"I was asleep."

"Ah, yes," she murmured vaguely, and went out.

It occurred to Mrs. Pollifax that at such a pace the quietness of the Clinic might be illusion. She had been here in her room three hours, and had already received a nurse, a small boy, a dietician, a waiter, and a secretary. Tomorrow there would also be a doctor. Quickly she changed from her traveling suit to a dress and went downstairs to discover where lunch would be served, and to do a little reconnoitering before anyone else interrupted her.

She found solariums everywhere, all of them empty at this season of anything but jungle-like rubber plants. There were two more of them on the Reception floor, as well as a pair of television rooms side by side. The dining rooms lay at the far end of the corridor—Mrs. Pollifax could see the waiters moving past glass-paneled doors. She paused at what looked to be the library and glanced in at more dark, heavy furniture and rich oak paneling.

One piece of dark furniture was occupied by a handsome, deeply tanned young man who appeared to be examining the crease of his trouser. He glanced up and saw her, lifted an eyebrow and said, *"Bon jour, madame,* but that's the limit of my French."

"It's just about the limit of mine, too," she admitted, and decided this was an opportunity to meet her first adult guest. She sank into another large, overstuffed chair and wondered if she would ever be able to get out of it. "You're waiting for lunch, too?"

"I am waiting," he said gloomily, "for something to happen in this place. After eight days here I would consider the dropping of a spoon almost intolerable excitement."

Mrs. Pollifax looked at him with amusement. He just missed being impossibly handsome by a nose that had been broken and still looked a little stepped upon; she liked him the better for it because it gave humor to a face that was otherwise all tanned skin, sleepy green eyes, white teeth, and blond hair. "You do look as if you're accustomed to a faster pace," she admitted frankly.

"You're staring at my purple slacks and red shirt," he said accusingly. "I thought—I actually believed—Montbrison might have a touch of Casino about it. After all, it's patronized by many of the same people, except when they come here it's

to repair their livers. How was I to know that repairing the
liver is almost a religion?"

"I had no idea," said Mrs. Pollifax, fascinated by the
thought. "Is it?"

"My dear lady," he sighed, "I can only tell you that when I
saw the Count Ferrari at Monaco in April he had a blonde in
one hand and a pile of chips in the other. The count," he
added, "is seventy-five if he's a day. Here at Montbrison he is
suddenly mortal and positively devout about it. He carries
pills. A whole *bag* full of pills. He dines across the room from
me, and I swear to you he comes in every evening with a
plastic bag of pills. You can see them: red, green, blue, pink."

Mrs. Pollifax laughed. "You're very observant but should
you talk about your friend so loudly?"

"Oh, he's not a *friend*, he doesn't speak English," the young
man said dismissingly. "We only say good evening to one another. I may not be a linguist—I confess to being stuffily British in that sense—but I can say good evening in approximately
fifteen languages. Rather handy, that."

"Unless you meet them in the morning," she pointed out.

He grinned. "That, my dear lady, is a season of the day I
avoid at any cost."

"If you're so bored—and if no one obliges you by dropping a
spoon—and since you look so extremely healthy," she said,
"why do you stay?"

"Because my doctor sent me here." He hesitated and then
added crisply, "I'm recovering from the Hong Kong flu, you
see. And you?"

Mrs. Pollifax also found herself hesitating and then she said
without expression, "Actually I'm recovering from the Hong
Kong flu, too."

This ought to have produced instant commiseration, a few
chuckles or a lively comparing of symptoms but it brought
instead a flat, curiously awkward silence. I wonder why, she
thought, and tried to find something to say. "I hear it was a
particularly virulent strain last winter," she ventured.

"Uh—yes," he agreed, and suddenly aware of his clumsiness he began to speak when the doors of the dining room
swung open. "Lunch!" he cried, springing to his feet. Very

thoughtfully he helped her out of her chair. "You have to watch these chairs," he said sternly. "They're geared for sleep and that sort of thing. *Everything* is geared for sleep here, you can disappear forever in one of these damn things. Try the couch next time."

"I'll remember that," she told him gratefully. "By the way, I'm Mrs. Pollifax."

He bowed elegantly. "How do you do. And I'm—*Bon jour, mon General*," he called out to an old man leaning heavily on a cane as he negotiated the hall to the dining room. "May I help you?" He was off like an Olympic runner to help the general, leaving Mrs. Pollifax with no name to attach to his acerbic personality.

In the dining room Mrs. Pollifax was guided to the table reserved for the occupant of room 113; the number was discreetly displayed on the shining damask cloth between the vase of wild flowers and the oil-and-vinegar tray. The table itself was placed in a corner of the first dining room, which gave her a strategic glimpse of those sharing her ell but no view at all of the other two rooms. The general was helped to a single table across from her in the center of the room and then her tanned young friend wandered off to his own table. Presently a subdued Hafez was brought in by the sallow woman in black and Mrs. Pollifax was surprised to see that they went to the long table for six by the window. It suggested a large party; he had mentioned a grandmother but the woman with him was not old enough, and gave every evidence of being a maid or companion. She wondered who the other people could be, and where they were.

She saw nothing of Marcel. Apart from Hafez and the general, only one other guest looked familiar and that was the man in the wheelchair whom she'd seen in the hall opposite Hafez's door. He wheeled himself to a solitary table nearby but facing the window so that she saw only his profile. It was not a particularly inspiring profile. His skin was dark but with a pallor that turned it to an unhealthy shade of gray. A thin black mustache decorated his lip, as if he reached for some longed-for sophistication that eluded him. His shoulders were massive and his business suit wrinkled. He looked out of place but indifferent to it; he ate quickly, with concentration, and wheeled himself out before Mrs. Pollifax reached her dessert.

Much more charming was the young girl who came in and sat opposite her across the room, and an older couple, the man with a London *Times* under his arm.

"I must learn something about all of them," she reminded herself. Marcel had mentioned the garden; she would spend the afternoon in the garden.

Chapter Four

The garden was bright with sun and flowers. With a professional eye Mrs. Pollifax inspected the beds of begonias along the paths and then headed for a chaise longue and sank into it, hoping that she wouldn't fall asleep. Just to be certain of this she climbed out of the chaise and attempted to elevate it to a sitting position.

"You're pushing all the wrong things," said a voice behind her, and a young woman in a bikini, body glistening with sun oil, put down her towel and books and leaned over the chair. It sprang back and up immediately.

Mrs. Pollifax smiled. "How efficient you are!"

"I am, yes," the girl said with a touch of rue in her voice. "Do you think that's an affliction or a gift?"

"A little bit of each, I should think," hazarded Mrs. Pollifax. "You're British?"

She shook her head. "Belgian."

"I saw you in the dining room, you sat opposite me," added Mrs. Pollifax by way of introduction. "I'm Mrs. Pollifax."

"How do you do," the girl said, and extended a thin brown hand. "I'm Court van Roelen." Her face was all cheekbones and angles, with a pair of eyes that blazed like blue jewels in her tanned face. It was a breathtaking combination.

Over the girl's head—she was surprisingly small—Mrs. Pollifax saw that her nameless male friend of the library was standing in the center of the lawn staring open-mouthed at the girl. He too seemed to find her breathtaking. He was now wearing yellow slacks, an orange shirt, and a polka-dotted cravat but the effect was entirely spoiled by his gaping. Closing his mouth he strolled toward Mrs. Pollifax. "I think a spoon just dropped," he said.

"I could hear the reverberations," she told him.

He grinned. "Don't let me interrupt anybody's sun bath, I'll just pull this young lady's chair closer and we can turn this into a cozy threesome." Beaming at Mrs. Pollifax he added, "Numerologically, you know, three is a number of great strength." Leaving no time for a reply he drew up a third chair, into which he settled complacently. "You were about to introduce us?" he asked Mrs. Pollifax with a lift of his brow.

"I will if you'll tell me your name."

He looked startled. "Oh, sorry about that. Burke-Jones is the name. Robin Burke-Jones."

Mrs. Pollifax gave him a quick glance; she had made a better choice than she'd realized in her first adult encounter. Performing introductions she settled back to see what would happen next.

"I haven't seen you before," Burke-Jones told the girl. "You've just arrived?"

"I've been here for ten days," she said coolly, "but I've been on the mountain every day hiking."

"Hiking," he echoed. "What do you mean hiking? There's nothing restful about hiking."

"I don't come here to rest," she said. "It's my vacation, and I prefer to avoid resorts, they're always so full of—" For just a second her glance rested on his exquisitely arranged cravat. "So full of playboys."

"Well, well," he said, beaming at her, "we must discuss this further."

"I don't see why," she retorted and turned over on her stomach to tan her back.

"Speaking of playboys," added Mrs. Pollifax wickedly, "what do you do, Mr. Burke-Jones?"

"Spend my time envying playboys," he said virtuously. "Actually, since you ask, I'm in the import business. Curios and knickknacks." He lifted an arm to wave at the general, whom a nurse was helping into a chair not far away. "A shop in Brighton, another in Dover, branches here and there," he added vaguely. "And you, Miss van Roelen? You are not, I take it, a playgirl?"

Her voice was muffled against the towel on which her cheek rested. "Administrative assistant, UNESCO."

"Oh, very worthy," he murmured, and lifted a brow at Mrs. Pollifax. "Wouldn't you say so, too?"

He was really impossible, she thought, and also rather nice but he was going to have a problem with Miss van Roelen. "Extremely so," she told him, and wondered what he really did. She did not for a moment believe in his import business, and considering Marcel's warning she saw no reason why she should.

The glass doors to the garden had opened and Hafez was arriving, dressed in a fresh pair of shorts and white shirt and carrying a shiny black box. The servant appeared like a shadow behind him and took a chair under a tree. Hafez placed his box on the glass and began fiddling with knobs and a small microphone. From this distance it looked like a tape recorder.

Abruptly Court sat up and called out to a woman strolling down the graveled path. "Oh, Lady Palisbury—"

This woman too had shared Mrs. Pollifax's dining room but she had been with her husband then. Mrs. Pollifax watched her pause and her face brighten at sight of Court. "Hello, there," she called, cutting across the lawn toward them. "I've been walking in the ravine." Under a huge sun hat a pair of deep-set wise eyes smiled at them.

"I just wanted to ask, did you find your missing diamond?"

Lady Palisbury shook her head. "No, my dear, but it will turn up, I'm sure."

"I almost inquired at lunch, but your husband—"

"Quite thoughtful of you, dear. No, I don't want to worry him, his blood pressure would skyrocket. John is a very impulsive man," she added, her mouth curving humorously.

"Lady Palisbury, this is Mrs. Pollifax and Mr. Burke-Jones."

She nodded pleasantly. "But I'm not going to join you, no

matter how comfortable you look. I'm on my way in to wake up my husband. He has a massage at four."

"Boom, boom, boom," shouted Hafez suddenly, streaking across the garden toward the glass doors. "Monsieur?" he shouted to a waiter. *"Un Coca-Cola!"*

Lady Palisbury strolled away. As she passed Hafez he held up the tiny microphone, the tape recorder cradled under his arm, and spoke to her in French. Lady Palisbury smiled, graciously took his microphone and spoke into it before she disappeared inside.

"Does his grandmother ever keep him company?" asked Mrs. Pollifax, watching Hafez fly off in another direction.

"Whose grandmother?"

"The boy's."

"Didn't know he had one," said Burke-Jones.

"It must be terribly dull for him here," Court said, sitting up and hugging her knees. "What would he be, ten, eleven?"

"He's so small it's difficult to guess. He said he was here with his grandmother, who's a patient."

"I suspect he's rather brilliant," said Court thoughtfully. "I don't know when he sleeps—he's all nerves, isn't he?—because he's one guest I met consistently at six o'clock in the morning, when I was leaving for my walks. He told me yesterday about pulsars. Stars, you know—or planets, I forget which."

"Mmm," said Mrs. Pollifax, watching the boy approach the general under the tree.

The general, too, was being kind; he spoke into the microphone and Hafez laughed. There was a shrill note to his laughter and Mrs. Pollifax studied the boy as he implored the general to say more.

Court laughed. "He has persuaded the general to say, *'Ici la police—sortez, les mains en l'air!'* which means 'Come out with your hands up, this is the police speaking.' The general," she added, "was once head of the Sûreté."

Robin looked startled. "I thought he was just a regular military general."

"He was a general during World War Two, under de Gaulle. Then he become head of the Sûreté."

"So he's a French police chief," murmured Mrs. Pollifax, watching Robin's face speculatively.

He said crossly, "How do you happen to know so much about everybody, Miss van Roelen, when you don't know anything about me?"

Court actually smiled at him. "I came here last summer and liked it, you see, and the general was a patient here then, too. He's very old and very alone and he hasn't much longer to live."

But it was now their turn with Hafez, who was suddenly in front of them thrusting his microphone at each of them in turn and shrilly demanding that they say something.

"I'll volunteer, Hafez," said Mrs. Pollifax, and he came eagerly to her side. She lifted the microphone, thought a moment and then recited an old nursery rhyme.

"Edward Lear!" exclaimed Court, delighted. "Here, Hafez, take me next." And into the microphone, with a smile at Mrs. Pollifax she recited, " 'There was an Old Man with a beard, who said It is just as I feared! Two Owls, and a Hen, Four Larks and a Wren, Have all built their nests in my Beard.' "

"I prefer the general's announcements to your frivolous limericks," said Robin, and grasping the microphone he called, "Come out with your hands high—the jig is up!"

But Mrs. Pollifax's glance had returned to Hafez because there remained something puzzling about him that she could not explain to herself. His eyes were far too bright, of course, his gestures quick and nervous but there was more to it than this; she realized his gestures were curiously without meaning. *He doesn't really know what he's doing,* she thought, watching him; *he doesn't care, either, he acts for the sake of being in motion.* Her gaze fell to his hands as he returned the mike to the tape recorder and she saw that they were trembling. She realized that the boy was living under an intolerable weight of tension.

"Tiresome brat," said Robin when the boy had dashed off to intercept others in the garden.

"Overactive thyroid?" suggested Court, lying down again.

"No," said Mrs. Pollifax slowly, "no, it's more than that. Much more, I think." She was remembering her own children,

and a time when Roger was six and booked for a tonsillec-
tomy, and a playmate had told him the doctor would smother
him with a pillow in the operating room. Roger had lived with
that terror for two days before he had entrusted it to her but
even now she did not care to remember those two days.

Both heads turned to her expectantly. "I think he's frightened," she said, and was startled to hear herself say it.

"Frightened?" echoed Court doubtfully. "What could possibly frighten a child here?"

"Frankly, it's he who frightens me," said Robin with a grin.

Mrs. Pollifax only shook her head and said nothing, but
now that she had identified the emotion that possessed the
boy she felt that she might even have underestimated it. He
was not just frightened, she decided, watching him, he was
desperately, nightmarishly afraid.

Dinner that evening was something called *sauté de veau
marengo*, which turned out to be veal, and Mrs. Pollifax began
to think of buying a French dictionary. In her youth she had
studied Latin and a smattering of Greek, neither of which
seemed to be of much help to her in contemporary life. From
each she had learned something of the beauty and history of
language but she had forgotten every scrap of her Latin with
the exception of the phrase *Fortes fortuna iuvat*, or Fortune
favors the bold. It was a phrase that contained a certain
amount of comfort for her now, as she considered at what
nocturnal hour she should begin her prowlings.

"You're new," said Lady Palisbury as the two of them sat in
the library, Mrs. Pollifax over her demitasse, Lady Palisbury
knitting as she waited for her husband to join her for dinner.

"This morning, yes. Ever so early. Straight from the plane."

"You come so far," murmured Lady Palisbury with a curious glance at her over her knitting.

"I have an internationally minded son-in-law," Mrs. Pollifax told her with a smile.

Lady Palisbury brightened. "Oh, how nice. We have four,
and all darlings. They're so soothing after a household of
daughters, all of whom are darlings, too, but given to shrieks
and squeals and quarrels and so forth." She had an amiable

way of talking, with frequent glances into the hall. "I fervently hope Women's Lib will give my daughters what I couldn't. When one has never been afraid of frogs and mice and spiders —and begets four daughters terrified of them—one begins to question chromosomes." She glanced up anxiously. "I do wish John would come before we get involved with the yodelers."

"Yodelers?" said Mrs. Pollifax, startled.

"You didn't see the sign in the hall? It's Friday night, you see, and the clinic arranges"—her mouth curved—"little weekend entertainments for us. Tomorrow there will probably be a film in the dining room, Sunday, of course, is visitors' day and tonight there are yodelers from the village."

"How very neighborly," commented Mrs. Pollifax. She had been watching the hall and her attention sharpened as Hafez and his companion left the dining room.

"You're curious about the boy," said Lady Palisbury, following her glance.

"He looks tonight as if he'd been crying," explained Mrs. Pollifax. "Do you know anything about him?"

Lady Palisbury turned over the sweater she was knitting and counted stitches before she replied. "I know they're Zabyans," she said, "but don't ask me which country Zabya is, I get those Arabian countries terribly mixed up. Oil, I think—yes, it's one of the oil countries, and there's a king. He was in the news recently, something about a birthday party and giving away all the royal land to his people."

Mrs. Pollifax nodded. "I remember that. A nice little man. At least he seemed to be *trying*."

"Very short in stature," nodded Lady Palisbury, "but long in courage. Oh dear, the yodelers are here."

The yodelers had indeed arrived, a group of plump, embarrassed, beaming villagers, the women in brightly embroidered dirndls and the men in high socks, shorts, and feathered hats. Lady Palisbury's husband stood in their midst looking equally as embarrassed and quite helpless. He separated himself from the yodelers and presented himself to his wife. "My dear, who *are* they?" he whispered.

"There you are, darling," said Lady Palisbury, putting away her knitting. "This is Mrs. Pollifax, John."

"Splendid," he said absently. "But Jane—"

"Yodelers, dear," she whispered, and as they moved into the dining room the group of performers followed; seconds later the sounds of strident yodels filled the air.

"Good God, have we been invaded?" asked Burke-Jones, strolling in from the solarium.

"Only by folk culture," she told him. "I think it's rather endearing."

He shuddered. "Not to me. Look, I'm driving down to the village for cigarettes—I have my car with me here—and I'll be gone only ten or fifteen minutes. Would you care to come?" He added casually, "I thought I'd ask Court, too."

Mrs. Pollifax smiled faintly. "It's half-past eight and I'm getting sleepy after losing a night's sleep on the plane. I think she's in the dining room."

"Who?"

"Court, of course."

Barely smothering a yawn she bid him good night and went upstairs.

She had left the doors to her room closed; there were two of them, a thick one padded with quilted fabric for soundproofing and an inner conventional one that could be locked. Both stood ajar now, and seeing this Mrs. Pollifax quickened her step. It might be only a chambermaid turning down the bed, or it could be Marcel.

It was neither. It was the boy Hafez, sitting in front of the glass-topped desk and hunched over something in his lap.

"Hafez," she said indignantly, "you simply mustn't walk in and out of rooms when people aren't in them."

His hands quickly returned something to the desk; whatever it was she heard it click against the glass top before he jumped to his feet to face her. "But, madame," he said, "I have been waiting for you. You did not say if you decided to be my friend."

"I would be delighted to be your friend," she told him, "but friends always knock before they come into a room."

"But, madame, I did knock," he protested. "It's just that I received no answer."

"Because I wasn't here."

"But where else could I have waited?" he asked, a desperate note creeping into his voice. "Serafina would have been very angry, she would have taken me off to bed if she saw me in the hall."

"Do you like Serafina?"

The child shrugged; whatever troubled him it was not Serafina. "Must you tell her I came inside?"

"No, but only because we're going to be friends, except you simply mustn't come in uninvited or we can't be friends."

He considered this and nodded. "Thank you," he said, and astonished her by walking out and closing both doors behind him.

Mrs. Pollifax stood looking after him, completely baffled, and then she sat down at the desk where Hafez had been sitting. Its contents were meager: a hairbrush, a jar of cold cream, a small bottle of aspirin, an address book, a lipstick, and the magazines she had read on the plane but not yet tossed into the wastebasket. She shared Court's impression of Hafez's intelligence and she did not feel that his visit had been entirely impulsive. She wanted to know which of these objects had caught his attention and which had clicked against the glass as he put it back.

She picked up the lipstick and examined it but it appeared untouched. She leaned closer to the aspirin and then she picked it up and held it to the light. She had bought it just before leaving, a small supply of twenty-five tablets in case of emergency. It looked only half-filled now. She removed the plug of cotton and poured the tablets into the palm of her hand. There were only twelve left. As she returned the bottle to the desk it clicked against the glass with a matching familiarity. Of course—glass against glass.

She shook her head. In a clinic where any nurse could supply aspirin, why did Hafez feel compelled to steal thirteen tablets, she wondered. Did he just—take things, like a kleptomaniac? She sat and frowned at the bottle, exasperated by her bewilderment; she realized that she would have to make a point of meeting Hafez's grandmother soon.

And then she found herself wondering what sort of grandmother would bring a small boy to the Clinic—a clinic of all places—when he ought to be at home playing with children of his own age. The old could be very selfish, she conceded, but it was possible the woman had no idea the child was disturbed.

I wonder, she thought idly, and glanced at her watch. It lacked a few minutes to nine and she did not have to signal with her flashlight until ten. Downstairs the yodelers were still at work, their lusty high notes penetrating the building, so obviously the social hour remained in force. I'll just pay a neighborly call, she thought. I'll make no judgments, I'll just *see*.

Resolutely she left her room and walked down the hall to knock on the door that Hafez had entered that morning. Hafez opened the door and a look of utter astonishment passed over his face. "Madame?" he faltered, and astonishment was followed by alarm. "Madame?" he repeated.

"Since we're friends I thought I'd pay a brief call on your grandmother," she told him cheerfully, and walked past him. "I trust she's well enough to—but where?" she asked, seeing that she was entering an obviously unoccupied room. Her glance swerved to an open door on the left, and then to an open door on her right.

Hafez said, "But, madame—" His glance leaped anxiously to the left, and Mrs. Pollifax followed it.

Somewhere a man's voice called out sharply in another language, and Hafez replied. There was the sound of glass falling to the floor, and an oath, followed by movement. Mrs. Pollifax reached the threshold of the adjoining bedroom and stopped. She had time to meet the shocked glance of Serafina, and time to glimpse the occupant of the bed in the darkened corner, and then she was seized from behind. A man grabbed her left elbow, another her right elbow, and lifting her off the floor she was carried, still erect, to the door. It happened so quickly that her breath was literally taken away from her, and with it her voice.

"*Ukhrujee,*" said the one burly attendant. "*Maksalamah!*"

She was shoved roughly outside. Across the hall the man in the wheelchair sat and watched with narrowed eyes. She noticed that his hands gripped the arms of his chair so tightly that the knuckles were white. He muttered something, re-treated and closed the door.

Mrs. Pollifax groped her way to one of the chairs lining the corridor and sank into it, shaken by the experience. After a few minutes she made her way down the hall to her room and closed the door behind her. She did not know whether to feel shocked, angry, or penitent. At the moment she felt a little of each and wondered which would triumph. "This isn't New Brunswick, New Jersey," she reminded herself, and then fiercely, "All right what could you expect, Emily? Of course they were outraged. Obviously the woman isn't well and these servants or relatives, or whoever they are, have come to see that she has the best of care and of course they're shocked to find a stranger bursting into the room without invitation."

Of course.

So much for penitence.

The woman had lain in bed, very pale and fragile in her sleep: long braided gray hair, a slightly curved nose, a good jaw, eyes closed. Serafina had been sitting near her but half out of her chair at sight of Mrs. Pollifax. The two attendants apparently stayed in the farther room, and Hafez had been given the middle one. The grandmother, in the third room, had not even known of Mrs. Pollifax's arrival—hadn't even stirred—but the man in the wheelchair across the hall had known. It had never occurred to her that he might be a member of the party.

And Hafez . . . he had been astonished to see her, and then alarmed, but he had made no move to stop her and as she had been carried out of the room she had glimpsed his face and he had looked pleased. Pleased by what, her coming to pay a call, or by her ejection?

She had expected—admit it—a querulous old woman, spoiled, vain, and doting on a grandson she needed but could neither entertain nor supervise. Instead she had found a still white face lying on a white pillow, and two angry attendants. She must ask Marcel; perhaps he could explain this.

She glanced at her watch and walked out to her balcony into a velvety stillness. Far below the lighted garden the lake was black and silent except for a lone steamer making its way to port; it trailed behind it ribbons of gold. It was peaceful

here, it steadied her. The curving shores on either side twinkled with the lights of casinos and villas. On her left the adjacent hillside was no more than a brooding silhouette. She held
her wrist to the light and checked the time.

At precisely ten o'clock she switched on her flashlight,
counted to three, turned it off, then on, then off, and was
startled and pleased to see that a pair of headlights sprang into
life on the hillside. They illuminated the road like twin beams
from a lighthouse so that she could see bushes, the trunk of a
tree, the texture of the rough dirt road, and above all the angle
at which the road dropped, and which the car now proceeded
to follow down, dipping lower and lower until it vanished
behind a stand of trees.

Whoever you are, she thought, it *is* nice to know you're
there.

In the garden below, one of the gardeners was turning off
the spotlights hidden among the flower beds. One by one they
died, and darkness joined with the stillness. The Clinic was
being put to bed.

It was time for her to get to work, she realized, and time to
forget her impulsive and abortive call on Hafez.

Chapter Five

*I*n Langley, Virginia, it was half-past four in the afternoon and Carstairs was only finishing his morning's work. He had begun the day with a tightly organized schedule but in midmorning the State Department had urgently requested a report on one of the smaller oil countries in the Middle East. It seemed the King of Zabya was celebrating his fortieth birthday on Tuesday, and a good many heads of state were attending the day-long festivities. Was the country stable enough for America to send the Vice-President, or should an expendable diplomat be dispatched in his place? Carstairs's comments on this during the afternoon had become increasingly unprintable but the report had been completed and delivered: the Vice-President could be sent but he would have to expect boiled sheeps' eyes on the menu.

Bishop wandered into the office smothering a yawn. "Schoenbeck's outside," he said.

"I thought you'd left."

"I'm leaving now. Schoenbeck's flying back to Geneva in two hours, he wants to wrap things up before he goes."

"Right. I don't suppose there's coffee?"

Bishop brightened. "As a matter of fact it's the only thing that's kept me intelligent, charming, and alive these past hours. Shall I bring in Schoenbeck?"

"*And* the coffee," added Carstairs.

Schoenbeck was Interpol, a rather pedantic little man with a lined face. He came in now, murmuring a thousand apologies for the intrusion and when courtesies had been dispensed with Carstairs offered him coffee and sat down.

"Gervard's going to be in charge at the Lake Geneva end," began Schoenbeck. "He's the man to contact if anything comes up. I won't be seeing you again, I'll be in Geneva."

"Anything changed?"

"My friend, everything changes," said Schoenbeck. "It is the law of life. I have just learned that it is useless for me to go to England for any new interrogations, the Dunlap man committed suicide this morning."

Carstairs swore gently. "How the hell could he commit suicide in a prison cell, wasn't he being watched?"

Schoenbeck shrugged. "The cessation of life, my friend, does not take long. He hung himself swiftly with a bedsheet. A frightened man, obviously. Suddenly more frightened of life than of death."

They were both silent, contemplating this. "No," said Carstairs, shaking his head, "more frightened of *them* than of us. Two ordinary working men, one in England, one in America, and nothing in common except they happened to work in a nuclear reactor plant—and succumbed to stealing two buttons each of plutonium."

"There is another thing they had in common, my friend," said the man from Interpol. "Both wanted very much to live— at least greed always disposes me to think thus—and both have killed themselves before we could discover any other links to this chain."

Carstairs nodded gloomily. "And their widows are richer. Anything yet on the money?"

Schoenbeck shook his head. "Not a thing, except that— voilà!—each has a bank account that is magically bulging. It must have been dealt over in cash. A dead end."

Carstairs sighed. "Well organized."

"Indeed yes." Schoenbeck, looking stern, put down his coffee cup. "It pains me, my friend, that we know so little, that all of it is based on scraps. We know that in each case the plutonium was tossed over the wall during working hours by a workman. We learn that in England a green sedan was seen by a farmer parked beside that wall about the right time, and the same green sedan was seen twenty minutes after the theft parked in front of the village post office—"

"But Stokely-on-the-Merden *is* a small village," pointed out Carstairs.

"Oh yes, small enough so that the postal clerk recalls a stranger mailing a crate to Switzerland that day to a clinic near St. Gingolph named Mont-something. But everything we have is based on the word of a farmer plowing his fields, two housewives gossiping in front of a post office and the vulnerable memory of a postal clerk."

Carstairs smiled forgivingly at his friend. "You're feeling discouraged, Monsieur Schoenbeck. How often do you have more solid leads? What do we ever work with but scraps and pieces? Yet the world lurches on."

"It is my concern over its continuing to lurch that troubles me," remarked Schoenbeck. "This is a dangerous time to have plutonium drifting about loose in the world, there is too much hate. Your agent is now joining ours at Montbrison?"

Carstairs glanced at his watch. "Yes, as a matter of fact she would have been there for some hours now."

Schoenbeck nodded. "Good. We have discovered, by the way, a clinic called Montrose some forty miles to the south, and we are putting an agent in there as well, whom Gervard will supervise. We will, of course, continue to follow every small possibility concerning the two men who stole the plutonium. The dead can no longer speak but their friends have not lost that power. What I want from you, my friend—"

Carstairs lifted his brows. "More?" he asked with comic despair.

"There is always more. I want from you an alert, a query, transmitted to all your agents around the world, barring none. It troubles me deeply that we hear no hints of this in the marketplaces of the world. In Beirut, Marseilles, and New York we hear not a whisper. This is most exceptional, a group this organized turning to this type of crime and no informants, no leaks, no tips."

"Queries everywhere?"

"Everywhere, if you please. The plutonium has to find a market eventually, does it not? And we *must* know who is buying it. Otherwise, my friend," he said flatly, "the balance of power will tip, slide, and perhaps send us all into oblivion."

"You still believe it's one of the international crime syndicates, forsaking drugs for plu—" The telephone interrupted Carstairs and he reached over to pick it up and bark his name into it. "What? Yes, he's here," he said, and handed the telephone to Schoenbeck. "You keep your office well-informed," he commented dryly.

Schoenbeck, smiling, took the phone. He listened, replied in rapid French, listened again and seemed to visibly sag in his chair. "*Qui,*" he added, and hung up. "Well, my friend, I must go," he said, standing up. An ironic smile played over his lined and weary face. "That was Geneva calling. There has been a third theft of plutonium."

"What?" thundered Carstairs.

"Yes, a third. In France this time. Two how-you-call-it metal buttons of plutonium, each weighing a kilogram." He leaned over and picked up a pencil. "A kilogram in pounds is 2.2046 for your edification, my friend. Six kilograms are now missing." He was figuring with the pencil and paper, and at last he held it out to Carstairs.

Carstairs reached for it and whistled. "Thirteen pounds and two ounces altogether," he said.

Schoenbeck nodded. "They now have their atom bomb," he said. "I leave you, my friend, but I think you will find me in France, not Geneva. In the meantime—*c'est la guerre*. Literally."

He went out, leaving Carstairs thoughtful and depressed.

*C*hapter *S*ix

E arlier, during dinner, Mrs. Pollifax had mentally compiled a list of what to avoid: the elevator, of course, which purred almost silently but still sent out vibrations of movement and whispering cables; the night concierge or whoever manned the counter and telephones at night; and she supposed that someone—somewhere—must be available for patients who were restless. She would have to discover for herself where the pockets of activity lay at night.

She changed into pajamas and robe and checked the jewelry box, leaving the tray inside but removing the jewels and tucking them into her pocket. "Fortune favors the bold," she reminded herself as she looked out on the dimly lighted, deserted hall. For one overwhelming moment she longed to retreat and go to bed and then she remembered Fraser. She walked down the hall to the elevator and took the broad, carpeted stairs beside it to the Reception floor. The switchboard was unmanned and the concierge's counter empty. She stood a moment listening and heard a low murmur from the television room; the night porter had forsaken his post for a program. Quietly she followed the stairs down and around to the ground floor. This was the unknown, a rabbit warren of therapy and equipment rooms, offices, baths and pools and the kitchen. It was also, she felt, the most likely place in which to

hide anything illicit, especially if it had been labeled MEDICAL
SUPPLIES.

Down here the lights had not been dimmed and the brightly
lighted hall alarmed her; before doing anything else she looked
for a hiding place. An unmarked door concealed a utility room
that was mercifully dark, and she slipped inside. Her flashlight
moved across tubs, pails, brooms, mops, and a wall filled with
fuse boxes and circuit breakers. From this vantage point she
opened the door a few inches and waited, listening.

To her right, far down the hall, someone had begun to whistle monotonously through his teeth. The sound came from the
kitchen but the frosted-glass doors remained closed; a pastry
chef, she decided, baking for the next day. Turning on the
Geiger counter she slipped back into the hall and tiptoed to
the wide swinging doors at the far end labeled HYDROTHERAPIES.

HYDROTHERAPIES was a large room, dark and almost gymnasium-size, and occupied by two round tile pools filled with
water that gleamed under her flashlight. Whirlpool baths, she
guessed as she moved slowly around the sides. A glance at
the luminous dial of the counter showed the needle quiet. She
opened a door in the wall and walked into an office; here she
spent several minutes investigating the closets. A second office stood next to it, followed by a room marked UNTERWASSER
MASSAGE. With some curiosity she entered the latter and found
a large, rectangular green tub standing in the center of the
room, raised on a platform. Pipes and formidable-looking
tubes surrounded it, and over the faucets a series of dials added
to the impression that she had stumbled into a medieval torture chamber. Here, too, water stood in the tub, very still and
filled with moving light. It was strange how alive and sinister
water could look at night, she thought, and with relief opened
the door to the hall.

She had now completed the east wing of the ground floor,
which was separated from the opposite wing by the lobby containing the staircase, elevator, and entrance doors to the garden. As she peered into the lobby from the Unterwasser Massage door she drew back hastily, surprised at discovering that
she was not the only prowler in the night. Barely six feet away
from her someone was trying to get into the building from the

garden. She could hear the click and rustle of tools at work; the intruder was picking the lock. Mrs. Pollifax turned off her scintillator counter and waited.

There was a last muffled click and the door swung open. Marcel slipped inside.

"Marcel!" she gasped in relief.

He jumped and crossed himself before he saw her standing in the shadows of the Unterwasser Massage room. "You scare the devil from me, madame!"

"Sorry—you frightened me, too. Whatever are you doing picking the lock?"

His face turned wry. "Waiters are not allowed keys, madame—and I am a waiter. It makes for much difficulty, especially when I am off duty." He moved away from the glass door to the garden and joined her in the darkness. "I have spent the last hour seated in the garden, in the darkness, watching. Have you been down here long? Have you seen or heard anyone?"

"Only the person in the kitchen working. Why?"

"I swear to you I saw someone on the roofs of the building a few minutes ago." He frowned. "It is very dark out there, with no moon, but still—" He shook his head. "I do not like it."

"And you want to look around," she said approvingly. "But first—really it's providential, meeting you, Marcel. I can borrow you for a minute?"

He grinned. "For eternity, madame! I may be of service?"

"Yes. You know Hafez?"

He sighed. *Mon Dieu,* who does not?" He lifted his eyes heavenward.

"He seems very upset, even frightened. I tried to pay a call on his grandmother less than an hour ago, to speak to her about it." She shivered. "I was carried bodily out of the room by two men."

He whistled faintly. "That is surprising and not very hospitable. Let me think. The Zabyan party," he said thoughtfully. "They occupy rooms 150, 152, 154. Their meals are served to them in their rooms with the exception of the boy and the maid. I have myself delivered some of the meals, but only to room 154, where a man in white jacket accepts the trays." He closed his eyes. "Their names are—yes, I have it—Madame Parviz and grandson Hafez, Serafina Fahmy, Fouad Murad, and Munir Hassan." He opened his eyes. "Other than this, I know nothing. They were not investigated further because, you see, they were not guests here when Fraser was killed."

It was Mrs. Pollifax's turn to frown. "You're quite sure of that?"

"Quite, madame. They arrived that same day, shortly after, but they were not here at that time. I will, of course, make inquiries further."

"Oh please do," she told him. "And there's one other thing: When can I get into the kitchen?"

His glance fell to the jewelry case and he smiled. "Ah, yes I see. But tonight no. Saturday—tomorrow—yes, there will be no one here then." He glanced toward the stairs. "I must go," he said. "Give me five minutes to get past the night porter. Technically I have been off duty four hours, and should be in my room in the village."

He moved to the stairs, listened a moment, and then with a wave of his hand to her vanished.

She reflected that she had at least learned the name of Hafez's grandmother, and that Marcel was vigilantly on guard outside the Clinic. She turned on her scintillator counter and crossed the hall to the door marked LABORATORIES. Inside this door lay a long narrow hall with small rooms opening from it. Of particular interest was the large storage room at the end of the hall. Her flashlight roamed past crates of peaches, spices, chocolate, and coffee. Another row contained crates of sterile cotton and cardboard cartons from various drug laboratories of Europe, none of them causing any change on her counter. At the far corner she found an aluminum chute standing against the wall, and above it a window of an exact size to fit both the chute ar.d the crates. She realized this was where supplies were unloaded. The window would be opened, the chute locked in place, the crates taken from a truck and sent sliding into the basement. She stood on a box and peered out of the window; her flashlight picked out cement and a lattice-work trellis. Tomorrow she would look for the window from the outside.

She had given Marcel his allotted five minutes. Denied the kitchen she began to have pleasant thoughts of bed, and returning to the lobby ascended the stairs to the Reception floor. This time, however, she was not so fortunate. The night concierge stood at his post by the switchboard leafing through a magazine. Shocked, he gasped, "Madame!" and rattled off a string of words in French, all of them alarmed.

She said firmly, "I've been looking for someone to take care of my emeralds." She removed the pendant from her pocket and placed it on the counter between them. "I saw a sign while I was brushing my teeth—in the bathroom, you understand— that said all valuables should be placed in your safe. How could I possibly sleep after reading that?"

He understood English; he nodded but he had trouble removing his eyes from the play of light across the emeralds. "But, madame," he countered, "I have no key. Only the head concierge can open the safe. I am sadly sorry. At seven he is on duty."

"Oh," she said. "Oh well." She put away the pendant with regret. *"Bon soir,* then."

"Yes, madame—and try to sleep a little? At seven he comes."

She nodded and continued up the stairs to her own floor. As she opened the door to room 113 she glanced down the hall and saw Hafez standing silently outside his room watching her. He was too far away for her to see his face clearly; he simply stood there, still dressed in white shorts and shirt, and then he turned abruptly and disappeared.

It was 12:05. The Clinic, thought Mrs. Pollifax, seemed to have a hidden but vivid night life of its own.

Locking her door she climbed into bed, reflected that she had at least made a beginning, and on that note fell asleep, entering a dream where she wandered through a labyrinth of dark rooms, each of them colder by degrees until she reached a hall thick with white frost. In her sleep Mrs. Pollifax stirred restlessly, and shivered.

She opened her eyes to find that a cold wind had sprung up and was blowing through the door to the balcony, presenting her with the choice of getting up and closing the door or getting up to look for a blanket. Neither prospect appealed, she wanted only to sleep. As she lay and rebelliously considered these alternatives a curious thought occurred to her: she had not left the balcony door open, she had closed and locked it.

A moment later she realized that not only was the door open but that someone else was in her room with her.

Chapter Seven

Her awareness was a combination of sixth sense and of those nearly imperceptible but speaking sounds comprised of motion, faint rustlings, and haste. She remembered the lamp sitting only a few feet away from her on the night table and tried to slowly disengage her right hand from its tangle of sheets. If she could reach the lamp before her unknown guest heard the rustling of the covers—

Over by the desk a thin beam of light appeared down near the floor, a light scarcely broader than a hairline. Caution vanished. Mrs. Pollifax freed her hands, swept back the sheets, switched on the light and stared in astonishment. "You!" she cried.

Robin Burke-Jones slowly rose to his feet from the floor. "Damn it, yes," he said, looking shaken.

"And through my balcony door—"

"Sorry about that. I suppose you want my hands up and all that?"

"If you'll feel more comfortable that way," she told him, groping for her slippers and wondering exactly where and how he fitted into this. Marcel had warned her, of course, but still she admitted a deep sense of disappointment because she had liked this young man. "At the moment I'd prefer to know just what you're doing in my room at"—she glanced at the clock—"at half-past one in the morning."

Defiantly he said, "I'll be damned if I'm going to tell you."
"And you'll be damned if you don't," she reminded him.
"A typical double-bind situation, I believe, but you don't have to rub it in." His voice was reproachful. "Look here, I don't suppose if I promised to leave the Clinic first thing in the morning, ever so discreetly—"
She ignored him; she had just seen that her jewelry case stood open on the desk. "Have you a gun?"
He looked actually offended. "Of course not."
"I think I'd rather see for myself if you're telling the truth. Do you mind keeping your hands up?"
"Of course I mind," he said snappishly. "Have I any choice?"
"None at all." She approached him gingerly, noticing for the first time his clothes, a startling contrast to his daytime costumes, being entirely and soberly black: black pullover, black slacks and black rubber-soled shoes. Patting him she found no gun but there was an oddly shaped bulge in his left pocket. "Out," she said sternly. "Empty it."
"A scandal's not going to help the Clinic," he warned her. "If I go quietly—if I swear to you—"
"Out," she told him.
He sighed. From his pocket he drew a small black object that looked like a truncated binocular. "One jeweler's glass," he said resignedly, and digging again he brought out her emerald pendant and two ruby necklaces. "The diamond pin dropped on the floor by the desk," he told her, and added bitterly, "I suppose you know that every damned one of these pieces—for which you can send me to prison for years—is a blasted fake?"
Mrs. Pollifax stared incredulously at the display and then lifted her glance to him accusingly. "But you're only a jewel thief!" she cried.
"What do you mean 'only'?"
"Why didn't you say so at once!" she demanded. "I thought —I can't tell you how relieved I am."
He backed away from her in astonishment. "Relieved? I don't think my hearing's been affected but you said *relieved?*"
"Yes, terribly. It makes *such* a difference." She crossed to

the windows, closed the balcony door and drew the curtains, really pleased to discover that her instincts had been sound after all. "Are you what they call a cat burglar?"

He sank into a chair. "I've never really thought about it. God I wish I had a drink," he said with feeling.

"Why were you going to steal my jewels if you knew they were fakes?"

"If you must know, they're damned good fakes and there's a market for good fakes. Look here, are you going to call the police?"

She considered this thoughtfully and shook her head. "On the whole, I think it wiser not—provided, of course, that you return Lady Palisbury's diamond."

He gaped at her. "Good God, you're clairvoyant!"

"It's simply a matter of listening and putting things together," she told him reassuringly. "Lady Palisbury had lost her diamond and now I discover a professional second-story man on the premises. You *are* a professional, aren't you?"

"I was," he said bleakly. "Until tonight."

"So you've never been caught before! You must be very good then?"

"Oh, one of the best," he told her dryly. "God, I wish I had a drink."

"I'll get you one." She patted him on the arm and went to her suitcase from which she removed two envelopes of instant mix and a pair of paper cups. "I always like to travel prepared," she told him. "Excuse me a minute." She went into the bathroom, filled the cups with hot water and returned, stirring them with the handle of a toothbrush.

"*Cocoa?*" he said disbelievingly.

"It helps to settle the nerves," she told him, pulling up a chair tête-à-tête. "You do realize, of course, that stealing jewelry is dishonest."

He managed a feeble smile. "I'm surprised it's just occurred to you."

"Have you tried more conventional work?"

He shrugged. "On occasion, but never with zest. I'm afraid I like the danger. I especially enjoy working alone."

She considered this and nodded. She could appreciate his point. "It's been remunerative?"

"Rather." She received the flash of a smile. "I've managed to salt away a few choice pieces of real estate. Clothes of course are a huge expense, and I drive a Mercedes convertible." He sighed. "The thing is, it takes a damnable lot of money to be rich."

"Mmmm," she murmured, studying him. "There's no import business, either?"

He shook his head.

"And I don't suppose Robin Burke-Jones is your real name?"

"Sorry about that," he apologized. "Actually it's plain Robert Jones." He sighed. "It's taken a damned lot of work turning myself into Burke-Jones and I wish the hell you'd tell me what you're going to do about me."

"I'm thinking about that myself," she admitted. "For the moment I wish you'd tell me how you arrived at my balcony without any noise. The gravel—how did you keep it from crunching like popcorn under your feet?"

"With the proper equipment—in this case padded runners —it's no bother." His glance suddenly narrowed and his face changed. "Look here," he said, "there's something wrong about this. About you, I mean. Surely you ought to be in hysterics or tears over finding a burglar in your room? Most women would have screamed or gone into shock by now, and you should never *never* be sitting here plying me with cocoa and inquiring about my techniques."

"I am always interested in people who do things well," she said with dignity.

He put down his cup. "I don't believe it. You shouldn't have given me cocoa, it's bringing me to my senses. Those jewels being fake—" He scowled at her. "You're not in desperate straits, are you? I mean I could lend you a hundred pounds if you're in trouble." A thought struck him and he added politely, "Or give you them."

She laughed. "I'm really very touched, but thank you, no."

"You're not going to blackmail me, and you're not going to inform—"

Mrs. Pollifax put down her cup and said crisply, "On the contrary, I said nothing about not blackmailing you."

He drew in his breath sharply. "I see. Yes, it would be that, of course."

"I propose an agreement," she suggested. "Terms, shall we call them? I shall say nothing at all of tonight's events, and nothing of your—uh—career so long as I hear sometime tomorrow that Lady Palisbury has found her missing diamond."

"Those are your only terms?" He looked taken aback.

"Almost. Have you robbed any other people here as well?"

He shook his head. "It's not my technique. I never commit myself until just before I'm ready to leave a place—it's too dangerous—but by that time I know precisely who to rob and how. I do my rehearsing ahead of time," he admitted. "Like tonight. As a matter of fact I've spent the last three nights out on the roofs—"

"Roofs!" she exclaimed.

"Yes, testing exits and entrances and generally getting the lay of the land. If you must know," he went on, "I overheard you telling the night porter a few hours ago that you had emeralds to put in the safe. Your voice carried, and I was in the solarium. I decided I'd better pay a visit ahead of schedule and see what you have. Most people don't bother with safes, they never believe anything will happen to their jewels."

This had the ring of truth. "And Lady Palisbury?"

He sighed. "No sense of property, that woman. She left her diamond out on her balcony two nights ago. Simply left it on the table." He shook his head disapprovingly. "Not even sporting of her. I ask you, what was a man to do?"

"Yes, I can see the temptation," said Mrs. Pollifax, nodding. "Tell me, how did you happen to choose this particular profession?"

"Is this part of the deal?" he asked darkly.

"No, but I'm terribly curious," she confided. "I'd feel so much more satisfied knowing."

He made a face. "There's no point in going into it, it's an extremely dull and vulgar story."

"But I enjoy dull and vulgar stories," she told him.

He shrugged distastefully. "If you insist, then. To be perfectly blunt about it, my name is not only *not* Burke-Jones but my father was a locksmith. Soho in London. Oh, very low caste," he said with a scowl. "As the eldest of six children—I can't possibly describe the accent I spoke with, the English very properly say that speech is breeding—my father taught me his trade so that by the time I was fifteen I could pick a mean lock." He sighed. "He went crooked just once, my father. For the sake of the money and God knows he needed it. Somebody offered him a small fortune to open a safe and—well, he was caught and died in jail. Of grief, I think. And that, dear lady, stirred in me a hatred of all 'systems'—that an honest trade brought debts and one fall from grace brought death and ruin."

"Life isn't fair, no," she agreed. "So it's anger that motivated you?"

"A very typical juvenile anger," he admitted, "but serving its purpose. I left school, totted up my assets—negligible—and decided to change myself. Went to acting school. No Oxford or Eton for me. No Hamlet, either. Acting school trimmed off the rough edges, put the h's back in my speech and removed the accent. Then I went off to the Riviera in borrowed clothes and made my first heist. But you see by the time the anger wore off I was too damned good at my trade to do anything else. There's nothing else I *can* do."

"Overspecialization," said Mrs. Pollifax, nodding sympathetically.

"A certain amount of hedonism, too," he admitted.

"I have often thought," she said idly, "that police and criminals have a great deal in common, the only difference being that they're on opposite sides of the law."

"Rather a large difference," he pointed out dryly.

She shook her head. "Purely one of intention, I'm sure. Both live by wit and deduction, don't they, and share a common isolation? It's always struck me that Sherlock Holmes took far more pleasure in talking to Professor Moriarty than to Doctor Watson."

He gave her a quizzical glance. "You've rather an unusual way of looking at things, haven't you?"

"I'm only thinking that you have invaluable talents," she told him thoughtfully.

He glanced at the clock on her night table. "Which I'd jolly well better put to work if I'm going to get Lady Palisbury's diamond back before dawn. You're really not going to call the police?"

She shook her head.

"And you'll let me—just walk out of this room?"

"You may consider yourself a free man."

He held out his hand and grinned at her. "I say, this has really been awfully pleasant. A bit strange but pleasant."

"It has," agreed Mrs. Pollifax, getting to her feet and beaming at him. "Actually it's been delightful. Which door will you leave by?"

"I'll feel much more secure leaving the way I came," he assured her. "And look, if I can ever do anything for you in return—my room's directly above yours, number 213."

"Number 213," she repeated, and watched him vanish over the railing of her balcony. Although she listened very closely she could hear nothing, not even a whisper of gravel. A fantastic performance, she thought, and as she turned off her light—there seemed no point in bothering with locks again—she reflected that Robin could prove to be something of a jewel himself.

Chapter Eight

In the morning there was a doctor, a large, hearty man named Dr. Lichtenstein. While he poked and prodded her they made polite conversation about America; Mrs. Pollifax obligingly coughed for him and he poked and prodded her still more. "Very good," he said at last, and prescribed a metabolism test, a lung X-ray, three blood tests, and an electrocardiogram.

"All this for Hong Kong flu?" she protested.

"At your age," he hinted delicately, and then, shrugging, "Why else are you here?"

Mrs. Pollifax sensibly did not reply to this but it was exasperating to say the least. She repressed her crossness, however. She was waiting to ask him a question.

"In the meantime," he concluded, removing his stethoscope and placing it in his bag, "enjoy Montbrison. Walk in the gardens. Feel free to visit St. Gingolph, and over at Montreux there is the Castle Chillon, where Byron visited." He closed his bag and stood up, saying to the nurse, "You will please schedule the tests?"

Mrs. Pollifax also stood. "By the way," she said casually, "you are certainly the one person who can tell me how Madame Parviz is today. She wasn't well enough last night to see me." When the doctor looked blank she said, "Hafez's grandmother."

"Hafez?" he repeated, and turned to the nurse, who explained the question to him in French.

"Oh, the Zabyan group," said the doctor. "I know nothing about it, Madame Pollifax, they bring with them their own doctor."

Mrs. Pollifax sat down in astonishment. "You allow that? Isn't it very unusual?"

"Of this I do not approve," he admitted with a shrug. "But it happens sometimes, it happens. In a Clinic like this certain adjustments are made, you understand? It is handled entirely by the Board of Directors."

"You don't know why they're here, then?"

He turned with his hand on the doorknob. "I understand the woman is very old, very tired, she wishes to see Switzerland again but with no wish to be examined by foreign doctors. Good day, madame."

She nooded, scarcely aware of his departure. But this was very peculiar, she thought, frowning, and his statement, added to the reception given her last night by the Zabyans, threw an entirely different light on the situation. If no one ever saw the woman—"I *must* talk to Marcel," she realized, and picked up the phone to order her breakfast.

But when her breakfast arrived it was brought by a young apprentice waiter. Marcel, he said, was on late duty today and would not be in until after lunch. This was frustrating news, and Mrs. Pollifax found herself very cross about the odd communication system set up by Interpol. Still, she knew the hours Marcel kept, having seen him here at midnight. There was nothing to do but wait.

She breakfasted on her balcony, only a little charmed today by the birds and the stillness. After breakfast she went down to the garden to sit in the sun.

"I was utterly taken aback," said Lady Palisbury, speaking to Court. They stood on the graveled path and her voice carried across the flower beds. "We breakfasted on the balcony as usual, John and I, and John had no sooner sat down in his chair when he winced and jumped up again. He said he felt as if he'd

sat on a golf ball. And there it was, my diamond, buried where
the two chair cushions met. It had been there all the time!"

"Oh, Lady Palisbury, I'm so glad for you."

"My dear, you have no idea how glad I am for myself. John
gave me that in ring in 1940—"

Several feet away, ensconced in the sun, Robin turned to
Mrs. Pollifax and murmured, "I'm actually blushing. It's
downright embarrassing being such a benefactor."

Mrs. Pollifax smiled. "Painful, too, I should imagine. A
good deed shining in a dark world—"

He groaned. "Please—spare me your clichés. And *don't* try
to reform me."

Mrs. Pollifax followed his gaze to Court, whose long,
straight brown hair gleamed in the sun. She looked remarkably wholesome and healthy, her bright pink dress emphasiz-
ing her sun-tanned face, and Robin's eyes were fixed upon her
with hunger. "I may not have to," she said with a smile. Beyond Court the doors swung open and a nurse pushed out the
man in the wheelchair. She thought idly what a shuttered face
he had, a cruel one, too. She had never felt that suffering
necessarily ennobled people; it could but more frequently it
didn't. It depended on attitude. "But I notice that you didn't
pack up and bolt this morning," she reminded Robin, "and
you're actually out of bed before noon."

"I decided to stay on a few days. You know, have a vacation
—like honest people?" He succeeded in wresting his gaze from
Court and flashed a wicked grin at Mrs. Pollifax. "Besides, if
you leave the Clinic first—if I outstay you—"

"It was a particularly virulent strain of flu," she reminded
him.

"About that flu," he said. "It reminds me that after I left
you last night I began remembering things. That jewelry case
of yours, for instance. I didn't pick it up but I pushed it across
the desk and I've never known a jewelry case to weigh so
much. About ten pounds, I'd say."

"Perhaps that's where I keep my genuine jewelry," she told
him pleasantly.

Court was moving toward them across the lawn and Robin
jumped to his feet. "Miss van Roelen," he said happily. "I was

wondering if you'd care to join me in a walk to the village before lunch."

Court looked at him with steady blue eyes. She hesitated and turned to Mrs. Pollifax. "I'd like to very much. The three of us?"

Mrs. Pollifax shook her head. "I'm having tests this morning."

Court glanced helplessly at Robin and Mrs. Pollifax realized that she was actually very shy. She wondered, too, if the girl hadn't sustained a few inner wounds recently that left her frightened of men. "But I'd certainly appreciate your bringing back four postcards for me," she said briskly. "It would be so terribly kind of you."

Court looked relieved and persuaded. "Of course," she said warmly. "Of course I will. Shall we go then?"

"Four postcards," Robin said gravely. He positively glowed with chivalry as he led her across the lawn, and Mrs. Pollifax, who had no need at all of postcards, saw them go with a sense of satisfaction. She began to look around the garden for Hafez but he had not appeared yet, and her roving glance caught the eye of the general sitting across the path from her and leaning on his cane. He bowed courteously.

"Good morning," she called.

His reply was too low for her to hear, and she left her chair for the empty one beside him. "Mrs. Pollifax," she told him, extending her hand.

"General d'Estaing, madame." His hand was dry and warm.

"A beautiful morning. You are feeling well today?"

He had surprising eyes in his strong pale face. They had remained alive and now they twinkled shrewdly in his lined face. "That is not a logical question to ask a very old man, madame. I have survived another day, that is all, neither triumphant nor particularly moved by the fact. I am, after all, eighty-nine."

"Eighty-nine!" exclaimed Mrs. Pollifax.

"The particular problem of being eighty-nine," he continued, "is that one has time to reflect upon a well-lived life but no friends with which to share the sweep of perspective. Have you ever come near to death, madame?"

"Yes," she said, nodding. "Near enough."

"Then you know that its terrors are exaggerated," he said simply.

"I think I should mind the waiting," she told him thoughtfully. "It must be rather like the last months of pregnancy, with no possible way to back out or change one's mind."

"You mean the irrevocability," he said, smiling. "Birth and death—no, we've no choice there." His gaze looked out upon the garden reflectively. "These young people, I find it ironic that they are learning how to live while I am learning how to die."

"Do you wish you could tell them how to live?"

He chuckled. "One cannot tell the young anything, madame."

She laughed. "Very true. General, in your work—I hear that you were head of the Sûreté—you learned a great deal about human nature?"

"Too much," he said dryly.

She hesitated. "You have met, perhaps, with real evil?"

"Evil," he mused, and she saw his eyes flash beneath the heavy brows. "You ask a Frenchman that, madame? I had the interesting experience once of meeting Hitler—"

"Ah," she breathed.

He nodded. "He impressed me, madame—this man who sent millions of Jews to their death and changed the course of history—with his ordinariness. Success encouraged his madness, of course, but that was the thing, you see: he was so ordinary. This is what astonished and alarmed me, that evil can be so commonplace. It is not in the face or in the words but in the heart, in the intentions. In my experience I have found only one form of evil to leave its visible mark."

"And what is that?"

"In general the act of murder leaves no mark on a man but I have found this is not true of the professional killer who murders more than once, and in cold blood. It is a curious fact that it shows in the eyes, madame, which I believe the poets call the windows of the soul. I have found the eyes of the habitual murderer to be completely empty. An interesting revenge by Nature, is it not?"

"Indeed yes," she murmured.

"The soul can be annihilated, you see—one must not trifle with it." He glanced at the nurse who had entered the garden bearing a tray of medicines and when she headed toward them he sighed. "Just as I thought, the medicine is for me. They must try to keep me alive a little longer, madame."

The nurse addressed him in French and they exchanged a few jokes before her eyes fell on Mrs. Pollifax. "Oh, but madame," she cried, "you are the one they search for, it is time for the tests. You go, eh?"

Mrs. Pollifax bid the general a good morning, and went.

After lunch Mrs. Pollifax stationed herself in the garden to wait for Marcel. She chose the gazebo, because it was secluded and discouraged company, and she fortified herself with a paperback novel and a discarded *International Herald Tribune* that she had found in the library. The sun grew hotter and the shadows longer. Two of the younger waiters appeared and moved among the guests, taking orders, but it was a long time before Marcel appeared. When she saw him she stood up and waved. "Oh, *garçon!*" she called, summoning her newest French word.

Marcel made his way cautiously toward her, his eyes wary. "*Oui*, madame?"

With a smile pinned on her lips, and speaking through clenched teeth she said, "Are you a good actor, Marcel? I have to talk to you."

He grinned. "All Frenchmen are actors, madame." He unfurled an order pad and held a pencil poised above it. "Now, madame. I shall smile, you shall smile, and we can speak."

"It's Madame Parviz again, Marcel. Have you any information yet?"

"It was requested last night by phone, when I returned to the village, but the information will have to come from Zabya. There should be something by tomorrow morning."

She nodded. "But there's more, Marcel. Did you know that none of the doctors have visited or examined her?"

He looked surprised. "This I did not know."

"Dr. Lichtenstein told me. I asked. He said it was cleared by the Board of Directors, and he explained it by saying that Madame Parviz—or so he was told—is very old and wants no foreign doctors examining her. But she isn't that old, Marcel, I saw her."

He looked doubtful. "Madame, I do not wish to be tactless but are you forgetting what we are here for? An invalid woman and a child, it seems most unlikely that they are involved—"

"Of course they're not," she said impatiently, "but there is something very peculiar there. Can you get me a list of the Board of Directors?"

He shrugged. "I have this already in my files, of course."

"I'm also curious, Marcel, about the man in the room across the hall from Madame Parviz. I should have asked you about him last night. He's in a wheelchair, I see him in the garden and in the dining room. I'm wondering if he isn't a member of their party, too."

Marcel sighed. "I can assure you that he is not, madame, because he did not arrive with them, he has been here for some time. Nor is he Zabyan." He frowned. "Room number 153 . . ." He shook his head. "I do not remember his name without referring to my list but I can find out his name in half an hour."

"I'd appreciate it if you could find out a great deal more."

He looked at her and smiled. Perhaps he found her amusing. "Very well, madame, I will do very thorough detective work on this man and by tonight I will have information for you, okay? But I would prefer better to hear something of Robin Burke-Jones, of whom I am most suspicious."

"And rightly so," she said, smiling back at him. "Actually I can tell you a great deal about him, almost all of it, I think, reassuring. He's—" She paused. Over Marcel's shoulder she saw Robin making his way across the lawn to her. "So if you'll make it crumpets with tea," she said in a normal voice.

He leaned forward. "I go off duty at midnight, madame. Can you meet me on the ground floor at that hour, by the elevator?"

"I'll be there. And lemon with the tea," she added, lifting her voice.

"And you can bring me a Scotch and soda," said Robin,

collapsing into the chair beside her. "Do you know that walking is strictly for the birds?"

"They fly," pointed out Mrs. Pollifax. "Are you just getting back from the village?"

He nodded. "We lunched there. *I* have returned but not Court. Oh no, she's still playing the organ in that old Anglican church by the café." He shuddered. "The organ, for heaven's sake."

"But how charming," said Mrs. Pollifax, smiling at him. "What a gifted person she must be. What in particular bothers you about that?"

"What bothers me is that she doesn't even know I *left*." In his indignation he was virtually gargling his words. "We stopped in the church on the way back, and the rector, or whoever he was, made conversation with us about the age of the church and its flying buttresses and then about music, and Court said she played and he begged her to try their new organ. She forgot about me," he concluded in a strangled voice.

Mrs. Pollifax nodded. "Yes, I thought you might find that a problem but I hoped not. She strikes me as being quite self-sufficient, you know." In the silence that followed she added tranquilly, "I've heard it makes for the very best marriages, actually."

"What does?" he asked suspiciously. "Organ music?"

"Self-sufficiency. So many marriages are parasitic, don't you think? The one party living through the other. Such a tragic waste of potential."

He regarded her with exasperation. "Look, I'm not planning to marry her or anyone. In my profession can you even imagine the complication of a wife? All I ask is a decent show of interest. I've got money, I'm not bad looking, I've been around—"

Mrs. Pollifax nodded. "Ego."

To her surprise he said humbly, "You really think it's that?"

"Yes, I do. You're quite accustomed to having your own way, I imagine. Especially with women, isn't that true?"

"I suppose so," he admitted forlornly.

"What draws you to Court, if I may be so presumptuous?"

"I've never met anyone *more* presumptuous." He hesitated as Marcel brought them drinks on a tray, removed them to the table and withdrew. "She's different," Robin said, scowling. "She's little. Small, I mean. And cool but warm underneath. She needs caring for, you can see that at once."

"Oh at once," agreed Mrs. Pollifax gravely.

"But she doesn't realize that. There's a vulnerability about her—" He caught himself up, frowned and said briskly, "Of course she's impossible. Do you realize that for the first eight days of her stay here she left her bed at five-thirty in the morning to *walk?* The girl's obsessed, it's unnatural."

Mrs. Pollifax considered him with sympathy. "There are people like that, you know. My neighbor at home, Miss Hartshorne, is one." She said thoughtfully, "I think it arouses guilt feelings in the rest of us. Certainly Miss Hartshorne's not very popular but," she added loyally, "she's ever so healthy."

"Exactly," said Robin. "And you called her Miss Hartshorne. She never married?"

Mrs. Pollifax shook her head.

"Well then, you see?" He was triumphant. "That's just what will happen to Court. She's beautiful—breathtakingly lovely—and she'll never marry."

Mrs. Pollifax beamed at him happily. "Then you needn't worry about falling in love with her, need you? She's no threat at all."

Robin glared at her. "You're expecting me to be rational."

"Surely consistent?"

"Consistent, rational, stable and well-adjusted?" He threw up his hands. "I give up." His glance turned accusing. "You're watching something, you're not paying the slightest attention suddenly. Damn it, this certainly doesn't seem to be my day for capturing anybody's attention."

"I'm watching Hafez," she told him. "He's up on the third-floor balcony outside his room. He hasn't been outside at all today and I've been wondering why."

"He really continues to trouble you?" asked Robin.

"Yes." She hesitated and then—it scarcely betrayed any secrets—she added, "I tried to pay a call on his grandmother last evening to look over the situation."

"Breathing fire, I suppose, and looking very stern, and she told you it was none of your business?"

Mrs. Pollifax put down her cup of tea and shook her head. "I caught only a glimpse of her in bed and then I was literally carried out of the room by two men of the party."

"Strong-arm stuff, eh?"

She realized that this was exactly how it had struck her at the time; it was the sickroom atmosphere that clouded her perceptions and created doubt. "Yes, and I intend to find out why."

He grinned. "I'll bet you will, too."

"Hello!" called Court, approaching them and looking radiant. "I've been playing the organ all this time, it's been delightful.

"Yes," said Robin, "I know."

Mrs. Pollifax arose. "And now I'm going to excuse myself before I become welded to this chair. I think a small nap is in order before dinner."

"Oh, but I was looking forward to talking to you!" Court protested. "I have your postcards, too, you know."

They exchanged postcards and centimes but Mrs. Pollifax could not be dissuaded. "I'll see you later," she said, and left.

As she entered the lobby she passed Marcel carrying a tray. "Madame, you dropped this," he told her, extending a hand with a slip of paper in it before he walked through the door.

On the slip of paper he had written: *In room 153, Ibrahim Sabry. Egyptian passport, age 51. Owner small munitions factory. Religion, Islamic. Destroy. More later.*

Chapter Nine

There was a film after dinner that evening, at nine, and Mrs. Pollifax was reassured to see that Hafez was going to be allowed to attend it. "Oh, *madame*," he cried in a raptured voice, meeting her in the hall. "Madame, a *film!*"

His eyes shone. He tucked his hand into hers and led her into the dining room where a screen had been erected and the chairs rearranged in a half circle. "It is all in French but I shall explain everything to you—every word," he told her passionately.

"Where have you been all day?" she asked. "I looked for you in the garden, and I looked for you at dinner. Hafez, I'm terribly sorry if I upset things last night by trying to pay a call on your grandmother."

He turned and looked at her with huge eyes. "But, madame, I know now that you are a true friend. I think it was very kind of you."

"But you were in your room all day?"

"Oh, that is nothing *now*. Look, madame, the picture is going to begin. I will translate."

He did indeed translate; he read aloud to her even the credits on the screen, and then as the story began he faithfully recorded every word. It did not make him popular with the handful of other people present, among them Ibrahim Sabry and the Palisburys. Mrs. Pollifax leaned over and suggested he lower his voice. "Oh, *oui*, madame," he said, and for two minutes he did. Mrs. Pollifax decided the only way to restore tranquillity to the group was to withdraw. It was nearing her Flashlight Hour, anyway.

"You can tell me the plot tomorrow, I'm going to leave now," she whispered to him.

His disappointment was huge, but glancing back from the door she noted that it was fleeting. He was once again immersed in the show, eyes round, lips parted. She smiled at his enthrallment. It was good to see him a child again. Court and Robin were sitting in the library talking, their heads close together; she waved at them and went upstairs.

At ten o'clock, and feeling rather like Paul Revere, she went again to her balcony to signal that she had survived a second day at Montbrison. Again the car lights flicked on in reply and again she watched her unknown friend disappear down the hill. Still she lingered; it was warm this evening, with a feel of rain in the air. The lights along the shore of Lake Geneva were gauzy, like smudged yellow fingerprints on a dark canvas. She realized that she still had not seen the mountains that rimmed the lake.

At 11:55, after practising her Yoga for half an hour, she checked the scintillator counter and tested her flashlight and prepared to learn what Marcel might have discovered. Closing her door behind her she moved softly down the stairs. Again the concierge's station was abandoned; the elevator idled there, brightly lighted and empty. She descended to the ground floor. Marcel had not arrived yet but it still lacked a minute to the hour.

It was awkward waiting here by the elevator in the brightly lighted hall. The doors to the garden stood across the lobby opposite her, two rectangles of opaque black glass shining like eyes. She felt extremely conspicuous. The ground floor was quiet except for the sound of water running in the Unterwasser Massage room next to the garden doors. There was no whistling tonight from the kitchen, which she would explore once she left Marcel. She moved away from the staircase toward the shadows behind it, and the movement was reflected in the glass doors, a pale wraith mocking her with perfect synchronization.

She checked her watch; it was precisely midnight. The running water was annoying because someone would be coming back soon to turn it off and she could not imagine how she would explain her presence. The sound was insidious, like two gossips murmuring and whispering in another room. Otherwise the Clinic was silent and there was in this, too, an odd quality of restiveness. There was no sign of Marcel.

In the Unterwasser Massage room something dropped to the floor and Mrs. Pollifax stopped pacing and became still. An object had fallen but objects did not drop by themselves. She placed the jewel case in the shadow of the stairway and moved across the lobby to the door of the Unterwasser Massage room. There she hesitated, listening, and then turned the knob. The room was in darkness; she switched on her flashlight as she entered. Across from her the door that led to Hydrotherapies was just closing. Its latch clicked softly and she saw the knob released from the other side by an unseen hand. She opened her mouth to call out but as she stepped forward the beam of her flashlight dropped and she gasped in horror.

Marcel lay in the pale green tub, his eyes turned vacantly to the ceiling. Blood spattered the sides of the tub and ran in zigzag lines across his white jacket. His throat had been cut from ear to ear.

"Oh dear God," she whispered, like a prayer, and sagged against the wall. Turning off her flashlight she groped for a chair and sat down and gulped in deep breaths of air. He could not have been dead for long, perhaps only seconds before she had descended the stairs. While she had been hurrying down to meet him here there had been stealthy movements in the dark, small animal sounds and sudden death. There had not even been time for him to call out.

The water still gurgled obscenely into the tub. After a moment—driven by a stern sense of duty—she switched on the flashlight again and crept back to Marcel. One trembling hand moved to his bloody jacket and waited but there was no flutter of a heartbeat, no possibility of survival. She rinsed the blood from her hand under the faucet and then found the spigot and angrily stilled the water.

At once she knew that she had made a dangerous mistake.

Her mind was clearing. Marcel was dead—murdered—and someone had left this room as she entered it.

She switched off the flashlight and stood up. The darkness was engulfing, and with the cessation of running water the silence proved to be as taut and alive as a scream. Somewhere in the three offices that lay between her and the Hydrotherapies room this silence was shared by another human being. Someone else listened to the emptiness and knew he wasn't alone: she had just told him so by turning off the water.

Marcel's murderer.

She stood irresolute. Into the silence there crept the faintest stirring of movement in the next room, a whisper of cloth against cloth, of protesting floorboards. He was returning. Marcel's murderer was coming back to see who was here.

She shivered. She did not believe she had been seen or heard earlier. She had come downstairs silently. The stairs were heavily carpeted and on her feet she wore the heavy knitted bedsocks that Miss Hartshorne tirelessly made for her every Christmas. She doubted that he even realized she had entered the room as he left it, but certainly he had heard the water stop splashing into the tub. He was coming back to learn who was here, and a little knowledge was a dangerous thing. For her.

She looked around her. She was isolated in this small room next to the brightly lighted lobby. Behind the murderer, on the other hand, lay three offices and a gymnasium-size room, giving him considerable space in which to move about and hide. Apparently his curiosity outweighed his caution and he felt impelled to search and to identify. She did not care to explore the reasons behind his logic because if he discovered her, then she discovered him as well. She did not believe he would accept such mutuality.

She must not be found here.

Quietly she backed to the door by which she had entered the room. She opened it and assessed the distance across the lobby to the staircase. Impossible, in such a bright light he would clearly see her before she gained the stairs. She turned back and pointed her flashlight at the door across the room, waiting for him to enter. A very small idea had occurred to her.

Slowly the knob began to turn. Matching her movement to his she left as he entered, fleeing into the hall—but not to the stairs, she rushed headlong to the utility room around the corner and flung herself inside. There she ran her flashlight over the fuseboxes: they were labeled in French, in English, and by number. She tugged at the circuit-breakers for the ground floor and a second later saw the light under the closed door vanish.

The silence was frightening. A door closed. Footsteps moved across the lobby to the foot of the stairs, and for that moment the two of them were separated only by the wall of the closet. She held her breath. He would be holding his breath, too, she thought, scarcely daring to expel it lest he miss some small, stifled sound. He was going to begin stalking her now like prey in an attempt to flush her out of hiding. And while they both waited, their thoughts screaming in the emptiness, he moved again.

He walked past the closet and down the hall toward the gymnasium, giving her just one fragile unguarded moment of hope. When she heard the doors to Hydrotherapies swing open she slipped out of the closet and raced to the stairs, snatching up the scintillator counter from the floor where she had left it.

When she reached the Reception floor level her heart was thudding ominously and her throat ached from dryness. She felt almost sick with horror. She stopped to catch her breath and saw the elevator still idle; on impulse she entered it. For a second she hesitated over the panel and then she punched the button for the floor above her own. *He must not learn which floor was hers.*

But he had heard the sound of the elevator in motion, for as she ascended with frustrating slowness she recognized the sound of feet pounding up the stairs below her. She realized he was racing up to cut her off, and his determination to find and identify her was terrifying. Slowly the elevator rose toward the fourth floor and slowly the doors opened. She stepped out. Another moment and she would be trapped unless—

Robin, she thought. Robin had said he was in the room exactly above hers. She ran down the hall, found room 213, discovered the door unlocked and stumbled inside.

Robin was sitting up in bed with a book on his knees. He looked at her in astonishment. "My dear Mrs. Pollifax," he said, and then seeing her face he gasped, "My God, what on earth?"

She shook her head, placed a finger to her lips and retreated into the darkness of his bathroom. There were advantages in appealing to a cat burglar; Robin responded at once by reaching for his bedside lamp and plunging the room into darkness. In silence they listened to footsteps walking down the hall toward the solarium. Softly the footsteps returned. After a short interval the elevator doors slid closed and the elevator hummed as it descended.

Slowly Mrs. Pollifax expelled her caught breath.

Robin went to the door and opened it, looked up and down the corridor and then closed and locked the door and walked across the room to draw the curtains of the window. Turning on a light he said pleasantly, "We're having a party in my room tonight?"

She left the darkness of his bathroom and found him rummaging in his wardrobe closet. "There's a bottle of Napoleon brandy here somewhere," he said. "Ah, here we are. Beautiful. I have never felt that cocoa measures up to brandy in a crisis." He poured an inch into a bedside glass and handed it to her. "Drink it down, you look like hell."

She nodded gratefully.

"And while you're thawing out," he continued pleasantly, "you'll no doubt think up some outrageous lie to explain why you've been playing hide-and-seek with someone in the halls at this ungodly hour, but don't—don't try—because I won't believe you. When you stumble into a man's room in the middle of the night, looking as if you'd just seen a corpse, and carrying of all things that damn jewelry case—" His eyes narrowed as he sprang to his feet.

"Robin!" she cried sharply.

He picked up the box and carried it to the light. "Sorry,

milady," he said. "Curiosity killed the cat but never a cat burglar, as you call it. I've been curious about this thing all day, and obviously you're not what you appear to be. Let's see what you really are." She sat mute as he opened the case. "Let's see, if I designed this—oh, it's very well done—I'd put the lock in one of these hinges, I think, and—" He triumphantly pressed the hinge on the right and removed the tray.

There was silence as he peered down at what he'd unearthed. "Good God, *not* the Queen's jewels. A—surely not a *Geiger* counter?" He stared at her disbelievingly.

She sighed and put down the emptied glass of brandy. "As a matter of fact, yes. Did you really expect stolen goods?"

He looked bewildered. "I don't know, I expected something illicit, although you don't *look* illicit. But a Geiger counter? What on earth are you looking for, uranium?" He thought he was making a joke.

Mrs. Pollifax considered him, hesitated and then made a decision. "Plutonium, actually."

"Plutonium?"

"Yes." There was a welcome impersonality about plutonium. It did not bleed, it was a metallic object without hopes, dreams, fears, or a throat that could be cut. At the moment plutonium seemed much less dangerous than Marcel's body lying in the Unterwasser Massage tub, and she did not want to speak of Marcel. She had sought sanctuary in this room, and Robin had saved her from being discovered and possibly killed. For this she owed him something, even truth, but if Robin was to be involved then let him be involved in an abstract without personality. Marcel's murder was too dangerous to share.

"Interpol is in this," she told him gravely, "and my government is in this, and yours, too."

He shuddered. "That's a bit thick." He stared ruefully at the scintillator counter in his lap. "My God, I've opened Pandora's box, haven't I? You're involved with my mortal enemies and I'm sitting here listening to you." He shook his head. "Damn it, I wish I'd allowed you to think up that outrageous lie."

"You didn't give me time," she reminded him.

"Plutonium . . . It would have to be stolen plutonium, of course."

"Yes. Presumed to have been sent here."

"Pretty damned clever sending it *here*." He began to look interested. "Not a bad drop-off point at all. I don't have to ask what your precious authorities are afraid of, of course, but they're not going to relish your telling me this, are they? Why did you?"

She thought about this a moment, a little startled herself at her openness. "I find no evil in you," she said at last, very simply. "It's true that you have a somewhat distorted sense of morality in one area but I'm looking for someone with no morality at all. Someone"—she shivered—"completely amoral, without scruples or fear or compassion or decency."

"Here?" he said in astonishment. "Among the patients?"

"Perhaps."

He looked at her. "So that's why you were relieved to find me only a thief. And tonight? What did you find tonight? Who was it out there?"

"I wish I knew. I wish I'd had the cunning to find out." The memory of Marcel intervened and she steadied herself. When she replied it was casually. "I was downstairs on the ground floor when I found myself playing cat-and-mouse with someone in the dark. I reached the Reception floor and the elevator was standing there and so I slipped inside, planning to walk down a floor to my room, you see, but I could hear whoever it was running upstairs after me, so I was cut off and—"

"And popped in here." He studied her face shrewdly. "If that's your story I won't do any more prying, but to be perfectly frank with you that little anecdote doesn't begin to match the look on your face when you burst into my room. Do you think whoever it was is still out there waiting for you?"

He had caught her off guard; she realized that she'd not thought of this yet.

Robin shook his head. "You don't have a poker face tonight, Mrs. Pollifax, I frightened you with that question." He regarded her curiously. "All right, I said I wouldn't pry but let's proceed as if you've stolen the Queen's jewels and the police are lurking. Can you manage a drop of eight feet on a rope?"

She brightened. "Over the balcony?"

He looked amused. "Yes, my dear Mrs. Pollifax, but don't look so eager. Have you ever before gone up or down a rope?"

"Yes, once in Albania—" She stopped. "Oh dear, I *am* tired, I should never have said that."

He looked her up and then down, taking in her height, her weight, her flyaway hair, the voluminous robe and woolly bedsocks, and he grinned. "I didn't hear you say it. I wouldn't believe it if I did hear it, especially knowing that Americans are not allowed in Albania. Who would believe it anyway, I ask you." He removed a coil of efficient-looking rope from his suitcase. "Mountain climbing rope," he explained, patting it lovingly. "The very best. By the way, there's nothing to this, there's no ledge at all on this floor but a perfectly splendid one on yours below so there'll be something under you all the way. I'll go first and check you out." Over the coil of rope he studied her and frowned. "You know, it terrifies me discovering who you are, but it's equally alarming to think your superiors may have sent you here alone and unprotected. I daresay it's the most absolute affrontery to offer my services but if anything comes up—" He looked embarrassed. "Well, hang it all, I'm already indebted to you, and if you should need a gentleman burglar—"

"I can't tell you how much I appreciate that," she said warmly.

"Oh?" He looked startled. "Well, do keep it in mind, then. By the way, is your balcony door locked?" She nodded and he added a circle of keys to his belt. "Full speed ahead then." On the balcony he tied the rope to the railing, fussed over the knots, tested the railing and glanced up. "All set?"

It was dismayingly dark out here but she reflected that this had the advantage of blotting out the garden four stories below. "I'm ready."

"Good. Give me your jewelry case. Once over the railing lean out a bit, rope in hand, and then slide down and *in*."

"In," she repeated.

He disappeared and Mrs. Pollifax found herself hesitating until she remembered the lighted halls and the shadowy solariums where anyone could hide. She climbed over the railing and grasped the rope. Closing her eyes she murmured a brief prayer and let go.

"Good girl," said Robin, catching the rope and guiding her in close to the balcony. "With a little training you'd make a splendid burglar." He helped her over the railing, turned his pencil-thin flashlight on the door to her room and a moment later it stood open. "I trust you locked your other door, the one into the hall?"

She shook her head. "No, I thought I might have to retreat in a hurry."

"Then I'd better take a look around and make sure nobody else used it for a hasty retreat." He followed her inside and while she put away the scintillator counter he glanced under her bed, into her closet and then disappeared into the bathroom. She heard him swear softly and then he sputtered angrily, "What the devil!"

She turned questioningly toward the door just as he reappeared pushing a frightened Hafez in front of him. "Behind your bathtub curtain," he said grimly. *"Hiding."*

Chapter Ten

Hafez stood very still in front of her but there was no quietness in him; he was taut with anxiety. He had been crying, of this there was no doubt, because his eyes were red-rimmed and his cheeks still damp. "Where have you been?" he cried despairingly. "I came to find you and you'd gone and I waited for you so long."

"Behind the shower curtain?" inquired Robin dryly.

"No, no, monsieur, in that chair over there—for fifteen minutes—but then I heard your voices on the balcony and I was afraid."

"But why?" asked Mrs. Pollifax softly. "Why aren't you in bed asleep?"

He hesitated, looking at Robin.

"I think you can regard him as a friend," Mrs. Pollifax told him.

Hafez looked doubtful.

"Try," begged Mrs. Pollifax.

"If you say so, madame." He turned back to her. "I have come to take you to my grandmama. She is awake now. Please," he urged, "you will come with me quickly?"

"At two o'clock in the morning!" exclaimed Mrs. Pollifax.

Robin said flatly, "Nonsense, lad, Mrs. Pollifax isn't going anywhere except to bed."

Watching Hafez, Mrs. Pollifax realized that she had heard of people turning white but she had never seen it happen before. The color literally drained from Hafez's face, as if his whole world depended upon her coming with him and Robin, as judge and jury, had turned down his appeal. She was touched and astonished. Rallying, she said, "On the contrary, it needn't take long." Turning to Robin she explained, "It's not as if his room is on another floor, it's just down the hall at the other end."

Robin said angrily, "Are you mad?"

"Probably."

He sat down in the chair by the desk and mutinously folded his arms. "Well, I'm staying right here, I'm not leaving until I see you settled for the night. Damn it, that's why I escorted you, remember?"

She gave him a forgiving glance. "I won't be long."

He added furiously, "If you're not back soon I'll turn the whole Clinic upside down. What's the room number?"

"It is 150, monsieur," said Hafez, regarding him with awe.

Robin nodded and Mrs. Pollifax gave him a last thoughtful glance as she gathered up her skirts. His attitude struck her as exaggerated, considering how little he knew about the events of her evening, and she wondered what caused it. "Let's go, Hafez," she said quietly, and heard him sigh with relief.

The hall was mercifully empty. Hafez tiptoed ahead of her and Mrs. Pollifax, who had only slightly recovered from her last venture into the halls, was happy to tiptoe with him. Down near the end of the hall Hafez stopped and drew a key from his pocket. Unlocking the door he beckoned her inside the dimly lit room. Somewhat nervously she stepped across the threshold and hesitated.

The normality of the scene reassured her. This time there was no Serafina, and the door to the adjoining rooms was closed. A small lamp burned at the night table, throwing shadows against the wall and a circle of light across the bed in which Madame Parviz sat braced against a number of pillows. She wore a rough homespun robe with a hood that shaded her face but even at a distance Mrs. Pollifax could see an uncanny resemblance to Hafez. A pair of brilliant dark eyes watched her approach; in the dim light they glittered under deeply cut lids but as Mrs. Pollifax drew closer she was shocked to see dark shadows under the eyes, like bruises. It was a ravaged face, once exotic, still handsome but drained of all vitality now. Only the essence of a strong character remained, and a certain imperial air that she shared with her grandson.

"Grandmama," said Hafez quietly, "here is my friend Madame Pollifax."

"*Enchanté*," murmured the woman in a low voice, and one hand lifted to indicate the chair next to the bed. Her voice when she spoke was filled with exhausted pauses, as if a great effort was being made. "I understand you—paid me—a call yesterday. When I was—asleep."

"Yes, Hafez and I have become friends," said Mrs. Pollifax, smiling. "You've a very charming grandson, Madame Parviz, I've been enjoying him." Her own voice sounded alarmingly healthy and she lowered it.

Madame Parviz did not respond to the pleasantry; her eyes remained fixed upon Mrs. Pollifax with an intensity that was embarrassing. "May I—ask a favor, then, Mrs.—Pollifax?"

The abruptness was startling in a woman so obviously gracious. Mrs. Pollifax glanced at Hafez, standing at the foot of the bed, and saw that he was watching her with the same intentness. "But of course," she said, suddenly very still and alert. "Of course."

"If I may ask—one thing Hafez—cannot do. A cable—sent from the village?"

"A cable," repeated Mrs. Pollifax.

"*Not* from—the Clinic."

"I see," said Mrs. Pollifax, almost holding her breath now. "You'd like me to send a cable for you but not from the Clinic." Turning practical she reached for her purse. "I've pencil and paper. If you'll dictate what you'd like—"

Hafez said quickly, "It is already prepared, madame."

And this was true: from beneath her blanket Madame Parviz drew a sheet of Clinic stationery and offered it to Mrs. Pollifax. "Please—you will read it?"

The silence as Mrs. Pollifax accepted it was heavy with suspense and she realized it was because two of the three people in this room were holding their breath. The mood was contagious and she heard herself read it aloud in a low, conspiratorial whisper. "To General Mustafa Parviz, Villa Jasmine, Sharja, Zabya: HAFEZ AND I SAFE AND WELL LOVE ZIZI."

Having read it Mrs. Pollifax was struck by its normalcy and curious at its necessity. "But it's not to be telephoned from the Clinic," she repeated.

"Please—no."

From the adjoining room, behind the closed door, there came an abrupt human sound resembling a snore; it *was* a snore, decided Mrs. Pollifax, hearing the sound move down the scale and then repeat itself and she saw Hafez and his grandmother exchange a warning glance.

"Is something wrong?" asked Mrs. Pollifax quietly.

"Wrong?" Madame Parviz turned quickly toward her and produced a laugh that was high and unnatural. "But—of course not!" Having managed this she leaned back exhausted against the pillows. "But—of course not, madame," she echoed.

"She is tired," Hafez said in a low voice.

The audience had ended. "Yes," agreed Mrs. Pollifax and arose and moved with him to the door. There she stopped and looked at Hafez thoughtfully. "You and your grandmother are very close, Hafez."

He nodded. His eyes were wary.

On impulse she leaned over and kissed the top of his head. "I like you very much, Hafez, and I think you're an ingenious young man."

"I beg your pardon, madame?"

She shook her head. "Never mind. Good night, I'll go to my room now."

She walked down the empty hall and entered the sanctuary of her room with a sense of relief. Robin sat in the chair by the desk, arms still folded across his chest. "Well?" he said, glowering at her.

"Well," she said, taking a deep breath.

"You finally met the vampire grandmother? You're satisfied?" A close look at her face and he sighed. "All right, you're not satisfied."

"It's been—a strange night," she admitted.

"You're reckless," he said. "Good God but you're reckless. Upstairs you were frightened of the halls, pale as a ghost, and then thirty minutes later you're tootling off on impulse with a small boy whom *anybody* could have sent. Anybody."

"Yes," she said absently.

"I get the feeling you're not hearing me."

"It's just turned Sunday," put in Mrs. Pollifax, frowning. "Where can one send a cable on Sundays, Robin?"

He gestured toward the night table. "You pick up the telephone, and provided the night porter's at the desk, and providing he's the one who speaks English—"

She shook her head. "I mean where does one go to send one personally, from an office."

He sighed. "You'd have to go to Montreux for that, to a PTT building. The telegraph is open on Sundays—8:30, I think, closed most of the afternoon and open again in the evening. I'll take you down in my car if you'd like."

She gave him a skeptical glance. "At 8:30 in the morning?"

He climbed to his feet. "Yes, at 8:30." He studied her face a moment and then said quietly, "Suppose you meet me at eight beside my car, which is parked around the corner from the main entrance. It's a dark blue Mercedes convertible. Will you do that?"

"It's very kind of you," she said, surprised.

"Not at all." He paused with one hand on the knob of the door to the balcony. "It's certainly been interesting seeing how the other half lives—the respectable half," he added with irony. "Sleep well, milady."

"Thank you."

"Oh, and by the way," he added, "I'd advise your taking a close look at that robe of yours before you wear it again. There's rather a lot of blood on it in the back, as if you'd knelt in a puddle of the stuff."

She stared at him in astonishment.

"I didn't notice it when you first popped into my room but when I saw it I had a fair idea of what frightened you tonight, and frankly it scares the hell out of me. See you at eight." He went out, carefully closing the door to the balcony behind him.

Considerably jolted Mrs. Pollifax stared after him and then she moved to the door and locked it behind him. His remark explained the reason behind his sudden protectiveness—he *knew*. She took off the offending robe, eyed it wearily and dropped it to the floor. There was suddenly a great deal to do, and a great deal to think about, but she was exhausted. Setting her alarm clock for seven she fell across her bed and sank into a sleep interrupted only spasmodically by small Unterwasser nightmares.

Chapter Eleven

The next morning Mrs. Pollifax breakfasted in the dining room and discovered that at 7:15 she was the only patient to do so. She found no unusual activity on the Reception floor, and the waiter who served her gave no indication that one of his colleagues had met with violent death during the night. When she had finished her coffee she left and descended to the ground floor, ostensibly for a stroll in the garden but actually to see what had been happening in the Unterwasser Massage room.

She discovered to her surprise that nothing appeared to be happening at all. The halls were deserted and the door to the massage room stood open. She moved toward it cautiously and stopped on the threshold. Inside, the pale green tub gleamed spotlessly. Sunlight poured through the frosted windows, striking the faucets and dials with silver and illuminating an immaculate and freshly polished floor. There was not so much as a hint that only hours ago a murder had taken place here, and for just a moment Mrs. Pollifax wondered if she might be losing her mind and had dreamed the murder.

Odd, she thought, frowning, and found it strange that no police were on duty here. Very odd, she mused and went upstairs to see if any police could have taken refuge in the offices behind the switchboard. But the offices were shuttered and locked and although she leaned against the door and listened she could hear no voices. Certainly the discovery of a body in the Unterwasser Massage room was an embarrassment but at the moment the Clinic's discretion seemed excessive and inhuman.

"Madame?" said the porter, peering around the corner at her.

She opened her mouth to speak, closed it and shook her head. It was nearly eight o'clock; she went out to find Robin in the turnaround.

Nothing was said as Robin backed his car and drove it up the narrow entrance to the Clinic and along the ravine. Emerging from the woods into bright sunlight he maneuvered his dark blue Mercedes through the streets of the village and headed it down the mountain toward Villeneuve.

"This is extremely kind of you," Mrs. Pollifax said at last.

As if a few hours had never intervened he said harshly, "All right, whose blood was it?"

She had been expecting the question; it had stood like a wall between them ever since she had stepped into the car. "The waiter, Marcel's," she told him quietly.

Looking appalled, Robin braked the car and drew it to a stop by the side of the road. "Hurt or dead?"

"Dead."

"Good God, do you mean murdered?"

She studied his face and nodded. "Yes, in the Unterwasser Massage room, in the tub. Did you know him, Robin?"

"Damned right I knew Marcel, he waited on my table and we had a bet on today's French bicycle race." He sat staring at her incredulously. "You found him there dead and—Was that all, or was there really someone else down there?"

Remembering, she shivered. "As I went into the Unterwasser Massage room by one door someone was just leaving by the opposite door. I almost called out, but then I saw Marcel lying there in the tub, all bloody and—" Her voice broke and she steadied it. "Yes, there was someone else down there, and someone very curious about me."

"His murderer?"

"I think so, yes."

"Good God, were you seen?"

She shook her head. "I'm quite sure I wasn't." She added wryly, "You see, I'd been reconnoitering the basement just as you've been reconnoitering the roofs. I knew where the fuseboxes were and that, I suppose, is what saved me."

He slowly shook his head. "That was cutting it a bit thin. Good God! But look here, why on earth Marcel? Why would anyone go after a perfectly innocent waiter—" A thought struck him and his eyes narrowed. "Or wasn't he a perfectly innocent waiter?"

"Actually he wasn't," she admitted. "He was an Interpol man looking for the same thing I am. Oddly enough you seemed to be his chief suspect."

Robin whistled through his teeth. "Good Lord, I hope you told him—no, I hope you didn't."

"I was going to tell him last night except—except—"

"Yes, *except,*" he filled in grimly. "Well, at least they didn't send you here alone, which lifts my respect for your superiors a notch. Look here, I told you before if there's anything I can do to help—"

"You're helping now, Robin, and I appreciate it."

"You mean by taking you to the telegraph office." He nodded and eased the car out into traffic again. "This cable you're sending is for Hafez's grandmother, of course?"

She smiled. "How wasted you are on petty crime, Robin. Yes, it's for Madame Parviz. Would it be against your scruples to help me do some balcony spying on room 150 when it's dark tonight?"

"Against my scruples!" He laughed. "Bless you for being so delicate about it, my dear Mrs. P., I'd be delighted to do some spying with you. What exactly did you find in room 150 last night?"

"On the surface, nothing," she said soberly.

"Ah, but under the surface?"

"A great many undercurrents." She was silent, staring ahead of her as they entered Montreux and Robin threaded the car through quiet streets. "Madame Parviz looked very ill and she was still quite weak. She asked me to send a cable for her announcing their safe arrival, to a man with the same name in Zabya. A General Parviz."

"That sounds normal enough."

She nodded. "Yes, until one remembers that Hafez and his grandmother have been at the Clinic for a week, and that she insisted the cable *not* be sent from the Clinic. There were only the three of us in the room but someone was asleep in the adjoining one—again very normal considering the hour—but when the sound of a snore was heard through the walls both Madame Parviz and Hafez looked alarmed. There was a kind of—of hushed urgency about our meeting."

"You mean you had the impression no one must know you were there?"

"Exactly. I'm trying to be very clear in my thinking," she told him earnestly. "Hafez has been frightened ever since I first met him, and I've not wanted to exaggerate or be melodramatic but I've felt he was trying to tell me something. Not consciously, you understand, but with every gesture and every expression. He's an unusually intelligent child, and I think he's been trying desperately to—"

When she faltered Robin gave her a quick glance. "To what?"

"To cope," she said softly. "Cope with something quite beyond him. I've been getting little messages consistently, without a word spoken. It's what I've felt from the beginning." She hesitated, feeling for words. "Everything matters terribly to children, you know, they're fresh and unformed, but of course they can exaggerate, too, so I had to be sure. Now I'm finally beginning to understand."

He stopped the car and backed it into a parking space and Mrs. Pollifax saw that across the street a large building bore the sign PTT. "Understand what?" asked Robin, turning off the ignition.

"I think I'd better send the cable first," she said. "It's half-past eight?"

"Just."

Mrs. Pollifax nodded and climbed out of the car and crossed the street. Entering the echoing, cavernous room she went to the telegraph window and copied out Madame Parviz's message, hesitating only when she reached the space for the sender's name. Since privacy seemed to matter very much to Madame Parviz she stood a moment, reflecting, pencil in hand. Inspiration arrived at last and feeling quite resourceful at keeping the Clinic out of it she wrote the name of William Carstairs, The Legal Building, Baltimore, Maryland. With that accomplished she paid for it and left.

"You were beginning to understand something," said Robin when she rejoined him, "and I hope you're not going to leave me hanging in midair."

"Oh, that," she said. "Yes, I'm beginning to understand why it's been impossible for Hafez to tell me anything. He *can't*. I'm also beginning to understand to what lengths he went to arrange my visit last night with his grandmother. It wasn't easy."

Robin looked startled. "You're implying a great deal wrong indeed."

"Yes, I am. Can we go back now? I want to sit in the garden and think, preferably over a pot of very hot coffee."

He started up the car. "I've nothing against thinking. I don't suppose I should ask about what in particular?"

"About thirteen tablets of aspirin, and what I report at ten o'clock tonight when I make my rather primitive contact with Interpol, about Marcel's death and what I tell the police when they make their inquiries."

"Which explains everything and nothing but I've already learned enough to scare the hell out of me. I wish it would scare the hell out of you," he said with a sidelong glance at her face. "I think I'm going to keep a very close eye on you today if you don't mind."

"I don't mind at all," said Mrs. Pollifax imperturbably.

As they drove into the entrance road of the Clinic and past the greenhouse Mrs. Pollifax saw a man in a green apron sweeping the steps, and Hafez seated on the top stair with his chin in his hand, the very same scene that had met her glance when she arrived on Friday. Now it was Sunday and Marcel was dead. She thought it would have been very convenient on Friday to have been clairvoyant and to have seen the seeds of destruction waiting here for catalyzation. The workings of fate always struck her with awe, for on these small assignments she inevitably arrived just in time to meet the effect of causes sown recklessly long ago. Marcel had been sent here, and had died, and his death in turn was setting new influences in motion. Where it would lead she couldn't guess but she knew that at some point influences and coincidences would converge. Nothing, she felt, happened purely by accident; it was an unraveling process.

As she walked toward the door Hafez stood up, eyes anxious and inquiring. "It's been taken care of," she told him in a low voice.

"Oh, thank you, madame," he gasped. His hand reached out to touch her arm, trembled there a moment, and then he turned and ran off up the stairs.

"Where are you going now?" Robin demanded.

Amused, she said, "To my room first, to order some coffee for the garden and to put away my sweater, and then—"

"Okay," he said hastily, "I'll see you later."

He too went up the stairs but Mrs. Pollifax lingered, her glance moving over the head of the concierge to the office behind him. It was still empty. There were no secretaries, no directors, no police in plainclothes in consultation and she found herself uneasy.

"Madam is looking for someone?" asked the head concierge.

She shook her head.

"Perhaps madam would like a copy of yesterday's *Herald Tribune*," he suggested. "We were sent an extra paper."

She thanked him, tucked it under her arm and went upstairs. As she changed into a cooler dress she briefly scanned the front page of the *Tribune*. The Common Market had agreed upon new farm tariffs. The price of silver had hit an all-time high. A minor official had been assassinated in Syria. She turned a page and found a photograph of King Jarroud of Zabya, and because this was Hafez's king she ran her eyes down the column quickly while she zipped up her dress. On Tuesday the King was celebrating his fortieth birthday and his tenth year in power . . . A parade, lunch in the palace beside the beautiful

Arabian Nights pool, America's vice-president among the long list of luminaries invited to the daylong festivity . . . Jarroud an extremely popular monarch with the people but not without his enemies, mainly among those of the upper class who distrusted his sweeping reforms . . . Had already done much to narrow the huge gap between rich and poor . . . Illiteracy rate reduced from 89 percent to 21 percent after ten years of compulsory schooling, 80 percent of the people now owned some land . . . the country 60 percent desert.

"Mmm," she murmured, postponing details until later, and moved to the telephone to order coffee sent to the garden. Really, this life of luxury was infectious and she wondered how she would ever adjust again to washing dishes.

Fifteen minutes later she descended to the ground floor and again strolled past the Unterwasser Massage room, hesitating only a moment when she found it still deserted. She understood very clearly that a murder could empty the rooms of any establishment in a matter of hours but it was unbelievable to her that no traces remained of an event that must have shaken the Clinic to its foundations. Did a man's life count for so little these days?

She pulled a chaise longue into the sun and lay down, recalling Marcel's dancing blue eyes and his mock, comic gestures. When death came to the general, she thought, it would be a completion, it would be the closing of a circle on a fulfilled life but there were the other deaths, the ones that did violence to meaning by their abrupt and senseless interruption of life, and it was these deaths she mourned in particular. Why had it been necessary to sentence Marcel to death? What had he done? Most vital of all, *what had he known?*

The general was being helped into a chair by the nurse. The Palisburys, she noticed, had already arrived and were establishing themselves under the poplar tree. The man in the wheelchair, Ibrahim Sabry, sat beside a table with a pink umbrella and read a thick newspaper. The same tableau was arranging itself but Marcel was missing. Fraser, too, had been snatched away from this tranquil garden scene and no one had missed him, just as few people would notice Marcel's absence.

And someone among these people was a murderer . . . someone here *knew*.

The glass doors swung open and a white-jacketed waiter came out bearing a tray. Seeing her he crossed the lawn toward her, picking up a small table as he came. *"Bon jour*, madame—your coffee!"* he said.

Marcel had brought her tea yesterday with just such a flourish but now he was dead and in his murder lay the answer to a good many things if only she could find the right question to ask. "Thank you," she said absently, and as the waiter left she went back in her thoughts to yesterday. She had hailed Marcel and asked him if he was a good actor. He had taken out his order book while she told him of her anxieties about Madame Parviz. He had not thought highly of them but he had agreed to look into them. And he had told her—just before Robin arrived—that he would have information for her at midnight.

He had been safe at that hour yesterday, she was sure of it.

She thought, Whatever Marcel did after I saw him in the afternoon must have taken him closer to something, turned him in a new and different direction, toward territory someone had marked off as forbidden. The question was, what had Marcel done between half-past three in the afternoon and midnight, when he was killed? Whatever Marcel had discovered she must discover, too.

"I hate to disturb your thinking processes," said Robin, strolling up behind her, "but I've been looking for Court and I can't find her anywhere. Has she passed this way?"

"My thinking processes are behaving very poorly at the moment," she said, "and no, I've not seen her. Would you care for a cup of coffee?"

"I'd love one if you have a spare." He pulled up a chair and sat down. "Look here, shouldn't there be an air of repressed alarm here today, a few damp eyes, a policeman or two? I can't help noticing that business is very much as usual."

"I've noticed it, too," she said, nodding. "It bothers me."

"Yes, I thought it might. Of course things are very different for the rich, you know. They've got to be protected and they pay liberally for that when they come here. They're not supposed to be exposed to anything viler than an enema. It makes life in such a place a complete conspiracy." He grinned cheer-fully. "At the casinos they handle it very tidily, you know. A chap blows out his brains after losing his last shilling and three minutes later you can't even find traces of the blood. I should resent that very much if it were I, and come back at once to haunt them."

"You're being abominably flippant and you're not cheering me up at all," she told him.

"Well, then, I wish you'd—oops!" he said in a startled voice and ducked his head under the table.

Mrs. Pollifax looked behind her to see what had surprised him and saw walking across the lawn one of the handsomest men she had ever seen, which startled her, too, if for different reasons. *Gilbert Roland,* she thought, and then chided herself for such sentimental nonsense. Ibrahim Sabry was looking up from his newspaper and smiling—yes, the stranger was head-ing for Sabry—but everyone in the garden was watching as well. The man was wearing a dark pin-striped business suit but this scarcely succeeded in scaling him down to life size. He was a figure out of an epic, tall, lean, proud, a beak of a nose set in a swarthy face, his eyes gleaming under straight quizzi-cal brows, his smile a flash of white in his dark face. "Who," said Mrs. Pollifax with feeling, "is *that!*"

Robin slid back into his chair looking sheepish but she no-ticed that he moved his chair so that he could sit with his back to the newcomer. She, on the other hand, moved her chair so that she could watch the stranger shake hands with Sabry.

"Reflex action—sorry about that," confessed Robin. "I for-get that people I've lifted a few jewels from really have no idea I'm the culprit. That's Yazdan Kashan. Good Lord, I'd forgot-ten it's Sunday—this is Visiting Day."

"And you robbed that man?" said Mrs. Pollifax incredu-lously. "He looks extremely difficult to take anything from. Should I know who he is?"

"Well, I don't want you fainting, my dear Mrs. P., but he's a sheik, a bona-fide sheik."

"Ah," she said with pleasure, "they really do exist then! But no longer, I take it, on the desert?"

Robin grinned. "Not when they belong to one of the world's

richest families, although I think he still spends a good bit of the year with his people. But not in a tent. Kashan's at least a generation away from all that, it was his grandfather who rode camels with the wind. Kashan's father discovered he was encamped on some of the world's richest oil fields in the Middle East, and Yazdan's the new breed. Went to Oxford, as a matter of fact, and then became a playboy and left jewels lying around carelessly—at least he was damned careless in Paris when I ran into him in '65."

"And now?"

"Now he's nearly forty and I hear he's a nut on religion and doesn't leave jewelry around. He reads the Koran instead."

"He's not reading it now," pointed out Mrs. Pollifax. "He's come to Montbrison to visit Mr. Sabry. What country is Mr. Kashan from?"

Robin gave her a quick glance. "Frankly I haven't the foggiest, I'm afraid all those deserts are one big blur to me." He sighed. "I suppose I should feel sentimental about the chap— he was my first really big job and it went off like peaches and cream and gave me no end of confidence."

"Which deserted you rather abruptly a minute ago," pointed out Mrs. Pollifax.

"Well, I told you it was my first major job; I had to remind myself for months afterward that he could afford the loss." He added indignantly, "I hope you don't think I became a criminal *easily*."

"Not at all," she murmured, "but there must be some way to make an honest man of you."

Hafez walked slowly across the lawn toward them and when he reached them twined one arm around Mrs. Pollifax's chair and hung on it. "There's going to be Wiener Schnitzel for lunch," he confided. He addressed this information to Mrs. Pollifax but his gaze rested on the two men under the pink lawn umbrella.

"Do you know Mr. Sabry, the man in the wheelchair, Hafez?" she asked, watching his face.

"Yes, madame, he has the room across the hall from me."

"But did you know him before you came to the Clinic?"

He shook his head. "No, madame."

She hesitated and then she added, "And Mr. Kashan, the man visiting him, do you know him?"

Hafez's eyes blazed before he dropped his gaze to the ground. "I know him," he said tonelessly.

"Is he from Zabya then?"

"Yes, madame." He lifted expressionless eyes and added, "I will go to lunch now, I think. *Bon jour.*"

Robin watched him leave and then lifted an eyebrow at her. "I must say that was a strange bit of dialogue. You sounded rather like the Inquisition."

"And Hafez like a robot," she said thoughtfully, "which means, I think, that we just had a fairly important conversation."

Chapter Twelve

The sheik lunched with Ibrahim Sabry in the dining room. Their heads remained close together at the table as they engaged in energetic conversation, frequently with gestures, but all of it too muted for Mrs. Pollifax to overhear. Court arrived a few minutes after Mrs. Pollifax, calling breathlessly across the tables, "I've been playing the organ again. Will you be in the garden this afternoon?"

Mrs. Pollifax nodded; she had no intention of being anywhere else. For the genuine convalescent there was the gift of shapeless time: naps, sunbath, small walks, massages, but she could scarcely call herself convalescent and time was working against her.

It was, therefore, in the garden that Court found her after lunch. "I want to talk to you," she said, striding toward her across the lawn. "I have to talk to you. Do you mind awfully?"

Mrs. Pollifax had been watching Sheik Kashan wheel Sabry into the gazebo; the wheelchair was barely narrow enough to fit through the door so that for a moment the structure shuddered threateningly. It was not the sturdiest of gazebos, anyway, being fashioned entirely of bamboo. Now Sabry was safely within, and the Sheik had seated himself at the round table inside and was pulling papers from an attaché case.

She turned her attention to Court just as the girl slipped into a chair beside her. "I'm available," she told her, smiling.

Court looked close to tears. "I came back from the village
this morning," she said, her voice trembling, "and I packed my
suitcase and then after lunch I went up and unpacked it
again."

"For myself I'm not that fond of packing," put in Mrs. Pollifax mildly, "but I daresay it's a form of exercise."

Court grudgingly laughed. "I'm sounding the idiot, of
course." She pulled a handkerchief from her purse and blew
her nose. "I thought perhaps if I talked to you—I simply don't
know what to do, I ought to leave, I know it, but—"

Mrs. Pollifax said gently, "Perhaps if you'd tell me just
what seems to be the matter—"

"Oh," said the girl angrily, "I don't want to fall in love
again, that's what's the matter. And of all people with *him*."

"Ah," said Mrs. Pollifax, enlightened at last. "We're talking
about Robin. Are you about to fall in love with Robin?"

"Love," said the girl scornfully. "And he's so much like
Eric." She shivered. "I can't bear that."

Mrs. Pollifax understood that there was going to be nothing
rational about this conversation and adjusted herself to the
fact. "Eric," she said pointedly.

Court's chin went up. "I *could* say that Eric abandoned me
in every capital in Europe. As a matter of fact I *will* say it
because it's what he did. I've been so careful," she explained,
"I've gone to such lengths to avoid entanglements. I've dated
only simpletons, frauds and ridiculous creatures I couldn't
possibly care about, and then I come here and—" She turned to
Mrs. Pollifax angrily. "Last summer there wasn't anyone here
under forty. Not a soul. And this summer—I'm disintegrat-
ing," she wailed. "I'm usually so poised, so calm, so—so—"

"Controlled?" suggested Mrs. Pollifax, handing her a fresh
handkerchief. "You haven't told me who Eric is, by the way."

"My husband," said Court, blowing her nose again. "Or
was," she added, wiping her eyes. "I married him when I was
eighteen and we were divorced when I was twenty and that's
eight years ago. Mrs. Pollifax, I do want you to know I had no
intention of crying."

Mrs. Pollifax nodded. "One seldom does. So you were married very young, and it wasn't a happy marriage, and now Robin reminds you of Eric?"

She shivered. "The pattern's terrifyingly similar. Robin's so *attractive*, and there's all that charm and he doesn't work for a living, which means no character at all. What he does have is too much money and too much experience—he's been everywhere, done everything, and known everybody—and that's just how it was with Eric. They're both playboys. I hate love," she announced, and after a second's pause added ruefully, "it *hurts*."

Mrs. Pollifax smiled. "I daresay you've gotten the worst of it out of your system now and we can talk. But really love has nothing to do with hurt, you know, it's we who supply the wounds. Which—if I may risk offending you—seems to be just what you're doing now."

"Given the circumstances, how?" demanded Court.

Mrs. Pollifax said dreamily, "I've often thought the Buddhists are quite right, you know, when they say the root of all suffering is desire. We're so full of greed, wanting this or that— to love or to escape love, to be this or be that, to possess this or that. What do you think you'll accomplish by packing your suitcase and bolting?"

"I won't be hurt."

Mrs. Pollifax smiled. "I wonder if you can be sure of that. Of course you know very little about Robin but I wonder if you can be absolutely certain he's just like Eric. When you find out more about him there may be a few—well, surprises," she said, honestly enough. "For that matter you may not fall in love with him at all. Whatever makes you sure the future will be exactly like the past?"

"I don't know." Court shivered. "I don't know. But he— well, you see, he kissed me last evening in the library, while the film was being shown—"

"Ah," said Mrs. Pollifax, nodding.

"And—" She lifted her chin angrily. "And I thought—all right, I'll say it—I thought how wonderful it would be to marry and—and even have children. Which I can assure you was the furthest thing from my mind when I came here."

"Of course if you run away," pointed out Mrs. Pollifax, "you can't possibly have a baby."

"No," said Court miserably.

Mrs. Pollifax patted her affectionately on the arm. "What you need, I think, is a little bit of Zen."

"I beg your pardon?"

Mrs. Pollifax nodded. "Zen—tremendously refreshing. There's a great deal to be said for letting life just happen."

"Without *control*?"

"That's it, you see—without control."

"But—but that's *frightening*!" cried Court.

Mrs. Pollifax laughed. "On the contrary, it's much less painful than fighting every step of the way, and so much more delightful than trying to arrange life like a table setting, which one can never do, anyway. Really it's quite exciting to see what will happen along next," she added.

"At your age," said Court cautiously, "there are still surprises?"

Mrs. Pollifax beamed at her forgivingly. "Frequently, I can assure you, some pleasant and a few not at all pleasant, but of course one can't have the one without the other. It's impossible."

"Oh," said Court.

From the path behind them Robin called, "So there you are! I thought my two favorite ladies had vanished into thin air." He pulled up a chair and smiled at Court. "Where have you been all day?"

Mrs. Pollifax let Court reply while she glanced casually across the garden to the gazebo. The sheik had returned his papers to the attaché case and was standing as he talked to Sabry, delivering what looked to be an impassioned speech. Certainly Sabry was receiving it without his customary passiveness; his eyes gleamed and he looked almost exalted, yet even exaltation could not quite obscure the insensitivity of his face. How empty his eyes were, she thought idly; if he were not in a wheelchair, if he were not welded to it and helpless . . . if he were not confined . . . And suddenly the general's words yesterday slipped into her mind: *I have found this is not true of the professional killer who murders more than once, and in cold blood. It is a curious fact that it shows in the eyes, which I believe the poets call the windows of the soul. I have found the eyes of the habitual murderer to be completely empty. An interesting revenge by Nature, is it not?*

Sabry's eyes were empty, like stones.

Mrs. Pollifax suddenly sat upright in amazement, excited and a little breathless as she considered that wheelchair and the illusion it gave of immobility. If Sabry were not in that wheelchair . . . She thought in astonishment, "It's possible, it's terribly possible. He was even here when Fraser was here, Marcel said so. But how shocking that it's only just occurred to me." Doubt assailed her and she shook her head. "No, no, impossible—purest imagination," she told herself, but what a diabolically clever disguise it could be, she thought, and realized that even now she found it difficult, almost inhuman, to doubt a wheelchair.

Court and Robin were staring at her in surprise. "What on earth are you thinking?" demanded Robin. "You look as if you've just seen a ghost."

"Perhaps I have," she said, remembering the darkened hall last night, the sound of steps, and of heavy breathing in the stillness. "I was wondering what keeps Mr. Sabry in a wheelchair. What his particular illness might be."

Court looked taken aback but Robin's glance was thoughtful. "I see," he said softly. "Like Frankenstein you think he may—walk at night?"

"This is a day for wondering," she said.

"I heard it was multiple sclerosis," volunteered Court. "He came soon after I did, over two weeks ago. He takes whirlpool baths."

"Polio and strokes and broken limbs leave marks for doctors to see," mused Mrs. Pollifax, "but multiple sclerosis is a very slow disease, isn't it?" It made a good cover story. She was remembering Marcel's last words: *I will investigate thoroughly, I promise you,* and a picture came to her mind of Marcel entering Sabry's room, perhaps without knocking . . . Her eyes returned to the gazebo which was once again threatening to collapse as the sheik pushed Sabry's wheelchair through the arch. They moved to the shade of the poplar and a formal exchange of gestures took place, rather like two Frenchmen kissing and embracing. As he walked away the sheik turned and called over his shoulder, "I'll be back at six o'clock. Until then, *bkhatirrkoom.*" Smiling with the air of a man with many things to do, he walked quickly through the glass doors and vanished, leaving Sabry idle with a sheaf of papers in his lap. He began to sort and then to read them.

"What do you think?" asked Robin, watching her face.

"I think it's time I find out." She stood up. "Court, may I borrow Robin for a few minutes?"

"Of course," Court said, looking baffled.

Robin followed her across the grass to the ground-floor entrance. Inside the door she turned to face him. "I want to get into Ibrahim Sabry's room and search it, Robin. Can you unlock his door for me?"

He glanced quickly out into the garden at Sabry. "That's a damned fool idea."

She tapped her foot impatiently. "There may not be another chance, Robin, it's a warm afternoon, it's nearing tea time and he looks settled under the tree. I want to find out if he's really an invalid. There has to be something, some hint—a pair of shoes with worn heels, a snapshot, even blood on his clothes if he was downstairs last night. Robin, do hurry!"

"All right," he said with a sigh. "Take the elevator, I'll meet you." He ran up the stairs two at a time and Mrs. Pollifax entered the elevator. At her floor she stepped out to wait, and after several minutes had ticked past Robin rejoined her. "I'm protesting this," he said angrily, "and I insist upon going in with you."

She said flatly, "Absolutely not. If anything happens—if he has hairy monsters waiting in his room to devour people— then you're the only one who knows what I've been up to."

His mouth tightened. "The balcony then. I'll stand on his balcony and not even breathe until you've left. For God's sake, woman, I can't chat amiably in the garden when I know you're in here. You're an amateur at this!"

She looked at him with exasperation but it was his skill that would unlock the door for her, after all. "All right," she said, "the balcony then," and led the way down the hall. Robin bent over the lock of number 153, the door opened and they entered Sabry's room.

"Now please—out of sight," she urged.

He moved across the room, stopping only to unlock the two doors of the huge wardrobe, which was fortuitous because they had not occurred to her at all. Blowing a kiss he slipped through the balcony door and was gone.

There was silence, and Mrs. Pollifax looked around her. This room was darker than hers because it faced the mountain that hung over the Clinic but otherwise it was identical to her own. She hoped very much that it would yield something to support her suspicions. Going first to the desk she unearthed a number of papers, all of them written in Arabic. There were no snapshots. She turned to the right-hand side of the wardrobe that Robin had so thoughtfully unlocked for her and went through the five suits hanging there but she found no traces of blood on his clothes, nor were there any shoes in this side of the wardrobe. There was a suitcase, however, and Mrs. Pollifax removed it and carried it to the bed. It was a relatively small suitcase, 30″ in size and weighing roughly twenty pounds, she judged. An identification tag dangled from its handle and picking it up she saw to her surprise that it was not Sabry's suitcase. It belonged to the sheik, who must have brought it with him today. The tag read YAZDAN IBN KASHAN, and, underneath, a temporary address had been scribbled in pencil: *Suite 1-A, Hotel Montreux-Palace, Montreux, Suisse.* That was where he was spending the night, then, and at six o'clock he would come back and pick up the suitcase. She leaned over the lock but it had been made doubly secure by the addition of two small brass padlocks, which she found curious. She half-turned toward the balcony and then reminded herself of Sabry. The suitcase could wait. Leaving it on the bed she returned to the closet to open and search the left side. She turned the knob, tugged and drew the door open.

Marcel's body, the upper half wrapped in glistening transparent plastic, occupied the entire half of the wardrobe, his spine curled into the foetal position, his head turned to one side, his vacant dead eyes staring straight into hers.

Mrs. Pollifax screamed.

She could not remember screaming before in her life. It was involuntary, an outraged protest, a reply to those staring, sightless eyes and to the shocked realization that his body had never been discovered at all. In the charged silence that followed her scream she heard the handle to the balcony door turn and then she heard the sound of running feet out in the hall and the door to the hall was thrown open. Sabry stood gaping at her. There was no sign of his wheelchair.

His glance moved from the suitcase on the bed to the opened door of the closet and his pale face turned scarlet. With three long strides he crossed the room, lifted his hand and struck her across the cheek. "Fool!" he gasped. "Idiot! Imbecile! Who are you?"

Mrs. Pollifax wordlessly shook her head.

He drew a gun from his pocket and tested its weight in one hand, his eyes malevolent, and then without another word he stalked out of the room across the hall and knocked with the gun at room 154. One of Madame Parviz's white-jacketed attendants answered the knock and Sabry gestured mutely at Mrs. Pollifax standing in his room. The man's eyes widened and he sucked in his breath with a hiss. Behind him Hafez appeared, and then the second attendant, both trying to look past Sabry.

Mrs. Pollifax had begun edging toward the hall when Hafez saw her. His mouth dropped open in astonishment. "Madame!" he cried in a shocked voice. "Oh, *madame!*" Darting under Sabry's arm he ran arcoss the hall and flung his arms around her protectively.

"You know her!" accused Sabry, following.

"She is my friend Madame Pollifax," cried Hafez. "Don't you dare touch her, don't you dare!"

Sabry viciously slapped him. "You told her!"

The mark of the blow was livid on Hafez's cheek. "I did not," he gasped. "I did *not*. Monsieur, I beg of you. You think I risk Grandmama's life?"

Mrs. Pollifax stood listening and watching in fascinated horror. She made no move to speak or to act; a knot had just been untied and an unraveling had begun.

Sabry moved to the wardrobe and carefully locked both

doors again. "She has seen what is inside," he told them. "We must get her out of here."

"Injection?"

"No, no, too dangerous at this hour." He realized he was speaking in English and began to issue orders in Arabic. One attendant hurried down the hall and returned pushing Sabry's wheelchair, which he must have abandoned down the hall at the sound of her scream. To the second man, reverting to English, he said, "Get the car, Munir." To Munir's question in Arabic he said with a shake of his head, "No, no, we do nothing until we speak with Yazdan."

"What does he mean, the car?" whispered Mrs. Pollifax to Hafez.

His hand tightened convulsively in hers. "They are going to take you to the sheik, who left by car for Montreux fifteen minutes ago. They will ask him what to do about you. Madame, you are in great trouble."

"Yes," she agreed, nodding, but on the other hand she knew it was the price she had to pay for watching the pieces of the puzzle rearrange themselves.

Munir had vanished to get the car. She saw the second attendant emerge from Hafez's room wearing a sports jacket and slipping a gun into his pocket. Sabry sat down in the wheelchair and pointed to the suitcase lying on the bed. "Bring it to me, Fouad—place it on my lap with a blanket to cover it. Quickly! It's not to be left here again." To Mrs. Pollifax he said grimly, "You will be leaving the Clinic now for a pleasant little Sunday drive. The boy will go, too. You will walk quietly beside my wheelchair, looking as if you are pleased. If you make a move, if you call out, speak or try to signal anyone the boy will pay with his life, do you understand?" His eyes raked her face with a hatred that had all the impact of a blow.

"I understand," she said quietly. There was no need to speculate any longer about evil, she had just met with it, felt it, and it shook her.

"And you, Hafez," he continued softly, "you will recall your own situation and see that you behave. Serafina will remain with your grandmother. It needs only a telephone call—"

"I know," Hafez said in a strangled voice.

"Show them your gun, Fouad." He nodded as Fouad brought it from his pocket, displayed it and returned it to his pocket. "Good. We will go." His voice was contemptuous.

And so they began their exodus down the long, carpeted hall, a small, tightly knit group, a man in a wheelchair with a woman on one side, a boy on the other and an attendant behind; a kind of obscene Family Portrait for Visitors' Day, thought Mrs. Pollifax, and began to wonder what could be done. Nothing for the moment, she realized sadly. There was Robin. She was certain that he was safe but she had no idea how much he could have overheard from the balcony. Certainly he had heard her scream for she recalled the balcony door opening but then it had quickly closed, which—under the circumstances—had saved him. Had he heard the footsteps running in the hall? If he had heard that much then he could have heard everything, and that was hopeful.

The elevator reached the Reception floor and the doors slid open. Sabry nodded to the head concierge behind the counter, they moved to the huge main door and Fouad neatly maneuvered the wheelchair down the steps. Just out of sight beyond the entrance Munir sat at the wheel of a long black limousine with the motor running. *I ought to scream*, thought Mrs. Pollifax, but she was paralyzed by the knowledge of how casually Sabry killed; he would think so little of a child's life or hers. Sabry issued more orders in Arabic and after a swift glance around him he climbed out of the wheelchair to take Munir's place at the wheel while Fouad folded up the chair and placed it in the trunk. The other attendant pushed Mrs. Pollifax and Hafez into the rear, where Fouad joined them on a jump seat, his gun out of his pocket now and leveled at Hafez.

Slowly the car moved up the entrance drive past the greenhouse, entered the main road through the woods and headed toward the village. Mrs. Pollifax exchanged a glance with Hafez and tried to give him a reassuring smile that failed. She was wondering what Robin *could* do. She was realizing that the most obvious course, calling the police, would take an incredible amount of time and include complications and explanations beyond belief, and neither she nor Hafez had time.

She began instead to think of what *she* could do, which was
nothing for the moment, but when they reached Montreux,
and the Hotel Montreux-Palace, she thought there might be
possibilities if she kept her wits about her. She could not
imagine another Family Scene moving through another lobby.
Someone would be sent up to Suite 1-A—Munir or Fouad, she
presumed—to summon the sheik downstairs. That would re-
duce their captors by two, and no one in the group realized
that she knew karate. If she and Hafez acted together they
might overpower the remaining two men and escape. But not
without the suitcase, thought Mrs. Pollifax; she was growing
very interested in a suitcase with two extra locks that could
not be left behind.

"Two quick karate chops to disable them," she said to herself. "Hafez open the car doors and I snatch the suitcase—"
She fastened her gaze on the back of Sabry's neck and plotted
the precise route of her karate strike while she tried not to
think what would happen if she failed.

They reached Villeneuve and turned to the right along the
waterfront, heading for Montreux. On their left Lake Geneva
looked placid and washed of color in the late afternoon sun.
Returning her glance to the back of Sabry's neck she inadver-
tently caught his eye in the rear-view mirror and hastily
looked away, her glance falling to the mirror attached to the
side of the car. In it, to her astonishment, she saw the reflec-
tion of a dark blue Mercedes convertible following behind
them.

A dark blue Mercedes convertible . . .

Her heart began to beat faster. There was suddenly nowhere
for her eyes to safely rest and she began to study the floor of
the car and then the gun in Fouad's lap, snatching quick fur-
tive glances into the mirror before dropping her eyes. It was
impossible to see the driver of the Mercedes, or to read its
license plate. She told herself there must be thousands of dark
blue Mercedes cars in Switzerland, and dozens of them on this
shore of the lake. On the other hand, this car was definitely
dark blue and it was allowing other cars to pass while it remained at exactly the same distance behind them.

It was a wide road, with increasing traffic. Glancing past

Sabry she saw a castle up ahead on the other side of the road, and for a moment her attention was pleasantly distracted by the sight of turrets, ancient stone walls and pointed clay tile roofs. She was staring at it when Fouad suddenly cried, *"Hasib! Ookuff!"*

Mrs. Pollifax turned her head and saw a flash of dark blue passing on their left. She caught a quick glimpse of a familiar profile—it was Robin—and saw his car surge ahead of the limousine. What followed happened all at once: the dark blue Mercedes cleared their car and slowed, Sabry leaned on his horn and cursed, the Mercedes braked and jerked to a stop and Sabry's car rammed it from behind with a crash and a grinding of metal.

Robin had just sacrificed the rear of his Mercedes convertible. For him, she thought, there could be no greater sacrifice.

Furiously Sabry tried to start up the limousine again but there were only ugly rattling noises. "Out!" he shouted. *"Ukhruj!"*

Doors opened and Mrs. Pollifax and Hafez were hustled outside to stand under the rock wall that rose almost perpendicular to that side of the road. Fouad's gun prodded her in the back. Mrs. Pollifax saw that the accident occupied most of the westbound lane to Montreux and that cars were coming to a standstill behind them. On the eastbound side the traffic moving toward Villeneuve was slowing to watch. The castle stood across the highway and an exodus had begun from the gates; several more hardy souls had already hurried to the center of the highway. Framed behind them stood a modest sign identifying the castle as the Castle de Chillon, open for tourists from 9 to 5.

Sabry cursed viciously. Turning to Fouad he snarled, "Get them out of here. Take them into the Castle—quickly, before a crowd gathers. Take this, too," he said, thrusting the suitcase at Fouad. "Come back in forty-five minutes. Hurry!"

For just a moment Mrs. Pollifax weighed the possibilities of running, but although Fouad's gun had been pocketed he held Hafez tightly by the arm. She and Hafez were thrust around the back of the car and out into the road where Robin and Sabry were confronting each other in fury. "You're damned right I cut you off!" she heard Robin shout. "How could I do anything else when you swerved out and accelerated at the same time? Somebody call the police!" he called across the road. *"Gendarmes! Polizei!"*

Good thinking, she thought.

Fouad hurried them across the highway, up the graveled walk and over a wooden bridge to the ticket booth where he shoved coins across the counter and held up three fingers. Just as the sound of a police siren rent the air they walked through the huge ancient gate and into an open, cobbled courtyard.

Chapter Thirteen

The rock on which Chillon stands," said the guide, "was occupied by men of the Bronze Age and later by the Romans. The ancient road from Italy over Great St. Bernard was widened at the beginning of the eighteenth century. Chillon was built to guard the narrow defile between the lake and the mountains and to collect taxes on all merchandise that passed."

"I hope there are dungeons," said Hafez.

They stood in the courtyard at the edge of a tour group, and at Hafez's words Mrs. Pollifax turned to look at Fouad. Her impression was that he was angry and bored at the necessity of guarding a boy and an old woman. He gripped the suitcase with one hand while his right hand remained in his pocket curled around the butt of the gun but he looked cross and shifted frequently from one foot to the other.

"*Are* there dungeons?" Hafez asked Fouad.

With a martyred air Fouad handed each of them the printed map and leaflet that had been distributed at the gate without cost. She could sympathize with his predicament; he had hoped they might enter and sit somewhere for forty-five minutes, but it was Sunday, and the few benches in the courtyard were filled with people. There could be no entrusting Hafez to so intimate and lively a scene. It was necessary to keep them separated from the tourists and he had shrewdly guessed that the only way to accomplish this was to join the tourists. They were to remain just behind the tour group and speak to no one, he had told Hafez, and Hafez had obligingly translated his words to Mrs. Pollifax.

"There *are* dungeons," said Hafez, consulting the diagram, "but not yet. Not until we finish with the underground vaults." He lifted innocent eyes to Mrs. Pollifax. "Isn't it tremendous that there are dungeons?"

"Tremendous," she said gravely and wondered if he was receiving signals from her as clearly as she was receiving them from him. Yes but *wait*, she tried to tell him with her eyes.

They passed under the windows of the caretaker's apartments and into the basement chamber of the castle, into a dim and medieval world of vaulted ceilings, ancient pillars and a floor of earth worn smooth by centuries. It was cool and dark in here; an arsenal, Hafez read aloud from his leaflet. The outside walls were striped with loopholes and through them Mrs. Pollifax could look out, almost at water level, and see Lake Geneva stretching flat and pale to the horizon, its waters gently lapping against the walls. "The dungeons are next," Hafez said, ignoring Fouad and speaking directly to her.

"Bonivard's Prison," said the guide in English after completing his first recitation in French.

"Dungeons," added Hafez triumphantly.

"This room dates from before the thirteenth century, when it was transformed and vaulted. It is here, in the fourteenth century, that Bonivard, Prior of St. Victor's in Geneva, remained chained to this fifth pillar for four years."

"Four years!" A murmur of incredulity swept through the group but Fouad took this moment to yawn. The pocket of his thin sports jacket sagged with the weight of the gun but his hand remained welded to it. The yawn was deceptive, she thought, stealing a quick glance at his face. He was stolid and gave every evidence of stupidity but he would be intelligent about his job, which was all that interested him. His dark eyes were alert and aware of every movement in the room. He knew she was watching him now and he turned and gave her a level, expressionless stare. She smiled vaguely and leaned nearer to hear the guide.

". . . because he was favorable to the Reformation, you
see, which he wished to introduce to Geneva. He was freed in
1536 by the Bernese, and was immortalized by the English
poet Byron, who has scrawled his name on this third pillar."

The group swerved toward the third pillar and Hafez started
to go with them but Fouad reached out and pulled him back.
"La!" he said flatly.

Certainly this was a grim place to spend four years, thought
Mrs. Pollifax: a cold earthen floor, a low ceiling—he couldn't
even have seen the water from the pillar to which he'd been
chained. Recalling the equally grim circumstances that might
await her and Hafez she glanced at her watch: it was 4:25 and
they had been in the castle for twelve minutes. Fouad would
return them to the highway at five o'clock—but that was the
closing hour, she remembered soberly. She glanced at Hafez,
who said quickly, "Next we go through the second courtyard
and then into the Grand Hall of the High Bailiff."

He was offering her possibilities, she realized, but all of
them were limited while they dogged the steps of the tour
group. She knew what Hafez had not yet learned, that groups
were unwieldy, slow to react to sudden jolts and frequently
composed of people who did not appreciate having their peace
disturbed. Fouad already knew this. There was no appeal that
either of them could make to a group. As to separating themselves from it Hafez could outrun Fouad but Mrs. Pollifax
could not. Fouad, for the moment, held all the cards: a gun and
a crowd of tourists.

Hafez was looking disappointed in her. She, on the other
hand, had begun to feel hopeful. A small miracle had occurred,
their trip to a distasteful unknown had been interrupted and
she saw no reason to be led back to Sabry like a lamb to the
slaughter. No rational alternative presented itself but waiting
did not bother her: it would give Fouad more time in which to
grow bored. And so, having a gift for enjoying the moment, she
gave herself over to medieval history and the enchantment of
the castle. And it really was enchanting . . . They moved up
a narrow wooden staircase to the next level and into the Grand
Hall of the High Bailiff.

"Savoy period," Hafez read aloud. "In 1536 the Bernese divided the hall into three, their 'Grand Kirchen' being to the north. The separating walls were removed in 1836."

Again Fouad yawned.

They moved on, through the Coat-of-Arms Hall, the Duke's Chamber, several apartments and then a chapel, where they lingered before they filed through a passageway up and into the Grand Hall of the Count. "Now called the Hall of Justice," recited Hafez, consulting the leaflet. "In the Middle Ages used for receptions and banquets. The tapestry hangings are all thirteenth century, the fireplace and ceiling are fifteenth century."

The hall was large, high-ceilinged and uncluttered but what impressed Mrs. Pollifax more than its history was its immediacy to the lake. Casement windows stood open to the sun and to the breeze from the water, and window seats had been built under each window so that she could imagine the lords and ladies of the castle contemplating the sun's rising and setting with a tranquil heedlessness of time. The windows were the real furnishings of the room, which was empty except for the ancient tapestries on the wall and huge carved, wooden chests placed here and there in corners.

Chests . . . Mrs. Pollifax felt a quickening of interest. Pausing beside one she ran her hand over its carving, noting the interstices in its serpentine design, and then casually placed one hand under the lid and discovered that it opened without resistance. It was empty except for a coil of thick rope, and she quickly closed it. Standing next to Fouad, Hafez had followed her investigation and he tactfully glanced away. Turning to Fouad he said, "It's like the old castle at home, is it not, Fouad? Look, madame, next comes the torture chamber and then what they call here a *Latrinehaus*, and then—" Fouad gave him a bored glance that silenced him.

It was now fifteen minutes to the hour. Lingering in the torture chamber, which Fouad seemed to regard with relish, she heard someone up ahead call out in English, "Latrines! Oh, do look!" Fouad pulled himself out of his reverie and signaled them to follow the group out of the torture chamber and into the high-ceilinged room adjoining it. The group pushed into one corner before it dispersed but when Fouad beckoned her on, Mrs. Pollifax firmly shook her head. "I want to look, too," she told him. "I've never felt that history books satisfactorily explained the hygienic arrangements of the past."

Reluctantly, with a martyred sigh, Fouad led her and Hafez to the corner and Mrs. Pollifax lifted a heavy wooden cover. She found herself looking straight down a cobble-stoned, chimney-like chute, long since sanitized, to the shallow water of the lake below. "Why—how astonishing," she said. It was almost dizzying to look down from this height at water lapping against the rocks. "And how ingenious," she murmured.

She stood without moving, suddenly alert as she realized that the tour group had moved on to the next room—she could hear their voices grow fainter—leaving her and Hafez alone with Fouad. It was now or never, she reflected, and tentatively, hopefully, flattened her right hand, waiting.

"We go now," said Fouad, and moving up behind her he tapped her on the shoulder.

Mrs. Pollifax turned. With the velocity of a coiled spring her hand struck Fouad in the stomach. He gasped, dropping the suitcase. As he doubled over clutching his middle she stepped back and delivered a karate chop to the base of his skull. He staggered to his knees, lingered a moment and then slowly fell to the floor unconscious.

"Mon Dieu!" gasped Hafez. "That was karate!"

"I don't think I killed him," Mrs. Pollifax said earnestly. "Quickly, Hafez, that chest in the corner over there, hurry—before anyone comes."

He sprang into action with joy, propping open the chest and running back to help. "But he is big, he is heavy, madame!"

"He certainly is," she gasped as they dragged him across the stone floor. Lifting and pushing they succeeded in rolling him over the side until the rest of him fell in, too.

"Will he still breathe?" asked Hafez.

"If this chest is like the ones in the other room—yes, it is, see? There are holes among the carved decorations for ventilation."

"So there are. Don't forget his gun," pointed out Hafez, and retrieved it from Fouad's pocket and handed it to her. They closed the lid of the chest just as the next tour group entered the adjoining torture chamber, and, by the time they crossed the threshold of the room, Mrs. Pollifax and Hafez were sitting on the chest talking amiably, the suitcase between them.

"How long will he be—uh—indisposed, madame?" asked Hafez politely.

"I'm trying to remember. It's so difficult, a matter of pressure points and degrees, and of course no one gets hurt in class. I hit him in the right place but I don't know how hard," she explained, frowning over it, and then gave up. "Anyway, let's not wait and see, let's *go*."

They caught up with the original tour group and passed them at the entrance to the Defense Tower. Instead of joining them, however, they hurried down wooden stairs and across the open drawbridge to the steps leading into the courtyard. "We left Fouad in *Latrinehaus XIII*," Hafez said, squinting at the diagram.

"May he rest in peace," she added piously. "Here's the courtyard, Hafez, put away your literature and let's see if we can get out of here without being seen."

From behind a low wall they assessed the main courtyard and the entrance gate. The little souvenir house beside the gate was being locked for the night by a guard, and on the other side of the courtyard a second guard was closing the small dark entrance to the castle proper and drawing bars across the door. Closing time was two minutes away, realized Mrs. Pollifax with a glance at her watch. She took a step forward, looked beyond the gate and ducked back.

"What is it?"

"The other one, the thin one, Munir. He's just outside the gate watching everyone leave."

"But it's closing time!" cried Hafez. "What can we do? Where can we go?"

Mrs. Pollifax's eyes raked the courtyard but a castle that had stood guard against attack for centuries had not been built with a variety of entrances in mind, and according to the tour guide the few secret exits had long ago been sealed. There was only the one entrance through which to funnel the castle's pilgrims.

"If we can't go forward we'll have to go back," she said, and grasping his hand she hurried him across the courtyard and up the wooden stairs to the drawbridge. A guard called out to them. Mrs. Pollifax shouted back, "We've left our raincoats inside!"

"Impermeables!" called Hafez blithely, and they hurried across the drawbridge, passing both tour groups on their way.

"Closing time!" bawled the guide.

"Impermeables!" Hafez called back, giggling, and they plunged ahead through room after room until they reached the Grand Hall of the Count. When they stopped here to catch their breath the silence was sudden and disconcerting; a long shaft of late-afternoon sun reached the middle of the room and their haste had sent dust motes swirling up the golden beam. "The chests," Mrs. Pollifax said breathlessly. "This is the room with two chests. Climb inside, Hafez."

"I really don't want to but I will. What do we do after this?"

"For encores?" she said tartly. "We'll try again to get out when the castle's settled down." Crossing the room she lowered herself into the companion chest.

It was not a pleasant enclosure: it smelled of mildew and had the dimensions of a tomb. She was soon grateful for its protection, however, because some ten minutes later a guard entered the Grand Hall of the Count whistling cheerfully. He walked around the room, closed and locked the windows and went on to the next chamber. Mercifully there was no sound from Fouad in the room beyond, and soon both footsteps and whistling died away.

Half an hour later voices drifted up to them from the level below, and Mrs. Pollifax raised the top of her chest to listen. "But, monsieur, I cannot take you farther, as you can see the castle is empty and locked up for the night. I myself have inspected it. Nobody is here."

It was Sabry who replied but she could not hear his words. The guard's answer was impatient. "Monsieur, it is out of the question, it is against the rules. I cannot allow you upstairs, the castle is closed for the night." A door slammed, followed by silence.

The silence expanded and deepened, became drowsy with the somnolence of late afternoon's hush. Mrs. Pollifax closed her eyes, opened them and closed them again. The mildew seemed less potent, the warmth hypnotic. Over by the closed windows a trapped fly buzzed against the panes, endlessly, indefatigably . . .

Mrs. Pollifax awoke with a jolt and pushed open the chest. It was still daylight; she saw by her watch that it was six-fifteen. *I mustn't do that again,* she thought, and climbed out of the chest to rouse Hafez. He looked up and waved a tiny flashlight at her as she lifted the top, and she saw that he'd been lying on his back playing tick-tack-toe on the lid of the chest with a piece of chalk. "What else do you carry in your pockets?" she asked with interest.

He stood up and from the pocket of his jacket drew out three marbles, a roll of tape, a jackknife, his tape recorder and a slice of Wiener Schnitzel in a soggy paper napkin. She smiled. "You might as well add Fouad's gun to your collection," she suggested. "I'll carry the suitcase. Let's take a look around now, shall we?"

He said doubtfully, "Do you really think they are convinced we're not here, madame?"

"No," she said, "but they might go away for a while. After all, if they had to consult the sheik once about us they may decide to do it again."

Hafez climbed out of the chest and pocketed the gun. Together they tiptoed through the cool, high-ceilinged rooms to the stairs by which they had gained the floor, but now they found the stairs concealed behind a closed door. Mrs. Pollifax rattled its latch but it did not budge. She ran her hands over the wood but it was a strong thick door with an ancient lock and no key. Hafez whispered, "It must have been locked from the other side, madame, or from this side with one of those old-fashioned big keys. Or perhaps it is barred?"

Mrs. Pollifax felt a sense of foreboding. This door, so huge and impregnable, was a surprise to her. She wondered how many other doors she had passed without noticing their existence. She and Hafez hurried back through the rooms toward the exit by which they had reentered the castle at five o'clock but here, too, their way was barred by a stout door, closed and locked. "Oh dear," said Mrs. Pollifax.

Hafez turned to look at her, his eyes huge. "We are locked in the castle, madame?"

"Yes," she said, and it seemed to her that her *yes* reverberated up and down the empty corridors and through all the empty rooms. Except the castle wasn't empty, she remembered. "Fouad!" she gasped.

They turned and ran back to the room where they had left him. Opening the chest Hafez said with relief, "He is still here, madame, may Allah be praised!"

He was still breathing, too, noted Mrs. Pollifax. He lay on his back, knees lifted, his eyelids fluttering as if he dreamed deeply. He gave no apparent signs of returning consciousness but she did not enjoy the thought of being locked in the castle with him. "There was rope in one of those rooms," she told Hafez. "We've got to bind his wrists and ankles or he'll spoil everything."

"I do not like him much," said Hafez, staring down at him. "If this was war I would shoot him, even if I am ten years old."

"Don't be bloodthirsty," she chided him. "Come, let's find the rope and tie him up—a gag might be in order, too—and then we'll have supper."

"Supper?"

"Well," she pointed out hopefully, "I was thinking of your Wiener Schnitzel, cut into equal portions with your jackknife. *If* you'd care to share it," she added politely.

Chapter Fourteen

In Langley, Virginia, it was midafternoon. Carstairs inserted the key into the lock of his office door and entered with a sigh of deep relief. He felt he had been excessively well-behaved today. He had risen at dawn, driven bumper-to-bumper to the golf club, awaited his turn in a milling crowd and played eighteen holes of golf under a humid, 90-degree sun. His doctor had told him the fresh air and exercise would rejuvenate him but instead he felt hot, irritable, and betrayed. To a man accustomed to deploying live human beings around the world he could think of nothing more idiotic than mindlessly pushing an inanimate ball around a green sward in the sun.

Shrugging off his jacket he sat down at his desk and realized that with two hours of work he could clear away last week's minutiae and begin the next seven days with a minimum of encumbrances. His office was quiet and refreshingly cool. He could order coffee from the commissary and later his dinner and in time he might forget his hysterical attempt to be normal. Normalcy, he decided without a flicker of regret, was simply not for him.

His buzzer sounded and he flicked on the switch. "Mr. Carstairs, sir?" said the bright young voice from the covering office in Baltimore.

"Afternoon, Betsy," he said. "They've stuck you with Sunday this week?"

"Yes, sir, and I was afraid you wouldn't be in the office this afternoon. I've a *most* peculiar call on the switchboard, sir. A Mr. Parviz insists on talking with you but he's not on our list at all. He's calling from Zabya."

"From *where?*"

"Zabya. Something about a cable you sent him. His English is either a little primitive or he's very upset, it's difficult to say which—and I might add that on top of that the connection's dreadful, too."

"He's certainly not one of ours," said Carstairs, frowning. "How the hell could he have gotten our unlisted number?"

"I've already asked him that, sir. Apparently he had the address, he turned it over to the Zabyan Embassy in Washington and they came through with the telephone number. Is the telephone company bribable, sir?"

"Not to my knowledge, and I can't imagine an embassy going to so much trouble, either. It'll be a damned nuisance if we have to change the number. Put the chap on my line so I can find out who the devil he is."

"Right, sir. A moment please."

Carstairs leaned over and switched on the tape-recording machine and sat back. There was a series of pops, followed by a peculiar underwater sound that occasionally accompanied transatlantic calls, and Carstairs heard a harsh, accented voice say, "Mustapha Parviz speaking. I am connected with Mr. William Carstairs, please?"

"You are, sir. What can I do for you?"

"I am calling in reference to the cable I received from you early today. You have just arrived back in America?"

"Just arrived back?" echoed Carstairs.

"Yes, I received your cable at noon here by Zabyan time. This is Mr. William Carstairs of the Legal Building in Baltimore Maryland, of the United States, who sent to me the cable from Europe?"

"Ah, the cable," said Carstairs craftily.

"Yes. It is most urgent, sir—I must learn the circumstances

under which you saw them. Are they safe? Did you actually see them? Are they in Montreux?"

Carstairs stiffened. "Montreux!" he exclaimed. "In Switzerland?"

The man at the other end of the line drew in his breath sharply. "You are playing with me, sir. I implore you—you must know this is of the gravest urgency, a matter of life and death. Where are they?"

Carstairs said swiftly, "I think we might clear this up very quickly, Mr. Parviz, if you'll just read me the cable."

The voice turned cold. "If you sent it, sir, I scarcely need read it to you."

"But you say that you received a cable from Montreux today, and in tracing it you discovered it was sent by—"

"You don't know." The voice broke. "You did not, then, after all—oh my God," the man said, and hung up.

Carstairs stared at the telephone in astonishment. After a moment he leaned over and switched on the recording machine and played the tape, listening carefully. Mustapha Parviz—the name struck him as vaguely familiar. *Where are they? Are they safe? Did you actually see them?* . . . Parviz had lost or misplaced something, documents or people, and it had something to do with Montreux. A matter of life and death . . . There was no mistaking the desperation in that voice; it had been studiously disciplined to the point of curtness but there were the revelatory small breaks, the quick intakes of breath, culminating in that bleak cry, *You don't know—oh my God.*

It was obvious that Parviz had no idea to whom he was speaking. It was equally obvious that he didn't care; he wanted only one thing, information, but without volunteering any in return. He'd been given the Baltimore address, but with neither explanation nor telephone number, and he'd desperately hoped—but how could he have gotten the address? Who would have sent him a cable bearing Carstairs's name?

He picked up the telephone and put through a call to Bishop on the off chance that he might be spared an hour's hunt through the files. Bishop wasn't at home but he was given a

Georgetown number and presently he captured him on the phone.

"It's Sunday," Bishop reminded him. "Day of rèst and gladness, remember? I'm at a party with a stunning blonde."

"Congratulations," Carstairs said dryly. "Now can you possibly tell me why the name of Mustapha Parviz sounds familiar to me?"

Bishop sighed. "Because he's in the Zabyan report we did for the State Department last week, file Z1020 if I'm not mistaken. Except it's not just Mustapha Parviz, it's *General* Mustapha Parviz. He's head of the Zabyan army."

"Good God," said Carstairs.

"Don't you remember the Jonathan and David bit? Parviz, son of a poor tentmaker, brought to the palace to be schooled with Jarroud so that the future king would rub shoulders with the poor? Later there was a commission to military school and then he saved Jarroud's life in '60 by taking a bullet in his shoulder intended for Jarroud. Now Jarroud's the king and Mustapha's General of the whole shebang."

"A fact he neglected to mention," mused Carstairs. "One more question, Bishop. If someone—and I can assure you it wasn't I—sent a cable from Montreux giving the sender's address as William Carstairs, the Legal Building, Baltimore—"

Bishop interrupted. "That could be only one person, sir— Mrs. Pollifax."

"You're quite sure?"

"Oh yes, we've only two investigative agents in Switzerland this week and one of them has no knowledge at all of the Baltimore covering address. Interpol doesn't have it, either; they contact us directly."

Carstairs sighed. "I don't know why I resisted thinking of it but of course it's just the sort of thing she'd do."

"Is Mrs. Pollifax into something, sir?"

Carstairs said testily, "For heaven's sake, Bishop, she's been there only two days."

"Three days now, sir," pointed out Bishop with maddening precision, "It's already Sunday evening in Europe. Do you want me at the office?"

"No, but you might stay available while I contact Schoenbeck in Geneva. I'll call you back."

He hung up, consulted his file and asked that a call be put through to Schoenbeck's office. While he waited he used another phone to order a pot of coffee and then drew out file Z1020. He was studying it with concentration when his call to Geneva came through. "Schoenbeck?" he snapped.

But Schoenbeck was out. A cool, formal voice explained that this was his assistant speaking and that Schoenbeck had left Geneva several hours ago. Could his assistant be of help?

"The biggest help you can give me is to tell me how I can reach him immediately. This is Carstairs in Washington, about the Montbrison business."

"Ah yes, of course," said the assistant in well-modulated tones. "It is the Montbrison case, monsieur, that has taken him from Geneva today. He left in midafternoon to confer with M. Gervard. Unfortunately he is not returned yet."

"What time is it over there?"

"Nine o'clock, sir, in the evening."

"And he's not back yet?"

"No, monsieur."

Carstairs said abruptly, "Something's happened then. Look here, we've an agent at Montbrison, too, and I've had a most peculiar telephone call—"

The voice was soothing. "No, no, monsieur, it had nothing to do with your agent Mrs. Pollifax. It is our agent who has disappeared for the moment. We are making inquiries."

"Disappeared!" exclaimed Carstairs. "Marcel?"

"It will be cleared up, I am sure," the voice went on with the blandness of a doctor reassuring a terminal patient. "It is M. Schoenbeck's urgent hope that cover need not be broken and so he consented to help with inquiries, very discreetly."

"When did you last hear from Marcel?" demanded Carstairs. "And what was on his mind?"

"His last report was yesterday—Saturday—at the usual hour of five o'clock, monsieur. As to what was on his mind—" The voice hesitated and then turned silky. "He mainly expressed some doubts about your agent, sir."

Carstairs's voice became even silkier. "May I ask why?"

"But of course, monsieur. He had requested her to make the acquaintance of a man named Burke-Jones, about whom serious suspicions have been aroused, and she did this. But she became quickly distracted by a small child staying at the Clinic. Marcel had begun to feel the maternal instincts had blunted her—uh—shall we say perceptions?"

Carstairs said curtly, "You may tell Schoenbeck that Mrs. Pollifax is distracted by everything that comes her way but never to the detriment of the job. Her distractions are notorious but never without point. When was Marcel's next contact to be made?"

"He should have telephoned this morning, monsieur, before going to work at the Clinic."

"But that's nearly fifteen hours ago!"

"Yes, monsieur. Naturally we have made discreet inquiries. He did not return to his room in the village last night."

"Has my agent been told about this?"

The voice was polite. "A call was attempted, sir. I put it through myself, after working out the code for it and asking her to make inquiries about Cousin Matthew. Unfortunately your agent had just left for a little drive with friends."

"What friends?"

The voice was disapproving. "I'm sure I cannot tell you, sir, but Monsieur Schoenbeck will contact you upon his return."

"Do that," said Carstairs. "I'll wait for his call." He hung up and swore steadily. He was still swearing when Bishop telephoned, and when he had finished, Bishop said mildly, "You're upset."

"You're damned right I'm upset. I've been talking with a Pollyanna in Schoenbeck's office who informs me that Marcel hasn't reported in for fourteen and a half hours but everything's all right."

"It doesn't sound all right to me," said Bishop.

"Bless you for that," breathed Carstairs. "Well, there's nothing to be done for the moment except wait for Schoenbeck's call. You can return to your day of rest and gladness, Bishop."

"Thank you, sir. Are you worried?"

"I don't know," fretted Carstairs. "It's maddening not to be in charge myself, and still more maddening to think how easily they could blow this. Schoenbeck is so damned cautious, so damned discreet. It inhibits him."

"Well, sir, my blonde is gorgeous but not quite so diverting as Mrs. Pollifax. Give me a ring if something comes up."

"Yes," said Carstairs and hung up with a sigh, knowing that if one of his agents had been out of contact for nearly fifteen hours in a closed situation like this he certainly wouldn't be driving off to a rendezvous to discuss it, he'd be tearing the Clinic apart and to hell with everybody's cover stories. "Too damned polite," he growled and began to consider a few things he could do from this end that, hopefully, wouldn't irk Schoenbeck. He could, for one thing, telephone Mrs. Pollifax and make certain that she was all right, and he could discover just why she had sent a cablegram in his name. Schoenbeck wouldn't care for his meddling but Mrs. Pollifax was *his* agent, after all.

He put through a call to the Hotel-Clinic Montbrison and it was placed before he had finished his cup of coffee. Whoever was on night duty over there spoke a disjointed English, and guessing the man's accent Carstairs switched to Italian. Even in Italian, however, he couldn't reach Mrs. Pollifax because there was no answer to the telephone in her room. This was worrisome because if it was nearly ten o'clock in the evening over there she ought to be getting ready to signal from her balcony. He asked a few questions about schedules at the concierge's desk and the porter replied, adding a few complaints as well.

"Who was on duty this afternoon?" Carstairs asked. He nodded and wrote down the name and home telephone number of the head concierge, thanked the porter and hung up.

Consulting the code given Mrs. Pollifax he picked up the telephone and asked that a cable be sent to her at Montbrison. "Take this down," he said and dictated: URGENTLY REQUEST EXPLANATION CABLE SENT IN MY NAME SUNDAY STOP UNCLE BILL ON THE LOOSE AGAIN IN FRANCE STOP WHERE IS COUSIN MATTHEW STOP ARE YOU RUNNING A TEMPERATURE STOP LOVE ADELAIDE. Got that?"

"Yes, sir."

"Now get me Switzerland again." He frowned over the

name of the head concierge. "A Monsieur Piers Grundig, in St. Gingolph." He began to feel the satisfaction of working through some of his frustrations and was just congratulating himself about it when Bishop walked in. "What on earth!" he said in surprise.

"Couldn't help it, sir," said Bishop cheerfully. "Something's up, isn't it? It was beginning to interfere with both the rest and the gladness. What do you *think* is up?"

Carstairs shrugged helplessly. "I wish I knew. Marcel disappeared from view sometime between five o'clock Saturday and seven o'clock this morning their time, and in midafternoon today Mrs. Pollifax went for a drive—with friends, I'm told—and she doesn't seem to have returned yet. Marcel's missing and I'm beginning to think Mrs. Pollifax is missing, too. And I had that damned mysterious call from Parviz. Hello?" he barked into the phone. "Is this Piers Grundig, head concierge at the Hotel-Clinic Montbrison?" He waved Bishop to sit down.

His questions to the man were concise and organized. He had seen Madame Pollifax leave? She had gone for a drive with people from the Clinic? She had left at what hour? And the names of the friends, he inquired as he reached for pencil and paper.

"Monsieur Sabry, yes," he said, writing busily. "Two gentlemen not familiar to you, and the boy Hafez. Hafez what?" He looked astonished. "Parviz," he echoed in a hollow voice. "Yes, I see. Thank you very much, Monsieur Grundig, I'm obliged to you."

He hung up, and seeing his face Bishop said, "Trouble."

"Trouble or a very remarkable coincidence," growled Carstairs. "I don't like it."

"Your intuition's usually right. And no Schoenbeck yet?"

"No Schoenbeck yet." Carstairs looked grim. "I gave Mrs. Pollifax to Interpol like a gift and they give every evidence of having discarded her like a boring Christmas tie."

Bishop said soberly, "Well, you know she doesn't look like a gift at first glance, sir. She confuses people by looking the nice cozy grandmother type."

"This time she seems to have confused the wrong people,"

Carstairs said harshly. "She's confused Interpol but I'm beginning to have the acute feeling that *someone* has seen through
the façade and discovered she's dangerous. And Interpol is the
last to guess this." He lifted his glance to Bishop. "There's a
damned busy week ahead, Bishop, but it's time someone translates Mrs. Pollifax to Interpol. Is your passport available?"

Bishop brightened. "In my desk, sir."

Carstairs nodded. "I'll call a taxi for you. I want you to take
along the tape recording of Parviz's call, and I want you to give
it to Schoenbeck, but first—I repeat *first*—you're to find out
where the hell Mrs. Pollifax is." He glanced at his watch. "It's
half-past four, Bishop, you've just time to catch the six o'clock
plane to Geneva. It will get you to Geneva—given the time
differences—by seven-thirty tomorrow morning."

"On my way, sir," said Bishop, snatching up the tape and
his jacket.

"Oh and Bishop—"

He turned at the door. "Yes, sir?"

"For God's sake keep me posted."

"Yes, sir," he said, and the door slammed behind him.

Chapter Fifteen

I t was nearing midnight and it seemed to Mrs. Pollifax that it had been dark forever. In fact it had grown dark inside the castle long before the last rays of sun fled the lake and the sky outside. Around eight o'clock they had divided Hafez's small hoard of Wiener Schnitzel but that, too, felt a long time ago. After a sojourn in each of the rooms they had settled in the Hall of the Count, where Mrs. Pollifax sat on the floor, her back against the wooden chest. Odd little noises punctuated the silence: the scurrying of mice, the explosive creak of wood as the temperature dropped, the sound of waves from a far-off boat lapping against the outer walls. From time to time she lighted a match from the package that Bishop had given her in New York and when she did this, to glance at her watch, the flare of light would pick out the suitcase beside her and the small arsenal in her lap: Hafez's jackknife, Fouad's gun and a segment of the rope that wound up to the pile she had placed on the chest. At the moment Mrs. Pollifax would gladly have traded them all for a warm coat and some food. "What are you doing now?" she called softly to Hafez.

"I am at the window, madame, looking at the stars. I can see the head of Ursa Major, the Great Bear, and also the Chair of Cassiopeia. Oh, I wish you could see the stars in the Rub' al Khali, madame, they shine so clear, so bright." He came back to sit down again beside her.

"The Rub' al Khali?"

"It's called also the Empty Quarter—except it is not empty, you know. Sometimes—sometimes my father has taken me there, and we camp out at night under the stars and they come near enough to touch. There are desert gazelles there, too. I shall be an astronomer when I grow up," he said firmly.

"Then we must make certain that you grow up," she said lightly. "Go on with your story, Hafez, I want to know everything."

"Yes," he said with a sigh, "but it is all so unpleasant and the stars so beautiful. Where was I? Oh yes, after finding me in the bazaar Munir drove me to the Zabyan airport but my father was not there at all, as you can guess. Fouad kept saying, 'He is inside the plane, they're giving him oxygen until the doctor comes.' So I ran across the runway to the plane and up the steps but my father was not there at all. Instead Grandmama lay stretched out on three seats, quite unconscious."

"Drugged," nodded Mrs. Pollifax.

"Yes. And as I went to her they closed the door to the plane and that's when I understood they had tricked me and nothing at all had happened to my father. The plane took off two minutes later."

"How many of them were there?"

"There were two pilots but I did not see them again. There was Serafina, who seems to be a nurse. There was Fouad and Munir, and a man I think was a steward and belonged to the plane because he wore a uniform and served food to me. We had one meal and I think it was drugged because I fell asleep afterward. When we landed I could scarcely believe we had flown all the way to Switzerland. That was when Mr. Sabry came on board to—to—" He sighed. "To explain."

"That you were hostages," said Mrs. Pollifax, nodding.

"Yes, madame. He said we were going to a very nice place, a Clinic, and I would be free to walk around and enjoy myself but my grandmother would be kept prisoner in her room. If I breathed a word of it, if I begged help or confided in anyone my grandmother would be given an injection that would kill her at once. He said Fouad and Munir would always be with her and that whether she lived or died would be up to me."

" 'An intolerable tension,' " remembered Mrs. Pollifax aloud, and her shiver was not from the cold. She could believe their threat; they really would dispose of Madame Parviz—and still could—with a quick and ruthless indifference. "And so your grandmother has been kept drugged ever since you came."

"Yes, madame."

Mrs. Pollifax smiled faintly. "Until you stole thirteen aspirin from me, Hafez?"

"You saw that, madame?" He turned and looked up at her, his face a pale oval in the darkness.

"I saw. I guessed that after the initial injections they must be giving your grandmother pills that looked just like aspirin. You planned a little sleight of hand."

"It was all I could think to do," he said, his voice trembling a little. "There were thirteen pills in the bottle next to Grandmama's bed. I replaced them with thirteen aspirin. I thought if Grandmama could once wake up we could talk of what to do. And she did wake up," he added proudly, "She said we must be very brave and cable my father that we are safe—even if we are not safe—and then place our lives in the hands of Allah. But, madame—" She saw the flash of his smile. "She did not know that you would help, too. Do you think Allah sent you?"

"The CIA sent me," she said dryly, "and I've never heard them accused of god-like qualities."

"But she is unprotected now," he went on in a troubled voice. "Madame, I am very worried about her."

She groped for his hand and squeezed it. "I think she'll be all right while they look for you, Hafez. They're not desperate yet and two hostages are better than one. But what's behind all this, Hafez, have they told you?"

He sighed. "No, but I am sure it has something to do with my father being general of the Zabyan army."

"You mean *the* general?" Her knowledge of army hierarchies had never been clear and it had always seemed to her that generals tended to multiply like corporative vice-presidents or rabbits.

"Yes, madame. It's always been said that no one could ever use the army to overthrow the government as long as my father is general. Because he is very loyal, very dedicated to Jarroud's cause."

"They have found a way to divide his loyalties now," she pointed out softly. "I wonder what they're up to." A coup, probably, she thought. One began by blackmailing a general, who would then turn over his army or not turn it over, depending upon how vulnerable he was—but Parviz was vulnerable now, indeed. It was true that he could compromise by agreeing to keep his army out of the arena, but that would be just as effective for the coup-makers as joining them. In any direction he turned he would be rendered helpless. He could save his family or his king but it was unlikely that he could do both. It was a diabolical trap. It was also very well-planned, she realized, because Parviz would have had a week to search for his family and that was long enough to scour the Middle East but who would think of looking for them in a quiet convalescent clinic in Switzerland?

But although Mrs. Pollifax worked hard at picturing a coup d'etat in Zabya it remained an abstract for her, a geometry problem lacking flesh and bones. She had no passion for making or unmaking history. Rulers came to power and rulers lost their power through votes, old age or violence. They had their brief fling at immortality and departed; it was history's victims for whom she felt compassion. What mattered the more to her at this moment was keeping Hafez and Madame Parviz alive while the actors played out their intrigues on a stage elsewhere.

"This isn't a fair question, Hafez," she said, "but when your father receives the cable sent this morning what do you think he will do? What manner of man is he?"

"Well, he is a man of much integrity, madame. I cannot imagine his turning over the country or the king to wicked people." He sighed. "I do not know what he will do, madame. If he thinks me safe, and if they promise not to kill the king— why, then, to save bloodshed he *might* do as these people ask. But only to avoid a great bloodletting. I don't know, you see."

If they would promise—she tried to think of what promises a man like Sabry would keep. "What influence has your mother?"

"Oh, she is dead, madame. When I was a child she died."

"You're the whole family then?" She was startled. "You, your grandmother, and your father?"

"Yes, madame."

Mrs. Pollifax shivered, and her list of victims expanded. Even King Solomon, she thought, might have a little trouble with this one.

"My father loves the king, they are like brothers," went on Hafez in a low voice. "My father says Jarroud thinks of the people and wants them to be less poor, which really they should be because the oil belongs to them. My father was very poor once, too, madame. They say it is my father who always reminds the king of the people." He hesitated. "Madame, I cannot answer your question."

She nodded. "Of course you can't. Tell me instead about the sheik. He's involved in this somewhere?"

"Oh yes, madame. It was his private plane that brought us here to Switzerland. His plane has been pointed out to me many times so I know this."

So there it was, thought Mrs. Pollifax, as the remaining pieces of the puzzle slipped into place. She was remembering the king's birthday party on Tuesday—oh, perfect, she reflected. The army would be much in evidence, out in force and proudly displayed, yet every attention would be diverted to the festival and to the visiting heads of state. Given the right coincidences, careful planning and shrewd arrangements the day would end with the king deposed or dead and the government taken over by—

By the sheik, of course, she thought. Of *course* the sheik. She remembered the flash of his smile, the dark handsome face of the man whom Robin had called one of the richest men in the world. She thought, *What does one do with so much money? He's already explored the world of the senses—of women, cars, jewels—and now he's moved on to the world of the ascetic, and he is still young. What next?*

She knew the answer because it followed a logical pattern: he would want power. Given power, he would be able to manipulate, to create and to change. It was the ultimate toy, the deepest psychological lust of all because it held within it all the satisfactions of the sensual as well as the ascetic.

Her hand moved to the sheik's suitcase behind her that had been so important to Sabry that it couldn't be left behind. I have Hafez and I have this, she thought, and wondered what they would do to get them back.

In the adjoining room Fouad moaned, and Mrs. Pollifax put away her thoughts and nudged Hafez. "We'd better look at Fouad," she told him, and distributing the contents of her lap she led the way into the next chamber. They bent over the chest with a lighted match. This time Fouad's eyes lifted to stare without intelligence at the pinpoint of flame above him. Another half hour or so, she guessed, and he would remember who they were and why he was in the chest.

She groped for a place to sit. "I have Hafez and I have their suitcase," she repeated . . . It must be one o'clock by now, already Monday morning. The caretaker of the castle would be asleep in his apartment by the gate, and the highway would be nearly empty of cars but she did not believe for a moment that Sabry had abandoned his post outside. At first he would have been angry, and then he would have been puzzled because Fouad was strong, shrewd, and armed with a gun. It would be inconceivable to him that Fouad could disappear in the company of an elderly woman and a boy. But that incredulity would have returned to anger by now, and given time to check and double-check she thought that Sabry must be quite certain the three of them were still in the castle. *Someone* would be on guard outside—waiting, watching . . .

Hafez tapped her on the arm. "What is it, madame, you sigh so heavily! And don't you prefer a chest? You are seated on the latrine."

"Latrine?" She was startled, and one hand moved to the ancient, splintery surface to discover that he was right, she was sitting on the long bench-top that concealed the latrine, while below—"Hafez!" she said in a surprised voice and began to smile in the darkness. "Hafez, I've been waiting for inspiration and you've just given it to me. *Think*, Hafez! Think what's below me!"

"Lake Geneva," he said doubtfully. "And rocks."

"No, no, a way out of the castle, Hafez. A way *out*."

"Down that chimney?" he said incredulously. "But, madame—how could one get down? It is two floors high, surely?"

"I'm thinking of the coil of rope," she told him eagerly. "I managed a rope once, over Robin's balcony. It will all depend on the strength of the rope. We must be resourceful, Hafez."

"Rope . . ." Hafez said reflectively, and his voice suddenly quickened. "Oh, *yes*, madame! Here, try it, feel it. Do you think—?"

"Let's tie it to the suitcase and drop the suitcase down the chute and see what happens," she urged. "Give me a hand, Hafez. Light a match."

Matches flared briefly, one after the other. They secured one end of the rope to the iron bolt of the window shutter on the wall nearby, and the other end she knotted to the handle of the suitcase. Gently they lowered the weight down the chute; it bumped softly here and there against the stones, and hung suspended, swaying back and forth.

"It didn't break," whispered Hafez. "How far down do you think it went?"

"I don't know," she said. "Twenty feet, thirty. It's a long rope." She was assessing twenty pounds of suitcase against Hafez's weight and her own and she was not sure that she liked the odds. To entrust their lives to a rope that had lain in a damp chest for days, months, even perhaps for years—

Hafez abruptly placed his hand on her arm. He said in a low voice, "Madame."

She heard it, too, and stiffened. Not far away—it came from one of the rooms nearby—a voice had lifted in momentary anger.

"Munir's voice," whispered Hafez. "Madame, they're *inside the castle*."

Inside the castle . . . Her astonishment fought against the chill of terror. How *could* they be inside, what entrance had they discovered that she and Hafez had missed? She tried to think. A ladder? The thought of a ladder jarred her out of paralysis. If they had a ladder they could scale the outside wall and gain the lower roofs, and from there—yes, they could do it if the ladder was long enough—they could reach one of those barless windows on the stairs to the Defense Tower and this would bring them into the corridor two rooms away. There was no magic about it, then; they had brought equipment and were coming in after them.

She turned quickly to Hafez, her decision made for her, and placed the end of the rope in Hafez's hand. "Go first," she told him sternly, "hand over hand, not too fast. If I can't make it, take the suitcase to Robin. The walls will be near enough to touch with your feet if you panic."

"I do not panic," Hafez whispered scornfully, and she saw his shadowy form step over the side and vanish. The rope groaned a little, and behind her the shutter creaked as it felt his weight but the knots held, the rope remained steady.

In the chest across the room Fouad groaned and moved, one knee hitting the top of the chest with a thud. In the corridor beyond the chest a beam of light flashed across the stones, lifted and vanished. A low voice said, "Fool! Keep the light away from the window!" It was Sabry's voice. She climbed over the side of the opening and waited, holding her breath. When she felt two tugs on the rope she thought—madness!—but she didn't hesitate.

It was dark and cold in the chute. The rope strained at her weight. She placed a hand under her to check her descent but even so she went down in an insane rush. The weight of the suitcase had turned the rope into a plumb line so that it moved in slow giddy circles between top and bottom. Her hands burned from the coarse hemp. Down—down—Something brushed past her, wings fluttering, and then she reached the suitcase and dangled there uncertainly. "Jump, madame," whispered Hafez excitedly. "You've made it! It's not far."

She let go, slid across wet rocks and promptly sat down in the water, head spinning dizzily. "Please, madame—do hurry," gasped Hafez, cutting away the suitcase with his knife. "Quickly, madame!"

She stumbled to her feet. Hafez handed her the gun and the knife, lifted the suitcase and waded out of the opening into the shallows of Lake Geneva. She followed. The water was up to her knees. She had neglected to remove her shoes and the rocks underfoot were slippery with lichen. As they moved slowly around the castle in the direction of the shore she alternately stumbled, rose, slipped and fell again. She was drenched when they reached the cobbled shore and as she waded out of the water she stopped and looked up at the dark castle serrating the skyline. Suddenly a thin beam of light impaled her and vanished. Out of the darkness a familiar voice said, "Good God, it's really you?"

It was a voice from another world. Mrs. Pollifax stood uncertainly at the water's edge, caught in the act of wringing water from her skirts. "Robin?" she faltered.

"Over here—in a rowboat," came his stage whisper, and she heard the creak of oar locks and a muted splash of water. "Climb in," she heard him say, and then he added flippantly, "Whatever kept you so long?"

Chapter Sixteen

A nd now let's get the hell out of here," Robin said, steadying her as she fell into the boat. "They've good ears, those two, they're at the gate." He sat down, picked up the oars and began to row.

"Monsieur, they are not at the gate," whispered Hafez, "they're inside the castle."

"Good Lord," he said, and rowed faster.

The darkness was thinning and shapes were beginning to separate themselves from the opaque blackness of night. She could see the point of land toward which Robin rowed, and then the silhouette of rocks through which he threaded the boat as he headed toward a more distant cove. He spoke only once. "Are those *teeth* I hear chattering?"

Hafez giggled.

"Yes," said Mrs. Pollifax with dignity. They rounded the point and a minute later the boat hit the graveled shore and ground to a stop. The castle could no longer be seen; it was hidden by trees.

"I've got a car," Robin said. "A rented one. It's up there off the road, straight ahead through the trees."

"You're a miracle, Robin," she said. "It's the greatest piece of luck your being here."

"Luck!" he growled, helping Hafez out with the suitcase. "It was getting too damned crowded at the front of the castle, that's all. The lake was the only place left for me. Could you hurry a little? The sooner we get out of this place the happier I'll feel. There's a blanket in the back seat of the car," he added. "Get moving while I tie up the boat."

When he joined them in the car Mrs. Pollifax and Hafez had already found the blanket and were huddled under it together. Climbing in behind the wheel he turned and gave her a stern glance. "Look here, I've never felt so helpless in my life," he said. "I've spent the whole night debating whether to go to the police, telling myself I'd call them within the hour, then postponing because I didn't want to upset your applecart, but don't you think it's time I drive like hell now to a police station?"

"Now?" gasped Hafez, and turning to Mrs. Pollifax he said desperately, "Madame, my grandmother—"

Mrs. Pollifax nodded. "Hafez is right, we *must* get back to the Clinic, Robin, it's where Sabry will head as soon as he discovers Fouad and learns how we've gotten away. There isn't time to go to the police."

Robin said incredulously, "We can be there inside of ten minutes."

"Yes and spend the next fifteen explaining to them. Robin, we must hurry to Madame Parviz—please!"

He angrily started the car. "Then you'd better explain to me what you found at the Clinic that's so important you go back. What *did* happen in Sabry's room?"

"Everything, and all of it ominous," she said grimly. "Hafez and his grandmother are hostages—"

"Hostages!"

"Yes, and Sabry's a murderer, and your old friend the sheik is heavily involved—"

"Yazdan!"

"And Serafina is guarding Madame Parviz, who's been kept drugged, and just one telephone call from Sabry could end her life and—"

"But this is incredible," protested Robin.

"Yes, isn't it? And Marcel—" Her voice broke. "Marcel's body is in Sabry's closet. That's why I screamed."

"Good God," he groaned. "You mean nobody knows he's dead except us?"

"Yes," she said, and sitting up saw that her words had at least effected a change in their speed for they were already entering Villeneuve. "We left Fouad tied up in a chest inside the castle but he was already beginning to stir and groan, and once they find him they need only telephone the Clinic, you see."

"I'm not sure they'll reach anyone—that night porter sleeps most of the night," Robin said dryly.

"Let's hope he's sleeping now!"

"But what are these demented people up to?" protested Robin as he guided the car at top speed through narrow streets and headed toward the mountains.

"I think a coup d'etat in Zabya," said Mrs. Pollifax. "The king is celebrating his fortieth birthday on Tuesday."

"But that's tomorrow."

"My goodness, yes," she said, glancing at her watch. "But what time is it?" she faltered, staring at a watch that said half-past midnight.

"Nearly four o'clock."

"Good heavens!" She held the watch to her ear and shook it. "My watch has stopped, I've lost three hours!"

"Be grateful, they were damned tedious hours, believe me."

She conceded this and sat back. It was no wonder, then, that Sabry and Munir had risked going into the castle after them. They were obviously running out of time if they planned to return to the Middle East today or tonight to await a triumphant entry into Zabya tomorrow. If they were leaving the Clinic so soon perhaps they had planned to bury Marcel somewhere on the mountainside before they left. She had certainly been naive about Marcel's death: of course they couldn't risk the discovery of a murder so soon after Fraser's questionable death. She had assumed that employees of the Clinic had concealed the tragedy when instead it was Sabry who had returned to the Unterwasser Massage room, carried the body up to his room and gone back to scrub away the blood.

And so neither the police nor Interpol knew that Marcel was dead, and there was nothing to warn them of anything wrong except that she had not signaled last night from her balcony. She wondered what they were doing about that. She tried to think what she would do if she were Interpol but she was too tired, and anyway she had begun to suspect that Interpol did not expect a great deal of her. It was Marcel who had direct lines of communication with them, and from her they apparently wanted only reassurances that she was all right. This was gallant of them if one enjoyed playing Boy Scout games with a flashlight at night but it was of no particular usefulness when, as the expression went, all hell broke loose. Possibly a touch of male chauvinism there, she thought; Swiss women had only just won the vote, after all.

"Really," she said aloud in an exasperated voice, "nothing seems to be going as they expected. I think Interpol has taken far too many precautions to keep everything undercover. There's also this suitcase," she added, looking at it speculatively.

"What suitcase?"

"You'll see it presently," she told him. "It has two padlocks on it beside the regular lock and I'm hoping you'll open it for me, Robin. It belongs to the sheik, at least it has his luggage tag on it, and Mr. Sabry seems to regard it as terribly important. Obviously it has something to do with the coup d'etat or whatever they're planning."

"I can hardly wait," Robin said lightly.

They had entered the village on the mountain, and turning the corner at high speed they surprised an old man sweeping the sidewalk with a broom. He jumped back from the curb, shaking his fist in indignation, and then they turned and drove down the narrow road along the ravine to the Clinic. It was still night here but the rising sun was dusting the mountain peaks with gold. The lake below was wrapped in a mist that drifted lazily with each stirring breeze.

Hafez said in an anguished voice, "We're almost there, but how shall we ever get inside the Clinic?"

"That you can safely leave to Robin," she told him wryly.

"But Serafina mustn't hear," he protested. "She'll be waiting for Mr. Sabry, and if she sees us without him—" His voice trembled. "You understand, monsieur, they kill so easily."

"That," said Robin grimly, "I'm beginning to understand."

He turned off the engine of the car and coasted it down the incline past the greenhouse. Abreast of the main door it came to a halt. "Don't slam the car doors," he whispered. "Watch the gravel—stick with the flower beds. Tiptoe around the Clinic to the garden door."

A few minutes later they stood inside the Clinic on the ground floor next to the Unterwasser Massage room. "Now here's what we do," said Robin, taking charge. "No sense taking the stairs and all three of us creeping past the concierge's desk. We'll go boldly up in the elevator, each of us pressed against the wall. With luck he'll think the elevator's going up empty."

Mrs. Pollifax offered him the gun. "Would you like this?"

"No, but I daresay it talks louder than I do." He shoved it into his pocket. "Hafez, what will Serafina do when I knock?"

"She'll ask who's there."

He nodded. "Be sure and tell me if she says anything else." He reached out and ruffled Hafez's jet black hair. "You're quite a lad, Hafez, your father must be damned proud of you."

The elevator carried them past the night porter and up to the third floor. Here they tiptoed down the hall to room 150 and Robin gently tapped on the door.

There were muted footsteps and then a low voice. *"Meen?"*

"She asks who you are," whispered Hafez.

In a thick voice Robin grunted, "Sabry."

The door opened a few inches and Serafina's face peered out. Quickly Robin placed his foot inside and leaned against the door. Serafina's obsequious smile vanished, she gaped in horror, then turned to flee. Robin seized her, placed a hand across the mouth and dragged her to a chair. "I say—someone bring me a curtain cord and a gag. Hurry, she's slippery as an eel."

Hafez produced both. Robin gagged her and then wound the cord round and round her and under the chair as well. "Not bad," he said in a pleased voice. "One could become accustomed to this sort of thing. Now what?"

"I think we move Madame Parviz to my room while I telephone the police," decided Mrs. Pollifax. "I don't like this room, it's not safe."

Robin said, "I couldn't agree with you more." He joined Hafez by the bed and looked curiously at the slender figure lying there unconscious. "So this is the mysterious Madame Parviz. Not quite the dragon I imagined, she looks more like a fallen eagle. Well, steady does it." He lifted her slight body easily. "If someone will open the door—"

She was carried down the hall to Mrs. Pollifax's room and placed on the bed. Mrs. Pollifax put down the suitcase with a grateful sigh and then remembered that its contents were still a mystery and turned to Robin. "Open it," she said.

"Now?"

"Now."

He took one look at her face, sighed and brought out his pocket-sized kit of keys. Carrying the suitcase to the desk he examined the padlocks and set to work grimly. The first padlock was quickly removed and discarded. "The second's a combination lock. Be very quiet while I listen for clicks. Look, can't you be calling the police while I do this?"

"In a minute," she said impatiently.

The second padlock was removed and Robin bent over the conventional lock. It snapped, and with a grunt of triumph he opened the suitcase. Sand-like grains of filler spilled across the desk. The suitcase was lined with small plastic sacks of the stuff, some of which had split open during the jolts of the night. Puzzled, Mrs. Pollifax reached down and pushed them aside to discover a layer of shredded newspapers. She peeled this away and suddenly stepped back in horror.

"What on earth!" exclaimed Robin.

"But what is it?" whispered Hafez.

Mrs. Pollifax was staring incredulously at the contents of the suitcase, at two innocent-looking drab cans suspended in a birdcage-like contraption and placed in a nest of newspaper and cotton. She had seen two such cans before but when she had seen them they were projected on the wall of a room in the Hotel Taft in New York. There was a world of difference between phantoms on a wall and the real and tangible thing. She could not remember when she had felt so shocked. She said in a shaken voice, "It's plutonium—I've just found the plutonium."

The intrigues of Sabry and the sheik abruptly took a dark and ominous turn and she was caught breathless and frightened by it. She had the stricken sensation of one who has taken time out to catch a minnow and has unexpectedly reeled in a whale.

Chapter Seventeen

I must telephone," she said in a dazed voice.

Hafez leaned over the suitcase looking awed. "This is PU-239?"

"Don't touch it!" she said sharply. "Not without gloves."

"But it belongs to the *sheik!*" pointed out Robin, reading the label.

"Yes. Astonishing, isn't it?" She was remembering how Marcel had deplored her interest in an old woman and a boy, reminding her that they couldn't possibly be involved in the search for plutonium, and she recalled, too, her reply: of course not, but there is something peculiar there. They had each of them been blind; the two puzzles had always been one and she was incredulous at how easily they fitted together.

She replaced the shreds of newspaper, the sacks of filler and headed for the door with the suitcase. "I'm going downstairs and call the police and then Mr. Carstairs in America. I shall never make the night porter understand unless I'm face to face with him."

"I'll go with you," said Robin.

"Me, too," echoed Hafez.

Ignoring the elevator Mrs. Pollifax hurried down the flight of stairs to the Reception floor with Robin and Hafez in her wake. The night porter rose to his feet, looking startled at such an exodus. "Madame?"

"I want you to put through two telephone calls for me," she said. "First to the police, and then—"

"*Police?*"

"Police," she repeated firmly.

He shrugged. Dropping a colored envelope on the desk in front of her he moved to the switchboard and plugged into the board. Mrs. Pollifax glanced at her watch—it was nearly 6:30 —and then at the envelope. She discovered that it was addressed to her and she opened it, bringing out a cablegram that had arrived for her during the night. She read:

URGENTLY REQUEST KNOWLEDGE CONCERNING CABLE SENT IN MY NAME SUNDAY STOP UNCLE BILL ON THE LOOSE IN FRANCE STOP WHERE IS COUSIN MATTHEW STOP ARE YOU RUNNING A TEMPERATURE STOP LOVE ADELAIDE.

Her immediate reaction was one of intense gratitude—at least *someone* guessed that something was wrong—but since Carstairs was several thousand miles removed from her this was of small comfort. Where were Marcel's people? She had just found Uncle Bill, and she had already found Cousin Matthew if only someone would come to the Clinic and ask. She glanced impatiently at the porter, who was swearing in Italian into the mouthpiece. "Are you speaking with the police?" she asked.

He shook his head. With a bewildered look he removed the headpiece and turned to her. "The line—she is dead."

"Line?"

"Switchboard." He stood up and moved to the rear of the board, checking knobs and outlets. "Dead," he repeated in surprise.

A chill crawled up Mrs. Pollifax's spine. Turning to Robin she met his equally startled gaze. She said quietly, "Try the lights."

There were no light switches at hand; Robin turned instead to the elevator and pushed the button. Nothing happened. No lights twinkled on the board overhead, there was no whispering of descending cables. The elevator, too, was dead.

They're coming, she thought, *they're on their way,* and she drew a deep breath to calm her skidding heart.

Hafez tugged at her arm. "Madame—it cannot be coincidence, surely?"

"I don't know." To the night porter she said, "Does this happen often?"

He sucked in his lower lip judiciously. "In the winter, two or three times, madame. Sometimes. In summer, only with the storm, but—" He shook his head. "No, no, fantastic."

"Where is the director of the Clinic? Can you call him?"

There had to be a director, even if she had not seen him, but after a few skirmishes with the porter's clumsy English it became apparent why she had not seen him. His family was on holiday in France, and he had left Thursday night to bring them back today. The secretary was in charge but she lived in Villeneuve.

Mrs. Pollifax found herself remembering the aerial view of Montbrison that Carstairs had projected on the wall of the Hotel Taft. The Clinic was surrounded by woods, isolated and alone in the center of seventy acres of forest and ravine, its narrow gardens carved out of the hillside with only the one road entering the property from the village a mile away. It would be very easy to lay siege to it. "There are only three of them," she reminded herself aloud.

"Four if you count the sheik," said Robin grimly. "And don't say 'only' four. It's like saying there are 'only' four copperhead snakes on the loose in a small room. I say, if we lock all the doors in the building—"

"With so many windows?" She pulled a memo pad from her purse and began writing. "Robin—" Handing him the slip of paper she said, "One person ought to be able to get away. Don't take your car, go by the path down the mountain and after you've called the police, telephone this number in Baltimore."

"And leave you here alone?" he said incredulously.

"I'm scarcely alone."

"You might just as well be. If they've succeeded in cutting the wires then they'll put up a roadblock and walk in the front door and—"

"Making it all the more important that you get help, Robin!" When he still hesitated she added fiercely, "Have you forgotten Madame Parviz—and Hafez—and the suitcase?"

He sighed. "All right." He pocketed the memo and gave Hafez a tap on the shoulder. "Take over, friend," he said and raced down the stairs to the ground floor and the exit into the gardens.

Mrs. Pollifax turned to Hafez. "Go upstairs to my room and stay with your grandmother, Hafez."

"But you, madame?"

"I've something important to do first. Have you still the toy flashlight in your pocket? I want to borrow it."

Wordlessly he handed it over to her.

"I want you to lock yourself into the room with your grandmother. Lock everything and let no one in, you understand?"

"Very clearly, madame." His eyes were anxious but she saw a glint of excitement in them as he turned and raced up the stairs.

Mrs. Pollifax picked up the suitcase, walked to the stairs and descended to the basement floor. Turning to the right she opened the door marked LABORATORIES and entered the X-ray room. After opening and closing several drawers and cabinets she found what she wanted: a pair of surgeon's gloves. Carrying them and the suitcase she walked down the hall to the storeroom, closed the door and turned on the flashlight. With Hafez's pocket knife she ripped a corner off a carton labeled peaches and then a corner from a carton labeled tomato juice. She studied them critically and then opened up the suitcase to observe its contents.

Drawing on her gloves she cautiously removed the two cans of plutonium from the suitcase, and then from the fragile cages into which they had been inserted. After carrying them carefully to the darkest corner of the supply room she dragged a sack of charcoal in front of them to conceal them and then returned to the cans of fruit. Clearly the cans of peaches were the proper size but each was adorned with a paper label bearing a garish picture. She began to chip away the labels with the pocket knife. This took time. From the kitchen she could hear sounds of movement, an occasional voice and then someone whistling *Marlene*. After a few minutes, deploring the time this was taking—the labels appeared to have been cemented to the tins—she carried them into the X-ray room and dropped them into a sink she filled with water. Alternately scraping and cutting she at last removed all but the smallest fragments. Returning to the store room she rubbed down their shining exteriors with charcoal, inserted them into the cages, packed both cans in the suitcase and replaced the filler and newspapers. Finished, she disposed of the gloves in a wastebasket and hurried upstairs with the suitcase.

There was no one at the concierge's desk. She passed it and hurried up the next flight to her own floor, glancing at her watch as she went. She had been downstairs for fifteen minutes—far too long—but the third level was quiet. No waiters had intruded yet on its silence with trays, and there were no sounds of conversation in the nurse's room. The electrical failure had interrupted the quiet, unchanging routine.

She turned the corner and abruptly stopped, one hand at her throat. The door to her room stood open. She was so astonished—Hafez had promised to lock it—that she forgot caution and hurried toward it without hesitation.

The room was empty. Madame Parviz no longer lay across the bed. The curtains had been opened and the door to the balcony stood wide. There was no sign of Hafez.

"Hafez?" she whispered, and then, "Hafez!" Moving to the balcony she leaned over the railing and looked down into the garden. "Hafez?" she called.

She turned and hurried down the hall to room 150 and opened the still-unlocked door. Serafina remained bound to the chair, her eyes screaming silent hatred at her. Mrs. Pollifax absently patted her shoulder as she passed her to search the other two rooms. There was no sign of Hafez, or even of Munir and Fouad. If Sabry and his two men were not in the Clinic then why had Hafez bolted, and where had he taken his grandmother? *What had happened while she was in the Clinic basement?*

She ran back to the staircase.

"Good morning," said Court cheerfully, descending from

the floor above. "You're certainly up early. There's something wrong with the elevator, have you noticed?"

"Yes. Have you seen Hafez?"

"No, I haven't. Is something wrong?"

But Mrs. Pollifax had already placed one hand on the banister and was hurrying down the stairs to the Reception floor. In her haste she caught the heel of one shoe in the carpet and kept her balance only by dropping the suitcase and clinging with both hands to the railing. The suitcase bumped and slid ahead of her and was retrieved by the head concierge, who had just started up the stairs. "Madame—you are all right?" he called.

She nodded and slipped back into her shoe.

"I was just coming up to knock on your door," he said. "Madame, there are two policemen here inquiring for you."

"Thank heaven," she said, walking down the stairs.

"They would like for you to go with them to the headquarters. A small passport misunderstanding, I am sure."

"Passport misunderstanding?" She stopped on the bottom stair, her eyes on the backs of the two men in uniform standing in the hall and she did not like those two backs at all. Taking a step backward she said, "Where's Robin? Where's Mr. Burke-Jones?"

One of the policemen slowly turned. It was Fouad, looking very continental in uniform. "Good morning, madame," he said pleasantly.

"Good morning," said Munir, walking swiftly to her side.

Mrs. Pollifax turned but it was already too late; each of them held her by an arm. "But these aren't policemen!" she cried to the head concierge. "Don't you recognize them? They came with Madame Parviz, they belong in room 154!"

The head concierge looked startled. "Madame?"

"I said they're not *policemen!*" she cried. "Surely you've seen them before, they came with Madame Parviz! Help me!" she called to Court, who stood transfixed on the staircase.

Gently but firmly Fouad and Munir were pushing her ahead of them to the main door. "Help—help!" cried Mrs. Pollifax as the pressure on her arms mounted. The head concierge gaped at her so blankly that she was forced to remember Fouad and

Munir had never stirred from their rooms. "Please!" she gasped, and then as they reached the door she turned and shouted to Court, "They're *not* the police—get help!" For just a moment she succeeded in grasping the knob of the door and hung there, sending a last desperate glance at Court, who stood baffled and uncertain at the foot of the stairs. Then Fouad and Munir lifted her over the threshold and she was carried beyond it, down steps and up the driveway toward two cars that were blocking the entrance.

The sheik jumped out of the nearer car, looking relieved. "Was it necessary to use my name?"

"*La,*" said Fouad.

"*Isri.*"

They carried her, still struggling, past the small car—it was a red Volkswagen—and Mrs. Pollifax glanced inside and with a sinking heart recognized the figure collapsed on the rear seat: it was Madame Parviz. She was picked up again and hurried along to the black Rolls-Royce. Her hands were pushed behind her back, roped painfully together, and then she was shoved inside so roughly that she fell across the trousered legs of the man already occupying the back seat. There was something familiar about those trousers—they were purple, she saw in dismay—and as she was plucked from the floor by unseen hands and hurled into the seat Robin said grimly, "They caught me, too—about five feet from the edge of the garden. A bloody rout, I'd say."

Chapter Eighteen

After leaving Mrs. Pollifax downstairs in the hall, Hafez had gone up to her room and locked himself inside with his grandmother. He had also locked the door to the balcony and drawn the heavy curtains. When he heard the footsteps in the hall he was sitting quietly beside the bed. He might not even have noticed them except that the steps paused at Mrs. Pollifax's door and a board creaked. Hafez stood up to face the door, expecting at any moment to hear Mrs. Pollifax call, "Hafez?"

But Mrs. Pollifax did not call. The quilted outer door was drawn softly open and he watched the knob of the locked inner door turn slowly to the right and then to the left. His heart hammering, he moved back to stand beside his grandmother. He heard a low, sibilant whisper and words spoken in Arabic. "It's locked. Hand over the skeleton key."

It was Fouad at the door.

Hafez's heart thudded so violently that he thought it must surely burst through his shirt. "Grandmama," he whispered, but his grandmother did not stir. He began to search for a weapon—anything, a pair of scissors, a paperweight—but there was nothing at hand. He thought of the pockets of his windbreaker jacket but he already knew their contents: several inches of rope, his tape recorder and spare tapes, a pencil and a few exotic stones collected for their color but not their weight. As the key rattled in the lock he backed farther and farther from the bed until he reached the door to the balcony and stood pressed against it. He realized with an acute sense of grief that he was going to have to abandon his grandmother. He had no alternative, it was either leave or be taken by these men and, if taken, there might be no hope at all for either of them.

He slipped behind the curtains, tugged at the door and stepped out on the balcony just as the door to Mrs. Pollifax's room opened. As the two men walked inside he climbed over the railing onto the ledge. The adjacent balcony was unoccupied and he crouched there a moment out of sight, trying to think how to escape. There were many exits on the ground floor but there was no way of reaching any of them without passing the concierge's desk. Robin had gone for the police. The important thing was to find out what Fouad and Munir planned to do with his grandmother so that he could inform the police when they arrived. He had to find a way to keep an eye on the two men without being seen himself.

In his eight days at the Clinic Hafez had followed the code of every ten-year-old: he had explored all the corners and unmarked rooms that adults accepted as out-of-bounds or of no interest at all. Now he recalled the dumbwaiter in the utility closet next to room 148 and he wondered if he could reach it without being noticed. He cautiously made his way along the ledge. At this hour there was no one in the garden below, and apparently the occupants of the rooms he edged past were still asleep. He reached the balcony of room 154 and climbed over the railing. The door stood open and he walked through the room to the hall door and peered out. The corridor was empty. Taking a deep breath he raced down the hall and ducked inside the utility room. Opening the door of the dumbwaiter he tugged at the ropes and brought the box up to the third floor, climbed inside and began to lower himself hand over hand. It reminded him of the chute at the Castle de Chillon and he remembered Mrs. Pollifax saying that they must be resourceful.

Well, he thought, they had been resourceful at the castle

and they had not been caught. Now it was up to him to be even cleverer because he was alone.

There were voices in the kitchen, waiters grumbling over the loss of electricity and the tediousness of a wood-burning stove. The dumbwaiter reached the bottom of the shaft and Hafez pushed open the door, stared at three startled faces and climbed out. *"Bon jour,"* he said brightly, and walked past them to the door and outside into the maze of trellises that concealed the exit. This brought him to the greenhouse and he ducked around it, climbed the high bank to the road, ran across the road and took refuge in a clump of bushes from which he could see the front door.

He hoped it was the front door that he should watch.

He stared at the walls of the Clinic, thinking of all the people inside asleep but this only made him feel lonely. Even if they were awake, he thought, they wouldn't know, and if by some chance they learned what was happening they wouldn't *believe.* It was the first time he had understood that a conspiracy existed among the living to wall out and reject what was disturbing. It took special people like Mrs. Pollifax and Robin to understand, he thought, and he supposed it was because they were in some way outsiders. They had stepped out of the circle long enough to see the shadows. They had dared the loneliness.

He felt a wave of infinite gratitude toward them and he thought, "I will be like them when I grow up, I swear I will."

A movement at Sabry's window caught his eye. He saw the balcony door open and Fouad walk out, peer to his left in the direction of the road and then wave a hand. A moment later Sheik Yazdan ibn Kazdan strolled down the driveway and entered the Clinic. Several minutes later Fouad and Munir stumbled out of the door carrying his grandmother. They were obviously in a great hurry, which meant they must barely have made it past the concierge's desk without being discovered. This was something the sheik must have arranged.

Where are the police, wondered Hafez impatiently.

The two men with their burden walked up the driveway past the greenhouse. As they came abreast of Hafez in his hiding place he ducked his head and began to move with them parallel to the road, taking care to walk carefully. At the top of the incline he saw two cars blocking the Clinic's entrance drive, one a small red Volkswagen, the other a long black Rolls-Royce. Sabry emerged from the latter and helped the two men place Madame Parviz inside the Volkswagen. The three then stood beside the car, talking and smoking.

Hafez had no paper but he did have a pencil. He drew it out, wet it with his lips and tested it on the inside of his nylon windbreaker. It wrote, and he carefully copied down on his jacket the license numbers of the two cars. He had scarcely finished doing this when the sheik came out of the Clinic. He and the three men began an argument, during which Hafez heard his name spoken several times, and then Fouad and Munir stripped off their jackets and stepped behind the cars. When they reappeared Hafez saw that they wore uniforms of some kind. The sheik opened the trunk of the Rolls and tossed their old clothes inside.

Why didn't the police come, Hafez thought desperately. He watched Fouad and Munir walk down the driveway in their matching uniforms and he guessed they were going into the Clinic now to find Madame Pollifax. There was no reason to believe they wouldn't capture her, too, and then he would be the only one left.

He would be the only one who knew—but what could he give Robin and the police except the license numbers of two cars that might have already vanished by the time they came? It was not enough.

He had seen the sheik open the trunk of the Rolls and toss clothes inside. It was a large trunk, and he knew it was unlocked. Now the sheik had climbed inside the car and he and Sabry sat talking in the front seat. It was very quiet except for the low murmer of their voices and birds chattering in the tall trees.

We have to be resourceful, Madame Pollifax had said.

Hafez moved swiftly. Once behind the Volkswagen he slid to his knees and crawled around it to the back of the Rolls and crouched there. Ever so gently he lifted the door to the trunk and opened it half way. It creaked a little but the murmur of voices continued. Climbing inside he lowered it softly behind him and stuffed a corner of Fouad's jacket into the opening to leave a crack for fresh air.

Chapter Nineteen

When the sheik's car reached the village it did not turn to the left to head down the mountain, it turned to the right to begin a precipitous climb upward. Mrs. Pollifax looked at the sheik seated opposite her on the jump seat and said, "Where are we going?"

His dark eyes were friendly as he smiled. "In due time we separate. I go far, madame, but you and the other two will go no farther than I wish you to go. You have been, you know, a very naughty lady."

That sounded patronizing and she told him so.

His eyebrows lifted. "How so? You have been only a minor inconvenience, no more than a buzzing gnat. Can one give to a gnat obeisance or importance?"

"I can't speak for Mrs. Pollifax," said Robin, "but I resent being called a gnat and a minor inconvenience, damn it."

The sheik laughed. "Well said, Burke-Jones, I'd feel the same way myself. Your face is familiar to me, by the way. Have we met?"

"Paris—'65," Robin said shortly. "Le Comte de Reuffe's weekend party. Gabrielle's ball. The races at Deauville."

"Ah yes, I remember now. Have you news of them? . . . '65 was a gay year, it lingers in my mind like vintage wine on the palate. I understand that Jackie has married?"

"Twice since then," said Robin.

Mrs. Pollifax only half-listened. She was looking around her as the road narrowed and the houses thinned. They were moving now up a steep slope through thick dark woods, they rounded a curve and suddenly they were at the top of the mountain on which Montbrison rested. But this peak was negligible, no more than a foothill, a steppingstone to what lay beyond, for they were surrounded by even higher peaks that merged into other, taller mountains stretching ahead like an endless cyclorama. Patches of forest broke up the quilt pattern here and there, and each seam of green on these lower slopes boasted a small village or cluster of chalets. Far off on another rock projection Mrs. Pollifax could see a tiny train chugging along like a slug, its smoke almost transparent against the pale blue sky.

"No, I can't believe that," Robin was saying. "Really I can't. Gabrielle a nun? I thought she married Roger."

It was too civilized for Mrs. Pollifax. "Where are we going?" she asked again.

"No, no, it was Danielle who married Roger," protested the sheik.

This name reminded Mrs. Pollifax of the film on Saturday evening—the heroine's name had been Danielle—and this in turn reminded her of Hafez, who had promised to confide the plot to her and had never done so. She realized that she was very frightened for him because he had been guarding his grandmother, and Madame Parviz was in the car behind them. What had happened to him? She recalled her impressions of the back seat of the Volkswagen and what she had seen in that quick glance inside. There had been only the one crumpled figure with head against the window and eyes closed . . . but if they had found Madame Parviz they must have found Hafez, too and he was not in the Volkswagen. If they had killed him—"Where is Hafez?" she demanded.

The sheik turned to look at her with interest. "Hafez?" He shrugged. "I don't think we need to worry about Hafez."

"I should like to worry," she told him.

Again he shrugged, this time with a pleasant smile. "But Hafez is—shall we say, expendable?" Over his shoulder he called, "Ibrahim, are we nearly there?"

"We are nearly there, Sayyid."

Expendable, thought Mrs. Pollifax, and felt a little sick.

They had been climbing all the time and now they had reached a bald, wind-swept plateau which ran like a spine across the mountain they'd left to the mountain ahead. Patches of thin grass grew wherever they found a little earth but there was little earth that had not been swept away by the winds. Mrs. Pollifax looked out of the car window and down, and caught a glimpse of Lake Geneva far, far below. The car slowed, and up ahead she saw a seam in the stony earth, a narrow cart track winding off toward the stony knob of a hill to the right. The car turned off the paved road and jolted and leaped across the ground with the Volkswagen following behind them.

They approached the knoll on a bias, winding around boulders and fields of dead earth littered with pebbles. There were no trees, they must be too high for trees, decided Mrs. Pollifax, and she began to feel the total hopelessness of their situation. It would be better to take each moment as it came, she told herself, and acknowledged for the first time that not many moments might lie ahead.

The car cleared the knob of the hill and Mrs. Pollifax looked ahead and saw a chalet, a weatherbeaten, closed-up Alpine cottage perched absurdly up here among the rocks and the clouds, its shuttered windows overlooking what must be a spectacular view of the country miles below. A single stunted tree was its only companion. As she watched, a cloud of mist drifted lazily toward them across the stony meadow. It obliterated the gnarled old tree, stroked the chalet with long ghost-like fingers and then swirled toward them. A moment later it had surrounded the car, damp and sunless and gray. When they emerged from its clutch the car had reached the chalet.

Robin peered out. "I say, this doesn't seem up to your standards as a *pied-à-terre*," he said, still playing the *bon vivant*.

"This?" said the sheik, startled. "Oh my dear fellow, this was rented only last evening when it became apparent that you and your friend were becoming nuisances. A pity, too, for it amused me to use the Clinic."

"Amused you?" said Robin.

"It's so much more dangerous," he explained simply. "There was the irony of it, too. I happen to be a member of the Board of Directors, you see. I am so very welcome there."

I don't think we're going to get out of this, thought Mrs. Pollifax bleakly, and turned her head as the Volkswagen pulled up beside them. Fouad climbed out and went up the steps of the chalet to unlock the door. With the door open he waved them in. The sheik uncrossed his long legs and stepped out of the car. "Sabry?"

Sabry nodded and brought out a gun. "You will go inside the chalet," he told them without expression.

Robin climbed out first, and as he turned to face her for the first time she saw that the right side of his face was scratched and torn, and his right eye swollen almost closed. "Oh Robin," she said sadly.

"I've obviously lived much too sedentary a life," he said lightly. "A fact that I intend to rectify at the earliest possible moment if I ever get out of this in one piece." His hands were also tied but as she climbed out he succeeded in lifting them to touch her arm reassuringly. At the moment it only made her want to cry.

They moved across the rocks to the wooden steps. Mrs. Pollifax turned for one last look around her but the empty, windswept landscape was so distressingly bleak that she did not linger; she entered the chalet almost gratefully.

Inside it was midnight, every window shuttered and barred. Fouad was lighting an oil lamp and as it flared up to illuminate the room he looked at her once, briefly, and she saw the hate in his eyes. Then he lifted the lamp and carried it to a table in the middle of the room, his face impassive.

"Cheerless place," said Robin behind her. "Rather like a cottage at Brighton in the off season."

It was precisely what it did resemble; it still held within it the bone-chilling damp of winter, the furnishings were shabby and dusty and the grate in the fireplace empty. There was a strong smell of cooking oil and mothballs.

"Planning to stay long?" quipped Robin.

The sheik moved away from the door as Munir carried in Madame Parviz and lowered her, none too gently, to the couch in front of the fireplace. Because Sabry chose this moment to glance at his watch, Mrs. Pollifax glanced at hers too; it was eight o'clock, which was difficult to realize in this lightless room. Sabry and the sheik began talking amiably in Arabic. The sheik brought out his wallet, counted an enormous number of Swiss francs into Sabry's palm and wished him well. Sabry went out, closing the door behind him.

"I wish I knew where he's going," Mrs. Pollifax said to Robin in a low voice. "I wish Hafez were here to translate that for us."

The sheik heard her and smiled. "But I have no secrets from you," he said, his eyes twinkling at her. "Ibrahim has gone to bring back a helicopter. You may have noticed that the terrain here is quite suitable for its landing. I've no intention of lingering any longer in Switzerland and since I've no idea what little hints either of you may have left behind at the Clinic I shall proceed as if the Clinic—as if all of Switzerland!—is looking for me." He appeared delighted at the thought. "To outwit them—oh superb sport, that."

"You're quite a sportsman," Robin said dryly.

"But of course—I am a Bedouin," he said with dignity. "Sit down, there is no need to stand on ceremony. The chairs are dusty but far more comfortable than standing. Munir—we'll have food now."

Mrs. Pollifax lowered herself into a straight chair near the fireplace, her tied wrists extended awkwardly in front of her. Across the room she met Robin's gaze and recognized the question in his eyes. She spoke it aloud. "What do you plan to do with us—with Robin, Madame Parviz and me?"

The sheik walked to the fireplace and rested a hand on the mantel. "I'm sorry you ask," he said regretfully. "I thought we could enjoy a rather charming picnic here together while we wait. It may be a wait of several hours and unfortunately—" He sighed. "Unfortunately Fouad and Munir have never developed the art of conversation. They remain distressingly utilitarian." He sighed. "In such bleak surroundings a little conversation helps to smooth the passing of time. Surely we need not discuss such a painful thing as your futures?"

"They are," pointed out Mrs. Pollifax, *"our* futures."

"Were," he corrected gently, with a smile. "Now of course they belong to me. We have a proverb that says 'If you are a peg, endure the knocking; if you are a mallet, strike.' I hope that you will endure with fortitude the consequences of your meddling."

"Haven't you been doing a little meddling of your own?" inquired Mrs. Pollifax.

He laughed. "It is all in the eye of the beholder, is it not? However, to answer your question as tactfully as possible, let me say that the helicopter, when it arrives, will have no room for you and Mr. Burke-Jones. There will be space only for Fouad, Munir, Ibrahim, myself and Madame Parviz, who—as you may have guessed—is still of some importance as a hostage. Now please, let us say no more, it becomes distasteful to me. There are always a few who have to be sacrificed for the greater good. We also have a saying 'What is brought by the wind will be carried away by the wind.' Ah, good—good," he said happily as Munir came in carrying firewood.

Quickly and efficiently Munir arranged the wood in the fireplace and lighted a fire. Once it was ignited he spread a rug on the floor in front of it—a gorgeous Persian rug, Mrs. Pollifax noted—and distributed cushions around it. Incense was placed on the mantel, a match applied to it and the scent of sandalwood met her nostrils. Then Munir retired to the kitchen off to the left and the rattle of cups could be heard. Mrs. Pollifax stood up and walked over to the fire, holding her bound hands out to warm them but it was uncomfortable standing so near the sheik and she retreated to the couch and sat down at the end of it, near Madame Parviz's feet. The poor woman was still unconscious, her eyes closed, but a second later Mrs. Pollifax glanced again at her and was not so sure. She thought a gleam of light showed between the fringe of her lashes and the bone of her cheek. She did not look again.

"For the greater good of what?" she asked the sheik. "If we're to be so lightly sacrificed perhaps you can tell us the great benefit the world is going to gain?"

"The benefits are Allah's, I am only the instrument," he told her sternly.

Munir returned carrying a tray. On it were tiny cups and a

large, beak-nosed brass coffeepot which exuded a spicy fragrance and a cloud of steam. The fire flickered across the rug,
picking out its jewel-like colors and the patina of brass. A
dusty Brighton cottage was rapidly turning into an Arab tent,
she thought, and she couldn't help but admire this imposing of
will upon a shell of a house.

Robin said stiffly, "If you're planning to feed us—in the
interest of fascinating conversation—we can't possibly manage with our hands tied."

"Quite so," the sheik said amiably. "They will be untied
once Munir has completed his chores." With a twinkle for
Mrs. Pollifax he added, "But you will please notice that Fouad
is at the door with his gun."

She had already noticed him squatting by the door in the
shadows; she took note and glanced away. "These plans you
have," she said to the sheik, looking at him steadily. "You're
responsible for the death of Marcel and you're responsible for
the death of a man named Fraser, and now you would kill us as
well. This is what you call being the instrument of Allah?"

He shrugged. "In war many people are killed, men and
women, children, soldiers, and onlookers. But I am surprised
that you know about Fraser. How is this?"

Robin, too, was watching her curiously. "You can't possibly
mean the English chap who was injured at the Clinic last
week! Do you mean he was murdered?" he asked the sheik,
turning to him. "And it had something to do with you?"

The sheik smiled. "He was a professional British agent, my
dear Burke-Jones. Unfortunately most of his work had been
done in the Middle East so that he and Ibrahim had met before.
So long as Ibrahim convalesced quietly and took the sun there
was no harm in sharing the Clinic. But of course once the
Parvizes arrived the situation would have been intolerable.
Fraser would have guessed something was up at once. He had
to be removed."

Robin thought about this for a moment and then said
coolly, "I happen to be a British agent, too, you know, and
since Mrs. Pollifax has absolutely nothing to do with any of
this I insist that you let her go at once."

Before Mrs. Pollifax could protest this wasted act of gallantry the sheik laughed. "I don't believe you for a moment, Burke-Jones, and I couldn't possibly allow her to go free. It's she, after all, who was found in Ibrahim's room. She knows too much. Enough of such nonsense." As Munir poured coffee from the pot into tiny cups he said, "Have you tasted *herisa* before? It's an herb coffee, I think you'll enjoy it. Munir, you may cut their ropes now. It is better there be no marks on their wrists."

No marks on the bodies, thought Mrs. Pollifax, and as a second tray was brought in bearing pastries and dates she experienced an almost hysterical urge to laugh. A Persian rug, tiny cups of herb coffee, incense, and a sheik—it was too much. She controlled her wild upsurge of laughter and abruptly felt like bursting into tears. "You travel with originality," she managed to say.

The sheik flashed his white smile at her. "We have a proverb, 'He who has money can eat sherbet in hell.' Anything is possible with money."

"Including the buying of armies and lives?" she said tartly. She held up her wrists to Munir, who carefully severed the bonds around her wrists, and when he had done this she rubbed them, wincing. But she could eat now, and she was grateful.

The sheik paused with his cup halfway to his lips and smiled. "Only a means to an end, Mrs. Pollifax. You spoke of meddling. Your meddling is destructive—it's in my way—but mine is constructive."

"In what way?"

"You have a saying, 'They shall beat their swords into plowshares.' " He turned his face to her, his eyes remote. "A rabble of men cannot do this, they are insufficiently enlightened but one man can accomplish what has never been accomplished before. I shall bring peace to the world, to the entire world."

"If only you could," she said longingly. "But bloodlessly?"

He smiled. "We have a saying that first it is necessary to build up the inside of the mosque and then the outside. No, not bloodlessly, because men are children and must have their quarrels."

Mrs. Pollifax sighed. "I should have guessed not."

"It will be a quick bloodletting, though. I have my own army in the desert, you see, they have been training secretly for some time, as well as collecting other certain—uh—instruments of power. I have scientists, a laboratory, munitions, all hidden away in the desert. All that is lacking now is a country, a base, but it is astonishing how easy it all is. In this materialistic world men will sell their souls for a few dollars. When one has money one can buy anyone."

"Apparently you couldn't buy King Jarroud," pointed out Mrs. Pollifax.

"Ah, but I have undermined him," he said with the flash of a smile, "and that has been far more enjoyable. General Parviz will be no trouble to me, the road to the throne is wide open." His smile became radiant. "One of the five pillars of the Moslem faith is the people's willingness to participate in *jihad*. Do you know what *jihad* is, madame?"

"A holy war," said Robin in a bleak voice.

"Quite so, yes," said the sheik. "The redress of wrongs is an act of religious obedience in Islam. I have had a vision—Muhammed came to me in a dream one night—telling me that the time has come, and that I am sayyid."

Mrs. Pollifax put down her cup and stared at him, caught by the play of emotion, a look almost of ecstasy on his face. She confessed herself moved by the passion in his voice and the almost hypnotic quality of his words.

"The Moslems have waited a long time," he went on, the fire illuminating the fierce profile and flashing eyes. "Nasser promised hope at first but it was Allah's will that he be struck down. Now Moslems quarrel among themselves. There is Quadaffi and there is Sadat and Hussein and Jarroud and we are all divided but I shall unite us in *jihad*—with one stroke—and when we are truly united we will be soldiers together, and when we have won back what is ours we shall impose peace on the whole world."

"Impose?" There was silence until Mrs. Pollifax, already guessing the answer, said softly, "How?"

"By the means given me to impose it." His smile deepened. "That, dear lady, is too great a secret to divulge but I have the means, never fear, the means to the glorious end promised me by the Prophet Himself. I can assure you the world will pay attention. *Allah Akhbar!*"

From Fouad came a resounding, *"Allah Akhbar!"*

"Your plans include much more than Zabya, then."

He laughed. "Of course. I'm surprised that you didn't see that at once. Zabya?" He shrugged. "A small desert country with a tiresome, idealistic little king. Who could possibly settle for Zabya? For me it shall be the beginning, a base in the center of an oil-rich continent, a foothold, a foundation on which to build an empire. Mohammed himself began with only the town of Medina, yet before he died he had changed millions of people's lives and had given us Mecca. After his death his followers carried Islam as far as France."

"And so you will be the new Alexander," said Mrs. Pollifax quietly.

He leaned forward, his eyes intense. "You must confess—if you consider it honestly and realistically—that what the world needs now—before it destroys itself—is one ruler. One law. One government. It is the only way to survive."

"Good God," put in Robin deflatingly, "you mean one damned bureaucracy to botch things instead of dozens? The red tape staggers the imagination."

The sheik ignored him. "The key to it all—the key to the master stroke—lies in that suitcase," he said abruptly. "You see it standing on the table? You broke open the locks but you couldn't possibly understand what you saw. I have already tested myself—myself and my cunning—by making fools of high men all over the world. It has pleased me a great deal. It was my first adventure, my beginning."

This had the effect of cheering Mrs. Pollifax's flagging spirits because she was the only one in the room who knew that he was addressing two cans of peaches instead of a suitcase bearing several kilograms of plutonium.

"You can't possibly succeed, it's too outrageous," Robin said.

The sheik smiled at him benevolently. "A thief is a king until he is caught." He rinsed his fingers in a bowl of water and dried them on a towel that Munir held out to him. Rising he said, "Join me, Munir, it's time." To Fouad he added, "Remain attentive. Keep your distance and shoot if they move."

He and Munir disappeared into another room and she exchanged glances with Robin across the Persian rug. Over by the door, some fifteen feet away, Fouad rose to his feet and leaned against the door, his eyes bored as he watched them. There was silence except for the crackling of the fire until Robin said, "I'm beginning to take him seriously."

"Yes," said Mrs. Pollifax.

"All this business about peace—it doesn't sound very peaceful to me."

"It's the latest style of peace," she said dryly. "It's called waging peace with limited-duration reinforced protective reaction strikes, low kill-ratio and no incursions."

"I see. But not war," said Robin gravely.

"Oh, no, not *war*. Good heavens no."

From the next room the sheik intoned in a powerful voice: *"La ilaha illa llah, Muhammed rasul allah."*

"He's praying," Robin pointed out. "I daresay we should be praying, too. I mean, it does begin to look a bit final, the three of them against the two of us. And when Sabry gets back with a helicopter there'll be four of them. Look, there's something I wanted to mention, not important, I daresay, but something funny about the boot of the car we came in—or trunk, as you Americans call it."

"And something I have to ask you," she told him.

Each stopped, waiting for the other, and in the silence a low voice from the couch between them said, "Not two against four. Three."

Mrs. Pollifax turned to look at Madame Parviz lying there, her eyes closed.

Robin said, "Did she—?"

"Yes," said Mrs. Pollifax.

Lips barely moving and eyes still shut Madame Parviz said, "There is a poker on the hearth."

"We'd better not look at her," Mrs. Pollifax advised Robin.

"A bit of luck having her conscious at last," he pointed out in a low voice. "I'm not sure I can reach the poker without Fouad seeing me. Have you noticed how carefully they keep their distance from us? It's like a planned choreography—downright obvious."

"They're aware that I know some karate," explained Mrs. Pollifax.

"So that's it!" said Robin, brightening. "I must say that until meeting you I seem to have led the most commonplace life. You might have told me you knew karate. If that's the case Madame Parviz can be armed with the poker and all we need are some brass knuckles for me. Stay with us, Madame Parviz!"

"But there has to be some way to get near them," pointed out Mrs. Pollifax.

"It's what we've got to wait for," Robin said. "Just one mistake, just one slip and we might be able to jump them. Damn it, I refuse to give up without protest." He was stretching out one leg so that his foot extended across the Persian rug to the hearth. Very carefully he prodded the tip of the poker, and when his foot only pushed it farther away he swore under his breath.

"It's a break not having our hands tied," Mrs. Pollifax pointed out. "How long do you suppose we have?"

"You heard the man, until Sabry brings back the helicopter. It's not hopeless, you know. If we can stall, somehow catch them off balance—"

Stall, mused Mrs. Pollifax, and it occurred to her there might be a way to confuse the sheik and his men, even to persuade them to postpone their escape. If she could say enough but not too much—Aloud she said, "There's one thing I could do that might give us a chance to get nearer them."

"What?"

"I don't think it's wise to tell the sheik we know about the plutonium, do you?"

"Good God, no," said Robin. "Keeping it secret seems to feed his superiority. He'd probably kill us on the spot."

"That's what I felt. But I can tell the sheik I replaced the two cans in the suitcase with two cans of peaches from the Clinic."

The glance Robin gave her was withering. "That's a singularly uninspired idea and not at all up to your usual standards. Do you take him for a fool?"

. "But that's exactly—" She stopped as the sheik returned, rubbing his hands together with satisfaction. As he looked from one face to the other they all heard it: the sound of a helicopter's blades beating the air at some distance away. Fouad opened the door. "Sayyid," he said eagerly.

"Allah be praised, he's early. Munir—" He gestured toward the rug. "Pack up our things, we'll be leaving in a few minutes. There's no point in your killing them, Sabry will do it."

The sound of the helicopter filled the room; a gust of air blew in through the open door, lifting ashes from the fireplace and scattering them. The noise abruptly stilled, and a minute later Mrs. Pollifax heard the crunch of shoes on the pebbles outside. Her heart began to hammer sickeningly against her ribs. As Sabry entered the room she stood up and said in a clear loud voice, "I have something to say to you."

Chapter Twenty

The sheik glanced at his watch. "Very well—say it, but be quick."

She lifted her head and said steadily, "There are only cans of peaches in your suitcase."

"I beg your pardon!" he said in astonishment.

"For God's sake," groaned Robin.

Her head went higher. "I think you should know that just before you brought me here I removed the two original cans and substituted two cans of fruit for them. The real ones are back at the Clinic."

He looked amused. "Which means that really we should not kill you yet, is this correct? Instead we should all drive back to the Clinic and play hide-and-seek again?"

"Whatever you feel necessary," she said calmly. "But I wanted to stress that if you kill us now you'll be sorry later for very practical reasons, if not moral ones. You won't know how to find the original two cans."

"That's very true, of course," he said politely, watching her face. "Munir," he added briskly, "bring us a can opener."

"Now you've done it," murmured Robin.

Mrs. Pollifax waited. Munir went into the kitchen and returned bearing a small metal can opener. "Give it to her," ordered the sheik.

"Sayyid," said Sabry in protest.

The sheik waved his protest aside. "No, no, this amuses me, Ibrahim, let us see what she dares."

Munir handed Mrs. Pollifax the can opener and she moved to the table in the center of the room. Opening the suitcase she slowly removed the plastic bags of filler and then the layers of shredded newspaper. She had at least gained the middle of the room, and she hoped that Robin would realize this. Detaching one of the cans from its cage she set it on the table, gripped the handle of the can opener and bent over it.

Abruptly a hand was placed over hers and she looked up into the cold dark eyes of the sheik. "That will be enough," he said curtly. "You are a very good actress and it's a clever trick on your part but do you really believe I would allow you to injure the contents of this can?"

"But it's only a can of peaches," she protested. "How can I persuade you unless I open it?"

"Shoot her, Ibrahim," he said in a bored voice and turned away. "Kill her, she grows tiresome."

"You bloody coward," cried Robin, stepping forward.

"Back!" snarled Ibrahim Sabry, lifting his gun. His sharp command was echoed by a shouted command from outside the chalet and Mrs. Pollifax saw Robin stop in midstride. Everyone stopped, it was like a game of Statues, Robin with one foot off the floor, the sheik with arm lifted, Fouad by the door with his mouth open, Sabry four feet away from her with his gun leveled at her head. And when the scene unfroze, she thought, Robin would place his left foot on the floor, the sheik would lower his hand, Sabry's finger would squeeze the trigger and she would die. The moment felt endless, she wanted to scream, "Get it over with!" and then she realized that what had turned them into stone was that all of the sheik's men were inside this room but the voice had come from outside.

"*Ici la police.——Sortez, les mains en l'air!*" called the voice.

No one moved. The moment stretched out interminably. She stood dazed, not understanding the words and wondering why the voice sounded so familiar, wondering why a picture flashed into her mind of a sunny morning in a garden and an old man leaning on a cane, and then she understood that it was the voice of General d'Estaing that she heard. She thought incredulously, the general *here*?

And then a second voice called, "Come out with your hands high—the jig is up!"

Robin's voice. *Robin's voice on a tape recorder.*

"Hafez," she whispered. He was alive.

"What the devil!" cried the sheik, and at once the spell was broken. Mrs. Pollifax threw herself at Sabry and knocked the gun out of his hand. As the gun clattered to the floor she slashed at him with her other hand and he staggered to the floor. Turning she saw that Robin had hurled himself upon Fouad and was struggling for his gun. As she stepped back Munir ran across the room to pluck Sabry's gun from the floor. He dropped it, bent to pick it up again and she kicked him. He grasped her leg and brought her down to the rug with him and they rolled over. The gun went off and sent a searing hot flame up her left arm. Just as Munir reached for her throat with both hands a figure in a long white robe rushed across the room and hit him over the head with a poker.

Mrs. Pollifax sat up. Her head was spinning dizzily and she felt a little sick. Madame Parviz was standing over Fouad and Robin was sitting on the floor brushing dust from his trousers. The sheik was nowhere to be seen, nor was the suitcase. Mrs. Pollifax stumbled to her feet, swayed a little, and made her way to the door.

The sheik was climbing into the helicopter that sat like a bloated dragonfly among the rocks outside. She saw the blades begin to rotate, churn, and then blur, and as she limped to the top step the helicopter lifted from the ground and she and the sheik exchanged a long glance through the Plexiglas window. The helicopter turned, lifted, and soared away over the hill, and as its noise diminished she heard the tape recorder call over and over *the jig is up the jig is up the jig* . . .

She sat down weakly on the top step and said "Hafez?"

The droning mechanical words seemed to come from the solitary tree on the hillside. "Hafez?" she called again, louder.

Hafez emerged from behind the tree. He hesitated until he saw her and then came bounding over the rocks toward her, a small intense figure radiating joy. "Madame!" he cried. "Oh madame, it *worked!*"

"Hafez," she said with feeling, "you've just saved our lives. However did you find us!"

"Find you? But madame, I never left you," he cried happily. "I hid in the trunk of the limousine. Don't you remember you said we must all be resourceful?"

"Resourceful," repeated Mrs. Pollifax, and frowned over a word that sounded familiar to her but held no meaning at all. "Resourceful," she said again, and looked up at the sun which had suddenly begun to skid across the sky.

Hafez gasped. "Madame—there is blood dripping on the stair!" His glance lifted to her arm and his eyes widened in horror. She heard him shout, "Grandmama! Robin! She has been shot!" and then, "Monsieur, she is fainting!"

Someone leaned over her, words were spoken, she was lifted and carried to the car while over and over the tape recorder called out *the jig is up the jig is up the jig is up the jig* . . . In the darkness that followed she heard a strange variety of voices—Bishop's first of all, but that was impossible because Bishop belonged in America—and then she thought she heard General d'Estaing speaking, and Court's reply, and then Dr. Lichtenstein commanded them to be quiet and there was silence. A long black silence.

Chapter Twenty-One

Mrs. Pollifax opened her eyes to find that she was lying in bed in her room at Montbrison. She stared at the ceiling, puzzled, and then her glance moved slowly down the wall, which an evening sun had striped with gold, and when her eyes focused on the face of the man seated beside her bed she said, "Whatever are you doing here!"

Bishop looked up from a magazine and grinned. "Is that any way to welcome me? Good God, when I arrived this morning I thought I'd arrived in time for your funeral. Carstairs sent me. He had a strong hunch things were going wrong."

She said dreamily, "They went wrong for me in the right way. Or right for me in the wrong way." She frowned. "Why do I feel so peculiar, Bishop?"

"You've just had a bullet removed from your arm," he explained. "You were bleeding like hell so Dr. Lichtenstein gave you a whiff of something and removed it in his office. They don't have an operating room here."

"Oh," she said, and tried to make sense of his explanation, which seemed very odd to her until she peered at her arm and discovered it swathed in gauze and bound to a splint.

"It's still Monday—only seven o'clock in the evening," he assured her. "Interpol has been here all day putting the pieces together and worrying like hell about you. They found a woman tied to a chair in room 150, and Marcel's body in the closet of room 153. I take it you've had a rather busy week-end?"

"Yes," she said, looking back on it from a vast distance and then the distance abruptly telescoped and she struggled to sit up. "The sheik?"

Bishop shook his head. "He got away. His private plane took off from Geneva airport at twelve noon."

"But the *coup d'ètat*—?"

"Firmly squashed—we *think*—but here's Schoenbeck," Bishop said, rising. "He's the man who can tell you about it. Mrs. Pollifax, it's high time you meet Henri Schoenbeck of Interpol."

Monsieur Schoenbeck advanced into the room looking a little shy, a little prim, his lips pursed but his eyes warm as they encountered hers. "And I, madame, am in your debt," he said, giving her a long and searching glance as he grasped her right hand. He returned it gently to her bed. "It is my loss that we meet only now, madame."

"Are you the person to whom I signaled?" she asked.

"No, no, that was Gervard." His lips curved faintly into a smile. "It may amuse you, madame, to learn that after al-lowing you to become settled at Montbrison over the weekend we had planned to pay a call upon you today and set up a more suitable contact. We had wanted," he explained, "to give you the weekend to become oriented. A plan, I might add, that has nearly cost you your life."

"Well," said Mrs. Pollifax politely, "it all appears to be over now, so there scarcely seems any point in post-mortems."

"Then allow me to tell you that I have just returned from the chalet on the Wildehorn. Burke-Jones and Hafez accompa-nied me, and on the way they told me a great deal of what happened. It may console you to learn that at this moment the sheik's three men are entering a nearby prison."

"It consoles me," she admitted, "but the sheik has flown away, I hear, with his peaches?"

Schoenbeck frowned. "I beg your pardon?"

"With the peaches."

Schoenbeck and Bishop exchanged glances. "Probably the chloroform," suggested Bishop.

Schoenbeck nodded. "The head becomes light." He said gently, "There is no need to pretend any longer now, madame. I have been told that you tried to persuade the sheik that he did not have the plutonium but you are quite safe now, you know."

Mrs. Pollifax sighed. "I suppose there *is* something absurd about peaches, Monsieur Schoenbeck, but I can assure you that what I said was true. The plutonium never left the Clinic. It's here."

"I think I believe her," said Bishop in an astonished voice.

"Never left the Clinic!" echoed Schoenbeck. "But then the French consignment—the French plutonium—is no longer in the hands of the sheik? Madame, if you would tell me precisely where it is—"

Mrs. Pollifax ignored the question and instead smiled at him dazzlingly. "What do you think of Robin, Monsieur Schoenbeck?"

"Robin? He has surprised me, that much I will say."

"If you mean Burke-Jones, isn't he the chap you all suspected of killing Fraser?" asked Bishop.

Schoenbeck looked pained. "Unfortunately, yes. Of all the guests at the Clinic he persisted in remaining a mystery. It appears that the man is nothing less than a jewel thief."

Mrs. Pollifax said calmly, "Yes, and a very *good* jewel thief. I'm delighted he's told you about himself but you must see that by being honest with you he's completely ruined his career." She looked at Schoenbeck sternly. "Is there anything you care to do about that, M. Schoenbeck?"

His glance moved to hers and he smiled faintly. "Yes, madame, there is, but I am wondering how you guessed it."

"It's an idea that frankly occurred to me several days ago," she said. "Perhaps you're reading my mind, M. Schoenbeck."

"Mon Dieu, one hopes not!"

"He's tremendously efficient about picking locks and he enjoys working alone, he's surprisingly clever in emergencies and he has gorgeous clothes."

Schoenbeck said dryly, "The clothes would do it, of course. As a matter of fact, madame, I am not such a fool as to allow such talent to slip through my fingers. I have already made certain approaches and he appears most interested." He added ruefully, "I can only wish that young Hafez could work for Interpol, too. Now there's a promising young brain."

"I think he prefers to become an astronomer," put in Mrs. Pollifax. "Where is he?"

"He and his grandmother are still talking to his father on the telephone, I believe, but he is anxious to see you when I have finished with you."

She shook her head in wonder. "It's incredible how resourceful he's been. If it hadn't been for Hafez—"

"Please," Schoenbeck said firmly. "Please, it is better, as you say, to have no post-mortems. Allow me instead to conduct them and to brood over how near Kashan came to pulling off his coup and completing his matched set of plutonium."

"What will happen to him?" she asked.

Schoenbeck sighed. "Very little, I fear. It is an unfortunate fact but—so far as I can see—no crime has been committed by the sheik except that of conspiracy, and this King Jarroud will have to deal with on a local level. The shiek paid others to kill for him, and it is they who will be punished. It is a pity but I think he will suffer only a little embarrassment and—one hopes—a few grave doubts that Allah personally spoke to him."

"Even when he planned to threaten the world with an atom bomb?" protested Mrs. Pollifax. "He said he had an army in the desert, and laboratories—and obviously he had a network of people available to him if he succeeded in stealing plutonium."

"We can only hope, madame," said Schoenbeck, "but we have discovered that before he left Switzerland the sheik had time to make a telephone call to Zabya. I fear that we may find only empty laboratories—if we find them at all—and as for a secret army I suspect the sheik has already ordered it disbanded or moved."

"Moved!" cried Mrs. Pollifax in a dismayed voice.

"Naturally he will not dare to try his *coup d'ètat* tomorrow but he still has several pounds of plutonium, madame. Dreams die hard."

"Oh dear," said Mrs. Pollifax.

He nodded. "I am not overly optimistic that Kashan's ambitions have been deflated. I can assure you that the sheik will be closely watched but I must tell you that the desert is enormous, madame, and much of it uncharted." He sighed. "When I grow depressed—as one does—about the frailties of civilization and the absence of saints, it is men like the sheik who give me patience. A number of governments muddling along give us a thin margin of error but it is nevertheless a margin against oblivion."

She said reluctantly, "He impressed me, you know."

Schoenbeck smiled. "But of course, Madame—the sheik would make the perfect anti-Christ."

"I beg your pardon?" said Bishop, startled.

Schoenbeck's mouth twisted humorously. "You do not know your Bible? It is prophesied that after the Jews regain Jerusalem—as they did several years ago—there will come the anti-Christ, a man who will perform miracles for the people and bring peace to the world. And—how does it go?" His eyes narrowed thoughtfully. " 'And when the people shall say— peace and safety!—then suddenly destruction will come upon them as travail upon a woman with child, and they shall not escape.' Thessalonians, I believe." He bowed to them and strolled toward the door.

"Monsieur Schoenbeck," Mrs. Pollifax called after him softly. "The plutonium is in the basement supply room, in the farthest corner hidden behind a sack of charcoal."

He smiled. "Thank you, madame."

"Odd duck," said Bishop when he had gone. "On the whole, I believe Carstairs was a bit rough on him." He, too, arose. "Well, Mrs. Pollifax," he said, walking over to kiss her lightly on the cheek, "it's time for me to fly away again. You've orders to stay through the week until you've thoroughly convalesced, you know. If you don't, Carstairs will have my head for it."

"But I'm delighted to stay," said Mrs. Pollifax, "and actually quite relieved that I may. Can you imagine Miss Hartshorne's reaction if I should go back to New Brunswick with my arm like this?" She shook her head at the thought. "She'll be very difficult, at least until Christmas. She'll say it's exactly what I deserve for spending a dull week in Baltimore visiting an old friend." With a small twinkle she added, "Miss Hartshorne feels I lack a sense of adventure."

"Good God," said Bishop with a shudder. "And if you're still in a sling when you go home what will you tell her?"

"That I tripped over Adelaide's cat, I think, and broke my arm."

"A very large cat?" suggested Bishop, grinning.

"Oh, very," she told him, smiling.

"Then I needn't worry about you any more. By the way, I think you'll find yourself in good company this week. Hafez and his grandmother will be staying a few days until Madame Parviz feels better. General Parviz will fly over on Friday to take them home and I imagine the general will be eager to meet you."

From the door Hafez said, "Please, may we come in now, monsieur?"

"She's all yours," Bishop said, and blowing Mrs. Pollifax a kiss went out.

Hafez, Robin, and Court tiptoed in and stood at the end of the bed beaming at her while she in turn beamed at them. She saw that Robin and Court were holding hands and she guessed that Robin, having unburdened himself to Interpol, had unburdened himself to Court as well. Mrs. Pollifax said mischievously, "*Ici la police. Sortez, les mains en l'air!*"

Hafez broke into a laugh and hurled himself across the bed to sit near her, his face shining with happiness. "Madame," he said, "we are all alive."

"Isn't it surprising?" she agreed.

"And, madame," he continued eagerly, "I have been speaking to my father on the telephone—twice we have talked—and you will meet him on Friday because they say you cannot travel yet, and he wishes to thank you in person and—"

"Hafez is back to normal," pointed out Robin, grinning.

"—and he is bringing from King Jarroud the Shepherd Isa Medal of Peace—"

"*Shepherd* Medal?" asked Court, sitting down.

"Yes, mademoiselle, named after the shepherd Isa, who saved our country from invasion in 1236. He threw himself from a cliff to warn the people in the valley that the enemy was on the hills, and when they saw his fall, with the enemy's arrow piercing his heart, they knew their country was in danger. And my father says on Friday we will have a small party here at the Clinic to present to you this medal, the highest given in my country. Isn't that magnificent, madame?"

"And you didn't even have to throw yourself off a cliff," pointed out Robin.

Court shivered. "You have all—the three of you—been in such danger and I didn't even know. I didn't *know*."

Hafez turned and looked at her and was glad to hear the sadness in her voice.

Robin, too, turned to look at Court. "If I'm going to work for Interpol—now that Mrs. Pollifax has succeeded in making an honest man of me—you'll have to grow accustomed to a spot or two of danger, you know. That is, if you're going to marry me."

Court said softly, "*Am* I going to marry you, Robin?"

"I'm damned well hoping so."

Her cheeks turned pink. "Well," she said thoughtfully, and then, "yes . . . I believe I am!" she said in astonishment.

"Bravo," said Mrs. Pollifax.

Robin leaned down and kissed the top of Court's dark head. "The wisest decision you've ever made, my dear, and it gives me a perfectly brilliant idea. If Hafez's party is Friday it gives us just time to get a special license. We can be married right here at the Clinic."

"And Mrs. Pollifax can be the matron of honor," cried Court. "Oh you simply must be my matron of honor, Mrs. Pollifax. You will, won't you?"

Mrs. Pollifax considered this with pleasure. "I can't think of anything I'd enjoy more," she confessed. "I can wear my drip-dry purple robe and my prayer beads. It's been *such* a disappointment that I've been too busy to wear either of them."

"That I can't wait to see," Robin said fervently.

"But who could be the best man?"

"Oh, no problem there," Robin said, and placed a hand on Hafez's shoulder. "There's only one person at the Clinic or anywhere else who could possibly qualify."

Hafez looked up at Robin and grinned.

With a blissful sigh Mrs. Pollifax leaned back against her pillows to watch them. She acknowledged that her arm was stiff and uncomfortable, and that ahead of her lay the greatest ordeal of all—Miss Hartshorne—but what is brought by the wind, she remembered, will be carried away by the wind. With this she dismissed all thoughts of the sheik and settled down to enjoy a really genuine convalescence.

Mrs. Pollifax
on Safari

For Marjorie Bell Fritz

I would like to thank Mr. Xen Vlahakis and Ms. Jeanne Harris of the Zambia National Tourist Bureau in New York for their generous help in providing material about Zambia, none of which included the Moses Msonthi School, which is purely fictional and does not exist.

Chapter One

It was barely eight o'clock in the morning when the telephone call came in from Algiers, but Carstairs was already at his desk high up in the CIA building in Langley, Virginia. With his left hand he switched on a tape recorder, with his right he buzzed for his assistant while he listened with narrowed eyes. At one point he interrupted, saying, "Mind repeating that?" and scribbled several words on paper. When Bishop hurried into the office the call had just been completed.

"Sorry," Bishop said breathlessly, "I was in the men's room, sir. I've missed something?"

"You have every right to be in the men's room," Carstairs told him reproachfully, "but you've missed an important call from Algiers. We may—just may, Bishop—have the first whisper of a breakthrough on the Aristotle case."

"Good God," said Bishop, staring at him incredulously. "After all these months?"

"It's possible. Remember that fabric shop that Davis' department placed under surveillance in Algiers? The stolen bank-note job," he added helpfully. "Bennet photographed some messages that were left out on a desk overnight and he decided, bless him, that one of them would interest us very much. Bright lad, Bennet. The cables and memos were in French and Arabic and he's only just finished translating them." Carstairs reached over and turned on the tape recorder. "Here we are," he said, and accelerating and then slowing the machine, he signaled to Bishop to take the words down in shorthand.

They both listened carefully as Bennet's clipped voice told them, "The original message, translated from the French, reads as follows: CONFIRM ORDER SEVENTY YARDS BLACK ARISTOTLE SILKS TO ZAMBIA THREE BOLTS COTTON DUE KAFUE PARK TWO BOLTS CHUNGA MUSLIN TEN YARDS FIVE-DAY SAFARI DESIGN CHINTZ DELIVERABLE JUNE NINE REPEAT CONFIRM RE-CONFIRM. CHABO."

"Right," said Bishop, puzzled. "Any more?"

"Yes, if you've got that down." Carstairs pressed the button and the voice resumed . . . "and when the clutter words have been extracted from the fabric order, using their usual decoding technique, the message becomes: CONFIRM ARISTOTLE TO ZAMBIA DUE KAFUE PARK CHUNGA FIVE-DAY SAFARI ON JUNE NINE REPEAT CONFIRM RE-CONFIRM. CHABO."

"Beautiful," said Bishop with feeling.

"I rather like it myself," said Carstairs. "Very promising indeed."

"Aristotle," Bishop mused, and shook his head. "I'd really begun to believe the man invisible, you know. All these assassinations and no one's ever noticed him in the crowd or come up with a description. How does he do it? It took us four months just to learn he has a code name and he's still a faceless, nameless Mr. X."

"He may have the reputation of being invisible," said Carstairs, "but damn it he's not supernatural." He pulled an atlas and a pile of maps from his desk drawer and began sorting through them. "Eventually *somebody's* had to refer to him through channels accessible to us, and it's possible that finally, at long last—" He pushed aside the atlas and began on the maps. "Here we are," he said abruptly. "Take a look at this. Central Africa in detail."

The two men bent over the map of Zambia and Carstairs pointed. "There's Kafue National Park, twenty-two thousand five hundred square kilometers in size, six hundred varieties of game. Note the names of the safari camps."

Bishop read aloud, "Ngomo, Moshi, Kafwala and Chunga."

He glanced at Bennet's message and nodded. *"Due Kafue Park Chunga . . .* Chunga camp, that would mean. I must say it's a rare day when something falls this neatly into our laps."

"It hasn't yet," Carstairs reminded him, "but it's certainly an exhilarating possibility." He leaned back in his chair, his face thoughtful. "We do know a few things about our mysterious Aristotle. We know first of all that he's a mercenary, up for hire to whoever bids the highest price . . . Look at his record: Malaga was a Liberal in Costa Rican politics, and Messague in France was a Communist. There was that British chap—Hastings, wasn't it?—who was making some headway in Ireland on negotiations when he was assassinated, and the colonel in Peru whose politics were strictly middle-of-the-road, and then of course there was Pete." His face tightened. "Our agents may be fair game these days, but no man deserves to be shot as he walks out of church with a bride on his arm."

"No, sir," said Bishop. "However, there's just one point—"

"Something bothering you?"

Bishop was frowning. "Very much so, now that I've caught my breath. What I mean is, a safari? An assassin going on *safari?*"

"We also know," continued Carstairs, appearing to ignore this, "that Aristotle is intelligent, he has a strong instinct for survival, and he's a complete loner or someone would have talked long ago. Tell me, Bishop," he said, leaning forward and pointing a pencil at him, "if you were Aristotle, how would you negotiate your assignments? How would you make contact with your next employer?"

"How would I—" Bishop was silent, considering this. "Russian teahouse?" he said at last, flippantly. "Turkish bath? A funicular railway in the Swiss Alps? I see your point, sir. Tricky. Very, very tricky, and probably a hell of a lot more dangerous for him than actually shooting down politicians."

"Exactly. It's this touch that encourages me very much. Damned clever idea, choosing a safari, it's perfect for a rendezvous. He'd have the chance to look over his potential employer before identifying himself, and then it gives them both plenty of leisure to haggle over terms and price. He'd be far removed from cities, with access to a wide area in case negotiations blow up, and what better protective cover than a small group moving through remote bush country? The man definitely has a flair for the artistic."

"You sound as if you're painting a portrait."

"One has to," Carstairs pointed out, "and then crawl inside it and puzzle out what he'll do next, and at that stage you've pretty well got your man, Bishop."

"Do we share this with Interpol?"

Carstairs shook his head. "No, definitely not. We first insert one of our own people into that safari. If we can pin down this man, find out what he looks like, identify him, learn where he comes from—"

"Not catch him?" said Bishop, startled.

Carstairs looked amused. "My dear Bishop, would you have us ask the Republic of Zambia to arrest everyone on next Monday's safari? And on what charge? Uh-uh. This calls for the purest kind of old-fashioned intelligence-gathering, and don't underestimate it."

"I never have, sir," Bishop said meekly.

"In fact, if you consider the world's population at this given moment," pointed out Carstairs, "you can understand how it narrows the field if Aristotle turns up at Kafue Park next Monday and we capture photographs of everyone on the safari. Instead of looking for a needle in a haystack, we'll have pictures of perhaps a dozen people to sort through, identify, trace and verify. Exposure does wonders for invisible men," he added dryly, "and Interpol can take it from there. What's the date today?"

"June first."

Carstairs nodded. "We've got to move fast, then. We've barely time to find the right agent and get him over there. Set up the computer, Bishop, will you? We'll run through the possibilities."

"It'll only take a minute, sir." Bishop walked over to the closet where the machine they referred to as the Monster was housed. He punched MASTER LIST, fiddled with knobs, fed it classifications like *Africa, Zambia* and *Tourist* and called to his superior. "Here you are, sir. Beginning with A, right down to Z."

"Always reminds me of a damn slot machine," growled Carstairs, gazing up at the screen with its myriads of blinking lights, and then he said, "John Sebastian Farrell! What the hell's he doing on this list when he hasn't worked for us in three years?"

Bishop, who had a memory to equal any computer, said, "Hmmm . . . Well, I could hazard a guess, sir. In that letter of resignation he sent us three years ago from South America —scrawled, if I remember correctly, on a torn sheet of wrapping paper—he said he was off to Africa to reclaim his soul or some such thing, and we could send any sums owed him to Farrell, care of Barclay's Bank, Lusaka, Zambia."

Carstairs frowned. "Something about cleaner air and a cleaner life, wasn't it? That still doesn't explain what he's doing on the computer list."

"A mistake, I think." Bishop left the computer, went to the phone, dialed a number and rattled questions into it. When he hung up he looked pleased. "Called Bookkeeping, sir. They tell me they've been regularly mailing Farrell's pension checks to Zambia for three years, and apparently that's what the computer picked up. They're terribly sorry and his name is being removed at once."

"He's still there? Those checks are being cashed?"

"That's what they tell me."

"Farrell," said Carstairs musingly, and returned to his desk and sat down. "Damn it, Bishop," he said, scowling, "I've known Farrell since OSS days, he worked for this department for fifteen years, yet why is it I can no longer think of Farrell without thinking of Emily Pollifax?"

Bishop laughed. "That was her first assignment, wasn't it? After she'd turned up in Mason's office to naïvely apply for work as a spy? And you'd been looking for a cozy grandmotherly type for your courier job and you took her on, and when all hell broke loose you thought—"

"I know what I thought," Carstairs said, cutting him off, and suddenly grinned. "Do you remember, Bishop? When it was all over they sat right here in this office. Farrell was in bandages, looking like death itself, and Mrs. Pollifax was in that damn Albanian goatherder's outfit . . . they'd just been pulled out of the Adriatic and I'd given her up for dead, I'd given them both up for dead—and she sat here pulling rabbits out of a hat—"

"Out of her petticoats, wasn't it?" said Bishop, smiling.

"—and it turned out that a complete amateur had duped all the professionals." He stopped smiling and said abruptly, "Mrs. Pollifax, of course."

Bishop, reading his mind, was shocked. "Tangling with a cold-blooded assassin, sir?"

"She's tangled with them before," pointed out Carstairs, "but this time she doesn't have to tangle with anyone at all, just take photographs. Most of these safaris nowadays are camera-shooting, not hunting safaris, and there'll be cameras in everybody's pocket."

"Maybe," said Bishop grudgingly, and then, smiling, "Of course she'd be marvelous at it. Ingenuous, artless, the sort everyone confides in . . . Do you think Aristotle might confide in her, too?"

Carstairs gave him a sour glance. "Try not to be naïve, Bishop," and then as his gaze moved to the clock, "She'll need a yellow-fever shot and someone will have to pull some strings to get her a visa in a hurry, and if that safari's booked solid there'll have to be more strings pulled, although thank heaven it's early June and not the high season yet in Africa. Bishop—"

Bishop sighed. "New York, I suppose?"

"Right. Get the first plane over and start things moving. The Zambia National Tourist Bureau's on Fifty-eighth Street, I think, and so is the embassy that will produce the visa. While you're phoning about a plane reservation I'll call Mrs. Pollifax and see if she can take this on. God, let's hope so," he said fervently. "After your business in New York you can go on to New Jersey and brief her."

"Right. Oh, by the way," said Bishop, pausing at the door. "If she's available do I mention Farrell being in Zambia?"

Carstairs considered this judiciously. "You'd better, I suppose, just in case—heaven forbid—they accidentally bump into each other at the wrong time. It could give the whole show away." He hesitated and then added, "Hold on a mo-

ment." Smiling almost mischievously, he said, "I'll go even
further. Ask her to give Farrell a ring on the telephone when
she arrives in Lusaka. He must be in the book. There might
not be time for a reunion before her safari, but they could
certainly get together afterward."

Bishop looked at him curiously. "That's a bit unusual, isn't
it?"

"Highly irregular but also crafty," admitted Carstairs. "I'd
like to know how our old friend Farrell is doing. Damn it,
Bishop, I miss that man," he said indignantly. "I can name half
a dozen jobs in the past three years he would have done a hell
of a lot better than anyone else. He must be bored to death
with retirement."

"It's possible," said Bishop.

"Of course it's possible. Definitely get her to Lusaka early,
Bishop, and ask her to look him up before she flutters about
photographing everyone on safari. Now go away and let me
tackle Mrs. Pollifax before she slips through our fingers. . . ."

At that particular moment Mrs. Pollifax was standing in
the middle of her living room practicing the karate on-guard
stance. One could never be too prepared, she thought, adjust-
ing her balance so that her weight was placed equally on both
feet, and when this had been accomplished she curled each
hand into a fist and attempted a quick horizontal slash. More
than this she dared not risk. Lorvale, her instructor, was cur-
rently enthusiastic about attacking with blood-curdling
shouts of *"Ki-ya!"* but it seemed reasonable to suppose that
this would bring her neighbors down upon her head.

The telephone began ringing and Mrs. Pollifax reluctantly
disengaged her stance to answer it. She could tell at once from
the rustling sounds in the background that the call was long
distance. A muffled voice said, "Hold please," and then a familiar one said, "Carstairs here. Mrs. Pollifax, could you leave
for Africa this weekend?"

Mrs. Pollifax reflected that karate did help; this somewhat
startling query did not unbalance her at all. "Yes, I think I
could," she told him. "How *are* you, Mr. Carstairs?"

"Understaffed and terribly busy," he snapped. "You did say yes?"

"It slipped out," she said, "but if I can find someone to water my geraniums, yes I could go to Africa this weekend."

"Then start looking," he said, his voice a shade less harassed. "Although not for a few hours, because Bishop's on his way to New York, or will be in a few minutes. He'll make all the arrangements for you. Who's your doctor?"

Startled, she told him.

"Good. Bishop will be around to see you. Sometime between one and two o'clock?"

"Either will be fine," she told him, hung up and at once felt a shock tremor move inch by inch down her spine to her toes. *What* had possessed her to say yes? She couldn't possibly leave for Africa this weekend, the idea was preposterous. Africa was halfway around the world and one prepared cautiously for such a trip, announcing it to friends, reading guidebooks, making lists in advance. That was how her neighbor Miss Hartshorne traveled, and at the moment it appeared to Mrs. Pollifax a very luxurious and sane way to do such things.

On the other hand, she could remember feeling exactly this way at other times when her tranquil world had collided with Carstairs' rough and dangerous world, and acknowledging this she let her mind run back over past adventures. She was, miraculously, still alive and sound, with dimensions added to her life that brought a chuckle at rare moments, such as when the garden club had shown a prize-winning Colin Ramsey film on Turkey and she had recognized two of the women in baggy pants and veils drawing water from a well. This time it was to be Africa.

She said it aloud—"Africa"—and at the sound of the word her heart began to beat faster and she realized that she was smiling. Africa, the dark continent. Tarzan. She remembered that when her son Roger was a boy she had taken him to see every Tarzan film that came to the Rivoli theater, and when his tastes had begun to veer toward Rita Hayworth she had gone to see Tarzan alone, enchanted by the animals, the steamy jungles, poisoned arrows and roar of lions . . . Lions, she thought with a gasp. Even if Carstairs sent her to a bustling African city she must find a way to see lions. She would *demand* lions.

How dull her life had been growing lately, she thought, and how exciting to realize that she was going to see Africa. There suddenly seemed a great many things to do. She would have to sort through her entire collection of *National Geographics*, and there was all that material on game conservation in her desk drawer . . .

With a guilty start she realized that it was nine o'clock and the breakfast dishes were still unwashed. Bishop would be coming in a few hours too, and she wondered if he was still partial to chocolate eclairs—she would have to visit Mr. Omelianuk's delicatessen at once. She reached for her coat, tucked her hair under a floppy straw hat, and went out.

It was a brilliant June morning but she walked carefully nevertheless, for the ground beneath her might be covered over with cement, and her eyes shaded by straw, but in Mrs. Pollifax's mind she wore a cork helmet and moved soundlessly through tall grasses, her ears alert for the sound of native drums.

Chapter Two

Bishop arrived precisely at two o'clock, and although he looked harassed he had lost none of his insouciance, which, considering the years he'd spent as Carstairs' assistant, always astonished Mrs. Pollifax. "Why don't you look older?" she protested, taking his coat. "You never do, it's disconcerting."

"Nor do you," he told her gallantly, giving her a kiss on the cheek, "but in my case I *know* I'm older because my pushups are growing lazier and when Carstairs loses his temper at me I sometimes feel an overwhelming urge to cry. Is that for me?" he asked, staring fascinated at the table in the living room set with damask linen, china teapot, flowered Haviland cups and pastries.

"*Especially* for you. Sit down and I'll pour. There are five eclairs."

"I count six."

"One," she told him reproachfully, "is for me. I suppose you're understaffed and overworked because of last year's congressional investigations? Which, I must add, was very shocking indeed. Even *you* need some checks and balances, you know."

"*We* are not and were not being investigated," he said, sitting down and picking up an eclair. "Carstairs asked me to tell you very firmly that his department has remained scrupulous to the letter in all its undertakings." He hesitated and then said dryly, "At least as scrupulous as can be expected when our business is to gather information by nefarious means, hit troublesome people over the head, and indulge in other interesting forms of skulduggery."

Mrs. Pollifax, recalling certain people that she herself had been forced to hit over the head, did not comment: it was a very modest number, of course, but one of which she was sure neither her garden club nor her pastor would approve. She continued pouring tea, noticing that Bishop was already devouring his second eclair. "You've not had lunch?"

"Clever of you to guess," he said, swallowing. "Carstairs packed me off at eight forty-five with a thousand errands to do, and presently you'll have your share to do too. I don't suppose he told you anything?"

"Not a thing, except it's Africa."

"He wants you to go on safari."

"On safari!" Mrs. Pollifax stared at him in astonishment. "Safari?" she repeated incredulously.

Bishop watched her eyes subtly shift focus as if she gazed at something unseen to him and very far away. She looked, in fact, as if she were experiencing a beatific vision, and understanding the processes of her mind, he shook his head. "No, Mrs. Pollifax," he said firmly, "they don't wear cork helmets in Africa any more."

She forgave him this underhanded remark but not without an indignant glance. She said with dignity, "I would be *delighted* to go on safari, cork hat or no. But why? Surely there's more?"

"Naturally. It's a very specific safari starting out next Monday in Kafue National Park in Zambia. That's in Central Africa, and if you're not up on your African countries, it was called Northern Rhodesia before it gained its independence in 1964. You can read all about it because I've brought you lots of pamphlets. It's good safari country, not as well-known, perhaps, as Kenya or Tanzania just to the north, but it's rapidly getting discovered. Less touristy, more relaxed and unspoiled . . . Actually, Kafue Park is one of the larger game parks in the world—half the size of Switzerland—and of course the Victoria Falls are in Zambia too."

"Of course," said Mrs. Pollifax, "and the President of Zambia, Kenneth Kaunda, recently visited Washington."

He looked impressed. "I'd forgotten that. Well, we'd like you to hurry over there, join the safari, get acquainted with your companions and take pictures of them—every one of them—either openly or surreptitiously."

"Is that all?" asked Mrs. Pollifax, puzzled.

"Believe me, it's frightfully important," he told her. "We want everyone on safari observed and recorded, and for this we need someone who has always dreamed of a safari, someone utterly charmed by a lioness in the bush, fond of birds and flowers, and of course given to compulsive picture-taking. In fact," he said with a smile, "I'd urge you to carry along a stupefying number of snapshots of your grandchildren, and if you don't have any, rent some. You know how to operate a camera?"

She nodded, and he slit open the mysterious package he'd brought with him. "Here's a very good normal camera," he said, handing it over to her. "Nothing fancy, you can buy it in any drugstore, easy to operate, small enough to tuck into your pocket. And here," he added, bringing out a jeweler's box, "is a different sort of camera, in case one of the group is camera-shy."

"This is a camera?" said Mrs. Pollifax, opening the box and staring at a brooch inside. "It can't be, surely."

"A bit vulgar, isn't it?" he said cheerfully. "But you have to admit it doesn't look like a camera."

"It certainly doesn't." She lifted the lapel pin out of the box and examined it. It had been designed as a miniature clock with a pendulum, its total length about three inches, which included the pendulum from which hung two small gold balls. The face was a sunflower with gold petals surrounding it, and two glittering eyes were set into the center with a curved smile below them.

"Lacks only a cuckoo," pointed out Bishop. "You pull on the chain to take a snapshot. Just a slight tug will do it, and then you touch the hands of the clock to move the film along for the next shot. The lenses are in the eyes. Takes forty snapshots, and then you bring it back to us and we smash it and remove the film."

"Very ingenious," murmured Mrs. Pollifax, and then with a thoughtful glance, "Just who is going to be on this safari, Bishop?"

"It's purest intelligence-gathering," he assured her blithely. "Someone of interest to us may be popping up there. You know how it is, a rumor, a whisper . . . all in the name of the game."

Mrs. Pollifax's smile was gentle. "I've never heard you lean so heavily on clichés before, Bishop. In the name of the *game?*"

"Well, I can't tell you *much* more," he said candidly, "because Carstairs won't allow it. But it won't hurt to point out that there have been a number of assassinations in the past seven months that have never been solved. The most publicized were Malaga in Costa Rica and Messague in France."

She nodded.

"According to the particular netherworld we're in touch with—made up of criminals, spies, informants and hangers-on —they were accomplished by one man with the code name of Aristotle. We don't know anything more about him but we've intercepted a message leading us to believe he'll be on this safari Monday, and that's all I can tell you." He brightened. "But I *can* tell you what the computer announced this morning when we fed it a list of possibilities for the job. It seems an old friend of yours is in Zambia. He doesn't work for us any more but you know him very well."

"I do?"

Bishop grinned. "I'd assume that after sharing a cell together in Albania for two weeks you'd know each other pretty damn well."

"Farrell?" gasped Mrs. Pollifax. "John Sebastian Farrell?"

"None other."

"But what's he doing in Zambia, and why doesn't he work for you any longer?"

"We haven't the foggiest idea what he's doing in Zambia,"

said Bishop, "and he isn't working for us any more because he
resigned three years ago. All we know is that his pension—"

"His what?"

"We do pay pensions," Bishop said, amused by the look on
her face, "and his payments are being sent to Farrell in care of
Barclay's Bank, Lusaka, Zambia. Better make a note of that.
Carstairs suggests you look him up when you get to Lusaka
and see if he's missing us as much as we've missed him. He
should be in the phone book if he's settled down."

"Farrell," said Mrs. Pollifax, her eyes shining. "That dear
man. A scoundrel, of course, but I'd trust him with my life,
you know. Although not," she added thoughtfully, "with my
daughter. No, definitely not with my daughter."

"Mothers always trust me with their daughters," Bishop
said wistfully, and then, pulling himself together, unzipped
his attaché case. "There's a lot to be done," he said briskly.
"I've already visited the Zambia National Tourist Bureau today, as well as the Zambian Embassy. Mercifully, the tourist
bureau has room for you in next Monday's safari. Kafue Park is
opening only this week—the rainy season's just ended, you see
—so luck was with us. As for your visa, it took persuasion, but
if you'll let me carry your passport back to New York with me
this afternoon they'll issue you one immediately and return
your passport to you by special delivery. That leaves your yellow-fever vaccination. Your doctor is being sent the vaccine
and you're to see him at four o'clock tomorrow afternoon. You
leave Saturday night for London, and Sunday night for Lusaka,
and here are your plane tickets," he said, placing them on the
table. "Here are also booklets and pamphlets and brochures
about Zambia—" He placed these on the growing pile and
glanced up at her. "Are you still with me? Am I forgetting
something?"

"Clothes," pointed out Mrs. Pollifax.

Bishop understood at once; it was why mothers trusted
him. "Go to New York early on Saturday before your plane
leaves, if you can't make it sooner. Slacks, a bush jacket, a
sweater, good walking shoes . . . Abercrombie's will be just
the place for you. And oh yes, here are antimalarial tablets,
good God I almost forgot them. Start taking them at *once*." He

glanced at his watch and sighed. "I hope that's all because damn it I'm already an hour behind schedule and I've got to be running along."

"Oh Bishop, so soon?"

He nodded. "It's one of the deficiencies of my life with Carstairs that I never see anyone for more than half an hour, and always on the run. Beautiful chocolate eclairs," he said fervently. "All five of them." Collecting his attaché case, he arose. "Now I need your passport."

She found it in the desk drawer and gave it to him. "I'll send you a postcard from Zambia," she told him.

"Better not," he said regretfully. "Just take lots of snapshots for us—of everyone on that safari, barring no one—and have your reunion with Farrell and see if he's bored yet. He called you the Duchess, didn't he?"

"It seems a century ago," admitted Mrs. Pollifax, following him to the door. "Do you remember how naïve I used to be?"

"No, really?" said Bishop, amused. "Yes . . . Well, I don't find you particularly hardened even now, but there's always hope, isn't there? Don't forget that yellow-fever shot tomorrow and stay out of trouble, you hear?"

"Of course," she told him, and watched him hurry down the hall to the elevator. When he had disappeared she closed the door, walked back into the living room, and remembering how her morning had begun, she nostalgically assumed the karate on-guard stance again. So much had changed, however —even to the slant of the sun through the windows—that as she cut the air with a horizontal slash she tried a small and daring *"Ki-ya."* This proved unsatisfying. Drawing a deeper breath she braced herself and shouted triumphantly, *"KI-YA!"*

Chapter Three

On Saturday Mrs. Pollifax left early for New York to spend an afternoon at Abercrombie's before her plane departure. She was already flushed with triumph at finding a new hat for traveling. It was not precisely a cork helmet but it looked so remarkably like one that she no longer felt deprived. It was a bulbous white straw with a single red feather that began in the back and ran up and across the top of the crown and down to the tiny brim in front, where it was held in place by a clip. The narrow line of scarlet relieved the hat's austerity and added a dashing touch to her two-year-old blue-and-white-striped suit.

Nothing had prepared her for Abercrombie's, however. It was true that she had once or twice poked her head in the door out of curiosity, but she had never before entered the store with purpose, or with a safari waiting in the wings. Now, given *carte blanche*, she lost all inhibition, especially after discovering that the five pounds she'd lost during the winter placed her unexpectedly in a pair of size 12 slacks. In only half an hour she dealt with her wardrobe: two pairs of khaki slacks went into her suitcase, a trim bush jacket, a heavy turtleneck sweater, and a long pale-blue cardigan with a sash. Her remaining creativeness she saved for Abercrombie's accessories, which left her in a state of ecstasy. She succumbed immediately to a pair of enormous tinted round sun-goggles which gave her the look of a Martian; she found herself wondering how she could have survived for so long without them. She bought a flashlight and then a pencil flashlight. Regretfully she decided against a set of aluminum dishes that folded one inside of another until they fitted into a small pouch. She bought a dust veil because there was always the chance that she might be caught in a dust storm; she added a silk kerchief with zebras racing across it, and believed that she had concluded her purchases until she saw the umbrella.

"It's rather large," the clerk pointed out, watching her with a fascinated eye.

"Yes, but isn't it beautiful?" she said in an awed voice, admiring its rainbow effect of scarlets, yellows, blues, pinks and oranges.

"I believe the rainy season has ended in Zambia."

"True," she said reflectively, "but then it's really a matter of semantics, don't you think?"

"I beg your pardon?" he said, startled by the *non sequitur*.

"I mean that an umbrella could just as easily be called a parasol, don't you think? If the rainy season's over there'll be sun. A great deal of sun, I should imagine."

"Yes," said the young man, intrigued. "Yes, that's certainly true. Sun and dust."

She nodded. "And I shall have my dust veil and a parasol."

"Yes you will," he said, beginning to follow her line of reasoning.

"And then if one falls in love with something," she confessed, "one is always sorry later one didn't buy it."

"Exactly," he said warmly. "Of course you must have it then."

Mrs. Pollifax agreed, and bought it, and was not even sorry when the airline classified it as a weapon and she had to watch it dropped down baggage chutes all during her trip. It was, she thought, a very minor inconvenience when it was such a glorious umbrella. Or parasol.

And so at ten o'clock that evening Mrs. Pollifax set out on her flight to London, suitably vaccinated and carrying her suitcase full of drip-dries, khaki and other small treasures. Not for her the luxury of magazines: once in flight she efficiently brought out her book on Central Africa animals and read, "The roan antelope is, in general color, a pale reddish brown, slightly darker on the hind quarters, the hair short and coarse," and then she fell asleep. Upon waking she read, "The sable antelope is rich deep brown, the old males jet black," and fell asleep again. At Heathrow airport she napped for a few hours in a day room, and at eight o'clock in the evening she boarded the Zambia Airways plane and resumed her trip to Lusaka.

Here she met with her first disappointment. Since Zambia was a new country, roughly a decade old and developing fast— the Third World, she thought solemnly—she had expected a few exotic companions on her flight, but instead she appeared to be surrounded by British families on holiday with babies and small children. The only bright notes provided were the lovely black stewardesses in their orange minidresses.

Mrs. Pollifax dozed and woke, determined not to miss her first glimpse of Africa. Very early in the morning, at first light, she opened her eyes and looked out over a floor of wrinkled clouds to see a bright-orange sun slip out of the dusk and trail a line of soft pink behind it. All drowsiness vanished as she sat up in anticipation. Gradually the clouds brightened and dispersed, the sun shed a warm clear light over the sky, and Mrs. Pollifax, looking down from the plane, saw Africa.

Africa at last, and not a dark continent at all, she thought exuberantly, staring at the strange world below. From this height it looked as if the earth's skin had been peeled back and cooked into a dull-orange crust and then lightly sprinkled with green lichen. Oddest of all were the upheavals appearing here and there in the earth. Really, she thought, they looked just like bubbles in a thick stew on the stove.

Soon the view grew softer, and the pale dusty green turned into rich chenille, defined by narrow red-clay roads like seams in a garment stretching to the horizon. Once she leaned forward, certain that she saw a village of huts below, and it thrilled her to think of natives waking to the dawn without realizing that she saw them from the sky. She began to grow excited about landing on this earth spread out below her, she began to consider what lay ahead . . . In her purse she carried vouchers sent her by the tourist bureau in New York, and she recalled that she was to be met at the airport by a tourist guide and whisked off to the hotel ("Transfer from Lusaka International Airport to Hotel Intercontinental: $6.60"), and she would remain in Lusaka for roughly six hours ("1430 departure Hotel Intercontinental to Chunga Safari Village, KT/3"). But before she left for Kafue Park at half-past two this afternoon she had every hope of contacting Farrell, and this gave an added fillip to her arrival.

Ever since leaving New York she had found herself wondering what Farrell might be doing in Zambia, and now she tried once again to fit what she knew of him into the rust-colored terrain below her. She remembered that when she'd first met Farrell he'd been running an art gallery in Mexico City, but he'd also been a bona fide painter himself. He'd mentioned smuggling guns to Castro in the early days of the revolution, and she knew that at one time he'd operated a charter boat out of Acapulco, and somewhere in there he'd also begun to work for Carstairs. Now he was retired.

Zambia was a land-locked country, so there would be no charter boats; its revolution had ended in 1964, so there were no guns to smuggle. What would Farrell have found here? "Perhaps an art gallery," she thought, and as she turned this over in her mind she began to like it very much. He would collect Zambian art, she decided, specializing in wood carvings, thumb-pianos and spears, which he would sell to tourists; but of course he would paint his own pictures, too, and she would buy one. Definitely she would buy one and carry it home and hang it in her apartment. She continued weaving pleasant little fantasies about his new life in Zambia, adding a beautiful wife because he would, she felt, make an excellent husband—retired rakes so often did—and perhaps there was a child by now.

She realized the *No Smoking—Fasten Seatbelts* sign had been blinking at her for some time, and now a voice interrupted her speculations to announce their imminent landing. Mrs. Pollifax tucked away her book, fastened her seatbelt and tried to discipline her excitement. This was not easy, because after two nights spent on planes the effect of her arrival on a new continent was rather like an overdose of adrenalin laced by large amounts of caffeine.

The 707 descended, taxied past a line of Zambia Airways DC-8s and came to a stop before a handsome modern terminal building. Mrs. Pollifax disembarked and immediately learned that African mornings could be cold. Shivering, she moved through Passport Controls, where she filled out a tiresome number of forms in a room hung with signs that read PRACTISE HUMANISM, and HUMANISM MUNTU UZYI BANTUIVYINA ULALEMEKA BACEMBELE. She then walked out into the waiting room to a wall of people waiting behind ropes. One of these people detached himself and moved toward her, a smiling young black man in a blue zip-up jacket tossed over a plaid shirt. "Mrs. Pollifax?"

"Yes," she said in relief.

"I'm Homer Kulumbala. Welcome to Lusaka."

"How do you do," she said, beaming at him.

They waited for her suitcase, and then for her umbrella, which appeared to startle Homer. After one look at it he said sternly, "This could be easily stolen. You must guard it carefully while in the city. It is very beautiful."

"Yes, isn't it?" she agreed happily.

A few minutes later they were speeding toward town in a VW bus emblazoned with the tourist bureau insignia. Mrs. Pollifax's first impressions were of space and newness, and a great deal of bougainvillea, and when they drew up to the hotel—which was also spacious, new and surrounded by bougainvillea—Homer told her that it was he who would be driving her to Chunga camp at half-past two, and that she would see more of the capital later, on the trip out of town. She thanked him and gave her suitcase to the porter, but the umbrella she carried herself.

As soon as Mrs. Pollifax reached her hotel room she did not stop to relax; she paused only long enough to extract her striped flannel pajamas from her suitcase and then she reached for the telephone directory on the shelf under the phone. Sitting down on the bed with the book on her lap—she was surprised to see by its cover that it encompassed the entire country—she eagerly turned the pages until she found Lusaka.

"A . . . B . . . C . . . D . . . E . . . F," she murmured,

and running a finger down the list of F's she ticked off Farmer's Co-operative Society of Zambia Ltd., Farmers Prime Butchery, Farmers Produce Association, Fashion Mart Ltd. . . . the name of Farrell was conspicuously missing.

Impossible, she thought, frowning, and resolutely began again, attributing the oversight to tiredness: Farmer's Co-operative Society of Zambia Ltd., Farmers Prime Butchery . . .

There was no Farrell listed among the F's.

Thoroughly frustrated now, she began thumbing through pages at random, checking out F's in towns with names like Chingold, Kazimuli, Kitwe, Kabwe. There seemed to be very few family names listed, and a vast number of government offices and co-ops. In small towns with only a dozen or so entries she noticed that telephone service was available for only a few hours each day, but none of these listed a Farrell either. Extensive research lay ahead, and she realized that in only six and a half hours she would be leaving for Chunga.

This time she began at the very beginning of the directory, but after an hour's diligent study she had still found no John Sebastian Farrell. Yet Bishop had reported that he was *here*, and that all of the checks sent to him in Lusaka had been picked up and cashed.

Barclay's Bank, she thought abruptly and, reaching for the telephone, dialed the front desk to ask what hours the banks were open. From eight o'clock to twelve, the desk clerk informed her.

It was half-past eight now. "And the afternoon hours?"

There were no afternoon hours.

Mrs. Pollifax thanked him, and with a wistful glance at her pajamas she picked up her purse and went out.

Cairo Road was a bustling main street lined with modern shops. A strip of green divided its double roadway, and there were pleasing, tree-lined cobbled spaces inserted between the buildings, restful to the eye. Women in long bright skirts, blouses and turbans mingled with women in smart frocks and sandals. Almost all of the faces were black, and almost all of the voices she overheard had unexpected and very charming British accents. It was a noisy, cheerful scene, with a great deal

of tooting from the small cars, motor scooters, Land Rovers
and bicycles that streamed up and down Cairo Road.

Mrs. Pollifax paid her driver and walked into Barclay's Bank
to the window marked INQUIRIES—MAIL. The man behind the
counter looked forbidding, his black face buttoned into bu-
reaucratic aloofness. She cleared her throat to gain his attention. "This is where mail is picked up?"

"Yes, madam," he said, regarding her with expressionless
eyes. "Your name is—?"

She shook her head. "I'm not looking for mail, I'm looking
for a man who receives his mail here. For three years his mail
has been directed to him in care of Barclay's Bank, Lusaka. I
don't have his address," she explained, "and I've come all the
way from America and I find he's not listed in the telephone
book."

"This is rather interesting," he said politely.

"His name is John Sebastian Farrell," she told him. "I
thought perhaps after three years you might be forwarding his
letters to an address?"

His gaze remained aloof, but after a moment he turned and
called, "Jacob?"

The beaming young man who appeared was of a different
generation; his tie was flaming red and his face eager. Mrs.
Pollifax repeated her query to him, and he promptly said, "No
address, he still gets his mail here."

"Personally?" asked his superior, who suddenly gave evidence of understanding exactly what Mrs. Pollifax wanted.

"I've never seen him," said Jacob. "A boy picks it up."

"Always?" faltered Mrs. Pollifax.

"I have never seen this man either," said the older clerk.
"There has been some curiosity about him, of course. I too
have only seen a boy ask for Mr. Farrell's mail. Not often,
sometimes not for three months. A different boy each time."

"Oh," said Mrs. Pollifax, her heart sinking. "Oh dear. Are
there—perhaps I shouldn't ask—but are there any letters waiting for him now, so that someone might be picking up his mail
soon? I could write a note," she explained.

Now they were both gripped by her problem, touched by
her dismay, their eyes sympathetic. "It would be good for you

to write a letter to your friend," Jacob said earnestly, "but only two weeks ago Mr. Farrell's mail was collected. I myself gave it out—a small boy again, with the note authorizing him to gather it—"

"I see," said Mrs. Pollifax. "Yes—well, I thank you very much, both of you."

"You must write him," the older man said firmly.

"Yes," she said. "Yes, of course."

She walked outside into the sun again, crossed the road to the center strip and sat down on a bench under a tree. She felt almost inconsolable, and very close to tears, which was probably the result of two nights of spasmodic sleep, but it was also due to a sense of acute loss. It was not just that Farrell was part of her assignment, it had nothing at all to do with her assignment. She was genuinely fond of Farrell and she had anticipated seeing him.

A newspaper lay beside her on the bench and she picked it up and opened it to conceal her tears. She saw that it was this morning's *Times of Zambia,* and out of some vague hope that she might find Farrell listed in it she turned to the back page and prepared to read the entire paper. On this last page, however, she found herself staring at CLASSIFIED ADVERTISEMENTS, and at a column marked *Personals* in particular. She read:

GOOD SAMARITAN: befriend suicidal and despairing. Write Box 1–A or telephone . . .

LOST: Mercedes keys left on counter National Commercial Bank Ltd. 10:30 Monday. Finder please return to . . .

Mrs. Pollifax turned thoughtful; she hadn't lost any car keys but she'd lost Farrell; she wasn't suicidal, but at the moment she felt disappointed almost to the point of despair. She glanced at the masthead of the newspaper and made her decision. Taking the paper with her she retraced her steps to the bank and inquired the way to the *Times* office. Directions were given her, and ten minutes later she entered the *Times of*

Zambia building, only a few blocks down Cairo Road, and was given a form to fill out.

She wrote her name and her address in the United States, and then:

> JOHN SEBASTIAN FARRELL: here for safari, love to see you. Back June 16 Hotel Intercontinental. Duchess.

As she completed this she became aware that a man had begun writing out a similar form across the desk from her, and glancing up she found him staring at her. He was a big man, several inches over six feet tall, with a seamed, deeply tanned face and a thatch of white hair. Meeting her glance he nodded. "Good face."

"I beg your pardon?" she said, startled.

"Good face," he repeated in a voice that marked him as American. "Look old enough to not mind my saying so."

"Old enough, yes," she said, smiling at him.

"Lost my wallet," he explained with a huge gesture encompassing the desk, his pencil and the office.

"I've lost a friend," she said, and carried her message to the young man at the counter. "How soon can you put this in your newspaper?" she asked him.

The young man accepted her copy and annoyingly read it back to her in a loud, clear voice. " *'John Sebastian Farrell: here for safari, love to see you. Back June 16 Hotel Intercontinental. Duchess.'* " With a glance at his watch he assured her that it would be in tomorrow morning's paper without fail, and that it would cost her one *kwacha* and twenty *ngwee*.

"Roughly two dollars American," put in the huge American, waiting beside her, and peering into her change purse he pointed to one of the larger silver coins. "There's your *kwacha*, the little one's the twenty *ngwee*."

"Yes—thank you," she stammered, gave the coins to the man and hurried toward the door. Behind her she heard the American say, "Morning. Cyrus Reed's my name. Lost a wallet."

Out on the street she found a taxi discharging a passenger at the building next door and firmly captured it. Once back in her hotel room again, she climbed into her pajamas and resolved to put all thoughts of Farrell aside for the moment. She had done all that she could; if he was still in Zambia he'd see the advertisement, and the rest would be up to him. In the meantime, she thought, animals and Aristotle lay ahead of her. Smiling, she fell asleep.

Chapter Four

Her alarm clock awoke Mrs. Pollifax at one, and she jumped out of bed and eagerly approached her suitcase. She opened it lovingly and removed the new bush jacket and the new slacks, reached for a drip-dry blue turtleneck blouse and brought out her comfortable walking shoes. There was a small delay while she fumbled with price tags, but once she was in her safari clothes the effect was dazzling: the old Emily Pollifax, vice-president of the Save-Our-Environment Committee and secretary of the New Brunswick Garden Club had vanished along with the straw hat she'd packed away in her suitcase. She looked—swashbuckling, she thought, admiring herself in the mirror, yes, definitely swashbuckling. Tarzan, she felt, would have approved.

There was a further delay while she tried on the khaki hat, the sun-goggles, the dust veil, and unfurled her parasol, but eventually she was packed and ready to leave. She descended in the elevator, paid her bill at the desk, left her bag with the porter at the front door and, still carrying her umbrella, headed for the Coffee Hut for lunch before her departure for Chunga. She was hesitating at the door when a man's voice behind her said, "Ha—found you again. Lunching now?"

Mrs. Pollifax turned and found herself staring into a kelly-green shirt. Lifting her gaze she identified its owner as Cyrus

Reed, last seen at the *Times of Zambia*. "As a matter of fact, yes."

"Good. Have it with me," he said, and taking a firm grip on her elbow he piloted her into the patio and seated her efficiently at an umbrella-shaded table. "Don't give you a chance to refuse," he said, taking the chair opposite her.

"No, you didn't."

"Don't often ask women to lunch," he said gruffly. "To dinner either, for that matter. Nuisance, that sort of thing. You aren't, I hope, a real Duchess? Couldn't help overhearing your classified advertisement in the news office."

"He did read it in a loud voice," she admitted. "Actually I'm Emily Pollifax. Duchess was a—a sort of nickname."

He extended an arm across the flowers and they gravely shook hands. He was certainly a large man; big was the only word for him, she decided, looking at him, but it seemed a matter of frame and muscle rather than fat. He moved and spoke slowly, as if stricken by lethargy, but he had whisked her to a table in seconds, and his smile, drowsy as it was, was singularly warm and responsive and his eyes shrewd. There was something very oriental about his eyes, she thought; it was because they were set into his face on the same plane as his brows, like almonds pressing into a snowman's face. Those Chinese lids increased his sleepy look and gave him the appearance of a large and slightly rumpled mandarin.

He said now, observantly, "Eyes had a faraway look when you explained the nickname. Good friend, this Farrell?"

"A very good friend, yes."

"Only kind to have," he said, nodding. "Imaginative idea, advertising. Cyrus Reed's my name, by the way. Lawyer, Connecticut. Care for a drink?"

Mrs. Pollifax smiled at the hovering waiter but shook her head. "I've not a great deal of time," she explained. "I'm being called for at half-past two."

"Then we'll order. I can recommend the chicken because I've had it every day since my arrival. Tirelessly, one might say."

Mr. Reed, it seemed, had been in Lusaka for four days. "My daughter," he explained, "is exhausting. Insisted on our stopping in Rome on the way here, and now she's gone off to Livingstone to see Victoria Falls while I catch my breath. Insisted on renting a car for the trip, said she'd see more of the country."

"I expect she will," said Mrs. Pollifax cheerfully.

"Already late returning. Due back three hours ago. What brings you here?"

"I'm leaving on safari this afternoon," she told him.

His sleepy gaze sharpened. "This afternoon? Not by any chance the five-day Kafue Park safari starting officially tomorrow morning?"

She looked at him in astonishment. "As a matter of fact, yes. You don't mean—?"

He nodded. "Exactly. Arrival at Chunga camp in late afternoon, with game-viewing on the river tomorrow morning, followed by Kafwala camp in the afternoon?"

"Yes, with pickup at two-thirty here by Homer?"

He shook his head. "Sorry about that. We're driving. Lisa's idea." He looked at her and added frankly, "Damn sorry about that, actually, but if I'll see you again the fates are smiling. You're—uh—what's the word they use these days, unattached?"

"A widow."

"Ought to say I'm sorry but can't. I like you."

She looked at him and began to laugh. "I really like your directness but I'm not accustomed, you know, to such—such—"

"Unabashed admiration? Can't think why not. You look alive," he said firmly. "Can't stand dull people."

"I'm very dull," Mrs. Pollifax told him sincerely. "I do volunteer work—not very efficiently—and raise geraniums and really—that is, in *general*," she added conscientiously, "live a very quiet life."

"Doesn't mean a thing," he said. "You look interested, a sense of wonder lingers. True?"

"I feel like a witness being cross-examined on the stand."

He nodded. "Bad habit of mine, the trouble with being a lawyer. My two children call it a deficiency—or rather, when they're pleased with me they say I'm direct, when they're angry I'm blunt."

"You have two children, then?"

He nodded. "Boy's thirty, the girl—that's Lisa—twenty-six. Raised them myself since their mother died, which happened when Lisa was three years old, and then said hands off, at least until two years ago. You've children?"

Mrs. Pollifax nodded. "Also a boy and a girl, both of them grown up and parents now. But what happened two years ago?"

"Had to rescue Lisa," he said, leaning back for the waiter to deposit dishes in front of them. "You can't imagine from what squalor," he added, "which wouldn't have mattered a tinker's damn if she was happy. Found her living in the East Village in New York doing social work, weight down to ninety-six pounds and crying her heart out over a chap she'd been in love with." He snorted indignantly. "Loved him, she said, because he cared. Trouble was the chap seems to have cared indiscriminately—about women mainly, I gather—and led her a merry chase. Considering Lisa graduated *magna cum laude* from Radcliffe it seemed very unintelligent of her."

"Emotions have nothing to do with intellect," pointed out Mrs. Pollifax.

"You understand that," he said, nodding. "Lisa didn't."

"What's happened to her since then?" asked Mrs. Pollifax.

"You'll see her," he reminded her. "Cool, brisk, business-like, that's Lisa. Liked her better when she tumbled for every cause that came along. Warm-hearted, ardent child."

"Then of course she still is," put in Mrs. Pollifax.

"Somewhere, yes, but in the last two years she's grown a shell three feet thick. Thought the trip might do her good. Not healthy for either of us, living together. Exhausting."

Mrs. Pollifax put down her fork and smiled at him. "Is there anything that doesn't exhaust you?"

He directed a sleepy glance at her and smiled. "As a matter of fact a few things . . . good food, good talk, collecting rare books . . . still play a decent game of tennis and I've been known to rouse myself at dawn for bird-watching."

"That's hard to imagine. Are you," she asked sternly, "ecology-minded?"

"Passionately," he said with a straight face.

Mrs. Pollifax laughed and decided at that moment that if she had been deprived of Farrell's company during her few hours in Lusaka, then Cyrus Reed made a rather fair replacement. She also found herself hoping that Mr. Reed's lethargy was genuine, his daughter bona fide, and that he had not acquired a nasty habit of assassinating people in his spare time.

"Dessert?" suggested Mr. Reed, offering her the menu.

She glanced at her watch and shook her head. "I can only thank you for a delicious lunch," she told him, picking up her umbrella, "and see you next at Chunga."

They said goodbye and she removed herself to the lobby, where she chose a chair in sight of the front door. There she sat, gazing with interest at a party of dark men in turbans. A porter walked past her ringing a bicycle bell and carrying a chalkboard on which were scrawled the words "Mr. Kaacha wanted at desk," and then suddenly Homer Kulumbala appeared before her, smiling.

"Good afternoon, you are ready for Chunga?" he asked.

"Ready and waiting," she told him.

"Your luggage?"

She pointed to her suitcase next the door and he picked it up and led her out to the hotel drive. The same VW bus was parked among the bougainvillea, and again she chose the front seat next to the driver. Homer went off to round up other members of the safari and presently returned escorting a narrow man in a pair of slacks and a bush jacket. "Oh dear, we're twins," thought Mrs. Pollifax ruefully, glancing from his bush jacket and slacks to her own, and wondered if everyone on safari would wear identical khaki clothes. "Hello," she said as he reached the bus.

He was a prim-looking little man, perhaps forty-five or fifty, his one notable feature a reddish-brown goatee. He seemed an odd candidate for a safari: he looked fastidious and a trifle pinched about the nostrils, as if the world had a slightly rancid odor to him. At sight of Mrs. Pollifax he looked even more disapproving, or perhaps he resented her occupying the front seat. He stepped carefully into the rear and in faintly accented English called to Homer to be careful with his two suitcases. Only then—and after wiping the seat with his handkerchief—did he turn to Mrs. Pollifax and say peevishly, "They throw them, have you noticed?"

"No," said Mrs. Pollifax, and introduced herself.

"Oh. Yes. Well." He extended a thin dry hand and shook hers. "Kleiber here. Willem Kleiber." He did not exactly wipe his hand after touching hers but she had the impression that he wanted to, and that the gesture was aborted only because he thought better of it.

"German?" she asked.

"No, no, Dutch," he said firmly.

If Mrs. Pollifax had feared that all bush outfits might look alike, this idea was quickly dispelled now as Homer escorted a third member of the safari to the bus. The woman walking beside him made Mrs. Pollifax feel suddenly dowdy and not at all swashbuckling. In her forties, she wore her long platinum hair tied in the back with a scarlet silk kerchief. Her bush jacket and slacks were cut out of pale-beige gabardine that very nearly matched the color of her hair, and they had been tailored to outline every curve of her figure. Diamonds glittered on several fingers, and a stunning turquoise was pinned to her black turtleneck shirt. Everything about her was striking, from her outfit to her cool sapphire eyes, the clear-cut features, pale-pink mouth and subtly tanned face.

". . . very nearly didn't stop, you know, and I was afraid I'd not be here in time, and then—oh, two already here, isn't this super," she said, stopping by the bus and smiling at Mr. Kleiber. "I think we'd better introduce ourselves, don't you?" Her voice was caressing, with a somewhat affected British accent, so that the word *better* emerged as *baytor*, spoken through the nose with a not unattractive nasal quality. "I'm Mrs. Lovecraft," she said. "*Amy* Lovecraft."

At this moment a tall, good-looking young man walked out of the hotel, shouted to Homer and then strode toward the bus, calling, "I say, is this the transportation to Chunga camp for the KT/3 safari?"

"What a lovely man," murmured Mrs. Lovecraft appreciatively.

"Yes, yes," said Homer. "You are—?"

"John Steeves." He was dressed very casually in a heavy
turtleneck sweater and shabby twill slacks; he looked, thought
Mrs. Pollifax, like a man who would know that African mornings were cold. He looked seasoned. His voice marked him as
an Englishman, the patina on his boots marked him as a hiker.
His face was long and intense, with a thick brown mustache
and interesting dark eyes.

Homer's face lighted up at the name. "Of course—yes, I was
inquiring for you. Have you luggage?"

"A duffelbag, but Tom's bringing it. He's one of the party,
too, we met in the Coffee Hut. Tom Henry." He turned and
gestured vaguely toward the hotel entrance. "There he is," he
said.

Mrs. Pollifax turned and saw a solid-looking young man
walk out of the hotel carrying a suitcase and a duffelbag, followed by a barefooted black boy carrying a second suitcase.
Tom Henry looked cheerful and uncomplicated, with sandy
hair and a pair of level, candid gray eyes. No nonsense about
him, thought Mrs. Pollifax, liking him at once; relaxed, stable
and efficient. The boy walking beside him suddenly looked up
at him and smiled. It was, thought Mrs. Pollifax, the most
adoring glance that she'd ever seen a child give an adult, and
she realized that the two belonged together.

"Henry?" said Homer, puzzled, and then, "Ah, this is *Doctor* Henry? Dr. Henry from the mission hospital?"

"And Chanda," the young man said firmly. "Chanda
Henry."

The three men and the boy moved to the back of the bus to
stow away their luggage, and Mrs. Lovecraft climbed in beside
Mr. Kleiber, saying, "Isn't this fun?"

Glancing toward the hotel Mrs. Pollifax saw Cyrus Reed
walk out, looking vaguely concerned. He had exchanged his
seersucker suit for a pair of new bluejeans that made his legs
look very long indeed, and over this he wore a shirt and a
shabby jacket. After noticing the bus he came toward it, and

looking extraordinarily pleased at seeing her in it, he leaned over and spoke to her through the window.

"She's five hours late now," he said. "Difficulties mount."

At that moment a small red Fiat raced into the drive of the hotel and came to a sudden stop, its tires protesting shrilly. A voice called, "Dad!" and a young woman as petite as Reed was enormous jumped out of the car and waved. "I'm here, Judge!"

"That," said Cyrus Reed resignedly, "is Lisa."

"Judge?" asked Mrs. Pollifax.

"Retired."

She turned to look again at the young woman who was now opening the door of the car. She was slim and long-legged and difficult to overlook because her hair was bright auburn, the color of a new penny, and her face was round and pixie-like, with a dimple in the chin. Mrs. Pollifax said, "She doesn't look at all cold and businesslike."

"She doesn't, does she," said Reed. He looked surprised. "Something's different. Like you to meet her. I'll bring her back."

Mrs. Pollifax watched as Lisa spoke to someone inside the car, and then from its confining interior crept a woman with a baby in a sling over her shoulders, followed by a small black man in a business suit and spectacles, three grinning bare-footed boys, a bent old man carrying a crutch, and at last a young man in purple slacks and pink shirt. It was rather like that old circus act, thought Mrs. Pollifax, where dozens of people kept emerging from a tiny car, and she wondered how on earth they had all fitted inside. Lisa shook hands with each of them and then allowed herself to be led off to the minibus by her father.

". . . a flat tire," she was saying, "but Kanyama helped me change it and Mbulo was carrying firewood when I picked him up, so we had a jolly fire by the side of the road and cooked a breakfast. Really neat—and you should have seen the Falls!"

"I suppose you had to give rides to everyone?"

"Well, but wasn't it providential that I did? Otherwise I'd still be down near Penga somewhere with a flat tire. It's not at all like the States, Dad. Nobody asked for a ride, but how could I drive by them when I had a car and they didn't? Hello," she said, smiling warmly at Mrs. Pollifax. "Hello," she added, nodding to Mrs. Lovecraft and Mr. Kleiber.

"Well, you've not made it with much time to spare," said her father, sounding like fathers everywhere.

"Yes, but I made it, didn't I?" said Lisa, grinning. "And who's holding us up now? See you all later," she called over her shoulder, and began propelling her father toward the hotel.

On the way to the entrance they passed Homer carrying luggage for another guest. The Reeds stopped to speak to him, leaving the newest member of the party waiting patiently, a faint smile on his lips. He was a man of average height, perhaps fifty, carrying an attaché case and a battered trench coat over his arm. He was still dressed for traveling, Mrs. Pollifax noted, in a light suit that must once have been well-cut but was wrinkled now. He wore his hair rather long; it was jet black, with streaks of pure white.

The group abruptly dissolved and Homer came toward them smiling. "We now have Mr. McIntosh," he said, gesturing at the man beside him. "We go. Gentlemen, if you will be so kind as to get in the bus now?"

The two men and the boy Chanda climbed into the seat in the far rear, next the luggage. Mr. McIntosh crawled past Mrs. Lovecraft to sit in the space between her and Mr. Kleiber. Homer closed and locked the doors and a moment later they were off, driving on the left side of the road like the British.

They passed the National Assembly building with its roof sheathed in copper and gleaming in the sun. They passed neat rows of government housing and then a shantytown with thatched-roof huts, and finally, leaving the city behind, a satellite station that had been built by the Japanese, Homer told them. As the traffic thinned they sped past fields of cotton, sunflowers and maize, and the pedestrians along the side of the road increased: women walking with loads of firewood balanced carefully on their heads, a few men wheeling bicycles. Then these, too, vanished and they settled down to the long road ahead, moving steadily toward the Mungwa mountain range. The sun began to look surprisingly low on the horizon to Mrs. Pollifax, and when she commented on this she was startled to learn that in Zambia the sun set at six o'clock.

She began to understand some of the urgency behind Homer's driving; certainly he drove like a man pursued by *something*, and now it was heartening to realize the something was darkness, because she had no desire to be caught among wild animals in the dark either. The excessive speed rendered conversation almost impossible, however; everything rattled and it was necessary to cling to one's seat.

An hour later Mrs. Pollifax was still clinging to her seat when Homer placed his foot on the brake and nearly sent her through the windshield. Up ahead she saw a roadblock, a gaily striped red-and-white pole extending from one side of the road to the other.

From the rear Mr. Kleiber called, "And what is this?"

"The bridge," said Homer. "All our bridges are guarded by the police."

"Good heavens why?" asked Mrs. Pollifax, turning to look at him in surprise.

"Rhodesian spies," he said with a shrug. "They try to bomb our bridges. We have three in Zambia, all of them over the Kafue River." He pronounced it *Ka-fooey*.

"Rhodesian *spies?*" repeated Mrs. Pollifax.

"Yes, spies. They are everywhere." With a jerk of his head to the left he added, "The police live over there."

Mrs. Pollifax glanced to the left and saw a cluster of corrugated tin houses down near the river, shaded by a circle of acacia trees. She started to speak but Homer's attention had turned to the guard who walked toward them, looking very official with a rifle strapped across his back. He wore a felt cavalry hat, blue khaki shorts and tunic, and around his legs a wrapping of heavy cloth from ankle to knee that could only be puttees, decided Mrs. Pollifax, remembering Kipling. He peered into the car and then shook hands with Homer and began talking in an incomprehensible language that Homer seemed to understand. At last the guard saluted, the bus was put into gear and they moved across the modest bridge over the river. "What language was it that you spoke back there?" asked Mrs. Pollifax.

"Nyanga," said Homer. "I speak Tonga, he speaks Luvale

but we both know Nyanga. All the government people know Nyanga."

"Those spies you mentioned," began Mrs. Pollifax, and then found it even more difficult to be heard as they turned off the paved highway onto a dirt road marked by a sign that read CHUNGA CAMP. "Those spies," she shouted above the rattles and bumps, hanging onto her seat with both hands to keep from hitting the roof of the bus.

"What?" shouted Homer.

"Spies," she shrieked. Just as she decided that the road had been cut out of a pitted lava bed it changed to brown dust beaten hard into corrugated stripes that placed her more firmly in her seat but vibrated her spine like a massage.

Homer neatly steered the bus around a hole and shouted back, "They spy on freedom fighters. In the Southern Province they used to cross the border from Rhodesia and kidnap people, set land mines and kill. There is not so much there now, but still they sneak in. A month ago they set a bomb in Lusaka, at private home, and killed Mr. Chitepo, Rhodesian black nationalist in the African National Congress."

"Who did?" shouted Mrs. Pollifax. "Who would do such a thing?"

Homer shrugged. "Mercenaries. Rhodesian police agents. Spies."

Mrs. Pollifax rested her voice while she attached this diverting piece of news to certain facts casually mentioned in the pamphlets that Bishop had deposited with her last week. She remembered that until recently Zambia had been a lonely bastion of black independence in the center of Africa, bounded on the east by Portuguese-ruled Mozambique, on the west by Portuguese-ruled Angola, with Rhodesia flanking its southern border, backed up by South Africa below it. That had been Zambia's situation when it finally threw off the last shackles of white rule in 1964.

At the time of its independence, however, Zambia had found itself still bound to Rhodesia by roads, electric power, rail routes and economic ties. A man who loathed apartheid and who dedicated himself to working against it, President Kaunda had set out at once to loosen those ties, enlisting the help of the Chinese to build a railway to the north, and the Italians to build a new dam. The price of rejecting any dependence on Rhodesia had been severe: during one crisis the country had been forced to export its copper by trucks over a road that came to be called the "Hell Run." Zambia had survived, however, and she supposed that it was proof of President Kaunda's genius that it had not only survived economically but had remained involved in and supportive of the liberation movements in her neighboring countries. Those were the words the pamphlet had used: *involved* and *supportive*. *Embroiled* sounded more appropriate, she thought dryly; certainly nothing had been said about spies, land mines and kidnapings.

Now of course, both Mozambique and Angola had won their independence after years of guerilla warfare and bloodshed, and Rhodesia and South Africa stood alone as rigid defenders of white supremacy. But she had forgotten—it came back to her now—that sometime during the worst of the infighting Rhodesia had angrily closed her borders to Zambia, precipitating even more strains on the Zambian economy. A pity, she thought, that taking a stand on moral issues had to prove so lonely these days, but apparently the closure was only a formal one if spies streamed back and forth. She remembered that the phrase "freedom fighters" had been mentioned, too, in one of those pocket histories.

"Freedom fighters," she shouted at Homer's profile. "Who are they?"

"Liberation leaders," he called back at her. "Refugees. They escape to Zambia with a price on their heads, or prison sentences. They stay, they train, they go back. Quietly, you understand?"

"Yes," said Mrs. Pollifax, nodding. "I just didn't realize it was still uh—continuing."

He nodded vigorously. "But the leaders begin to talk now. South Africa grows very worried, she fears a race war in Africa and pushes Rhodesia to talk, loosen up. We have a saying: *'Ukupangile nsofu kano uli ne fumo.* Before you can talk of killing an elephant you must first be equipped with a spear.' " He grinned and slowed the minibus. "And speaking of elephants, there is your first elephant, everyone. You wish pictures?"

Exclamations rose from the rear, but Mrs. Pollifax could only gasp and stare. Her first elephant stood scarcely fifteen feet away, grazing contentedly on the leaves at the top of a tree, his huge gray frame bleached by dust, his flaplike ears cocked as if he knew very well they were there. Slowly he turned his ponderous head and looked at the minibus with beady interested eyes. Mrs. Pollifax was certain that he stared directly at her. She gave him a delighted, grateful smile before she lifted her camera and snapped his picture.

They drove on, reaching another road barrier, this one manned by an amiable young park guard. After slowing down to allow a family of baboons to cross the road, Mrs. Pollifax glimpsed the thatched tops of buildings ahead. They entered a clearing, passed a gas pump, a cluster of rondevaals with thatched roofs, and coasted to a stop near a sloping riverbank.

"Is this Chunga camp?" called Mrs. Lovecraft.

Homer shook his head. "This is noncatering section, for weekend campers only. We wait now for the boat. There should be a boat," he said, frowning, and climbed out and stared across the river at what looked to be an island.

Mrs. Pollifax opened the door beside her and jumped down to stretch her legs. The others stirred too, and climbed out, smiling at each other a little uncertainly. Mrs. Lovecraft strolled over to join Homer, and after a moment Mr. McIntosh and Mr. Kleiber followed her. The sun had disappeared behind a cloud, draining all color from the landscape, and Mrs. Pollifax felt suddenly very small under the huge silvery sky as she waited for a mysterious boat that showed no signs of appearing on that vast flat expanse of silky gray water.

"There," said Homer suddenly, pointing. "The boat."

A small speck had appeared on the gray water, looking almost spectral as it rounded the point. It veered, grew larger, became an object totally unlike a boat, and then as it moved toward them, one man at the stern, she began to hear the sound of its motor and she realized it was a pontoon boat, nearly flat and propelled by an outboard motor.

"Good, let's help with all this luggage," Dr. Henry said, and

walked around to the back of the bus and began handing suitcases to Chanda. There was a whispered discussion between
them and then he said, "No, no, you give it to her." Holding
up Mrs. Pollifax's gay umbrella he said, "Chanda tells me this
is yours?"

"Yes, but how on earth did he know?" she asked in surprise.

Dr. Henry laughed. "I couldn't possibly tell you, but he
always knows these things. He says he looked inside of you
and saw colors to match. *Mukolamfula* was the word which, if
the little Bemba I've learned is right, means rainbow."

"I'm very touched," she said, smiling at Chanda.

The boy handed her the umbrella, grinned, ducked his head
shyly and went back for another suitcase. Behind her the boat
had just landed, the slant of its bow dovetailing perfectly with
the slant of the riverbank. Homer said, "The boat will come
back for the luggage, it is very safe here. You will get in now,
please?"

They distributed themselves on packing cases; the boat was
pushed away from the shore, the motor sputtered, they turned
and began the trip toward the distant shore, any conversation
rendered frivolous by the awesome silence of the river. The
only sounds were of the water streaming past the bow, leaving
a frothy wake behind them, and the murmur of Homer's voice
as he spoke quietly to the boy at the wheel. The air was cool,
full of fragrances, and as they chugged their way toward the
opposite bank the smell of a wood fire became distinct.

Suddenly the sun reappeared, very low on the horizon now,
and as the boat rounded the point Mrs. Pollifax had her first
view of Chunga camp. She saw another sloping riverbank cut
out of the trees, with a narrow wharf jutting into the water.
Smoke from a campfire drifted lazily across the clearing,
threading its way through the palms. Off to the left there was a
long white building with a thatched roof, and behind this,
spaced at intervals up and down a gently sloping hill, stood
narrow cabins built of reed and thatch.

The sound of the boat had brought a handful of people down
to the landing, all of their faces black. One in particular stood
out from the others, a broad-shouldered young man in forest-
green tunic and shorts. His smile as the boat reached the

weathered gray dock was as broad as his shoulders, a brilliant slash of white that met and warmed two laughing eyes.

"Welcome to Chunga," he said as the boat slid up to the wharf. "I'm Julian, your safari manager. If you will come in and register—?"

Mrs. Pollifax was the first to enter the small office near the landing. Julian handed her registration forms and a pen and she brought out her passport and copied down its numbers. Over her shoulder Julian called instructions to the boy who had brought them in the boat, and a moment later she heard the sound of the motor on the water. "Besides the luggage," he explained to her, "there are two more guests coming soon from Lusaka."

"Yes, I know," she said, "I met them."

His huge white smile blossomed again. "Then you have already two friends, good. Moses takes you up now, you'll be in Leopard cabin."

Moses wore dusty sneakers and bright-blue slacks. She turned and followed him up a gravel path. The reborn sun was meeting the horizon now, its light no longer clear gold but a hot amber that rusted the soil a deeper red. Along the path leaves crackled underfoot like dry parchment, and Mrs. Pollifax shivered in the sudden coolness. When they reached the cabin marked Leopard, Moses carried her suitcase up four wooden stairs and placed it beside the door, and then he stood and explained that there was a shower and pointed vaguely off into the distance. Mrs. Pollifax, her mind now on sweaters, blankets and hot coffee, shook her head, thanked him and scurried up the steps into the cabin. As she turned to close the wooden door behind her the sun slipped over the horizon with finality. Homer had been absolutely correct: it was just six o'clock.

Chapter Five

*I*t was dim inside the cabin. Two small screened windows were heavily shaded by the thatch roof but an electric-light bulb dangled over the night table and Mrs. Pollifax snapped it on. The pair of narrow beds looked oddly bridelike: they were sealed inside of white mosquito netting that flowed like bridal veils from the ceiling and were tucked firmly under each mattress, rendering each bed nearly inaccessible. Frustrated, she deposited her suitcase on the floor until she saw a luggage rack behind the door and placed it there instead, and then, looking around her she said aloud, "Well—I'm *here.*"

And so, presumably, was Aristotle, she reminded herself.

It was incredibly, starkly quiet . . . Something fell to the ground outside her cabin; it sounded like fruit dropping from a tree. A faint breeze rustled the reed walls and then subsided, and she could hear the distant hum of a generator. Presently voices inserted themselves into this bottomless quiet; she heard a girl laugh, a man reply and recognized Cyrus Reed's voice: so he and Lisa had arrived. She opened her suitcase and quickly changed into a heavy sweater, combed her hair, checked the film in her camera and picked up her jacket. When she opened the door a lizard slid across the step and vanished under the cabin. Carrying her flashlight she walked down the path toward the water, hesitated, and then passed through an empty, brightly lighted bar into the dining hall.

Just beyond its low wall a campfire was burning in the cleared area overlooking the river. A dozen chairs encircled it, and one of them was occupied by John Steeves.

Seeing her he rose and gave her a quick, rather shy smile that lighted up his serious face. "I don't believe I know your name," he said, holding out a hand. "I'm John Steeves."

"Emily Pollifax," she told him, shaking hands with him. "Do sit down. I love this fire. I'm going to sit as close as I dare because actually I'm freezing."

"I know," he said, nodding. "It's really early spring here, and a rather late rainy season too, they tell me, which is why the roads haven't been graded yet. As perhaps you noticed," he said with a grin.

She realized that he was much older than she'd thought at first. Everything about him was boyish—his relatively unlined face, his slouch, his vitality—except for his eyes: there was something haunted about his eyes, as if they'd seen too much. They were what her son Roger would call the eyes of an old soul, so that she now added quite a few years to her original impression and guessed him to be in his middle thirties.

"Looking forward to the safari?" he asked, and Mrs. Pollifax realized that she'd been staring at him.

"Oh yes indeed," she told him warmly. "And you?"

He nodded. "Bit of a rest for me. Too much traveling spoils one for resorts and the really plush places."

"You travel a great deal, then?"

He nodded, extended one lean leg and poked at the fire with his shabby boot. "Write travel books," he said.

"Steeves," she mused. "I'm afraid—"

"I know," he said with that sudden blaze of a smile that so transformed him. "People never remember authors' names."

"Tell me the titles of your books, then."

"Mmmmm . . . *Lost in the Himalayas, At Home in the Andes*, followed by *Over the Chinese Border* and *One Hundred Nights in a Mongolian Yurt*."

"But of course," she exclaimed. "I read *Over the Chinese Border* and enjoyed it tremendously. You disguise yourself and live among the natives."

He grinned. "You might say disguise is the main ingredient

of my success, yes. A bit of the actor in me, you know, I love fooling around with makeup. Actually I began as an actor, but it's much more fun applying it all to dangerous situations."

"You like danger?" she asked curiously.

"It certainly beats the humdrum routine of ordinary living," he said ruefully.

"Yes," agreed Mrs. Pollifax, smiling faintly. "The exhilaration. The things one learns about oneself. The total immersion in the moment."

He looked at her in surprise, as if he'd not expected this from her. "You seem to have experienced something of it—" His glance moved beyond Mrs. Pollifax and he stopped speaking, a curious expression on his face. She turned and saw Lisa Reed walking toward them, her father just emerging from the dining hall behind her.

Steeves rose to his feet, looking impressed. "I say—good evening. You weren't on the bus with us, are you in the safari group too?"

Lisa had changed into bluejeans and a denim shirt and in them she looked younger, more vulnerable, her fashionable leanness replaced by a fragile quality. It occurred to Mrs. Pollifax that she was blushing; certainly her gamine face had turned a darker color but her voice when she spoke was impersonal. "Yes, we came by car from Lusaka. I'm Lisa Reed."

"And Cyrus Reed, parent," added her father. Sinking into the chair beside Mrs. Pollifax he smiled at her and said, "Good to see you again."

Steeves looked pleased. "Americans, are you? I do wish you'd sit down over here—I've not met an American in years. Perhaps you can explain to me what's been happening in your country."

"Lisa can if anyone can," said Reed. "A biased account, naturally."

Steeves flashed his quick, radiant smile. "But all accounts are biased, surely? You had something called a watershed affair?"

That won a smile from Lisa. "No, no," she said, sitting down next to him, and began speaking with quick gestures, her face very serious, her slender hands cutting the air with incisive slashes.

Her father turned to Mrs. Pollifax. "Thought you'd like to know, by the way, that someone was asking for you at the hotel when I checked out."

"Asking for me?" gasped Mrs. Pollifax. "Was he tall, with dark hair and blue eyes and—"

Reed shook his head. "Zambian. Short black chap. Dressed in a kind of —well," he said, looking pained, "it had hibiscus all over it. Or bougainvillea. That sort of shirt, with black trousers and sneakers."

Puzzled, Mrs. Pollifax said, "And you're quite sure he was asking for *me?*"

"Clearly," nodded Reed. "Couldn't help but overhear. Asked for your room number, the clerk said you'd already checked out, he left."

"How very odd," said Mrs. Pollifax, frowning. "There's that advertisement, of course, but it won't be published in the *Times of Zambia* until tomorrow morning."

Her companion nodded. "Unless the typesetter knows someone who knows someone who knows your friend. Or perhaps the travel bureau sent a chap along to make sure you'd gotten off on time." With a gesture toward the other two he said, "Damn glad to see there's someone young and male for Lisa."

Mrs. Pollifax wrenched her thoughts away from the mysterious man at the hotel. "I thought," she said, "that your daughter blushed when she saw him."

His brows lifted. "Thought so, did you?" He turned and gazed at Lisa with interest. "Amazing. I missed that."

"You were standing behind her."

"So I was. Seems an engaging fellow, Steeves."

John Steeves was certainly being very attentive, thought Mrs. Pollifax, glancing at the two across the campfire: those haunted eyes of his were fixed intently on Lisa's face as he listened, his quick smile occasionally transforming their sadness. It was a rare person who listened like that, reflected Mrs. Pollifax, and thought it a quality difficult for any woman to resist.

"And you?" asked Reed, directing his quizzical glance at her. "Always travel alone?"

"Oh yes," she said simply. "At least—"

"At least you start off alone," he said with his slow smile, "and then collect people like a Pied Piper? Ah, here comes whatsisname. Dour fellow you rode out with."

"Mr. Kleiber," she reminded him. "Willem Kleiber."

Mr. Kleiber approached the fire hesitantly, sat down two chairs removed from Cyrus Reed and said distastefully, "There is a complete absence of running water here. Exactly how does one wash?"

"The word safari," said Reed in an offhand voice, "means camping, you know."

Lisa had turned at the sound of his voice. "There are shower pipes behind those reed fences, you know. Hot water too."

Mr. Kleiber's nose looked, if anything, even more pinched; he had the most active nostrils of anyone she'd met, thought Mrs. Pollifax. "Anyone can walk in," he said coldly. "Anyone. There's no door, there's no roof."

In a rather amused voice Steeves said, "I really don't think anyone would want to, you know. Try singing loudly while you're under the tap."

"That's just what I did," said Amy Lovecraft, strolling into the circle and joining them. She was looking very elegant in snug black pants, a cashmere sweater and a short suede jacket. She chose the seat on the other side of John Steeves and sat down, placed a hand on his arm and smiled into his face. "I do hope we're on a first-name basis now so that I can call you John."

"Please do," he said politely. "Have you met Lisa Reed?"

"No, duck," she said and, leaning forward, gave Lisa a much less enthusiastic smile. "I've not met that lovely huge man over there, either."

"We're both Reeds," Lisa said shortly. "I'm Lisa and he's my father Cyrus, and that's Mrs. Pollifax next him."

"Delighted, Cyrus," said Mrs. Lovecraft, giving him a warm smile and ignoring Mrs. Pollifax. "And here comes Tom Henry. I think it's super our having a doctor with us as well as a noted travel writer, don't you?"

This was tactless, thought Mrs. Pollifax, and quite enough to antagonize the remaining men, but if she decided to reserve judgment on Mrs. Lovecraft for the moment she could welcome Dr. Henry wholeheartedly. He sat down next to her, crossed his legs, gave her a cheerful smile and said, "I hope dinner's soon, I'm starving."

"About five more minutes," Mrs. Pollifax told him after a glance at her watch. "Or just enough time to ask what Homer meant when he said you're at a mission hospital. Does that mean you live here in Zambia?"

He wrenched his eyes from Lisa Reed and turned to give her his full attention. "Yes it does—the hospital's over on the Zambesi River near the Angolan border. I came out from Canada three years ago and I'm sure all my friends expected me back in Windsor a week later." He gave her a sidelong boyish smile. "Needless to say I'm still here."

"You like it."

"Love it," he admitted. "So much so that I wanted to try a safari on my seven days' leave. There's so much about the bush I've been too busy to learn, and a great deal about wild animals I want to learn."

"Including *Homo sapiens?*" said Cyrus Reed, leaning forward to enter the conversation.

"Well, I see a good many of *them*," said Dr. Henry, smiling back, "but aside from several missionary families at the hospital it's been a long time since I've seen a group like this. I'd forgotten," he said dryly, "what a lot of nonsense people talk."

Cyrus Reed smiled. "I agree with you completely."

"What do you talk about at your hospital when you're relaxing?" asked Mrs. Pollifax.

He grinned. "Oh—life, death, septicemia, who's due to boil the next drinking water, or what the village witch doctor said that day."

Mrs. Pollifax laughed. "Scarcely small talk."

"God, no." He looked chagrined. "Obviously I'll have to brush up on that." He smiled at Chanda as the boy walked into the campfire circle and came to stand beside him. "*Bweleniko,*" he said. "*Mwapoleni.*"

"*Kuntu kuli kusuma,*" the boy said, smiling.

"Endita." Turning to Mrs. Pollifax he said, "Chanda talks
Bemba but he speaks a little English now and understands it
very well. When we first met I was struggling to learn Nyanga,
and now I'm having to learn Bemba, and it all grows rather
confusing. Chanda, you've not met this gentleman yet. He's
Mr. Cyrus Reed."

Chanda stepped forward and shook hands with Reed and
then, to their surprise, clapped his hands three times. "That's
the Zambian greeting," explained Dr. Henry with a grin.
"Chanda's given you only the modified version. When it's
done properly it's repeated three times . . . a handshake followed by three claps and then another round or two. Quite a
ceremony."

"Certainly feel thoroughly greeted," admitted Reed.

Somewhat removed from them, Willem Kleiber said in
alarm, "He's not—uh—yours, is he?"

Tom Henry's smile was friendly. "He is now. He was
brought into the hospital half-dead, his entire village wiped
out by fighting on the Angolan border. Freedom fighters
brought him in."

Overhearing this, Lisa gasped, "You live there?"

He nodded.

"But that must be fascinating."

"It is," he said, meeting her glance with a faint smile.

At that moment a drum began beating to announce dinner.
Mrs. Pollifax turned and saw that in the open-air dining room
behind her a huge tureen was being carried in by a boy in a
white jacket. She also saw Mr. McIntosh standing on the step,
hesitating between them and the dining hall. He had changed
into khaki slacks over which he wore a white shirt open at the
neck and a black V-neck sweater, and she wondered if he was
going to appear late at every meal and leave early, like a
shadow. Intuitively she felt that he was an intensely private,
introverted man, but having decided this she wondered how:
was it the manner in which he looked out from under his
brows, head slightly bent? or was it that his smile, which was
surprisingly sweet, never changed or wavered? He simply
stood and waited, smiling, while they left their chairs and

moved toward him, and then, still smiling, he turned and walked toward the buffet table and placed himself in line.

With the arrival of McIntosh Mrs. Pollifax realized the safari group was now complete and she wondered, not for the first time, which of these people could be an assassin. Now that she'd met them all she found this a very jarring thought because they all looked so normal, even wholesome, and certainly all of them were—well, explainable, she reasoned, reaching for a word that eliminated the existence of sinister motives and façades. She could not imagine any of them a professional killer standing in a crowd with a gun in his pocket, waiting, measuring, judging, whipping out the gun and firing, then vanishing into the crowd. In the first place, none of these people looked capable of such brutal violence, and in the second place she couldn't imagine any of them managing such a thing without being noticed.

Cyrus Reed would certainly be noticed, she thought with an amused glance at him towering over the soup tureen. It was possible that without his goatee Mr. Kleiber might look sufficiently nondescript; it was also possible that Tom Henry was not a doctor at all. McIntosh, she thought, would certainly melt into a crowd—he was doing so right now; John Steeves was too distinguished to melt, but she knew from his books that he was a genius at disguising himself.

If Carstairs was right, she thought, one of them had to be wearing a devilishly clever mask . . . and then she recalled with interest Carstairs' telephone call to her the evening before she left New Jersey. She had assured him that yes, her passport had been returned safely to her and that yes, Bishop had explained the importance of the snapshots, and then she had asked him the question that had begun to exasperate her. "I realize this is an insane world," she had told him, "but can you please tell me why an assassin would go on a *safari?*"

"Why, to meet someone, I imagine," Carstairs had said pleasantly. "Plan the next assassination, perhaps, or be paid for the last one. Certainly not for *fun.*"

If this was true—and Carstairs' suppositions nearly always proved sound—there could be two people wearing masks on this safari, each watching the others and wondering, as she was doing . . . and this meant that eventually they would have to go off together for a good little chat, didn't it? It occurred to her that if she was very observant and very discreet she might be able to do a little eavesdropping . . .

Of course Carstairs had made it very clear to her that she was to do nothing but take photographs, and she planned to do a very *good* job with her picture-taking, but now that she thought about it, it seemed incredible waste for her to be here on the spot and not do a little spying as well. After all, it was taxpayers' money that was paying for her safari, she thought virtuously, and as a taxpayer herself she abhorred waste.

Besides, she added, dropping all pretense at justification, it would be such fun to surprise Carstairs and catch Aristotle.

Chapter Six

*I*n the morning the safari officially began with the game-viewing excursion up the river before leaving for Kafwala camp. Mrs. Pollifax came to breakfast early and still a little sleepy, for it was barely seven and she'd not slept with any continuity. The walls of her cabin had rustled all night—she was convinced that some small animal lived in them—and at one point she had awakened to a loud animal cry, followed by a soft whistle and the pounding of feet. After this another fruit had dropped from the tree outside her cabin, and the reeds had begun to whisper again . . . At breakfast Julian told her that animals roamed freely through the camp at night, that a hippo had been heard and that pukus, who liked the safety of the camp at night, made soft whistling sounds. It was just as well she'd not known, she reflected, or she might never have dared fall asleep again.

"I want you to meet Crispin now," Julian said as they rose from the breakfast table. "I will be staying at camp to make final arrangements for our trip at noon, and Crispin will take you game-viewing. He's assistant safari manager and he'll be with us for the entire safari."

Crispin was not in uniform, and looked surprisingly like an eager schoolboy in his flowered shirt, dark trousers and sneakers. He had a long slender face and bright, interested eyes. He actually looked excited about taking them out game-viewing, and Mrs. Pollifax found this rather endearing.

John Steeves said, "Crispin's even more English than Julian. What are your Zambian names?"

"Mine?" Julian laughed. "You want it all at once? Milimo Simoko Chikwanda."

Steeves grinned. "I'll call you Julian. And Crispin's?"

"Wamufu Chinyanta Muchona."

Steeves nodded. "Definitely Julian and Crispin."

"I think so," Julian said in amusement.

There was a charming picnic air about the excursion up the river. The sun was soft and golden, the river full of morning sounds, and they traveled on a splendid breakfast of bacon and eggs, sausage, toast and coffee. Mr. Kleiber, sitting next to Mrs. Pollifax, went so far as to confide that he would like to see a crocodile. Across the aisle Amy Lovecraft had blossomed out with a professional-looking camera loaded with all kinds of attachments that she tried to explain to John Steeves. The Reeds sat together in front, both looking sleepy; Tom Henry and Chanda stood in the stern of the boat and McIntosh by himself in the bow; he too bristled with cameras and light meters.

Abruptly Crispin called out to the boy at the wheel, gestured, and the launch headed across to the opposite bank, at which point Mrs. Pollifax lifted her camera and took a picture of the river ahead, managing to capture several profiles at the same time. She had already taken a snapshot of everyone climbing into the boat and no one seemed to have minded except Cyrus Reed, who had glanced at her reproachfully, as if he'd not expected this of her.

"Hippo," said Crispin in a low voice, and pointed.

Every head turned to the left, the launch slowed and they coasted toward a cleft in the tangle of roots and trees that lined the riverbank. Slowly they drew abreast of a dark, secret-looking inlet of water that flowed into the river, and as they reached this narrow tributary Mrs. Pollifax looked deep into its shadows and saw enormous shapes moving through the trees, and suddenly heard a thunderous roar as the first hippo plunged into the stream. Patches of sunlight glinted across

monstrous black heads as the hippos floated and bobbed out
into the river. She counted five, six, seven hippos and gave up
counting at eleven. They kept coming, whole families snort-
ing and cavorting with ponderous mischievousness, one of the
bolder ones swimming out near the launch to give them all a
curious stare.

Mrs. Pollifax laughed, and when the launch resumed its trip
upriver the others were smiling too and began to talk and
move about the boat. McIntosh peeled off his jacket and came
to stand next to Mrs. Pollifax, his camera at the ready. Without his jacket, only a short-sleeved polo shirt remained and
she thought it made him look rather flat-chested. His posture
was not good but then, she thought forgivingly, it would be
impossible for anyone to stand erect if they insisted on peering
out at the world from under their eyebrows; a certain amount
of slumping was compulsive. She noticed that his longish
black hair badly needed a shampoo but the threads of white in
it were dramatic against his tanned face.

"I hope you don't mind," he said with his faint smile, and
sat down on the edge of the bench next her, his eyes on the
shoreline.

"Not at all," she said. "That's a handsome camera you
have. I've been admiring it."

He glanced at her, his smile deepening, and told her what
kind it was.

"Lovely," she said, not understanding a word, and then
with a bright smile, "Where do you make your home, Mr.
McIntosh?"

"Pretty much out of my attaché case," he said, smiling.

"But you're American, aren't you?"

"An American citizen, yes."

"Then do you," she asked reasonably, "live in the United
States?"

"Not really," he said, smiling. "I come and go." He lifted
his camera and snapped a picture of the riverbank, and then as
Crispin called out "Egret!" he slipped away from her to the
rear of the boat.

Behind her Amy Lovecraft leaned forward and said, "He's
impossible to talk to, isn't he? I couldn't even get a direct yes

or no from him on whether he's married. I mean, surely that's something you could answer yes or no to? A man either has a wife or he hasn't."

Mrs. Pollifax turned to smile into her vivid sapphire-blue eyes. "You have a point there, although of course these days such matters are sometimes—"

"What's more," said Mrs. Lovecraft, lowering her voice, "I don't think McIntosh is his last name at all."

At this Mrs. Pollifax turned completely to face her. "Good heavens," she murmured, "really?"

Mrs. Lovecraft nodded. "When we registered at Chunga," she said, her voice becoming conspiratorial, "I was standing next him and I caught a glimpse of his passport. McIntosh is his *first* name. There was an entirely different name following it, something that began with an M too, but I couldn't make it out. And," she added indignantly, "I've never seen an American passport with the last name first. Julian may have accepted him as Mr. McIntosh because he doesn't *know*, but take a look at your own passport sometime: the last name *doesn't* come first."

"Amy," called Steeves from across the aisle, "you wanted to see some impala, take a look over here."

Mrs. Lovecraft jumped up, leaving Mrs. Pollifax to digest this interesting piece of information. *Not* a sensible woman, thought Mrs. Pollifax, watching her leave; stupid of her to go about saying such things, indebted as Mrs. Pollifax was to her for the news. She might have thought it exposed McIntosh, but it also betrayed her spitefulness at being ignored by him. She wondered if Amy Lovecraft's life had been difficult: she was a very attractive woman and must once have been lovely, but so very often beautiful women grew up lopsided or didn't grow at all. She thought there was a curious hardness about her, as if her beauty was a deceptively rich topsoil, thinly spread over rock. . . . Finding that no one was looking in her direction, Mrs. Pollifax reached into her purse and surreptitiously examined her passport. Mrs. Lovecraft was absolutely right: there was no juxtaposition of names, the given name came first.

"Having fun?" asked Cyrus Reed, walking up the aisle.

"Oh yes," she said, beaming at him, and then, thinking of what Mrs. Lovecraft had just told her, she added, "and I'm learning so much, it's really so educational."

At midmorning they stopped briefly at an abandoned ferry crossing where the remains of a road cut like a knife through the tall grass. Crispin allowed them to climb out for a moment and walk a few cautious paces down the road. "But not far," he said firmly. "Not without a guard."

"Why should we need a guard?" protested Mrs. Pollifax.

"It's dangerous."

She looked out upon the peaceful scene, at bright petunia-like flowers blooming by the roadside, at a landscape empty of all movement, and she was incredulous. "But it looks so safe!"

Tom Henry grinned. "It does, doesn't it? But we're near the river, you know, which means if you left the road you might stumble across a crocodile sunning itself in the mud. Failing that, there are puff adders, pythons, black mambas and bushwangers, not to mention the possibility of a rhino or hippo who might be in an ugly temper."

"Oh," said Mrs. Pollifax, taken aback.

Crispin said, "You treat many snake bites at your hospital, Doctor?"

"Maybe not so successfully as your village medicine men," said Tom, "but we save a few. Speaking of medicine men, it's certainly humbling to realize that people here evolved their own vaccine centuries before we did in the laboratories."

Crispin said modestly, "We are in the position to learn, you know. We see the mongoose fight with a poisonous snake, he is bitten, he runs to a certain bush and eats the leaves and lives. The medicine man studies all these signs."

Steeves said, "And which do you visit, Crispin, when you feel ill?"

Crispin grinned. "I would go first to the medical doctor," he said, his eyes laughing, "and then I would visit the medicine man just to be sure."

"Covering all your bets," chuckled Dr. Henry as they climbed back into the boat.

Lisa, standing on the bank next to Mrs. Pollifax, said in a

low voice, "Care to bet whose arms Mrs. Lovecraft is going to fall into?"

She had misjudged her, however; Amy Lovecraft graciously accepted Crispin's hand, stepped onto the bow of the boat and remained there for a long moment, her profile turned to the sky, before allowing John Steeves to help her inside.

"What's your deadliest snake?" Reed asked Crispin, which brought a laugh from Lisa.

"Oh the viper," he said. "You are bitten, and in ten minutes you die."

"Good heavens!"

"The black mamba is second, killing in ten or fifteen minutes. If you go to the zoo in Lusaka the snake man will tell you all about it. He will also tell you snakes neither see nor hear, they only sense vibrations." He grinned. "Therefore if you meet a snake and stand perfectly still it won't find you."

"I couldn't possibly stand still," said Lisa, shivering. "I'd run like blazes."

Mrs. Pollifax looked at Crispin, and then she looked at the dark, jungle-like banks of the river lined with twisted roots like claws, deep shadows, tangles of brush and palm and the white tracery of dead roots. She thought of the disciplines needed in this country to avoid sudden painful death and she acknowledged ruefully that survival here was a trifle different from crossing on the green light.

Some forty-five minutes later they reached Chunga camp again. They had seen an egret, a cormorant and a group of impala and hippos, and Julian was waiting on the dock to tell Mrs. Pollifax that a policeman from Lusaka had arrived to ask her questions.

"He arrived fifteen minutes ago," Julian said, helping her out of the launch, "and I told him I will bring you to him. He's seated over there in a chair behind the trees, very private."

There was no curiosity in Julian's candid gaze; in Mrs. Pollifax, however, there was considerable curiosity and she admitted to being startled. "You're quite certain it's me he wants to see?"

"Oh yes," said Julian simply, "he has driven all the way from Lusaka to see you."

"That's a long drive."

"Anything wrong?" asked Cyrus Reed.

Mrs. Pollifax realized that she had been the first person off the boat and now the others had arrived behind her and were listening. She smiled, shook her head and followed Julian to the appointed place, which was indeed private, being nearly encircled by palms. A slender young man in a dark-blue uniform rose. He looked self-contained and very polite, his black face thin and intelligent. "Mrs. Pollifax?"

She assured him that she was Mrs. Pollifax and sat down.

A small table had been placed in front of him on which rested a half-finished Coke and a notebook. He now placed the notebook on his lap and drew out a pen.

"I have come, madam," he said, pronouncing the word m'domm, "to inquire about your advertisement in this morning's *Times of Zambia*. A most curious advertisement, surely?"

"My adver—oh," she said, comprehension dawning, "it's been published today? I'm so glad. The young man said it would be, of course, but I've completely lost track of time, and—" She stopped, aware that her interrogator was waiting patiently for her to finish. "I'm sorry," she said. "I hope I didn't break any law?"

He looked as if he were seated at a garden party balancing a cup of tea on his knees instead of a notebook but his eyes were very watchful. "This man John Sebastian Farrell." He pronounced the name precisely and carefully. "You know this person?"

She nodded. "Yes, of course, or rather I used to. I'm trying to find him. You haven't—haven't come to tell me where he is, have you?"

"No, madam."

"For that matter," she added thoughtfully, "my name wasn't mentioned in the advertisement at all."

"The *Times* office gave me your name, madam, after which I contacted the tourist bureau to learn your itinerary. Now this man," he continued, courteous but resolute. "What causes you to believe he is in Zambia?"

Mrs. Pollifax started to reply and then stopped, suddenly anxious. "Is there something wrong? I don't understand—"

"If you will just answer—"

"Yes, of course," she said. "A mutual friend told me that he's living in Zambia and that he receives his mail in care of Barclay's Bank in Lusaka. I looked first in the telephone directory, but since his name wasn't listed I went to Barclay's Bank, where they told me his mail is collected very seldom and they had no forwarding address for him. So I thought of advertising." She paused, waiting, while he wrote this down. "Why?" she asked. "You surely haven't driven all the way from Lusaka to—"

"May I ask the name of your friend?"

"Friend?" she repeated blankly. "You can't possibly mean—"

"The mutual friend who told you this man lives in Zambia."

This sounded serious indeed. She said after a moment's hesitation, "Bishop. William Bishop."

"His address, please?"

"*Bishop's* address?" She was astonished but struggled gamely to remember where she sent Bishop's Christmas card. "Georgetown, in the District of Columbia," she said at last. "The Laurel Apartments, I believe. In the United States."

"Thank you," he said.

"And now that I've told you all this," she said firmly, "you will tell me, please, why it's so important?"

He put down his pen and folded away his notebook. "You are aware, madam, that you register and show your passport everywhere you go, so that no one may enter this country illegally."

"But I didn't enter—" She stopped in dismay. "You mean Mr. Farrell may be in your country illegally?"

"I did not say that, madam," he said politely. "I am checking into this matter."

"I see," she said, and then added accusingly, "Farrell is a very fine man, Lieutenant—"

"Lieutenant Bwanausi. Dunduzu Bwanausi."

"Lieutenant Bwanausi," she repeated bravely, and won a

faint smile from him; in fact, he looked considerably friendlier as he rose from his chair. "That is quite possible, madam. We will see. I hope you enjoy your safari. Good day, madam."

She watched him go, her face troubled as she thought of the long dusty trip he had made here from Lusaka, and the long dusty trip back; it certainly did not imply any casual interest in Farrell. She felt, too, that there was something that she had missed during the interview, something wrong about it that she couldn't put her finger on. She sat and tried to reconstruct the interview.

A flock of tiny brilliant birds pecked at the earth around her. She heard the palms behind her stir once, convulsively, and then the sound of the launch starting up, followed by the steady putt-putt of its motor as it backed and headed down-river to return Lieutenant Bwanausi to his car. The sun was growing intense on the back of her neck, the air was dead-calm with a complete absence of wind or breeze.

There was no breeze, she thought, and yet the palms had rattled stridently a moment or two ago, a fact that her mind had registered without her being aware of it. Very odd, she decided, and swiftly, soundlessly left her chair. The palms were silent now, and quite empty. She moved in among them listening to the sound made as her shoulders brushed against the brittle dry fronds. She tried tapping a single branch with her fingers to see if a small bird or animal could have rustled them, but she found this quite impossible; someone human had to have disturbed the palms to make the sound she'd heard, someone standing and listening to Lieutenant Bwanausi.

She pushed through the bushes and out to the earthen path behind them and looked toward the dining hall. The distance was not far, and anyone could have reached it from this point in a matter of seconds. There was no one in sight. Walking quickly she passed the office and saw Mrs. Lovecraft leaning over the desk talking animatedly with Julian; she continued through the bar to the dining room and counted heads: the rest of the party were seated there waiting for lunch, relaxed, sprawling in their chairs, laughing at something Chanda had said.

She withdrew before she could be noticed, realizing that it could have been any one of them. It could have been Cyrus Reed, who seemed to be keeping a very firm eye on her, or it could have been Amy Lovecraft, who had already ferreted out something to gossip about in McIntosh. But Amy so much preferred males that it was difficult for Mrs. Pollifax to imagine her curiosity extending to any female in the party.

Or it could, she reflected, have been the one person among them who would find the arrival of a policeman disturbing: *Aristotle.*

She did not like this thought. Remembering they were to leave for Kafwala immediately after lunch, she turned and hurried up the path to Leopard cabin to finish packing her suitcase.

Chapter Seven

The *mwamfuli* I could carry," Chanda said as Mrs. Pollifax prepared to board the pontoon boat after lunch.

Mrs. Pollifax was about to say that one multicolored parasol was no bother at all for her, but seeing the look on Chanda's face she promptly handed it over to him, and then demonstrated how it worked. The pontoon boat set off with them once again sitting on packing cases, but Chanda made the trip standing in the bow under her umbrella, a broad grin on his face.

There were three Land Rovers waiting for them when they reached shore. Mrs. Pollifax, who had not yet considered the logistics of supplying a safari, stood and watched as their luggage was piled into one of the Land Rovers, followed by a sack of potatoes, a huge bag of green beans, two cases of beer and an insulated box filled to the brim with frozen chickens and steaks.

"Looks as if we'll eat well," Mr. Kleiber said in a pleased voice.

"Yes, doesn't it?" said Mrs. Pollifax, and recognizing the moment as an auspicious one—they were all standing in clusters watching—she lifted her camera and took a close-up picture of Mr. Kleiber.

"My yogurt lunches back home seem pathetic here," Lisa

told Dr. Henry, and Mrs. Pollifax snapped a picture of them too, smiling at each other in the sun.

It was not the first time that she had noticed them smiling at each other. It had happened during the trip upriver this morning, and again at lunch, yet so far as she knew Lisa and Dr. Henry had exchanged no more than a few pleasantries, and Lisa was nearly always in the company of John Steeves, who seemed quite stricken by her. Mrs. Pollifax waited now for Tom Henry's response to this remark. He said, "Yes," and continued looking at Lisa until her smile deepened and she turned away—as if, thought Mrs. Pollifax, an entire conversation had just passed between them.

"I hope you're going to take my picture too," said Steeves.

"Oh, especially yours," Mrs. Pollifax told him, hating herself for gushing, "because my children will be so thrilled." She was conscious as she said this of Cyrus Reed turning and observing her with some astonishment. Really, she thought, Mr. Reed's attention, or rather his expectations of her, were going to prove extremely difficult on this trip. In a spirit of defiance she pointed her camera at him and took his picture too. She was completing her collection with a snapshot of Julian standing beside the Land Rover when he gestured to her to climb inside.

"You'll ride with me," he said, and helped her to climb up to the front seat.

She was joined almost immediately by a guard with a long rifle, the same guard who had opened the gate for them the day before, lean and graceful, dressed in khaki shorts and the same moth-eaten gray sweater. Then Lisa strolled over, followed by John Steeves, McIntosh and Amy Lovecraft. The Land Rover with their luggage had already started; Julian shouted at Crispin, climbed in, waved, and they too were off, leaving the others still arranging themselves in the third vehicle.

"Will they have a guard too?" asked Mrs. Pollifax.

Julian turned and looked at her with amusement. "Yes, of course. You still do not believe?"

Lisa leaned over and said, "Well, it *is* a park."

"I've heard," said Mrs. Lovecraft, "that Americans are accustomed to feeding the animals."

Julian grinned and shook his head. "It is safe most of the time so long as one remains on the roads, and in daylight, but even on the road—one of the guides at Luangwa Park was driving along like this three years ago when he was charged by a wounded buffalo. There was not much left of the Land Rover, I can tell you, and if the buffalo had not been quickly shot by the guard there would have been not much left of my friend either."

"I see," said Mrs. Pollifax, blinking. "What—uh—happens if you do have an emergency out here in the bush?"

"Oh, we have marconis," he explained, deftly steering the car around a hole. "At Chunga there is a first-aid station too."

"Marconis?"

"Radio. Already this morning guests have used it. You sent a message to Lusaka, didn't you, Mrs. Lovecraft?"

"Yes," she said curtly.

"I did too," volunteered McIntosh.

"And if there is a serious emergency a Flying Doctor comes, but with Doctor Henry here—"

"*Nyalugwe*," said the guard sharply, and Julian braked.

"He says 'leopard.' " Julian stopped the Land Rover, and the only sounds were of McIntosh and Amy Lovecraft bringing out cameras and checking them; Mrs. Pollifax already held hers in her lap.

"There," said Julian, pointing, and on the crest of a small hill they saw a leopard standing in a tangle of thorn bush, his spots melting perfectly into the background. He turned and looked at them for a long moment, and then he lifted his magnificent blond head and walked away into the bush.

"My God how beautiful," whispered Lisa. "When you think that some silly woman would turn that fabulous creature into a fur coat—"

"Thank heaven for game parks," said Mrs. Pollifax. "Did you see his eyes, did you see those muscles when he moved?"

"Splendid specimen," said Steeves. "I've seen panthers before but never a leopard walking free."

"I believe I caught him on film," McIntosh said with satisfaction.

"Me, too," added Mrs. Lovecraft. "Thrilling."

"I missed," said Mrs. Pollifax sadly. "I was too busy looking."

They drove on along the dusty, shadeless road, of necessity driving slowly. Ahead of them a dozen black-and-white pin-striped fowl broke into a hurried trot. "Guinea fowl," said Julian, and honked the horn, which only caused the guinea fowl to scurry faster, their plump rear-ends registering their indignation until a second beep from the horn persuaded them to the right, and off the road. The Land Rover did not stop again, and as the road grew bumpier the interior of the car grew warmer; the guard in the rear slapped uninhibitedly at tse-tse flies and no one spoke. They came eventually to an intersection marked *Kafwala 11 km.* and headed down a new dirt road. Its surface was dotted with elephant droppings, and the Land Rover rattled ominously as it hit the holes left by their crossing during the rainy season. The terrain was becoming heavily wooded now, with trees on either side of the road.

It was nearing three o'clock when they reached Kafwala, entering it from the rear where a man stood patiently ironing clothes on a slab of wood with a heavy old-fashioned iron. Half a dozen men lazed around a fire watching him and talking; they looked up eagerly at the sound of the Land Rover, which bumped past them and came to a halt in the middle of a grassy compound encircled by tents and white cement huts with thatched roofs. Directly ahead of them stood a long white building with an arcade in its center; beyond it the earth sloped sharply down to the river. As soon as Julian cut the engine Mrs. Pollifax could hear the sound of rapids.

"This is Kafwala," announced Julian, and jumped down from the Land Rover. "Here we stay for two days, game-viewing, before driving north to Moshe."

"Now this looks like a real camp," said Lisa with satisfaction. "Primitive. I think I'm going to like Kafwala very much." She turned and gave Mrs. Pollifax a hand. "Can you still walk? I feel as if I've been massaged all over. Crispin said there's a bathtub here, can you imagine? How on earth do you suppose they manage it?"

"They manage it," said Mrs. Lovecraft, climbing down, "by heating the water in a Rhodesian oven." She glanced around and pointed. "There it is, do you see? There's a drum of water inside that huge square of cement, they light a fire under it and the pipes carry the hot water to the tub or shower."

"Damned ingenious," murmured MacIntosh. "I'll have to take a look at that."

"Yes, but how do you know such things?" asked Lisa.

"Oh my dear," she said in her slightly nasal voice, "I'm what you'd call a Colonial, I've lived in Africa all my life. In the Sudan, in South Africa, in Zambia, in Kenya."

Mrs. Pollifax looked at her with interest; she thought this explained her air of being British without being English. "Army?"

Mrs. Lovecraft turned and looked at her. "My father, yes. Not my husband. We had a tobacco farm until his death. Not far from here, farther south."

"I'm sorry."

"Oh—sorry," said Mrs. Lovecraft, and a scornful, bitter look crossed her face. "But you're a widow, too, aren't you?" She turned away abruptly and smiled at McIntosh. "I'm ready for a drink, ducks, aren't you?"

The Land Rover carrying their luggage bumped its way into camp and the Zambians surrounded it, laughing. Julian waved and then turned to Mrs. Pollifax. "Let me show you your room," he said, leading her toward the arcade set into the center of the long building. "Here," he said, pointing to a door set into the passageway, and then throwing open the opposite door he gestured to Lisa. "You and your father will be here, across from Mrs. Pollifax. Tea is at four, ladies," and with this he hurried off to distribute the others.

Lisa said, "Care for a look at the river?"

Mrs. Pollifax had opened the door to her room—there were no locks or keys—and was peering inside. It was dim because of the tall trees surrounding the building, but she saw the usual two beds shrouded in netting with a chamber-pot under each, a nightstand with a candle, but, most delightful of all, frosted glass windows and thick white walls. There would be no rustling noises tonight.

"A bit dark but very snug," said Lisa, looking over her shoulder. "I wonder if you'll have a roommate?"

"There's only Mrs. Lovecraft," pointed out Mrs. Pollifax.

She and Lisa exchanged a doubtful glance and Lisa laughed. "She's rather awful, isn't she? All that jewelry and pseudo-helplessness but under the fluff I'm beginning to sense the iron-hand-in-the-velvet-glove syndrome. My father had the effrontery to tell me last night that I'll end up just like her if I'm not careful."

"Now, that," said Mrs. Pollifax firmly, "is utterly impossible."

Lisa laughed. "That's because you didn't meet me in my executive phase. I've really been quite a trial to Dad, I confess. He's an absolute dear but a great worrier. Heaven knows I've given him cause, though. There was a man, you see, and until he decamped I thought he'd solve all my problems."

"As no man can, of course," said Mrs. Pollifax.

Lisa nodded. "Yes, I see that now but for a long time I blamed myself, I felt so—so unlovable, you know? So I went to the opposite extreme and—and amputated every emotion that bubbled up, but of course that was ridiculous. It's taken me forever to understand that I'm still myself, and really a rather nice person, and that I just picked a lemon. I'm glad now," she said, smiling warmly at Mrs. Pollifax. "I don't know why I'm telling you all this—probably because I'll burst if I don't tell someone, and you look so—so human—but Africa's having the most tremendous impact on me. Ever since we arrived I've been having the strangest dreams at night, and seeing life and myself in the most astonishing perspective. This country's returning me to something I lost, it's disinhibiting me. Do you find this alarming?"

"No," said Mrs. Pollifax, smiling as she considered it. "No, because I've been here just long enough to see what you mean. Time seems very different here, as if it stopped and has only just begun again, and everything's new. And yet at the same time it's very old, pre-Biblically old, as if the world itself began here." She stopped and laughed. "Obviously I can't put it into words."

"One can't," Lisa said eagerly as they began walking down the path to the river under huge, ancient trees. "Not important emotions. And yet, you know, under the surface there seems to be a great deal going on here. I had a very spooky thing happen to me yesterday when I was driving back to Lusaka. I thought I'd deliver this woman and her child directly to their village, which was about a mile off the main road, but after dropping them off I must have made a wrong turn because I couldn't find my way back, not even to her village." She paused and added with a shiver, "I kept driving until I was really lost, and then I came to a road-block on this dusty, deserted road and—really it was terrifying—I was suddenly surrounded by soldiers or police, I don't know which they were."

"Good heavens," said Mrs. Pollifax, startled.

Lisa nodded. "About twenty of them, all with rifles. They were terribly nice but at the same time they checked everything, my passport and visa, my luggage, the car. They must have kept me there for nearly an hour answering questions: why I was on that road, and where I was going, where I'd been, how long I was to be in Zambia and why I'd come to Zambia in the first place."

"Where did this happen?" asked Mrs. Pollifax.

Lisa frowned. "Somewhere down in the Kafue Flats area—that's what the map said, anyway."

"The driver who brought us to Chunga," said Mrs. Pollifax, "spoke of spies—Rhodesian spies—infiltrating Zambia."

"Probably," said Lisa. "There have been guerilla raids all along the Rhodesian border—except Africans call it Zambabwe, you know—and deep inside the country too. Not by Zambians but by revolutionaries crossing through Zambia, so I suppose the Rhodesians send people into this country as well. But if I lived next door to an *apartheid* country," she said hotly, "I don't think I'd sit on my hands either. I think it's terribly unfair that a minority of two hundred and fifty thousand white people have absolute power over six million natives and *squash* them. After all, it's their country."

"In general," said Mrs. Pollifax mildly, "the Golden Rule seems to be the last rule applied to any situation these days." They had reached the riverbank and she thought how incongruous it was to speak of violence in such a setting. On their left the water raced over great primeval boulders, shooting up plumes of spray and caressing the ear with its stormy descent. Once beyond the rocks the water gentled, sending small ripples to the shore at their feet until on their right it flowed smoothly around an island and became almost a backwash before it continued on its way south, to Chunga camp and beyond. There were several rough chairs placed near the bank, and a circle of them at the empty campfire site. "Rhodesia *is* very near," she said, sitting down in one of the chairs, "and Zambia used to be Northern Rhodesia, didn't it?"

"Oh yes," said Lisa, "but until you've visited Livingstone you've no idea *how* near. Half of Victoria Falls is in Rhodesia. I took one of those sundown cruises out of Livingstone, and one side of the river was Zambian and the other Rhodesian. The guide said we were under observation the entire time, because the river's the only barrier, and people can cross at night. In fact—"

She stopped as a voice hailed them from the top of the hill: the third Land Rover had arrived and John Steeves was descending, followed by Amy Lovecraft, Dr. Henry and—very gingerly—Willem Kleiber. A multicolored parasol next came into view, with Chanda under it. A moment later Cyrus Reed and McIntosh began descending the hill too, as well as a young man wearing a white linen jacket and carrying a tray of glasses.

Dr. Henry sat down near Lisa and smiled at her. "We saw a water buffalo, a number of puku and some impala."

She said, "We saw a leopard."

"I think," said John Steeves, taking the chair next to her, "that if you look very quickly into those palms to your left you can add a monkey to your list."

"Never mind the monkey," said Amy Lovecraft deflatingly. "Mrs. Pollifax, Julian asked me to tell you there's hot water now, and because there are so many of us we have to stagger our baths."

"And he's giving me first crack?" said Mrs. Pollifax. "Except I haven't the faintest idea where the bath is."

Chanda looked up and said eagerly, "I know where the *bafa* is, I will show you."

"Good, let's go," she told him, and rose from her chair to

follow him up the hill. He chose to ignore the path and to leap gracefully from rock to rock, and for the first time she noticed the long puckered seam of a scar that ran up the back of his leg from the ankle to his thigh. She remembered Dr. Henry saying that he'd been nearly dead when he was brought into the hospital, and she wondered how many more scars there were. At the top of the hill he turned and waited for her, his eyes as luminous as if incandescent bulbs shone behind them.

"I move fast, like monkey," he said, grinning.

"You certainly do." Pausing to catch her breath she noticed a small chamois bag suspended about his neck on a string. "What's that, Chanda?" she asked, pointing.

He looked down in surprise, stuffed the bag quickly inside his shirt again and gave her a thoughtful look. *"Cumo,"* he said guardedly. Suddenly his enormous smile was back. "You like to see? It is my treasure."

"Love to," she told him. "Is it secret?"

"Very secret," he said, and seemed grateful when she opened the door of her room and beckoned him inside. First he gravely returned her parasol to her. *"Santi mukwai,"* he said, and then he removed the chamois bag from around his neck and knelt beside her bed to empty its contents across the blanket.

She found herself both touched and amused at what emerged, remembering her son Roger's similar collection at this age, except that a more sophisticated society had rendered Roger's treasures obsolete. In the bush, Chanda's collection still had immediate value.

"From *cifulo,"* Chanda said, pointing past the wall of her hut. *"Mushi.* My home."

"Do you mean your home before you met Dr. Henry?"

"Before this," he said, pointing matter-of-factly to his scarred leg, and picking up objects from his collection he explained them one by one. *"Munga—* thorn," he said.

"Munga," she repeated, nodding.

"Bulobo—fishhook. *Mwele*—knife." *Mwando* was a ball of string. *Lino* was a tooth—his own, she suspected, although his were white and gleaming. "And *cibiliti,"* he added, holding up two safety matches.

"Yes, and a snake," she added, pointing to a dried skin.

"*Nsoka*," he said, smiling and nodding. "My father give me *nsoka*. He was hunter, very big man. He track game—*Ishanda Ionshe nama*. He teach me."

"So you'll be a hunter too?"

"Already a hunter," he said, grinning. "Very good one." She watched in silence as he returned his treasure to the chamois bag, his touch loving.

When he stood up she said quietly, "Thank you, Chanda."

"You *nunandi* now," he told her. "Friend. You and Dr. Henry. And now you have *bafa*," he said with his charming smile. "I show you."

Ten minutes later Mrs. Pollifax was seated in a hot tub in a small thatched hut, contentedly humming a song and reflecting that she was having a very good time on her safari and taking some very good pictures. Twenty minutes later, dressed again, she returned to her room and sat down on her bed to do a little planning about those pictures. Yesterday, for instance, she had completed her first film, tucked away now in her suitcase, and this morning she'd begun her second. That left four untouched cartridges, which meant—she made rapid mathematical computations—ninety-three more snapshots, many of which would have to be spent on animals and scenery. She was quite certain, however, that she'd already captured each of her traveling companions at least once on film, and this pleased her very much. Some of the pictures might not come out well, of course, but statistically it was a good beginning, and she thought that by tomorrow she could relax and become more casual about her filming. She happily touched the four sealed yellow boxes of film lined up in her suitcase and then she slipped her hand into the pocket of her folded bush jacket to check the completed cartridge she'd packed away this morning.

The cartridge wasn't there.

Startled, Mrs. Pollifax picked up the jacket, turned each pocket inside out, shook the garment, tossed it across the bed and began digging through her suitcase. She could find no metal cartridge. She crawled under the bed and searched and then checked through her purse: no film. Thoroughly alarmed now, she picked up her suitcase and dumped the contents all over the bed and began a frenzied hunt.

Still there was no cartridge. Be calm, she thought, and sat down on the bed in the middle of bright sweaters, cold creams, slacks and sneakers, but there was no evading the fact that the film was missing. Yet she'd packed it this noon at Chunga camp before coming here, and several minutes later when the boy had come for her suitcase she'd reopened the bag to add her toothbrush, and the exposed film had still been there: she could see it now in her memory, sticking out of the pocket of her folded bush jacket. And since her suitcase had been locked during its journey to Kafwala there could have been no accident that would jar open the suitcase and scatter its contents. The film had been locked inside her suitcase when it left Chunga, and her suitcase had remained locked until she had opened it half an hour ago to extract a bar of soap for her bath. She'd reached inside without looking because she knew exactly where the soap was, but she'd had to unlock the suitcase to do so, and the lock had not been tampered with then . . .

But if the film wasn't lost—and it couldn't have been, she thought grimly, going over and over it—then it had to have been stolen, and stolen while she was taking a bath.

She sat without moving, allowing the shock of this to catch up with her, and it was a very real shock, with implications that left her a little dizzy. How frightfully arrogant she'd been, she thought, dashing about taking her snapshots so openly while all the time someone on this safari didn't want to be photographed. Someone had allowed her to snap as many of them as she pleased, and then her film had been quietly taken away from her. She had been discreetly and firmly put in her place.

Score one for Aristotle, she thought.

Brazen, of course, but so easy . . . an empty room with only an inside bolt on the door and no way of locking it on the outside, her suitcase unlocked and she in the bathtub . . .

A flicker of anger stirred in her, grew, and at last triumphed over her alarm: it appeared that she now had a definite adversary, faceless, nameless and observant. She could assume that her burglar knew nothing about her except that she preferred faces mixed in with her scenery, but her unknown antagonist was clever, she knew that now. He had moved in early, counting on her not noticing, counting on her being a dithery, rather silly woman addicted to snapshots. He would do better next time, she thought, to leave an unexposed film behind him, because even silly dithery women noticed when too many exposed films disappeared.

But in the meantime she had lost twenty valuable pictures, and unless she could outthink her burglar she was doomed to see her completed films picked off like flies. It was also disturbing to realize that her collection was reduced to the six or seven snapshots still in her camera . . . or had these been tampered with too? The camera still registered seven snapshots on its gauge, and the cartridge looked untouched, but just to be certain she removed the film, put in a fresh one and dropped the half-completed one in her purse. The sealed boxes she hid: one in her totebag, one in the toe of a sneaker, the last inside her purse.

Defiantly she decided that she would continue her snapshot-taking with an enthusiasm certain to annoy her adversary, but it was time now to turn to her lapel-pin camera. She had worn the latter pinned to her sweater and by now her companions must be accustomed to seeing her wear it, incongruous as it looked with casual clothes. She would continue to wear it doggedly.

Still shaken by her discovery she repacked her suitcase and locked it. As she left her room she found Cyrus Reed opening the door of the room on the other side of the arcade. He turned, looking genuinely surprised. "You're there?" he said. "Good, we're neighbors."

Even if it was he who had stolen her film, she thought it might be wise to mention her discovery of its disappearance. "If you've been down by the river," she said, "I wonder if you could tell me—or remember—just who left the group to walk up this way past my room?"

Reed looked from her to the door behind her and his brows lifted. "Something missing?" he asked quietly.

She nodded. "Yes, while I was in that building over there taking a bath. But I don't," she added, "want to cause a fuss."

"Quite right," he said. "Very sensible. And you want to know who left the party . . . Have to say nearly everyone," he said regretfully. "Let's see . . . good lord, even I left. Spilled some beer on my slacks, came up to change. Steeves ran out of film—passed him coming up as I went back. McIntosh left to take a nap—still gone. Kleiber came up for a map to prove some point or other, Lisa for a sweater. Chanda went with you and didn't return. Yes, I'd say the only two who stayed by the river were Mrs. Lovecraft and Dr. Henry. Nothing too valuable, I hope?"

"Fairly so, yes. To me."

"Don't like to hear that. You gave a thorough search? But of course you would." He placed the emphasis on *you* very flatteringly.

She gave him a smile and took a few steps toward the path. "A very efficient list, Mr. Reed. Thank you."

"No," he said firmly.

She turned in surprise.

"Not Mr. Reed. Call me Cyrus."

"Oh." She hesitated and then nodded. "And my name's Emily." As she descended the hill, leaving him behind, she realized that she felt obscurely better and was even smiling. A rather fatuous smile, she guessed, but still she was smiling.

By half-past six there was a crackling fire down by the river, the sole illumination except for a lantern hung from a post. They sat in a circle around the fire, drawn closer by the darkness beyond them and by the feeling of being very small under the huge trees and beside the roaring river. They sat and talked and sipped beer. The only activity came from two people: one the grave-faced young man in a white jacket who came down the hill bearing silverware, napkins and plates, then went up again and returned with cups and saucers, more beer and glassware. The other was Mrs. Pollifax who, with a flashcube attached to her camera, knelt, hovered, stood, sat and wickedly took picture after picture.

"Why do you bother," asked Mr. Kleiber curiously, "when you don't have a good German camera like Mr. McIntosh or Mrs. Lovecraft?"

"Oh, but this camera is just fine for an amateur," she said. "I snap pictures just for my children, you know. They'll be fascinated, and then of course my grandchildren will love seeing the animals. I always try," she told him firmly, "to create a total background, so that they can step into the adventure and experience it too."

"And do you," asked Cyrus Reed dryly, "show slides?"

She gave him a level glance and without batting an eyelash, for she loathed slides, said, "Of course."

"Incredible," he said, staring at her.

On an inspired note she added, "As a matter of fact after dinner I'll bring down pictures of my grandchildren to show you. They're very *lovely* grandchildren."

"Really?" said Amy Lovecraft coldly.

The young waiter had just arrived bearing a large tray, followed by two young men carrying steaming dishes, and he chose this moment to announce that dinner was served. Mrs. Pollifax jumped up immediately and became the first to approach the food spread out on the table. She was not surprised when she returned to her chair to find herself something of a pariah after her announcement about snapshots. Mr. Kleiber chose a seat as far removed from her as possible, and Mrs. Lovecraft, who had shown no real interest in Mr. Kleiber before, eagerly took the chair next him. Lisa, assuming a more neutral corner, was joined by Steeves as usual. Tom Henry found a seat not far from Lisa, and McIntosh, still smiling enigmatically, sat beside Julian.

Only Chanda and Cyrus Reed showed signs of not being infected. Chanda sat down cross-legged on the ground beside Mrs. Pollifax and gave her a dazzling white smile. "I sit here. You *nunandi.*"

"Damn awkward eating from one's lap," growled Reed.

"Try a corner of this little table," suggested Mrs. Pollifax. "After all, the word safari means camping."

"*Touché,*" he said, smiling. "Thanks. Incredibly good food. Can't imagine how they do such a *cordon bleu* job out here without electricity."

"There is big wood stove," Chanda told him eagerly, "and very fine cook. Julian calls him a—a chef."

Reed nodded. "That's it, then. Saw you up there poking around. Anyone else speak Bemba here?"

"*Cimo*," said Chanda, holding up one finger. "There is good life here in park, maybe I not be hunter."

"Tom said you're damn good at hunting and tracking and only twelve years old," pointed out Reed, deftly spearing a piece of steak. "Said you went off to see what's left of your old village on the Angolan border this spring, and hiked fifty miles through the bush alone."

Chanda's smile deepened. "Yes, that. He tell you about the lions?"

"Lions!" exclaimed Mrs. Pollifax.

"Three of 'em," said Reed, nodding, "but how did you know they were following you, Chanda?"

"Because—" Chanda hesitated. "I do not know name for *cula*."

Several chairs away, Julian said, "Frogs, Chanda."

"Ah! Yes. I hear them, you know. They make a frog sound, and then I cross *kamana*—"

"Brook," called Tom Henry.

"Yes, brook, and frogs are very noisy talking to each other. I walk more, and then—" He lifted one hand and cut the air dramatically. "*Cula* sound stop. So I look for big tree to climb because it becomes dark, like now, and I know something follows me or the frogs would be making noise."

"Good heavens," said Lisa. They were all listening now.

"Three lions try to climb tree for me, but I am too high. I sit all night for them to go away."

"I take it they did eventually," said Steeves.

"But not until morning," put in Tom Henry.

"Yes, I climb down from tree but cannot walk. *Mwendo* become like tree too."

"He means he'd lost all circulation in his legs," explained Tom. "His limbs had become like the tree."

Chanda nodded. "So I hunt sticks and dry grass and after long time make fire rubbing sticks. This is very hard to do. For many hours I sit to warm myself at fire, and then I go."

"Something I can't imagine any American twelve-year-old doing," said Reed.

"Still, Africa's a shade more hospitable a country than Mongolia," put in Steeves. "There you've panthers and tigers, but even if the sun shines three hundred days a year you get tremendous winds and a horrendous wind-chill factor."

"Tigers we don't have," said Julian, "but tomorrow we look for lion for you."

"Oh, I do hope we see one," cried Lisa eagerly.

"What time do we start?" asked Mrs. Pollifax.

"Directly after breakfast, about half-past seven."

"Early," said Amy Lovecraft, making a face.

The white-jacketed waiter had brought down a new tray which he set upon the table. Now he bowed, his face grave, and said, "Pudding is served, please, ladies and gentlemen."

It was after the pudding that Tom Henry reminded Chanda he was tired today and it was time for him to invest in some sleep. The boy arose from his cross-legged stance on the ground, and at the same moment Mrs. Pollifax had a sudden, dazzling idea. She, too, arose. "I'll go up with Chanda," she said. "It's so dark I couldn't bring myself to go alone, but if we're breakfasting at seven—"

"What, no snapshots of your grandchildren?" asked Reed mischievously.

"I'm still catching up on my sleep," she said, ignoring him and picking up her purse. "Good night!"

A chorus of farewells followed her as she turned away from the fire. It was very dark outside the circle of light and Chanda took her hand and guided her. Pebbles slid underfoot; the sound of the rushing water behind them made a low musical backdrop, rather soporific, she thought, like the murmur of voices heard from a distant room. There was a lantern waiting at the top of the hill, placed on a table in the center of the arcade. She turned and looked back at the campfire, counting heads. They were all there, no one had left. She said, "Chanda . . ."

"Yes, madam."

"Chanda, I wonder if you'd hide something for me—keep something for me—in your *cumo* bag."

He stared at her, eyes clouded now, opaque, mysterious, so that she wondered if he understood.

"It's something important and quite small. Only until the safari ends," she added quickly. "It needs—needs hiding." She walked around the corner of the passageway out of the lantern's light and opened her camera and removed the film that she'd completed down by the campfire. When she held it out to Chanda he remained impassive, the expression in his eyes chilling, as if he looked into, through and beyond her into something she couldn't see. Then abruptly the mask splintered into smiles, the strange effect was gone and an enormous smile lighted up his eyes.

"Yes, secret," he said, nodding, and taking the cartridge from her hand he loosened the string of his chamois bag and dropped the film inside.

She realized that she had been holding her breath; she exhaled now in relief. "You're a real friend, Chanda."

"But of course—*nunandi*," he said, laughing, and raced off into the darkness, calling over his shoulder, "Good night, madam!"

She stared after him thoughtfully. She did hope he understood but at least in giving him one of her films she felt that she had diversified, and this lifted her spirits. Her glance moved to the fire at the rear of the camp where the silhouettes of half a dozen men crouched talking around the blaze. She turned to go to her room and jumped when she saw Cyrus Reed standing in the arcade watching her.

"Oh—you startled me," she gasped, and wondered how long he'd been standing there and how much he'd seen.

He held out her sun-goggles and her umbrella. "Left these behind you," he said, handing them to her, and then, "Care for a stroll around the compound before turning in?"

She hesitated. "I do feel rather unexercised," she admitted.

"Good. Damn good display of Orion and the Pleiades if we can get away from the light of the fire. Tiresome down below after you left. Can't help noticing that Mrs. Lovecraft talks through her nose and Mr. Kleiber sniffs a great deal through his, and Steeves was running on about Mongolia, which is all very well but this is Africa."

She laughed. "You poor man."

"Not at all," he said amiably, taking her arm. "Decided to look for better company."

"I think your daughter Lisa's a darling, by the way."

"She is, isn't she? Seems to be thawing out now. Damn glad to see it."

"And you," she said, "are really a judge?"

He brought out his flashlight, checked it and nodded.

"A *phungu*, Julian tells me. The Nyanga word for judge or counselor."

"Phungu," she repeated, trying it out on the tongue. "Sounds a little like fungus. What sort of *phungu* were you before you retired? Did you have hundreds of exciting cases?"

"Strictly routine," he said, "except for the Rambeau-Jenkins case."

Mrs. Pollifax stopped in her tracks and stared at him. "Oh," she gasped, "do you think she murdered him?"

He had been staring up at the sky; now he turned and looked down at her and smiled his sleepy smile. "That, my dear, only God knows."

"But you were there, you presided, and I've so often wondered—"

"Ha—common fallacy, that," he told her. "We *phungus* never judge guilt or innocence, we judge evidence. The law isn't emotional, you know, it's cold and impersonal. Has to be."

"But you're not," she told him indignantly.

She could see his smile in the light of the campfire. "Don't ever tell anyone, my dear." He stopped and said, "With you the 'my dear' just slips out."

"Well, *I* think Nina Rambeau was innocent," she said, and hoped he wouldn't notice that she was blushing. She wondered how long it had been since anyone had called her "my dear." "Have you found Orion yet?"

He shook his head. "Glow from the men's campfire bleaches out the stars. Daresay if we wandered a little way up the road we could see better."

"Oh, do let's," she said.

He nodded pleasantly to the men around the campfire as

they passed. "Just looking at the stars," he told them, pointing at the sky.

The men burst into smiles and nods.

"Damn lot livelier up here than down by the river," he said mildly as they left the fire behind and entered the road beyond.

They had ventured a few paces into the darkness when Mrs. Pollifax looked back and sighed. "It's the guard," she told Reed. "He's *following* us, isn't that ridiculous?"

"Not at all," said Reed thoughtfully. "Can't have it both ways, my dear."

"Can't—what do you mean by that?"

"Well," he said in his mild voice, "if you want to observe wild animals in perfect safety you capture them, bring 'em back to our world and look at them behind bars in a zoo. Here we're their guests," he pointed out. "Trespassers, actually. They run free, wild and protected, but we do *not*."

"Of course you're right," she said reluctantly. "It's just that it's so *confining* not to be able to leave camp without being followed."

"Doubt if anyone could confine you, my dear. Ought to mind his presence far more than you since I've every intention of kissing you."

She turned and looked at him in astonishment, which placed her in the perfect position for him to make good his intention. "Orion be damned," he said, and swept her into his arms.

Mrs. Pollifax gave a small squeak of protest, resisted briefly and then discovered that she fitted very nicely into the curve of his arm and that she enjoyed being kissed very much. When he let her go she promptly dropped her sun-goggles, her kerchief and her umbrella. "Oh," she stammered. "Oh dear."

He patiently retrieved them and handed them back to her. "And there," he said, grasping her hand and firmly holding it in his, "is Orion."

"Yes," she said, feeling very disoriented and breathless as she realized that she was not immune, after all, to huge and charming *phungus*. It was all very disconcerting, she thought —at her age, too—and then she lifted her gaze to the sky and was struck breathless all over again. "Oh," she whispered.

It was like standing in the center of a planetarium, the sky a huge bowl turned upside down and fitted snugly to the horizon and then filled with thousands upon thousands of stars. This, surely, was infinity, she thought, gazing up in awe, and slowly became aware of the silence surrounding them, a silence like the beginning or the end of the world.

It was interrupted by a cough from the guard some distance behind them. Cyrus said dryly, "I think we're keeping him, he's been patient with us long enough."

Without speaking they turned and walked back to camp.

When Mrs. Pollifax entered her room again it was already very cold and she paused only long enough to slip a new cartridge of film into her camera and to hide the camera under her pillow for the night. Blowing out the candle beside her bed she inserted herself between the blankets, tucked the mosquito netting around her and was surprised to find her room still filled with light. She noticed now what had escaped her by daylight: the wall of the room over her door rose only to a height of eight feet. Between this and the inverted V of the rafters there was only mosquito netting, so that she could see the glow of the lantern in the passageway outside.

She lay gazing up at this light and thinking about her strange day, about her film being stolen and then about Cyrus Reed, who was proving very distracting indeed. She realized that she was going to have to discipline herself very severely; after all, for her this was no ordinary safari. She was here for a purpose, and if she was not attentive and very clever, then Aristotle would continue wandering around the world negotiating contracts to shoot more people and this would never do.

Never, she thought, and resolved to put Cyrus Reed completely out of her mind. She closed her eyes and then opened them when she heard voices and footsteps outside on the path. A moment later she recognized Amy Lovecraft's high-pitched laugh.

"I would have fallen, Mr. Kleiber, if you'd not rescued me like a knight in shining armor, you dear man. This path—"

Amy Lovecraft, thought Mrs. Pollifax, was definitely hunting something more than game.

"I do not understand," Mr. Kleiber said in his pedantic, humorless voice, "why one bulldozer could not be assigned to this hill. They have the bulldozers, I know. They use them on the roads, and with only one hour of work—"

"Are you in the construction business, Mr. Kleiber? You seem to know so much about machinery."

"Heavy machinery, yes. I sell worldwide. It's—"

Their voices blurred as they passed from the arcade into the compound; she heard one more brittle laugh pierce the stillness and then there was silence. Mrs. Pollifax had closed her eyes again when she heard fresh pebbles crunching underfoot outside the building. "Really beautiful," Lisa Reed was saying. "I love it, don't you?"

It was Tom Henry who replied. "Absolutely." A comfortable silence followed and then Tom said, "John Steeves is certainly very distinguished."

Lisa said carelessly, "Oh—distinguished, yes."

"As a matter of fact we've one of his paperbacks at the hospital. *One Hundred Nights in a Yurt,* I think. The chap who read it—"

"Tom."

"Mmmm?"

"Don't be a goose."

Tom Henry laughed. "Have a good sleep, my dear."

Mrs. Pollifax heard him walk away and Lisa open the door of the room opposite hers. A very interesting exchange of words, she thought, smiling, very interesting indeed, and wondered on whom she might eavesdrop next.

She was not kept waiting long: McIntosh came next through the arcade, talking to Cyrus, and for a man of smiling silence McIntosh had suddenly become very articulate. ". . . Monetary Fund, of course. You simply can't cure inflation unless nations stop going to the printing press. The world is being drowned in worthless paper . . . Irresponsible. Expedient, of course, but disastrous. No discipline without paper being backed by something."

"Gold?" inquired Cyrus.

"Probably, yes. We've not been on a gold standard since 1901. Governments sneer at it, of course, because it would force discipline on them. But mark my words, Reed, whole civilizations have become graveyards by corrupting their currency."

"You do considerable business between countries?"

"Oh yes, quite international, but of course multinational's the word these days. But I don't want to hold you up, we can continue this another time. Good night, Reed."

"Yes . . . Lions tomorrow. Good night."

The last to pass by her door were Julian and John Steeves, and they were walking much faster. ". . . oh, much better here," Julian was saying. "Too many young men of my country head for the cities, and this is bad. Lusaka is full of thieves and spies."

"Excellent sense," said Steeves. "I'm not very big on cities myself. I like your bush, it has a mystique . . ."

Mrs. Pollifax did not hear the rest because they had left the arcade and their voices faded. In any case she was growing warmer now, and with this came a voluptuous drowsiness: she closed her eyes and slept and dreamed of masks. In her dream she sat in a theater and one by one each member of the safari walked out on stage to form a single line facing her. It was only when they moved up to the footlights in unison that Mrs. Pollifax saw they were holding masks to their faces. At a given signal each mask was swept away, but underneath lay another mask, and then another and still another . . .

Chapter Eight

When Mrs. Pollifax woke at half-past six the next morning it was bone-chillingly cold. The young waiter who brought coffee to her room on a tray said, "Good morning, madam," and it was so cold that wisps of vapor curled from his lips to match the steam rising from the coffeepot. Mrs. Pollifax put one foot out of bed, poured coffee into a cup and carried it under the blankets with her, wondering if she would ever be warm again.

"I thought Africa was t-t-tropical," she protested at breakfast, which was served down by the river in the morning mist.

"We're four thousand feet above sea level," Julian reminded her with a flash of white teeth. "You are ready for lion? Perhaps it will warm you to hear that Crispin took the Land Rover out at dawn and found lion tracks six miles north of camp."

"Oh how wonderful!" gasped Mrs. Pollifax.

Almost as exciting was the news that overnight two of the Land Rover roofs had been removed so that they could ride standing up and scan the savannah for game, like professionals. Mrs. Pollifax could scarcely wait.

But in spite of her excitement she had not forgotten her resolve of the night before, and between breakfast and departure time she retired to her room to make a list for the day and contemplate it. *Find out*, she wrote, *who's traveled widely during the past eight months (France—Costa Rica).* To this she added: *Try McIntosh again, could be opening up. Mr. Kleiber: if good at machinery ask about guns. John Steeves: what disguises preferred?* She studied this memo and then lit a match and burned it.

They set out shortly afterward in the two Land Rovers, the sun higher now and promising warmth soon. For this excursion Mrs. Pollifax had arranged her clothing in layers so that as the day advanced she could remove first her bush jacket, and then her heavy sweater, and then the pale-blue cardigan until eventually—it was rather like peeling an artichoke, she thought—she would be resplendent in striped shirt and kerchief before the process reversed itself. She also carried her bright parasol and two rolls of film for her camera and wore her lapel pin.

As they left Kafwala camp behind and headed for the open savannah Mrs. Pollifax realized that, like Lisa, Africa was having its charismatic effect upon her: the road wound ahead of the Land Rover like textured brown ribbon, the high grass tawny on either side and the earth flat under the incredible arc of blue African sky. There were also the surreal notes: a candelabra tree, its limbs perfectly splayed, its blossoms a dull orange; a baobub tree smooth and silvery in the warm morning light, and when Mrs. Pollifax inquired of Julian what the cement posts along the road meant, Julian laughed. "Not cement —termite nests." Bringing the Land Rover to a halt he jumped out and kicked at the top one, exposing holes like a honeycomb.

It was Mrs. Pollifax who spotted the elephants first. "Oh look," she cried, and in both Land Rovers heads swiveled to the left. At some distance away from them a line of elephants was moving across the savannah, an entire family with three young ones among them.

"Baby *nsofu*," said Chanda, pointing and grinning.

"I count nine," volunteered Cyrus, standing beside her.

Mrs. Pollifax stood up on the seat and took three pictures in rapid succession, and then somewhat reluctantly slid down in the seat and snapped a close-up shot of John Steeves as he watched the procession.

"Can we get out?" called Amy Lovecraft, who was all beige and white today, with a green kerchief around her hair.

"Better if we drive ahead down the road," said Julian. "They're heading for water, we'll see them closer farther along."

The two Land Rovers inched ahead for half a mile and stopped, after which everyone climbed out and stood in a group waiting, cameras ready.

"This light," said Mrs. Pollifax, gesturing widely toward the sky. "It so reminds me of the light in southern France. The same luminous quality. Has anyone been in France lately?"

No one appeared to pay her the slightest attention; John Steeves stared inscrutably into the distance; McIntosh was busy with his light meter; Mr. Kleiber grunted noncommittally, while Amy Lovecraft simply ignored her. Only Cyrus turned and looked at her. "No," he said. "Have you?"

Having never visited France in her life, Mrs. Pollifax found herself figuratively pinned to a wall and was happy to be rescued by the elephants. "Here they come," she cried.

The elephants emerged from a copse of trees and lumbered toward them, trunks swinging. They crossed the road only twenty feet away from them without so much as a glance at their audience. The baby elephants brought a laugh from Lisa. "They're *darling!*"

Satisfied, they climbed into the Land Rovers and drove on. Gradually the topography began to fold in upon itself, nurturing seams and hollows and small hills. The Land Rover coasted down an incline to a dried-up brook bed surrounded by tangles of thorn bush and twisted roots. It stopped and Julian climbed out. "Here," he called, beckoning, and when they joined him it was to see the imprint of a lion paw in the dust.

The Land Rovers drove ahead in low gear, no one speaking now. Cautiously they rounded a wide curve, slowed as they approached a grassless area beside the road, and—Mrs. Pollifax caught her breath in awe—there lay two lions stretched out sleeping in the sun. The Land Rover coasted to a stop only eight feet away from the lions; beside Mrs. Pollifax the guard leaned forward and swung his rifle into horizontal position, his eyes watchful.

"A lioness and a male," whispered Julian.

As the second Land Rover drew up behind them the lioness lifted her magnificent head, yawned and rose to her feet. She stretched, looked them over without interest and sniffed the air. The male stirred and rose to his feet too, massive, nearly nine feet in length, and Mrs. Pollifax held her breath as he stared unblinkingly at them. Remembering her camera just in time, she snapped a picture only a second before the two beautiful tawny creatures slipped away into the grass and vanished.

"Lion," breathed Mrs. Pollifax, and felt that her cup was full to the brim.

At noon they came to Lufupa camp, which was small—for weekend people only, Julian said—and not yet open for the season. The camp occupied a point of land where the Kafue River curved and broadened, smooth as a millpond in the noon sun. They were to lunch here, Julian said, pointing to a picnic table under the acacia trees.

Mrs. Pollifax had now removed three of her layers of clothing and was happy to sit in the shade. It was a tranquil scene: not far away two men were painting chairs a bright blue in the grass, and mattresses were being aired in the sun. Up on the roof of the largest hut an old man was spreading out fresh thatch and tying it down with wire, like shingles. Finding herself next to Mr. Kleiber at the picnic table, she turned to him with a warm smile. "Do you know much about guns, Mr. Kleiber? I'm wondering if you can tell me what sort of rifle our guard carries."

The man serving them their lunch chose this moment to place in front of Mr. Kleiber a plate of chicken, mashed potatoes, gravy and fresh tomatoes. McIntosh, seated across the table, answered instead. "A 3006, I'd say."

"Oh—you know guns," she said brightly.

"Or possibly a 3004," Kleiber said with his mouth full.

"A 3004," Crispin told them from the end of the table.

Very inconclusive, thought Mrs. Pollifax, and decided there was something far too relaxing about all this fresh air and that an evening campfire might be the better place for tactful interrogations.

After lunch they strolled upriver a short distance, with guards at their front and rear, and watched hippos bathing in the shallows. This especially pleased Cyrus because there had been no ox-peckers on the backs of the hippos they'd seen at Chunga camp.

"Ox-peckers?" echoed Mrs. Pollifax.

"Tick-birds," he explained, and pointed. "Find them on rhinos' backs too. Feed on their ticks and conveniently warn them of danger." His glance moved to John Steeves, who was helping Lisa remove her sweater, and he frowned. "Chap really seems to be zeroing in on Lisa. Very confidently too."

Mrs. Pollifax smiled. "If there's one thing John Steeves has, I'm sure it's confidence."

"Seems a decent enough chap," said Reed. "Just difficult to picture as a son-in-law. I mean—yurts?"

"Oh, I don't think you need worry about that."

"No?" said Reed, looking surprised. "Together all the time."

"There are," said Mrs. Pollifax, "undercurrents."

"I'm overlooking something?"

"You've been watching Steeves and not your daughter. He's with her, but she's not with him, if you follow me. It's a matter of the eyes. Glances."

"You astonish me," said Cyrus, and turning to her he added accusingly, "Matter of fact, you've astonished me ever since we met."

Mrs. Pollifax found herself blushing—really it was very tiresome, she'd not blushed in years—and fielded this statement by turning to Mr. Kleiber, who was looking distinctly bored by the hippos. "Still no crocodiles, Mr. Kleiber?"

He looked startled. "Not yet, no. Dear me, I hope soon, though. What a hot sun, I think I've had enough of walking."

She thought that Mr. Kleiber had begun thawing out a little today; the pinched look was no longer so pronounced, and occasionally he smiled at something said by the group. He appeared to like McIntosh, whose reticence matched his own, and when something unusual occurred he would look first to McIntosh, rock a little on his heels while he waited to catch his eye, and then deliver himself of a pithy comment in his dry, sarcastic voice. He had begun to tolerate Amy Lovecraft too, no longer looking frost-bitten when she took his arm and asked if he minded her walking with him.

"Crocodiles you will see at Moshe tomorrow," said Julian, overhearing him. "The camp is very open, right on the river, and the crocodiles sun themselves on the banks."

They turned to go back and Mrs. Pollifax fell into step beside Cyrus. Never having walked behind Mr. Kleiber before, she was amused now to see what an odd walk he had: a strut, she thought, with a stutter. He walked with his shoulders rigid, back straight and head high, but his right foot toed in slightly and threw the rhythm just a shade off balance, like one instrument in a band playing a beat behind the others.

"Looks like company up ahead," said Cyrus.

A shiny beige Land Rover was parked next to the safari jeeps, and three men, all black, were talking to the workmen. As they drew nearer, one of them climbed back into the car and the other two could be seen shaking hands and saying goodbye. The man in the car leaned forward and gestured to them to hurry.

Reed said abruptly, "Chap on the left in the green shirt is the man who was asking for you at the hotel. In Lusaka, when I was checking out."

Startled, Mrs. Pollifax said, "Are you sure?"

"Never forget a face. Shall I give him a shout?"

"Oh yes, do," she said, hurrying.

Reed began to shout, and Mrs. Pollifax waved frantically, but the two men gave them only a quick glance and then jumped into the Land Rover and the car sped away. A moment later it had vanished among the trees.

"Had his chance," said Cyrus. "Muffed it."

"But they must have heard you," protested Mrs. Pollifax, "and if they were deaf they would have seen me waving, because they turned and looked."

Approaching the Lufupa workers Cyrus said, "From the city, were they?"

"Oh yes, sir," the elder said, beaming. "They did not know the camp is closed. Three gentlemen from Lusaka."

"Didn't they wonder what we're doing here?"

"Oh yes, missis. I told them you are all from Kafwala camp, on organized safari."

Odd, thought Mrs. Pollifax, frowning, very odd, and could not quite shrug off the sensation that if Cyrus was accurate, then forces were in motion that she did not understand. Turning to him she said stubbornly, "I don't—I really don't—see how on earth you can be so certain it was the same man."

"Could be wrong," he said fairly.

She looked at him quickly. "Are you often wrong?"

"No. Study too many faces in court. Habit of mine."

She nodded. Nevertheless he'd admitted that he could be wrong and she clung to this, because otherwise she was left with the uneasy mystery of a man who wanted to see her in Lusaka and then, catching up with her, jumped into a car to avoid being seen.

Some hours later Mrs. Pollifax, happily showering back at camp, was tempted to break into song again. Life in the bush, she thought, certainly stripped one of inconsequentials: she had been hot and dusty for hours and now the cold water splashing over her heated skin brought a delightful tingly sensation. She had been out-of-doors since dawn, and soon there would be a feast around the campfire for which she already had a ravenous appetite. She wondered when she had felt so free . . . perhaps never . . . and running through her mind like a melody were little vignettes of the road at midday: the hot sun, dust, the orange trunk of a thorn tree as well as another tree they'd seen bearing long torpedo-shaped gray fruit that Julian had called a sausage tree. She had also learned to say thank you in Nyanga—*zikomo kuambeia*—and at Lufupa . . .

But it was better not to think of Lufupa, she reminded herself. The memory of it raised disturbing questions because they set in motion doubts that eventually, no matter how she reasoned them away, returned full circle to Cyrus. It was Cyrus, after all, who had told her that a man had asked for her at the hotel after she had left, and it was Cyrus who insisted now that it was this same man they'd seen at Lufupa camp, but she had only his word for there being such a man at all. What was she to make of it? If Cyrus was Aristotle . . . she shivered at this demonic thought and turned off the water and reached for a towel. But if Cyrus was Aristotle, it didn't make sense his manufacturing a Mr. X who was looking for her, and if he had *not* fabricated this stranger—if there really was such a man . . .

"There you are!" said a man's voice suddenly, and Mrs. Pollifax jumped.

Outside the shower hut Lisa's voice replied. "Hello, John, I was just looking for a sunny spot to dry my hair."

"Where is everyone?"

"Oh—around." Lisa's voice was vague. "Mrs. Pollifax was waiting to take a shower when I came out but she's gone now. Dad and Chanda are over at the kitchen watching the chef start dinner on that funny stove they have here. Mr. Kleiber pricked a finger and Tom is assuring him that he's not going to get a rare African disease. McIntosh is napping and—"

"Enough, enough!" he said with mock despair. "What I really came to ask you is why you've been avoiding me since lunch. It made me wonder. Look here, was it a shock to you when I said I'd been married once, very briefly, years ago?"

"A shock? Good heavens, no, John!"

"What *did* you think?"

Mrs. Pollifax, torn between announcing herself and listening, opted for the latter and continued dressing.

"I thought," Lisa was saying slowly, "if I remember correctly, that I wasn't surprised it lasted only six months. I thought you must be a rather difficult person to be married to."

"A rather difficult—! And here I was hoping—what on earth makes you say that?"

"Well—there's something secret about you, isn't there, John? Something concealed, a little room somewhere marked 'Keep Out'?"

There was a long silence and then Steeves said lightly, "This is rather a setback for me, Lisa, I was hoping to ask you to marry me when the safari ends."

"*Me?*"

"Did you really think I went about squiring beautiful young girls so attentively every day?"

"No—that is, surely you were just being friendly? John, I'm terribly flattered but let's not talk about this any more. We shouldn't do at all, you know."

"Why wouldn't we 'do at all,' as you put it?"

"Because . . . well, you don't really have room in your life for marriage, do you?"

"I could change, you know," he said. "I don't have to go batting around the world forever."

"Change into what?" she asked, and then, indignantly, "And why should you? You're a beautiful person, John, just as you are. You give a great many people pleasure by doing all the wonderfully dashing things they daydream of doing. It's marvelous."

"And very lonely," he pointed out.

At this moment Mrs. Pollifax decided that it was more than time to announce herself: she dropped her shoe on the cement slab and said, "Oh dear!" and continued dropping things and picking them up again to give Lisa and Steeves time to adjust to her presence. When she walked out of the shower hut John had vanished and Lisa was folding up her chair. She turned and smiled faintly. "I suppose you heard all?"

"It was impossible not to," admitted Mrs. Pollifax. "I waited as long as I could, but it was growing very damp and cold in there. It's nearing sunset time, I think."

"Yes, time for sweaters again. Thank you for—well, rescuing me." She fell into step beside her, absently carrying the chair along with her. "Isn't life strange?" she asked. "I read John's latest book this winter and his photograph occupied the entire back of the bookjacket and I used to look at it—those sad eyes practically stabbing my soul—and I'd say, 'Now there's a man, if only I could meet someone like that.' "

"And now you have," said Mrs. Pollifax, giving her an interested glance, "and you find a room inside of him marked 'Keep Out'?"

"You really did hear everything." Lisa sighed. "I wonder what made me say that. John strikes me—now that I've met him—as a character in a very contemporary novel, the kind that begins and ends in the same way, with the hero staring into his scotch and soda and about to leave another woman behind as he goes off to a new adventure. He seems—caught by something. And terribly sad about it."

"Caught," repeated Mrs. Pollifax musingly. "A strange word to use."

"People do get trapped, I suppose. Inside of images, all kinds of things. But he is a lovely person, isn't he?"

Mrs. Pollifax nodded. "A very unusual man, yes, very charming and—as you suspected—very much a loner. But I think you're looking for someone a little cozier, aren't you?"

Lisa burst out laughing. "Cozier?"

"Someone warm and caring and devoted. Less complicated." She reached her door and opened it. "It is sometimes," she said, "very difficult to remain faithful to *oneself*."

"Oh, I do hope you like Dad as much as he likes you," Lisa blurted out, and then stopped, blushing. "Oh dear, I didn't mean—What on earth am I doing carrying this chair with me?" she asked, noticing it for the first time. "I really must change for dinner. Which in this case," she added, laughing, "means removing one sweater and adding another, or changing from jeans to corduroys!"

The sun had already set when Mrs. Pollifax descended the hill to join the group around the campfire, and the single lantern hanging from the post had been lighted. The flames of the fire held shades of blue in them tonight, and the wood crackled merrily.

"You missed an egret," Cyrus told her with a welcoming smile. "Incredible sight."

"And a family of monkeys scolding us from the trees," put in Tom Henry. "They were certainly cross at finding us here again, this must be their playground."

"A dozen at least," added Lisa.

"God I'm hungry," said Amy Lovecraft. She was wearing still another new outfit tonight, a blue Jacquard turtleneck and dark-blue slacks over which she'd thrown a fleecy red jacket. Mrs. Pollifax wondered how many suitcases she traveled with, and decided it was better not to know.

Julian said, "I've given orders that dinner be served early tonight—before seven—because everyone is so hungry."

"Marvelous," said Amy, pronouncing it mav-lus.

"And what time is it now?"

Julian glanced at his watch and frowned. "The men are late, they should have begun setting the table by now. I'd better go up and see what the matter is."

"Yes, do," said Amy. "Frankly we're all starving."

Julian half rose from his chair and then froze and fell back in astonishment. Following his gaze Mrs. Pollifax saw three men move out of the darkness toward the campfire, silently, like phantoms rising out of the mist. At first she didn't understand, thinking them Kafwala workers whom she'd not seen before, and then the firelight picked out the long barrel of a rifle, and as the three black men moved to surround them she felt the first taste of fear in her throat.

Steeves said with a gasp, "I say, who the hell—what *is* this?"

They had arrived so silently, their steps muted by the sound of the rapids, that Mrs. Pollifax found it difficult to believe in their reality. It was like opening one's door in July to find Halloweeners on the doorstep. Then Julian, looking grim, said, "*Nguti!*" and she knew these men were real and dangerous.

In excellent English the leader said, "If you move we shoot. We wish only hostages. You," he said, pointing to Mrs. Pollifax. "You—walk over here."

"Now wait a minute," said Cyrus, starting to rise from his chair, but one of the men reached out and pushed him down.

"And you," said their spokesman, pointing to Amy Lovecraft.

Mrs. Pollifax stood up, acutely aware of how snug the circle around the campfire looked. As she reluctantly crossed that circle, about to leave it, she became equally aware of each person she passed: of John Steeves looking furious, of Willem Kleiber shrinking back in his chair as if to make himself invisible, Lisa open-mouthed and plainly frightened, and Tom Henry studying the faces of the men with guns. When she reached the leader and turned, she saw that Cyrus was looking so outraged that she would have smiled if she hadn't felt so much like crying. It was, after all, dinnertime, and she was hungry and cold and she had the distinct feeling that she was not going to be fed.

And then Amy Lovecraft came up behind her and the leader said to his confederate, "Take them—quickly," and turning back he spoke across the fire to Julian. "You will remain very still, please. Your men on the hill have all been locked into the kitchen, your marconi is broken and your Land Rovers put out of action. I will have my gun on you, watching. I warn you, don't try to follow. Don't move."

"You're not Zambians," Julian said curtly, watching him. "How did you get into the park?"

"That's our business."

Whatever else was said, Mrs. Pollifax was not destined to hear because she was being pulled away from the scene by one of the men. He gripped her tightly under one arm and dragged her in among the trees and along the river, then pulled her up a steep hill until she came face to face with a Land Rover waiting in the darkness. A rope was tied around her wrists, binding them together tightly behind her back, and then she was shoved into the rear of the car and a rifle held at her chest. The rifle was lowered for the arrival of Amy Lovecraft, who was pushed in beside Mrs. Pollifax, and then one of the men climbed into the driver's seat and started the engine, the Land Rover backed, turned and waited.

"This is terrifying," whispered Amy Lovecraft. "Isn't there something we can do?"

"With our wrists tied and a rifle pointed at us?" said Mrs. Pollifax dryly, and concentrated on catching her breath after the rush up the hill.

She heard footsteps, a muffled laugh, and the third man swung into the seat behind them. "Let's get out of here—fast," he said. "Turn on the headlights and move it, we can't keep Sikota waiting."

Chapter Nine

*I*t was astonishing, thought Mrs. Pollifax, how furious she could feel at Aristotle as they bumped along the road in the darkness. It seemed to her the height of injustice that because of him she had come to Africa and now she was being carried off into the night while he remained back at the camp-fire safe, warm, unidentified and—most outrageous of all—looking forward to his dinner. Certainly Carstairs could never have foreseen such an ironic ending to her mission. Her first reaction to being abducted struck her now as tiresomely pious: she'd actually thanked heaven that Chanda had been given a film so that if anything happened to her there would be a record left behind for Carstairs. Her reaction now was much less noble: she felt that she would resent very much anything happening to her, she *thoroughly* resented being lifted out of her safari, and under no circumstances did she feel that a few snapshots were an adequate exchange for a life. She was also hungry.

She turned and looked at Amy Lovecraft in the dim light from the dashboard and noticed that her hands were tied in front instead of behind her, and Mrs. Pollifax resented this very much too. In fact the depth of her indignation surprised her. Her own hands were tied in the back, which made it impossible to lean against the seat or to relax for even a second; it also demanded a great deal of effort from her just to remain on the seat, which was slippery. It was depressing, too, to reflect that of all the people on safari Amy Lovecraft was the last person she would have chosen as companion in such a situation. The woman was incalculable.

Having brought out her grievances and inspected them, Mrs. Pollifax began to feel better. About her abduction and her hunger she could do nothing, but she could at least try to like Mrs. Lovecraft. There had to be something lovable about her, she thought, and if they were going to be captives together she'd jolly well better find it now. She said in a comforting voice, "They'll come after us, you know, it will be all right."

Amy Lovecraft turned and looked at her. "After us?" she said, her lip curling. "Yes, but when exactly? And what the hell do you mean by 'all right'?"

Well, nothing lovable yet, thought Mrs. Pollifax, and decided to postpone any fresh attempt for the moment. Besides, she had discovered that by wedging herself sideways into the corner she could maintain a precarious balance, which was providential because the Land Rover suddenly turned off the road and plowed through the tall grass. They jolted ahead for several hundred feet and then came to a stop, went into reverse and backed out into the road again.

"I wonder what that was all about," said Mrs. Pollifax.

"I know a few words of Nyanga," said Mrs. Lovecraft, and leaned forward and spoke to the driver. She appeared to know quite a number of words, and the driver to speak Nyanga, because he replied at some length.

"He refuses to say," Mrs. Lovecraft told her, sinking back into her seat. "He doesn't want us to talk either."

"It was probably an attempt to confuse anyone following us," said Mrs. Pollifax sagely. "I hope that at some point he'll tell us why we're hostages."

Amy Lovecraft shrugged. "It's usually money, isn't it?" she said indifferently.

Mrs. Pollifax moved out of her corner and tried bracing herself with both feet against the floor. The road ahead was empty even of guinea fowl tonight, and she could see nothing on either side: there was only the dim light from the dashboard silhouetting the two men in front of her, and beyond this the bright twin beams of light combing the rough road. She and Amy Lovecraft huddled in the rear in darkness, with the third man crouched behind them; at times she could feel him breathing down her neck.

They were heading north, she knew, because they had made the same turn to the right after leaving camp that Julian had made this morning when he took them north to look for lions. She tried to recall her map of Kafue Park and, closing her eyes, remembered that it was shaped roughly like the state of Florida, that it was large and it was long, and that there were police posts at various intervals along its border. Only two roads entered it. The road that ran the length of the park from top to bottom, or south to north, was the road on which they were driving now, this narrow dirt road gutted with elephant holes which, for all its simplicity, remained the supply line that laced together the camps at Kafue Park.

The second road ran from east to west and was the paved Lusaka–Mumbwa highway by which they had entered the park on Monday, with its police stations at either end. Thinking about this, she decided that her abductors were either mad or uncannily shrewd, because they were heading precisely where they shouldn't go. They had Lufupa camp somewhere ahead of them—the camp at which they'd picnicked at noon—and Moshe camp above that, near the top of the park, while behind them they had Kafwala camp and the Lusaka–Mumbwa highway. This left them with only one large tract of land in which to maneuver, and she wondered how they proposed to get out of it. She also began to wonder why they'd chosen to snatch their tourists in a park since there must be tourists in far more accessible places . . . Lusaka for one, or Livingstone. It was all very illogical and baffling.

She opened her eyes to discover that the Land Rover was leaving the road again and stopping. This time one of the men climbed out and walked back through the tall grass, and during the interval he was gone the driver had time to light a cigarette and smoke it. When the man returned, the driver snuffed out his cigarette and started the engine, but this time he didn't slip the gear into reverse, he drove ahead into the bush, leaving the road behind. With this act something unal-

terably changed. It had been a modest road, thought Mrs. Pollifax wistfully, but it was a road that led back to Kafwala camp
or ahead to Lufupa, or even indirectly to the city of Lusaka.
Leaving it was like cutting an umbilical cord.

The ground was smoother now, but they drove fast and
there were small hills and hollows to unsettle Mrs. Pollifax, so
that at one point she ended up on the floor. Somewhere off in
the distance a hyena howled, and Mrs. Pollifax longed to join
with it and howl too. They drove on and on, it seemed interminable, the men occasionally exchanging sharp grunts or
pointing up to the stars. It was a long time before they bumped
to a halt, and before the headlights were extinguished Mrs.
Pollifax glimpsed the shapes of two abandoned, crumbling
huts inside a circle of trees.

The man sitting behind her said sharply, "Set up the radio,
Reuben, we're ten minutes late."

"But Simon—"

"Later. Set up the radio—anywhere—but fast."

From one of the huts the two men carried out a heavy dark
object, set it down on the grass and leaned over it. A candle
was lighted, Simon squatted down in front of it, slid up an
antenna and began fiddling with dials. His voice when he
spoke was quite clear in the still night. Mrs. Pollifax heard,
"Simon to Green-Bird, Simon to Green-Bird . . ."

Simon to Green-Bird suddenly broke off. "Got him," Simon
said triumphantly, and then, "All okay here, Green-Bird,
couldn't be better. What about your end?" He chuckled, listening. "Perfect. We follow through then as planned? My
watch says 9:05 . . . Right. Twenty-one hours from now at
Location B. Last contact, Green-Bird. Signing off."

He slid the antenna back and nodded with satisfaction.
"Smooth as silk, Mainza. You and Reuben take the candle and
hide the radio." He paused, glancing around him. "I'll take the
hut on the right. Reuben, you guard its door."

Turning back toward the Land Rover, his voice exhilarated,
he said, "Out, ladies. Climb out and follow me."

They were led inside, and when a lantern had been lighted
its illumination proved beyond any doubt that the men had
been here earlier, for besides the radio that had been magically

produced, there were sleeping bags in the corner, two boxes and a tarpaulin. The hut was small, perhaps eight feet square, and only three of its walls remained standing. Simon unfurled the tarpaulin and hung it over the fourth wall, which had crumbled away leaving only the wooden framework.

"Who are you?" asked Mrs. Pollifax as the lantern shone on Simon's face.

"It's of no importance," he told her.

"But you're not Zambians?"

He laughed. "No, not Zambians." Unrolling a sleeping bag he tossed it to Amy Lovecraft. "You—over there. Sit quietly, I wish to question this lady."

Amy Lovecraft carried the sleeping bag to the corner and sat down, her back against the wall, her bound wrists held out in front of her. She had been silent for a long time, and she remained silent, her eyes watching Simon intently. Perhaps she was weighing the possibilities of using feminine wiles on him, thought Mrs. Pollifax, but this was pure conjecture: at least she was subdued and not hysterical.

Simon carried one of the two boxes to the center of the hut and gestured to her to sit down. She ignored this, saying stiffly, "My wrists hurt. You tied Mrs. Lovecraft's wrists in front of her and I don't see why mine can't be tied that way too."

Simon shot a quick glance at Amy Lovecraft and shrugged. He called, "Reuben?"

"Yes, Simon."

"Come in and guard this woman while I change the ropes on her wrists."

So much for that, thought Mrs. Pollifax, thinking wistfully of a back strangle, a front choke or a forearm slash; nevertheless, she was grateful to have her arms no longer pinned tightly behind her, and the relief to her shoulder muscles was exquisite.

"Now," said Simon. He produced the other wooden box and sat down opposite her, so close that their knees touched.

"Yes, now," said Mrs. Pollifax dryly. "What is it you want of us? What kind of ransom are you asking, and why?"

He brushed this aside indifferently. "The ransom requirements have already been delivered to the television station in

Lusaka, madam. They became known at the precise moment we removed you from Kafwala camp. Now all you need do is co-operate. We wish information from you, it is a matter of photographs."

"Photographs," echoed Mrs. Pollifax, suddenly alarmed.

He did not notice her reaction, which was merciful, because a second later he was sliding four glossy six-by-ten-inch photographs from a crisp manila envelope, and Mrs. Pollifax could see at once that they were not hers.

"These," he said, and placing his gun on the floor he handed her the pictures. "You will tell me which of these men is familiar to you."

"Familiar?" she said blankly. "But you must know I can't help you, I arrived in Zambia only Monday. It's ridiculous to think I could identify—"

"You will look at the photographs," he said flatly. "They are large and quite clear. We wish your impressions."

As she picked them up he leaned closer, his eyes on her face, and she thought, *Be careful, something is important here.* Because of this, instead of rifling through them quickly she kept them one on top of the other and approached them warily. The first was a color photograph of a long-faced man with a sweeping handlebar mustache and curly gray hair. Nothing there. The second was of another mustached man, very swashbuckling, with a bold look. She eyed him politely and then turned to the third picture, which was of—of John Sebastian Farrell, she realized in astonishment—*Farrell!*— and with a desperate concentration she forced herself to look into his face without expression before she wrenched her gaze to the last photo, a black-and-white picture of a plumpish hard-faced man.

She said, "They all have mustaches. I'm supposed to know one of them?"

"You *do* know one of them," he said, anger creeping into his cool voice. "You advertised for him in the *Times of Zambia.*"

She allowed her surprise to show; it was genuine but not for the reason he supposed. "I advertised for a man named John

Sebastian Farrell," she told him. "Is *that* why you abducted me? You've just told us it was for ransom."

He shrugged. "The ransom scarcely matters. You know this Farrell, you can identify him for us, and that is what matters. The ransom is only—what do you call it, the red herring?"

This was rather staggering news. She gasped, "You amaze me," and then, accusingly, "Why was it necessary to kidnap two of us, then? Why Mrs. Lovecraft as well?"

"Two are always better than one," he said with a faint smile. "She will be hostage to *you*."

Over his shoulder Mrs. Pollifax glanced at Mrs. Lovecraft to see how she was taking this news of her expendability, but she appeared to have withdrawn into a world of her own, her brows knit together, her eyes blank. In the dim light of the lantern she looked bloodless, her face the same shade as her pale hair. "I didn't realize Farrell was such an important person," she said, turning back to Simon. "Why?"

"That is *our* business. Which of these four is he?" He leaned forward, his eyes narrowed. "You understand we know one of these men is Mr. Farrell, we *know* this, so you will now tell us which he is."

"But none of them *is* Mr. Farrell," she lied.

He hit her hard across the face with the back of his hand, brutally, without emotion. "I don't think you understood the question."

She looked at him, blood running from her cut lip into her mouth, her anger matching his as their eyes met. She said steadily, "And you are not a very nice person."

"You see that? Good. Now look again at these pictures."

"No," she said, turning away, "because those men are strangers to me."

"Look at them," he shouted, and held the first one in front of her eyes, one hand encircling her neck and forcing her to look. "This one?"

"No," she gasped.

He held out the second. "This?"

She shook her head.

"This one, then?"

"I told you—none of them," she cried, her fury outweighing her terror.

He hit her again, this time so savagely that she fell off the box to the floor. Behind him Mrs. Pollifax heard Amy Lovecraft begin to cough, and impatiently Simon leaned over and pulled her to her feet.

"Listen to me," he said in a hard voice. "To me you are so much carrion. We do not leave this place until the sun rises tomorrow morning and there will be more of this, much more. I will drag this information from you the hard way or the easy way, but *you will give me what I want*. Think about this, it is your choice."

He stalked out.

There was a long silence, and then in the corner of the hut Mrs. Lovecraft stirred and sighed, her trance ended. She lifted her head and looked at Mrs. Pollifax and she said, "You were absolutely super, you know. I hope I wouldn't have told them what they want, either."

Licking the blood from her broken lip, Mrs. Pollifax said angrily, "It's ridiculous, I really believed we'd been kidnaped for money."

"Yes, but what will you do when this Simon comes back?" she asked, looking at her curiously. "How long do you think you'll be able to trick him?"

Mrs. Pollifax had been wondering why Simon chose such a strange moment to break off his interrogation when a few more blows might have broken her; it was odd, she thought, his giving her this time to convalesce. Now she reluctantly turned her attention to Amy Lovecraft. "Trick him?" she said. If Amy believed that she could identify Farrell then this was a notion that had better be dispelled at once. Mrs. Lovecraft was speaking in a low voice but one of the walls was of canvas, and Simon—yes, Simon had definitely chosen a very curious moment to leave. "Trick him, Mrs. Lovecraft?"

"Oh call me Amy," she said impatiently. "Of course you were tricking him, it's what I would have done too, but you can't keep it up forever. The man is frightening. What are we to do?"

"There's nothing we can do," she said, and sat down and faced her. "None of those men was Mr. Farrell."

"Simon seemed certain of it."

"That's his problem."

"But you must see that we're in this terrible mess together," cried Amy. "It's so unfair. You have something to bargain with, but I—" She lifted her bound hands helplessly, her voice trembling. "I've nothing. I have to depend entirely on you because of this mysterious man they called Farrell. Who is he anyway? And how do you happen to know a man who lives in Zambia?"

"If he *does* live here," pointed out Mrs. Pollifax, and hoping that Simon was listening behind the tarpaulin she said in a clear voice, "Actually he's a man who lived next door to us years ago in New Brunswick, New Jersey. That's in the United States," she added parenthetically. "A very delightful young man except of course he can't be young now, for it must be twenty or twenty-five years since I've seen him. I'll tell you how nice a person he is," she confided. "He helped my son build a soapbox car when he was twelve years old. He was devoted to Roger."

She saw that Mrs. Lovecraft—Amy—was regarding her with astonishment and she began to expand on this further, developing a touching story of boyhood escapades, of families moving and losing touch, and then, "It was Mr. McGilli-cuddy," she said, beginning to enjoy herself. "I ran into him on the street in New Brunswick several weeks ago. He'd known the Farrells very well, and he was amazed to learn I was going to Zambia on safari. He said John Sebastian was living here; he knew because they still exchange Christmas cards, and for the past few years he'd sent his in care of Barclay's Bank."

Amy's mouth, which had dropped open, closed with a snap. "And because of this you advertised for him in a newspaper? How could you be such a fool? How could you do such a thing? Just see what it's led to!"

"Well, I certainly didn't expect it to lead to this," pointed out Mrs. Pollifax reasonably. "But what Simon doesn't understand," she added, "is how very difficult it is to identify a man one hasn't seen for years. Perhaps I'd recognize him if he walked into this hut, but from a photograph, after twenty-some years?" She hesitated and then added warmly, "He used to call me the Duchess, you know—quite teasingly, of course —but he was that sort of child, very affectionate with adults, and so aware. Such a nice boy," she concluded, and her nostalgic smile was genuine enough: she was hearing Farrell roar with laughter at her story.

Amy appeared unmoved. She said, "I don't know why you can't trust me. I think you're telling me a lot of nonsense. You were very brave with that terrible man Simon but you're not talking to Simon now. I think you're playing games with me."

Mrs. Pollifax began to wish that Amy were a little more perceptive so that she would understand the situation. She said, "My lip is bleeding and my jaw hurts and I don't feel very much like games, I can assure you."

"But you must know one of those men," said Amy, "and I mind very much your not being frank with me. My God, it's my life too, you know. We ought to talk—make plans—because once you identify this man they'll let us go free, they'll return us to the safari, we'll be out of this nightmare."

Mrs. Pollifax doubted this very much but she thought that to say this would imply a working knowledge of evil that had best be concealed for the moment; it seemed far more sensible to maintain the façade of a woman who had never met with anything more violent than a snub from her garden club president over the identification of a knotweed. She felt it rather naïve of Amy to believe that Simon would return them to the safari if she identified Farrell. He had said the ransom was only a red herring; how would he explain this if she and Amy were returned to camp? It was more likely that he would simply abandon them in the bush and let them fend for themselves, and even this, she thought, was the happiest alternative; she could think of others far worse. She had not, for herself, detected any signs of altruism in the man. She said crossly, "That's all very well but I can't tell them what I don't know."

She stood up and began to walk restlessly around the hut, Amy's eyes following her, and then she moved to the corner and pushed aside the tarpaulin with her bound hands and looked outside.

The first thing she discovered in the moment before the guard saw her was that Simon was not, after all, glued to the canvas listening to their conversation. She could see this clearly because two lanterns hung suspended from the branch of a tree, creating a circle of light in which Simon and Mainza were siphoning gasoline from a drum into the tank of the Land Rover. Above the lanterns a tarpaulin had been clumsily rigged to conceal the light from above, suggesting that it was search planes that worried them.

But it literally staggered Mrs. Pollifax to realize that Simon had not been eavesdropping on them. When the guard turned and lifted his rifle threateningly she dropped the edge of the tarpaulin and returned to her orange crate, but she remained shaken by this discovery. Why hadn't Simon been listening? He struck her as a very clever young man, and she simply couldn't conceive of his missing such an opportunity. He'd left behind him two frightened women, alone together for the first moment since they'd been snatched from Kafwala camp. He'd made his demands and then he'd hit her and then he'd walked out, leaving behind him the perfect climate for confessional. He must have known that something would have to be said about Farrell, but he'd not even troubled to listen. He was either very sure that he had all the time in the world to extract information from her, or he was not so clever as she'd thought him, or—

"I'm going to get some sleep," she said abruptly. "Simon said we'd be here until dawn, didn't he?"

"Sleep!" cried Mrs. Lovecraft.

"Yes, sleep. I'm really very tired, and not as young as you are," she pointed out, tugging at a sleeping bag. She pressed it flat with her bound hands, sat down and inserted herself into it. "If you wouldn't mind extinguishing that lantern—"

"I would mind," snapped Mrs. Lovecraft.

Mrs. Pollifax only nodded and turned her face to the wall away from the light. She stretched one leg and then the other; the ground was very hard and her bones sharp, but she had no intention of sleeping. Outside she could hear one or two murmurs from the men, and somewhere very far away the haunting cry of an animal. She attempted a gentle snore, moved and then settled down to the business of pretending sleep, surprised at how difficult it was.

What she wanted to think about in particular—and think hard—was the sobering fact that she had not, after all, been selected for this abduction at random. This needed growing used to, it changed every premise and, above all, her prospects. The kidnaping had been arranged exclusively for her, and because it was due entirely to her advertisement in the *Times of Zambia* on Tuesday morning it must also have been arranged very hastily. But this in turn led her thoughts to Farrell, and to the most pressing question of all: who was Farrell now, and what had he become that he was the object of a policeman's inquiry and the motivation behind this insane abduction?

She tried bringing back into her mind the photograph of him she'd just been shown, but all she could remember of it was her response, the shock like a whiplash that had hit her. It had not been the clearest of pictures, she recalled, but she'd recognized him at once, for what was recognition, after all? Certainly it was not the shape of a nose or mouth or jaw but a matter of essence and of memory that stemmed from an organ far different from the eye. It was instant and it was inexplicable. And now, whatever he was up to, she was going to have to protect him for as long as she could, while she waited for deliverance or an opportunity to escape. It was not a pleasant thought.

She had been feigning sleep for perhaps fifteen minutes when she heard the sound she'd been waiting for. Amy Lovecraft rose from her sleeping bag, blew out the lantern and stood quietly in the middle of the hut, listening, and then she moved noiselessly to Mrs. Pollifax's side and leaned over her. Hearing no change in her breathing, Mrs. Lovecraft tiptoed across the hut, lifted the tarpaulin and walked outside.

There was no outcry.

"She's asleep," Mrs. Lovecraft told the guard in a low voice, and then, "Where's Simon?"

Mrs. Pollifax pushed back her sleeping bag and sat up.

"She's asleep," she heard Amy repeat.

"She's talked? She's told you everything?"

It was Simon speaking, but in so low a voice that Mrs.

Pollifax left her sleeping bag and crept across the earth floor to place her ear against the tarpaulin.

". . . some improbable story I don't believe for a minute. How long do we have before we kill her?"

"Until Sikota comes. We meet him at nightfall across the Lusaka–Mumbwa road at an old burial ground. I have compass instructions. That gives us twenty hours and we'll need them if they begin a search. But she could be useful, *Tsa*, like tethering the goat to capture the lion."

Mrs. Lovecraft said impatiently, "We can't linger, you know that. By Saturday I've got to be far away, and so must you. We can't take her with us, she has to be disposed of inside of twenty hours whether she talks or not. I thought by now—"

"This was your idea, *Tsa*."

"Don't be impertinent," she snapped. "If you do your work well she'll talk, I promise you. She's a fool, but she could be a clever fool. Hit her harder, Simon, and then I suggest . . ."

Their voices receded as they walked away and Mrs. Pollifax crept back to her sleeping bag and sat in it shivering. *If you do your work well she'll talk, I promise you* . . . the words hung still in the air. It was not pleasant to realize that her wildest guess had turned into fact: there had been no need for Simon to eavesdrop because Amy Lovecraft had never been a hostage at all, she was only pretending to be one in the hope that Mrs. Pollifax might confide to her what she refused to tell Simon.

She ought to have realized the complicity earlier, she thought, considering this, and perhaps a part of her had, for she had minded *very* much—with an astonishing anger—that Mrs. Lovecraft's wrists had been bound together in front of her, giving her so much more comfortable a ride. There had been a curious lack of alarm in her attitude too, and surely her exchange of words with the driver on the road had proven a lengthy one, considering the size of her query. There was Mrs. Lovecraft's persistence in not believing her about the photographs . . . her performance had been convincing but her skepticism had continued for perhaps a shade too long in a situation where they both were victims. More than this, though, there had been a growing awareness in her that Simon had known just whom to abduct at Kafwala camp, which implied that someone on the safari had been involved.

She remembered now the palms rustling at Chunga camp after her interview with Lieutenant Bwanausi, and Mrs. Lovecraft in the office as she passed. There was the radio message that Julian had mentioned her sending too. Not your typical tourist, thought Mrs. Pollifax angrily, a woman who traveled on safari and then casually called in cutthroats from Lusaka for an abduction. Her talents as an actress had been superb too; in retrospect there seemed a downright innocence about Amy's lusting after every man in the party.

But for how long could she hold out against torture, she wondered now, as she objectively examined a situation that was more hopeless than she'd realized. Simon had announced that they would stay in this hut until dawn, and soon he would come back primed by Amy to hit her harder, and with whatever fresh suggestions Amy had made after they passed beyond hearing. Twenty hours lay ahead of travel, alternated with torture, and at the end of them she was to be killed.

And no one but herself would ever know why. As a bona fide hostage there had always been hope, because many hostages survived, but she saw now that it was going to be Mrs. Lovecraft who survived this particular ordeal. She could even guess at a scenario: after she had been killed tomorrow night there would be Sikota to smuggle Simon, Reuben and Mainza out of the park by some clever means, and then, following a suitable length of time, Amy Lovecraft would stumble out of the bush in a state of hysteria. There would be a few artful scratches and bruises, a terrifying tale of how Mrs. Pollifax had been murdered while attempting to escape. And who would not believe her? Amy would be a heroine.

And for so long as these wrists of hers remained bound, thought Mrs. Pollifax, that scenario was going to proceed very smoothly toward her murder and Amy Lovecraft's elevation to sainthood. She minded this very much, but even more, she realized, she mourned the comfortable illusion that she'd just lost of having a confederate of her own here, however unstable. Until a moment ago she'd believed they were three men against two women. Now there were suddenly four people against one—and she was the one—and it felt lonely.

The tarpaulin opened—Mrs. Pollifax could see the dark sky and the stars beyond it—and Mrs. Lovecraft tiptoed back to her sleeping bag. She had just settled into it when someone outside gave a startled cry.

Simon called, "Ssh—no, leave the lights. Reuben?"

"Here, Simon."

"Be silent. Wait."

The shout did it; Mrs. Pollifax rose from her sleeping bag and went to the tarpaulin, leaving Amy to her own dissembling, which consisted of sharp gasps and, "What's that? What woke me?" Ignoring her Mrs. Pollifax pulled back the flap and looked out. The lanterns were still lighted under the tree, but Simon and Mainza stood rigid now, both staring out into the bush. Following their gaze Mrs. Pollifax saw a large shape moving through the grass toward the camp, too tall to be a lion, too slender to be an elephant. The apparition moved steadily and noisily toward them, a bulky, man-shaped silhouette against the night sky, and then as it drew closer the farthest projection of the light picked out a pair of ragged sneakers, then a pair of bluejeans followed by a sweater and jacket until it reached the face of Cyrus Reed.

She had to be dreaming, thought Mrs. Pollifax.

He came to a stop and stood there, looking big and wondrously normal and not at all ruffled. "Hello," he said amiably, blinking at the sudden brightness. "Saw your lights. Damn tiresome wandering about out there in the bush. Mrs. Pollifax around somewhere, and Mrs. Lovecraft?"

Chapter Ten

Standing just behind Mrs. Pollifax, Amy said furiously, "Oh, the *fool!*" and then she recovered herself and added with less heat, "Now he's a hostage too!"

"Yes," said Mrs. Pollifax dazedly, "but how do you suppose he ever found us?"

Reuben turned and saw them and waved his rifle menacingly. Mrs. Pollifax dropped the tarpaulin and retreated to her orange crate and sat down to wait, her heart beating very fast, her thoughts in a turmoil. Several minutes later the tarpaulin lifted and Cyrus stepped inside the hut with his wrists tied together. He stood in the improvised doorway, blocking it completely, and Mrs. Pollifax thought that she'd never been so glad to see anyone before in her life. His glance took in Amy Lovecraft, lingered a moment without expression on Mrs. Pollifax's torn lip, and then he said in his mild voice, "Damn good to see you."

"Oh Cyrus," she said simply, "how on earth did you get here?"

"More to the point," interjected Amy sharply, "did you come alone?"

"Sorry about that," he told her. "No U. S. Cavalry racing to the rescue but there should be soon. Chanda's gone to get help."

"Chanda?" said Mrs. Lovecraft incredulously.

Cyrus nodded, looking pleased. "Damn clever boy, Chanda, or *ba na mâno*, as he puts it in Bemba. Damn clever at tracking too. We were only half an hour behind you. Slowed us down a bit, that false turn off the road you made, but it took Chanda only a few minutes to look over the signs and guess the trick. Learning a lot on this safari," he said, smiling at Mrs. Pollifax.

"But tell us how you got here," cried Amy, looking as if she wanted to shake him. "You can't have walked, and the Land Rovers—they said the Land Rovers—"

She had almost given herself away there, thought Mrs. Pollifax, watching her.

"Oh, yes, all the tires were slashed," Cyrus told her cheerfully, "but these ruffians who carried you off didn't realize there were spares in the storage hut. Julian took off in a great hurry for Chunga in one of the cars. Wanted to radio the police, he said . . . organize search parties. Seemed a damn shame nobody thought of following you while the trail was hot. *I* thought of it, and Chanda thought of it, so we had a little talk and stole a Land Rover."

"Just like that," said Amy with a hollow laugh. "How—how original! Then you've brought a Land Rover here?"

"Not exactly here," he conceded. "Got mired in a swampy piece of land half a mile away. Thought we'd have to sit there until dawn, the two of us, but then we saw the light here. Chanda gave me escort—just to be sure I didn't tangle with any lions—and then took off into the night for Kafwala."

"On foot?"

"On foot," nodded Cyrus, giving her a curious glance. "Something wrong?"

"No, not at all, but what a story," said Mrs. Lovecraft. "Then Chanda will be coming back with help very soon?"

Mrs. Pollifax wanted to cry out, *Don't say any more,* but she sat helpless and irresolute, not wanting Amy to learn that her connivance was known.

"Afraid not soon," confessed Cyrus. "Not *that* many spare tires. Julian's got four on his Land Rover but he's down at Chunga camp now. Other four are on the Land Rover stuck out there in the bush. Only a matter of hours, though."

"How—how comforting," said Mrs. Lovecraft, attempting another brittle laugh.

If Amy was laughing, Mrs. Pollifax was struggling against tears. Her emotions had never felt so battered; at sight of Cyrus her spirits had gone skyward, but now they were plummeting as she realized with a sense of horror what his arrival meant for him. She was touched by his courage, appalled by his recklessness and comforted by his reliable and enormous presence. At the same time—just to complicate the tangle— she wanted to laugh at the comic note he was introducing into the situation. For instance, he was blocking Simon's entrance into the hut now, which became more and more obvious from the rude noises outside. Cyrus turned, looked down, said, "Oh —sorry," and Simon emerged from behind him looking very much like an angry puppy riding herd on a Saint Bernard.

Simon said sharply to Mrs. Lovecraft, "Out—quickly. I separate you now. Into the other hut."

Mrs. Pollifax had wondered how they would confer about this development, and she thought that Simon managed it very convincingly; in turn, Amy Lovecraft managed to look convincingly frightened as she walked out ahead of him. As soon as the tarpaulin fell in place behind them Mrs. Pollifax whispered, "Be careful what you say, he's really taking Mrs. Lovecraft out to confer with her."

"*Confer?*" said Cyrus, staring at her in astonishment.

She nodded. "When Amy thought I was asleep she walked out and began talking to them about me. It turns out that she's in charge of the whole thing, except for someone called Sikota in Lusaka."

"Good God," said Cyrus, looking appalled. "And I was about to ask if we ought to worry about her being taken off alone like that. Glad you told me. Damn glad I came."

"Yes, because if Chanda hurries—how long do you think it will take him to reach Kafwala on foot?"

Cyrus shook his head. "Too long," he said uneasily. "And they'll know it. Shouldn't have told Amy about Chanda."

"But how could you have not told her when you thought she was a hostage too?" protested Mrs. Pollifax. "And they would have insisted on knowing how you found us, Cyrus. If you'd refused to tell them they would have followed your tracks to the Land Rover."

"Shouldn't have mentioned there being so few spare tires, either," Cyrus said gruffly. "Very bad. Who's this Sikota chap you mentioned?"

"He must be the man who delivered a ransom note to the television station in Lusaka at the same time we were captured. They talked to him by radio," she explained.

"Oh?" said Cyrus, digesting this. "Pity Julian couldn't have known that before he went dashing off to get the news out. Done better, I'm thinking, to have followed you."

"As you did," she said, smiling.

"Yes." He gave her a thoughtful glance. "Suppose you realize these are the same three men we saw at Lufupa camp this noon. Which of them hit you?"

"It doesn't matter, Cyrus."

"Try hitting you again," he said sternly, "and they'll have me to deal with."

She said unsteadily, "You should never, *never* have come after us like this, Cyrus. It was madness."

"Only thing I could think of to impress you, my dear."

"Impress me!"

"Well," he said with a boyish grin, "couldn't believe you'd give me a thought, coping with this bunch of hoodlums. Rather hard to overlook if I'm here. Too big."

She began to laugh, which tore open her cracked lip again and sent a stab of pain across her cheekbone, but it was amazing how much better she felt for it, and almost light-hearted. It fortified her for Simon's reappearance.

He walked in and gave Cyrus a nasty glance. "We do not wait for dawn to leave," he said coldly. "Because of you we go now."

"Afraid of that," sighed Cyrus. "Sorry, my dear."

"It's all right," she said, but of course it wasn't. For just a few brief moments there had been a flicker of hope that Chanda might be able to bring rescue before dawn. And really it was so unfair, she thought helplessly, to see all of her plans to uncover Aristotle aborted like this. By now, back at camp, who knew what arrangements were being made to assassinate some unknown and unknowing victim?

"Mainza—" Simon's voice brought her back to the present, and she realized that her worries over Aristotle were a luxury just now. She had to resist distractions; her life and Cyrus' life depended upon it.

"Mainza, remove all but this lantern."

Mainza nodded and began rolling up the sleeping bags. "And while the car is being packed, we begin again," Simon told her, looking grim. "Sit, please, and you—" He pointed at Cyrus. "You will stand in the corner over there where I can observe you."

"Think not," said Reed mildly. "Bigger than you are. Don't plan to budge an inch."

Simon gave him a long, measuring stare. "You prefer that we shoot you instead?"

Cyrus shrugged. "No need to, you know. Only came to keep the ladies company. I'll stand where I am and watch—like a UN observer," he added helpfully.

Perhaps it was Cyrus' size or his mildness or a lingering sense of authority from his years on the bench, but it became obvious now to Mrs. Pollifax that Simon didn't know how to handle him. Cyrus was large, he was amiable and he exuded kindness, but he had an air about him of being immovable. Simon eyed him with resentment and then apparently decided to ignore him because he turned away and gestured Mrs. Pollifax to sit down.

"As I started to say, we begin again." He was forced to step back as Mainza passed him, his arms filled with sleeping bags. When Mainza had gone he sat down on the other box. "Now you will tell me *exactly* how you met this Mr. Farrell."

"*Farrell?*" said Cyrus, lifting an eyebrow in surprise. "So that's it!"

"Yes, Farrell," Mrs. Pollifax said, nodding, and then, "all right," and began her story again. She explained about the house in New Brunswick, New Jersey, her son Roger and the soapbox car, but this time she embellished the story with small artistic details. She added a soapbox derby in which Roger won a first prize of five dollars, and she gave Farrell a mother who played the piano and a father who owned a department store. "And then the father died," she added, tiring of the story. "That's when they moved away."

Mainza tiptoed in again and then went out with the remaining sleeping bags and a lantern. Simon did not comment on her story. He drew out the four photographs again and held up the lantern for her to examine them by. "Which?" he demanded, handing them to her. "Perhaps it will improve your memory if I tell you that your life depends on it."

Mrs. Pollifax examined them one by one, frowning appropriately while Simon studied her face. She noticed that numbers had suddenly appeared in pencil on the bottom corner of each photograph; Mrs. Lovecraft's idea, no doubt. "I don't recognize any of these men," she said again with finality.

"Mind if I look?" asked Cyrus, and when Simon only shrugged he took the pictures, glanced through them and shook his head. "Absolutely impossible," he said flatly. "None of these men could have lived next door to Mrs. Pollifax."

"I may ask why?" Simon's voice was biting.

"Look at her, look at them. Tough-looking chaps. You think she'd know such a person? None of them," he added with authority, "built a soapbox car in his life."

Smiling at him, Mrs. Pollifax thought, *You dear man, there are so many things you don't know about my friends, but you've become one. Solidly.*

Simon leaned closer to her. "I do not believe you understand me. If you remain stubborn we kill you—like that," he told her, snapping his fingers. "We kill this man too."

"Stay as stubborn as she pleases," said Cyrus. "Why this passion for having Mr. Farrell identified?"

"So we will know which of these four men he is," he said, exasperated. "Ah—Mainza, the Land Rover is ready?"

"Everything is inside, Simon."

"Then we go. Take them out, Mainza, I'll bring the lantern and tarpaulin. As for you," he told Mrs. Pollifax, "we talk again, but if you do not talk for me, Sikota is the man with a genius. For him *everyone* talks."

They climbed into the Land Rover. Apparently Amy's role

of innocent hostage was to be continued because she was led out of the second hut by Reuben, her wrists still bound, and inserted between Mrs. Pollifax and Cyrus on the rear seat. A rope was threaded through each of their bound wrists and secured to either side of the car, giving them a primitive check against falling; evidently some rugged driving lay ahead.

Amy spoke only once. She turned her flawless profile to Cyrus and said coolly, "It was terribly sweet of you to come, Cyrus, but I hope you'll realize what you've done. Now we're both hostages to Mrs. Pollifax. They'll kill us first to persuade her to talk, and believe it or not this woman seems very willing to sacrifice us. She doesn't give a damn at all."

"Ha," was Cyrus' only response.

The Land Rover started with a jolt, and following this, in proportion to the distance they covered, all sense of time diminished for Mrs. Pollifax. It was not that the Land Rover drove so fast but that a relentless speed of fifteen miles per hour over rough ground abused every bone in the body. The headlights had been taped so that only the immediate ground could be seen, and frequently the Land Rover swerved to avoid a rock, and once a startled wild beast. At some point during the first hour—she supposed it was an hour—Cyrus observed that they were heading west, and then after an interminable length of time he announced that they seemed to be veering south, but except for these comments no one spoke. Mrs. Lovecraft remained silent and Mrs. Pollifax reflected that if Kafue Park was half the size of Switzerland, this gave Simon a great deal of space in which to maneuver, and any search parties vast difficulties in finding them.

It was kinder not to think of Aristotle. She began to think instead of how far she could go in protecting Farrell's life from whatever dangers these people represented, and she thought the dangers must be considerable if they would go to such lengths as an abduction. But there was Cyrus' life too . . . He had wandered after her, heroic and innocent, and it was unthinkable that he might have to pay for it with his life. She felt responsible for him even if he would snort indignantly at such an idea. How could one choose? One could say that Farrell was the younger, with more years ahead of him to live, but balanced against this was the fact that Farrell had survived to his forty-some years by outwitting just such people as Simon, and how could she assume that he wouldn't survive her identifying him? And on that score there rose the doubts—oh God, the doubts, she cried silently, those niggling, poisonous doubts that were perfectly logical but which she would do well to face now, and with honesty. Chance had brought her and Farrell together once in a very rare intimacy, but there was no overlooking the fact that their values had been different even then, and that four years had intervened since she'd known him. He might be smuggling drugs, or involved in something equally abhorrent to her. She could vividly remember her shock at first meeting him—that hard-bitten face and those mocking eyes . . .

She discovered that she was smiling as she remembered those first reactions of a refugee from the New Brunswick, New Jersey, Garden Club. What a sheltered life she'd led before she met him, and how she must have amused him! It was preposterous to think he could change that much. He was a man who'd not broken under torture, and when he believed he was going to his death his first thoughts had been of her. No, she couldn't betray him, she simply couldn't . . .

She realized that she couldn't betray Farrell and that she absolutely couldn't sacrifice Cyrus. She was going to have to wait and trust to her instincts hour by hour, and in the end—if they weren't found in time by a search party—there might be no choice at all, or very little, because even if she identified Farrell it might not save Cyrus' life. She would simply have to wait, and in the meantime, just because it was night and she was cold and hungry, she mustn't lose hope. In fact, if she could just get these ropes off her wrists, the bush country of Zambia would ring with her shouts of *Ki-ya*.

"Growing light," said Cyrus, lifting his bound wrists and pointing toward the horizon. "Must be nearly four o'clock."

Mrs. Pollifax looked up and for the first time since her capture saw the world around her. The light that he'd pointed out was murky, no more than a subtle diminishing of darkness, but it was enough to define thorn trees and tall grass and the slope of the ground. She felt totally unequipped for this new day, but slowly and softly a warm golden light stole over the earth, dissipating pockets of mist in the hollows, and then abruptly the sun spilled over the horizon, huge and orange, and Mrs. Pollifax's spirits rose with it.

Simon and Mainza began chattering together in the front, and at length called in their own language to Reuben in the back. Mainza pointed to the left, they swerved in that direction, entered a copse of trees and came to a stop.

"We rest," said Simon, turning off the ignition.

They climbed stiffly out of the Land Rover and were led to a cleared area which, mercifully, received the warmth of the sun. Reuben brought them sleeping bags which they spread on the ground, after which bathroom privileges were extended to them and they took turns going off, with Reuben as guard.

Simon and Mainza remained beside the car. As soon as Amy had gone, leaving her alone with Cyrus, she looked at him and said firmly, "It's absolutely imperative that we get these ropes off our wrists."

"Logical, my dear, yes," he said, nodding, "but for the moment impossible."

"Then, failing that," she said earnestly, "there ought to be some way for us to capture Amy and use her as a shield or hostage."

"Thought had occurred to me," admitted Cyrus, "but not with any solution. Have to add I'm not very good at this sort of thing."

She smiled. "It may surprise you what you can accomplish if your life depends on it."

"Yes, but say, for instance, I approach our friend Amy from the rear," he said, "and fling my bound wrists over her head and hold her as a shield, what then?"

"Then I stand behind you—"

"Two of us hiding behind Amy?" He smiled faintly. "Bit of a stalemate, I'd say."

"Why? They wouldn't dare to shoot us," she protested. "If they did they'd hit Amy."

"Could stand facing each other for days, though," pointed out Cyrus. "Or they'd circle us. Three against two, and they've guns."

Mrs. Pollifax bit her lip. "You have a point there, unfortunately. Oh, if only there were some way to free our *hands!*"

"What then?" he asked, looking at her with amusement.

"Well, you see I'm rather good at karate."

This startled him but there was no overlooking his gleeful appreciation of this. *"Damned* astonishing woman," he said. "Enough to goad me into chewing off your ropes with my bare teeth."

"I wish you could," she said wistfully. "They plan to kill me when we reach the burial ground, you know."

"Burial ground? Nothing," protested Cyrus, "has been said about a burial ground."

"That's what I overheard . . . it's across the Mumbwa–Lusaka highway, which we'll have to cross at some point, apparently, and around darkness they meet Sikota there."

"So," mused Cyrus. "The longer it takes us to reach the burial ground—a macabre meeting place to say the least—the longer we have to exercise cunning, I take it?"

She nodded. "Why is Mainza climbing that tree now?"

He turned to look. "Could be lost. See better from a tree."

"But they have a compass and maps."

"Simon's been poring over both since we sat down," he told her. "Very heavy frown on his face."

"I think it would be lovely if we're lost," she said, watching a scarlet butterfly hover over Amy's sleeping bag, touch down and then twinkle away. "I'd like to see it happen to them, they deserve it."

"Not so sure *we* deserve it," he pointed out. "Very tiring sort of thing, being lost. Makes men like Simon irascible and insecure. Better sleep now, my dear, it may be your only opportunity."

She nodded and lay down, and thinking how pleasant it was to be called *my dear*—and how fortifying Cyrus was—she closed her eyes and then opened them to watch Mainza climb down from his tree. Amy was returning from the bush—she could hear the crackle of dried leaves and the snap of twigs—with Reuben's heavier footsteps behind her. The sun and the warmth of the sleeping bag combined to soothe her aching muscles and help her forget her hunger; she closed her eyes a second time, felt tiredness wash over her in waves and then engulf her, and she slept.

When she opened her eyes the clearing was empty of voices and she saw that Cyrus' sleeping bag was unoccupied. Without moving her body she turned her head and saw Amy burrowed deeply in her sleeping bag with only strands of pale hair in sight. Over near the Land Rover, Simon and Mainza were stretched out asleep in the sun. Reuben sat dozing with his back against a tree, the rifle across his lap, his eyes closed, but of Cyrus there was no sign until a sudden stealthy movement from the Land Rover caught her eye. It was Cyrus, creeping around the back of the vehicle on hands and knees. Mrs. Pollifax glanced at the dozing Reuben and then at Cyrus, and held her breath in horror.

Chapter Eleven

She had no idea what Cyrus had been doing behind the Land Rover but he was in plain view of Reuben: only Reuben's closed eyelids—a fragile barrier—lay between him and discovery, and Cyrus' stealth was proof that he was up to something. She dared not lift her head lest the movement wake Reuben, who was obviously supposed to be thoroughly awake and guarding them. She lay very still and held her breath. Cyrus was still on his hands and knees, but when he reached the side of the Land Rover he slowly rose to his feet, glanced once at Reuben and then tiptoed soundlessly toward her, testing the ground underfoot at each step. Only when he had dropped to his sleeping bag did she sit up, and as she did so Reuben gave a start, opened his eyes and instinctively reached for his rifle.

"Feeling better?" asked Cyrus without expression. "About four hours' sleep, I think."

"Much better," she said politely.

The others were stirring now too, sitting up, and stretching, yawning, their faces cleared of tension and hostility, so that for a moment they might have been a picnic party waking up from a nap out in the bush. Simon called out something to Reuben, who laughed and replied, and then Mainza and Simon both laughed, completely relaxed. Only when Simon's glance fell on the map and the compass did his frown return. He picked them up and tension was visible again on his face.

Amy Lovecraft sat up and pushed back tangled hair with her tied wrists. "Oh God, how I'd love a bath," she said.

But the only water they were to see this morning was brought to them by Reuben in a canvas bag. They took turns drinking from it, and then he opened his palm and revealed a handful of peanuts. "Ground nuts," he said, dividing them equally among them.

"So that's what they're called here," said Mrs. Pollifax. He had thoughtfully shelled them and she tried to chew each one carefully—there were only eight—because they were both last night's dinner and today's breakfast as well. In fact, if this was Thursday she remembered that it was time for another malaria tablet, but she supposed it was trivial to worry about malaria when she might not even survive the day. Perhaps it was also trivial to worry now about Aristotle . . . Cyrus was conspicuously silent; he looked tired, and she realized he'd probably not slept at all, and again she wondered what he'd been doing crouched behind the Land Rover. She turned her head and glanced at Amy, and not for the first time speculated about her motives in this insane abduction. She wondered if Amy could possibly be Aristotle. Women *were* assassins, and clever at disguise, but Aristotle—Aristotle, she felt, was different. Bishop had described him as a professional and a mercenary, with no ties to any particular country. She simply couldn't imagine him involving himself in an abduction, and then there was the fact that Amy knew these men, and Aristotle always acted alone.

Her thoughts were interrupted by Simon, who shouted, "Up!" and once again they were herded to the Land Rover and loosely roped in place. They set off in the warm morning light, and Mrs. Pollifax noticed they avoided open spaces now, which she thought showed more faith in a search party than she could muster at the moment. Shortly after leaving they skirted another clearing and surprised a herd of zebra standing motionless in the sun. The herd took flight at once, their stripes dancing and blurring as they swept across the plain in a cloud of graceful motion, and then as they reached the edge of the clearing the Land Rover swerved and they came to a stop.

"Flat tire," said Simon.

They climbed out and sat on the ground while Mainza jacked up the Land Rover and removed the tire. The spare was taken from its mounting on the hood and inserted on the rim, the jack was disengaged and the Land Rover lowered until it came to rest on the new tire, which slowly, comically, went flat too.

It was at this moment that Mrs. Pollifax sensibly added two and two together and glanced with interest at Cyrus. He was looking exceptionally sleepy and he refused to look at her. Deep inside of herself she smiled; really, she thought, Cyrus was going to be extremely useful now that he was getting into the swing of things. Simon, Reuben and Mainza were looking incredulous; they began talking accusingly among themselves, examining the two tires and gesticulating. She gathered that both tires had lost their valve caps but that the men found it difficult to understand how this could have caused so much leakage of air. Several suspicious glances were sent in their direction, but since no one could recall a moment when they were unguarded no one accused them.

"Into the car," Simon said at last, his voice surly.

They climbed inside and bumped along on the naked rim of the wheel for several hundred feet until they hit a half-buried rock that bent the rim. The Land Rover at once acquired an unhealthy list that sent Amy and Mrs. Pollifax into Cyrus' lap, and the car out of control. With a shout of frustration Simon fought the Land Rover to a stop. "We walk," he said furiously.

"Sorry about this," whispered Cyrus as he helped her down from the Land Rover.

She gave him a frankly admiring glance. "You make a lovely fly in the ointment."

"You saw?" When she nodded he grinned. "Damn nuisance, walking, but makes me feel better. Vented my spleen, so to speak."

"Do vent it again," she shrugged over her shoulder as Simon commanded her to be silent and take her place in line.

They began their march with Simon in the lead. The terrain

was a mix of flat ground and clusters of thorn trees, a combination not at all unpleasant for walking. What Mrs. Pollifax minded was the silence in which they walked; a little conversation, she thought, would be a happy distraction, but Simon had placed her behind him and she was followed by Mainza; Amy and Cyrus came after him, and Reuben brought up the rear. It was so quiet that she could hear the swish of their trousered legs and the thud of Mainza's rifle as it slapped his hip at each step; occasionally twigs snapped underfoot. As the sun rose higher, however, she became increasingly aware of a hollowness in the pit of her stomach that only food could alleviate, and the sun, which felt no warmer to her skin than a June sun in New Jersey, began to have a curious effect on her; her head felt light, but whether this was from hunger or the sun she didn't know or, at the moment, care. She developed a nagging thirst, and after they had walked for an interminable length of time she suspected that she was also developing a blister on her right heel. The tse-tse flies gathered, and with her hands tied she could only swat at them blindly, but Simon showed no signs of halting for a rest and she found herself lacking even the energy to complain. It seemed simpler to plod dreamily along, her eyes mesmerized by the ground in front of her, her head floating along somewhere behind her, like a balloon on a string.

"Rest," said Simon suddenly, and they sank to the ground under a tree, too tired to speak.

Mainza brought out the canvas bag of water and gave them each a few sips.

"Boiled, I hope," said Cyrus.

Amy sniffed at this remark. "Even boiled water here can cause gastric trouble. If you'd only tell them what they want to know," she snapped at Mrs. Pollifax, turning to face her, "we could be back on safari with the others now, instead of— of *this!*"

Mrs. Pollifax, feeling better, snapped back. "Nonsense. I don't believe my telling them *anything* would free us now, because we can identify Simon and Mainza and Reuben, and why should they allow that?"

Amy moved closer and lowered her voice. "I've been trying to make friends with Simon, you may have noticed?"

"No," said Mrs. Pollifax.

"Well, I have, and I think—" She smiled disarmingly and a little ruefully. "I think they might not kill *me*. It's possible I could divert the three men so that you and Cyrus could get away. Not now but later."

Shot while trying to escape, thought Mrs. Pollifax. For just the briefest of moments she looked at Cyrus, who was listening to this, and then she turned to Amy and said in a shocked voice, "Oh, I don't think that would be sensible, do you? I suppose you mean an *escape.* I shouldn't care for that at all, would you, Cyrus?"

"No indeed," he said blandly. "Exhausting. Besides, our hands are tied."

"So are mine," said Amy, "but I might be able to persuade Simon to untie them."

I'll bet you could, thought Mrs. Pollifax. She said earnestly, "Well, it would certainly be lovely to have our hands free—it's so difficult walking with them tied—but as for escape—" She shuddered. "I don't know, the idea fills me with terror." She realized that Cyrus was looking at her with a puzzled frown and she wondered what she'd just said that made him suddenly look so suspicious of her. "But if you could persuade him to free our hands," she added wistfully.

"Yes," said Amy, "but you simply *must* consider getting away if the occasion arises. You have to be more resolute."

"Yes," sighed Mrs. Pollifax.

A moment later Simon announced that it was time to move on, and she learned the reason for Cyrus' peculiar expression. Helping her to her feet he said, "Beginning to wonder if you *do* show slides."

"Slides!" she gasped. "Cyrus, what on earth—!"

"Same voice," he said. "Both times. Been worrying about those slides."

She stared at him in astonishment. "Oh—*slides,*" she said, realizing how alarmingly observant he was.

He added in a kind voice, "Try wrapping your bush jacket around your head. They didn't wear cork hats for nothing here in Africa. Very strong sun." He tugged loose the jacket that was knotted around her waist and she thanked him. Incapable of tying it around her head with her hands bound, she placed it there like a basket with trailing fronds and hurried off to obey Simon's peremptory summons.

They resumed walking, they stopped . . . they walked, they stopped. She was becoming very familiar with the African soil, she thought; it was a vivid rust color, with the coarse-grained texture of an anthill, and although the rainy season had only recently ended it was dry, very dry, providing only a vaguely hospitable surface to the stalks of grass. The earth was in fact kinder to her than to the vegetation, for she rested on it, and when Simon ordered them up again her only anticipation was to sit on it again. It was level enough for walking but it was important to watch out for snakes, and so she walked with her head down, which was tiresome. The tse-tse flies kept biting, and when they stopped for a break the meager sip of water doled out to them was no longer enough, and at each stop Simon examined both compass and map with the same frown teasing his brows. Then it was up again to resume walking, the monotony of it interrupted only twice—once by a herd of impala racing in panic across their path, and once by the sight of a dead buffalo lying on its side under a tree, with only the shell of its carcass untouched.

"Lion kill," said Reuben from the rear.

Sometime after that Mrs. Pollifax became aware that Simon had stopped. She had been stumbling along behind him when she looked up to see that Mainza had left his place in line and was grasping Simon by the arm, pointing behind them.

"Something is following us," Mainza said in a low voice.

"I see nothing. Animal or man?"

Mainza shook his head. "I don't know, it moves when we move, stops when we stop. If I go ahead to that hill, Simon, and circle back—"

"Do that. Be careful. We will rest behind the hill."

The word *rest* was all that mattered to Mrs. Pollifax and she followed Simon eagerly now. Mainza soon disappeared behind the swelling in the earth, and when they came abreast of it

Simon led them around it and signaled them to stop. "Sit," he said, "but not on the hill, this is an anthill."

Mrs. Pollifax sank gratefully to the ground and applied herself to resting with enormous concentration. Her shoulder bones, subtly hunched together by the pull of her tied wrists, were acquiring strange aches and pains; her feet hurt and her eyes felt like bruised grapes. This was having an effect on her thought processes that was alarming, and yet she felt incapable of any discipline at all; it was rather like watching oneself fall asleep in the snow and not caring. There would be no decent rest for her until they reached the burial ground, and she reminded herself that once they reached that destination her longed-for rest could very well become an Eternal Rest, but this reminder met with no response at all. It occurred to her to wonder if she was suffering from sunstroke. She saw Simon and Reuben level their rifles, suddenly tense, but she was only mildly interested when a man trudged unseeingly past them. She was grateful that he was not a lion, but the day held such a surrealistic quality that she found nothing surprising about their encountering a man here. Besides, he looked as if he belonged here and he was certainly not prepossessing. He was a native wearing torn black pants, cut off at the knee, a ragged pair of old sneakers on his feet and a brilliant plaid wool cap on his head that made him look ridiculous. A sweater had been rolled up and tied around his waist by the sleeves, and on his back he carried something wrapped in a bloody newspaper; it had weight to it, and there were a number of flies buzzing around it. The man noticed them only when Simon stepped forward with his rifle, but he looked startled rather than frightened. He gave Simon a radiant, uncertain smile and then his gaze dropped to the rifle and he gaped at it, fascinated. Apparently the rifle was more amazing to him than the sight of five people crouched behind an anthill.

Mainza came up from the rear and pointed his gun at the man, searched his pockets and sniffed at the bloody package.

"Jonesi," the young man said, beaming and pointing to himself. "Jonesi. Good evening."

"Good evening," however, turned out to be the only English that he knew. Mrs. Pollifax gathered that Nyanga was tried on him, as well as a few words of Luvale and Bemba, but these produced only excited nods from him and the words, "Jonesi. Good evening."

"Don't think he has all his wits about him," suggested Cyrus.

Mainza peeled back a corner of the bloody package and said accusingly, "He's been poaching, Simon. He's a poacher, his name is Jonesi, and what do we do with him?"

"I don't like him," Amy said suddenly in a cold flat voice.

Simon shot her a quick glance and without appearing to answer her said to Reuben, "He knows the land, he could help us find the burial ground."

"Ah," said Mrs. Pollifax, coming to life, "you don't know where the burial ground is?"

"Of course we know," snapped Simon, and then spoiled the effect by adding, "It's only that we've never traveled this way before."

"So you're lost?" said Amy sarcastically. "How thoughtful of you to tell us all about it, Simon."

"Don't see how this Jonesi's going to help if you can't even communicate with him," pointed out Cyrus.

But Mainza, having captured the poacher's attention, sat down cross-legged on the ground and began digging in the earth with a stick, forming a series of small mounds. When he had created half a dozen of these he placed a twig on one, a button on another, and a shred of cloth on a third. The poacher squatted beside him, watching doubtfully, until suddenly he nodded and burst out talking, pointing to the south and laughing. After more sign language Jonesi took the stick from Mainza and drew the rough outline of an animal, after which they made more sign language and Mainza stood up. "He knows the burial ground," he told Simon. "He'll take us there if we don't report his poaching. It's antelope meat in his sack."

Mrs. Pollifax thought about this carefully, aware of something there that she'd been too tired to catch. Antelope meat . . . She applied herself to this diligently: antelope meat, burial ground, poaching . . . but of course, she thought dizzily, Jonesi's meat was butchered meat, and if it had been

butchered, then it had to have been cut from the carcass with a
knife . . . a *knife.*

Her tiredness fell away from her like an old coat that had
been ready for the Salvation Army anyway. Hope was all that
she'd needed, and now it began flowing through her blood-
stream like adrenalin. A knife. With a knife they could assert
themselves and get away. A knife would free their hands for
all kinds of gloriously hostile purposes.

"You look," said Cyrus as they rose to go, "like someone
who's just found the Holy Grail."

She gave him a dazzling smile, and in the brief moment
before Simon separated them she whispered, "Cyrus . . . the
poacher has to be carrying a *knife."*

Chapter Twelve

Mrs. Pollifax reasoned that her first efforts, now that she was aroused, ought to go into establishing some kind of relationship with the poacher. Under the circumstances she felt she could at least extend to him a small but heartfelt welcome, and then slowly hope to impress on him the fact that she and Cyrus were captives. If sign language had succeeded once with him, she could see no reason why it shouldn't succeed again.

She began to walk faster, accelerating her pace until she drew abreast of him. When he turned his head to look at her she smiled at him and won a huge and vacant grin in return. He was certainly the tallest Zambian she'd seen, probably six feet tall if he stood up straight, and so thin that his ribs could be counted under his flesh. His face was long and bony, and, combined with his protruding teeth, his senseless wide grin and that absurd green-and-black plaid wool cap, it gave him the look of a man definitely lacking in intelligence. Nevertheless he was not one of *them*, she had just deduced that he must be carrying a knife, and he was their only hope.

After they had exchanged a number of eager smiles, she felt that she had paved the way for a subtler message. When he turned again to look at her she lifted her tied wrists to his gaze. She did this discreetly. His eyes dropped to her hands, his

smile broadened, and then he startled her by throwing back
his head and laughing.

This was certainly depressing. The laugh drew a backward
glance from Simon, and she had to pretend that she was lifting
her wrists to push back her hair. She decided that making a bid
for Jonesi's friendship at this point could be dangerous, and
she fell back behind him in line.

This left her with her second challenge: where did a man
who wore only sneakers, cap and shorts carry a knife? She
guessed it would have to be in one of the pockets of his disreputable shorts until she remembered that Reuben had searched
both of Jonesi's pockets and had seemed satisfied that he carried no weapons. If it wasn't in his trousers, she decided, then
the knife would have to be concealed either in the rolled-up
sweater around his waist or in his cap, and of the two she
thought that she would vote for the cap: there was an elemen-
tal logic in this because the cap was obviously a prized possession, and the knife would be equally valued. She began to play
with possibilities for getting the cap on his head and discovered that this happily removed all thoughts of hunger and
thirst from her mind.

In midafternoon they came to the road. Simon signaled
them to stop, and once they had straggled to a halt Mrs. Pollifax heard the unmistakable sound of a truck in the distance.
It soon passed. Simon waited for them to form a circle around
him, rather like a Boy Scout leader preparing to give instructions to his troop. "The road is just ahead," he explained. "We
go two by two across it, and very quickly, you understand?"
Pointing to Mrs. Pollifax he said, "You will go first, with Reuben and Mainza. Reuben, you will come back for the man, I
will follow with the other woman. Listen before you cross, the
wind blows from the west."

Mrs. Pollifax was led forward through a screen of trees until
they came to the road, a two-lane macadam highway stretching from east to west. It was depressingly empty of traffic now.
Reuben grasped one of her arms, and Mainza the other, and
they hurried her across and into the shelter of trees on the
opposite side. When Reuben went back for the others Mrs.

Pollifax sat down, hoping it wasn't on an anthill, and tried not to think how near they must be to the burial ground now. *How long before we kill her? Until Sikota comes, we meet at the burial ground across the Lusaka–Mumbwa road.* It ran through her head like a macabre nursery jingle.

Seeing Reuben escort Cyrus to her through the trees, she thought now what an astonishing person Cyrus was and how comfortable he was just to look at, for nothing about him seemed changed. He might be tired but he remained completely unruffled, with the air of a solid man who knew exactly who and what he was even in the center of Zambia. It struck her suddenly that she would feel very lonely if she never saw him again.

"You look like a judge even here," she told him, smiling.

"Feeling very unjudgelike at the moment," he said, sitting down beside her. "I'd give each of these people six months in solitary. No bail, either. They walk too fast."

"I think," said Mrs. Pollifax in a rush of warmth, "that it's terribly selfish of me, but I'm awfully glad that you came, Cyrus. You *are* hard to overlook."

"Told you so," he said in a pleased voice.

"It was so—so very gallant," she explained. "Except that— if you should have to pay for it with—"

"No need to be tedious, my dear," he interrupted quietly. "Entirely my own choice, you know, didn't have to come. More to the point," he added lightly, "is the dinner I plan to buy you when we get back to Lusaka. Menu's been occupying me for hours."

She realized in a sudden spasm of perceptiveness that Cyrus was only too aware of how near they were to the burial ground. "I think it has to be in either his sweater or cap," she said in a lowered voice. "The knife, I mean—if he has a knife."

"Mmmm," murmured Cyrus. "Let's hope it gets cold then, and soon." He held up his wrists and scanned his watch. "Nearly four o'clock."

"Oh dear, and dark in two hours?"

"Must have walked about twenty miles. Saw a data bird, by the way. Pity I couldn't have pointed him out to you." He broke off as Simon strode toward them, apparently tireless, with Jonesi loping along beside him and Amy a pace behind.

"On your feet," said Simon, and that was the end of any further conversation.

It was perhaps ten minutes later that Jonesi called out sharply and pointed to the left, jabbering away in his language that no one understood. He appeared to know the terrain now because, once they veered off to the left, they encountered a narrow, hard-beaten path through the grass and soon came upon the ruins of several huts, their scaffolding lying in crazy patterns like jackstraws.

And then quite abruptly they reached the burial ground.

It lay in the sun at the edge of a broad savannah, and if Jonesi had not led them it was difficult to see how it could have been found. It was not large. Perhaps it marked the site of some ancient battle, or it was where chiefs or medicine men of this village were buried, for Mrs. Pollifax counted only twelve low mounds. There had once been the village, and people had lived here and guarded the graves, and then the villages had been moved when the land became a game park, but in the people's minds the burial ground still existed, still mattered, for the stakes at either end of each grave stood erect and undisturbed, and no one had touched the round earthenware pots that had been broken at death and lay scattered between the sticks. She liked that touch, thought Mrs. Pollifax, it seemed so much more personal than flowers. A pot would be something of one's own, used every day of one's life, and what better symbolism than to end its existence along with the life of the man who had carried it, drunk from it, cooked in it and eaten from it.

Cyrus interrupted her trancelike musings with a nudge. She turned and, following his gaze, saw that Jonesi had sat down and was removing the sweater from around his waist. She watched with Cyrus as the man carefully unrolled the sweater, picked a dried leaf from it, blew on it, smoothed it out and then pulled it over his head and shoulders. There was no knife, which left only his cap as a possibility.

"We wait for Sikota now, he will come within the hour," Simon said, and turning to Mrs. Pollifax, with a triumphant note in his voice, "No one has ever held out against Sikota. He knows many tricks, I promise you." The menace of this unpleasant statement was only slightly undermined when he added, "You are now extended bathroom privileges."

"Please," said Amy, and jumped to her feet and followed Simon in among the trees.

When the two of them were out of sight, Mrs. Pollifax looked down at Jonesi, seated cross-legged on the ground, and then at Cyrus, sitting with his back to the tree. Not far away Mainza and Reuben sat talking earnestly together, their rifles beside them. She thought, *It's now or never for the cap,* and meeting Cyrus' glance she said aloud, "It's now or never."

"Oh?" he said, puzzled.

She walked around Jonesi, and when she was behind him she pretended to stumble. She thrust forward her bound wrists, fell against him and shoved his cap from his head. It dropped to the ground in front of him, and just as she recovered her balance a second object fell with it, making a solid *plunk* as it met the earth.

It was his jackknife, stained with blood.

Both Jonesi and Cyrus reached for the knife at the same time. "Hope you don't mind," Cyrus said courteously, picking it up with one hand, and with the other handing Jonesi his cap. "There's a little matter of ropes, if you'll bear with us for a moment. Emily?"

She sat down next to the poacher and held out her wrists to Cyrus. With his hands bound together it was slow work—"like sawing through a redwood tree with a handsaw," he said grimly—but presently her bonds fell from her wrists and for the first time in twenty-four hours her hands were free. She flexed them with a sense of wonder and then took the knife from Cyrus and went to work.

"Of course they're going to notice our hands when they come out of the woods," murmured Mrs. Pollifax, hacking at his ropes. "We've not much time, you know."

"Jonesi is shielding us beautifully from the other two, but I wish he'd stop grinning at me," complained Cyrus. "What do you suggest I do, my dear, take on Simon?"

"Oh no," gasped Mrs. Pollifax. "Amy, *please.* Just move her

out of the way somehow. Oh dear, they're coming back now.
Cyrus—"

"Yes, m'dear?"

"Good luck or goodbye, I don't know which, but—"

"Steady there," he said gravely, and climbed to his feet,
keeping his wrists together as if they were still bound.

Mrs. Pollifax, too, arose, and stood beside the tree, her heart
beating tumultuously.

"Who's next?" asked Amy, walking toward them with Simon close behind her. She came to a stop and smiled up at
Cyrus.

Casually Cyrus leaned over and encircled her with his freed
hands, turned her around to face Simon and held her in front of
him with a viselike grip. "Well, Simon?" he said.

Simon's eyes dropped to Cyrus' wrists and one hand moved
toward his gun. Before he reached it Mrs. Pollifax stepped out
from behind the tree and delivered her very best horizontal
slash to the side of his throat. A look of utter astonishment
passed over Simon's face, he lifted a hand toward his throat
and then sank to the ground like a crumpled paper bag.

"Incredible," said Cyrus.

Amy said, "My God, what do you think you're doing?" and
then she looked toward Reuben and Mainza, who had seen
none of this, and began screaming.

Mrs. Pollifax snatched up Simon's rifle and called to Reuben and Mainza, "Don't touch your guns or we'll shoot!"

The two men gaped at her across the clearing, too surprised
to move. Amy stopped screaming. Holding her tightly in front
of him, Cyrus slowly advanced across the clearing toward the
two men. Mrs. Pollifax followed with the rifle and Jonesi
danced along beside her laughing.

"Feel like Jack Armstrong the all-American boy," growled
Cyrus halfway across the clearing. "Damned if it isn't working
too. Pick up their rifles, my dear."

"Gladly."

Amy, struggling in Cyrus' grasp, cried, "You're fiends, both
of you, they could have shot me."

"Oh stop," said Mrs. Pollifax crossly, "you know very well

they'd never have shot you, Amy. *I've* known it since last night when you thought I was asleep."

"Oh," gasped Amy. *"Oh!"* and a string of expletives poured out of her, followed by a number of references to barnyard animals which Mrs. Pollifax thought showed a great paucity of imagination on Amy's part.

"Amy's wrists are still tied," said Cyrus, ignoring the stream of obscenity. "Need rope now for Reuben and Mainza, and as soon as possible, I think." Looking beyond them he called out, "Jonesi, be careful with that rifle."

Jonesi had picked up Mainza's gun before Mrs. Pollifax could reach it, and was cradling it lovingly in his arms. Hearing his name spoken, he backed away and sat down on the ground, the rifle across his knees, his face defiant.

"So long as he doesn't accidentally pull the trigger . . ."

"Let him play with it for a few minutes, we can get it later," Mrs. Pollifax told him. "We need that rope most of all."

This problem occupied them for some moments, because there was no alternative but to knot together the sections of rope they'd cut from their own wrists. It was tedious work. When Reuben and Mainza had been rendered inactive Cyrus stepped back and said in a pleased voice, "Very, very good," and then he asked, "Now what, my dear?"

Mrs. Pollifax looked at him in dismay. "Now what?" she faltered. She realized that his question exposed a dilemma that seemed too distant an hour ago to ever become real. She was confronted with the fact that Sikota was still to be anticipated, they were lost in the bush, and the sun was already very low on the horizon and withdrawing light from the savannah. It would soon be dark. "Now what?" she repeated.

"I can answer that for you, madam," said a voice behind them. "You will please drop the guns and lift your hands in the air."

They spun around in astonishment. *"Jonesi?"* gasped Mrs. Pollifax.

"Yes, madam," said Jonesi the poacher in excellent English. "You have been most helpful to me, I thank you." Bringing a small object out of his pocket he put it to his lips and blew. A piercing whistle filled the air, and from the copse of trees several hundred yards away a number of men came running. In the growing dusk it was difficult to count heads but she thought there were six or seven of them, all carrying rifles.

"Police?" gasped Mrs. Pollifax.

"Not police, no madam," said Jonesi, looking amused. "The police are in Lusaka far, far away. You are *our* captives now."

"Oh *no*," protested Mrs. Pollifax. "I thought—I hoped—"

"This," said Cyrus, blinking, "is exactly like being swallowed by a shark, who's then swallowed by a whale, who's then swallowed by a—my dear, what is the matter?"

"I'm not sure," whispered Mrs. Pollifax, staring at the men who had emerged out of the dusk and were fanning out to encircle them. One in particular among them had caught her eye, a man taller than the others, in khaki shorts, puttees, a thick sweater and a felt cavalry hat that heavily shadowed his face. Something about the way he moved. . . . He strode toward them now with a rifle slung across his shoulder, stopped to give Amy Lovecraft a long hard look, and then continued on to Jonesi.

Deep inside of her Mrs. Pollifax began to smile. The smile surfaced slowly, arriving on her lips at the same moment that the man saw her. He stopped in his tracks, appalled. "My God I'm hallucinating," he said.

"Absolutely not," she told him, tears coming to her eyes.

"But—Duchess?" he said incredulously. "Emily Pollifax from New Brunswick, New Jersey? *Here!*"

He began to laugh. "I don't believe it. Duchess, what in the name of all that's holy are you doing in the middle of Africa with this bunch of cutthroats? Or to put it more bluntly," he said, sweeping her off the ground in an exuberant hug, rifle and all, "what the hell are you up to now, Duchess?"

Chapter Thirteen

hen Farrell joined them some minutes later they were seated at a campfire, built for them by one of his young men. Farrell sat down, crossed his legs under him, and said, "There—business taken care of." He looked at Cyrus and then he looked at Mrs. Pollifax and he grinned. "Never saw you look better, Duchess, except for the bruise that's rapidly blossoming on your right cheekbone."

"A souvenir from Simon," said Mrs. Pollifax. "Did I hear them call you Mulika?"

"It's a name they've given me." His smile was breathtaking, a flash of white in his tanned face. She'd forgotten how handsome he was. He looked ruddy and healthy, and his mustache was infinitely more dashing than she remembered. "And by the way, Jonesi begs me to apologize to you both. He asks you to remember that you traveled in bad company and if your hands were tied, so were the hands of the other lady."

"Has a point there," admitted Cyrus.

"He found it a damn puzzling situation. Sorry, incidentally, that we've had to postpone dinner—"

"Food?" breathed Mrs. Pollifax.

"—but we're expecting Sikota, you know, which is why you've been moved out of harm's way. Now for heaven's sake, Duchess, *talk*. Tell me how in hell you and Cyrus got here, and why."

Mrs. Pollifax obligingly talked. She referred briefly to her arrival in Lusaka and then she concentrated on a description of their last twenty-four hours. When she had finished, Farrell looked stunned.

"I can't believe it," he said. "You just walked into the *Times of Zambia* office and placed an advertisement for me in the personals column?"

"It seemed very logical," she told him. "I couldn't find you."

He shook his head at her. "That directness of yours, Duchess, is going to cost you your life one of these days."

"Nearly did," said Cyrus. "Apparently."

"And you didn't even see the advertisement," lamented Mrs. Pollifax. "I thought—just for a moment, you know—that you might have come to rescue us! Farrell, what *did* bring you here in the nick of time? And why shouldn't I have advertised for you? And how do you come to be called Mulika?"

He hesitated and then he said flippantly, "Believe it or not, *mulika* means 'shedder of light' in the Nyanga language. Surprise you?" He looked at her and added soberly, "So help me I've tried to shed some, Duchess, because I've fallen in love with this country. You've heard of middle-age passion? Well, mine is directed at Africa in general—uncluttered, still unpolluted—and at Zambia in particular. Actually I came here to farm—"

"Not an art gallery," said Mrs. Pollifax, nodding.

"—and I do own two hundred acres in the Southern Province, but I don't see them very often these days because I've been helping train and instruct freedom fighters."

"Freedom fighters!" exclaimed Mrs. Pollifax. "So that's it . . . But surely—" She frowned over this, puzzled. "Surely that's not enough to explain Simon's abnormal interest in you? He and Amy were ready to commit murder to find out what you look like. There must be other men doing this who don't—"

"Don't have a price on their heads?" He grinned. "A pity you see that, Duchess. Yes, of course there's more, because with passion one always gets involved. You see, it's all very exciting to watch Zambia grow and develop, but next door you have Zambabwe—or Rhodesia, as you probably know it—and the people over there straggle across our border, some of them having been handled roughly, to say the least, most of them just out of prison or about to be arrested and sent off to prison, and the contrast isn't very nice. These people want autonomy too, they wither under *apartheid*—God, it's such a waste—and they need to be listened to.

"And so," he went on, his eyes gleaming in the firelight, "I got involved. With my background and my white skin I became something of a spy. You've heard of spies?" he asked, his smile mischievous. "I began traveling back and forth across the border as a fake tourist, oh-ing and ah-ing at Zambabwe's natural wonders, which are considerable, and I helped Jonesi set up a damn good underground escape route. Even lived briefly in Salisbury. Unfortunately it came to be known that a man named Mulika was guiding men out of Rhodesia, and then eventually that Mulika was a white man, and after that they learned my real name, I knew that. But your advertisement, Duchess, so direct and so naïve—" He shook his head. "It must have caused a number of tidal waves in more than a few small ponds."

"Including the Zambian police," she told him. "I was interviewed by a—oh," she gasped, "*now* I realize what was wrong with that interview. How blind of me! He didn't want to know anything about you at all, only how I came to know that you were in Zambia."

"Who?"

"A Lieutenant Dunduzu Bwanausi," she said.

Farrell burst out laughing. "Dundu? God, you must have alarmed him. I'll bet he thought you were a Rhodesian agent. I'll have to radio him all's well."

"You know him?"

"A very good friend of mine. His brother Qabaniso happens to be half owner and partner in my farm."

Their campfire was small, far removed from the burial ground, and on an incline from which they could watch a larger campfire being built some five hundred yards away. Mrs. Pollifax found her attention distracted now by Jonesi's activities. Amy Lovecraft and her confederates had been placed around the fire, their wrists still bound, and Mrs. Pollifax saw that Jonesi was tying gags across their mouths.

Following her glance Farrell said dryly, "The goats are being tethered to catch the lion, Sikota being the lion. And a rather big one, I suspect, well worth catching."

"Rather hard on Mrs. Lovecraft, isn't it?" asked Cyrus.

"No harder than for Simon and Reuben and Mainza," pointed out Farrell, "but of course you're still laboring under the illusion that she's Amy Lovecraft, aren't you. She's not," he said, his voice hardening.

"Who is she?" asked Mrs. Pollifax.

"A Rhodesian by the name of Betty Thwaite. She's given us a hell of a time catching up with her, because from what we've been told she certainly didn't come to Zambia to abduct anyone, and the bush country is the last place we thought of looking for her."

"It's Amy you were hunting for, then?"

"Desperately," he said. "Night and day and around the clock for the past six days."

"Why?" asked Cyrus.

"Well, to give you her background, she's the intelligence behind a fanatical right-wing group in Rhodesia, one of those situations where a group takes a more extreme stance than the government, and then, like the *Herstigte Nasionale Party*, breaks away to form its own party, which in turn provokes several more spinoffs, and by this time you're deep among the fanatic fringe. That's where you find Betty Thwaite's group, all gung-ho for slaughtering anyone who suggests compromise or reason. Even the Rhodesian Government doesn't claim Betty. All we knew," he said, "was that she'd been smuggled across the border into Zambia last week, either by boat at night across the Zambesi River near Livingstone, or through the swamps into Botswana and then into Zambia. We also knew that she'd left Rhodesia with a forged Kenya passport and a change in name and in hair color, but why she decided to switch horses in midstream and kidnap you, Duchess, I just don't know. It certainly wasn't her purpose in coming here."

"But she did kidnap me!"

"Yes, and that's what baffles me," he said, scowling. "Oh I

have to admit there was some sense in her madness, because if you'd given them what they wanted it would have been a real coup for her, and she's a very ambitious woman. The next time I crossed the border into Zambabwe—" He circled his throat with a finger. "Curtains."

Cyrus said, "But she didn't arrive here with that in mind?"

Farrell shook his head. "That's what's so damn puzzling. According to our informant—and he's never been wrong before—she was coming to Zambia for the purpose of assassinating President Kaunda."

"Assassinating?" said Mrs. Pollifax, suddenly alert.

"Good God," said Cyrus. "Why?"

"Why assassinate Kenneth Kaunda? Because KK, as he's affectionately called, is a gentle but insistent force against *apartheid*, Cyrus. He's been making behind-the-scene appeals to both Rhodesia and South Africa for diplomatic talks on compromise, and what's more, they've begun listening to him."

"Assassinate," repeated Mrs. Pollifax, frowning.

He nodded. "You can understand our panic. We had only an old photograph to work with, and time's been against us. We batted zero until we found a waiter at the Livingstone airport restaurant who remembered her, and that's when we learned she was a blonde, after which we linked her with the flight to Ngomo airstrip traveling as a Mrs. A. Lovecraft. She stayed a few nights at Ngomo Lodge and then flew to Lusaka, where we discovered that she arrived just in time to join—of all things—a safari party." He shook his head. "But it doesn't make sense," he said. "It simply doesn't make sense, her going off on a *safari*."

"It could," said Mrs. Pollifax softly, trying to control the excitement that had been rising in her. "It could, Farrell. It's possible that Amy Lovecraft came on safari to meet the *real* assassin."

"Meet the—*what?*" said Farrell.

"Because that's why I'm here," she told him, nodding. "I don't know about your Betty Thwaite, but I do know about assassins. It's why *I* joined the safari." She glanced pointedly at Cyrus and then back at Farrell. "I was sent," she added, "by a mutual friend of ours named Carstairs."

"Good heavens," said Farrell, and now they both turned and looked at Cyrus, who regarded them benignly but lifted one eyebrow, waiting.

Farrell said, "Do you tell him, or shall I?"

"Tell me what? That you didn't," said Cyrus, "live next door to Emily in New Brunswick, New Jersey, or build a soap-box car for her son? Already guessed that, young man. How *did* you two meet?"

Farrell grinned. "Would you believe tied back to back in Mexico, after being doped and carried off by the—"

"Farrell!" she gasped. "You're overdoing this."

"Nonsense," said Farrell. "My dear Reed, if you're so obtuse that you believe this charming but terribly resourceful lady does nothing but raise geraniums, then you're not at all the man for her, and it strikes me from the way you look at her—"

"Farrell!" sputtered Mrs. Pollifax.

Cyrus said in his mild voice, "Certain—uh—arts have become apparent to me. A persuasive bending of truth, shall we say, and then there was the karate—"

"Karate!" It was Farrell's turn to be surprised. "Duchess, you astonish me, you're becoming a pro?"

"Pro what?" asked Cyrus quietly.

"She had this little hobby," Farrell said blithely. "As CIA courier. Sandwiched in between—if I remember correctly—her garden club and hospital activities. That's how I met her, except that three years ago I resigned from the CIA and wrote finis to that chapter. But if you don't mind assimilating this little bombshell later, Cyrus, I want very much to learn about this safari. Enlighten me, please, Duchess. And fast."

She told him all that she knew. "But Carstairs was certain enough of his informant to send me here. I was simply to take pictures of everyone on safari, nothing more, so that every member of the safari could be traced—"

She stopped as Cyrus let out an indiscreet roar of laughter. "Sorry," he said, subsiding into chuckles. "Not really amusing except—those snapshots!"

Mrs. Pollifax gave him a reproachful glance before she added, "Carstairs seemed very sure that Aristotle would be on the safari to meet someone and discuss his next project, and if Amy Lovecraft's been heavily involved in her Rhodesian group all this time I can't see her wandering around the world shooting people. I'm only assuming, of course, but putting our two stories together—"

Farrell said abruptly, "I'm going to break radio silence and call Dundu. I'm stricken by the same assumptions, Duchess, because your story fits into mine like the one missing piece of a jigsaw puzzle." He nodded. "It certainly explains why Betty Thwaite headed for a safari of all things, and if she'd already concluded her business with Aristotle, it also explains why she could go off on a tangent and take on an abduction. She eavesdropped on your interview with Dundu and realized that one of her traveling companions was a woman who actually knew and could identify me. She couldn't resist. The abduction must have been done on impulse, and of course it was terribly unprofessional of her, but she thought she could handle both. Yes, very ambitious woman, Betty Thwaite. But I don't like using the radio, damn it."

"Why?" asked Cyrus.

"Because that's how we discovered and pinpointed *your* party," he said. "We'd left Chunga camp for Kafwala and stopped on the road to radio our whereabouts to headquarters, and that's when we overheard Simon calling Green-Bird in Lusaka. The code name Green-Bird was not unfamiliar to us," he went on, "so while we continued to Kafwala to look for Mrs. Lovecraft, Jonesi set out alone to track you down. Very good at that sort of thing, Jonesi. He wore a homing device in his cap so that we could find him again."

"As a fool, Jonesi was certainly convincing," commented Mrs. Pollifax.

"Oh God yes, he can go anywhere with that act, it's saved his life innumerable times. But Duchess, let's get back to basics: which of those people on safari do you suspect is Aristotle?"

"I've no idea," she said truthfully. "I'd say none of them, except that my first film was stolen from my room at Kafwala camp, which implies that my picture-taking bothered someone a great deal. It had to have been Aristotle who stole the film because Cyrus told me that Amy Lovecraft and Dr. Henry stayed down at the campfire while I was gone. Amy could tell you who Aristotle is, of course."

"I wouldn't bet on that," he said dryly. "So we can assume that Aristotle's still with the safari, and the assassination's already been scheduled?" He shivered. "I'm not sure that Zambia could survive as a country without President Kaunda. He's a damn strong leader and a beloved president. Any leader's a genius who can hold together a country of at least seventy different tribes speaking sixteen major languages and make it all work." He stared into the fire, frowning, and then he looked up and said sharply, "All right, this is Thursday night. Where's the safari now?"

"Camp Moshe," said Cyrus promptly. "Tomorrow they make their way back to Chunga camp, remain there over Friday night, and then end the safari in Lusaka on Saturday."

Farrell nodded. "Then I've definitely got to get a message to Dundu so the police can put everyone on safari under surveillance until they leave Zambia. Give me their names. It may save time to radio them now." He drew pencil and paper out of his pocket.

"There's Cyrus' daughter, Lisa Reed," began Mrs. Pollifax.

"And Dr. Tom Henry," added Cyrus.

Farrell looked up. "Not the chap from the mission hospital over near the Angolan border?" When Mrs. Pollifax nodded he said, "Small world. Go on."

"John Steeves, travel writer, and a very charming man. Willem Kleiber—Dutch I think he said, very prim and hygienic and in heavy construction work, whatever that means. And then there's—well, McIntosh."

Farrell stopped writing. "Yes?"

"According to Amy Lovecraft, that's only half his name. She peeked at his passport. Of course anything she said is suspect now, but I can't see any ulterior motive in her saying that unless it was true."

Farrell put down his pencil. "What sort of person is he?"

"Secretive," said Mrs. Pollifax.

Cyrus cleared his throat and said cautiously, "Reserved, in my estimation. Businessman. American."

"But always traveling," added Mrs. Pollifax.

"All right, who else?" asked Farrell.

"Chanda," said Cyrus. "Dr. Henry's protégé, who, I might add, tracked down Emily's abductors for me, and then went back to camp on foot to guide any search parties. Age twelve."

"Yes, and where are those search parties?" asked Mrs. Pollifax.

"No idea, Duchess. I'm sorry, but it's a damn big park." He gave her a rueful smile. "When you were taken west they undoubtedly went east, and now that you've headed south they're probably combing the north. That's usually the way, isn't it? Okay, we've Lisa Reed, Dr. Tom Henry, John Steeves, Willem Kleiber, the mysterious McIntosh, and young Chanda. Anyone else?"

"Amy Lovecraft, Emily and myself," said Cyrus. "Nine in all."

"Right." Farrell pocketed the memo and rose to his feet. "I'm going to radio Dundu now. Sit tight and I'll send a man over to guard you while I'm gone because this campfire has to be extinguished in a few minutes."

Mrs. Pollifax looked at him in astonishment. "Guard us? Sit tight? But surely you want me down at the campfire with Amy and the others. Sikota will be expecting to see me there. He'll count heads."

Farrell shook his head. "Too dangerous for you, Duchess."

"Dangerous!" she gasped, standing up. "Farrell, this is an assassination we're trying to stop! Of course I'm going down there."

Farrell sighed. "Look, Duchess," he said patiently, "you're tired, you need a rest. There are only seven of us men, and three are out scouting for Sikota, and anything could happen down there in the next hour."

"Absolutely right," agreed Cyrus. "Sit, Emily."

"I refuse," she told him, and grasping Farrell by the arm she turned him toward the campfire. "Look at them—four mannequins in a store window," she pointed out hotly. "No movement at all, no one talking, eating, smiling or lifting their hands. Sikota isn't a lion, he's a man with a brain that reasons. Those people abducted me and I'm missing, and then he'll wonder why nobody moves, but if Cyrus and I—"

"Ha," snorted Cyrus.

"If Cyrus and I sit with them we can talk and—and pass things around, as if we're eating, which heaven only knows I wish we *could* do, having eaten nothing all day."

Farrell turned to Cyrus. "Well, Cyrus? Damn it, I've got to send this radio message."

"Both of you absolutely right," said Cyrus judiciously. "Dangerous place to be down there. Crossfire and all that if he slips past your men." He considered this, sighed and climbed to his feet. "Have to admit Emily's right, too," he added, "and if all this helps—don't happen to have a pistol, do you?"

"Take it with my blessing," said Farrell, unbuckling a holster at his belt and handing over a gun. "Take this, too," he said, reaching into his pocket, and gave him a chocolate bar.

"Food?" gasped Mrs. Pollifax.

"Food," said Cyrus. "You go along and send your message, Farrell, we'll wander along down."

"Yes, but plain or almond?" asked Mrs. Pollifax happily.

Their move to the campfire had its ludicrous aspects; Mrs. Pollifax could see this at once. She sat down on one side of Amy Lovecraft, and Cyrus on the other side, while Amy made loud gurgling protests deep in her throat, and across the fire Simon glared at them both with bloodshot, outraged eyes. From five hundred yards away the campfire had looked brilliant but now that Mrs. Pollifax sat beside it the fire seemed astonishingly small, and the darkness around it like a black curtain. She felt exposed and horribly vulnerable.

"I believe we're here to supply motion," Cyrus reminded her. "What's the matter—second thoughts, my dear?"

"You won't," she said in a small voice, "say 'I told you so'?"

"Emily," he said with a sigh, "this is no moment to become rational. I've walked twenty miles in the bush today, helped you turn the tables on these villainous creatures, I've been captured by guerillas and am now sitting here a target ripe for any passing gunman, and do you really think—can you have the effrontery to think—I would say 'I told you so'?"

"You really are a darling, Cyrus," she said, smiling.

"Thank you. Eat your chocolate."

The moments passed slowly, each one seeming interminable. She and Cyrus passed twigs and pebbles back and forth and made flippant, imaginative conversation with a silent Amy, and then in turn with Simon, Reuben, and Mainza. In fact, as Mrs. Pollifax pointed out, they behaved like idiots, to which Cyrus replied that pantomime had always attracted him and that he enjoyed talking with people who couldn't answer back.

It was twenty minutes later that Mrs. Pollifax became aware of Amy suddenly stiffening beside her. She turned and looked at Mrs. Lovecraft and found her staring off to the left, her eyes opened very wide and filled with alarm. Mrs. Pollifax followed her glance and she too saw something move: a shadow paler than the darkness of the trees. She said in a hushed voice, "Cyrus—over there," and fell silent, suddenly afraid, because if this was Sikota then he had slipped past Farrell and Jonesi and the others without being seen. She saw the shadow pause and then start toward them from a new angle . . . the lion approaching the tethered goats, she thought, her throat suddenly dry, and at that moment he seemed exactly like a wild beast stopping to sniff the air for danger. She guessed that he was uneasy and felt a fleeting sense of pity for him, as if he really were a beast being drawn into a trap, and then her pity dissipated as she recalled that this was not a lion but Sikota, for whom everyone talked, which meant he was a man skilled in torture. He was entering now on the farthest reach of the firelight, which began to give his pale shadow some substance. Leaning forward to peer through the dusk, she saw the outlines of a short, grotesquely fat man stuffed into a pale business suit and carrying a long rifle under his arm. She realized in astonishment that he must have arrived by car—he *had* to have come by car in a suit like that, and Jonesi and Farrell had expected him on foot. Then as he took several new steps toward the fire she lifted her eyes to his face and saw that his skin was a dingy white, with a thin mouth almost drowned in pouches of fat.

He had stopped, his hand caressing the trigger of the rifle, still half in shadow but his pale suit gleaming in the dusky light. *He knows something is wrong,* she thought, feeling her heart beat faster. There was a terrifying intelligence about his stillness, as if he was sending out tentacles to weigh and test the atmosphere. And then, as he hesitated, he did the one thing that nobody had anticipated: he called out sharply in a clear, imperative voice, "Simon?" and then, angrily, *"Simon?"*

And Simon, bound and gagged, could neither turn nor reply.

There was an uncomfortable, suspenseful moment of silence during which a hyena howled in the distance, and then abruptly Jonesi stepped out of the bush off to the right and shouted, "Drop the rifle!" From the opposite side of the clearing Farrell called, "Drop it, Sikota, you're surrounded!"

The man slowly turned toward Jonesi, and then he slowly turned toward Farrell. When he moved his action was sudden, all in one piece, and incredibly fast and graceful for a man of so much flesh. He lifted his rifle to his cheek, peered through the telescopic lens, pointed it at the campfire and pulled the trigger.

"Down!" shouted Cyrus.

Mrs. Pollifax agreed completely with this suggestion and rolled off to one side. Two other shots followed the first, but when she lifted her head she saw that it was not Sikota who had fired them. He lay crumpled on the ground, looking like a very large soft pile of laundry.

"Are you all right, Duchess?" shouted Farrell, and she heard the sound of running feet.

Mrs. Pollifax looked at Cyrus and he looked at her. He said unsteadily, "Well."

"Yes," she said, called to Farrell, "He missed," and stood up, brushing the dust from her clothes.

But Cyrus was shaking his head. "He didn't miss," he told her, pointing.

For a moment she didn't understand, and then she followed the direction of his pointing finger and gasped, "Oh no! Farrell? Jonesi?"

It was Jonesi who reached them first, and it was Jonesi who stepped carefully over Simon's feet and knelt beside Amy Lovecraft. Amy looked as if she'd grown tired of sitting upright and had lain down to sleep, but when Jonesi lifted her head there was a bullet hole in the precise center of her forehead; her eyes were sightless.

"Damn," exploded Farrell, coming up behind them, and he began swearing softly and relentlessly under his breath.

"Incredible shooting," said Cyrus, looking a little sick.

"He had a telescopic lens. He got past us somehow, you know. Damn it—both of them dead!"

"He thought she would talk, Mulika."

Cyrus snorted at this. "Couldn't have known our Amy, then."

"Perhaps he didn't," suggested Mrs. Pollifax, and turned away with tears in her eyes. "Sikota's a white man, Farrell, I saw him."

"Let's have a look," he said brusquely, and they followed him back to the crumpled body of Sikota. One of the men had turned him over and was staring down into his face.

"You know him, Patu?"

Patu nodded. "I know him, Mulika. He is the Portuguese who runs the curio shop on Cairo Road. Who would have thought he was a spy? He came in a truck, Mulika. Joshua is in the truck now, he says it has a false floor with space to hide people in it."

"So that's what he planned . . . Not exactly Betty Thwaite's type," Farrell said, staring down at the man, "but politics makes strange bedfellows." He straightened, his face grim. "But we've no time for postmortems. I've talked to Dundu by radio, and as soon as I give him the all-clear he's sending a helicopter for you both." He turned to Mrs. Pollifax and said angrily, "Dundu told me over the radio that President Kaunda's opening a new school in Lusaka on Sunday afternoon, the day after your safari ends. It's his only public appearance until August, and it's been heavily publicized."

"Oh-oh," said Cyrus.

"Yes. And if your Aristotle really exists," he said, his face hardening, "then I can't imagine his returning to Zambia at a

later date when he's already here now. Sunday would have to
be the day."

"Sunday?" said Mrs. Pollifax in horror. "So soon?"

"It gives us forty-eight hours." He turned to look at Amy's
body and sighed. "Cover her with one of the sleeping bags,
Patu. In her own way—I scarcely care to admit it—she was a
warrior. At least she wasn't a paid mercenary like Sikota and
the rest of this unholy group."

"Lieutenant Bwanausi has the list now?" asked Cyrus.

Farrell nodded. "He has the list and he's probably circling
now over Kafwala camp waiting to hear from me. Chanda's
been of enormous help to them, but unfortunately they didn't
make contact with Chanda until this morning, and his information was outdated by then because you'd headed off in this
direction. Incidentally, Duchess," he added, and a faint smile
softened the grimness of his face, "Dundu reports they asked a
ransom for you of fifty thousand *kwacha*."

"Now that's positively insulting," said Cyrus. "About
thirty thousand in American dollars, isn't it?"

"Never mind, I'm alive," said Mrs. Pollifax, wrenching her
gaze away from Amy's shrouded figure. Her eyes moved from
the dying fire to the sky overhead, and then to the burial
ground hidden by darkness, and back to the man at their feet.
She said bleakly, "The helicopter will come, then, and whisk
us away from all this, but what happens next, Farrell?"

He nodded. "You go back to Lusaka and wait," he told her.
"Spend tomorrow and Saturday recovering. Do a little sight-
seeing and try to forget tonight, because it's been a shock for
you both. But I promise you this," he said in a hard voice.
"There'll be no assassination, Duchess, and KK will safely
open his school on Sunday afternoon. I'll promise you another
thing, too," he added. "I'll meet you and Cyrus for lunch at
your hotel on Sunday and I'll deliver to you the name and
identity of Aristotle."

"Just like that?" said Cyrus.

"Just like that," promised Farrell, and turning to Patu he
said, "Get me the radio now, Patu, we have a long night of
work ahead."

Chapter Fourteen

*I*t was Sunday morning and Mrs. Pollifax stood outside the hotel entrance watching Dr. Henry pack his ancient Land Rover. It was already filled to the roof with cartons of medical supplies and bolts of brightly colored cloth, and Cyrus was strapping the last suitcase to the luggage rack. The two days of hedonistic pleasure that Farrell had prescribed for them had never materialized. Much of Friday had been spent at police headquarters making and signing statements, followed by a highly censored interview with a *Times of Zambia* newsman and a great deal of picture-taking. She and Cyrus had briefly shopped for souvenirs yesterday, but it had been impossible to forget what was going on behind the scenes. The safari party's return at midday, escorted by Lieutenant Bwanausi, had been a sufficient reminder, and Cyrus had not been allowed to see Lisa until late afternoon. Nor had she been able to sleep well: her dreams were haunted by fears that Aristotle would kill again and that the assassination, already set in motion, would somehow—in some mysterious way—take place in spite of the police.

Lisa, standing beside Mrs. Pollifax, turned and gave her a radiant smile. "It's all so incredible, isn't it?" she said. "Do you think that as soon as I arrived in Zambia something inside of me *knew?*"

"I think it's wonderful, and just right for you," Mrs. Pollifax told her warmly.

"And to think that it hit us both the same way," Lisa told her in an astonished voice. "And frightened us so much we kept our distance, not trusting it. I know how *I* felt . . . I sat at the campfire that first night talking to John and thinking we were going to have a very pleasant safari flirtation, and then I looked up and saw Tom and I thought—I just thought, *Oh, my God.* Like that."

Listening to her, Mrs. Pollifax could almost forget—but not quite—that in a few minutes she would be meeting Farrell. She smiled at Chanda, who was playing with her multicolored parasol, opening it and closing it and grinning, except that it was no longer hers because she had given it to Chanda at breakfast. "It's a *bupe*," she'd told him after conferring with Tom on the Bemba word for gift. Now she asked Lisa, "Will you be married here or in Connecticut?"

Lisa laughed. "All I know is that Tom, the scrupulous guy, insists that I first see his hospital—and the funny house with a tin roof we'll live in—and then we'll make plans and I'll fly home and tell Dad."

Her father, joining them, looked at his watch and said to Mrs. Pollifax, "Nearly time, my dear. Ten minutes to twelve."

Lisa gave them each a curious glance. "You have a lunch date with that mysterious Mr. Farrell, haven't you. Will you tell us someday—you and Dad—what really happened to you out in the bush?"

"I'd tell you now," said Mrs. Pollifax, "except that it's not our story to tell. Not yet, at least." *Not until we've seen Farrell*, she reminded herself, and put this thought aside as Chanda came to say goodbye to her, the glorious multicolored parasol held high over his head.

"Goodbye, Chanda *nunandi*," she told him, gravely shaking his hand. "It's been a very real joy knowing you, and I hope —oh dear," she gasped, feeling a spoke of the umbrella become entangled in her hat.

Cyrus began to laugh.

"What is it?"

Cyrus and Tom surrounded her, and the umbrella was carefully disentangled from her hat. Lisa giggled. "It's that red feather," she told her. "It's sticking straight up in the air, all fifteen or twenty inches of it. You look like an Indian chief."

"Very charming Indian chief," Cyrus said, grasping her arm. "No time to mend it, either. Goodbye, Tom . . . Lisa, keep in touch."

"You too," she called after them.

Hurrying through the lobby toward the Coffee Hut, Mrs. Pollifax, aware of a surprising number of glances directed at her, said, "Cyrus, my hat—?"

"Very eye-catching," he told her truthfully. "Sets a new style. There—made it," he said, seating her at a table and taking the chair opposite her. "Nervous?"

"Of course I'm nervous," she told him, placing her sun-goggles and her purse on the table. "I've been nervous ever since Farrell telephoned to say they've arrested Aristotle and he'd tell us about it at twelve."

"Should think you'd feel relieved, not nervous. Satisfied, happy."

"Of course I'm not being *logical*," she conceded, "but I find it so difficult to dislike people. I know they're frequently selfish or opinionated and egotistical, or dull or contrary and sometimes dishonest, but if one expects nothing from them it's astonishing how fascinating they are, and always full of surprises. You see, I liked everyone on our safari, which makes Farrell's message very worrisome. It means I can expect to be upset soon."

He said accusingly, "Couldn't possibly have liked Amy Lovecraft."

"No, but she—I do feel sorry for her, you know."

"Ha," snorted Cyrus. "Got herself into it. Who was it said 'character is destiny'?"

"But that's just it," Mrs. Pollifax told him eagerly. "Life is so much a matter of paths chosen and paths not taken, and Amy seems unerringly to have chosen all the paths that would lead to her appointment with Sikota the other night. I can't help feeling cosmic undertones, Cyrus. It's like watching *A* lead to *D*, and then to *M*, and eventually to *Z* for all of us."

"*All* of us?"

She nodded. "Yes, because six days ago at this hour Amy was still alive, and although we didn't know it, Farrell was down south looking for her, and you and I were sitting here having lunch together—"

"—and Aristotle, whoever he is, was buckling on his moneybelt?"

"Oh, I don't think so," she said earnestly. "It would be a numbered account in Switzerland, wouldn't it?"

"Whatever you say, my dear," he told her blandly, "since you're so much more accustomed to this sort of thing than I. About that quiet life you said you lead . . . raising geraniums, was it?"

"I said that in *general* I live a very quiet life," she reminded him virtuously. "I do think there's a difference between living a quiet life and in *general* living a quiet life."

"Splitting hairs, my dear."

"Well, but—yes, I am," she admitted, giving him a dazzling smile. "And you noticed, didn't you."

"Sorry to keep you waiting," Farrell interrupted, pulling up a chair and joining them. "I'm afraid I can't stop for lunch with you, either, damn it, because I've got to head south and meet Jonesi in—" He stopped in midsentence, staring at Mrs. Pollifax. "Good God, Duchess, your hat?"

"Never mind the hat," she pleaded. "Who is Aristotle?"

"John Steeves."

"*Steeves?* Good heavens," said Cyrus.

"Now I really do feel upset," murmured Mrs. Pollifax. "I'm glad Lisa isn't hearing this. Farrell, are the police sure? Has he confessed?"

"I don't think you can expect a confession only hours after an arrest," Farrell told her, and with a glance at the hovering waiter, "Later, if you don't mind, we're not ordering yet . . . No, Steeves hasn't confessed, in fact he's refused even to give his home address or next of kin. The man's being completely unco-operative, which seems almost as incriminating as the parts of a gun and a silencer that were found in his luggage—apparently smuggled past Customs somehow—and the fact that, according to his passport, he was in France on the day that Messague was assassinated."

He hesitated, and Mrs. Pollifax said, "There's more?"

He nodded. "A notebook with scribblings in a code we've not been able to puzzle out yet, but on the last page—sorry, Duchess—a list of four names with dates: *Messague,* September fifth, which happens to be the day he was assassinated, *Malaga,* October thirtieth, and the names Hastings and O'Connell, which mean nothing to us at the moment but are being checked out. We think the last two were assassinations, too."

"Unbelievable," said Cyrus.

Farrell shrugged. "Perhaps, but would you have believed Amy Lovecraft was a Rhodesian named Betty Thwaite, or that the Duchess here was snapping pictures hoping to record an assassin's face?"

"Steeves," repeated Mrs. Pollifax, trying to assimilate this. *A room with a door marked Keep Out,* and Lisa saying, *He seems caught somehow—and terribly sad about it.* "Farrell, he had to have been blackmailed into it," she said. "There's no other explanation. Have you met him?"

Farrell looked amused. "Those sad spaniel eyes of his, you mean? I'm told women always want to mother a man who looks as if he's suffered, and perhaps he has, but I'd have to cast my vote for a troubled mind. Yes, I've met him."

"I wonder why he doesn't defend himself," she said, frowning, "although I suppose if he's Aristotle there's not much he can say. He's in prison?"

"Definitely in prison, yes, or President Kaunda wouldn't be dedicating the Moses Msonthi School at one o'clock today. Duchess, you've too soft a heart, it's time you retired too."

"It's just that he seemed genuinely fond of Lisa," she pointed out, "and it's so difficult to imagine any assassin being attracted to a woman and looking as if he cared."

"Someone," said Cyrus, "undoubtedly made the same remark about Jack the Ripper, my dear."

"Yes, but—all right," she conceded. "I'm sorry, it's probably the shock. What will happen to him now, Farrell?"

"For the moment, not a great deal," he said. "The man's safely tucked away, which is the main thing, booked for illegal possession of a weapon, and for smuggling that weapon into the country. It was all very discreetly handled after the safari ended, and now they've gained time to collect further evidence. Your McIntosh, by the way, turns out to be McIntosh Magruder—I thought that might interest you."

"The billionaire recluse?" said Mrs. Pollifax, startled.

*"Multi*billionaire recluse."

"Thought he never came out of seclusion," said Cyrus.

"Apparently even the Magruders of this world listen to their doctor. Magruder had been ill and his doctor advised some travel and a change of scenery. That's who McIntosh is, while Willem Kleiber jets around the world selling earthmoving machinery to developing countries."

"Very appropriate for a man who is anything but earthshaking," commented Cyrus.

"Yes. Prim little man, isn't he? Duchess, have you been in touch with Carstairs since you came out of the bush?"

She shook her head. "It costs twelve dollars to call the United States for three minutes," she told him. "I asked. So I thought I'd wait until I could present him with Aristotle's identity, which I *think*," she added, "he'd find well worth a twelve-dollar call."

"Frugal to the end," said Farrell, "except for those hats of yours. Duchess, what happened?" He stared fascinated at the feather that shot into the air like an antenna.

"Sorry you mentioned it," Cyrus said in his mild voice. "Been trying not to notice it myself."

"I had a small accident with a parasol," she explained with dignity, "and I will presently find a safety pin and tie the feather down, since it's the only real hat I brought. Farrell, do you think Carstairs will have heard about our abduction?"

He smiled. "Don't sound so wistful, Duchess, I doubt it. You were in and out of the bush too fast to reach the American papers. Front-page news here, though. I can't help noticing how the waiters are staring at you. Unless, of course, it's the hat." He glanced at his watch and sighed. "Duchess, I loathe goodbyes, but there's this long drive ahead of me—"

"I know," she said, nodding. "We've scarcely had time to talk, but I can't complain when you and Jonesi saved our lives."

"I owed you that, you know. It makes us even," he told her with his quick smile. "Duchess, you'll have to come back to Zambia soon. With Cyrus, perhaps, to visit Lisa? Only, for heaven's sake don't advertise for me in the newspaper next time, Duchess, or it'll cost me my head. You can always reach me in care of Qabaniso Bwanausi at our farm, I've written down the address for you." He opened her purse and slipped a piece of paper inside, and then he pushed back his chair and stood up. "Goodbye, Cyrus, I certainly like your style . . . As for you, Duchess, one of these days—oh to hell with it, I'll just give you a quick kiss, a God bless and go."

He leaned over and hugged her, and with a nod and a wave to Cyrus he walked away.

"Oh—Farrell!" called Mrs. Pollifax after him.

He turned. "Yes?"

"I was to ask you very formally and very officially if you'd like to return to your old job. Carstairs misses you."

He grinned. "I'll take care of that myself, Duchess. Same cable address?"

"Same cable address."

He waved and walked out, and Cyrus said, "Damn decent chap, your Farrell, even if he doesn't know a soapbox derby from a horse race."

"Yes," she said, blowing her nose, and then she gave him a distracted smile and said, "Cyrus, would you mind terribly if we don't have lunch now? I think I've lost my appetite."

"I don't wonder," he said, helping her up from her chair. "A walk should do us both good."

"Thank you. I can't say that I even arrived with an appetite," she told him as they walked out of the restaurant into the lobby of the hotel. "The suspense made me edgy all morning, and now I simply can't eat when John Steeves—when he —and then Farrell going, too—"

"Perfectly understandable," he said.

He steered her through a crowd of people waiting for the elevator and came to a stop as the door of a descending elevator slid open and discharged a fresh crowd of people into the lobby. They stood patiently while the two groups exchanged places, the one swarming into the elevator, the other pushing their way through. Once in motion again, she and Cyrus fell into step behind a tall man in a turban who was hurrying toward the hotel exit. Just to one side of him walked a shorter man whose erect posture caught Mrs. Pollifax's eye next, and she transferred her gaze to him. There was something very familiar about that walk, she decided, and then she thought, *Of course—a strut with a stutter.* She said to Cyrus, smiling, "That's Mr. Kleiber ahead of us, Cyrus, let's catch up with him and ask—"

She stiffened as the man glanced off to the right and she saw his face. It wasn't Mr. Kleiber, it was a black man wearing gold-rimmed spectacles, and so it couldn't be Mr. Kleiber, and yet—and yet it *was* Mr. Kleiber, she realized in astonishment, recognizing his nose and forehead, except that it was a Willem Kleiber without a goatee and changed, somehow, into a Zambian. She saw him walk through the glass-doors and signal to a taxi and she gasped, "Cyrus, it *is* Kleiber—run!" and breaking free she raced after him.

"Taxi!" she cried as Mr. Kleiber drove away. A second taxi slid up to her, she fumbled with the door, jumped inside and gasped, "Please—follow the car that just pulled away. Hurry!"

The taxi shot ahead just as Cyrus reached the curb. Through the open window Mrs. Pollifax shouted to him, "Call Dundu—call someone! Help!"

Chapter Fifteen

Cyrus, suddenly bereft of his lunch partner, stared after the vanishing taxi in horror. One moment Mrs. Pollifax had been with him, and the next not. He'd distinctly heard her say, "Cyrus, that's Mr. Kleiber ahead of us," and then the man had turned his head and revealed a gleaming black Zambian face, and obviously the man wasn't Kleiber at all. But Emily had gasped, "It *is* Kleiber—run," and had left his side with the speed of a gazelle and now she was gone, heaven only knew where, shouting something about Dundu and help.

He walked back into the lobby and sat down, mourning the slowness of his reflexes and reminding himself that six days with Emily Pollifax should have proven to him that he had to be on his toes every minute. No slides, he thought, grateful for this, but instead a woman who gave sudden shouts and vanished. He wished fervently that he'd reached the taxi in time to go with her.

Again he wondered why she'd jumped into that taxi, because there had to be a reason for it. What *would* Kleiber be doing wearing gold-rimmed spectacles, a charcoal pin-striped suit and a black skin? He supposed that some sort of dye could be injected into the veins, or perhaps there were pills for that sort of thing, but the idea was insane. Still, Emily had believed it was Kleiber. Possibly she was overwrought after hearing the news about Steeves, but Emily, he decided, wouldn't be overwrought. If nearly being killed by Amy and Simon hadn't done the trick, he really didn't suppose anything could. And of course she knew now that Steeves was Aristotle, so why—?

He sat considering this until he felt a chill run down his spine, and then race up again, and when it hit the base of his skull he rose and walked over to the desk. "Look here," he said, "I want to put in a call to the police."

"Something wrong, sir?"

"Don't know but I want to call the police."

"This way, sir." The desk clerk led him into a private office and pointed to a telephone on the desk. "There you are, sir. Ring the operator and she'll connect you."

A moment later Cyrus was struggling to pronounce a name which he'd never seen spelled, and had only heard in passing. "A Lieutenant Dundu Bonozzi," he said. "Have to speak to him right away."

"Sorry sir, he's not here," said the man at the other end of the line.

"Could be a matter of life and death," Cyrus told him, feeling damnably awkward at saying such a thing. "Any way of contacting him?"

"He's at the Moses Msonthi School—guard detail, sir. You can leave a message and we'll try to get it to him if he phones in."

"Yes," said Cyrus, feeling this was reasonable and at the same time trying to think of a way to express his unease. "All right, let's try this one. Ready?"

"Ready, sir."

"Here we are: 'Are you certain you have the right Aristotle? Kleiber left hotel as black man, Mrs. Pollifax in pursuit.'"

"A very odd message, sir."

"Indeed it is," said Cyrus uncomfortably. "Look here, anybody else there I can speak to?" But even as he said this he realized how entangled he could become in trying to explain a European in blackface to a stranger; Dundu was the only person who would understand. "Never mind," he said, "what's the name of that school again?"

"The Moses Msonthi School, sir. Manchichi Road."

"Right. I'll look for him there."

He hurried out to the entrance to find that, perversely, there were no taxis now. He paced and fumed, considered the state of his blood pressure and consulted his watch: it was 12:40 and Farrell had said the dedication ceremonies began at one o'clock . . . When a taxi finally arrived it was 12:45 and he was too grateful to express his sense of aggrievement. He climbed in and directed the driver to the school.

"Oh yes, sir, yes, sir," the driver said with a big smile. "Our President opens the school today. Very nice, very beautiful school for girls."

"Yes . . . well, see if you can get me there fast," he told him, and tried to think of what he'd do when he reached the school. There'd be crowds, he supposed; a big event opening a new school, probably speeches, perhaps not, but certainly crowds. He hadn't the slightest idea how he'd find Dundu, or whether Emily would turn up there too. Perhaps by now she'd discovered the man was a bona fide Zambian, except that if it really was Kleiber . . . Better not think about that, he decided, and practiced taking deep breaths to remain calm. The streets were relatively empty of traffic since it was Sunday and the shops were closed, but as they neared Manchichi Road the traffic increased. Cyrus paid off the driver a block away from the school and set out to find Dundu Bwanausi, not even certain that he'd mastered the man's name yet.

Mrs. Pollifax sat on the edge of her seat watching the taxi ahead and contributing frequent comments to spur the driver on. "He's wanted by the police," she confided, feeling that some explanation was becoming necessary and hoping that what she said was true but hoping at the same time that it wasn't. "Not too close, driver, we mustn't be noticed. Have you any idea where they're heading?"

"We are very near Manchichi Road, madam, perhaps he goes to watch our President dedicate a school."

Oh God, she thought, and said aloud, "Do you mean the Moses Msonthi School?"

"Yes, madam. This is Manchichi Road we turn into now, and the taxi ahead is going to the school, see? It stops now."

She began fumbling in her purse for money. "I'll get out

now, I hope this is enough," she said, thrusting *kwacha* notes on him, and as he drew up to the curb she added, "But will you do something important for me, driver? Will you call the police and tell them—tell them Aristotle is at the Msonthi School? *Aristotle.*"

"Aristotle. Yes, madam." He gave her a curious glance.

She climbed out and gave him a long, earnest look. "I'm depending on you, I'm depending *desperately* on you."

"Yes, madam."

Up ahead she saw Mr. Kleiber strolling around the edge of the crowd looking for a place to enter it. She hurried toward him, mentally rehearsing what possible karate blow might fell him before he could shoot President Kaunda, because of course that had to be the only reason he was here in his masquerade, which meant that her instincts about John Steeves had proven sound after all, except that Steeves was now in prison and here was Aristotle still free, and no one knew . . .

It was frightening.

The sun was glittering, and shone on women in colorful blouses and skirts with babies slung over their shoulders, on barefooted children and men in overalls and in solemn Sunday best. A very neat avenue had been left clear for the President, she noticed. She saw Kleiber examine it and then, before she could reach him, he slipped into the crowd and vanished from sight.

Lieutenant Bwanausi was idling near a police car at the southern corner of the crowd, waiting to see his President, whose photograph hung on every wall of his small home. One of his friends passed and called out a greeting, and then came over and shook hands with him, asking how things went with him. Dundu thought back on his week's work, recalled how close an assassin had come to threatening the life of his President, and said that life went very well for him indeed. His friend strolled on, and hearing the crackle of static from the car radio behind him, Dundu reached for the microphone. "Bwanausi here."

At first he didn't understand what Soko was saying. "How

is this, your speaking the name Aristotle, Soko," he said. "Two messages?"

First, it seemed, there had been the message from a man at the Hotel Intercontinental, which Soko now read to him. "But Dundu," he protested, "I thought the man was drunk. Now a second call has come in from a taxi driver. He says he and a woman chased a taxi to Manchichi Road, and this woman pleaded with him to call us and say that Aristotle is at the school."

Dundu felt a spasm of fear. Was this possible? Could John Steeves not be Aristotle after all? Yet how could this be, given the evidence? "Man, this is bad news," he told Soko. "Is it too late to reach KK's party? Aristotle is the code name of the assassin we thought we jailed last night."

There was a stunned silence. "Oh God," said Soko. "I'll try, Dundu, I'll try."

"Do that, send out a—" He stopped as he heard the sirens. "Too late, the President's here, Soko." He dropped the microphone and began running . . .

Mrs. Pollifax pushed her way through the crowd trying to find Mr. Kleiber, but now in her panic everybody had begun to look like Mr. Kleiber and she couldn't distinguish one face from the next. She stopped and forced herself to be calm, and instead of elbowing her way deeper into the crowd she turned and pushed her way toward the avenue down which the President would walk. Reaching the front row, she thanked a man who had let her pass and leaned out to look down the avenue. One glance was enough: she saw the President climbing out of a limousine and shaking hands with a number of people grouped around the car. She turned her head and looked to her left and saw Kleiber standing in line only twenty feet away from her, one hand in his pocket, a faint smile on his lips, his face remote, almost dreaming. Mrs. Pollifax turned and began to struggle toward him.

Cyrus had given up trying to find Lieutenant Bwanausi. He had withdrawn to a playground behind the crowd and had climbed to the top of a convenient jungle gym, from which he could sit and keep an eye out for a familiar face. He held little hope of finding one now, and if he didn't he wondered if Emily would expect him to throw himself across the President's path. Probably, he thought, and hearing a sudden ripple of cheers from off to his right, he realized that it was one o'clock and that President Kaunda must have arrived and that he'd better do something. Before climbing down he took one last look at the knots and clusters of people on the fringe of the crowd, framed against the wall of heads beyond, and then he realized that for several minutes he'd been absently watching something—a red stick or a pennant—move determinedly from a point on his right toward an unknown point on his left. Staring at it intently now, his eyes narrowing, it stirred his memory.

Emily's feather, he thought in astonishment, and taking a quick fix on it he climbed down from his jungle gym and hurried to the edge of the crowd, entered it at some distance ahead of where he judged Emily to be, and alternately pushed and shoved his way inward. He was in luck: the first time he stopped to look for the feather he spotted it some twenty feet away. Assuming that Emily was under it, he moved forward to intercept her, and at that moment the crowd shifted and he saw her. He also saw, not far away from her, the back of a man wearing a charcoal pin-striped suit: Kleiber.

Emily had seen Kleiber too. She crept forward, the feather at a ridiculous slant now, and when she moved in beside the man, Cyrus, thrusting aside several small children to reach her, guessed what she was planning to do. She had just lifted her right hand when Kleiber turned his head and looked at her. Cyrus saw them exchange a long glance, and then he saw the gun in Kleiber's hand and he caught his breath, appalled. Slowly Kleiber lifted the gun and pointed it at Mrs. Pollifax, who froze, staring at him in astonishment.

Cyrus gasped, *"Not* karate, Emily—judo now." Memories of long-ago gymnasium classes came back to him, of a dreary evening spent in throwing and being thrown to the mat, and with only a fleeting thought to brittle bones, Cyrus hurled himself across the twelve feet of space that separated them. His shoulders met solid flesh, there was a crunch of bone meeting bone, several sharp cries, and he and Emily Pollifax, Willem Kleiber and two small boys fell to the ground together.

Only Dundu Bwanausi, racing to them from the opposite side, knew that five people had not been accidentally pushed to the ground by the crowd. He leaned over Kleiber with a grim face, pocketed the man's gun and snapped handcuffs on his wrists. He picked up the two crying children and dusted them off. He gave Cyrus a hand, and then he helped Mrs. Pollifax to her feet and carefully restored her hat to her. Only when he looked into her face did his expression change. He said softly, fervently, "Oh madam, *zikomo—zikomo kuambeia*, ten thousand times *zikomo* . . ."

But Cyrus, too, had something to say. "Damn it, Emily," he complained, "only way to keep an eye on you is marry you. Think we could find a quiet corner and talk about that?"

Chapter Sixteen

In Langley, Virginia, it was Monday morning and Carstairs, returning from an early conference Upstairs, was scowling.

"Something wrong?" asked Bishop, looking at him curiously. "Or wronger than usual?"

Carstairs poured himself a cup of coffee before answering. "Not really," he said, "except that my ego's suffered a small blow."

"Oh?"

Carstairs made a face. "You know I've never enjoyed being outmaneuvered by the British . . . Upstairs asked for a review of the Aristotle file this morning, and damned if Liaison didn't report that British Intelligence has a man on Aristotle's trail too."

Bishop began to understand. He said with a grin, "You mean one of Emily's safari companions was an M1 agent?"

Carstairs nodded. "Some travel writer or other. Seems a damned waste of talent."

Bishop chuckled. "Think he was taking snapshots too?" He had a sudden vivid picture of Mrs. Pollifax and a British agent swarming over the safari with their cameras.

"It's no longer important," Carstairs said, shrugging. "The safari ended Saturday and we'll soon have Mrs. Pollifax's photographs, and we can pool the results with London and Interpol. The pictures are what matter, although I'm certainly hoping she'll bring us Farrell as a dividend. I wonder if they've had their reunion yet . . ."

"As a matter of fact they have, sir."

Carstairs put down his cup of coffee and stared. "You've heard from her?"

"No," said Bishop, "but this cable arrived from Zambia while you were in conference. It's from John Sebastian himself, no less, datelined 2 P.M. yesterday Zambian time."

Carstairs brightened. "Marvelous! Is he coming back to us?"

"No," said Bishop, and read aloud:

SORRY CHAPS BOOKED SOLID FOR NEXT FEW YEARS STOP SUGGEST YOU BOOK EMILY HOWEVER BEFORE CYRUS BEATS YOU TO IT STOP DELIGHTED TO FIND DUCHESS STILL INDESTRUCTIBLE ALTHOUGH NOT FOR WANT OF TRYING STOP RETURNING HER TO YOU ONLY SLIGHTLY BRUISED WITH LOVE AND KISSES FARRELL.

"Now what," said Carstairs, "is that all about?"

"I suspect he'd been drinking, sir," said Bishop, and tossed the cable into the wastebasket.

Mrs. Pollifax on
the China Station

With special thanks to David Ownby, China guide,
for sharing his knowledge of the country, and for his
translations and advice.

Chapter One

Mrs. Pollifax sat in Carstairs' office with a cup of coffee in one hand and a sandwich in the other, her hat an inverted bowl of blue felt with such a cockeyed twist to its brim that Bishop guessed it had been frequently sat on and squashed. He saw her glance at Carstairs, seated behind his desk, and then at him, and now she said gently, "Yes, the weather's been unseasonably cool for May, and my trip to Langley Field very pleasant, we've discussed my geraniums and how I met Cyrus Reed in Zambia, but I really do think—"

Bishop put down his own coffee cup and grinned. He thought this must be how she appeared to her garden clubs—a cheerful, cozy little woman with fly-away white hair and a penchant for odd hats and growing geraniums—and he thought it a pity he couldn't share with those garden clubs his first meeting with her in this office, just after she'd led an escape party out of Albania against incredible odds, and had been whisked back to this country by jet. She had sat in this same chair, wearing the voluminous clothes of a goat-herder's wife, her face as dark as a gypsy's after three days adrift in the Adriatic, and what she'd accomplished had staggered them all. He sometimes felt it was impossible to reconcile these two Emily Pollifaxes; his grin deepened as he said, "You're suggesting we dispense with pleasantries and get on with it?"

"Well," she pointed out, "it's difficult to believe you've

brought me here to discuss the weather. *Really* difficult," she added with a twinkle, "considering that you sent a private plane for me, which I must say was dashing of you."

"We do try to be dashing when we can," Bishop told her gravely. "It counteracts the soiled trench-coat image that—" He stopped, remembering Mrs. Pollifax's reproachful telephone calls to him when a scandal about the CIA surfaced. *But that wasn't our department,* he would tell her, and point out that he really couldn't relay her indignation to the White House. He supposed that it was this quality in her that led Carstairs to brief her more carefully than he did his other agents, but her responses were never more surprising to Bishop than the fruit cakes she sent at Christmas, which usually incapacitated the entire department, their brandy fumes lingering almost as long as the hangovers.

Suddenly he remembered why Mrs. Pollifax was here, and what Carstairs was going to propose to her, and he felt that old clutch of horror that always hit him when she sat innocently on the edge of her chair, all eagerness and delight at a new assignment, and always chiding him for his concern. It was rather like an attack of violent indigestion, and he wondered if Carstairs was feeling it too; if so, he gave no evidence of it. Not yet at least. He would eventually, of course; he always did.

"The job we have in mind," Carstairs began smoothly, "is innocuous enough on the surface, Mrs. Pollifax, but because of the country involved could be extremely dangerous—extremely—if you came under suspicion." He gazed at her thoughtfully. "Which is why I wanted you here personally, to make sure you understand this, and to ask whether you still feel—are still interested—"

"What country?" she promptly asked.

"The People's Republic of China."

She drew in her breath sharply. "But how incredibly exciting," she breathed, "and what an amazing coincidence! I've been so curious, so interested—"

"Extremely dangerous," Bishop heard himself say firmly.

Her eyes widened. "But you say that about all the assignments," she told him, "and surely we're friends with China now?"

"Exactly," Carstairs said lightly, "which makes it all the more shocking if any suspicions should be aroused. But we have some business there that simply can't be handled through diplomatic channels, and we've decided to chance it."

"Chance what?" asked Mrs. Pollifax cheerfully.

"Roughly speaking," he said, "we want to get a man *out* of China, but to do this we must first get a man *into* China—an agent, of course—to accomplish this. Your job, if you take this on, would be to provide cover for this agent, and at a certain point approach a certain native—*not* an agent—who's known to have some helpful information."

Mrs. Pollifax said warmly, "Well, that sounds easy enough to—"

Bishop interrupted her. "Of course it sounds easy and innocuous," he said indignantly, "because he hasn't mentioned that in making this contact in Xian you become absolutely expendable—all to guard the identity of someone else—and that this man in Xian, who is *not* an agent, could just as easily turn you over to the People's Security Bureau, for all we know about him."

Carstairs looked at him incredulously; in an icy voice he said, "My dear Bishop, all our people become expendable when they take on a job, you know that and so does Mrs. Pollifax. I've already told her it's dangerous." He turned back to her and said stiffly, "Bishop is right, of course, and you *would* be risking exposure at that point, but to this I would add that it's of value to us that you do not speak Chinese, and would not speak it either in your sleep or under drugs; that you've endured interrogations before, and have shown a remarkable ability to sustain the role of Aggrieved and Misunderstood Tourist. I have every hope that such talents wouldn't be needed, of course, but still—despite Bishop's inexplicable attack of sentiment," he said, giving him a quelling glance, "he is perfectly right."

"Sorry, sir," Bishop said lamely. "It's just that—"

"Yes," said Mrs. Pollifax, and drew a deep breath. "You've made it quite clear, I think—both of you—but of course I'd love to go. As soon as you said China—"

Damn, thought Bishop, *she's going to go: Carstairs' blood*

pressure will be up for days, and I'll have to resort to tranquil-
izers. This is always what happens after she goes because all
hell usually breaks loose around this woman and we have to
sit here in Langley Field, Virginia, and worry about her. How
could we have forgotten this?

"Good—we did hope you'd take this on for us," Carstairs
was saying heartily, "because I can't think of anyone who
would provide a better aura of—well, respectability, but at the
same time be resourceful enough to make a contact that is *not*
going to be easy. You can leave in ten days, on June first?"

Mrs. Pollifax smiled. "You once gave me exactly one hour's
notice. Yes, I can leave in ten days."

"And Cyrus Reed," put in Carstairs. "I hear that it's turned
into quite a romance between you two, and that you've been
seeing a great deal of each other since you met. Will he object
to your doing another job for us?"

"Cyrus," she said, neatly fielding both comment and question, "is in Africa until June sixth. He left last week to visit his
daughter. The daughter," she reminded them, "who was on
safari with us last summer and met and married a doctor
there."

Both of them nodded. In any case, thought Bishop, the question had been a mere courtesy; both he and Carstairs knew
very well that Cyrus was safely out of the country and could
make no objections.

"But what is it," asked Mrs. Pollifax, "that you do have in
mind?"

"We'll get to it, shall we?" said Carstairs, and left his desk,
moving to the opposite wall where he pulled down a large map
of the People's Republic of China. "Our particular problem, as
I said," he began pleasantly, "is that it's almost as impossible
to get an agent into the country as it is to get someone out.
Especially since the man we want to rescue—let's call him X
for the moment, shall we?—is in a rather inaccessible area.
Actually," he added casually, "in a labor camp."

"Labor camp!" exclaimed Mrs. Pollifax.

"Labor *reform* camp, and roughly in this area." Picking up a
pencil he described a circle that enclosed a startling number of
miles in the northwest corner, a region colored yellow-brown

on the map, denoting desert and other inhospitable possibilities, with only the names of a few cities or towns interrupting
the space.

"But that's a great deal of country," pointed out Mrs. Pollifax, taken aback. "And you don't know exactly where?"

"Not precisely, no," said Carstairs. "That's what we hope
you'll find out from the man you contact in Xian, who spent
several years in that same labor reform camp. His name, by
the way, is Guo Musu. He's a Buddhist, and they suffered
rather extravagantly during the Cultural Revolution. Many of
their temples and monasteries were taken over or destroyed,
and the monks sent off to communes or labor camps, where in
either case they were given massive doses of Mao's thinking
. . . gems such as book learning can never be considered genuine knowledge, and how heroic it is to give oneself totally to
one's Motherland—and of course to Mao. Because of this we
hope he'll prove sympathetic enough to pinpoint the location
of that camp for you."

"He's a barber now," put in Bishop.

Carstairs nodded. "Yes, in Xian. He also speaks enough English to communicate," he added parenthetically. "We gleaned
this information from his brother, who fled China for Hong
Kong, where refugees from the mainland are habitually ques-
tioned. It's the right camp—Ching Ho Forestry Camp—which
means Clear Stream in English. They have a penchant for giving camps and prisons delightful names," he said dryly. "And
contacting Guo Musu will be your job."

"I see," said Mrs. Pollifax, looking dazed. "But if Mr. Guo
chooses not to pinpoint the location, or can't be found in
Xian?"

"We're not entertaining thoughts of failure," Carstairs told
her firmly. "This Mr. X has got to be found and brought out
before the Russians get to him."

"Russians!" exclaimed Mrs. Pollifax.

"Yes." Leaning against the corner of his desk he said, "One
of our agents who works for the Soviets—a double-agent,
needless to say—has brought us information of X's existence
and of the Soviets' interest in him. Before summer's end the

Russians will be mounting a major undercover operation to
get this chap out of China, too."

"But—one may ask why?"

"Because our friend X knows a great deal about China's
fortifications along the Russian border," Carstairs said. "In
fact, he designed a good share of them—the below-ground sections added in the late sixties and early seventies, at least. By
our good fortune no one in the government has remembered
him yet. Apparently somewhere along the way, through some
error in the records or through being mistaken for a prisoner
who died, our Mr. X has acquired the name and identity of
another man. I don't want to confuse you with names, but if I
tell you that X's true and proper name is Wang Shen, and that
his current name is Wong Shen, then you can share speculations on what happened."

Mrs. Pollifax nodded. "I see . . . He's an engineer, then.
But how did he end up in a labor camp?"

"That we don't know," Carstairs said. "Some indiscretion
or other, a confidence shared with the wrong person, a banned
book seen in his possession—it scarcely matters; it happened
to so many people during Mao's time." He nodded toward the
map. "What matters is this seven hundred miles of shared
border between the two countries, between Russia—her for-
mer mentor and big brother, now an uneasy and threatening
neighbor—and China, struggling to assert her rightful position
in the world. It's worth a great deal to the Soviets to learn in
precise detail what booby traps face them along that frontier—
and no one in China realizes that Wang Shen, with all that
information in his head, is still alive."

"Astonishing," said Mrs. Pollifax, blinking at this.

"It's especially important to prevent Wang from falling into
the Russians' hands," went on Carstairs. "We could, of course,
notify the Chinese of the Russians' interest in the man, but
frankly we're not sure what the government would do about
it. He is presumably listed as a counterrevolutionary, a revisionist, a capitalist-roader, or some such, or he wouldn't be in
a labor reform camp. He's also thousands of miles from Peking, in a country still heavily weighted with Mao bureau-

crats. Someone just might decide that killing him would be the simplest solution."

Mrs. Pollifax, considering this, could see his point.

"And," he continued, with a faint smile, "lest you think we're being altruistic here, we'd be delighted to have a chat with Mr. Wang ourselves in the interest of preserving the balance of power on this fragile planet." He sighed. "Very touchy thing, that border. Our satellite photos can't tell us very much because so many of China's defenses are underground. The Chinese military can be charmingly frank about being years behind in defense, but they can also be charmingly vague about what they have over there to hold Russia back—other than a billion people, underground shelters, and anti-aircraft on every hill, of course."

"I begin to understand," said Mrs. Pollifax dryly.

"Yes. A great deal depends on China's being strong enough to keep the Russians in check. Since *we'd* never attack through Russia, it's obviously a matter of reassurance for us, but there's also the fact that if Wang is valuable enough for the Russians to want we'd like to take a whack at getting him ourselves."

"But with difficulty," she pointed out.

"Good Lord, yes. Travel in China is very circumscribed. China watchers we have, and compilers of statistics, and news from any Chinese who leave by way of Canton for Hong Kong," he explained, "but our Embassy people in Beijing—the new name for Peking—are still pretty much confined there, except for carefully arranged inspections of communes and factories. The country is *extremely* security conscious. The Chinese themselves can't travel at all unless they're given special permission by their units—which, when you come to think of it," he said thoughtfully, "is a damn clever way of keeping track of a billion people."

Mrs. Pollifax, frowning, said, "Then how—?"

He nodded. "Exactly. What we're up against here is China's hinterland—Xinjiang Uygur Autonomous Region, thousands of miles from any official points of entry. High mountains. Desert land that's being reclaimed by irrigation. A region of minority peoples, and X—Mr. Wang—hidden somewhere in the middle of it. Remote, to say the least.''

"To say the least," murmured Mrs. Pollifax, startled.

"However, the area *is* being visited by occasional tourists now, looking for the unusual and the offbeat—always, of course, led by a China Travel Service guide, but nevertheless a pleasant way to reach the area.''

"Ah," murmured Mrs. Pollifax, leaning forward now attentively.

"It's too risky, sending you and another agent together, just the two of you, with a guide. What we're putting together for June first is a small group of what are known in the tourist-agency trade as 'wait list' people. Markham Tours here is cooperating without knowing the real reason. 'Wait list' people are those who signed up too late with Markham Tours, and have been placed on a waiting list, and would be willing to forego an American tour guide with the group in order to go there. Bishop, the brochure.''

Bishop stoically handed Mrs. Pollifax the glossy colorful booklet whose words he already knew by heart . . . an extraordinary tour of Marco Polo's Silk Road presented only by Markham Tours . . . archaeological sites, among them the Yunkang Caves of Datong, the Imperial Tomb in Xian of Qin Shi Huang . . .

"The Imperial Tomb of Qin Shi Huang?" gasped Mrs. Pollifax, scanning the first page. "But I've read about that—all those life-sized terra-cotta warriors and horses they found! How thrilling—and the Silk Road, too?"

"Yes," said Carstairs. "Miss Markham was one of the first to visit China when it opened up, and to arrange for visitors. This won't be one of their regular tours, but they'll make the arrangements and use their considerable connections to make sure it's a bona fide sight-seeing experience for you all. What they *can't* provide at such short notice, however, is one of their own American guides to accompany you, so you'll be in the hands of a native guide, which may or may not be limiting, depending on his or her command of English.''

And which, added Bishop silently, *is not at all accidental, my dear Mrs. Pollifax, no matter how contrite and apologetic Carstairs may sound.*

"I see," she said, and was silent, thinking about all that he'd said. "What occurs to me—"

"Yes?"

"What I don't understand—seeing that you're sending in an agent to find Mr. X, or Wang—is how that person will be able to smuggle Mr. X out of China and—"

"That," intervened Carstairs smoothly, "will be *our* problem."

"—and also," she added relentlessly, "how that agent will have any freedom of movement to even contact Mr. X, or Wang, especially traveling in a group and under the eyes of a government guide."

Good for you, Emily, thought Bishop, *you're getting close to the heart of the matter which is exactly why I'm having chills.* He waited patiently for Carstairs to field this with his usual tact.

"That will also be our problem," Carstairs said silkily. "It's much safer if you know nothing about it, not even which member of your party will be the agent."

Caught off balance by this, Mrs. Pollifax gasped. "Not even who—!"

"Not until you've contacted our Buddhist chap Guo Musu in Xian," he told her firmly. "Believe me, it will be best for both of you. After all, it will be a very small tour group," he said, "and we want you to treat everyone openly and equally. After you've visited the Drum Tower in Xian—Guo's barbershop is in its shadow—your coagent will contact *you.*"

Bishop watched her struggle with this, and then he turned his head and glanced at Carstairs and saw that his face had suddenly tightened. Bishop guessed what he was thinking; a moment later Carstairs proved it by saying in a surprisingly harsh voice, "There's one other instruction for you, Mrs. Pollifax. If anything unusual happens on this trip—*no matter what*—I expect you to get that tour group the hell out of the country, you understand?"

Mrs. Pollifax smiled. "Which means, of course, that you're expecting something unusual to take place?"

Carstairs gave her an unforgiving glance that was totally unlike him, and when he spoke again his voice was cool. "On the contrary, we trust it will be happily uneventful, and I believe that will be all for now, Mrs. Pollifax. Bishop can fill you in on the missing details and give you a visa application to fill out, and for this perhaps you wouldn't mind waiting out in his office for him? In the meantime we're delighted, of course, that you're taking this on."

He didn't look at all delighted; he looked rather like a man who had just swallowed a fish bone and was going to choke on it, and deep inside of him Bishop chuckled: it had finally happened, he had simply underestimated the time it would take for Carstairs to realize all the things that could go wrong, and how devilishly fond he was of Mrs. Pollifax. *Ah well,* thought Bishop cheerfully, *I've already passed through it and been inoculated, I'll just have to shore him up.*

Watching Mrs. Pollifax leave the office he waited for the door to close behind her and then he moved to a panel on the right wall with a mirror set into it. "You can come out now," he told the man who had been listening and observing from the other side.

The man who walked out to join them looked furious. "Good God," he said, "you're sending *her?* I've nothing against the woman personally, but if that's who you're sending with me into China—"

"The perfect reaction," Bishop told him imperturbably. "Do sit down and let us tell you about Mrs. Pollifax—bearing in mind, I hope, that your reactions are exactly the same that we trust China's security people will experience, too." . . .

Mrs. Pollifax, returning to New Jersey, felt that her cup was running over. It had been startling enough to fly off that morning from Teterboro in a small private plane—how surprised her neighbors would be to know of that!—but this adventure paled now beside the fact that she was actually going to visit China. She was remembering the loving report on China that she'd written in fifth grade, and the triumph of the jacket she'd given it: gold chopstick letters on dark green construction paper. Land of Pearl Buck, too, she thought dreamily—how many times had she seen the film *The Good Earth?*—and of Judge Dee mystery novels, emperors and empresses and palaces and Marco Polo and silk. They all swam together happily in her mind.

But what felt the most amazing coincidence of all was the class in Chinese art that she'd taken during the past winter; it was true that she still had a tendency to confuse the Shang, Zhou, Han, Tang, and Sung dynasties, but the professor had so frequently referred to treasures destroyed during Mao's Cultural Revolution that she had looked up a great many things about modern China as well, accumulating names like The Long March, The Great Leap Forward, the Hundred Flowers, the Cultural Revolution—which certainly appeared to be anything but kind to culture—and the Lin-Confucius Campaign. Now she was going to see China for herself, which only proved how astonishing life could be.

She happily overtipped the cab driver, and reaching the seclusion of her apartment tossed coat and hat to the couch, adjusted the curtains to give her geraniums the last of the day's sunshine, and put water on to boil for tea. Only then did she spread out the brochures and maps and *Hints to Travelers* that Bishop had given her, but it was his page of notes that interested her the most: there was the name Guo Musu to be memorized, and a tourist's map of Xian cut out of a brochure, with an X penciled in near the Drum Tower—but what, she wondered, did a Chinese barbershop look like?—and there was also a tentative list of the people who would accompany her, subject to change, Bishop had told her. She eyed these speculatively:

Peter Fox/Connecticut
Malcolm Styles/New York
Jennifer A. Lobsen/Indiana
George Westrum/Texas

Next she carefully read her travel schedule: New York to San Francisco; San Francisco to Hong Kong; overnight in Hong Kong with instructions to meet the rest of the party the next morning in the hotel's breakfast room before departure by

train for Mainland China. The itinerary: Canton, Xian, Urumchi, Lanzhou, Inner Mongolia, Datong, Taiyuan, Peking; departure from Peking for Tokyo and thence back to New York,
arriving four weeks later.

While her peppermint tea steeped in its china pot she put
the notes aside and glanced through the photographs in the
brochure, fervently wishing she could pick up the telephone
and share her excitement with Cyrus. This was very selfish of
her, she admitted, because she knew that he must have been
bracing himself for just this occasion. How strange it was, she
mused, that Cyrus knew what even her son and her daughter
didn't know: the reasons behind her small travels, the risks
she met, and thinking about this she decided that in her next
letter to him in Zambia she would not mention China at all;
instead she'd write a separate letter that would be waiting for
him on his return. This would spare him at least one or two
weeks of worry—and he *would* worry, she conceded; he would
know at once why she was going, and there was no way to
reassure him that it was a routine assignment. "Routine?" she
could hear him say. "Went to Zambia on a routine assignment, didn't you, Emily? Just to take pictures, stay out of
trouble? All hell broke loose, nearly got killed, both of us, and
caught an assassin. Don't mention routine to me, m'dear."

And of course at the back of her mind, not ready for admit-
tance yet, lurked an awareness of the tension she had sensed
in Bishop. She thought now, uneasily, *He knows much more
than I've been told; he really hoped I'd say no.*

Lifting her eyes she glanced around at her safe, familiar
apartment—at the sunlight striping the worn oriental rug, the
books lining one wall, the tubs of geraniums at the window—
and she remembered the number of times she'd left it without
knowing what lay ahead of her, or if she would ever see it
again. She said aloud, "Yet I'm here. Very definitely still here.
Somehow." One had to have faith, she reminded herself, and
on impulse left the brochures and walked over to her desk and
removed from one of its drawers a collection of envelopes
bearing colorful and exotic stamps. *Maybe I keep them for just
such a moment,* she thought, knowing their contents by heart:
a recent letter from her dear friend John Sebastian Farrell in

Africa; a birth announcement from Colin and Sabbahat Ramsey in Turkey; a holiday message from the King of Zabya with a note from his son Hafez, and Christmas cards from Robin and Court Bourke-Jones, from the Trendafilovs, from Magda and Sir Hubert, all of them people she'd met on her adventures.

Last of all she drew out a soiled and wrinkled postcard that had reached her just last year, a card addressed to Mrs. Emily Pollifax, New Brunswick, New Jersey, the United States of America—no street address, no zip code—so that only a very enterprising postman had rescued it for her. On one side was the picture of a castle; on the opposite side the words: *You remain here still with me, Amerikanski. I do not forget. Tsanko.**

Yes, she thought softly, her life had become very rich since that day she found it so purposeless that she had tried to give it away. So many new experiences and so many new friends . . .

With a glance at the clock she put away the collection of cards and letters, and carrying her cup of tea into the bedroom she quickly changed into slacks and a shirt. An hour later she was in a back room at police headquarters, wearing her brown karate belt and making obeisances to retired police lieutenant Lorvale Brown before advanced instructions began. Presently shouts of *hi-yah* filled the air because Lorvale believed in attacking with sudden blood-curdling shouts as well as a slice of the hand.

The next day Bishop called and told her to add two more names to the tour group, that of Iris Damson of Oklahoma, and Joseph P. Forbes from Illinois.

"Is he my coagent?" she blithely inquired. "Or she?"

He said with equal cheerfulness, "I'm told it's raining today in Hong Kong."

"Then may I ask instead—now that I've had more time to go over the list you gave me—why I'm to carry with me four pounds of chocolate, two pairs of thermal socks, and such an incredible supply of vitamin pills and dried fruits?"

---

* *The Elusive Mrs. Pollifax*

"It's just a sneaky way to keep you from taking too many clothes," he told her. "Now don't you think you've asked enough questions?"

"Obviously," she said, and rang off.

During the next nine days Mrs. Pollifax addressed her Garden Club on The Care and Feeding of Geraniums, including their propagation from seed, studied maps and old *National Geographics*, bought a simple Chinese phrase book for the traveler, and began taking malaria tablets. She invested in a rough straw hat with a swashbuckling brim, notified children and friends of her departure, wrote several newsy letters to Cyrus in Africa, and a separate one to his home in Connecticut explaining that she was off to the Orient to do a very small job—nothing worrisome at all—for Carstairs. And on June first she flew off to Hong Kong for her great adventure—in China.

Chapter Two

Mrs. Pollifax picked up a spoon from the dazzling white tablecloth and beamed at the waiter who was filling her coffee cup. "Thank you," she said, glancing down at a plate that she had heaped with papaya and watermelon from the buffet, and as he left she thought happily, *It's begun, I'm here—and in only a few more hours I'll be entering China.*

She had arrived in Hong Kong the night before, after what seemed like days of travel, and her first glimpse of the Orient had been deeply satisfying. The plane had begun its descent over a fairyland harbor of boats outlined in delicate-colored lights; the shapes of mountains had drifted past the window, now and then exposing clusters of tiny white lights at their base—villages, presumably—before the harbor suddenly reappeared, enchantingly toylike from the sky. There had been a young woman to meet her at the Kai Tak air terminal, and this had also been a pleasant surprise: a representative of Markham Tours who introduced herself as Miss Chu, efficiently bundled both her and her suitcase into a car, and told her that she would personally appear in the hotel lobby at eleven the next morning to introduce them all to Mr. Li, their China Travel Service guide. It had been very soothing to be under the protective wing of Markham Tours because Mrs. Pollifax's major concern had been to find a bed and sleep in it for as long as possible. Two nights in the air—her body did not yield itself happily to plane seats—had reduced her senses to a state of numbness; after flying across the United States, and then across the Pacific, she felt that nothing could excite her except bed.

It was different this morning after ten hours of sleep; she looked upon the exotic scene around her with eager interest: at the fresh flowers encircling the hotel's buffet, at the refreshingly novel Asian faces. But there was one English or American face among them: she found herself exchanging glances with a sullen-looking young man of college age seated alone at a table nearby. The fact that he did not return her smile but only glowered back at her did not dismay her at all. She felt that she loved everyone this morning, even Sullen Young Men; a recovery from exhaustion tended to have this effect upon her.

Seeing that it was nearly eight o'clock she removed from her pocket the red, white, and blue ribbon that Miss Chu had given her last night, and pinned it to the collar of her shirt for identification purposes. This action appeared to catch the eye of a bearded, stocky man just entering the restaurant, and he changed his course to head for her table against the wall.

"Good morning," he said, arriving beside her to extend his hand. "Glad to see I'm not the first—my name's Joe Forbes."

It was on the tip of her tongue to blurt out, ah yes, the newcomer to the list, but she bit back her words just in time. "How do you do, and I'm Emily Pollifax," she said, smiling up at him as she clasped the proffered hand.

He certainly seemed likable: the two most noticeable features about him were his bristling beard and an amiable air of being at ease. He was strongly built, not tall but very fit, with a pleasant face. The brown beard was neatly trimmed and flecked with gray. His receding brown hair gave him a high forehead with only a few frown lines etched between the brows. He looked about forty, a seasoned traveler, dressed casually in a black turtleneck under a brown zip-up jacket, and corduroys and work boots. He placed a small duffle bag and a Chinese-American dictionary on a chair beside her, and with a nod at the book and a sleepy smile explained, "I'm learning Mandarin. You'll take care of these for me?"

"Of course," she told him, and watched him stroll toward the buffet, feeling very pleased about this Joseph Forbes who had made such a late appearance on the tour list, and who looked very capable and reassuring if he should turn out to be her coagent. She realized, too, that she'd forgotten the thrill of being out in the world—how small and insulated her corner of New Jersey looked from Hong Kong, crossroad of the Orient! She took another bite of papaya and:

"Oh!" cried a voice beside her. "I've found you! I'm Iris Damson!"

Startled, Mrs. Pollifax turned and looked up at the woman standing over her—looked up and smiled, and there was something about Iris Damson to make anyone's smile especially warm. She was tall and lanky and awkward, in her early thirties, perhaps, with a great deal of shoulder-length brown hair which, in spite of being tucked behind her ears, kept falling forward which led to still more awkward gestures as she pushed it back. Her clothes—*oh dear*, thought Mrs. Pollifax, *how totally and horribly wrong for her:* a fussy summer cocktail dress with huge white polka dots on black cotton and everything she wore shiny-new, right down to the brilliant white purse that she clutched in one hand. Yet there was something oddly endearing about the effect. *She looks as if she's arrived at a party*, thought Mrs. Pollifax. Her face was thin, with both the jaw and nose a shade too long, but her smile was radiant and exuded joy at being here, at having found Mrs. Pollifax, at having found Hong Kong; it was like being struck by a bolt of sunshine.

"I'm delighted to meet you and I'm Emily Pollifax," she told Iris warmly.

Iris Damson found the edge of a chair and perched on it, then abruptly jumped up, gasping, "It's buffet? Oh, I didn't notice." Snatching up her purse she swept a drinking glass to the floor, turned scarlet, and immediately disappeared under the table.

Before Mrs. Pollifax could rush to her aid or soothe her she became aware that someone else had stopped beside the table, and half out of her chair she looked up to find a tall, suave man at her elbow. "Oh," she gasped, feeling that Iris's confusion had become infectious. "How do you do, are you one of us, too?"

At that same moment Iris' head appeared above the snowy white tablecloth and the man, startled, said in an amused voice, "Well, hello—have you been there long?"

Iris Damson unwound herself to her full height, which nearly equaled the man's, extended a thin arm, fervently shook his hand, gasped, "It's *buffet*," and fled.

The man calmly sat down next to Mrs. Pollifax, his calmness a welcome antidote. "I'm Malcolm Styles," he told her, "and you?"

"Emily Pollifax."

"Thank you. And the young woman who—er—jumps out from under tables?"

Mrs. Pollifax smiled. "That was Iris Damson, pursuing a water glass."

A waiter appeared at his elbow, saying, "Coffee, sir?"

"Love some," he said, and as the waiter left he lifted the cup to his lips and over its rim gave Mrs. Pollifax the same frank appraisal that she was giving him.

She reflected that he was precisely the sort of man that a waiter *would* hurry to wait on, her own coffee having arrived much later, and without any sense of betrayal she put aside Joe Forbes and substituted Malcolm Styles because she thought that if Malcolm Styles was not a spy, he ought to be. He looked like a male model, or the star of any Hollywood spy film, or at the very least the head of some spectacularly successful computer firm. It was not just the flawlessly cut business suit, it was that thick black guardsman's moustache and the quizzical dark eyes that also, she realized, looked extraordinarily kind. One brow was tilting up a little now as he looked at her with amusement, while the moustache followed the tilt very becomingly—oh, charming indeed—as he smiled. If she herself had unnerved Iris, thought Mrs. Pollifax, then Malcolm Styles was surely going to chronically shatter Iris's poise. She smiled back at him, genuinely liking him for the kindness in his eyes.

"Finished inspection?" he asked, amused.

She laughed. "A very thorough one, wasn't it? I think you're very elegant."

His smile deepened. "Presently I'll be wearing a very red noisy sport shirt—"

In which, thought Mrs. Pollifax, *you will look equally distinguished, let us not kid ourselves.*

"—because I've only flown in this morning after a business stopover in Tokyo. And now if breakfast is buffet—as I have been told in no uncertain terms," he said dryly, "I hope you'll excuse me?"

"Yes, of course," she told him, and watched him stroll toward the buffet, pick up a tray and manage to look both friendly and unapproachable at the same time. She wondered who would appear next, thinking how much like the first act of a play this was becoming, with each person arriving singly, and on cue. She looked up from her coffee to see a young girl approaching with a red, white, and blue ribbon pinned to her collar, but her analogy was upset when the girl turned and spoke to the older man behind her. *Not* singly, amended Mrs. Pollifax, and waited.

"Are you China?" the girl asked, coming to her table and pointing to her identical ribbon. She had a pert young face, very friendly and gamine, almost overwhelmed by huge round glasses that made her face look even smaller; her upper lip was *retroussée,* not quite meeting the lower one and exposing square white teeth. She wore a purple shirt and pink cotton skirt that emphasized her dark hair and fresh complexion. "I'm Jenny," she said. "Jenny Lobsen." Glancing over her shoulder she added, "And this is George Westrum."

Mrs. Pollifax stood up to shake hands this time. "Hello to both of you. You're traveling together?"

Jenny laughed and vigorously shook her head. "Oh no, we spotted each other's ribbons in the lobby at six o'clock this morning, I guess we're both still on San Francisco time. So we went walking. It was great—we saw people practicing Tai Chi in the park."

Mrs. Pollifax extended her hand to George Westrum, amused by the difference in temperament between him and

Jenny. Although he wore a boyish cap tilted back on his head, George Westrum was a very dour-looking man in his fifties. His face was taciturn and weathered, with a tight mouth that looked like a purse snapped shut forever, yet as he gripped her hand and looked squarely at her Mrs. Pollifax swore that she saw a twinkle in the man's eye.

"Just George will do," he said.

A twinkle, a baseball cap, and a tight mouth—very interesting, she thought. "I'm Emily Pollifax," she told them, and mentally running over Bishop's list she added, "And now we're all here except for one person."

At that moment she became aware that Sullen Young Man from the nearby table had risen and was strolling toward them, still looking as if he preferred to be elsewhere, and also rather out of place in his ancient faded jeans and jogging shoes. Reaching them he said, "I've had my breakfast and I'm just leaving—I'm Peter Fox." He looked at each of them one by one, nodded, added, "See you later," and before anyone could speak he walked out of the breakfast room.

So much for him, thought Mrs. Pollifax, startled, as she gazed after him. She wondered whether his hostility was going to infect and effect the others; she thought, too, how unfriendly it was of him to have sat nearby for so long, watching but without declaring himself.

But there was research to be done on all of them, she remembered, and with a glance at her watch she excused herself, secure in the knowledge that at least she had met her six tour companions, however superficially. At the top of her research list, however, she now placed Peter Fox. Assignment aside, she found that she was intensely curious as to what had brought him here, and apparently so unwillingly.

Huge crowds surrounded the railway station, encircling it in lines ten deep until it looked, said George Westrum, exactly like a baseball stadium at World Series time besieged by eager fans. With Miss Chu and Mr. Li to run interference, they made their way through line after line to a smaller queue inside the building, where they waited with families gripping small portable fans in one hand and food packages in string bags in the other: visitors to Canton, bearing gifts to relatives.

"This must be first class," murmured George Westrum, standing just behind her.

"In a classless society?" said Mrs. Pollifax in amazement.

Again she surprised that twinkle. "It's a matter of semantics," he said. "They call them soft seats, as against the hard seats for the masses out there."

"You've visited China before, then?"

"I read a lot," he said simply.

She smiled at him. "And what do you think of our newly met China guide?"

"Mr. Li? Young and very organized," he said. "Put him in Western clothes and he'd be a junior executive anywhere. IBM, probably."

She laughed. In spite of Mr. Li's modest attire it was exactly that executive quality, with its sense of coiled energy, that had first struck her on meeting him, too. Or perhaps his attire wasn't modest at all, she thought, as she glanced around and compared him with the other Chinese waiting in line, for his sandals were of leather, not plastic; she had already glimpsed black silk socks with tiny clocks on them, and he wore a digital watch on his wrist. She only wished that she could be more confident about his English, which was spoken with enthusiasm at a reckless speed and with an explosive laugh at the end of each statement.

The crowd suddenly began to move and they achieved the train at last, said good-bye to Miss Chu, and climbed aboard the appointed car that would take them across the Lo Wu bridge into Mainland China. Mrs. Pollifax, entering the car last of all, chose to sit next to Peter Fox, from whom she received a swift, bored glance. Paying this no attention she gazed around in awe at the starched lace curtains at each window of the railway car, and the pale blue decor. Everything was immaculate; in fact no sooner were they all seated than a young woman hurried out from some inner sanctum to run a damp floor mop up and down the aisle and erase every hint of traffic. Music began; a small TV screen over the door sprang to life and as the train began to move, so did figures on the screen: a happy smiling young woman sang a Chinese song in a strident singsong voice; a handsome young man joined her and with large gestures and an even happier smile reinforced the suggestion of total bliss in Mainland China. Mrs. Pollifax watched in fascination, and then her attention moved past Peter Fox's impassive profile to the lush green countryside sliding past the window.

Eventually the stoniness of that profile challenged her. "Excited?" she asked Peter Fox, not without irony.

He turned and gave her a measuring glance. "Half and half," he said with a shrug.

Being direct by nature she refused such tiresome ambiguousness. "What made you come, then?" she asked. "What made you choose China?"

"I didn't," he said.

Mrs. Pollifax began to feel amused by this conversation. "I thought you seemed a little martyred," she said, warming to the game. "Of course my next question—naturally—is just why and what—"

But apparently he was not playing games. "I didn't mean to seem martyred," he said, with deadly seriousness and a scowl. "It's just I'm still making up my mind whether I'll like it. It's a college graduation present from my grandmother."

"Ah," said Mrs. Pollifax. "It was her idea then, China?"

He nodded. "She was born here—spent the first thirteen years of her life in China, so China it had to be."

"For you but not for *her?*"

He said with a shrug, "Well, she's been in a wheelchair the last eight years."

"Oh, I see. I'm sorry. So you had no choice," she said, nodding, and noticed how white his skin was at close quarters. A pair of too-heavy dark eyebrows emphasized this pallor, and when they drew together in a frown—as they were doing now —they dominated his face, with its high cheekbones and stubborn jaw.

"Well—since I've never traveled before," he said with another shrug, "China just seems a freaky place to start. I mean, I've never traveled even in the United States, let alone Europe where everyone seems to begin. I suppose you've been to Europe?" he asked suspiciously.

"Oh, here and there," she said vaguely, and watching that impassive face she asked on impulse, "Don't you ever smile?"

He turned and gave her such a suddenly shrewd and thoughtful look that she was taken aback; she realized that in some way she was amusing *him*. "That goes with it?" he asked.

Oh, very hostile, she thought. "I was also wondering how old you are," she told him with a smile. "A second impertinent question for you."

"Twenty-two," he said dryly.

In the seat ahead of them Malcolm Styles turned and said, "I heard that, and I'm sitting with Jenny here, who's twenty-five. Shall we change seats and let the infants have a go at each other?"

Jenny's piquant face surfaced beside his. "Infants!" she protested. "Why don't we just turn the seats and face each other?"

"You'll miss the scenery."

"We can see it backwards for a while. Where was your grandmother born in China, Peter?"

He reached into his duffle bag and brought out a small wrinkled map. "We go near it toward the end of the tour. I was told the guide could arrange a side trip so I can take pictures. A little village outside Datong," he said, handing her the map and pointing. "Not too far from Beijing."

Malcolm said gently, "I hope we can all see it. What was it like in those days?"

"Warlords," said Peter, and nodded. "Yeah, I guess it'll be interesting to see what's happened since then; it sure beats reading about it. Her father was a doctor-missionary, and I guess they saw terrible things while they were there. Droughts. Famine. Confiscatory taxes. Disease."

"I hear even flies have been eliminated now," said Malcolm, "although not the occasional drought, flood, and earthquake, unfortunately. What about you, Jenny?" he asked. "Why China?"

Jenny beamed at him. "Well, I'd done enough backpacking through Europe—sorry, Peter," she said, laughing at him, "and

China it had to be, even if I had to borrow half the money to get here, which I did, because second-grade teachers aren't exactly rich. Which is what I am," she explained with a lively gesture. "Not rich but a second-grade teacher. There's such a strong pull in me toward China that I just have to have been Chinese in a past life."

"The Empress of course," said Peter, and suddenly grinned at her, those relentless black brows lifting to wipe away several years and make him a believable twenty-two-year-old.

"A smile!" exclaimed Malcolm, with a humorous glance at Mrs. Pollifax.

"I see it," she said, smiling back at him. "Beautiful."

With the arrival of Peter's first smile came the young woman with mop and pail again, to walk up and down and leave glistening streaks of water behind her. Mrs. Pollifax's gaze moved beyond her to the window: to rice paddies with tender green shoots springing out of the water, a water buffalo plodding along a path behind an old woman, piles of mud-and-straw bricks and trimmed logs, and a house on stilts. She heard Jenny say, "Mr. Styles—"

"Malcolm, please."

"Okay. Malcolm, you haven't said what you do when you're not traveling."

Mrs. Pollifax watched the black guardsman's moustache tilt down as the brows rose humorously. "Now that will have to wait," he told her lightly, "because it's time for me to check out the men's room—if my walking up the aisle doesn't bring out that mop again."

Mrs. Pollifax gave him a thoughtful glance as he left, thinking how adroitly he'd sidestepped answering Jenny when it would have needed only a second to say *I'm in business, theater, or advertising.* She'd not expected him to be evasive; his voice had been quietly dismissing, and there was no overlooking his well-timed retreat. She wondered what he wanted to conceal and why he wasn't ready for that question. Perhaps, she speculated, he was taking refuge in the men's room to decide just what he did do when he was not traveling.

Or perhaps she was looking much too hard for her coagent, except that she felt it ridiculous that she not know.

The train was slowing. Joe Forbes strolled up the aisle and called out to them, "Mr. Li says we're reaching the border now, and box lunches for us in half an hour."

At once cameras were unfurled and the buffs sprang to their feet, everyone except Mrs. Pollifax and Iris, who remained seated up front. Gazing out the window she thought again, *So many people!* They stood in queues, waiting to board the rear cars that George Westrum had called hard seats, and the lines were serpentine: men and women in simple cotton clothes holding bundles and waiting, among them soldiers in khaki with red stars on their caps, and behind them a series of shabby buildings and the outline of low green hills.

Mrs. Pollifax left her seat and walked down the aisle to join Iris. "Not taking pictures, I see."

Iris looked up, startled. "Oh I'll take a few later, just for me." She smiled. "No matter what I do, though, they come out weird. Heads chopped off, and that sort of thing." With a gesture toward the window she said, "I was just thinking what my friend Suzie would say about all those huts and rice paddies we passed. Suzie loves glamour; she'd say, 'You're spending all that money to fly halfway around the world and see *this?*'"

Mrs. Pollifax smiled. "I suppose if you chose one of the city tours—Shanghai especially—you'd find nightlife and glamour. Were you tempted?"

"Cities are what I know best," Iris said ruefully. "But," she added firmly, "I wanted something different."

Mrs. Pollifax nodded. "I think you found it."

Iris grinned back at her. "I think so, too." She turned in her seat to face her. "Look, Mrs.—it's Pollifax, isn't it? This dress —it's no good, is it."

"No," said Mrs. Pollifax calmly.

"Damn," Iris said without rancor, "I knew I shouldn't trust Suzie. She's a go-go dancer," she explained, "and the only person I know who's traveled. Once to the Caribbean and once to Bermuda, so I let her choose for me."

"I've never met a go-go dancer," Mrs. Pollifax said thoughtfully.

"Really?" Iris bestowed her large radiant smile on her. "I

should keep my mouth shut, but since you've never met one I'll tell you that you're talking to one now. You wouldn't believe it, would you, with me being so clumsy, but when I dance I'm not. And how else would I know Suzie?" she asked candidly. "I did it full time for three years, and then when I started college I worked part time until I finished college last month."

"College last month," repeated Mrs. Pollifax, and realized that her instincts had been sound and that Iris was going to have ever-widening dimensions.

"Began college at twenty-eight," Iris said triumphantly. "Took a high-school-equivalency test and just started because I never did finish high school. Maybe it's a college nobody's heard of, but it was just right for me. And I happened to take a year's course on China," she added, "and was the only person in the class to get an A. So I decided you could have Paris and London, I was going to come to China. Except I *told* Suzie there'd be no cocktail parties or men, but she said, 'What's a trip without cocktail parties and men?' "

"What indeed," said Mrs. Pollifax, fascinated.

"So I reminded her men are what I don't need, having been married often enough, but Suzie—"

"Often enough?" echoed Mrs. Pollifax, regarding her with some awe.

Iris nodded. "At sixteen to a cowboy—that was Mike—and then to Stanley, who turned out to be a crook, and then to Orris. *He* struck oil, which is when he decided he was too good for me. He was nice, though, he gave me a really fair shake when he left, and I may be dumb about clothes but not about money. That's when I decided I'd had enough, though, and it was time to change my life."

"Yes," said Mrs. Pollifax, and waited.

"I mean," Iris went on eagerly, "we let men define who we are, right? That's Women's Lib. I went to some of the meetings at college and I could see how it had been with me. For Mike I ate beans and franks all the time and was a cocktail waitress. For Stanley I learned how to keep my mouth shut about his shady deals—'button up,' he was always growling. For Orris I lived in a trailer on the oil fields and was a go-go dancer until he struck it rich. And you know what?" she added, leaning forward and shoving back her mane of hair, "I did it all to please *them*, not me."

"I see exactly what you mean," said Mrs. Pollifax, admiring the passion of Iris' discoveries.

"Except now I've let Suzie influence me," she said, glancing ruefully down at the huge polka dots and stiff white collar. "What do I do? Will there be clothes in Canton, do you think?"

"Chinese clothes."

Iris scowled. "I'm too big, I'm nearly six feet tall."

"Didn't you bring anything to—well, relax in?"

"I stuck in a pair of old jeans at the last minute—something old and something blue," she said wryly. "In case I had a chance to ride horseback or something. And a denim shirt."

"Wear them," Mrs. Pollifax told her firmly.

Iris looked startled. "But Jenny's in that pretty little skirt and blouse, and look at you in—"

Mrs. Pollifax shook her head. "Wear them."

Iris sighed. "Gosh, the money I spent on all this stuff, enough to keep Vogue Boutique in business a whole year, I swear."

"You'll look splendid in jeans," said Mrs. Pollifax, paying this no attention. "Be yourself."

Iris considered this and sighed again. "There it is again, the hardest thing of all, don't you think? Being yourself? But if I should blossom out in my jeans tomorrow would you stick near me?"

"For the initial impact, yes, but after that you're on your own."

Iris grinned. "You're really nice. I thought when I first saw you, oh boy *she'll* be the one to cold-shoulder me—I mean, when I first saw you, before I spoke to you. And here I end up telling you the story of my life."

"Stanley," said Mrs. Pollifax, "would have told you to 'button up'?"

Iris laughed her joyous laugh. "You sure listened if you remember *that*. Oh-oh, here comes Mr. Forbes again. He's cer-

tainly no talker, he just keeps studying that Chinese dictionary of his."

"Yes, but I took his seat and I'll let him have it back now,"
Mrs. Pollifax told her. "I'll see you later, Iris."

As the others streamed back into the car the train lurched
and then began to move, and Mr. Li appeared carrying a carton
of box lunches for them. A moment later the railway station
and the border were behind them, and Mrs. Pollifax thought,
We're now in Mainland China. It begins at last.

Chapter Three

They dined late that afternoon in the Guangzhou Restaurant, just off the train and in another world. Their number had been increased by one, the local Guangzhou, or Canton guide who explained that the hotel was so far out of town that they must have their Chinese banquet now. The man's name was Tung, and Mrs. Pollifax began to understand now that only Mr. Li was to be permanent and *theirs*; the others would come and go, with names like Chu and Tung, leaving only vague impressions behind.

In any case, Mrs. Pollifax felt that her sense of inner time was still so confused that a banquet in late afternoon could scarcely be more difficult than breakfast at night over the Pacific. They were here, very definitely in China, on the second floor of a huge old wooden building in a room filled with large round tables, only one of which was occupied by a family of Chinese who ate and talked with enthusiasm in a far corner: a wedding party, explained Mr. Li.

With her chopsticks Mrs. Pollifax lifted a slice of sugared tomato toward her mouth and experienced triumph at its arrival. From where she sat she could look out across the restaurant's courtyard and see a line of clothes hung on a rope stretched from eave to eave: an assortment of grays, dull blues, and greens. She decided that it was probably not someone's laundry because the wide street outside had been lined with just such clothing too, hung like banners from every apartment above the street floor. Presumably it was an efficient solution to a lack of closet space, and remembering her own crowded closets at home she pondered the effect on her neighbors if she did this at the Hemlock Arms.

Mr. Li, seated beside her, chose this moment to announce, "It is important there be a leader to this group. You are oldest, Mrs. Pollifax, you will please be leader?"

Mrs. Pollifax, glancing around, said doubtfully, "I'm the oldest, yes, but I wonder if perhaps—" She stopped, aware that Iris' eyes were growing huge with alarm at the thought of her deferring to a man and betraying The Cause. She wondered if later it would prove convenient or inconvenient to be a leader, and Carstairs' words drifted back to her: *if anything unusual happens—if anything goes wrong—get that group the hell out of China.* Possibly, she decided, it might prove convenient. "Yes of course," she said, and smiled demurely at Iris across the table.

Mr. Li laughed merrily. "Good—okay! You can find for me out of each person what they most want to see. For the arrangements. We cannot promise them, it is the local guides who decide, but I struggle for you."

"Yes," said Mrs. Pollifax, and decided not to mention the Drum Tower in Xian just yet.

"For tomorrow," said Mr. Li, "Mr. Tung has arranged—" He bent his ear to Mr. Tung and surfaced, nodding. "We visit Dr. Sun Yet-sen Memorial Hall, the panda at the zoo, various other stops, and late in afternoon departure to Xian."

"The beginning of the Silk Road," pointed out Malcolm, nodding.

George Westrum, on her left, said gruffly, "For myself, I'll say right now that I want to see their farms, and the equipment they have. That'll be communes, of course."

"I'll make a note of that," she told him. "You're a farmer, George?"

"Have a few acres," he said.

Mrs. Pollifax gave him an exasperated glance. She had wrested words out of young Peter, and had witnessed Malcolm's evasiveness, and she was bored with all this modesty. She asked bluntly, "How many?"

"Several thousand," he admitted.

"Cows, horses, sheep, or grain?" she shot back.

"Beef cattle. And oil."

"Aha!"

He nodded. "A surprise to me, that oil," he said. "Retired early from government work—"

"Government work?"

"Yes, and bought a ranch, expecting to raise cattle, not oil. That young lady I saw you talking to on the train," he said casually, with a not-so-casual glance across the table at Iris. "She Miss or Mrs. Damson?"

Mrs. Pollifax's *aha* was silent this time. "I haven't the slightest idea," she told him cheerfully, "except that I do know she's not married now. Is this a thousand-year-old egg?" she asked, turning to Mr. Li.

"Oh yes, but *not* a thousand years old," he said with his quick smile and another merry laugh.

"It tastes like egg, it just looks rather odd, as if it had been left out of the refrigerator too long."

Jenny said, "I believe they're soaked in brine or something, and buried in the earth."

"The food's coming with frightening speed now," pointed out Malcolm across the table as the waiter brought still another platter to the table. "Sweet and sour something," he announced, spearing a piece between chopsticks and delivering it to his mouth before passing it on. "How many meals will be Chinese on our trip?"

"It is good, you all using chopsticks," said Mr. Li. "Very good. You, Mr. Fox—press fingers a little higher," he told Peter, receiving a hostile glance in return. "The food? After tomorrow no Western food."

"Not even breakfast?" gasped Jenny.

"Chinese breakfast."

"What fun," cried Iris with a radiant smile.

"I've been studying Chinese this last year," Joe Forbes told him across the table. "I'd like to try it out on you now and then. For instance, would I be called a *da bi zi?*"

Both Mr. Li and Mr. Tung burst out laughing. *"Xiao hua,"* cried Mr. Li enthusiastically.

"Meaning what?" asked Jenny.

Joe Forbes said, "I *hope* I asked if I'd be called a 'long nose' among the Chinese—except it's so damn easy to get the tones wrong. Did I?"

"You did, yes," Mr. Tung assured him, "and Comrade Li said *Xiao hua*, meaning 'a joke'!"

"Surely we're called round eyes, not long noses," asked Malcolm.

"Anyway not foreign devils anymore," contributed Jenny.

"Capitalist-roaders?" suggested Iris, grinning.

Mr. Tung gave an embarrassed laugh. Mr. Li lifted his glass of pale orange soda pop and said, "Let us toast to Chinese-American friendship!"

Mrs. Pollifax raised her own glass of soda. The others lifted their glasses of Chinese beer, which she promised herself she would try the next day, since water was advised against, the tea extremely weak, and the soda tasted rather like flavored water. In the meantime she waited to ask George Westrum just what his government service might have been. He was a silent man but he talked well when he did speak; his face was expressionless, even harsh, but there was that occasional twinkle of humor that suggested other dimensions. He must certainly have retired early—as CIA men often did, Bishop had told her—because he looked to be still in his fifties, and he was obviously strong. She felt that he was noticing everyone and everything—watching and alert—and she was amused that he had especially noticed Iris.

But there was no opportunity to question George Westrum further. Mr. Li, pleased that Forbes was learning Mandarin, at once grasped the chance to practice his English, and their exchange of words occupied the others. "Yes, I teach history," Forbes was saying, "in a small Midwestern university." He was smiling but Mrs. Pollifax realized that actually he did not smile all the time, it was merely an illusion caused by the arrangement of his features, but definitely smiling now, she could see the difference.

"Professor?" said Iris, and made a startled gesture that

struck a nearby bottle of beer and sent it rolling off the table. Iris turned scarlet. "Oh," she gasped. "Oh I'm terribly sorry." She dropped her napkin and started after it.

Malcolm placed a firm hand on her arm. "Please," he said with a smile. "Not again. Let me do the honors this time."

"Oh! Oh thank you," said Iris, her cheeks burning.

But a waiter had rushed to the table to wipe up the spilled beer, just as another waiter arrived bearing a huge soup tureen. "Now that looks too heavy for Iris to tip over," Jenny said, with a laugh.

"I understand soup means the end of a meal in your country," Joe Forbes put in. "In America we have it first, you know."

Mr. Tung looked appalled.

"We feel," explained Mr. Li gently, "that it belongs at the end. To settle the dinner."

"And don't forget," Malcolm pointed out, "the Chinese gave us silk, printing, gunpowder, and porcelain among other things."

"But obviously not the idea of soup to end a meal," added Jenny.

Mrs. Pollifax put down her chopsticks. It had been a lavish dinner—melons, rice, pork, shrimp, eggs, tomatoes, more courses than she could count—but she was glad to see it ending. *It's been a long day,* she thought, *and I miss Cyrus . . . I can't go through China missing Cyrus, I have work to do. I haven't managed Yoga for three days, perhaps that's it.*

They rose from the table, descended dusty wooden stairs, and left the restaurant to be assaulted by the life outside. Mrs. Pollifax revived at once and looked around her with pleasure: at the broad street dense with people and bicycles, at children stopping to stare at them shyly and then smile. Off to one side she saw a line of stalls piled high with shirts, plastic sandals, bananas, sunflower seeds, and nuts. A woman and child sat patiently beside a very small table, waiting to sell a few bottles of garishly bright orange soda pop. Across the street small huts had been squeezed on top of the roof of a long cement building from which the paint was peeling. Flowers in pots stood on ledges, or flowed down from roof dwellings and apartments to overhang the street. The colors were muted, except for the flowers and the flash of an occasional red shirt. Even the sounds were muted: the persistent ringing of bicycle bells—there were no cars—and the shuffle of feet. It was approaching dusk, and the day's heat had turned into a warmth that mingled pleasantly with the smells of cooking food. *This is more like it,* thought Mrs. Pollifax, drinking in the smells and sights, and it was with reluctance that she climbed back into the minibus.

This time it was Malcolm Styles who took the seat next to her. As he leaned over to place his small travel kit under the seat a pocket notebook fell out of his pocket and dropped into her lap. She picked it up and handed it back to him, but a solitary sheet of paper had escaped and settled into a niche beside the window. Retrieving this she glanced at it and gasped, "But how lovely!"

It was a sketch—a line-drawing in pen and ink—of a Chinese child, no more than a quick sketch but with lines so fluid and joyful that it staggered her with its delicacy, its aliveness. She looked at Malcolm with amazement. "You're an artist!"

His grin was rueful, those thick brows drawing together deprecatingly. "Of a sort."

"Stop being modest," she told him sternly. "What do you *do* with a gift like this?"

His eyes smiled at her. "I'm not at all modest," he told her. "Really I'm not. I just feel very uncomfortable when people learn that I wrote and illustrated the Tiny Tot series, and am now the author of the Doctor Styles' picture books, and—"

"The Doctor Styles' books!" she exclaimed. "Good heavens, my grandchild adores them, I sent him one at Christmas and—but that means you also wrote *The Boy Who Walked Into a Rainbow?*"

He nodded. "That's me."

She gazed at him incredulously. "I thought you were an actor or a fervent businessman," she told him. "Or a male model—you know, distinguished gentleman who drinks only the best sherry or stands beside a Rolls-Royce smoking a briar pipe and looking owlish."

"With attaché case?" he asked interestedly.

"Oh, *welded* to one," she told him.

He nodded. "Then you can understand the shock when people discover that I live in a world inhabited by rabbits that talk and mice who rescue small boys."

"Well—yes," she admitted, smiling. "Yes, that could be a shock."

"It is," he assured her. "Usually there's an instinctive withdrawal, then a look of suspicion, followed by a hearty 'By Jove that's nice,' and a very hasty retreat. I must say you've taken it rather well, though."

"Not a great deal surprises me," admitted Mrs. Pollifax. "Not anymore, at least. It must surely make for a very good life?"

"Oh yes I'm very fortunate," he said lightly. "I do only one book a year now, and that leaves six months for travel or for anything else that appeals."

Six months, she mused, turning this over in her mind; yes there were certain possibilities there, and his books made for wonderful cover. "Are you hoping for a book from this trip?"

He said softly, "Oh I think not, but it will refresh me. I'm looking forward intensely to the Qin Shi Huang Tombs—"

"Oh yes!"

"—and the museums and temples. And sketching, of course."

They had been driving through darkening streets—there were no street lights—and now as night arrived there were only dim electric lights shining yellow in the apartments along the streets. Glancing up she could look into the windows and see a single feeble bulb suspended from the ceiling, see the dark silhouette of a man standing at a window peering out, glimpse a face seated at a table reading, the light etching the face in chiaroscuro. Hong Kong's fluorescent lights had been stark clear white; here the color was a yellow that barely illuminated the dark caves of rooms.

"Surely those can't be more than twenty-watt bulbs?" she murmured to Malcolm, pointing.

"Twenty-five at most," he said.

Huge dark China, she thought, moved by the silence, the absence of cars, and the darkness.

The buildings thinned until the headlights of the bus picked out mud-brick walls, then lines of trees with only a solitary light to be seen at a distance—a commune, perhaps— and then at last the bus turned down a graveled road that ran through a thinly wooded area, lights gleamed ahead, and they drew up before a huge, raw, half-finished modern building.

"I hope," said Mrs. Pollifax with feeling, "our hotels aren't always going to be *this* far out of town."

"The question being," Malcolm said, extending a hand to her, "whether they're trying to keep us from meeting the people, or the people from meeting us."

They walked into a huge echoing lobby that was almost a parody of contemporary architecture: a few self-consciously Danish chairs, a very Art Deco cobblestone fish pond, with a fountain springing out of its base. They were the only people in the cavernous lobby except for a young woman behind a desk who passed out room keys to them.

"Bags outside rooms at half-past seven," said Mr. Li. "We do not return here to the hotel tomorrow, remember."

"It would take hours to get back here anyway," commented Iris, and received an answering smile from George Westrum.

Mrs. Pollifax entered room 217, found it bland but comfortable, with hot water running from its sink taps, and promptly ran a bath and climbed into it. She carried with her a book on China's history to read, but she did not read it. She was too busy wondering instead what lay ahead of her in this vast country; she wondered what the others were thinking, and who among them was thinking ahead to Xian, and then to Xinjiang Province lying to the north of them. She was remembering, too, the strange assortment of items that she'd brought into China with her, the stores of vitamin pills and dried fruit, the thermal socks, and chocolate. She remembered Carstairs saying, "It's almost as impossible to get an agent into China as it is to get a man out of China."

Out of China . . . this was the question that had occurred and reoccurred to her before her departure; how *did* they plan to get X out of China? It was a question that had sent her to the very good topographical map in her encyclopedia, and the result had chilled her because Xinjiang Province, thousands of miles from the sea, bordered Tibet and Pakistan and Afghanistan, its desert running like a flat carpet to the terrible mountain ranges of the Kunluns and the Karakaroms. Thermal socks, dried fruit, chocolate . . . the supposition she had drawn still shocked her.

But as she slipped into her robe and headed for bed she knew there was still another, even more shocking suspicion that she had consigned to the periphery of her thoughts, not allowing it entry, stubbornly resisting it because if she brought it out and looked at it, she would understand Bishop's fears for her. Turning out the lights she once again refused it entry and succeeded in pushing it far enough away to fall asleep at once.

Chapter Four

*I*n the morning Iris made her appearance in jeans, and after faithfully escorting her downstairs Mrs. Pollifax could see that emotional support would no longer be needed: Jenny whistled, Malcolm gave her a second calm glance, and George Westrum's eyes rested on her with a glow that Mrs. Pollifax hoped Iris noticed, but doubted that she did; Joe Forbes murmured, "Well, now," and even Peter Fox looked mildly appreciative. It was true that at breakfast Iris tipped a plate of peanuts into her lap, with half of them cascading to the floor, but—as Jenny cheerfully pointed out—peanuts were easier to recover than spilled beer. Iris, thought Mrs. Pollifax, was in danger of being assigned the role of comic in the group.

At breakfast and again at lunch Mrs. Pollifax pursued her responsibility of listing for Mr. Li what each person particularly wanted to see, and in this she found no surprises: Joe Forbes wanted to visit a university, Jenny the second-grade class in a school, and George listed only communes. Malcolm's priorities were more numerous and entirely cultural. Young Peter repeated his request for a side trip to the village where his grandmother was born, while Iris wanted to see the Chinese Opera but especially the Ban Po Village Museum in Xian because the artifacts reflected a Neolithic society run by women eight thousand years ago. Women's Lib again. For herself, Mrs. Pollifax wrote down the Drum Tower in Xian and hoped no one would ask why. After consulting her guidebook she added the Bell Tower for camouflage, and any Buddhist temples.

But Guangzhou, or Canton, she found, was mainly a waiting game. She enjoyed their trip to the bank to exchange travelers' checks for tourist scrip: she watched in fascination as four clerks hovered over her money, carefully checking the amount on an abacus. But tourist money, Mr. Li told them, could not be spent on the streets, at the bazaars, or free markets, only in the government-run shops.

Mrs. Pollifax at once rose to this challenge. "How can I get real money?" she asked him, thinking ahead to possible exigencies, and was told that the Friendship Stores would no doubt give real Chinese currency in change, whereupon she promptly asked for large denominations of tourist scrip, determined to collect as many of the authentic bills as she could. "My new hobby," she told Malcolm cheerfully.

Aside from this, the Dr. Sun Yet-sen Memorial charmed her with its gorgeously intense blue-laquered tiles, but it smelled musty inside; she obediently oh-d and ah-d at the pandas in the zoo, but the heat there at midday nearly felled her, and once again they lunched on the second floor of a restaurant, with the natives on the street floor below.

Only once was she fully startled out of her lingering jet-lag apathy. With an unexpected half hour of time confronting Mr. Tung, he offered them a pleasant stroll down a suburban road that held a mixture of older buildings among the brand-new scaffold-laced structures. One building in particular caught Mrs. Pollifax's eye, creamy-white against the dull cement facade of its neighbors, and of an architecture that she could only identify in her mind as tropical-colonial. Graceful arched windows, each one trimmed in a tender green, were set like jewels into the smooth creamy walls. Next to an open green door hung a vertical sign, and Mrs. Pollifax brought out her small camera and took a picture of the charming vignette: a courtyard, a door, a leafy green tree, a donkey cart parked next to the door.

"What does the sign say?" she called to Mr. Tung, pointing.

Moving to her side he looked at it. "People's Security Bu-

reau," he said, and abruptly turned away, his face expressionless.

People's Security Bureau . . . the Sepos, she remembered
from her reading, and she wondered if, since Mao's death, the
Sepos still knocked on doors at midnight to take people away,
or whether the new order had changed this. She hoped so.
Bishop had said, "You'll find many surprising changes happening there, but they've been taking place very cautiously, very
slowly." She lingered a moment gazing at the open door, trying to imagine what lay behind its innocent facade, and then
she turned and hurried away, made uneasy by a vague sense of
foreboding.

"What did he say that building was?" asked George Westrum, catching up with her.

"People's Security Bureau."

"Oh, cops. By the way, did you know Malcolm writes kid-
dies' books?"

The tone of his voice, she thought, would not have surprised Malcolm. "Yes, very fine ones," she told him. "Perhaps
your children—are you married, George?"

He shook his head. "Never had children, been a widower
for years. Tell me why in hell a man would write children's
books? Hasn't he grown up yet?"

Mrs. Pollifax glanced at George's baseball cap, tilted boy-
ishly at the back of his head, and smiled. "Do any of us?" she
asked dryly. "And should we—completely?"

He didn't hear her; he said abruptly, "There's Iris Damson
up ahead. Doesn't realize it's almost time to be heading for the
bus. Excuse me, I'll just hurry along and tell her."

She watched him march briskly toward Iris, passing Joe
Forbes photographing workers mixing cement, then Peter and
Jenny taking pictures of each other, and Malcolm aiming his
camera at children playing. She smiled, thinking George Wes-
trum was showing very definite signs of becoming addicted to
Iris.

In late afternoon they reached the airport, where they said
good-bye to Mr. Tung. Because there were no reserved seats on
the plane, not even for foreigners, there was a mad dash across

the tarmac once the plane was announced, and the group found themselves widely dispersed throughout the small two-engine prop plane. Mrs. Pollifax settled herself into an aisle seat with two men in Mao jackets beside her, and realized, now that she had sampled a little of China, it was time she began considering just how she was going to approach Comrade Guo Musu in his barbershop near the Drum Tower in Xian. She found that no inspiration occurred to her at all; she had no idea what the Drum Tower might be, and not even her wildest flights of imagination could conjure up the appearance of a barbershop, which in China would scarcely announce itself with a striped barber pole. It troubled her, too, that so far the tour appeared to be arranged to prevent even the most accidental of encounters with the Chinese, and up against these frustrations she began to reflect instead on just which member of the group might be her coagent. One of them—*one person on this plane*—knew what Xian meant, and why she was here.

One person, she reflected, and again asked, who? Which one?

From where he sat on the plane he could just see the back of Mrs. Pollifax's head several seats down the aisle, and as the plane lifted he wondered what she was thinking about as they took flight to Xian, and to Guo Musu, and he wondered how in hell she was going to extract information from a total stranger, given so little time and the watchful eye of Mr. Li. Once again he shook his head over Carstairs' choice; they had a very tight schedule, and if she failed in this contact it was highly doubtful that he would ever find the labor camp by himself. The distances were too vast, and their time too painfully limited.

He had programmed himself not to think ahead, but separated from the others now, with two native Chinese between him and the window, he allowed his mind to wander a little from the discipline he'd imposed upon it. He already knew how tough his assignment was going to be, and how the rescue of X—if it could be accomplished—was only the beginning of it. It brought a curious feeling to know so much intellectually about China and to apply this knowledge on arrival to the country's reality: it felt positively schizophrenic, for instance, to be listening with half his mind to the conversation between the two Chinese next to him, to understand every word they said yet pretend that he didn't.

In Guangzhou he'd been sorely tempted to buy a newspaper, a copy of *Zhong Guo Qing Nian Bao*—the *China Youth Daily*—which he was accustomed to reading weeks late, in America. This he had resisted, allowing himself only a glance at its headlines. The two men on his right were discussing production figures. They were both foremen in a factory returning home to Xian after a meeting of cadres in Guangzhou. He was curious about them. They were in their fifties; one had mentioned that he was born in Nanjing, while the other came from a village outside Beijing.

To live now in Xian, so far away, he thought, it would have been *shang-shan-xia-xiang* that wrenched them from their native towns and families, or what was called "up to the mountains and down to the villages," that great experiment of Mao's that sent intellectuals into the country to dig wells and plow fields, and peasants out of the villages to be trained and educated. He understood the need; there were too many people in China's cities, and it was vital to spread them out, except that usually only the peasants—the *jie ho*—were ever returned to their native villages. The educated young people, the *chi-shi qingnian*—found themselves banished forever to the countryside. He wondered how *he* would feel if, upon graduating from college, he were to be sent off to a remote Inner Mongolian commune, for instance, to be *tu bao zi*, a hick— literally a clod of earth—for the rest of his life. It had been one of the most astonishing leveling experiments in modern history, the attempt to reeducate nearly a billion people in the "correct" ideological way to think, as against an incorrect way . . . the turning over of one's heart and mind to the Motherland, the achievement of absolute trust in the parent-state. *Work without laying down conditions. Work without expecting reward. It is the work that counts, not the person. What helps our reform we should talk about abundantly, what is bad for reform we should not talk about at all. Education Through Labor.* Dui shi, bi dui ren—*it is the mistake we are after, not the man. Be grateful to the state by working with enthusiasm, without thinking of yourself.*

Except that for X it was not education through labor, but reform through labor, and what would Wang be like after his years in a reform camp? To survive he would have learned humility through self-criticism and confession; he would have been taught over and over that he must selflessly work for the greater whole, because whatever changes had occurred since Mao's death it was doubtful that they would easily reach a labor camp in a remote province. If by now Wang had not turned into a model prisoner, thinking "correct" ideological thoughts, he could just as easily have given up hope and have become a shell of a man. Would he even consent to leave, to escape?

Would he even find Wang? And if he found the camp, would he be able to recognize him? What if he had been altered beyond recognition? From some ancient file there had arrived that single blown-up photograph of a younger Wang . . . *Comrade Wang, engineer, greeting volunteer workers for our Motherland's defenses as they arrive in the north from villages and cities all over our country to joyously give of their labor.* There had been no date on the photo, just as there was no knowing what political tide had swept him aside, condemned of revisionist thinking or of being an anti-revolutionist.

There were the other unknowns and variables as well: the fact that the only information they had about the logging camp was its existence somewhere in the Tian Shan mountain range and surrounded on three sides by a stream of water so fast-flowing that it couldn't be crossed except on horseback. Not that the poor devils needed such barriers, he reflected, because if a prisoner decided to escape, where could he go? He needed identity papers, authorization for travel, and coupons for food and clothing, and wherever he went he would still be in China.

Such thoughts as these didn't undermine his confidence, they were merely parts of a logistics problem that would have to be solved as they left Xian and drew closer to Urumchi and to the Tian Shan range. He knew that he was well trained, that he was nerveless and capable, and he spoke the language fluently. The most aggravating unknown was Mrs. Pollifax. He objected very much to having the success of his assignment rest just now in someone else's hands, much less those of a foolish middle-aged lady. He had fought against this from the beginning, insisting he manage the contact himself, but Carstairs had said, "We can't risk you, the contact in Xian is too pivotal, too dangerous. If you should be caught—if Guo should betray you—we'd lose you, and you're irreplaceable because of your background in the country. The situation needs someone entirely different, someone so outwardly innocent that she'll deflect suspicion."

"She?" he'd repeated sharply.

And Carstairs had smiled pleasantly and said, "Yes, we have a woman in mind."

So here they were, the two of them, locked together into this situation for better or for worse, flying over mountains the color and shape of camels' humps, in a country whose culture was among the most ancient in the world. And he loved this country, which was a strange thing to discover because he loved so few things. Because of this he knew that he hated Mao for setting China back decades with his cultural revolution that wiped out intellectuals, closed universities, nearly destroyed art and science, and, in turn, brought only a new form of corruption out of the corruptions he'd intended to erase. Well, that was long since over; both Mao and the more liberal Chou were dead, and new leaders in command, but the country was still filled with Maoists. He thought wryly of the current political metaphor, "the two ends are hot and the middle is cold," a very Chinese way of saying that change was passionately wanted at both the top and the bottom of the society, but sitting squarely in the middle in many areas were Mao's bureaucrats, threatened by the progressive changes, indignant, clinging in fury to the old status quo. The reformers were listening, though: how could they help but hear the people at the Democracy Wall in 1979? The people still waited with infinite patience for the democracy that had been promised them once by Mao.

He turned and looked at the two men beside him, wishing

he might ask them a thousand questions. Seeing him glance toward them they smiled, eager to show their friendship.

"*Ni hao,*" he said, carefully avoiding any tonal pronunciation, rendering the greeting flat and drawling and clumsy.

The man next to him nodded vigorously; the second man by the window leaned forward to give him an eager smile and a thumbs-up gesture, and he was offered a Double Happiness brand cigarette, which he politely refused. As they returned to their conversation he glanced down the aisle and saw Mrs. Pollifax and her two seat companions stand up and change places with an extravagant exchange of bows and smiles: she was being given the window seat, and he wondered wryly how she had accomplished this without language.

He wondered, too, how much she guessed when she had been told so little.

He wondered if it had occurred to her yet that if Mr. Wang's rescue was a success, the man was going to have to be accompanied out of China—escorted, led, or dragged out, depending on his sympathies and his state of mind.

He wondered if she realized that in order to accompany Wang out of the country he himself was going to have to disappear from the tour group—and foreigners were simply not allowed to disappear into China. When would she recognize the fact that the whole purpose of the tour was to allow him to vanish—and that indeed all of them were hostages to his success in disappearing . . .

It was a woman guide who met them at the airport in Xian, and Mrs. Pollifax was amused by the look of awe and delight on Iris' face at sight of her. Apparently Mr. Li knew the woman from previous trips and greeted her cordially. "This is Miss Bai," he told them, introducing her.

She was a slightly built woman, older than Mr. Li, very serious and intense, in fact one could guess her efficiency by the way that Mr. Li subtly relaxed on finding her there. Noticing this Mrs. Pollifax experienced a sudden insight into the tensions behind Mr. Li's nervous laugh: the necessity to please not only the people he guided but also nameless faceless superiors who had selected him out of thousands to associate with foreigners.

"You will not be far out of town here," he told them cheerfully. "The hotel is in the middle of Xian."

"Hooray," cried Jenny.

Because they had all been separated on the plane Mrs. Pollifax noticed that they met now like long-lost friends. Even Peter looked less sullen, and as they headed for their next minibus she heard him asking Malcolm about his books—word had spread quickly, she thought dryly—while Joe Forbes was teasing Jenny about her hair, which she'd braided into a pigtail. "Going native, huh?" he said, pointing to a girl on the street with a similar thick braid down her back.

"I can't wait to buy a Mao jacket and cap," she told him. "Wait till you see me then!"

"You wish such purchases?" asked Miss Bai, overhearing her. "I will arrange for a visit to a department store tomorrow."

"Wonderful," breathed Jenny. "Thanks!"

Xian was the color of the mountains they'd flown over, terra-cotta and dusty, with patches of green only in the long lines of newly planted poplar trees and in an occasional rice field. New cement apartment houses were being built, but they were windowless and unfinished, still outnumbered by the old walled compounds along the road and the tiny mud-and-straw homes glimpsed behind them. Their bus drove toward the city through pedestrians and bicyclists, constantly sounding its horn. Entering Xian the landscape changed, the buildings drew closer together, they met with billboards lining each intersection where once Mao's thoughts must have been inscribed but which now advertised soap and toilet paper and toothpaste.

This time their hotel sat squarely in the center of town on a busy street. In Canton there had been lingering traces of the European influence, but here the architecture was Russian, a massive square hotel built of gray cement with a wall and a sentry at the gate. The Chinese spirit had asserted itself, however, with a huge scarlet sign on which gold letters in Chinese and English proclaimed THE THEORETICAL BASIS GUIDING OUR THINKING IS MARXISM AND LENINISM. MAO TSE-TUNG.

Iris regarded this in despair. "I've not *read* Marx," she cried. "What was his approach to women?"

"Cautious," said Malcolm.

"I'll bet yours is, too," Jenny told him.

"Naturally," he said, "or I'd not be a bachelor."

"Are you really!" Jenny exclaimed happily. "Not even one very *little* marriage somewhere?"

Mrs. Pollifax gave Jenny a sharp glance. On the surface she thought Jenny insouciant and lively, yet she'd begun to notice a strange bite to her words. It was present when she mocked Iris' clumsiness, and it was in the tone of her voice now, a curious recklessness, a sense of trying too hard. *There is a suggestion of desperation here,* she thought, and wondered why.

Mr. Li interrupted her speculations with an announcement. Dinner, he said, would be served in twenty minutes, and he pointed to the building where it would be served, and for the evening, if they wished, they could stroll to the People's Park together while he and Miss Bai worked out their schedule for Xian. Next he explained that there were no keys to the rooms at the People's Hotel—there was no need for keys—and he read out their room numbers.

"I don't like there being no keys," Jenny complained as they climbed the stairs to the floor above.

"I think," said Mrs. Pollifax, "one has to bear in mind that the hotel is run by the government, and there's a soldier on duty at the entrance, and as you can see," she added as they reached the second floor, "there's a chap at a desk to check people."

"But there are so many workers here," Jenny protested.

Malcolm fielded that one. "Plum job, my dear. If it even occurred to one of them to steal something—doubtful—where would they sell it? Don't be so suspicious," he chided, adding dryly, "this isn't America, you know. Who's for that stroll after dinner, by the way?"

After one look at her room Mrs. Pollifax decided very firmly to opt for the walk to People's Park. She could not conceive of an evening spent in a room so small, so unbelievably dark and hot, with a tiny air-conditioner that made chuckling sounds when she turned it on. She therefore set out with the others following dinner, and falling into step beside Iris she asked how things were going.

Iris did not fail her. "Oh isn't it *wonderful!*" she cried, turning to face Mrs. Pollifax and very nearly falling over a stone in her path. "I asked Miss Bai what her first name is. I have it written down somewhere, but in English it means Elder Fragrance, isn't that beautiful?"

"Really lovely, yes," agreed Mrs. Pollifax, "but I think you'd better watch out for the holes in this sidewalk, Iris."

"Okay. But what's with this Peter Fox?" she asked. "I sat next to him at dinner and I don't know when I've met anyone so grumpy—unless it was Stanley before he had his morning coffee. Is he going to be a real wet blanket?"

"He may thaw, given time," said Mrs. Pollifax generously. "It seems his grandmother gave him this trip as a present because she was born in China and can't come herself. I daresay he'd much rather be off backpacking somewhere with a group of friends."

"If he has any friends," said Iris. "Well, I can see how he feels, of course, but if somebody gave me a present—any kind of present—you wouldn't catch me sulking like that. And a free trip to China—wow!"

Mrs. Pollifax smiled faintly, noting the words *if anyone gave me a present, any kind of present,* and reflected that Iris would be too busy giving presents to receive any; the takers must flock to her like bees to a honey flower. A pity, she thought, and said mischievously, "George Westrum seems very nice."

Iris warmly agreed. "Oh, isn't he? And I think"—she lowered her voice—"I think he used to be an FBI man, isn't that intriguing?"

"FBI?" repeated Mrs. Pollifax alertly. "How very exciting!"

Iris nodded. "Now all we need is someone from the CIA."

"Yes indeed," murmured Mrs. Pollifax, without so much as a blink of an eye. "Quite horrid people, I'm sure."

"Oh there must be *some* nice people among them," Iris

conceded with her radiant smile and then, glancing ahead, "Look—that must be the park. We're here! Except why are the others huddling around the gate?"

"Because it costs money," shouted Malcolm, as Iris called out her query, crossing the avenue. "The real stuff. Either of you have any?"

"I have," Iris announced, joining them. "I bought those white jade cups at Canton airport, remember?" As the natives gathered to watch, she dug into her purse, brought out small wrinkled bills and then several coins and presented them to the man. He selected several *fen*, beamed at her, and issued them tickets.

"Now this," said Joe Forbes as they entered, "has to be the real China."

Mrs. Pollifax was inclined to believe him. There were paths to the right and to the left, but she was drawn instead toward a crowd straight ahead from which, even at a distance, she could hear roars of laughter. Joining it Mrs. Pollifax stood on tiptoe to peer over heads and found them gathered around a television set, a modest and perfectly normal television set plugged into some unseen outlet in the out-of-doors, with cartoons dancing across its screen. Amazing she thought, and looked instead into the faces of the people watching the cartoons, touched by their innocent excitement and joy.

The subtitles, however, were in Chinese, and presently— still smiling at the pleasure it was giving—she moved away to investigate a small growing crowd off to the left, and discovered Malcolm seated under a tree sketching. Not far away George Westrum was attempting sign language with a young woman, with Joe Forbes chuckling at his elbow. At once a young man spotted Mrs. Pollifax and hurried to her side. "You are American too," he cried eagerly. "I may ask questions?"

"Oh yes," she told him warmly. *"Ni hao!* Good evening!"

His boldness, his daring, immediately drew people from Malcolm's circle into his, and Mrs. Pollifax found herself smiled at and approved as the audience waited with attention for their comrade to address this visitor from a country half-way across the world. Their pride in him was palpable, and

Mrs. Pollifax waited too, her heart beating a trifle faster at the importance of this moment.

"In America," he said slowly, his brows knitted together by the seriousness with which he, too, regarded this moment, "you grow cotton?"

Mrs. Pollifax, a little surprised, nodded her head. "Yes. Oh yes. In our southern states."

"Suzzen states?"

"Warm places," she explained. "Like Canton?"

"Canton?" He looked bewildered, and she saw that they had suddenly lost their way; the eagerness still hung between them, tangible but severely threatened.

"No," she said, trying to retrieve direction, "in the United States, where I live. Where—" She was suddenly overwhelmed by the nouns, pronouns, verbs that separated them and with which she must frame a sentence, acutely aware too of the perplexities of *for* and *about* and *from*; the wall between them seemed opaque, the gulf immeasurable, and then with sudden inspiration she remembered the snapshots she had crammed into her purse at the last minute. She reached into her purse and drew them out: a photograph of her apartment house, with herself standing in front of it; several of her grandson opening packages at Christmas in her living room; one of Cyrus, and two of her geraniums. She offered them to this new friend. With great wonder her pictures were accepted, people crowded in to peer over his shoulder, they were then distributed by the young man, one by one, moving from hand to hand accompanied by murmurs of awe and surprise.

"*Snow?*" asked her friend, pointing to the picture of her standing in front of her apartment house.

"Yes," she said, nodding happily. "Yes, snow. Too cold there for *cotton.*"

"Ah—I see, I see," he cried in relief, understanding, and addressed his friends rapidly and with authority.

"Husband?" he asked, pointing to Cyrus.

She smiled. "A *very* dear friend."

"Aha," he cried joyously, and again addressed the crowd, but it was the photographs of her grandson that drew the most appreciative murmurs, and she was given glances of deep respect.

A picture, she thought, *was certainly worth a thousand words; hadn't it been the Chinese who first said this?*

Her friend was thanking her now with pleasure. "Now we see, yes," he said. He turned and spoke sharply to one of the men holding a picture and snatched it back, rubbing away a smudge of dirt before he returned it to her. One by one the snapshots arrived in her hands and she put them away. It seemed an auspicious moment to withdraw. "I go now," she told them all, bowing. "Good night and thank you! *Zai jian!*"

"*Good* day," they called, laughing with her, and as she left they surged again toward Malcolm and his sketchbook.

Mrs. Pollifax wandered on along the path, ignoring a charming arched bridge over a pond and drawn toward a mysterious bright light in the distance. Iris, catching up with her, said, "I'm ready to go back, it's growing dark."

"Hi there," called Jenny, emerging from a side path. "Going back?"

"Yes," said Mrs. Pollifax, "but not until I've investigated that bright light ahead. I'm curious—I noticed it when we entered the park and it's still there."

"Noises, too," contributed Iris as they strolled toward it.

"Of people?" asked Jenny doubtfully.

"Weird sounds," Iris decided. "People and engines. An adventure for us maybe?"

"Definitely," said Mrs. Pollifax happily. "Let's look and find out."

Out of the darkness, the light emerging from its interior, appeared a circular wooden structure with steps leading to the top and the silhouette of heads lining a platform that encircled the structure. "Yes, yes," said the solitary attendant leaning against a step, and untied a rope to allow them free entry. They mounted narrow precipitous wooden stairs—up, up, toward the suffused brilliant light—to find themselves peering down into an arena with gently sloping sides.

"Good heavens," breathed Iris, "it's like looking into a barrel, it's so small. Look—two motorcycles!"

As they watched, two splendidly dressed young men

emerged from a small door and mounted the cycles, the crowd murmured appreciatively, the young men bowed, grinned, rev'd up the engines to a roar, rode once around the floor, and then as they gained speed they sent their cycles upward and into the curve of the wall. Mrs. Pollifax braced herself as the cyclists circled higher and higher, engines roaring, the platform creaking and trembling and shuddering under her feet. The cyclists became perpendicular now, and for one moment she thought they might shoot out over the top, taking people and platform with them (headline: *Xian, People's Republic: In China today dozens were killed when two performing cyclists went out of control and careened into the audience. Among the dead, three American tourists, as yet unidentified.*), and then the engines slackened, the momentum was aborted and —perhaps most difficult of all—the two shining young gods guided their vehicles down, still spinning off the walls, reached bottom, and came to an earth-trembling stop. Off came the helmets; the cheers were thunderous and joyful.

Mrs. Pollifax joined the applause; it was over, they had arrived at the end. Slowly they descended the steps with the crowd, to the hard-packed earth where a single light now illuminated the path. "Now *that*," she said, "was slightly incredible."

"So was that platform," commented Jenny. "If felt like an upside-down bushel basket and just as frail. I was scared to death."

"Never mind, it was fun," breathed Iris, her eyes shining.

Already the lights were being extinguished all over the park; nothing was wasted, it was nine o'clock, the television screen was dark, the park emptying. They walked out onto the avenue where the small garish lamps of the vendors shone like fireflies in the darkness. People lingered, chatting, under the dim light of the occasional streetlamp, some strolling in pairs, some hurrying home, a few on bicycles.

"Now which way did we come?" asked Iris.

"Oh—down that road," Mrs. Pollifax said, pointing.

Jenny shook her head. "Uh-uh, that's where we saw George taking pictures, don't you remember? So we take the other street."

Mrs. Pollifax expressed her doubt. "I really don't think so."

"But I'm *known* for my bump of direction," Jenny insisted. "Really I am . . . trust me!"

"We'll trust you," Iris told her gravely.

They reached, eventually, the broad avenue on which they had expected to find the People's Hotel, but there was no hotel. Instead they met with a sea of people strolling down the center of a road in a silence broken only by the shuffling sounds of their feet. There were no cars. As they continued walking there was no hotel, either. They were looked at with curiosity; a few turned to stare.

"Still confident?" Mrs. Pollifax asked Jenny.

"Oh yes," said Jenny, and then spoiled such assertiveness by pausing to say to a young man, "Do you speak English?"

He smiled, shook his head, and hurried on. So did they, but after three more blocks Mrs. Pollifax's skepticism had turned into alarm; she decided the time had come to try that universal language of the hands. She stopped two men, and laid her head on her hands in a manner that she hoped denoted sleep. "Ho-tel?" she asked. "Hotel?"

The two men nodded happily and turned to point in the direction ahead of them.

"Xiexie," she said, bowing.

But another block still produced no hotel, and Mrs. Pollifax began to picture them sleeping in a doorway for the night, began to look down narrow alleys and into mysterious entrances that led to wooden doors, speculating on how long a tourist might be lost in Xian, and longing passionately for a real bed.

It was Iris who next said, "I don't see a damn thing ahead resembling a hotel. Let me try."

"But I'm supposed to have such a good bump of direction," wailed Jenny.

"Well, coming to China has dislocated it, I think," said Mrs. Pollifax.

"Ho-tel?" asked Iris, stopping three men and repeating Mrs. Pollifax's symbol for sleep.

At once Iris drew a crowd; they became surrounded by faces made dim and unearthly in the near-darkness, faces marveling at Iris' height, a few women tittering behind their hands; it turned into a party, and a few minutes later a dozen of the young men escorted them half a block farther, smiling and murmuring "hotel" and pointing, and there—at last—was the hotel, with its sentry and its gate.

Bows, thank yous, and smiles were exchanged, they passed through a deserted lobby, mounted stairs, and Mrs. Pollifax entered her small hot room with its chuckling air-conditioner. The temperature had dropped only a few degrees and she found the twenty-five-watt light in the lamp depressing. Kneeling beside her suitcase she unlocked and opened it to return the camera she'd extracted from it before walking to the park, and suddenly became very still, the movement of camera to suitcase arrested.

Her suitcase had been opened and searched while she was gone.

A long time ago she had worked out a formula for packing, and although efficiency had been only a minor reason for this she had automatically continued to pack in a certain way even when there was no necessity for caution. She had felt there was no need for caution on this trip, but apparently she had been wrong. Her suitcase had been unlocked very expertly, and very professionally and discreetly searched, but whoever had done the job couldn't possibly have known of her packing formula. When she had snatched the camera from her suitcase after dinner her bright red pajamas had as usual been folded up with the pajama bottoms underneath the pajama tops—that was the important detail—and her toothbrush and comb tucked into their folds. Now the pajama bottoms were on top, and both toothbrush and comb had vanished somewhere into her suitcase.

Now this, thought Mrs. Pollifax, abruptly sitting down on the floor, *is a pretty kettle of fish, and completely unexpected.*

Who, she wondered, *could have done this?* She could not believe it had been a worker in the hotel; opening a locked suitcase without leaving behind so much as a scratch was an art denied to the average person.

The police? But Mr. Li had handled Customs, and at the

border no one had felt any need to question her about her remarkable supply of vitamins and dried fruit.

Her mysterious coagent? But whoever he was there seemed no need for him to investigate her; he had the advantage of knowing who she was, as well as what she'd brought with her.

What a bewildering finish to a delightful evening, she thought, and realized that she felt thoroughly jarred by this. *I don't understand it,* she reflected, *and I don't like it. It's almost as if—* But she did not allow herself to complete that thought, and hastily drew out her pajamas.

Chapter Five

*M*ay we see the sketches you did last evening in the park?" Mrs. Pollifax asked Malcolm at breakfast.

He said ruefully, "I ended up giving them all away to my audience. We certainly attract crowds, don't we?"

He smiled across the table at Iris, who flushed as usual but managed one of her radiant smiles in return.

"Quite a schedule today," commented Joe Forbes, spearing a peanut between his chopsticks.

"Yes indeed," she said. Miss Bai had pinned to the dining room wall a calendar of events for their stay in Xian, presented in flawless calligraphy, but to Mrs. Pollifax the most important news was that after trips to the Bell Tower and to the Wild Goose Pagoda, they were going to visit the Drum Tower.

For the Drum Tower Mrs. Pollifax still had no plans. How very easy and natural the assignment had seemed to her when she was sitting in Carstairs' office in Langley Field, Virginia, and how very different it looked now that she was in Xian! She had absolutely no idea what obstacles were going to greet her, or even whether she would be able to find Guo Musu's barbershop. She dared not ask about a barbershop near the Drum Tower or she would be shown it—if it existed—in the company of Mr. Li or Miss Bai. She had finally accepted the fact that she could assemble no strategy whatever in advance, which was not the happiest way to approach such an important moment, or the Drum Tower either, or Guo Musu if he could be found, but Mrs. Pollifax had a great deal of faith: something would occur to her. A miracle would take place.

Yes, definitely a miracle, she told herself firmly.

In the meantime they were going to visit Ban Po Village this morning, which would please Iris, and a department store, which would please Jenny's desire for Mao cap and jacket, and Mrs. Pollifax tried to pretend that it pleased her too, that this was a perfectly normal day with the afternoon of no particular significance, and that her suitcase had not been searched the night before.

At Ban Po Village they were ushered into a briefing room and seated at a long table with a tea cup placed squarely in front of each chair, and while they sipped hot tea the resident guide delivered facts to them, translated into English by Miss Bai . . . the site discovered accidentally in 1953 . . . the foundations of forty-five houses with remarkably preserved pottery and tools . . . in existence from 6080 B.C. to 5600 B.C. . . . evidence of its being a matriarchal society . . .

Released from the tyranny of the briefing, Mrs. Pollifax considered those facts. She decided that facts could not possibly describe the drama of workmen starting to build a factory here and discovering instead the remains of an eight-thousand-year-old village. Strolling along the walkways of the building that sheltered the excavation, she tried to come to grips with eight thousand years of time and failed. Eight thousand was only a number, there was simply no way to cope with such aeons, but what did come to her—like a lingering fragrance across the years—was the intelligence at work here: the intricately worked out trenches between the houses, the playful designs etched into pottery, the burial of dead children in huge egg-shaped pottery urns, as if to return them, she thought, to the embryo from which they'd entered life. It gave her a pleasant feeling of pride in the human race. She wondered what archaeologists in the year A.D. 10,000 would find when they uncovered the relics of the twentieth century; would there, she wondered, be any signs of intelligence remaining? or only vestiges of folly and violence?

On the drive back to Xian she began to feel oppressively

hungry. Miss Bai was explaining to Peter and Jenny the government's current Five Stresses—civilization, morality, order, cleanliness, and manners, and the Four Beautifications—of thought, language, heart, and environment—and Mrs. Pollifax was ashamed of herself for yawning. "Why do I get hungry so early?" she complained to Joe Forbes, sitting next to her.

"Peanuts for breakfast?" he quipped amiably.

"But I also had a hard-boiled egg," she protested.

Malcolm called across the aisle, "I'd say it's the chopsticks. You may *think* you eat a lot—"

Iris turned around in the seat ahead and said, "But she's the most expert of us all, haven't you noticed?" She beamed at Mrs. Pollifax. "Wasn't Ban Po Village tremendous? I hope I didn't monopolize the guide, but honestly—eight thousand years! I mean the Qin Shi Huang Tombs we see tomorrow are only 210 B.C."

"Practically contemporary," put in Malcolm mischievously. "Possibly it's culture that's giving us an appetite?"

But Mrs. Pollifax's eyes were on George Westrum who was seated next to Iris, and who had turned now to give Iris a glance that startled Mrs. Pollifax. She thought: *George is on his way to adoring this woman . . .* It was a peculiar word to choose but it was the word that had slid into her head: *adoration,* she mused. *Devotion. Worship.*

The alliances that were beginning to form had already begun to interest her. The infants, for instance—as Malcolm continued to call Peter and Jenny—had at once formed a twosome. Iris talked to everyone, but Mrs. Pollifax noticed how often George Westrum managed to sit next to her, his face inscrutable, his eyes watching every play of expression across her vivid face. When Malcolm joined them George's eyes shifted to Malcolm's face, again without expression. Iris appeared to regard Malcolm with some caution and blushed a great deal, but Mrs. Pollifax wasn't sure whether it was his charm or his book writing that dazzled her.

As for Joe Forbes, Mrs. Pollifax admitted that she'd not yet fathomed him at all. He was always with them—smiling and amiable—and often contributing a brief comment or wisecrack, but he was oddly *not* there somehow. She wondered if anyone else had noticed this. Not consciously, she decided, but his personality had so little impact that once or twice she'd caught someone adding, "Oh yes, and Joe too."

She wondered if this meant that he was the agent who would eventually approach her after her attempt this afternoon at the Drum Tower. Her knowledge of professional agents was limited and theatrical, but she had heard that certain full-time agents took great pains to rub out their personalities and achieve anonymity; perhaps this became habitual, and the loss of personality irreversible. *Except, of course, for John Sebastian Farrell,* she thought with a smile, *who only heaped new layers of personality on his own to gloriously and cheekily distract.*

She was still smiling, still thinking of Farrell, when they drew up to the department store in Xian.

"A *real* department store?" asked Jenny skeptically.

Mr. Li assured her that yes this was a real one, where the Chinese people shopped. "But they will also take your tourist scrip here, and you have forty minutes to look."

"Forty minutes!" wailed Jenny. "To find a Mao cap and jacket? Peter wants to buy them, too. Oh yes, and Joe," she added.

"Miss Bai—?"

Miss Bai nodded. "I'll go with them."

"Anyone else?"

No one else had any pressing needs. They entered the store together to immediately veer off in different directions. The first floor was high-ceilinged and large and struck Mrs. Pollifax as curiously empty, which was puzzling to her because throngs of people lined the counters. She realized she was associating it with American department stores, which were all color, movement, and glamorous displays, and at once felt penitent. Turning right she began a tour of the broad and dusty aisles, hungering for color to relieve the dull greens and grays and blues, and was suddenly brought to a standstill by a wall that blazed with color.

"Books," she whispered in delight: books placed side by side against the wall so that their jackets bloomed like flowers. She moved toward them, and the people crowding around the counter made room for her. *"Xiexie,"* she said quietly, taking her place.

But she was a foreigner, after all, and the clerk hurried to her, smiling. Mrs. Pollifax thought, *I'll buy one, I'll buy a book as my souvenir here.* She pointed to a paperback with a jacket design that stood out from the others because it did not have an illustration of a soldier, or a girl and a boy. "That one," she said, drawn by its black and white lines splashed with abstract yellows and scarlets.

The girl's hands hovered, then dropped. She picked out a cream-colored book next to Mrs. Pollifax's choice and placed it in her hands.

"No," said Mrs. Pollifax politely. "No, not this one." She shook her head and then glanced down at the book and opened it to see what it was. She found maps inside: it was a purse-sized atlas of China, the cities and towns marked in Chinese with not a single English word to be seen, and therefore incomprehensible and useless to her. On the other hand, she mused, it could make a lovely souvenir for her grandson, who would be pleased and amused by it. "I'll take it," she said, nodding, "but I'd also like—" and she pointed again to the charming cover that had originally caught her eye. Several more books were picked up and put down before the one she wanted was achieved. It turned out to be a recipe book, also in Chinese, but with lavish color photos at the back.

"I'll take both," she said, holding up two fingers and smiling. Reaching for her purse the crowd drew closer while she and the salesgirl sorted through her Chinese currency for the *yuan* that would purchase one recipe book and one book of maps.

And then—suddenly jarred—she thought, *"Maps!"*

Maps, she repeated, the word tugging at her mind, and she picked up the atlas and looked again at its competently waterproof cream jacket. This time she opened it more thoughtfully. On page one she found a map of the entire country, with each province in a different color. She could recognize the Xinjiang Autonomous Region because of its size—enormous—and its location in the northwest corner. After studying the shape of it she turned the pages until she found the identical shape on page thirty-eight.

Which means, she thought in amazement, *that I'm actually staring at a map of Xinjiang Province with all its roads laid out in front of me and marked, and all its towns and villages identified, even if their names are written in Chinese, which I can't read.*

But Guo Musu—if she found him—could read them.

And standing there in the middle of China, in a department store in Shaanxi Province surrounded by eavesdroppers and interested spectators, Mrs. Pollifax began to laugh. Her laugh began as a chuckle that traveled up from her toes and emerged as a luxurious, Cheshire-cat smile that lighted up her face.

Her miracle had just happened.

"I'll buy two of these," she told the clerk, holding up the atlas, and reached into her purse for another *yuan.*

To the others, back in the bus, she showed only her recipe book. Peter, Jenny, and Joe Forbes were happily wearing their new Mao caps and jackets ("show and tell time," laughed Jenny); Iris had bought a bright enameled mug, Malcolm an ink stick, and George a handkerchief with Xian printed on it.

"A taste of the consumer life," commented Malcolm dryly, "to keep us from suffering withdrawal pangs."

They lunched. They visited a cloisonné factory where they had a long tea-and-briefing, due mainly to Iris asking far too many questions about workers' hours and wages; they were led through dark and dusty halls to watch cloisonné jewelry intricately crafted, and then to a Friendship Store for purchases. They visited the Bell Tower, and the Wild Goose Pagoda, except that by midafternoon it was so hot that only Jenny and Peter climbed the eight stories to its peak.

And then in late afternoon they came to the Drum Tower, and Mrs. Pollifax's moment of truth had arrived.

Chapter Six

Mrs. Pollifax descended last of all from the minibus, trying not to remember that she'd flown halfway around the world for this moment. She found that her heart was beating much too quickly, and she forced herself to close her eyes and remind herself that *que será será*, and that, after all, a thousand years from now—Following these incantations she opened her eyes and looked around her. They were parked in a dusty narrow alley, surrounded by earthen walls. Off to her left she saw the high, lacquer-tiled roofs of what had to be the Drum Tower. Between this and the bus lay a maze of mud-and-straw walls, interrupted here and there by alleys leading into a mysterious interior. There was no barbershop; in fact, there were no shops to be seen at all, there were only walls.

No panic please, she told herself, and smiled at a small round-faced child who grinned back at her. She called to Mr. Li, "I'm going to take some pictures of children, I'll catch up with you in a minute." Having said this she knelt in the dust and began dramatically snapping pictures with a camera that was completely empty of film. As the others moved away down the dusty lane she slipped into the nearest alley and, with several of the children trailing her, began to look for a barbershop.

She was soon completely lost and gave herself up to the

luxurious feeling of being on her own again, free of the group
but cherishing too the assumption that somewhere—somehow—there would be a way out of this maze of clay-colored
walls. In the meantime it was fascinating to be inside them
instead of looking at them from the outside: to glance into
dark rooms and tiny courtyards, assess the herbs hung in door-
ways to dry, watch children squatting in the dust to draw
figures with a stick or a stone. She passed two ancient men
playing cards, one of them with a marvelous wisp of goatee on
his chin, like a mandarin; she smiled and nodded to them and
received courtly bows in return. Threading her way through
one lane after another she turned left, then right, stopping now
and then to take a pretend-picture of a flower, a doorway, a
child, until at last she entered a much broader alley to find
herself virtually under the roofs of the Drum Tower but still
inside the compound's walls.

Here at least there were markets: stalls and shops carved
into the clay wall behind them, and people, far too many people. She walked slowly down this wider road, nodding and
smiling to passersby, trying not to notice the number who
came to their doors to watch her, or that slight edginess she
felt at being so conspicuous. She passed a bicycle repair shop;
she passed a stall in which an ancient sewing machine had
been installed, and then a vendor of steaming noodles.

And then—quite suddenly—she found herself passing a barbershop.

She tried not to stare. Her quick glance noted an exterior of
crumbling adobe that matched the wall into which it was set,
a large, very dusty glass window, an open door and a dim
interior filled with men. Only the chair placed near the window identified it, and the man with clippers bent over his
customer in the chair.

Here is a barbershop, thought Mrs. Pollifax, *but not where
I thought it would be, or where Carstairs and Bishop thought
it would be, either.*

She continued past it, glanced into a shop filled with
women working at a long workbench, and finding neither an
exit from this alley or another barbershop she stopped. She
thought, "If it's not Guo Musu in there—well, that's why I

was chosen, isn't it? Because I stand up well under police interrogations?"

But for a moment she thought indignantly of Carstairs and Bishop, neither of whom realized the quantities of people on the move in China in the daytime, and the total lack of privacy anywhere. People on the street, people crowded into a barber shop . . . they had certainly not considered the effect of an American tourist plunging in among the crowds to ask for information. It was outrageous and it might prove suicidal, but she was going to have to go into that shop.

She turned and retraced her steps to its door.

A dozen men seated along the wall gaped at her as she walked inside. She called out, "Does anyone here speak English?" The barber was intent on guiding clippers around the ears of his customer; he had scarcely glanced up at her arrival and her heart sank at the lack of response. She began again. "Does anyone here—"

The barber lifted his head and looked at her. "I speak a little." He was a nondescript, sallow man, his face devoid of expression.

"I'm so glad," she said with an enthusiasm she didn't feel. "I'm lost. I wonder if you could come to the door—" here she pointed, "and show me the way to the Drum Tower?"

The man spoke to his companions in his own language; heads nodded and the smiles blossomed so ardently that for a minute she feared they might all jump up to help her. But the barber had put down his clippers and he joined her alone in the doorway.

"Please—come outside," she said in a low voice. "Are you Guo Musu?"

He stiffened. "How is this, please," he whispered, "that you know my name?"

They were being watched with interest by a circle of bystanders in the alley, and by the men behind them in the barbershop. In spite of their being out of earshot she knew that she must be careful and protect this man, whether he helped her or not. She asked, "Which way to the Drum Tower?"

Automatically he pointed in the direction she'd been heading; she hoped this gesture established authenticity, but it was going to be difficult to remember appropriate gestures while she talked. "There isn't much time," she said quickly. "Your brother Chang, who reached Hong Kong safely, said you could tell me where the camp is located that you lived in for three years. The labor camp somewhere in Xinjiang Province."

"Chang!" he exclaimed. "Labor camp?"

Damn, she thought, and deplored this lack of time and privacy, *he's going to need time to adjust to this, the shock couldn't have been greater if I announced that I came from the moon.* "I'm visiting your country," she told him politely. "We're enjoying Xian very much. We saw Ban Po Village this morning, and tomorrow we visit the tomb of—"

Amusement flickered in his eyes; she had underestimated him. He said, "And you have somehow found me to ask—"

"I know what you think," she told him frankly. "You could be arrested for giving me this information but I can also be arrested for asking you."

An ironic smile crossed his face.

"I'm American," she told him. "It's Americans who would like to know."

"Americans," he repeated, turning the word over on his tongue. "And just what do you expect of me?" There was a very real irony in his voice now.

She said earnestly, "What I thought—what I hoped—I bought an atlas this morning in Xian, with Xinjiang Province on page thirty-eight. Let me show you." She turned to page thirty-eight and handed it to him. "If you decide to trust me I thought we might walk a little—away from your shop and your neighbors—and I could hand you a pen."

He looked at her, studying her with curiosity and interest. The irony slowly receded; he said at last, quietly, "I will walk with you to the end of the road and show you the way to the Drum Tower."

"Oh thank you," she gasped, adding quickly, "You're very kind."

He said politely, "Not at all."

As they walked he glanced down at the map of Xinjiang Province, whereas Mrs. Pollifax glanced back, relieved to see that only a few of the smaller children followed, but at a distance. Nearing the end of the alley he looked up from the atlas and met her gaze. Wordlessly she offered him the pen, leaning closer to him so that no one would see. He gravely accepted it.

"I'll keep talking," she told him as he made a mark on the map, and without watching him she began a pantomime of gestures and smiles. After a moment he slipped the atlas back into her hand, and she slid it into her purse.

Bringing out her identical copy she said, "In case any one saw us—"

His eyes widened in astonishment.

"No, this is a duplicate," she said, presenting it to him with a bow. "Look at page thirty-eight and you'll see."

He turned to that page, and she saw his relief. "Please take it," she told him. "As a gift. For showing me the way to the Drum Tower."

"For showing you the way to the Drum Tower," he repeated, and suddenly smiled, showing a number of teeth capped in steel. "And Chang?" he asked, his irony exquisite now. "He is well?"

"I am told he is very well," she said, smiling back at him, and suddenly she was aware of the immensity of what he had dared to do for her, and she seized the book he held and wrote her name in it. "Now each of us knows," she told him. "It's only fair. We're hostages now to each other."

"But there was no need for that," he told her gently.

Startled, she said, "Oh?"

"Your eyes speak for you, which is why I do this," he said. "I think it is possible that you also follow The Way."

She had forgotten that he was Buddhist. "I seek," she acknowledged softly, "but sometimes—oh, in very strange ways."

His smile was warm. "But there are no strange ways, *xianben*—only the search."

"Ah," she said with a catch of breath, and for a long moment they gazed at each other and she was mute, deeply touched by a recognition, a tenderness between them. She said at last, very softly, "Thank you, Mr. Guo, and—please—may you have long life and double happiness."

He nodded and walked away, once again a sallow nondescript man, no doubt wearing an ironic smile for the comrades who moved eagerly toward him. She watched him hold up the atlas she'd given him, and as his neighbors drew close to examine it she left. Presently she was mounting the steps to the Drum Tower.

Mr. Li was waiting at the entrance. "Where have you been?" he demanded. "Miss Bai has gone to search for you."

She only smiled at him, and moved past him.

She found the others in the small Friendship Store at the top of the building, looking into glass cases at ancient relics displayed for sale. Not one of them looked up at her entrance, and she commended her silent partner for being so controlled and disciplined an actor. But although she too concentrated on the relics with control and discipline, her thoughts remained with Guo Musu and on that curious sense of meeting that she'd experienced with him. *Nothing happens by accident,* she thought, and she knew that she would not easily forget that moment of tenderness between them.

And she had succeeded. Her job was done. She'd found and made contact with Guo Musu and there was exhilaration in this, and a sense of triumph.

They attended Chinese Opera that evening. Mrs. Pollifax, tired from the suspense and from the tensions of finding Guo Musu, found Jenny and Peter extremely irritating. In spite of being several years older, it was Jenny who seemed to be succumbing to Peter's hostile attitudes: they had moved from an early sharing of college jokes and anecdotes to a running patter of tactless criticisms of China that Mrs. Pollifax found deplorable. She had already overheard a few whispered flippancies about Mr. Li, and only that morning they'd been giggling about the questions Iris had asked at the cloisonné factory's tea and briefing.

Now it was the Shaanxi local opera that met with their unkind laughter.

Mrs. Pollifax herself was entranced. The theater was shabby and the audience in dull work clothes, but the stage shone like a jewel with the brilliance of the costumes—color for the eye at last, she thought, as she feasted on it. Mr. Li had explained

to them that the ancient tale was in serial form and had begun
three nights ago; it would last four hours tonight, but they
would depart at intermission. Mrs. Pollifax found no problems
at all in following it: the gestures were stylized but the meaning of each one, coupled with the droll and vivid expressions
on the actors' faces needed no words of explanation. There was
a marvelous humor in the story, and she laughed along with
the audience without the slightest idea of what was being said.

Jenny, however, was not content with this and demanded of
Mr. Li a translation of every word spoken, after which she
would repeat his explanation in a loud voice for the rest of
them.

"So this guy—the one in black," she was saying, "has come
down from heaven to avenge the death of—which one, Mr.
Li?"

"Get a load of the singing!" interrupted Peter, laughing.
"Straight through the nasal passages, vibrating all the si-
nuses!"

Jenny giggled. "Not to mention how the princess sniffles
into her sleeves, the one in bright red?"

Ugly Americans, thought Mrs. Pollifax sadly, and was
about to speak to them when George Westrum surprised and
impressed her by turning around and doing it first.

"Look here," he growled, "you're not giving this a chance,
and you're being damned rude, too."

Mrs. Pollifax glanced around and saw that Jenny had the
grace to blush but Peter's face only turned cold and stony
again. They stopped their chattering and Mrs. Pollifax returned to the opera, but something had gone out of the evening. She realized that the first rift had appeared in their
group, and the embarrassment of it hung in the air, an embarrassment for themselves, for Mr. Li, for China, and for Peter
and Jenny. It was not a comfortable way to feel, thought Mrs.
Pollifax, and when they left at the intermission there were no
comments about the opera on their way back to the hotel. The
silence was awkward, and only Iris and Mrs. Pollifax called
out good night to Jenny and Peter.

*   *   *

She had been alone in her room for only a few minutes when the door opened, startling her. She turned her head to see Peter walk in without knocking and she was appalled at this breach of manners; not even the assumption that he might have come to apologize dampened her sense of outrage. She said angrily, "Whether you realize it or not, Peter, it's customary to knock."

He stood there, arrogant, cold, and sulky. He closed the door behind him and without paying her words any attention he walked across the room and tucked the curtains more securely around the air-conditioner. Only then did he turn and say quietly, in a voice she'd never heard from him before, "I've come to ask if you made contact with Guo Musu today."

Chapter Seven

Mrs. Pollifax stared at him incredulously. "You?" she gasped. *"You!"*

He stood silent, watching her, waiting.

"You're too young," she flung at him. "You're only twenty-two, how could you possibly be one of Cars—" She stopped.

"One of Carstairs' people," he finished for her.

She stared at him in shock, her mind spinning in an effort to adjust: *not* Joe Forbes, *not* Malcolm Styles, *not* George Westrum. She said, feeling her way toward something concrete, "You can't possibly speak Chinese or—"

"Fluently. Mandarin as well as several dialects."

"There was that grandmother—"

"Oh yes, that grandmother," he said with a faint smile. "Born in Kansas City, Missouri, actually, and the closest she's come to China is Mah-Jongg."

"What's more I've *disliked* you," she told him angrily. "I didn't realize how much until you walked in just now without knocking. Spoiled, sulky, unappreciative—"

"That good, huh?"

Mrs. Pollifax began to laugh. "I see . . . yes. All right—*very* good, and I'm acting like an idiot." She held out her hand to him. "I'm sorry."

His handclasp was firm. "It was a shock for me when I first

saw you too," he conceded politely. "I won't say where it was, but definitely it was a shock."

"That bad, huh?" she mimicked, smiling at him. "Then shall we start all over again before getting on with the job?"

"If there *is* a job," he said quietly. "Look, the suspense has been damn hard to handle, I didn't see any barbershop at all near the Drum Tower."

She nodded. "Then I'm delighted to tell you that there was a barbershop and a Guo Musu, too."

"My God," he said, staring at her. "Where?"

"Hidden away in that maze of alleys."

"But were you able to—did he—"

She nodded. "It's in my purse, excuse me."

"What's in your purse?"

She reached across him to the bedside table, groped for the atlas and brought it out. "Page thirty-eight," she said, opening it and handing it to him.

He stared at it in amazement. "Where on earth did you get a Chinese atlas?"

"In the department store this morning," she told him. *"Quite* by accident. I pointed to what I thought would be a book of poems and they handed me this instead. It was a miracle."

As he leaned over page thirty-eight Peter's face was no longer impassive. "It's a miracle all right," he said, and glanced up at her. "Have you looked at this? Guo's not only marked the location of the labor camp but he's added notes."

"Notes?" she echoed, and Guo's face returned to her again, and that moment of sharing, of knowing. "He did that for us, too?" she said, with a catch in her voice.

"I'll say!" He showed her the page, excited now. "He's pinpointed the labor camp halfway between Urumchi, where we go tomorrow, and Turfan—just off the main highroad over the Tian Shan mountains. But what's even more fantastic, he's scribbled a footnote explaining the circle he's drawn, he says it marks a Red Army barracks some six or eight miles from the labor camp." He looked at her and shook his head. "How did you manage all this? You were missing for only about forty-

five minutes this afternoon. I mean, you're one hell of a surprise."

"Thank you," she said.

"No, I mean it," he told her. "To get all this in minutes
from an absolute stranger? Since reaching Xian I've been feeling damnably humbled, wondering how on earth I'd have
managed it. I wanted to, you know, I insisted on doing it myself but Carstairs refused. This morning I realized I'd have
behaved like a bull in a tea shop. Spoken Chinese probably,
alarmed Guo Musu thoroughly, even given the whole show
away and gotten nowhere. How did you do it?"

"It's probably why they sent me," said Mrs. Pollifax modestly. "The Chinese do have a deep respect for their elders,
after all, and I tend to look quite harmless."

He grinned. "That's for sure—you fooled *me*. And now—"
He hesitated, staring down at page thirty-eight. "It's incredible
but I think we're in business at last. I can even get down to
some serious planning now. Amazing."

She smiled at him. "Good—but did *you* by any chance
search my suitcase last night?"

He looked at her blankly. "Search your—why should I want
to search your suitcase?"

"Oh," she said with a sinking heart. "It wasn't you, then?"

"No of course not." Peter looked shocked. "Are you sure?"

"Oh yes. Somebody did. Was yours?"

He shook his head. "No, I take the usual precautions. I'd
have known right away." His brows drew together into a
frown. "I don't get it, who would do such a thing, and why?
And why *you?*"

"It was done very professionally," she told him, "and it
wouldn't have been noticeable at all if I didn't have my own
way of packing, too. The lock wasn't picked, and everything
was left in order—but not the right order." His scowl had
turned into such a look of alarm that she added softly, "Don't
look so jarred, it was probably some sort of random security
check." She didn't think at all that it was a security check, but
she saw no point in worrying Peter just now when he had his
plans to make. "In any case," she told him cheerfully, "I think
we should put it aside for the moment, there being other

things to think about, don't you agree? Which leads me to a
question I've been waiting for some time to ask you. With
enormous curiosity."

She had succeeded in distracting him; he smiled. "Be my
guest and ask, but I'll bet I know what it is."

She smiled back at him. "I'm sure you do: the one detail no
one's mentioned, and which didn't seep through to me until
too late to ask. You're going to be escorting our friend Mr.
Wang—X—out of the country, aren't you." She didn't even
bother to make it a question.

He nodded.

"Then as a bona fide member of a bona fide guided tour,
allowed to visit China as a tourist, how are you ever going to
manage to vanish from the tour and gain freedom for your very
risky undercover work? I can't believe that you'll just bolt.
You wouldn't have a chance, would you?"

He shook his head. "Not a chance in a million. No, there'll
be an accident."

"Accident," she repeated, watching his face intently.
"What kind?"

"That's up to me," he told her. "I've a few ideas boiling
around in my head but it depends on a lot of factors like terrain and circumstances and timing. I'll be killed," he added
casually.

"Killed," she repeated, and waited.

"In such a way there'll be no trace of a body," he explained,
adding soberly, "and it's growing on me fast that your help is
going to be very much needed."

"I see," she said musingly. "Yes, it would have to be that, of
course. The *only* way to vanish into China."

"Yes—become a non-person. Without the Sepos in hot pursuit. A dead person."

She shivered. "Not easy."

"No."

"And from the vitamins and dried food I'm carrying I de-
duce you'll be heading for the mountains?"

He nodded. "There's been the feeble hope that another
route might open up, but I don't think it will."

"Very *high* mountains," she said quietly. "And cold ones. Surely not through Tibet?"

"No, we can head around the Taklamakan desert toward Khotan and a pass over the Karakaroms."

"The very thought chills me," she admitted. "Literally as well as figuratively."

He nodded. "That's where I'll need your help, too; you can help me find warm clothing and carry some of it in your suitcase when mine's full."

"Like what?" she asked, and reached for paper and pencil, glad to move her thoughts toward the practical.

He frowned as he concentrated. "What I did smuggle in is small stuff. I've got thermal underwear, two heavy ski masks rolled up, fake papers, and a heavy sweater. The windbreaker jacket I brought has a second one zipped inside it. I've knives, flashlights and batteries, a good compass hidden in my camera, topographical maps, complete medicine kit right down to snake serum, and two collapsible canvas bags for water—"

"Plus the chocolate I brought, the dried foods, and vitamins—"

"Yes. And now what's needed is more of the big stuff. Blankets and sheepskins—anything that can be cut into vests and coats. We're heading tomorrow into nomad country where there ought to be sheepskins in the bazaars or Friendship Stores. Buy whatever you find, you can refuse to have it mailed home for you until we get to Beijing, make up some sort of story, rope whatever you find to the outside of your suitcase and keep it with you."

"Right," she said crisply, noting this down on paper.

"In the meantime," he added with a crooked smile, "I have my Mao cap and jacket, and they were very nearly top priority, believe me, because I shall have to become as Chinese as a native soon."

"How on earth did you learn fluent Chinese at such an age?" she asked. "It's unexpected."

"Very weirdly," he told her. "When I was into my freshman year at Harvard—yeah, Harvard," he admitted with a grin. "I started out hanging around bars in Chinatown in Boston. Coincidence? I don't know. And I began picking up the language bit by bit—with an ease that staggered me. Coincidence? I don't know. By the time I graduated from Harvard I could read and write Mandarin, and was already into dialects, and it's not true, either, that I've just finished my senior year. I'm in graduate school now—their Far Asian studies department—or was, until I took off to get in shape for this."

"And Carstairs?"

He grinned. "No, it was Bishop. I met *him* in a Chinatown bar in Boston, or perhaps—who knows?—he arranged to meet me there because he'd heard of me. A setup maybe."

She smiled. "Quite possibly. And here we are."

"Yes. And now I have this," he said, looking down at the atlas with astonishment. "I'll take it along to my room and figure kilometers from the map I brought, and do some calculations."

"Did anyone see you come into my room?" asked Mrs. Pollifax, remembering her searched suitcase, and still uneasy about it.

He shook his head. "The hall was empty." He thought a minute. "If anyone's in the hall when I make my exit I'll say I came to borrow a drinking glass. But tell me first—I'm curious —what was Guo Musu like?"

She told him, describing the barbershop and their meeting, and as she talked she became aware of several quick, perceptive glances directed at her, as if he understood much more than she was saying, and for this she was grateful.

When she had finished he nodded. "I wish I could have talked with him. It's been terribly frustrating," he added, with a rush of boyish candor. "The opera tonight, for instance. I really hated Jenny's running commentary when I could understand every word for myself, and I came near to hating her for demeaning it. I've also overheard and understood everything that Mr. Li and Miss Bai talk about together, and I feel like a bloody eavesdropper. Mr. Li," he said ruefully, "doesn't think very highly of me either." He stood up. "I'll go along now and study this map more closely."

Rising too she said, "It might be a good idea for us to become a shade friendlier inside the group. In case we're seen talking together, as we'll surely have to do from time to time."

"Good," he said, with a grin. "I'll begin sitting next to you at meals occasionally, and show signs of thawing. And look," he added almost shyly, "you've been great. I'm awfully glad to have finally met you. *Really* met you, I mean."

She smiled at him warmly. "That goes for me, too." As he moved to open the door she said, "Hold it a moment," and ducked into her bathroom. "Your water glass," she reminded him.

He whistled. "You really are a pro! I forgot, damn it." And glass in hand he made his exit.

Chapter Eight

They drove the next morning to the tomb of China's first emperor Qin Shi Huang, and if this had once promised to be the highlight of sightseeing for her, Mrs. Pollifax now found it difficult to think of anything but Peter's visit to her room last night.

For one thing, the very magnitude of the job that he'd been given nearly overwhelmed her: to devise his own death, to rescue a stranger from a labor camp and then travel what had to be hundreds of miles over desert and cruel mountain passes seemed incredible. The man whom Peter had been sent to rescue had to be very important indeed, she was thinking, and here, too, she decided there must be a great deal that Carstairs had not told her.

And then there was Peter himself . . . She still marveled at his being the agent sent in with her, and she was not at all displeased, but she wished that he'd not forgotten that drinking glass. It was a trivial omission, but it reminded her of his youth and the fact that this was probably his first job, and if so, a massive one. He was certainly a good actor, and he was intelligent. From her impressions of him she guessed there was a natural exuberance in him about what lay ahead, and that this would have been the quality that captured Carstairs' attention, for if she trembled for Peter, she was absolutely certain that Peter did not tremble for himself. Behind the impassive face that had softened only slightly last night she had glimpsed that sort of loner who had to climb mountains because they were there, as the saying went, and for whom danger was addicting, and ordinary life puzzling. It was the stuff of which the T. E. Lawrences and Richard Halliburtons were made, she mused, embryonic now in a cool twenty-two-year-old, and obviously invaluable for this particular job.

But as an agent, she thought, he should never have forgotten that water glass.

And this, she mused, was perhaps another reason why she'd been chosen to accompany Peter: to keep an eye on him and to steady him. It amused her to remember that this was precisely what she'd done by instinct last evening when he'd looked so alarmed about her suitcase being searched: she had reassured and distracted him, hiding her own alarm. Carstairs, she thought, must have done some rare chuckling when he tossed the two of them into this maelstrom—he was no fool about people—but at the moment she wished she might have a few indignant words with him. Obviously, her job in China was not to end in Xian, after all. It might even be just beginning.

She glanced toward the front of the minibus at Peter, who was seated next to Malcolm this morning, as if he'd decided to divest himself of Jenny for the day, and she wondered idly what they were talking about. The two guides sat in front of them, with Miss Bai occasionally interrupting her conversation with Mr. Li to pick up the microphone and point out a field of workers, a commune, or a factory. And then—abruptly —they were pulling into the parking lot of the archaeological site, and ahead lay a broad courtyard framed by low-lying buildings, the largest of which resembled an airplane hangar.

"No cameras allowed," called out Mr. Li.

"No—no pictures," echoed Miss Bai. "We meet here again in one hour, the Friendship Store on the left, a film theater next it showing history of this remarkable discovery, and soda pop to be found in souvenir building."

It was Joe Forbes with whom Mrs. Pollifax strolled toward the hangarlike building that had been erected over the remarkable discoveries. "But this isn't the tomb itself?" he asked pleasantly.

"I don't believe they've even started on the tomb yet," she told him. "These are the burial figures found on the periphery. He took an entire army to the grave with him, but mercifully not a live one, which I do think was kind of him, and very enlightened."

"Another discovery," he quipped, "when a factory was planned?"

"According to the guidebook, this time it was commune workers digging a well." *Pleasantries from behind plexiglass*, she thought, darting a glance at his pleasant, smiling, never-changing face, but knowing now that he wasn't Carstairs' man she felt little need to probe the mystery behind his lack of personality; there probably was no mystery at all, she decided; some people were simply born bland.

They walked together into the building, where Mrs. Pollifax promptly moved to the railing that separated them from the digging site, and here she caught her breath. She had been certain that she knew what to expect; she had studiously looked up photographs but now she realized that they'd been taken out of context, mere pictures in a magazine lacking environment and reality. The sheer impact of what she saw stunned her: hundreds of life-sized men standing below her in the broad trenches that honeycombed the earth floor, men like gray ghosts waiting patiently at attention, hundreds of them in battle formation lined up in rows as far as the eye could see, each face different and individual with here and there a hand lifted or a head turned slightly as if to listen. Silent and waiting they filled the hall, so alive in gesture and stance that surely, she thought, they must be breathing as they stood there, liberated from the earth that had held them for nearly two thousand years.

Malcolm, coming to stand beside her, said simply, "My God."

She smiled, liking Malcolm. "It's a mighty emperor who goes to his grave with—how many?" she asked.

"The latest count is five hundred terra-cotta warriors, six war chariots, and twenty-four horses, with thousands more expected."

Iris, joining them, whistled, and the three of them stood

there, staring down into the trenches, absorbed and awed until Mrs. Pollifax, recovering, began to be aware of a very odd sensation of tension flowing between Malcolm and Iris. Strange, she thought, standing between them. She glanced curiously at Malcolm, but he was staring at the figures below; she looked at Iris, but she too was staring straight ahead, her lips still pursed in a whistle, and then George Westrum came up to claim Iris and the tension snapped. But for just a moment Mrs. Pollifax felt that she'd stumbled into a kind of energy-force field, and since she was not accustomed to picking up vibrations so strongly it left her puzzled. *Perhaps this place is a little haunted,* she thought, and wondered what had happened to her.

Iris and George walked away together and Malcolm wandered on, his sketchbook in hand. When Mrs. Pollifax resumed strolling it was Peter who fell in with her.

"Seems a good time to get friendlier," he said with his wry half-smile. "We leave for Urumchi late this afternoon and I've been doing my homework."

"Productive?" she asked, trying not to look eager in case anyone was watching.

"Definitely." His voice was crisp, with an undercurrent of excitement. "It looks good—ideas begin to blossom. Nothing's jelled yet but I'm absolutely certain now that the thing can be pulled off, all of it." With a nod toward the excavations he added, "What do you think?"

"Incredible. Spooky, even, they feel so alive."

"He was a bit of a bastard, that first emperor," Peter said pleasantly. "Burned books. Executed his friends. Made some pretty severe laws. But," he added, "the laws he made were the first the country ever had, and one of them was to banish feudalism, even if it did pop back after his death. He pulled a lot of warring states together and gave the country shape and unity, and without all that China might never have tamed the *Xiong nu* during the next dynasty."

"Tamed who?"

"*Hsiung-nu*—the horse people, the nomads from the steppes who swarmed through the passes of the Altai and Tian Shan ranges to attack . . . Mongols and Turkic people. That's where we're heading later today, you know, into frontier country. Urumchi, Turfan, the Tarim Basin, the Tian Shans, the Taklamakan desert. Back in 221 B.C. it was China's wild west, the far frontier."

"Genghis Khan, perhaps?"

"Yes, eventually. What riders they must have been, sweeping down from the mountains into the desert, with towns changing hands at the drop of a crossbow!"

"And has it been tamed now?" she asked, picturing what he spoke of in her mind.

"It's not been made an Autonomous Region for nothing," he told her. "I gather the central government still has its problems there and has had to make a few compromises. Not easy trying to organize nomads into communes, and Moslems into good Communists. A great number of ethnic groups live there —it was the Silk Road, after all!—the Uyghurs being in the majority."

"Weegurs?" she repeated.

"Yes, but spelled U-y-g-h-u-r, which may give you an idea of the language you'll meet there, most of the words being pronounced with strange gargling sounds. For instance the word for good-bye is *hox*, which you pronounce horrssh, and *aromat* is thank you, but comes out *rock-met*, slightly gargled. In any case, Mao tried to solve the Uyghur majority by sending thousands of Chinese into the province to settle among them, but basically it's Moslem country and they've had their share of incidents, so-called."

"Uprisings?" asked Mrs. Pollifax in surprise.

"Passive resistance would probably describe it better. In fact, something like sixty thousand Kazakhs simply left China in 1962, going over the border into Soviet Kazakhstan."

"How absolutely fascinating," she said. "I wish Mr. Li could be this informative."

Peter shook his head. "You can't blame Mr. Li," he said soberly. "From his age I'd guess he was brought up during the Cultural Revolution, when education went into an ice age. You probably know more about his country and its history than he does, though he's learning fast." He shook his head again. "These abrupt changes must have been psychological hell for people, at one point raiding monasteries, closing schools, and sending intellectuals into the fields or to prison; the next decade opening the schools, retrieving teachers and scientists from the rice fields, and restoring the same buildings that were mutilated. It has a certain Alice-In-Wonderland quality, you know? Mao may have been a brilliant revolutionary, but he sure as hell lacked consistency for the long run. Oops, here comes Jenny," he said. "I'd better mend my political fences and talk to her. See you later," he added quickly, and strolled back toward Jenny, his face emptied of expression again.

In the afternoon they visited Huaching Hot Springs Guesthouse, from which Chiang Kai-shek had escaped capture by the Communists, leaving his teeth behind. It was a very charming place, with ponds and arched bridges, but Mrs. Pollifax only felt uncomfortably hot; her feet were tired and she sat down as often as possible and as close to the water as possible. Besides, she thought crossly, Chiang Kai-shek might have escaped from a window to climb the mountain behind his room, but he'd only been captured and eventually released again. Of much more interest to her was the young Communist who had hurried to Xian to negotiate with Chiang once he was captured. The young man's name had been Chou En-lai, and Mrs. Pollifax had long since succumbed to Chou's personality from seeing him on television. She completely understood the reaction to his death in 1976 when the people defied Mao and the police to pour into Beijing's Tian An Men Square and mourn Chou in their own way. It had been a spontaneous outpouring of national grief and love and worry that had been conspicuously missing when Mao died eight months later.

She was seated on a bench thinking about this when Peter strolled up the path and sat down beside her. His face impassive he said, "Jenny's gone to find a ladies' room so I've got to talk fast. Quick—have you pencil and paper?" She was amused to see that he was speaking out of the corner of his mouth, just like a film gangster.

She nodded and dug into her purse, bringing out her memo pad.

"I've been talking to Mr. Li about what we see in Urumchi, and it sounds good, as if we'll be visiting all the right places, but when he confers with you—and he will, because you're leader, remember?—make sure we visit the Kazakhs up in the grasslands *after* our overnight stay in Turfan. You can't possibly know what I mean, and there's no time to explain so just write it down, okay?"

Mrs. Pollifax wrote TURFAN, SEE FIRST. "Is there a name for the grasslands?"

"Yes, take a look at your Markham Tour brochure if you brought it—"

"Didn't."

"The grasslands have always been a part of their regular tours here, and we've got to insist on them, but *after* visiting Turfan. If I remember correctly the brochure reads"—he closed his eyes and quoted—" 'See the colorful Kazakh Minority Peoples demonstrate their superb horsemanship. A nomadic people, they live in summer in yurts on the grasslands of the Tian Shan mountains.' And," he added, "we simply *must* go there last."

"I wonder what reason I could possibly give Mr. Li for this," she asked pensively.

"Tell him *something*. Tell him you've heard how hot Turfan is . . . Well, it is," he said. "It's five hundred feet below sea level."

"Below!" she exclaimed.

"Yes you'll find it listed on maps as the *Turfan Depression.* It's also an oasis in the desert, and *hot*. You can tell Mr. Li you're feeling the heat, or someone is, and it would be lovely to cool off in the mountains after Turfan." He smiled faintly. "You seem to manage okay. As leader you've got clout—use it. And if it's any help," he added, "Jenny seems to be getting tourist tummy, or Montezuma's Revenge, or dysentery, whatever the current word is."

"Oh dear!"

"Yes." He nodded and as Jenny appeared from between two ancient buildings he added flatly, "But it's *absolutely necessary* we go to Turfan first. Totally. I'll explain why when we get to Urumchi."

"I'll look forward to that," she told him dryly, with the distinct feeling it would be much kinder if she avoided hearing that explanation.

It was a six-hour flight to Urumchi. The two-engine prop plane fairly bulged with passengers, a few even seated on their luggage in the aisles. A hostess occasionally negotiated her way among them, passing out candies or cups of tea, but for dinner they landed at Lanzhou and dined in an echoing hall of the air terminal, handed warm moist wash cloths as they entered, and warm moist cloths at the meal's end. The paper napkins, noticed Mrs. Pollifax, were steadily shrinking in size; they had not been large in Canton, but they were now approaching the shape of her memo pad, and were slippery as well. Following dinner they returned to the plane and in the hours before darkness Mrs. Pollifax looked down at stark, barren mountain ranges, golden-brown in color like dark honey illuminated by the sun's gold. Occasionally—surprising her— she saw terraces carved out of a mountainside, forming patterns like ripples in a pond but with no sign of villages or of human life anywhere in the incredibly empty landscape.

China, she decided, looking down at it, was all terra-cotta and dusty jade. Everywhere. Only the shapes changed, and the shades of beige and brown, and the presence or absence of any green at all.

It was night when they landed in Urumchi, and well past ten o'clock. Having said good-bye to Miss Bai at the Xian air terminal there was now a Mr. Kan waiting for them here, and while still in the air terminal Mrs. Pollifax placed herself squarely in front of Mr. Li and reminded him that she was group leader. "When do we discuss plans for Urumchi?" she asked.

If Mr. Li was surprised by this sudden aggressiveness, he concealed it. "In the morning perhaps?" he suggested. "Mr. Kan will tell us what he's arranged."

"No," said Mrs. Pollifax firmly. "Tell him tonight, please, that we all want to visit Turfan *before* we go to the Kazakh grasslands. I hear that Turfan is very hot, and we'd prefer the mountains later, to cool off."

"Cool off!" he repeated, and laughed merrily at the phrase.

"Yes—do please insist on it before any plans are made final."

"You wish Turfan soon," he said, assimilating this.

"Yes. Oh yes—definitely." From the blank look that came and went on Mr. Li's face she received the distinct impression that while he spoke English well he did not understand it with equal ease. "Turfan first," she repeated, and was made more comfortable by a confirming flash of comprehension in his gaze. *He saves face*, she thought as she climbed into the waiting minibus. *How much has he understood of our prattlings? How much would I understand if people spoke rapidly, injecting slang words, and in different accents?*

Once again the hotel was nearly an hour's drive out of town, but this time there were no complaints: there was an intimacy about the *Yannan* that had been missing in the Canton hotel's oversized Art Deco vulgarity, and in the Xian hotel's stark Russian frugality. For one thing there was only a very modest fishpond in the lobby, and through an opened french door a smaller, brighter dining hall could be seen. The guest rooms were at ground level, elevated a few steps above the lobby; Mrs. Pollifax found her own room spacious and cool-looking. Its walls were white, and on one of them hung a very charming watercolor, an original, with a subtly Turkish flavor to it. Obviously new and interesting influences had entered Xinjiang Province.

But although it was nearly eleven o'clock Mrs. Pollifax felt restless, and while she waited for her suitcase to arrive at her door she gravitated toward the lobby, passing the small gift counter on the way. It had been opened for their arrival—a young woman presided over it—and Iris and George were leaning over the counter examining its treasures. In the lobby she found Malcolm sitting on the edge of the goldfish pond. "Real fish," he told her, pointing. "How are you doing?"

"Surprisingly well so far," she told him.

"Jenny has a touch of traveler's tummy. I've given her two of my pills," he said. "Anyone else, do you know?"

"Not to my knowledge," she told him, "but doubtless there'll be more. It's my theory that somewhere along the line there's usually one rebellious new employee in a kitchen who just can't understand why the water has to be boiled for foreigners, and so they don't. One has to count on that, it's human nature."

He looked amused. "Very experienced of you—about human nature, I mean. And since Jenny's been drinking nothing but boiled water—"

"So-called."

"—it's a very rational explanation. If somewhat alarming," he added, his glance moving to Iris, who was walking toward them looking excited, with George following behind her, smiling.

"Look," she cried, holding out a hand, "just see what George insisted on buying for me!" In her palm lay a disc of antique white jade, intricately carved by hand. She was radiant as she displayed it.

"How exquisite," breathed Mrs. Pollifax, bending over it.

"Lovely," said Malcolm, giving it a brief glance and then looking at Iris.

Iris turned pink. "It's *very* old," she said almost defiantly.

Jenny called from the hallway, "Any suitcases yet?"

"How are you feeling?" called Malcolm.

Jenny walked over to join them and he made room for her on the wall of the fishpond. "Better, thanks, but I should never have stashed those pills in my suitcase, we don't see our luggage that often. Thanks for bailing me out, Malcolm. What's that?" she asked Iris.

"White jade, isn't it gorgeous?"

The wide glass doors swung open now, and Mr. Li, Mr. Kan, two hotel workers, and Joe Forbes appeared with their luggage.

Iris said, "That's what I've been waiting for—good night everyone, see you in the morning! George, thanks so *very* much—see you!"

George Westrum, looking somewhat startled, tugged at his baseball cap, lingered a minute, and then drifted away, too.

Jenny said, "Excuse me," and followed the men and the luggage down the hall.

Mrs. Pollifax, leaning comfortably against the fishpond, said, "I'm so glad to see Iris given a present, wasn't she excited? I have the impression that she's not received many gifts in her life."

Malcolm said calmly, "She'll be receiving a good many of them in the future."

Startled, Mrs. Pollifax said, "From George, do you mean?"

"No, not George," he said, and then, aware of her scrutiny he added, "or didn't I mention that I'm psychic at times?"

"No, you didn't," she told him sternly. "You only said that you live with talking mice."

"The two are not synonymous," he said dryly, "but I can be quite psychic at times. It comes in flashes, and I frequently get very clear intuitions about people. How are you on the subject?"

"Oh, a believer of course," she said. "How can one be otherwise? As a matter of fact I once spent several days with a Rumanian gypsy—a queen of the gypsies, actually—who had the gift of second sight, and who—" She stopped, aware that Innocent Tourists did not usually have their lives saved by gypsy queens when being pursued by the police through Turkey. She added lamely, "But we all have the gift, haven't we, simply covered over by rationalism and disbelief?"

He had been smiling at her discomfiture. "You must tell me more sometime about your friend the gypsy but I think I'll say good night now. Hi, Jenny," he said, as Jenny reappeared.

Jenny gave him a bright but abstracted smile, and at his departure walked over to the fishpond to sit beside Mrs. Pollifax. She said in a strangled voice, "That white jade. Did George give it to Iris?"

"Yes," said Mrs. Pollifax calmly. "Why?"

Jenny pushed out her legs and stared angrily at her blue and white sneakers. There was a long silence while she examined her shoes, scowled at them, pushed back a lock of hair, and picked a piece of lint from her skirt. "I hate that woman, I just hate her," she said furiously.

"Iris?" said Mrs. Pollifax, startled. "Why?"

Jenny turned and glared at her. "She's so bloody happy all the time, and everyone—oh, I should never *never* have come on this trip," she cried, and burst into tears.

A hotel worker, passing through the lobby to the dining

hall, glanced curiously at Jenny. Mrs. Pollifax said, "Come outside a moment until you feel better." She led Jenny through the glass doors to the front of the *Yannan,* where the bus had been unloaded and was just driving away, leaving the velvety darkness bisected only by splash patterns from the lighted guest rooms. Mrs. Pollifax identified her own room by her purse standing on the windowsill. In the room next to hers she saw Peter walk over to the window and pull the curtains together. Except that if it was Peter there was something odd about his face, she noted absently.

"What did you expect from your trip?" she asked, handing Jenny a handkerchief.

"I thought—I wanted—it was supposed to—" She broke into a fresh spasm of tears. "And it—" She shoved the handkerchief back into Mrs. Pollifax's hand, turned angrily and fled back into the lobby to disappear down the hall to her room. Following slowly, Mrs. Pollifax heard a door slam shut.

Peter might be able to comfort her, she thought. Peter knew Jenny best, and might be persuaded to talk to her. Since he'd not gone to bed yet—she had, after all, seen him at his window only moments ago—she went to his door and knocked. When there was no answer she knocked again, then leaned against the door and listened. She heard no sounds of running water; she heard no sounds at all. She called his name softly, so that he would know it was she, and when even this brought no answer she stood back and stared in exasperation at the door. He was simply not responding.

Or he wasn't there.

The thought of Peter not being in his room sent a chill down her spine, which struck her as a completely irrational reaction. Moving to her own door she carried in the suitcase waiting outside it, unlocked it and extracted toothbrush and pajamas. She thought, *He's just strolling around the grounds, not sleepy yet.*

But there had been something strange about his appearance when she'd glimpsed him in the window, something off-key that troubled her. She tried to think what it was, concentrating hard on reconstructing that moment. She realized that he'd done something to his eyes. The light behind him had thrown his face into shadow, but very definitely it had been his eyes that were different: their outer corners had been subtly drawn upward, giving him a native look. It had been Peter's shoulders and head that she'd seen in the window but the face of a Chinese.

So it's begun, she thought. *This is Xinjiang Autonomous Region, we've reached Urumchi and it's begun . . . he's gone out into the night to reconnoiter, to look for the labor camp.*

She wondered how far he would go and when he'd be back. She wondered if he'd be seen and—if he were stopped— whether his papers would pass examination, and she felt a clutch of fear for him. But it was going to be like this for the next few days, she reminded herself, culminating in his eventual death, and somehow she must remain calm.

I'd better begin doing my Yoga every morning, she thought. *Resolutely!*

Chapter Nine

In the morning Mr. Li knocked at her door at her door at seven o'clock, itinerary in hand. He said, "It has been difficult, Turfan first, Mr. Kan has had to change many plans, he was up very late." He didn't laugh merrily this time but he wasn't reproachful or accusing, either, and Mrs. Pollifax felt that she was meeting the real Mr. Li for the first time. "The plan," he added, "is now as you wish."

"Come in," she told him. "You can explain it to me and then I'll make a copy and hang it in the hall for everyone to see, the way Miss Bai did in Xian."

"Excellent," he said, businesslike and efficient, and walked over to her desk to spread out the papers. "As you see, we visit many places today in Urumchi—jade-cutting factory, carpet factory, museum, free market, department store, a hospital. Tomorrow morning we leave for Turfan and stay overnight. After that the Kazakhs and the grasslands—with picnic and horsemanship—and the following day Heavenly Lake, very beautiful, before leaving to begin trip to Inner Mongolia."

"Oh *very* good," she told Mr. Li warmly. "Very good indeed, I'm so grateful to you, Mr. Li. I'll want to thank Mr. Kan, too."

"Yes," said Mr. Li, looking down at the plans with satisfaction.

When he had gone she looked at the crowded schedule and wondered how and where Peter was ever going to find the space to make his own complicated plans and arrangements. She would have preferred to knock on his door at once to make sure that he was back in the Guesthouse, and to tell him that Turfan would come first, but instead she conscientiously found a Magic Marker and made a poster of Mr. Li's schedule. Carrying it out to hang in the lobby, the first thing she saw was Peter, sound asleep in a chair. She felt so infinitely relieved at seeing him that she could have kissed him but she only tiptoed past and taped the sheet to the wall.

When she turned, his eyes were open and no longer slanted. "Busy night?" she asked with a smile.

He grinned sleepily. "You don't miss much. You guessed?"

She nodded. "Jenny was upset. I thought you could talk to her so I knocked on your door." Pointing to the itinerary she said, "Turfan tomorrow, the grasslands later."

That woke him in a hurry. "Thank God," he said fervently, and sprang out of his chair to look. "Now we're really in business," he told her, removing a memo pad from his pocket and beginning to copy it. "Look, I've got to talk to you—"

He stopped as Malcolm and then George strolled into the lobby, followed a moment later by Joe Forbes. The doors to the dining room opened; Iris rushed in after them, upsetting a chair before she could sit down, and as Mrs. Pollifax began to attack roasted peanuts again with chopsticks Jenny walked in, her eyes still pink-rimmed, and across the table Peter winked at her. Another day had begun.

It was a crowded day. Although Peter remained upright and interested during the tours, Mrs. Pollifax was amused to notice how he dozed off during the tea-and-briefings. There were a number of these today because they preceded each inspection of a factory, and the scene was always the same: a bare utilitarian room with a photograph of Mao on the wall, a long table lined with tea cups in which lay dubious brittle twigs over which a young woman would pour boiling water from a thermos. Following an interval of five or ten minutes the tea would sink to the bottom of the cup so that the brew could be sipped without acquiring a mouth full of twigs, and the foreman or cadre would begin his talk about the factory or the workshop, halting frequently for Mr. Kan or Mr. Li to translate his words into English. When this had been done, questions were eagerly awaited. George usually wanted to know about machinery and methods, Joe Forbes asked for production figures and annoyingly checked them out on paper looking for flaws, and then Iris would begin. Mrs. Pollifax found it hilarious to watch the change in Iris when her turn came: her face lost all of its liveliness and every vestige of humor, as if knowledge was a matter too sacred for lightness. She turned deeply serious, the Conscientious Student personified in her pursuit of how women lived, what they ate and earned; her questions had a rooted intelligence behind them but they came out absurdly muddled.

Malcolm, with a quizzical twist to his brows, murmured, "Do you suppose there's a masters' thesis involved here somewhere?" Jenny's lips thinned angrily while Peter simply dozed and missed it all.

It was during the visit to the carpet factory that Mrs. Pollifax found Peter alone at last. George was determined to buy a rug in China and have it shipped home, and he was not a man to be cheated. While the others stood around listening and yawning and sprawled across piles of rugs, Mrs. Pollifax slipped away, her interest in carpets depleted.

Wandering outside she found Peter restlessly pacing up and down the alley, pausing to run his eyes over a huge chalkboard on which words had been printed in pink and white chalk. "Mao's thoughts for the day," he said, turning to her. "Thanks for getting Turfan fixed up so quickly. I hear that originally it was to be last, so you've really saved the day."

She waved this aside impatiently. "Where did you go last night?"

"Let's sit on the steps," he suggested. "I hiked. Walked and walked and walked. For one thing I found the Army barracks—bless Guo Musu for putting *that* on the map—and this gave me a bearing on where the labor camp has to be."

She stared at him, appalled. "But you must have walked *miles!*"

"Yes of course—walked, jogged, ran. All of it in total darkness, naturally, but there was only the one road to follow and I managed to stay on it. It was a pretty close connection, though, I didn't get back here until six this morning. But I also found a river, and it just *has* to be the one that flows past and around X's labor camp—I plan to follow it tonight and see."

She shivered. "If you find the camp will you try to make contact with X?"

"Good Lord no, just get the lay of the land," he said flatly. "I won't try to reach X until I've officially disappeared."

She glanced over their itinerary. "And when—when will the—uh—disappearance happen?" The words had stuck in her throat, she couldn't think why; it seemed a simple enough question.

"At the grasslands, directly after we've visited Turfan. On Thursday."

"Thursday," she repeated, nodding. And this was Monday . . . three more days. Until he officially died, leaving no body behind. She said carefully, "Why has it been so important that we go to Turfan first?"

He waited as a workman passed, wheeling a cart filled with bricks. "To hide things there. A cache," he explained. "If you look at your map you'll find Turfan's a desert oasis four hours by car south of Urumchi, and on the same route that X and I will take as we head for the mountains. We can collect food and blankets there on our way, since I can scarcely disappear with a suitcase."

He sounded pleased; she glanced into his face and found no hint of tension or fear. "That's very clever," she told him, adding dryly, "I forgive you here and now that forgotten drinking glass."

"Forgotten what?"

"Never mind . . . Peter, does it have to be the mountains, isn't there any other way? You must have brought identification papers that would take you anywhere."

"Forged identity papers," he pointed out. "Nice authentic forged ones, yes. Four of them, actually, to cover a variety of people and intricacies of disguise and destinations."

She said earnestly, "Then why can't you and X leave the country an easier way? Those mountains, Peter—even if it is summer!"

"What easier way?" asked Peter. "Easier how? Think a

minute. We're more than three thousand miles from Peking right now, and not much closer than that to Canton. To head for either would mean train, bus, plane, hiking, and remember X and I won't be traveling as American tourists, we'll be natives, subject to checkpoints and queries. No, there are too many variables," he said with a shake of his head. "Too many bottlenecks, risks, and cliff-hangers, whereas the mountains are only six hundred miles away from where we are now. And besides," he added mischievously, "we just might meet the 'Mother-Queen of the West' somewhere in the Kunluns."

" 'Mother-Queen of the West!' "

He nodded. "There are surviving records of an adventurous emperor back in 600 B.C. who liked to go exploring. His name was Wa Tei and he went off traveling in the west with his retinue—a large one, I gather—and he's said to have penetrated as far as the Kunlun mountains that divide Tibet and Khotan. That's where he met the Mother-Queen of the West—a kind of Queen of Sheba person—who ruled this strange top-of-the-world land. He was lavishly entertained and brought back stories that have turned into myths and legends, rather like Homer's tales. Except," he added, with a smile, "a good many of Homer's stories were assumed to have been myths and turned out to be real. Who knows, it could happen to me!"

"A Shangri-la," breathed Mrs. Pollifax, her eyes shining. "How absolutely wonderful!"

"Of course," he added, "it may have been a scruffy little mountain village full of dirt and lice—"

"Don't," she begged. "I demand a Shangri-la."

"Mrs. Pollifax, you're a romantic."

"I know," she told him happily. "I am, I insist on it—but so are you, I think?"

"Guilty," he acknowledged with a boyish grin. "But legends aside, it's true that it may be more rugged skirting the Tarim Basin and the desert but we can travel by night on donkeys, avoid people almost entirely, and go at our own speed. And there *is* a British weather expedition somewhere in those mountains if we can find it."

"As well as the ghost of the Mother-Queen of the West." She nodded. "Of course as soon as you mentioned *that* I knew there wasn't a shred of hope that you'd change your mind. A British weather expedition sounds rather persuasive, too."

"If it can be found," he said politely.

"If it can be found," she agreed politely, and thought how unreal it was to be sitting here looking out on a dusty alley lined with sheds, tools, and carts and discussing with Peter a mere six-hundred-mile stroll toward mountain ranges that peaked at 28,000 feet. *I wish Cyrus were here,* she thought suddenly, and wondered if he was back in Connecticut yet; it was so very difficult to know, given those time changes crossing the Pacific; her logic in this area had never been trustworthy, and speaking of logic she wondered why she felt like crying whenever she remembered that Peter was going to die in three days . . .

Iris wandered out of the building looking distracted. "Oh dear," she said, sitting down beside them and pushing back her hair.

"Oh dear what?" asked Mrs. Pollifax.

"I don't know. I hope the free market comes next, I like the sound of it, I must be feeling very confined. What is it, by the way—have we been told?"

Peter said briskly, "Flirtation with capitalism. People in the communes are being allowed small parcels of land of their own now. Instead of selling their produce or pig to the government, they can sell it in the free market and keep the profit for themselves."

Iris' eyes opened wide. "But that *is* capitalism!"

Peter grinned. "It would be tactful not to use that word, I think. Call it motivation instead. Actually *they* call it—" He abruptly stopped, looking stricken.

He had nearly used a Chinese word, and Mrs. Pollifax glanced quickly at Iris to see if she had noticed; she found her staring into space without expression. A moment later the others came out of the building and they climbed into the minibus, and Peter gave Mrs. Pollifax a rueful apologetic smile.

As he smiled at her Peter was thinking *My God that was a close one, this is growing really difficult, I've begun to think in Chinese and I almost spoke in Chinese in front of Iris.* As he passed Mrs. Pollifax, already seated, she glanced up; their eyes met and she winked at him.

He grinned, at once feeling better. *She's really something,* he thought, taking a window seat two rows behind her in the bus, and to his surprise he found himself wishing that she could go with him tonight, when he planned to follow the river to the labor camp. *She's getting to me,* he realized. *Me, the hard-line loner.* He wondered what it was about her that drew him, and for want of any cleverer insight decided that it was a kind of capable innocence, but that didn't fit either. There had begun to be a sense of kinship between them; he felt at ease with her, which astonished him.

At dinner Peter made a point of yawning a great deal, which proved tiring in itself for there were twelve courses through which to yawn. Because of their busy day there were no plans for the evening, which was merciful, for an early start mattered very much to him tonight. Jenny suggested a get-together in the small lounge for some singing, a suggestion aimed at him, he realized, but he only yawned and said he was going to catch up on his sleep.

Once in his room he quickly changed into the cheap plastic sandals and gray cotton pants he'd purchased in Xian, added a white undershirt and then—leaning over his canvas dufflebag —he divested it of the thin mountain-climbing rope with which he'd laced the bag. This he wound around his waist and chest before adding the khaki Mao jacket over the bulk to conceal it. Into pockets he thrust his jogging shoes and ID papers, and then brought out the very clever invention that tilted his eyes by ingeniously concealed tapes. Peering into the mirror at the effect, he grinned: he looked very much like the workers he'd seen all during the day. When he'd undergone his wilderness survival class they'd gone to great lengths to prevent him acquiring a tan; now he understood the thinking behind it because he'd seen very few dark Chinese. Both Mr. Li and Mr. Kan had complexions like bisque china, the skin very white and opaque. His own pallor, his heavy brows and slanted eyes certainly removed all resemblance to Peter Fox: he was Szu Chou now, as his papers proved.

Unhinging the screen at his open window he pushed it back, slipped outside, and became part of the night.

It was nearing midnight when he stumbled across the cave by accident. Only an hour earlier he had found the river, and in following it had left the road behind him, wading across at the only point where the stream narrowed. This brought him into difficult terrain where he had to use a flashlight. He disliked showing a light, but it appeared to be deserted countryside. Since leaving Urumchi only one truck had passed down the road—he had taken shelter in a hollow—and rather than stumble into trees and over rocks, wasting time he couldn't afford, he had to assume this area was equally as untenanted.

Half a mile after he'd forded the river the sound of rushing water grew thunderous, the river curved abruptly, and he met with a waterfall. Deprived of any means of crossing the river again he trained his light on the fall, judged it to be about thirty feet high, and stoically began climbing up the hill beside it, clinging to the roots of trees and to rocks and bushes. Once on the top he admitted—not without resistance—that a brief rest might be a good investment, a catnap would be even better, and he set his wristwatch's tiny alarm for thirty minutes. Finding a mossy patch among the rocks he sank down, leaned back, and promptly fell over. His assumptions had been wrong: the rock against which he thought he leaned did not exist; there were rocks to the right and to the left of him but he'd fallen into what appeared to be a cavity in the hillside.

Turning on his flashlight he parted the underbrush to examine what lay behind it, and his light picked out a hollow roughly twelve feet by eight, its ceiling a little over five feet, laced tightly with roots from the forest. In astonishment he stood up and trained his light on the ground above to see what had caused such a miracle. *Roots,* he decided: years ago a massive tree must have been struck down, leaving a space over which the surrounding root systems had slowly woven a carpet as they groped toward the support of the rocks on either side. On top of this network Nature had gradually deposited soil and moss, leaving the hollow untouched, and had then charmingly screened its entrance with underbrush.

There was suddenly no need for sleep. Excited, Peter checked his compass, crawled inside the cave, and sat looking around him in amazement. It was dry and warm inside. Bringing out his map he spent a few minutes computing his location, marked it in pencil and grinned: if his estimate was correct this cave was only a mile from the labor camp, and a perfect place to hide two people next week while the security police searched for X. It was better than perfect, it existed only ten feet from a rushing stream of water, and water was the most precious commodity of all.

Already in his mind he was making the commitment; now he backed it by groping in his pocket for the dried apricots and apples he'd brought with him for a snack tonight. These he deposited in the center of the cave, like a promise, and then he remembered the slab of chocolate from his previous nights' explorations, and added this to the fruit. With a glance at his watch he parted the underbrush and left, exhilarated by his discovery.

Continuing to follow the river upstream he arrived in a few minutes at a point where a second river joined with the first one to rush down toward the waterfall. From the pattern of it —the headwaters arranged like the crossbar of a T with the second stream dropping to waterfall and highway—he thought this had to be the river that led to the labor camp. Moments later he confirmed this when he shone his flashlight across the rushing water for a minute and its beam picked out piles of neatly stacked logs and cut trees waiting to be denuded of their branches. He had reached a logging area.

It was time now to find a way to cross the river and find the camp.

Peter began to reconnoiter, as yet paying no attention to the water racing past him but examining the trees on each bank, his flashlight twinkling on-off, on-off, like a firefly. Presently he found what he was looking for: a stout tree on his side of the river opposite several strong trees on the farther bank. Unwinding the rope from his waist he knotted it around the base of the tree next to him and knelt beside the river to study its currents. *Vicious*, he thought, *nasty and vicious*, exactly the sort of current that would sweep a man under before he had a chance to catch his breath. He sat down and removed his shoes and socks and hid them with his flashlight, compass, and papers under the tree. Then he tied the end of the rope around his waist and lowered himself into the water.

At once the rapids swept him away, the icy water knocking him as breathless as if he'd been given a blow to the solar plexus. The current tumbled him over and over, extracting what breath was left him while jagged rocks pummeled and bruised him. Only the rope saved him: considerably downstream it snapped him to a halt, threatening to cut him in half from the current bearing down on him, but it held and he was able to surface and breathe again. Now he began the fight to swim across the river, the rope holding him in place as he fought, struggled, dogpaddled, and at last fell across the opposite bank.

But the icy cold had invigorated him, and a moment later he was on his feet, slapping his arms and jogging-in-place to restore circulation. With the rope still around his waist he hiked back to the stand of trees opposite his starting point, and after untying wet knots with chilled fingers he secured the end of the rope around the base of the larger tree. Checking it he found just enough slack; the tree was well-rooted and the rope firmly engaged. When he finished it was still night but dawn was emerging almost imperceptibly from the darkness, the shapes in the clearing where he stood acquiring sharper edges: dawn was only an hour away. He was bone-chillingly cold and he was tired, but his reconnoitering was nearing an end, he would soon be on his run back to Urumchi with three days to complete his plans. He headed across the clearing for the shelter of standing trees where he suddenly stood very still, listening.

The rush of the water behind him was deadening to the ear but above it or below it he understood that he was sensing movement ahead of him. Human sounds: the murmur of voices, the shuffling of feet. Lowering himself to the ground he crept to the next stand of trees and came to a stop.

From his hiding place he looked out on a second clearing into which a dozen or more men were marching in a bedraggled fashion, dull shapes in a twilit world. Once in the clearing they stood passively, a few wandering off to lean against piles of wood, or to sit on logs while their leader—or guard—gestured to men unseen as yet. Peter saw the flare of a match; from the vaguely discerned movements he deduced the men—prisoners—were smoking, eating, or idly talking . . . a free moment before the day's work began, a precious moment.

One of the men left the others and strolled toward the cluster of trees behind which Peter hid. Quickly Peter dropped to the ground again as the man paused beside a low bush six feet away from him, fumbling at his trousers. He was so near to Peter that he could see the neatly mended patches in his drab shirt; from the ground he could peer up and into the man's face and see him clearly.

And seeing him clearly he thought in a rush of shock, *But this man is Wang Shen!*

He thought, *I haven't even found the labor camp and here is X . . .*

He was shaken and incredulous. He didn't want it to be X, some part of his shocked head insisted that it couldn't be X, searched wildly for discrepancies, demanding doubt, skepticism, second thoughts because this was not in his scenario . . . And yet it *was* X, he had memorized that face until he knew its very essence—the slant of the cheekbones, the shape of the pointed jaw and the blunt nose, the intelligent eyes, the rather sardonic mouth. This was Wang Shen all right, and he was standing only six feet away from him.

He thought, *Dear God, this is incredible—the cave and now this.*

He thought, *It can't ever happen this way again. Not like this.*

But he had no plans made yet, X was to be rescued later, after he had divested himself of the tour group, he couldn't possibly do anything now, it was too soon, this was a mere reconnaissance. In only a few hours the tour group was to leave for Turfan, and it was already perilously close to the time when he must race back to the hotel. He couldn't afford any rescue attempt now, it would make him late and then they would all be in the soup, including—and most of all—Wang Shen.

"There's the cave," an inner voice reminded him.

"The cave *now?*" he protested. "Leave X there for two days when everything could go hideously wrong and I never get back to him? Abandon him there with only a handful of dried fruit, a chocolate bar, and no ID papers should something happen and I never reach him again?"

He thought abruptly, *I wish Mrs. Pollifax were here.*

The devoutness of that longing staggered him. He had believed he could manage everything himself and originally he had thought her preposterous, and now he wished above all else that she was here to advise him. "What would she say?" he asked himself, and then, desperately, "What would *she* do?"

Words suddenly came to him that she had used describing her meeting with Guo Musu. "Oh, I had no plans," she'd said to his amazement. "There comes a time when one has to trust oneself and whatever presents itself. It's like that occasionally."

Like that occasionally . . . of course. He was nearly exhausted, he was trembling with cold and he hadn't planned this at all, but he had found a cave and now he had found X. *My God*, he thought, *Mrs. Pollifax is more flexible than I am, and I'm twenty-two.* And with the memory of her words a sense of her presence returned to him and he grinned: Mrs. Pollifax would simply get on with the job, matter-of-factly.

And so—matter-of-factly—Peter proceeded to get on with the job: he softly called out Wang's name.

The man had just begun to turn away; he hesitated now, startled. Some distance away his companions were huddled over a tiny fire, their faces turned aside. Peter moved slightly away from the tree, just enough to expose his presence, and then quickly popped back. But Wang had seen him; his face had turned astonished and baffled. Peter extended one hand, thumb up. A moment later the man shuffled over to the tree and stood in front of it, curious but perplexed.

"You're Wong Shen," Peter said from behind the tree.

"Who—?"

"Also Wang Shen."

Dorothy Gilman

"*Zhe shi shenme?* What is this? Who are you? Where did you come from?"

"*Wo jiang* Peter—American, *Meiguo ren*—sent with papers to take you out of the country. Can you decide quickly? Are you well enough? To go *now?*"

"You're testing me," the man growled. "Long live the great and correct Communist Party of China!"

"*Ta ma de,*" swore Peter, "the time is *now*. I've a rope across the river, it can be done before there's too much daylight, there'll never be such a chance again."

"Why?" he asked harshly. "How is anyone interested in me?"

Peter said impatiently, "Because the Russians have learned who you are and they'll be after you next. *Lai bulai*—are you coming or aren't you?"

There was silence. Peter waited in suspense for the man's friends to call to him, or for Wang to call out to the group and betray him, and then abruptly, calmly, the man moved around the tree to peer at him and his glance was searching. He said, "You look very young, with good food in you."

"I hope I also look American—my eyelids are taped."

Studying Peter's face the man's gaze seemed to come from far away, as if he drew on a part of him buried very deep, and then his eyes sharpened, he returned to this cold misty dawn and to the moment. He said with infinite dryness, "If you have found me—if you have managed to cross that river—what have I to lose? Let's go!"

Thank God, thought Peter. Wang glanced back once at the clearing, bent over to look at a root, dropped to his knees and crept behind the tree, his movements without haste, measured, as if he had long ago learned the art of blending into backgrounds to avoid attention. Peter dropped to the ground with him and they crawled together to the next copse of trees; reaching it they stood up and raced to the stream.

"You can do this?" Peter asked X, pointing to the rope which the dawn was illuminating now.

Wang's thin frame shivered in the cold. "*Shi,*" he said, and stepped forward. Testing the rope first—he seemed incredulous at its lightness—he lowered himself into the icy river.

Hand over hand, at times almost submerged by the current, he propelled his body to the other side, climbed out, shook himself, and stood up. Quickly Peter untied the rope from the tree on his side—there must be no signs of their departure—and once again knotted it around his waist. This time he leaped far out into the water and was better able to control his entry into the rapids so that when the rope pulled him up short he was within a maneuverable distance of the opposite shore. A moment later he was out, and joining Wang upstream.

"We can talk later," he said, pulling on socks, buckling on his sandals and stowing flashlight, shoes, and compass into his Mao jacket. "And the faster we go the warmer we'll be," he added, trying to still the chattering of his teeth, "although I'll say right now that your escape was planned for next week, not today. We must be resourceful!"

The man gave him a sharp glance but he said only, "Let's go then."

They reached the cave within the hour, losing only a few minutes searching for it. Pulling aside the branches concealing it Peter said, "This was the first miracle, Wang, the second was coming practically face to face with you when I was only reconnoitering."

Wang crept into the cave, amazed. "Truly this *is* a miracle."

"You're not so strong as you seemed at first," Peter said. "You couldn't run."

Wang's smile was kind. "We're given very little food."

Peter nodded. "And I've little to offer you—look."

Wang only shook his head. "What you have here—just to see fruit and chocolate—looks a feast to me. I am also expert by now"—his tone was humorous—"in foraging in the woods. What exactly is the situation?"

Briefly Peter explained it. By now he had begun doing rapid calculations for his own preservation, and he was worried and tried not to show it to Wang. It had taken him four hours to reach the cave, for instance, and it would take him at least another four hours to return to Urumchi . . . Already it was past four in the morning and breakfast for the tour group was to be served at 8 A.M., with a departure for Turfan at nine. He would be too late for breakfast and even his return by nine was now problematic: how he was to explain his absence was beyond his capabilities at the moment. He concluded his story to Wang by saying, "And so you must rest and grow stronger here, for the mountains. When the tour group returns from Turfan late tomorrow I'll bring you more food, but as you can see—"

Wang had sat down on the cave's floor and now he smiled for the first time. "Don't worry please, I will enjoy extremely this release from *jian ku lao dong,*" he said, using the word for hard physical labor. "It is enough to be free. *Wo lei le*—I'm tired."

"Okay, but watch any tracks you leave in the woods when you go out," Peter counseled. "Remember, they'll be searching for you soon. When I return I'll whistle like this." He gave a soft bird call and repeated it twice. "Got it?"

Wang was looking happily around him. "Yes, yes," he said absently. "Some apricots first, I think, and then I will sleep. I may even sleep for days!"

Peter said, "Good. Only wish I could . . . *ziajian!*"

"Ziajian," responded Wang, but by this time Peter was already outside and beginning the long hike back to Urumchi, a trip made all the more conspicuous and hazardous by the growing light of day.

Chapter Ten

By seven o'clock that morning Mrs. Pollifax had already guessed that Peter wasn't back—she had knocked early at his door, feeling obscurely troubled about him —and when they assembled in the lobby at eight for breakfast and Peter still didn't appear her worry sharpened and she prepared for the worst. They were to leave for Turfan in an hour, their luggage had already been collected and Peter's absence had become obvious and serious. The list of horrors that might have happened to him seemed endless to her: he could have been picked up by police as a local native for questioning; he could have been picked up as an American with fake ID papers; he could have met with an accident and be lying alone and helpless somewhere; he might have found the labor camp only to be discovered himself. Whatever had gone wrong he was not here, and he ought to be here.

The door to the dining hall opened, they walked in to breakfast and Mrs. Pollifax—feeling embarked on a roller-coaster ride whose end she couldn't foresee—sat down and without enthusiasm attacked a hard-boiled egg.

Mr. Kan, hurrying in, said, "I have knocked and he doesn't hear, the manager is to open his door with a key, he may be ill."

"Are *you* feeling okay?" Malcolm asked Mrs. Pollifax from across the table.

Jenny, seated next to her, turned and stared.

"Fine," said Mrs. Pollifax and gave them each a forced bright smile.

"Oh he'll turn up," said Iris cheerfully, earning a bland smile from Joe Forbes and an admiring one from George.

Mr. Li stuck his head through the door to call to Mr. Kan, "He's not in his room. He slept there but he's not there."

"Slept there," murmured Mrs. Pollifax: that meant bed turned down and sheets wrinkled . . . she was relieved to hear that Peter had thought of this, except of what use was a turned-down bed if Peter didn't reappear soon?

"But nobody has seen him," added Mr. Li, coming in to join them, and he did not laugh merrily; he looked anxious and puzzled.

"We don't leave for Turfan without him, do we?" asked Jenny.

The two guides launched an intense discussion in their own language until Mr. Li shook his head. "We must. The arrangements have been made. At nine we will notify security police, of course."

At nine o'clock when they filed out to the waiting bus, still speculating on Peter's absence, they were met by a sleek gray limousine pulling up in front of the hotel, a "shanghai car" as they were called, bearing white curtains at the windows to conceal its occupants. It looked very official and very menacing: *They've arrested Peter*, thought Mrs. Pollifax with a sinking heart. A gentleman in a soft gray Mao uniform climbed out of the car, followed by a smiling Peter.

"Hi," Peter called out cheerfully. "Sorry I'm late, everybody —went for an early morning jog and got lost until Mr. Sun rescued me. Very high official, speaks American!"

An early jog, thought Mrs. Pollifax, and her gaze moved to his outfit, the pants rolled to his knees, legs bared down to his running shoes, Mao jacket tied around his waist, and a T-shirt emblazoned with the words MOZART LIVES.

Beautiful, she thought, paying tribute to Peter's resourcefulness. Heaven only knew what he'd had to discard to present such a picture, but if one overlooked the absence of his ubiquitous blue jeans, he was the perfect jogger, face flushed, eyes bright, and even in China they must have heard of the American passion for jogging. She felt a leap of excitement, the very same feeling that overtook her at sight of one of her *pelargoniums* breaking through the earth: Peter, too, was blooming. He'd carried it off. Somehow. The tension had snapped; Mr. Sun was speaking benevolently to Mr. Li and Mr. Kan, who looked both pleased and honored, and Peter, giving Mrs. Pollifax a broad impish grin, dashed into the hotel to wash his face.

Several minutes later as he walked up the aisle of the bus he leaned over and whispered in Mrs. Pollifax's ear. "You *what?*" she gasped.

He nodded, grinning his triumph. "The job's done. Quite a night!"

"But how—what—"

"Later," he said. "Collect food, X will need it when we get back. Collect everything," he added and looked up as Iris and George walked down the aisle. Glancing at his watch he said, "Now I've got four hours to sleep—talk to you later." He continued to the rear of the bus and promptly stretched out across four seats. Jenny, following, looked affronted and abruptly sat down next to Joe Forbes.

X found . . . X already freed, thought Mrs. Pollifax in astonishment. What could have happened, and how could it have happened? What had taken place during this endless night?

The bus began to move—they were off to Turfan—and Mrs. Pollifax's thoughts moved with it: backward and then forward but no matter where they went they returned to the fact that Wang had been removed from the camp and hidden. How pleased Carstairs would be, she thought; how pleased *she* felt for Peter . . . suddenly it had been *done*, and she was smiling as she glanced out of the window at the hulk of an old bus they were passing, and then rough adobe houses with pale blue wooden doors.

"What does that sign say?" she heard George call to Mr. Li, pointing.

"It says, 'Protect our Motherland and Heighten Alertness,'" he called back.

As if to illustrate its message Mrs. Pollifax glanced up at a distant hill—they were leaving Urumchi behind now—and saw anti-aircraft guns silhouetted against the sky, and posts strung with barbed wire. *Against Russian invasion,* she reflected, *but it looks as if the Soviets won't find Wang now. He's ours.*

Now they were passing fields of yellow rapeseed, with clusters of commune huts in the distance. Off to their right the mountain range they followed had the shape and color of sand dunes, strange and surreal to the eye, and then the road straightened and was lined with poplar trees on either side, closing out the mountains. They began to meet trucks carrying laborers to the fields, but there was smaller traffic, too: handmade carts that hugged each side of the road and were put together out of wood with large old rubber tires for wheels, some pulled by one or two horses, some pulled by a man between the shafts. The poplars thinned and then vanished as they emerged into flat treeless country, and here Mrs. Pollifax became aware of the stone-lined irrigation trenches parallel to the road, with here and there women washing clothes in the water.

But having purred with satisfaction for a contented interval, Mrs. Pollifax's thoughts now approached certain new uncertainties, retreated from them, and then returned to face and examine them. It was all very well, she thought, to say that phase two had been triumphantly accomplished, but there was no getting around the fact that the rescue of Wang was to have been phase three, not phase two. X was tucked away now but with a long and dangerous wait ahead of him, and obviously with nothing to eat or Peter wouldn't have mentioned collecting food; and what if—perish the thought—Peter could never return to rescue him? *As soon as I see Peter alone,* she decided, *he must tell me where the cave is. Both of us should know . . . and in the meantime we must pray that he's not discovered by the Sepos.*

Her eyes went back to the land, to a long flat lovely valley they were crossing, the mountains a marvelous pastel blue in the distance. Far away her gaze picked out a walled clay compound, dusty beige against the dusty beige of the earth. The mountains drew closer here to them, incredibly wrinkled like very old faces, and then—suddenly—in the midst of nowhere they came upon a factory with nothing in sight but piles of slag, the sky, the road, and the distant mountains.

Such space, thought Mrs. Pollifax, *such enormous tawny space. But why a factory here, and how does anything arrive or be taken away?*

Her thoughts returned to Peter's message in the bus. She could collect food for X, yes, lining her purse with that plastic bag she carried and slipping food into it at the table, but this meant that Peter would have to make still another trip out into the night when they returned to Urumchi. This meant no rest for him; how long could he go without a decent night's sleep, she wondered, and still think clearly for what lay ahead?

Across the aisle Jenny was growing restive. "Let's wake him up," she told Joe Forbes in a loud voice directed at Peter in the rear. "He's slept long enough, don't you think? Hey Peter!"

"He looks very comfortable," pointed out Joe Forbes, smiling.

"But he went to bed early last night, right after dinner," Jenny said, pouting, "and jogging can't take that much out of anyone!"

Mrs. Pollifax turned and said politely, "I'm not sure that he went to his room to sleep last evening, he mentioned letters and cards to write."

Clearly Jenny didn't welcome this intrusion; she looked startled, mumbled, "Oh well," and subsided. It occurred to Mrs. Pollifax that it had been clever of Peter to use Jenny as cover during the early days of the tour, but his choice was showing signs of boomeranging. Jenny looked ready to cry again; she was not going to take his defection graciously. *A strange girl,* she thought, and wondered what caused this penchant for overreacting.

On either side of the road the country was flat and empty, with the consistency of gravel, but there were surprises: a sudden glimpse of rail tracks, of freight cars on the dusty horizon being loaded with crushed stone, and then of workers strolling along the road wearing dust masks, and then—abruptly—a huge body of water in the middle of this arid dead land, fed by runoffs from the mountains and dropped like a shimmering blue jewel into the warm dry panorama.

In midmorning they stopped beside a shallow irrigation stream and Mr. Li produced Lucky Kolas for them. After this they were off again through the Koko Valley to begin their descent into the Turfan depression, crossing an interminable valley of gray slag, the only signs of civilization the crisscrossing railroad and power lines. At times it gave the illusion of being a gray beach stretching toward a gray sunless sea in the distance.

"Very prehistoric," Malcolm said, leaving his seat to join her. "I hope by now you're a trifle bored with your thoughts, as I am with mine. Feel like talking?"

She smiled. "Yes there's a time for thinking and a time for talking." *And a time to stop worrying,* she added silently.

He said easily, "I find I can all too easily succumb to group mentality; it has a nice cozy hypnotic quality, rather sheeplike and very comfortable."

"Are you feeling refueled now, after being quiet?"

"Definitely. I don't feel that you're a group person, even if you do function well in one. George Westrum, for instance, is a group person totally, mainly because he lacks any original thoughts to entertain himself while alone."

Mrs. Pollifax gave him an amused look. "Rather hard on him, aren't you?"

Malcolm said simply, "He has been instructing Iris in the butchering of his steers and how they are sent to market, with side excursions into profit and loss. He sits behind me, I can't help overhearing. I doubt he's noticed an inch of the country we've been passing through."

"And where is Joe Forbes on your scale of ten?" she inquired.

He smiled. "Not the loner I first thought him to be. There's that need to please, and to smile all the time, plus that lamentable determination to practice Chinese on the guides and to ingratiate himself. I think in general he might be called an Ingratiator."

Mrs. Pollifax, finding his pithy comments almost as interesting as Cyrus' might have been, asked, "And Iris?"

He brushed this query aside impatiently. "Iris is simply Iris."

"Meaning what?"

He smiled, his quizzical brows drawing together. "Why, an original, pure and simple. A transformer and a transcender."

"You like her then," said Mrs. Pollifax. "Or appreciate her. Yet give every evidence of avoiding her."

He grinned. "I avoid George, to be blunt about it, and since he's in constant attendance on Iris, well—there it is."

"And Jenny?"

Malcolm stopped smiling. "A rather troubled person, don't you think? The trip seems to be putting her under enormous pressures. Nice little thing, a pity. I have the feeling—"

"Psychically or intuitively?" intervened Mrs. Pollifax humorously.

"Pressure," he said, ignoring this, "can go either way, it creates diamonds, it also creates explosions. What are your feelings on the matter?"

"At the moment—given her tears the other night—I think explosions."

"Followed, one hopes, by clearing skies," he said. "At the moment she seems extremely cross about Peter having a nap. Do I see green up ahead?" he asked. "Yes, a rather dusty green but definitely green. Do you think we're approaching Turfan?"

This seemed possible because Mr. Kan was unwinding his microphone and presently standing up to explain Turfan to them: a city with a population of 120,000, containing seventy farms and where, for about thirty days of the year, the temperature lingered at 113° F., and in winter descended to twenty below zero . . . Its irrigation system was unique, consisting of underground tunnels, some of them two thousand years old, through which the runoff from the distant mountains reached this desert city . . . And this afternoon they would be introduced to this underground system. Whereupon he promptly sat down.

"Short but to the point," said Malcolm, "and since the air

conditioning's just been turned on it's doubtless 113° Fahren-
heit right now."

"I see we're back to red clay," mused Mrs. Pollifax, looking
out of the window. "My goodness, I just saw a field of cotton."

Soon she was seeing grapevines, too, and mysterious green-
ery growing behind the walls of compounds, but here there
were wooden bars set into the clay windows, and large wooden
gates in the walls that showed the Turkish influence Peter had
mentioned. On this road it was small tractors that pulled the
wooden carts; presently they passed a traffic jam of army
trucks, and then a bazaar shaded by squares of canvas and
surrounded by parked donkey carts and bicycles. "And here
we are," announced Mr. Li as they swung down a broad dirt
road and turned left into a large compound of whitewashed
walls. "The Friendship Guesthouse. Lunch in one hour!"

A square hot room with cement floor and walls; two narrow
beds and a window; a huge round fan whirring at top speed on
the bureau; a bathroom with a shower tap, a dripping faucet,
and no tub or stall . . . Mrs. Pollifax went to her door and
called after the others, "Anyone want to walk to that bazaar
down the road before lunch?"

Iris poked her head out from the door of the room next to
hers. "I take it your room's as hot as mine? Count me in!"

Jenny said defiantly, "Joe and I are going to sit in that grape
arbor and check our cameras."

But Peter said, "I'd love a walk!"

Once in the bazaar Mrs. Pollifax bought recklessly for X:
several ripe golden melons, tiny apricots, raisins, nuts, and a
string bag in which to carry them, and for herself a pair of
cloth shoes and a kerchief. She was about to add some grapes
to the collection when she abruptly felt giddy and close to
fainting. The heat, she decided, a strange kind of heat because
the sun was only moderately bright. She looked at the man
from whom she had bought raisins: he sat solidly under a strip
of canvas wearing a white skullcap, his face shaded. Something in her eyes must have explained her dilemma because he

jumped up, grasped her arm, and sat her down on his box in the shade of the canvas.

She smiled gratefully. He offered her water but she shook her head, remembering that it wouldn't be boiled. Across the pathway from her she saw Peter talking to a young native who appeared to be enthusiastically practicing his English; George Westrum was taking a picture of the rows of rubber-tired carts that had been turned into selling stalls with the addition of canopies, boards, and boxes; Iris had crossed the irrigation trench and was trying to approach a water buffalo that had wandered into the scene. Mrs. Pollifax's sympathetic friend was still offering her water with a mounting insistence. Making no impression upon her he pulled off his skullcap and pantomimed the pouring of water over it and into it.

"Ah!" she cried, understanding, and brought out the kerchief she'd just purchased. He nodded eagerly and she held it out to him while he poured water over it; she placed it on her head, delighted by its coolness, and thanked the man profusely with gestures.

"That bad, huh," said Peter, joining her. "Look, I want you to meet my friend over there, he speaks a little English and I've got a deal going with him that includes you. In fact it seems to *depend* on you."

"On me!" she exclaimed, and as the sun struck her again she recoiled. "Peter—"

But he was already saying to the young man, "Sheng Ti, here is my grandmother."

Mrs. Pollifax gave Peter a reproachful glance. "Not *another* grandmother, Peter?"

"Ah yes," cried Sheng Ti, bowing and smiling, and she looked at him with interest.

His face was at variance with his clothes, which were disreputable: neatly patched pants, a sweat-stained dirty undershirt, and sandals repaired with string; his face, however, shone with intelligence, and his eyes were bright and eager.

"Now that you see my grandmother you will do this for us?" Peter asked him. "To win the bet—the wager?"

"Bet, yes. For the lady yes, I understand now," he said, nodding vigorously.

"Okay, then. Outside the Guesthouse. Wait down the street at the corner, okay? Very secret. Ten o'clock tonight." Peter counted out change and placed it in the young man's palm. "Ten o'clock, Sheng Ti," he added, holding up all of his fingers.

"Ten," repeated Sheng Ti.

As Peter led her away Mrs. Pollifax glanced back and said, "Peter, what on earth—what was all that about?"

"He wouldn't do it for me," Peter told her, "so I tried him out on you and it worked. An authority figure, that's you," he said, grinning. "I think he's what's called a 'hooligan'—no visible means of employment so I took a chance on him, he ought to be relatively safe."

"Safe for what? Peter, you didn't speak Chinese to him!"

"God no," he said. "I'm just a crazy American tourist wanting to win a bet, a bet that I could drive a donkey cart for a couple of hours without the guides hearing about it. I had a hunch he might be open to something illicit. We'll need to hide our foodstuff and sheepskins in the desert, and how else could we get them there? Besides, you're not used to missing all the fun, are you?"

She laughed.

"Disguises later, after we leave Sheng Ti behind tonight," he went on. "A kerchief for you, that quilted jacket you bought in Urumchi—"

"Very observant of you," she said dryly.

"—cotton slacks, and I'll slant your eyes for you after we've left Sheng Ti, in case we're stopped." He signaled to an ancient man with a seamed face sitting patiently over his cart and donkey. "Hop on, he's a cab driver, Turfan style, and you've got to get out of this sun."

She gratefully pulled herself onto the shelflike rear of the cart, smiled at the driver, and waved good-bye to Peter, thinking how confident and thoughtful he was becoming—and also quite dear, she added, startled by this realization. How unbelievable this would have seemed to her in Hong Kong and Canton, or even in Xian when he was being irresponsible and hostile, and with this there came a strange feeling, not unfamiliar to her, that all of this had been intended to happen, and that her meeting with Peter held a significance that was not apparent to her yet. She was delivered to the entrance of the Guesthouse, gave the driver a handful of *feng*, and returned to face the heat of her room, passing Jenny and Forbes seated talking under the luxurious grape arbor. She felt only a little giddy as she examined her treasures from the bazaar and put them away but when she left her room for lunch and sightseeing she wore a dripping wet towel wound around her head. She did not plan to nearly faint again under Turfan's sun, and if her day had just been extended by a cart ride into the country with Peter, it would at least be cooler by night.

There were no keys to the rooms here, so that when Peter knocked softly on her door at ten that night he followed this by quickly slipping inside. Speaking in a low voice he said, "We can leave by your window." He was carrying his dufflebag and he placed it now on her bed. "What do you have?" he asked.

"A second padded quilted jacket from Xian," she told him crisply. "In Urumchi I bought two sheepskin vests, one small blanket, and of course, there are the vitamins and dried foods I carried with me. And to fit all this into my suitcase," she reminded him, "I had to leave almost everything behind in Urumchi except my pajamas. Even," she added sternly, "my hairbrush."

"I'll lend you mine," he said dryly. "How are you carrying it all?"

"Rolled up in a bundle." She pointed to it sitting on the floor beside the chair.

"And may one ask what's happened to your two lower front teeth?" he asked with interest.

"Ah," she remarked happily, "that was a dental bridge. I noticed an old lady in the bazaar this morning with missing teeth, and I thought it would add an authentic note to my disguise." She knotted the plain cotton kerchief around her head, patted her cotton jacket and leaned over to adjust the buckles on her cloth shoes. "Shall we go?"

Peter unlatched the screen, removed it, helped her over the sill and followed, replacing the screen behind them. In single file they stole up the path in the darkness, passing the lighted rooms of the others and coming to a stop at a certain place in the wall where the top had crumbled, releasing the pointed shards of glass embedded in its cement to repel intruders. Tossing both dufflebag and bundle over the wall, they were soon outside the compound and moving toward the street's corner.

The cart was waiting with Sheng Ti beside it. A fuzzy moon dimly illuminated his features; he gave them and their luggage a glance that unsettled Mrs. Pollifax by its thoughtful speculations. He said, "I go with you?"

Peter smiled and shook his head. "No, we'll be okay. Back in two hours."

"I did not steal it," Sheng added, his eyes running curiously over Mrs. Pollifax's cloth shoes, pants, and quilted jacket.

"Good," Peter said and tossed their baggage into the rear, handed Mrs. Pollifax up to the seat with a flourish and squeezed in beside her.

Sheng Ti handed him the reins. *"Zaijian,"* he said, and stepped back into the shadow of the wall.

The donkey moved, the cart lurched, the wheels gave one outraged groan and they were underway; when Mrs. Pollifax glanced back Sheng Ti had vanished. A lone cyclist pedaled toward them in the darkness and called out a greeting; Peter returned it, slipping easily and gratefully into Chinese. "But I think we stop now and make our eyes slant before we run into anyone else," he said, and pulled up beside a vacant stretch of wall.

"What a peculiar contraption," said Mrs. Pollifax when he shone his flashlight once and very quickly, after inserting it under her hair.

"The amazing thing is that it doesn't hurt and it can't be seen—and now you are a true Han," he told her, and she saw the flash of his smile in the faint moonlight.

Slowly they proceeded down the road and out of Turfan, occasionally meeting cyclists as they returned from work or pedaled to work, the pale moon etching black shadows of walls and trees across the darkness of the road. A dog barked. A voice was heard from behind a wall. Other than the clip-clop of the donkey's hoofs and the movement of the wheels there was only the silence of the desert around them.

"How absolutely beautiful to be free for a couple of hours!" said Peter with a happy sigh.

Since Mrs. Pollifax was already experiencing this same reaction—a sense of elation at being out and into the space around her and free of Mr. Li, Mr. Kan, and the tour group—she said with feeling, "Pure bliss! It's safe to speak English now?"

He gestured around them at the empty pale countryside. "Who's to hear?"

And so they began to talk. Of families. Of what they had left behind to come to China. Of the desert. "The Taklamakan desert," Peter told her, "has been called a hungry and ravenous monster. It's considered far more treacherous than the Gobi, it eats people and cities, swallowing them whole."

"*Cities?*" she said incredulously.

He nodded. "Entire cities that flourished in the days of the Silk Road. They find them now and then, the archaeologists, and there are probably more treasures buried there still than you or I could ever imagine, as well as the bones of men and animals caught in its violent dust and earth storms."

She shivered. "We're not on the desert yet, are we?"

"No, and won't be. Only its rim."

"And you and X—you won't cross it, will you?"

"No—skirt it."

As they talked, their voices low in keeping with the rhythm of the plodding donkey and the clouded moon binding them in its spell, she thought and spoke of Cyrus.

"Why don't you marry him?" asked Peter bluntly.

"If we get out of—if I get out of this in one piece, I intend to," she announced with a firmness that startled her. "It seems to me now that I hesitated—oh, for all the wrong reasons. Foolish ones."

"Someone said that if the heart is engaged—"

"Yes," she said, nodding. "And mine is. I hesitated, wanting to be sure, feeling—oh feeling that life would be different, changed, if I married, and that I might have to give up—all this."

"All this," murmured Peter, and suddenly smiled. "So you're an adventurer, too!"

"Yes—no—yes, of course I am," she admitted, laughing. "But what I overlooked—"

"Yes?" he asked curiously.

"What I overlooked," she said simply, "is *change* . . . Meeting Carstairs and becoming useful to him changed me so that nothing was or ever could be the same again." *Like a kaleidoscope,* she thought, remembering that simile following her first adventure. "But meeting Cyrus also changed me so that nothing will or can be the same ever again. *Nothing.* Not even this," she added ruefully. "Which is what I didn't see clearly until now."

"You're not sorry you came?" he asked.

She shook her head. "Oh no! There were things I had to learn, as you can see. Important things. Even at my age!"

He said with a sigh, "I think my parents stopped learning a long time ago, which made me a misfit, a changeling, and restless. A very conventional middle-class family, except they did send me to Harvard where I didn't belong either but—"

"But where you learned to speak Chinese."

"Yes. Funny, isn't it? It came so easily to me, without any classes or lessons at all, as if I'd spoken and read it before and it was already etched in my subconscious waiting to be redis-covered. You must know the very Eastern theory that we've lived many lives; can you believe in that at all?"

"Easily," she said, nodding. "For a long time I've found it a very supportive, meaningful explanation for the curious things that happen to people: the tragedies, the uncanny res-cues, and coincidences in life." She laughed suddenly. "And Cyrus has a rather mandarin look about him; he's a large man and very American, but there's an oriental cast to his eyes that drew me from the beginning. Just as I've been drawn to the country of China itself," she added meditatively.

"Think we've known each other before?" asked Peter, with a chuckle.

She thought without saying it aloud: *yes it's possible, why else do I feel so connected with you—suddenly and inexplica-bly—and so alarmed about what lies ahead for you? There's*

an understanding between us, unspoken but familiar, that
I've experienced only with Tsanko and with Cyrus. Aloud she
said quietly, "It's quite possible, yes. A sense of fatefulness—
of stars crossing—happens rather frequently to me these days.
I lived a very prosaic life, you see, and then suddenly I too met
Carstairs, and I've often wondered if this strange new life was
waiting for me all the time during those years I lived so quietly. I've wondered," she added softly, "how much choice we
really do have about some of the large events in our lives. Is
Peter Fox your real name?" she asked abruptly.

He shook his head. "Peter's my name but not Fox." He
glanced down at his luminous digital watch and said, "We've
been in transit exactly fifty-five minutes, I think it's time we
stop and look for a place to hide all this gear."

She looked around her at the low, hunchbacked surrealistic
mountains off to their left. They had to be sandstone, she
thought, to have been whipped into such frenzied, angry
shapes by wind and rain, and to have created the gulleys and
earth cleavages among which they were riding now. "It's certainly a good place to hide things, but however will you find
your cache again?"

"By compass, by noting distance and direction of travel, and
by making a map of the shapes and contours. C'mon," he said,
bringing the cart to a halt. "I really need your help, we've only
a few minutes to do this. *You* pick the place. Take the flashlight."

Mrs. Pollifax said sharply, "No, Peter, no flashlight."

Startled he asked, "Why?"

"I don't know." She stepped down from the cart, gave the
donkey an absent pat on its flanks and moved off the road
toward three jagged rocks about six feet high. "I think here,"
she called.

Peter was already lifting out his dufflebag. She went back
and retrieved her own bulky package and when she joined
Peter she could see him nod in the dim light. "Good," he said,
and bringing out his knife he worked away at enlarging a hole
under one of the rock formations. Into this he pressed the
small items: vitamins, melons, two filled water pouches, the
dried fruit, and the socks, finally sealing the gap with a stone.

On the surface between two of the rocks he laid out the bulk-
ier items—the two pairs of boots and the sweaters—and then
covered them over with the sheepskins and at last the rug.
With his knife he scraped enough dust from the earth to scatter over the rug until it looked a part of the earth.

"Not bad," commented Mrs. Pollifax. "But let's not linger.
Please."

He gave her a sharp glance, found several loose stones to
weigh down the rug and nodded. "Okay, let's go. We'll both
pace off the distance to the road, okay?"

They each found it to be fifty-two feet.

"You drive while I make notes," he told her, handing her
the reins. "Or at least what notes I can manage without a
light. I don't understand you, why not a light?"

"Not yet—later, but not here," she told him, surprised by
the depth of her unease. With some difficulty she turned the
donkey around on the road and they began their return into
town. She noticed that Peter worked over his notes like an
artist, glancing up, holding out his arm to measure and to
squint, writing and drawing sketches into his notebook until
at last he lighted a match inside cupped hands and checked his
compass. "I hope you're not implying that someone's been
watching us," he said.

To cover the strange flash of alarm that she'd experienced
she said lightly, "Let's just say I'd hate to see you and X reach
that cache and find nothing. You'll be coming to it from
where?"

"*Not* from Turfan," he said and pointed over his shoulder.
"We'll start out from the cave in the mountains and head
southwest, bypassing Turfan, and after rescuing our sheepskins we'll move south toward the Bagrach Kol, or Lake Bos-
ten," he explained. "Then we'll roughly follow the oases
towns along the desert, keeping at a distance from them, naturally."

"Yes," she said, and was silent, feeling her dread for both
him and X.

They reentered Turfan, driving down the same broad road,
the cart intruding only lightly on the deep silence of the night.
When they reached the corner of the Guesthouse wall Sheng

Ti appeared suddenly out of the shadows, advanced toward them, put a finger to his lips counseling silence, and spoke directly to Peter in a low voice.

It needed a moment for Mrs. Pollifax to realize that Sheng Ti was speaking to Peter in Chinese. She said in alarm, "What is this? Why does he speak to you in—"

"He heard me greet that damn cyclist in Chinese," Peter said grimly, and swore. "What is it, Sheng, what's the matter?"

Sheng no longer troubled to speak English, he was obviously agitated, his voice breathless, his gestures quick.

Peter turned to look at Mrs. Pollifax. "How did you know?"

"Know what?"

"Sheng says we were followed on foot by someone from the Guesthouse. Very stealthily, very secretly. And seeing this he followed that person, whoever it was, and thus trailed *all* of us into the desert."

Chapter Eleven

At the ramifications of what Sheng had said Mrs. Pollifax gasped, "One of the guides?"

Peter turned back to Sheng. "No—no, Sheng says *not* a native, he is sure of this. He says this person wore some kind of cloak, so it could have been a man, it could have been a woman—I asked him—but he is certain it was a foreigner, very definitely, because of the way this person walked and acted."

She drew in her breath sharply, remembering her searched suitcase and realizing that it had never been far from her mind. *Something is wrong,* she thought. *Terribly wrong.*

She accepted Sheng's judgment, acknowledging his shrewdness and his street wisdom. "Where is this person now?" she asked.

"Back in the Guesthouse."

She turned her attention to Sheng Ti, realizing that he must be dealt with first of all. "What does he think or suspect about all this?" she asked. "Does he perhaps expect money to not speak of this to anyone?"

Peter spoke to Sheng in Chinese. "He says he wishes to talk with us alone somewhere about why we carry baggage out of the city and return without it. He feels that he alone saw the baggage we carried—which is probably reassuring if I ever find time to think about it. He also wishes to know why I concealed my speaking Chinese so well, and why suddenly you have two teeth missing and dress like a Chinese woman."

"Yes," she said. "Where can we talk?" But she was thinking, *Someone in this tour group knows about Peter and me. Someone among them knows why we're here. How could this have happened? Who else would know about Wang? Who else would even be interested in Wang?*

"Not far," Peter was saying. "You think we can trust Sheng?"

"For the moment I think we have no choice," she said dryly, but in examining her initial reactions to Sheng she added, "I believe we can trust him, yes, but in any case I have a brown belt in karate."

Peter laughed. "Wouldn't you know! Okay—he says we leave the cart and walk."

She thought, *There is no one—absolutely no one—who could know about Wang or be interested in him.*

Except the Russians, she remembered in horror.

Carstairs had said, "One of our agents who works for the Soviets—a double-agent, needless to say—has brought us information of X's existence and of the Soviets' interest in him."

Had brought them information of X's existence . . .

Information that came solely from the Russians, who badly wanted Wang for themselves . . . The same Russians who supposedly had plans to abduct Wang later in the summer . . .

Supposedly . . .

But what if instead, knowing themselves persona non grata in China, they chose to leak their information to the CIA and let the Americans find Wang for them instead? Let an American agent enter China and find the labor camp, find and release Wang and then . . . and then . . . *Oh God,* she thought in horror, *could Peter and I be walking into a trap?*

They were following Sheng through narrow alleys, turning left and then right; he stopped now beside an abandoned irrigation ditch spanned by a crumbling bridge. Sheng led them under the bridge and gestured to them to sit down.

Peter said in surprise, "He says he sleeps here; this is his home."

They squatted, knees touching. Sheng had been eating garlic which made for a powerful atmosphere; he was also anxious, and this too contributed an odor so that they hunched together in a cloud of garlic, sweat, and dusty earth. "But why is this his home?" asked Mrs. Pollifax. "Why doesn't he have a unit like everyone else?"

Peter began to speak to Sheng, and Sheng replied at length, and while they talked Mrs. Pollifax's mind flew back to Carstairs' mysterious counteragent. If all the information came from the Russians and they were being followed . . . She shivered a little, exploring the idea of herself and Peter being mere pawns because if her theory was correct and if the Russians were masterminding this operation, then it would be a member of the KGB who had been planted in the tour group.

To watch them. To snatch Wang for the Soviets once he was free.

And Carstairs doesn't know, she thought, trembling at the prospects should her suspicions be right. *He doesn't even guess and there's no way to communicate, to tell him that possibly . . . maybe . . .*

Peter turned to her and said, "He tells me that he's twenty-six years old and he's *hei jen*—it translates as being one of the 'black persons,' living without registration and without a ration card or employment. He lives off friends or steals and sells things in the black market."

"Good heavens," she murmured with a glance at Sheng.

"He says that you and I must have very good identification papers to have dared to go out tonight dressed as natives. He wants either my ID papers or yours. He says he can pay. He wants to use them to escape to Hong Kong."

Mrs. Pollifax considered this with interest. "So he won't betray us then," she said with some relief. "Not if he wants something from us." The word *betray* struck her forcibly and she thought, *Carstairs has in effect been betrayed by his double-agent, his counterspy, hasn't he? and doesn't know this either.* Aloud she said, "But how did he come to live under a bridge and be *hei jen?* He looks very intelligent, I'm curious."

She had to wait again for the reply, watching Peter's gestures and the changes in expression on his face as he listened: surprise, thoughtfulness, a frown, a nod, until at last he resumed. "He says it began for him with *shang-shan xia-xiang*—what they call 'up to the mountains and down to the villages' . . . the many young people sent down to the country to learn hard physical labor. Sheng was *cheng-fen bu hao*—bad background, meaning his family used to be rich peasants, landlords. Because of this he had no hope of school or a job in the city. He was sent to a commune in central China where the farmers hated these city youngsters foisted on them . . . this was ten years ago, when he was sixteen; he felt lonely and ostracized. He stood it for three years and then he ran away. For this he was given *shou-liu*—detention—and then he was sent to a commune near Urumchi where they work on the roads. Here he acquired more bad records—*tan*, or a dossier. What it amounts to—to sum up—is that he couldn't conform."

"I'm not sure I could have either," commented Mrs. Pollifax thoughtfully. "But how on earth does he survive?"

Peter said in a level voice, "He steals. People sometimes give him food. Once he stole a cartload of melons and set up a stall in the bazaar and sold them. With the profit he bought pumpkin-seeds and nuts and sold them, and then jars of honey . . ."

"Sounds a promising businessman," said Mrs. Pollifax, giving him a smile.

"He saved up money for a Flying Pigeon bicycle—one of the best—but being without a unit and without coupons he had to go to the black market to buy it. The man took his money but never produced the bicycle and since then he says his anger has given him much despair, he sleeps too much and has gone back to stealing."

Mrs. Pollifax said impulsively, "But there's such sensitivity in his face, and look at those eyes. He shouldn't be an outcast."

Peter said, "I've told him his country is changing now that Mao's dead, and that mistakes of the past are being corrected. If he just waits a little longer—"

"What does he say to that?"

"He asks how these changes can reach him. They are very slow, and even slower this far away from Peking. He says he has nobody to speak for him, nobody to say he is not bad, he says he is now an invisible person." Peter shook his head. "We could never sell ID papers to someone like him, not with his background, he's not reliable."

Mrs. Pollifax looked at Sheng, an idea occurring to her that she liked very much. He returned her glance, a sudden flash of anger illuminating those black eyes. "I do not beg," he said, thrusting out his jaw.

"If you should leave your country," she asked him gently, "what would you do, what would you want?"

He scowled at her. "To go to school. To work."

She nodded and turned back to Peter. "Well?"

"What do you mean 'well'?" he said indignantly. "As I just said, with a background like that he's scarcely reliable, he'd blow it. He'd be picked up and he'd blow the whole thing."

"Not if he left the country with you and Wang," she told him.

"If he *what?*"

She said slowly, "It's true there would be three of you if he joined you, and three are harder to hide in the countryside, but he's a master of hiding, isn't he?" *And if there is danger ahead*, she added silently, *three can fight better than two.*

Peter grinned. "Hearing you cracks me up, it really does."

She conveniently ignored this. "In the mountains you'll need help with X, who may not have your stamina. Sheng could turn out to be valuable to you, and how can he 'blow it,' as you say, if he's with you all the time? Frankly I feel he'd be extremely reliable if it helps him to get out of the country."

Sheng was looking at her intently; she could feel his tension as he comprehended what she was saying; she could hear the quickening of his breathing, as if he waited with an incredulous hope.

"You'd trust him?" Peter said.

"Yes," she said simply.

Sheng sat very still; it was as if he'd not heard her but very slowly she saw his shoulders straighten, and when he lifted his head it was to say with dignity, as one equal to another,

"*Xiexie.* Thank you." And then to Peter, "You sell me papers? I may go?"

Peter was silent and then he nodded. "Okay. But I give you papers, not sell them, and you go with me. To the south and over the high mountains." He translated this into Chinese.

When Sheng understood what Peter was saying he visibly trembled with emotion. Impulsively Mrs. Pollifax reached out and touched his hand and saw the gleam of a smile: it was the first time she'd seen him smile, and it was a smile of incredulous joy. He said fervently, "I will not fail you, I can die for this."

"It will be very hard going," Peter reminded him.

She said gently, "Peter—"

"Yes?"

"He knows what hardship is. He can somehow make his way to Urumchi, can't he? Give him papers and money and have him meet you somewhere near the hotel there."

"Yes," Peter said dazedly. "You don't think he'll—?"

"It's a good way to find out, isn't it?" She stood up. "Peter, I want to go back now, I feel very uneasy about our being followed. I want to think—to see—to check—"

He looked startled. "Oh—yes, of course," he said, and then, "I ought to be thinking about that, too."

Very tactfully she said, "I'll think about it now, you can think about it later." It had needed all of her will power to concentrate on Sheng Ti and his situation when instead she had wanted to cry out to Peter, *If what I think is true then someone in our tour group is here to find Wang, too. They've known who you are from the beginning and they've searched suitcases until they identified me as your cover because they knew just what to look for and they found it in mine: that preposterous hoard of dried foods and vitamins. Peter, don't you see what this means?*

In silence Peter and Sheng escorted her back to the compound and around the wall to the corner where they had scaled it earlier; she was boosted over it to creep stealthily to her window, where she removed the screen and climbed back into her room, securing the window behind her. For a moment she stood in the darkness, her mind checking and rechecking the thoughts that had dazed her during the last forty-five minutes, but her conclusion remained the same: someone in their tour group could be working for the Russians, and she and Peter could be in grave danger.

Hearing a faint sound beyond her door she tiptoed across the room and quietly opened it just in time to see a shadowy figure pause by the door next to hers, open it, enter and close it softly.

But that was Iris' room, she remembered, and she thought, "Iris?" and then in astonishment, *"Iris?"*

By the luminous dial on her bedside clock it was half-past one in the morning but Mrs. Pollifax did not feel like sleeping. She sat in the darkness for a long time, not enjoying her thoughts or speculations at all.

Chapter Twelve

rs. Pollifax awoke with a start to discover that both heat and daylight had arrived and that she had fallen asleep across her bed, still in the costume of the previous night. The huge electric fan was wheezing from exhaustion. Walking into the bathroom to wash her face she was confronted by a mirror over the washbasin that reflected a strange slant-eyed woman; she hastily disengaged the tape hidden under her hair and watched Emily Pollifax emerge again. The sense of pending heat was oppressive; she felt vaguely worried still, and jaded from those worries; she had not slept well. She stood on the slatted shower platform while a thin stream of lukewarm water poured over her, and she wondered what Cyrus was doing now. At this exact moment. He seemed very far away.

Having dressed in her thinnest and coolest clothes she walked out to the grape arbor to sit down and face her day. Putting her head back she gazed into the tightly laced green leaves above her and at the clusters of pale green seedless grapes grown in Turfan, Mr. Li had said, for fifteen hundred years. Presently a door in the long line of rooms opened and Malcolm emerged, glanced around, and strolled over to join her.

"I scarcely recognize you without a wet towel around your head," he said dryly.

"After breakfast," she promised him.

He nodded. "Breakfast in that incredibly hot little room with two fans, one of which doesn't work, and George Westrum manages to find the only place where the working fan stirs any air."

"Courage," she told him, "it's only half-past seven. Except —where is everyone?"

Two doors opened simultaneously: George Westrum emerged from his and Iris from hers; they smiled, greeted each other and walked together toward them. Jenny came next, followed by Joe Forbes, and then Peter hurried out looking surprisingly fresh and bright-eyed. They sat or sprawled under the grapes, their conversation desultory and idle as they waited for Mr. Li.

He joined them looking both serious and somewhat anxious, so that their greetings did not extract from him his usual beaming smile.

"What's up for today?" asked Forbes.

Mr. Li nodded. "We spend most of today in Turfan, of course. This morning we visit the Thousand-Buddha Caves, also an ancient tomb, and following lunch we look forward to Jiaohe—ancient city—and then return to Urumchi." He hesitated and then turned to look at Peter. "You were not in your room last night, Mr. Fox."

Mrs. Pollifax's heart skipped a beat. *Oh dear*, she thought in dismay.

"I beg your pardon," Peter said coldly.

"You were not in your room all night," Mr. Li repeated firmly.

"And how the hell would you know that?" asked Peter, rallying, while the others listened in astonishment.

"Because I looked in—there are no keys, as you know. I looked in and went back many times to look. You were not in your room all night."

Mrs. Pollifax thought, *I've got to stop this; I've got to think of something . . .*

"I don't know what business it is of yours," Peter told him.

"It is the business of myself and China Travel Bureau," he said formally. "I am responsible. You were not in your room, you were not anywhere in this compound. I have to ask, *where did you go?*"

They had all frozen into a tableau staring mesmerized at Peter, who stared back at Mr. Li; they had been made uncomfortable by some unknown quality in Mr. Li's voice, and by the rising suspense of a long silence that Iris broke at last by speaking.

"Actually," said Iris in a calm voice, "Peter spent the night with me. In my room. All night."

Every head swiveled toward Iris, and George Westrum gasped. Mrs. Pollifax looked quickly at Iris and then her glance moved to George who was staring incredulously at Iris, his mouth open; she saw that his face had turned white, as if he'd been struck. *How strange this is,* thought Mrs. Pollifax, *all of us simply sitting here and watching.*

Peter said, "Iris—"

"It's quite true," she said with a lift of her jaw. "He was with me."

George leaned forward, his eyes cold with anger and disgust. "You *slut*," he said, biting the words through his teeth and he rose to his feet and stalked out of the arbor, his back rigid.

His words seemed to reverberate, or was it the hate behind them, wondered Mrs. Pollifax—oh those tight thin lips, she thought, this had been there all the time. Even Mr. Li looked stricken. In an embarrassed voice he said to Peter, "If that is—I didn't—"

Malcolm said pleasantly, "Surely it's time for breakfast now, don't you think?" He stood and walked across the arbor to stand casually behind Iris' chair, and Mrs. Pollifax loved him for this. Iris herself sat very still, a flush on either cheekbone, her head high.

"Yes indeed," said Joe Forbes, as if coming out of a trance, and jumped to his feet.

Iris looked around, her face without expression, her glance resting lightly on Mrs. Pollifax, and then she too stood up.

Jenny, staring at her, said, "Well of all the—!"

Mrs. Pollifax heard herself say firmly, "I think we've had enough."

Jenny gave her a hostile glare and turned to Joe Forbes. *"Poor* George," she said dramatically.

"Poor *Jenny*," he said lightly. It was the first evidence that he'd given of being aware of the shifting alliances.

They moved across the compound in procession, Malcolm walking silently beside Iris, Joe Forbes and Jenny with Mr. Li. Peter, falling in at the rear with Mrs. Pollifax, said in a low voice, "I'm in shock."

"Accept, accept," she murmured.

"But—why did she do it?"

"I don't know," she told him. "I just don't know, Peter, but it's becoming terribly important that we talk in private soon. I think there could be more shocks ahead. Where's Sheng Ti now?"

"On his way by bus to Urumchi, I hope. I suppose you mean you're worried about what Sheng told us—that we were followed last night into the desert?"

"Yes."

He said with a frown, "You realize we have only Sheng's word for that, don't you? You and I haven't seen anyone, we have no proof. He could have made it up to hide the fact that he followed us himself."

"Possibly," she conceded.

"But in any case," he added, his face lightening, "tomorrow's the day for visiting the Kazakhs up in the grasslands, and at some point during the day I expect to vanish, which will take care of anybody's lurking curiosity." With this confident statement he held the screen door open for her to enter the dining room.

This time George did not capture the enviable spot in front of the one working fan; he did not join them at all for breakfast.

Mrs. Pollifax, with dampened towel wrapped around her head, forced herself to concentrate on sight-seeing for the next hours. There was nothing else to do, she decided: she was experiencing a sense of events moving inexorably now toward their conclusion and without any way to alter or color them. That word *inexorable* again, she thought with a shiver. X was hiding in his cave at the edge of the Tian Shan mountains, while Sheng Ti was somehow making his way to Urumchi, armed with his coveted ID papers at last; they too would head for Urumchi again toward the end of this day, and Peter had reminded her that in only thirty or so more hours he planned to disappear. In the meantime they had been mysteriously followed into the desert last night—she did not share Peter's skepticism about Sheng's tale—and Mr. Li had known Peter was gone. If one of the members of the tour group had told Mr. Li of Peter's absence, she could no longer believe that it was Iris. Iris had provided cover for Peter at a rather staggering cost.

Sticks and stones may break my bones, she thought, reflecting on that cost to Iris . . . *a good name is rather to be chosen than great riches* . . . Why had Iris leaped to protect Peter? What did she know, and how? She discovered as they embarked on their sight-seeing that she was carefully avoiding Iris, going to great lengths to neither walk with her, speak to her, nor catch her eye, and then to her chagrin she noticed that Iris was going out of her way to avoid her, too. It was as if each of them knew something about the other they didn't care to acknowledge, but what *had* Iris been doing outside her room at one o'clock in the morning?

Since there was no answer available to her—because she wasn't even sure just now of the question—Mrs. Pollifax philosophically gave herself up to the moment, and to their excursion into the desert to see the Thousand-Buddha Caves. This was not at all difficult: they had arrived at the heart of the Silk Road and it was an incredible countryside, totally emptied of colors to which the eyes were accustomed. It was a land of beige—beige, terra-cotta, cream, tan, and dusty gray, set into a valley of surrealistic shapes: harsh angles cut into sandstone cliffs, mesas pleated and wrinkled by wind and sun, and jagged tawny mountains climbing in tiers to a heat-seared washed-out sky. Nothing moved, nothing appeared to live except the shapes, which had a life of their own.

Yet it felt neither unfriendly nor desolate. The sense of space was glorious, and the palette of earth colors were as warm as if they'd been toasted by the nearly-suffocating sun.

Leaving the bus for the caves Mrs. Pollifax looked down in astonishment on an oasis of bright green, long and narrow like a knife-slit between the jagged sandstone hills, a miraculous ribbon of green threaded by a canal carrying sparkling water down from the mountains. Standing on the cliff overlooking this oasis Mrs. Pollifax was transfixed. In her mind's eye she saw a long line of camels, horses, donkeys slowly moving up this trackless valley to arrive at this oasis with its glacier-fed running water, so incongruous in the midst of the heat and sun and desert. In her imagination she could hear the tinkle of camel bells and voices calling to one another in the exotic languages of the Silk Road. If they were leaving China, they would be heading for Persia, India, Russian Turkestan, the camels laden with silk, furs, ceramics, jade, iron, lacquer, and bronze; if entering China they would be bringing gold and precious stones, asbestos and glass, wool and linens, and— perhaps most significant of all—the religion of Buddhism.

"Yes," she whispered, "this is *it*, this is what I came to see, what I hoped to feel." And she stood lost in the magic of it until Mr. Li's call to her broke the spell.

They lunched back at Turfan in the small hot room with its malfunctioning fans, with George again seizing the one promising spot for air. Mrs. Pollifax's returning cheerfulness was not altogether shared by the others, however; subtly they had now formed themselves into two camps. Although there was not the slightest acknowledgment of it by gesture, glance, or word, Mrs. Pollifax and Malcolm had tacitly united to protect Iris, and Peter along with her. The others, thought Mrs. Pollifax dryly, were being far more obvious in their allegiances, and in the case of Jenny even strident. Jenny had come into her own: she now had George and Joe Forbes in attendance, and although her voice was shrill all of her elfin charm had returned. Like a Lady Bountiful she offered everyone the raisins she'd bought in the bazaar the day before, not even affronted when Mrs. Pollifax and Peter refused them. George's baseball cap had taken on a more cocky angle, but his face remained a mask of tight-lipped coldness: he seethed with anger. Joe Forbes appeared to observe Jenny as if she were a precocious child, but Mrs. Pollifax thought that he was enjoying very much being in the center of things for a change.

After lunch they were off again to see the ruins of the city of Jiaohe, but they were growing accustomed now to the desert, to its tawny shades of cream and beige, to the far horizons and to the hints of Turkish influence as they passed through Turfan: the boots, the occasional sash around the waist, the kerchiefs worn around the head by the women, the higher slant of cheekbones, and rounder eyes.

"The city of Jiaohe," explained Mr. Kan, taking up the small hand microphone in the bus and looking very serious, "was once the location of the royal court of Che-shi. It is sixteen hundred years old, having flourished in the year A.D. 200. This was very important communication center on the ancient Silk Road. Of much strategy—and importance, too, as you will see by its locale."

"What do you mean by that?" asked Jenny.

"It is built on steep cliff with ravines all around."

"What happened to it?" asked Malcolm.

"It was destroyed by roving bands in fourteenth century."

"Roving bands?"

"Muslims. Genghis Khan maybe. Nobody knows. It *died*." He snapped his fingers and smiled.

"More ruins," sniffed George, looking very warm and flushed from the heat.

"Looks like some sort of dried-out maze," Joe Forbes said, as they swung past the solitary caretaker's house and headed up the dusty road to the top of a broad mesa.

"But a child's maze," said Iris eagerly, her head craned to look. "People lived where, Mr. Kan?"

"You will see," he told her. "In small rooms—oh very dark, very small—inside walls."

The bus came to a stop, the doors opened, and they met with desert heat again. Iris at once strolled off with Mr. Kan, who talked earnestly to her, delighted by her questions and her interest, but Mrs. Pollifax wondered if Iris didn't attach herself to him to avoid the others. Peter lingered to ask directions of Mr. Li, and George and Jenny moved off together. It was Malcolm who caught up with Mrs. Pollifax as they approached the walls that opened into a vista of lanes and alleys.

"Hot," she said, turning to smile at him.

"Very. Your towel dried out already?"

"I've timed it," she said. "It turns damp inside of ten minutes and dry in half an hour. Yes, it's now dry. You've been very thoughtful about Iris, by the way."

"Not at all," said Malcolm calmly. "I have plans for Iris—I intend to marry her, except I do rather hope she won't go around being so quixotic in the future."

Mrs. Pollifax beamed at him appreciatively. "Malcolm, you're wonderful," she told him. "I'm truly happy to have met you and I feel that I shall forever love your talking mice. You and Iris are a marvelously improbable combination, but now that I think of it terribly *right*. You wouldn't insist she stop falling over chairs or that she cut her hair?"

He smiled. "What, and lose that awkward flash of hands every few minutes? Not on your life."

"When did you decide all this?" she asked.

"Well, there's that psychic bit," he explained. "I had a nearly overwhelming reaction to her when I first saw her, which—as you may remember—was as she popped out from under a table in Hong Kong. I felt as if I'd been hit over the head, frankly. It took some time to understand what had happened, but there it was. . . . In any case I found her so funny, earnest, and unique that it scarcely needed any help from the psyche, although it's been very pleasant knowing all this time —really *knowing*—that she wasn't going to marry George, no matter how ardent he proved to be."

"But what about Iris and *Peter?*" she suggested mischievously.

He laughed and steered her to the left, down a slope toward a more intricate arrangement of walls. "Surely you know *that* was a lot of hogwash."

"George didn't," she reminded him.

"Well, George is a nerd, of course. He has excellent taste in women, but obviously he goes after form rather than content or he'd never have believed Iris for an instant. He has a small mind."

"Have you mentioned any of this to Iris?" she inquired.

"Good Lord no," he said, looking appalled. "Not being psychic she couldn't possibly know what I do. On the other hand," he added with a chuckle, "we have avoided each other assiduously for a week—suspiciously so—and I do hope I don't sound macho if I say there has been an intense awareness between us."

"I have been—not unaware," she told him, remembering the electricity she'd felt between them in Xian, at the tombs. "You're being very tactful, then."

"Oh no, just giving her time," he said, and suddenly stopped.

"What is it?" asked Mrs. Pollifax, alarmed by the look on his face.

He had become immobile, his head turned as if to listen to something she couldn't hear. He said, "I heard—thought I heard—"

She said sharply, "Malcolm, are you all right?"

"Yes," he said. "Yes, yes—let's keep walking."

"What did you hear?"

He shook his head. His face had paled, he looked strained, but seeing her concern he managed a smile. "I'm fine, honestly. No problem."

Mrs. Pollifax was already fumbling in her purse for the smelling salts she carried with her. "No problem except that frankly you look awful. Here." She held out the small vial to him.

He grasped both her arms and the smelling salts and propelled her into an open space. "Look at all the shards lying around," he pointed out. "An archaeologist's delight."

"And note the signs in English suggesting no one remove any. Malcolm, what's wrong?"

He placed both hands over his ears. "I'm trying, I'm trying, except that covering my ears doesn't help, I can still hear them." He reached for her smelling salts and unscrewed the cap. "This won't help either," he said fiercely. "I still hear them. Voices wailing in despair, the same lamentations I felt—heard—at Auschwitz, except here there are no screams, just unbearable despair. Something very sad happened here," he said, looking around them at the sun-baked empty mesa.

"I wonder what," she said, her gaze following his, believing him, believing that what he heard was something lingering here from the past.

"Not violence—that's the strange thing," he said. "Just weeping and wailing, lamentations, and a terrible sadness."

"Malcolm let's get out of here," she told him. "You do look horrid, you know."

Peter, following down the path and coming upon them said, "What is it, something wrong?"

"Malcolm."

Peter stared. "My God he looks absolutely wiped out."

They helped him to his feet and slowly retraced their route back to the bus. As soon as they left the walls behind them Malcolm straightened and lifted his head, the color returning to his face. "It's okay, I feel better now," he told them both.

"The heat," Peter said, nodding. "I'll go and tell Mr. Kan that it's bothering you. Sit and take deep breaths." He hurried off to look for the guide, filled with an energy that defied the heat and promised well for his desert travels, thought Mrs. Pollifax as she turned back to Malcolm.

"I always thought it must be quite fascinating to be psychic," she told him. "An added dimension to life, you might say. Now I see that it has its hazards and its price."

He gave her a twisted smile. "Hell sometimes. Sorry about this, you won't mention it to anyone?"

"You notice I didn't," she said dryly.

"Good of you not to assume I'd gone off my rocker. Hearing voices is one of the first signs, they tell me."

"You seem surprisingly sane to me," she said firmly, thinking that if he should be their KGB agent, he was at least a sane one. "When it happens in a ruin that's six thousand years old . . . Auschwitz, too?"

He nodded unhappily. "They had to carry me out. Most humiliating experience in my life. On a stretcher."

"Let's talk of something else," she announced. "I think we should. Iris, for instance? Or the heat? Or—" She suddenly wondered if he sensed or "saw" anything about her, or about Peter, and for just a moment felt endangered and uneasy.

The moment passed. Mr. Li, hurrying toward them in the heat, called out, "I have sent Mr. Kan to find all our people, the young lady Jenny is very sick."

Mrs. Pollifax sighed. "And a four-hour trip back to Urumchi ahead of us? As group leader, Mr. Li, I do think we must go."

Both Iris and Mr. Kan appeared from among the walls supporting a very white-faced Jenny between them. "Cramps," Iris explained, and accepted Mrs. Pollifax's smelling salts. Jenny was installed in the bus on the rear seat and a paper bag produced for her. Joe Forbes and George Westrum strolled in from a different corner of the city with Peter herding them like a shepherd rounding up a flock. The bus started, and Mrs. Pollifax took one last look at Jiaohe dreaming in the hot golden sun in its sadness. *What did happen to you,* she asked silently, and knew that she would always wonder.

Once again as they entered Urumchi they passed the anti-aircraft guns silhouetted on the hills outside the city, and the huge sign PROTECT OUR MOTHERLAND, HEIGHTEN ALERTNESS. Threading their way through the sprawling town they passed several factories belching sinister yellow vapors, and then as they approached the wooded driveway leading to their hotel Mrs. Pollifax looked from her window and saw Sheng Ti.

He was sitting by the road at the entrance, watching the oncoming bus with great interest. She saw his intelligent eyes focus on Peter, and then on her, and she quietly lifted one hand to him, and smiled. Somehow he had made his way to Urumchi. He was here.

The bus turned into the drive and Mrs. Pollifax, taking stock, found herself grateful, and almost happy. Sheng Ti had arrived to join Peter. They were back in Urumchi, and it was gratifying to realize that she no longer need wear a wet towel wrapped around her head and look like a berserk Arab. She was bearing leftover food from their meals in Turfan, all of it conscientiously, if wetly, stuffed into her suitcase, and behind her in the bus Jenny had fallen asleep at last after being actively ill a number of times.

But most of all, she thought as she looked back on Turfan, she knew that she would not easily forget her trip into the desert with Peter. They both carried back with them the ramifications of that night—the knowledge that someone had been watching them—but for herself she knew that she would never forget that sense of leaving time behind them for a few hours, of moving effortlessly, slowly, into another century. It had diminished barriers and touched them both so that perhaps the closeness she'd shared with Peter was the most important part of the memory, and what had moved her most of all.

And because of this she decided not to tell him of her suspicions, not to burden him with them yet. They drew up to the hotel, and it was Mr. Kan and Mr. Li who went to the back of the bus to look after Jenny. Mrs. Pollifax, leaving the bus with Peter, whispered to him, "You saw Sheng Ti on the street out there?"

"I sure did." He nodded. "I'm really pleased. He made it."

"Do you go off with food for X tonight?"

He nodded.

She had to say it. "You'll be terribly sure you're not followed?"

"You can bet on it," he told her grimly.

"Good. What about your plans for the grasslands, for zero hour tomorrow?" she asked, and discovered that the word *tomorrow* chilled her.

He turned and looked at her as they gained the lobby, and she saw that his eyes were distant and cold, as opaque as they had been when she first met him in Hong Kong. He said curtly, "I don't think that you ought to know."

She didn't take this as a rebuff, she merely nodded, understanding the need in him now to withdraw and to build up that lonely austere strength that was familiar to her from her own experience. One couldn't share, not in this business, not with other lives at stake, and perhaps, she reflected, it was this experience of altered selfness that was the meaning behind all of her own adventures: a sense of bringing to each moment every strength and resource hidden inside of herself as well as the discovery of new ones: a sense of life being so stripped to its essence that trivia and inconsequentials fell away. It was very akin to a mystical experience, as she had realized long ago.

And so she only nodded. There would be no more sharing unless Peter found that he could afford it; Turfan was behind them, they were agents, and Peter the cold professional that she would never be. With equal crispness she said, "Right—just let me know if there's anything I can do."

He stopped and looked at her. "There's one thing you can do, yes. With your experience in people, you trust Sheng Ti? Really trust him?"

She said simply, "Yes."

Peter nodded. "Then I'll take him with me tonight to the cave and let him hide there with X."

"Very good," she said. "And I'll leave my contribution of food for them both in your room when I go to dinner."

Due to their long drive back from Turfan it was a late dinner that evening, and for Mrs. Pollifax it was made even later by Mr. Li detaining her in the lobby as the others walked into the dining room.

He said, "There is this matter of Iris Damson and Peter Fox last night. As group leader, Mrs. Pollifax—"

"Yes?" she said without expression.

"It is most uncomfortable, and as group leader—"

"It *was* uncomfortable, wasn't it," she agreed, and remembering that the best defense was an offense she asked with great innocence, "However did you come to learn that Peter wasn't in his room? Who was it who told you?"

A curtain immediately dropped over Mr. Li's shiny black young eyes, and Mrs. Pollifax realized that she was experiencing oriental inscrutability; it did exist after all. She remembered that in Chinese society it wasn't the individual that mattered but the people. As group leader Mr. Li would expect frank information from her, he would assume her proprietary interest in the group as a mass while certainly not giving anything in return. He said again, stubbornly, "As group leader—"

She smiled at him. "As group leader, Mr. Li, I insist we go in for dinner. Believe me, I'll do everything in my power to make things less uncomfortable for you, but on an empty stomach, no."

He looked suitably young and chagrined at this subtle reprimand for detaining her, but she also sensed in him an iron determination to probe and to bring order because this was his group, his tour, his responsibility. He was troubled by the implications of that confrontation in the grape arbor—*as I am, too*, she thought, entering the dining hall and taking her seat with the others, *but not for the same reasons*. The dinner had already begun. She grasped a spicy dumpling with her chopsticks and looked around the table at the others, studying each one carefully, seeing them all as likable, explainable, good people and to all appearances precisely what they seemed to be and said they were.

As I am too, she thought with a rueful smile.

There was Malcolm, so debonair with his guardsman's moustache and quizzical brows, his talking mice, and his psychic talent: she disliked very much the thought that he might be dissembling, but he could very well be the cleverest of them all. Her glance moved to Joe Forbes, bearded, smiling and affable; she had met her share of college professors with that same innate blandness of personality, as if the world of academics stifled contact with the outside world and preserved them in aspic. And there was Iris . . . Iris had already proven herself a remarkably good actress when she had lied for Peter, but her rescue of Peter could just as easily be a diversionary tactic, a deliberate attempt to confuse and disarm, for after all Iris *had* been up and abroad that night, the only member of the group to be seen, and her knowledge of Peter's absence had been made obvious. She turned her gaze to George Westrum, tight-lipped and flushed, half-boy, half-man in his baseball cap; if he wore a mask it was surely to hide the truculent child that he'd so brutally unleashed at Iris in Turfan. And then of course there was Jenny with her bright smile and tart tongue, missing from the table tonight and presumed to be asleep.

When the soup arrived to complete their meal Mrs. Pollifax

excused herself, wanting very much to be alone. She told herself that following the heat, dust, and tension of Turfan the only thing that mattered at the moment was the gleaming white bathtub in her room. She did not want to speculate any longer on who had followed them into the desert, she wanted to forget and to rest, except that deep down she knew that what really caused her malaise was the knowledge that tomorrow night, if Peter was successful, he would not be with them anymore.

Zero hour.

Chapter Thirteen

At breakfast the next morning a very wan Jenny came to the table to sip a cup of tea; Malcolm's experience at Jiaohe appeared to have left him tired; George Westrum merely played with his food, eating almost nothing. Only Iris and Joe Forbes and Peter ate heartily, but Mrs. Pollifax thought that in general the group was approaching a nadir, as perhaps groups had to when moved about with increasing speed, without a free day to assimilate.

She herself had slept well, but on waking, and realizing that this was Thursday and grasslands day, her appetite had completely vanished. They were to spend the day in the mountains, with a picnic at midday, and under ordinary circumstances this would have sounded delightful.

Today, however, was not an ordinary circumstance. She ate three roasted peanuts, nibbled at a hard-boiled egg, and then excused herself. Peter, following her down the hall, caught up with her and said in a low voice, "You were right, Sheng's really okay."

"He's with X?"

He nodded. "They hit it off right away—a pair of bloody nonconformists, those two."

She said quickly, "Peter—"

"Mmmm?"

She stopped to face him, wanting him to know much more

than she dared to say to him in words just now. "Peter, listen and hear me, it's important. *No matter how successful today proves to be, don't relax your guard. Be careful!*"

He said impatiently, "Of course I'll be careful."

She shook her head. "You don't understand, Peter, I don't mean just careful, I mean you must expect—I don't know what—but assume—" She hesitated. "Assume that something could be wrong, very wrong."

The amused skepticism in his eyes died away in the face of her urgency. "All right," he said quietly. "I'll accept that, I'm hearing you."

"Good luck," she told him and entered her room, realizing that her major fear now was that Peter's sleight-of-hand, whatever it might be, might backfire and there be a corpse after all: Peter's.

"Let go," she told herself. "This is his problem, not yours. *Let go . . .*"

Once again they climbed into the minibus following breakfast, but this time they headed for the mountains surrounding Urumchi, climbing slowly, exchanging terra-cotta and dust for the green of spruce and fir trees. They passed a Red Army barracks, and Mrs. Pollifax wondered if this could be the one that Guo Musu had checked on their map; if so they must be quite near the labor camp from which X had been so surprisingly removed already. They turned right, stopping at a checkpoint—a hut from which a man emerged to examine Mr. Li's credentials—and then they headed up the narrow dirt road, passing a scattering of yurts on the hillside, surrounded by browsing sheep and goats. Already the air had become cooler, and Mrs. Pollifax drew on a sweater. The meadows grew more and more tilted and the trees moved in closer until after several miles of climbing the forest hugged the road. The bus slowed, they passed a shadowy glen lined with picnic tables and then came out upon a wild and forbidding area dominated by a waterfall.

Why it felt so forbidding Mrs. Pollifax didn't know, but certainly it did not strike her as hospitable. The waterfall was spectacular, as high as a three-story building, and its water fell like a silver curtain to the rocks below, making all the appro-

priate sounds, but there was no sun here, the mountain rose
steeply on the left, like a wall, and the narrow paths cut out of
the earth held puddles of water from the fall, and looked slippery and dangerous.

Mr. Li, showing it to them proudly, said, "This is where we
picnic after the horsemanship of the Kazakhs. We stop to leave
the beer here in the mountain stream to cool it for you." Mr.
Kan was already unloading cartons from the bus and carrying
them one by one toward the water.

"Will they be safe?" asked Jenny.

Mr. Li laughed. "Oh yes! On weekends there are many stu-
dents here from the university, but today, no." He added as an
afterthought, "Very dangerous walking here, the rocks extremely slippery. Only two weeks ago a student fell from
above and was killed."

Mrs. Pollifax's gaze sharpened and she glanced quickly at
Peter. She thought, *This is where it will happen, then, this is
where Peter disappears. A shoe, a jacket left behind, some
indication of a fall* . . . Peter was staring intently at the
rocks and at the rushing water, his eyes narrowed, his face
expressionless.

"But for now," said Mr. Li, gesturing them back into the
bus, "the show of horsemanship please. Too early for lunch!"

Herded into the bus they set out again, and soon met with
open space that slowly widened and broadened until they
drove up and into a breathtaking expanse of green meadow-
land that stretched as far as the eye could see, lined on either
side by mountain ridges. Mrs. Pollifax felt at once a sense of
relief to see the sky again, and the sun. She heard Malcolm
say, "This resembles Switzerland—it's amazing!"

Perhaps, yes, thought Mrs. Pollifax, except that several
yurts occupied this end of the long stretch of meadow, and the
faces of the men approaching the bus were swarthy and high-
cheekboned and they wore blue Mao jackets and scuffed boots.
Mr. Li conferred with them, announced that the demonstration would begin very shortly, pointed to elevated areas along
the meadow, and suggested that they stroll there and wait.

"Stroll and wait," repeated Iris, grinning as she jumped
down from the bus. "Have we been doing anything but?"

"Travel fatigue," suggested Malcolm sympathetically. "We'll all get our so-called second wind in a day or two and be off and running."

"Well, that will beat strolling and waiting," teased Iris.

Mrs. Pollifax said nothing; the picnic area and the waterfall had added a sense of oppression to the anxiety with which she'd begun her day, and she felt that her entire being had given itself over to waiting, waiting for Peter to engineer his disappearance. *I must stop watching him,* she thought, and seeing how cheerful he looked she felt almost cross with him. They reached one of the more inviting knolls and sat or sprawled on the grass while off to their right, in the distance, the Kazakhs began to group with their horses, talking and laughing among themselves.

"It looks terribly macho," said Iris suspiciously, watching them.

Joe Forbes had brought out a pair of binoculars and was peering through them. "Two of them are women, though," he told her, "and hooray, they're going to begin now."

The demonstration began, and proved so superb that Mrs. Pollifax almost forgot about Peter for the next half an hour: the Kazakhs galloped down the meadow to show off their splendid mounts, then held several good-natured races, followed by a game of tug-of-war over the pelt of a sheep. This, explained Mr. Li, had in older days been tug-of-war over a live sheep, but this they were spared.

"Terrific horses," Peter said. "Wouldn't mind trying one of them myself." It was the first time Mrs. Pollifax had heard him speak since they'd left Urumchi.

"Oh could we?" breathed Iris eagerly. "I've ridden all my *life!*"

Mr. Li looked shocked. "Oh—impossible," he said flatly.

Iris said, "The show's over, do let's try! Mr. Li, come along and translate for us, okay?"

Mrs. Pollifax lagged behind as the others surged down the slope to meet with the Kazakhs; she was beginning to feel bored and restless, which she knew to be the result of her rising suspense: since she found suspense difficult to deal with she simply wanted this day to be gotten through as straightforwardly and quickly as possible, and to see it interrupted by this distraction rather annoyed her. It seemed pointless and tedious, but of course she and horses had never enjoyed a warm or comfortable relationship. By the time she joined the group in the meadow she saw that Mr. Li's translating, and Iris and Peter's eagerness, had produced an effect: Peter was being allowed to mount one of the horses, a Kazakh holding on to the bridle. Cautiously the horse and Peter were led up and down the meadow and then with a laugh and a shout the Kazakh released them both and Peter effortlessly, joyously, cantered back to them on his own.

They all cheered his performance and the Kazakhs, huddled and watching, grinned their approval.

"Terrific!" shouted Iris. "Me next?"

"How about me?" asked Forbes.

Peter, still mounted, grinned down at Mrs. Pollifax. "Somebody give *her* a horse," he told them. "Group leader and all that. C'mon, we'll all take your picture, Mrs. Pollifax, what d'ye say? Ask for a horse for her, Mr. Li."

Mrs. Pollifax, laughing, shook her head. "No thanks!"

"Try," said Malcolm, as a horse was led over to her. "You can show your grandchildren the picture and—"

"Just sit on it," Peter told her. "C'mon, be a sport."

Mrs. Pollifax winced, recalling certain past incidents with horses and then decided to swallow her reluctance and opt for the role of Good Sport. Both Malcolm and Forbes boosted her into the saddle and there she sat, very stiffly, with Peter on his horse beside her and holding the reins for her.

"See? You've done it," he told her. "Not bad, is it? Take her picture fast!" he called to Malcolm.

He leaned over and adjusted something on the saddle of Mrs. Pollifax's horse, except that whatever adjustment he made did not appear to please her horse. It snorted, reared in alarm and took off—there was no other word for it, her horse took off like a jet plane in ascension—so fast there was neither time for Mrs. Pollifax to breathe or to scream, the problem of survival being immediate and consuming as she struggled to stay mounted on this huge creature gone mad.

Down the length of the meadow they flew, she and the

horse joined together by only the most fleeting of contact: Mrs. Pollifax hanging on in desperation, each thundering jolt an assault on her spine, her hands groping for the elusive reins, for the horse's mane, then for his neck, for any accessory available as an anchor to keep her from being tossed into the air and then to the ground. Behind her she heard shouts, Peter's voice, and almost at once the sound of Peter on horseback in pursuit. The words he shouted were unintelligible, blotted out by the pounding of horse's hoofs.

Mrs. Pollifax prayed: that she would not fall off the horse . . . that she *would* fall off, but gently . . . that Peter would reach her quickly and bring her to a halt. But the horror of it was that the horse had only one direction now in which to go, and that was straight ahead and *up*—up the steep and wooded ridge ahead of them—and—"Oh God," she prayed as the horse raced in among the trees and without faltering began to climb, so that instead of crouching near his neck she was suddenly sliding backward now, her hands clutching his mane, which— she thought wildly—was scarcely a way to soothe or to appease him. Up they went at a 90-degree angle, the crazed horse slowing a little but not, felt Mrs. Pollifax, from any change in his determination to destroy her, and certainly not from repentance, but due entirely to the steepness of the hillside.

Now, she thought as he slowed—*now* is the time to jump. To fall off.

It was at this moment of resolution that she discovered her right foot was entangled in a stirrup. She shook her foot impatiently but it refused to be freed; she dared not look down at her foot, it felt irrevocably captured, and then the moment of possibility had passed, they arrived at the top of the ridge and Mrs. Pollifax caught a fleeting glimpse of what lay ahead and abandoned all hope.

What lay ahead was *down* . . . down through forest to miles and miles of flat desert intercepted only by one deep slice cut out of the earth—a small canyon, too broad to cross— and inside of her she screamed. Screamed for Cyrus, for Peter, for some magical hope that was beyond her. She saw her life pass in front of her, prepared herself to relinquish it, and in one giddy moment foresaw their end. Down the ridge they plunged at breakneck speed, Mrs. Pollifax thrown forward again, fighting to keep from sliding in and under the horse's neck, her foot still entangled. They reached the bottom of the mountain and the horse's hoofs struck the hard flat surface of the desert. Lifting her eyes Mrs. Pollifax looked ahead and saw now that the deep cut in the earth contained a boiling racing mountain stream and that the horse was going to leap that canyon and that he was not going to make it. Nor would she.

And all because she had mounted a horse to have her picture taken . . .

In one last desperate frenzy Mrs. Pollifax applied herself to disentanglement. Hanging on recklessly by one hand to the horse's mane she slid her other hand down to the tangled stirrup, tugged, shifted, wrenched, and miraculously felt her foot slip free. Lifting her leg over the horse's back she sat sidesaddle for a fleeting second and then she kicked herself off and away from the horse, flew high into the air and went down.

She struck the ground hard, instinctively breaking the fall with her left hand, and lay there stunned, feeling the blessedness of the earth beneath her. After a moment she lifted her head, found her neck intact, rolled over on the ground and stared at her left hand lying inert on the pebbles beside her. *Odd*, she thought, wondering vaguely why she could neither lift it nor feel it as an appendage. She was still staring at it when Peter rode up to her, flung himself from his horse and ran to her side.

"My God, are you hurt?" he cried. "Believe me, it wasn't supposed to be like this."

Wasn't supposed to be like this . . . what an extraordinary thing for him to say, she thought.

"Mrs. Pollifax, are you *all right?*"

"It's my left hand," she told him. "It just lies there. Otherwise," she added with a return of spirit, "I'm basically fine. Perhaps a little in shock, perhaps a little dazed. Yes, definitely a little dazed." She placed her right hand underneath her left one and lifted it. Cradling it and supporting it, she sat up. "But what," she demanded, "happened to that damn runaway horse?"

Peter said, "Can you stand up?"

"Of course I can stand up, just give me a minute."

"But I can't give you a minute," he cried despairingly. "I can't, damn it—this is where I disappear, don't you see? Oh damn it, Mrs. Pollifax—Emily—I'm sorry, believe me I'm sorry. I stuck a burr under that horse's saddle so that he'd run away with you, poor devil. Except I was so sure I'd catch him long before the top of the mountain. I thought—oh hell, we don't have *time*. I never expected this, can you ever forgive me? Is your wrist broken?"

"Probably," she said calmly. "Where are the others?"

"I told them I could handle it—bring you back okay—but heaven only knows how much time we have before they—"

"Yes," she said, and told herself that she could put all this together and recover later; she could even understand the sense of what he'd done. "Help me up," she said, giving him her good hand. "I thought it was going to be the waterfall. What happened to that horse?"

He groaned as he helped her to her feet. "I feel like a murderer, he crashed down into the river. It's got horrible currents, it's the same one I had to cross to reach X's camp. I haven't looked but I saw the horse go down. *Heard* him, too, it was ghastly."

She nodded. "And now you disappear too?"

"Yes, supposedly drowned in this river and swept away while trying to rescue you but of course I was really going to backtrack into the mountain to the cave."

She nodded. "Then it's a very good thing the horse met with such an accident, I really have nothing personal against him but it will fill out the picture. Yes, definitely it supports your being drowned and swept away."

Peter looked at her in astonishment. "You're right, I hadn't thought of that; am I in shock too, I wonder? But I can't leave you like this. Does your hand hurt? It's swelling already."

Standing, she gave a shaky laugh. "Of course you can leave me like this. Yes my wrist hurts, but mostly it feels numb, as if a spring has broken inside—a very interesting feeling, actually, but never mind that. For heaven's sake, Peter, where's your professionalism? *Go!*"

Behind them a pleasant and very familiar voice said, "Nobody's going anywhere, at least not without me."

They wheeled to see Joe Forbes standing several paces behind them, still smiling, still looking affable except that in his hand he held a small snub-nosed efficient pistol. Far behind him at the foot of the hillside she saw a horse tethered to a tree and guessed it was his. Neither had heard him approach over the pebbles and gravel of the desert floor.

"*So you're the one,*" she said, nodding.

"The one what?" demanded Peter. "What the hell's the matter with you, Forbes, pointing a gun at us, have you lost your mind?"

"Don't," Mrs. Pollifax told him. "We've been working for the Russians without knowing it, Peter. I've suspected this ever since Sheng told us we were followed into the desert. It's been a trap, Peter."

"Trap!" he cried. "You mean Carstairs—"

"Carstairs doesn't know. The Russians simply leaked the information and sat back to watch us do all the dirty work, and now I believe you're meeting your first KGB man, Peter. Take a long look."

Peter stared at Forbes in horror. "KGB! *You!*"

"Held in abeyance," said Mrs. Pollifax. "A 'sleeper,' I believe they're called. Wonderful credentials, very American, too. Waiting for you to locate and free Wang, after which he was supposed to snatch the prize from you at the last minute and run with it to Moscow. The Russians never planned any attempt to free Wang, we were to do the job for them."

Forbes said dryly, "Only one thing wrong with that, Mrs. Pollifax—not Forbes *was* to snatch—*is* to snatch the prize. Right now." He made circular motions with his gun, directing her to move to one side. "It's Peter I have business with—get away from him."

"No," said Mrs. Pollifax, feeling all her senses giddily heightened by pain. "No I'm not going to move. Not one inch, thank you. You can't possibly expect Peter to tell you where Wang is."

Forbes smiled a lethal smile. "No, but he's going to *show* me where he is. I speak Chinese better than I let on, and I know the Sepos are searching these mountains for a prisoner who's missing from a labor reform camp somewhere nearby. Somehow you got him out and hid him, and I want him." He waved his gun menacingly again. "We're running out of time and—"

"Yes that *is* a problem for you," said Mrs. Pollifax cheerfully. "The lack of time. How are you going to handle *that?*"

He gave her a pleasant glance that held touches of a sneer in it. "Shut up," he said, and turned to address Peter. "Either both of you go with me now, taking me to Wang Shen—both of you—or I'll kill your friend Mrs. Pollifax here and now. In front of you, so that you can watch her die."

It was important that Peter not believe this. "How absurd," she told Forbes hotly. "You'd kill us both after we take you to Wang anyway, I'm sure that Peter can't possibly fall for *that.*" She gasped. "Oh damn—Peter—sorry—I think I'm going to faint." She stumbled backward toward a small mound of stones and sat down, putting her head between her knees.

Peter started to move toward her but Forbes stopped him. "You've already lost *her,*" he said contemptuously. "What a ridiculous accomplice they gave you, an old woman who faints at the drop of a hat. A boy and an old woman . . . typical American ineptness."

"To hell with you and your assumptions," Peter said angrily. "She broke her wrist, damn you, and—"

From her seat on the rocks Mrs. Pollifax cautiously lifted her head. She had only pretended to feel faint; actually she had never felt so keyed-up, or so alive, but it had seemed a convenient way to put distance between the three of them and now she saw that Peter and Forbes were confronting each other so intensely that she was forgotten. Her good right hand found and curled around a smooth stone under her foot. As Forbes opened his mouth to retort to Peter she lifted her arm and hurled the stone at Forbes.

It hit him on the shoulder, doing him no harm, but it threw him off balance. He fell back and before a startled Peter could move—before Forbes could even regain his balance—Mrs. Pollifax was on her feet and in motion, dealing Forbes a quick karate shin-strike and then a hard slash to his temple. Forbes collapsed to the earth without a sound, his arms outstretched, his eyes open and vacant.

"My God," gasped Peter, rushing to him and prising the gun from his slackened fingers. "My God, Mrs. Pollifax, only brown belt you said?"

"Yes," she said, kneeling beside Forbes, and abruptly she stiffened. "What's worse—oh dear—I believe he's dead, Peter."

"Worse?"

She said unsteadily, "I've only once killed a man—in self-defense, in a cornfield in Albania. I hoped—*so* hoped—" Her voice trembled; she pulled herself together and looked around them. "You'll have to do the rest, Peter, I can't."

"Can't what? Do what?"

Think, she told herself, *think*, be strong for a little longer. She said in a steady voice, "He made one mistake, Peter, he should have simply followed you when you disappeared, without declaring himself, and killed you when you led him to Wang. And now he's dead and you're not, thank heaven, but we have to think and act quickly." She stood up, drawing new strength from being erect. "We have to change how things look—everything," she told him. "They have to find Forbes' body here, you see that, don't you? The two of you disappearing is too much. There has to have been a fight between you both. A fight *here*." She nodded. "It may even be better this way, Peter, but *you've* got to do it."

"Do what?" he asked blankly. "Am I in shock? I can't think!"

She nodded. "My horse ran away with me—they all saw that. The horse is dead in the canyon. I have a broken wrist. You rescued me. Forbes followed and there was a fight and he killed you."

"But a fight about *what?*" he cried.

"Something—anything," she said impatiently, "it doesn't matter. What you have to do now is this." She pulled the long souvenir knife she'd bought in Urumchi out of her pocket and drew it from its sheath. "We need blood, Peter—lots of blood. Carry him to the edge of the water, and I think—yes, quickly, I'll smooth away the tracks from your dragging him . . . He should have your Mao jacket clutched in one hand, or the bloodied sleeve of your jacket. *Something* of yours. And his face should dangle down, as if he struggled to reach you as you went over the side into the rapids. But there has to be blood."

"God," said Peter so devoutly that she felt it was said in religious awe.

Peter removed his Mao jacket.

"Tear it a little," she told him as he dragged Forbes' body toward the gap in the earth. "And—I'm sorry—but please knife him in the heart now, while he'll still bleed. There *has* to be blood," she repeated passionately, stubbornly.

He gave her one quick incredulous glance as he grasped the knife and leaned over the body. "Better not watch," he said, and she was glad to turn away.

When she looked again there was a great deal of blood both on the ground and on the jacket. "Knifed him in the aorta, I think," Peter said curtly, pressed the sleeve of the bloodied jacket into Forbes' hand and then shrugged himself into the remainder of his jacket.

"Toss the knife into the river," she told him. "It has your fingerprints on it."

"What else?" asked Peter, deferring to her.

Mrs. Pollifax looked around, her adrenalin glands racing, her mind operating with a cunning she'd forgotten that she possessed. Forbes lay at the edge of the canyon, his head and one arm dangling over its side, the bloodied rag of a jacket clutched in the hand that lay at his side. Below him—quite horribly—lay the horse, sprawled across a rock just above the racing stream, and quite dead. "Fingerprints where they should be," she said with a nod, ticking off the details. "Your jacket but his blood. I think the picture's complete—now *go*, Peter—go fast."

Peter stared at her. "But—what will you tell them? Mrs. Pollifax, what will you tell them? Why did Forbes and I kill each other?"

"I'll say . . . I don't know what I'll say," she told him. "Leave it to me, Peter—just go. Hurry. Your job's only just beginning."

"But so is yours," he pointed out. "And you're stuck with—"

She said fiercely, "Peter, you're an agent, sufficiently christened and bloodied now, with Wang and Sheng out there waiting for you. Don't bleed for *me*, you've got work to do."

"Yes," he said, staring at her, "except—oh damn it, I want to say—to tell you—" He reached out his hand and gently touched her broken one.

"But you don't have to say or tell me anything," she told him, the tears rising to her eyes, and with her good hand she met his extended fingers and grasped them. She said shakily, "Oh Peter, I'm always saying good-bye to brave and courageous people."

The tension in his face dissipated as he smiled his very rare warm smile. "And I'm saying good-bye right now to a very brave courageous person. Except it can't be good-bye . . . If I ever get out of this—" He leaned over and kissed her on the cheek. "Say hello to Cyrus for me, and marry him, will you?"

He turned, gave a glance at the carnage around them, shook his head over it and began to run, toward the north and toward the deep forest.

"Say hello to the Queen of Sheba for me," she called after him, and then, in a whisper, "God bless you, Peter." She stood watching him until he disappeared among the trees, and only then did she begin walking tiredly toward the mountain down which she and the horse had catapulted. She had just reached the first line of trees and had begun to ascend when she was met by men with horses, Kazakhs who had come to look for her.

Chapter Fourteen

The corridors were broad and dusty—there seemed to be dust everywhere in China, she thought blurredly—but in the halls of a hospital it was unexpected. Everything she saw held a surreal quality, filled with intimations of violence: a young woman rushing up a staircase, her white jacket stained with blood; a young worker wiping up a pool of blood in a corner; a patient with a bloody bandage around his head being supported by two orderlies; Army guards stationed at the end of each hall, leaning casually against the walls, their faces blank.

She refused anesthesia. The doctor was a young woman, her soft dark hair plaited into braids, face serious, her white jacket worn over cotton pants. Consultations were held with others —she was still a tourist, Mrs. Pollifax noticed, wondering for how long she would be treated as one. A young man with a wide eager smile tried a little English with her. Again she refused anesthesia and a hospital bed for the night and hoped that no one would guess it was because she feared what she might say under anesthesia. She was given a local injection and her hand strung up on a traction bar while the young woman manipulated, kneaded, tugged, and pressed the bone into place.

"A *bad* break," the young man translated for her, and when the doctor had completed her manipulations she began winding gauze around her arm, finishing it off with wet plaster. She found herself encased to the elbow.

"No acupuncture?" she quipped, feeling that the numbing weight of her broken hand now dominated her entire body like an aching tooth that turned even her thoughts jaded.

"Pliss," he said, smiling his toothsome smile. "We treat you American way, all of us being most sorry you have had this accident in our country."

Mrs. Pollifax gravely accepted this apology and thanked them all. In the hall outside she found Malcolm and Mr. Li waiting for her, and at sight of Malcolm she promptly burst into tears. He handed her a handkerchief and hugged her. "You're still in shock," he told her. "Hang in!"

In shock yes, but not entirely from the wrist, she remembered, and knew that she didn't want to think yet about that horrible scene at the river, and of Peter leaving.

Malcolm said, "I wanted to come with Mr. Li and tell you."

"Tell me?" she repeated, and glancing at Mr. Li she saw that his poise was shattered, he looked distraught and anxious.

"Yes," Malcolm said. "It's your turn to be interviewed by the police and the fact that you're in pain and shock doesn't seem to move them at all. They insist on seeing you now."

"Yes," she said, quite understanding why. "You don't look terribly well yourself, Malcolm."

He smiled wryly. "We've all had a shock, of course, but I begin to suspect that Jenny's raisins are doing us all in." He made a face. "George is sick back at the hotel and Jenny's back in bed, and bed is where I'm heading next."

"And Peter and Forbes are dead," she added, wanting to make it real to her, wanting to fix it firmly in her mind that Peter too was dead, not just missing, not gone to meet X and Sheng, but dead. "Have they found Peter's body yet?" she asked.

"I don't think so," Malcolm said. "We've all given statements but we've not been told anything." Mr. Li made a sound in his throat and Malcolm added, "Oh yes, and we're not supposed to talk about it. I promised, we all did, because you're the only one who can tell the police what happened, you see."

She wondered what time it was and how many hours had

passed since she had stumbled toward the woods and had been met by the Kazakh horsemen. She dimly recalled being lifted up behind one of them and carried back to the long meadow where she had been delivered to Mr. Li and placed at once in the bus. There had been what seemed an interminable wait after that, until finally Mr. Li arrived with the others and told them stiffly that they must return to Urumchi now, there had been a bad accident and both Mr. Fox and Mr. Forbes were dead. She remembered that Jenny had screamed and then gone into hysterics until Malcolm slapped her face. She remembered Iris examining her wrist and giving her two aspirin and a bottle of warm beer with which to wash them down, and then Mr. Li had insisted that no one talk. After leaving the others at the hotel she had been driven to the hospital in a gray car with curtains at the windows—another shanghai car—and now she was being driven in still another gray car to the security police.

Not the same car, she decided, for there had been a cigarette hole burned in the upholstery of the other one; either the hole had been mended during her hour at the hospital or it was a different car, and she wondered why it mattered, but the smallest things seemed to be of vast importance just now, they kept her from being afraid.

My zero hour, she thought numbly. Peter had experienced his and acquitted himself, and this was hers, and this was why Bishop had been afraid for her, except that no one had known that she would have a broken wrist and feel so oddly dazed for this interrogation.

She was ushered into still another spartan room: a table, several folding chairs, and bare walls except for the ubiquitous photographs of Lenin, Chou, and Mao. It was very similar to all the other rooms they'd been ushered into, but there would be no tea-and-briefings here. The man sitting at the table looked incredibly young; an older man stood looking out of the window, his back to her; he wore a charcoal gray Mao uniform, while the young man facing her was in khaki, with two pockets in his tunic. She remembered that Peter had told her pockets were the only sign of rank in the PLA . . . *which Peter had told her* . . . The thought of Peter brought tears back to her eyes; she allowed them to remain, not hiding them, recalling—ironically—that they were appropriate for this occasion, if for the wrong reason.

She glanced at Mr. Li, who had taken the chair farthest away from her, as if to disassociate himself completely. He looked pale and rather miserable and she realized they must have been giving him a hard time. She thought drearily, *I'm going to have to fight for his future, too.*

Her interrogator was keeping her waiting as he shifted a number of papers in front of him. Where Mr. Li's face was round, this young officer's face was long and narrow. The horror of it, she realized, was that Peter and X and Sheng might already have been found, either in their cave or near it, and these two men know this. Certainly they must already have begun the search for Peter's body . . . Was the water deep enough to hold a body captive? If Peter had miscalculated, would the very absence of a body lift their suspicions about his death? At what point, she wondered, might they begin to search the mountain slopes instead?

If they knew too much, then every word that she spoke would be a recognizable lie, and they did not like spies here. Chinese jails . . . *oh, Cyrus,* she thought bleakly, and wished with all her heart that she wasn't so *tired,* wished that a broken wrist would radiate violent pain instead of this strange numbing ache that was exhausting her by its subtlety and consistency. It was hot in this closed-up dusty room, too, and the shock—"I've got to stop thinking like this," she told herself sternly. "Think of Cyrus . . . dear Cyrus . . . or Bishop. Or Carstairs. Or geraniums." Anything except what had happened back there by the stream, and of what could have gone wrong.

She wished the man by the window would turn around, but he remained obdurately at the window, his back to her.

The young officer put aside his sheaf of papers and looked at her. He said without expression, "I am most sorry that such a tragedy has occurred. I must ask you questions and discover how such a thing happened and who is to blame."

She said politely, "It has been—for all of us—a tragic loss, a terrible one, and I don't see how anyone can be blamed."

The officer said curtly, "Mr. Li—"

"Oh, certainly not Mr. Li," she said firmly. "Mr. Li has shown nothing but courtesy and kindness to us all. A very excellent guide."

Mr. Li gave her a startled glance and then returned his gaze to the floor; perhaps he had not expected equanimity.

"But Mr. Li and this riding of horses—"

She shook her head. "You don't understand how it was," she told him earnestly. "We all watched the Kazakhs perform, and they were magnificent," she emphasized, "but everyone except myself had ridden before, and could ride very well. And Americans"—she hesitated and then looked him straight in the eye—"Americans do tend to be assertive about things they want to do. Peter was the first to ask for a horse to try, and the Kazakhs were *most* polite and let him climb on one, and they obligingly led him up and down the meadow on a rope until they saw that Peter knew horses and really could ride." She stopped, aware that she was flooding him with trivia. "Anyway, they very courteously allowed him to gallop up and down by himself, and then the others pleaded for the same chance but Peter insisted I be put on a horse next. Because I'd never ridden one. Because he thought I should have a picture taken of myself on a horse."

With exquisite irony the officer said, "And did he take your picture?"

"I don't know, the horse ran away with me. And the Kazakhs were certainly not to blame," she put in quickly. "We were all laughing together, and they understood our having fun and were very obliging."

"And Mr. Li?"

"Standing and watching," said Mrs. Pollifax. "Helping to translate the interest in the horses and smiling at our pleasure." He hadn't been smiling, he'd been glowering, but never mind that, she thought.

"And so the horse ran away with you," pointed out the officer, glancing down at his notes.

"Yes."

"And Mr. Peter Fox followed you on horseback."

"Yes."

He waited and then said smoothly, "Yes. Now we come to
the important part, please. Your horse 'ran away' as you say,
and once over the mountain you came down to the flatland
with Mr. Peter Fox in pursuit."

His English was excellent; she wondered if he'd ever lived
in the United States but dared not ask. "The horse galloped, or
whatever they do," she pointed out, "and my right foot was
caught in the stirrup and when I saw the river ahead I knew I
had to—absolutely *had* to—jump off."

He was watching her very closely now. "Yes. You succeeded in freeing your foot?"

She nodded. "Yes, I'd been trying to for some time but—I
guess desperation helped. And I jumped off and broke my
wrist."

The man standing at the window abruptly turned to look at
her for the first time, and her glance swerved to meet his. At
once she was sorry that she'd looked at him because his gaze
unnerved her. The younger official had been observing her
with a professional efficiency, but the eyes of this man were
penetrating and alert. She thought, *He is very much the
younger man's superior and he's been listening to me, measuring each inflection and nuance, and now he is going to
watch my face, my eyes, my hands.* Yet he did not look unkind; his iron-gray hair matched his charcoal Mao suit, and his
face was that of a scholar.

She turned her attention back to the young man at the
table. "I see," he was saying politely, with a glance at the cast
running up her arm. "And where was Mr. Joseph Forbes?"

She shook her head. "Nowhere to be seen. It was Peter—
Peter Fox—who galloped up and slid from his horse and ran
over to me. I discovered my wrist was hurt and he helped me
up and we were standing there talking about what to do . . .
Actually Peter was apologizing."

"Apologizing?" he repeated.

"Yes, for insisting I mount the horse. And then very suddenly Joe Forbes was there, he'd left his horse in the woods and
walked, and this startled us."

"And then?"

She kept her eyes resolutely on the young man behind the

table. "He became very abusive to Peter. He called him names for allowing me to get on the horse, and he said—he also called him names for taking advantage, as he called it, of Iris Damson." She had thought about this and now she delivered it. "He called Peter an out-and-out—should I mention the word?"

"Please," he said.

"Bastard," said Mrs. Pollifax. "And that's when Peter hit him in the stomach and I fainted."

"You fainted," said the young officer, and gave her a thoughtful glance.

"I fainted," she told him firmly.

"I see. So you will presently," he said smoothly, "tell me that you do not know what happened during the next few minutes."

She met this with a lift of her chin and an edge to her voice. "I would like to point out that I had experienced a runaway horse, believed that my life was about to end, I'd thrown myself off and broken a bone, and although I daresay it affords you some amusement to hear that I fainted, faint I did."

"Yes," he said, with an appreciative smile. "And when you came out of this faint what did you see?"

"Exactly what I assume you saw if you have visited the area," she told him. "Peter was nowhere to be seen, and there was all this blood, and Joe Forbes was lying by the river. I limped over to him and saw that he was—quite dead." She shivered. "After a while I realized it was part of a Mao jacket Mr. Forbes was clutching in one hand, and Peter—Peter had been wearing one. That's when I had the horrible realization that Peter might be dead, too. Have you found him?"

"No," he said shortly.

She decided that she believed him. "What," she asked him, "do you want to find out? It's such a terrible thing, we're all very upset, and I don't understand—"

He said, "We have never had such an event occur. Naturally a tourist becomes ill now and then, but this is a murder."

"Yes," said Mrs. Pollifax, and was acutely aware of the man standing by the window watching her; she willed herself not to look at him.

The young officer shuffled his papers. "Mr. Li has told us

there was something between this young Peter Fox and Mrs. Damson that might have provoked the quarrel. Mr. Li said he found Peter Fox missing an entire night in Turfan, and the next morning Mrs. Damson explained that Mr. Fox had spent the night with her. This is true?"

Mrs. Pollifax winced. "I heard her *say* that, yes."

"Why do you wince?"

"I hoped it wouldn't come to this. I really know nothing about it. I just heard her say it."

"But you did hear it said. Did they spend much time together, these two people?"

Mrs. Pollifax shrugged. "No more than with any of us. We were usually all of us together."

"In this country such matters are frowned on. In your country it is different?"

She sighed wearily. Obviously it was different here—all those unisex Mao jackets, for one thing—but she felt too jaded to explain her own country, to point out the variables, the multitude of codes, the generation gaps, the sexual revolution, the mores and traditions of courtship. She said, "Not necessarily. Why don't you ask Iris—Mrs. Damson?"

He said coolly, "Already we have, I assure you."

"Good," she said in relief.

"She continues to weep," he added with irony, "and to say as little as you do, Mrs. Pollifax."

She said dryly, "I *feel* as if I've been talking forever."

He drew out a sheet of paper and read from it. "I quote Mrs. Damson. 'Yes Peter spent the night in my room. I don't suppose you'll believe me when I say it was perfectly innocent. He came in to talk, about nine o'clock I think it was. He said everyone else had gone to bed and did I have any books he could read. I didn't. He stayed, talking—on the other bed, curled up—and then he suddenly fell asleep. So I just brushed my teeth—I was already in pajamas—and left him in the one bed while I went to sleep in the other.' "

Dear Iris, thought Mrs. Pollifax, *magnificent Iris.* To the officer she said, "I can believe that, you know. Iris is a very casual person."

He said irritably, "But if this Peter was not in love with her why should he argue, fight, and kill Mr. Forbes over her?"

"Perhaps," said Mrs. Pollifax cautiously, "he felt a very warm friendship toward Iris, and Mr. Forbes said something insulting about her. But really I don't know, it has all been—simply awful. I wonder," she said truthfully enough, "if the explanation will ever be found."

He said sharply, "It is very surprising to me that none of you has any explanation at *all*. A man is dead, Mrs. Pollifax, and another presumed dead for the moment. None of you appears to have noticed anything between Mrs. Damson and this Peter, or between Mrs. Damson and Mr. Forbes. Only Mr. Westrum—"

Mrs. Pollifax looked up.

"Ah—a reaction, I see."

"Yes," she said, nodding. "I think George Westrum is or was in love with Iris Damson."

"Quite a *femme fatale*," said the officer with a touch of sarcasm.

Mrs. Pollifax smiled faintly. "Yes. But if there was any triangle, as we call it in America, it seems far more realistic that George Westrum would have been furious at Peter." She leaned forward and said with urgent sincerity, "Look, Mr.—Mr.—"

"Mr. Pi."

"Thank you," she said, and turned her gaze squarely on the man by the window. "And yours?" she asked coolly.

He bowed slightly, looking amused. "I am Mr. Chang."

"I want to point out to you both that we're all terribly tired, and I'm sure that none of us cares to go on with the tour now. When can we leave? As group leader I have to emphasize that several of us are ill, and all of us deeply upset . . ." *If anything happens get that tour group the hell out of the country*, she remembered, and looked challengingly at Mr. Pi.

He said quietly, "You will all remain here, of course, until Mr. Peter Fox's body is found."

She struggled not to show her dismay. "That will be soon, I hope?"

He said without expression, "But of course. You may go for

now, Mrs. Pollifax, but naturally this will continue tomorrow."

"Naturally," she said, and as she arose she really did feel like fainting, caught her breath, steadied herself, and then thought, *"Oh why bother?"* and sank to the floor, welcoming the oblivion.

It was nearly dark when Mrs. Pollifax was driven back to the hotel in the curtained gray limousine with a silent Mr. Li beside her. Reaction was rapidly overtaking her: since last entering the hotel she had killed a man, seen Peter vanish into the hinterlands of China and into heaven only knew what perils; she'd suffered a runaway horse, a broken wrist, a hospital, and her first police interrogation in China. She supposed that it was not particularly odd of her to want to find a dark corner and cry. Actually, she decided, to cry was not enough: she would prefer a scream.

She would not, of course, be allowed a scream.

She said good night to Mr. Li and walked alone into the empty lobby, turned down the long hall past the souvenir counter, and entered her room. She turned on the lights and stood there, waiting for tears, even a sob, and when none came she sat down on her bed and stared blankly at her white plaster arm and thought of Peter. Hearing a soft knock on her door she lifted her head, considered not answering and then called out, "Just a moment," and then, "Come in."

It was Iris, awkwardly tiptoeing and carrying a tray. "I heard you come in," she said. "I'm next door to you again. I brought you a pill."

Mrs. Pollifax shook her head. "I don't need a pill."

"Ah, but it's a codeine pill," Iris told her. "I've got this doctor back home who gave me supplies for every possible emergency, bless him. Very sensible man, insisted I bring a few pain-killers along in case I broke a leg miles from nowhere. You'll need it before long, you know, it'll hurt tonight."

"It hurts now," admitted Mrs. Pollifax. "How are the others taking this?"

"Oh forget the others," Iris said cheerfully. "It's you I've been worried about ever since the Kazakhs brought you back, you look as if you're going to freak out if you're not careful. I've got some brandy, too, and I think after the brandy you should wash down the codeine tablet with a cup of tea. Doctor Damson, that's me. I don't know how long you've been doing this sort of thing—"

Mrs. Pollifax stiffened. "What sort of thing?"

Iris handed her a glass. "Hold this while I get the tea steeping," she said, and became very busy. She poured hot water into cups from the sterilized-water thermos, ran her hands under the table, disappeared into the bathroom for a few minutes and returned with a second glass, became interested in examining the curtains before she pulled them closed, turned on the table lamp, peered inside and behind it, then glanced under both chair and bed, and finally poured them both brandy. "I don't think it'll hurt me to have some of this too," she announced. "Everybody's sick—*everyone*—Jenny with hysterics, Malcolm's just come down with the same cramps Jenny had yesterday, and George with some kind of dysentery."

She sat down on the edge of Mrs. Pollifax's bed and gave her a radiant smile. "Let's make it a toast, shall we?" and clicking her glass against Mrs. Pollifax's she said lightly, "Shall we drink to Peter?"

Mrs. Pollifax stared at her. "To—Peter?" she said, wetting her lips.

"To Peter," Iris said, and tipped her glass back and emptied it. Leaning over Mrs. Pollifax she pulled back the blankets, pounded both pillows, got up, and stirred the two cups of tea, tasted one, made a face and picked them up, leaving Mrs. Pollifax somewhat alarmed and very alert now.

"Peter is dead," Mrs. Pollifax told her carefully. "So is Forbes. They hope to find Peter's body tomorrow."

"Oh?" said Iris briskly. "They say the currents in that river are very treacherous, though."

"Yes."

Iris was digging out Mrs. Pollifax's pajamas from her suitcase. She said in the same brisk, conversational voice, "The thing is, you know, I once did some undercover work in Texas

. . . I was dancing in this place where they were selling drugs and porno under the table, so to speak, except I didn't know about that until I got approached by the law."

"How very interesting," said Mrs. Pollifax, watching her.

"Isn't it?" Her voice was oddly soothing as it continued without expression, simply stating facts as casually as if she were describing the weather. "I worked for the law for about eight months and I wasn't any heroine, believe me—and by the way, I've just checked your room here for bugs, so nobody else is hearing this—but it was all of it great training for somebody who'd breezed through life never noticing anything. I watched, snooped a bit where I wasn't supposed to, eavesdropped, reported to the undercover guys, and the place got closed up. Besides earning me a citation it left me marked, though. It taught me to notice things. Little things."

"Oh?" said Mrs. Pollifax cautiously.

"Yeah," said Iris cheerfully. "Little things, like a certain young man in our tour group who doesn't speak any Chinese but then one day he stands next to Mr. Li and Mr. Kan while they're telling jokes—or telling *something* funny, obviously—and this young man has to turn his face away to hide his own laugh because obviously he understood every word they were saying."

"How—amazing," said Mrs. Pollifax weakly.

"I certainly thought so. And then his doing so much yawning and napping after we got here to Urumchi, as if he never got any sleep at night . . . not to mention the two of you going over the wall together after we got to Turfan. I saw that, and saw somebody follow you, too, because you all passed my window, one by one. I was standing there in the dark doing my isometrics, and I think I can guess now who it was who followed you both." She grinned at Mrs. Pollifax. "You're a wonderful actress, no one would ever guess that you're not—but never mind."

Mrs. Pollifax looked at Iris thoughtfully. "You're a remarkable actress yourself, Iris, and now I can thank you for what you did in Turfan. Above all I'm glad to understand why you did it because—"

Iris nodded and handed her the codeine tablet. "I know—it

worried you. And believe me, I don't want to know anything more and I'm not fishing, honest." She held up her right hand to emphasize this, as if she were under oath. "Except I've got my own theories and I just want to make sure of one thing: we've been drinking a toast to Peter, right? To maybe long life and double happiness for him?"

Mrs. Pollifax smiled at her warmly. "Iris, I love you," she said, "and I thank you because finally I think I'll be able to cry now. To Peter, *yes.*" She emptied her glass of brandy, feeling it reach down to her toes, and then she leaned over and hugged Iris and allowed her to tuck her into bed.

Chapter Fifteen

The next morning, after a sleep filled with nightmares—all of them about Peter—Mrs. Pollifax discovered that she could neither tie her shoes nor comb her hair with her arm in a cast. Only she, Iris, and the two guides were well enough to appear at eight o'clock in the dining room, the others being still sick in their rooms, and after Mr. Li had tied her shoes for her—surely an act of contrition she thought, looking down at his sleek black head—and after Iris had brushed her hair for her she was borne off to visit security headquarters again, this time in the gray limousine with the cigarette hole in the upholstery.

Mr. Chang was there again with Mr. Pi, and now she was able to see how immaculately he was dressed, and how silky the fabric of his charcoal-gray Mao tunic. This time he sat at the table beside Mr. Pi but his eyes were no less penetrating. There was a tape recorder present for today's interview, and she was asked to repeat her story again from beginning to end. It was surprising how difficult she found this; yesterday she'd been keyed up, still in shock, her efforts focused with such intense concentration that she'd given a superhuman performance, even with Mr. Chang's distracting gaze upon her. Today her hand ached with dreary persistence, she'd not slept well, the plaster cast on her arm felt hot and uncomfortable, and her fingers were swollen. Today she realized, too, how very much Mr. Chang frightened her: she felt that he missed nothing, not even the blink of an eye.

When Mr. Pi had completed his endless questioning Mr. Chang said courteously, in flawless English, "And what were the last words you heard spoken between Mr. Fox and Mr. Forbes before you—er—lost consciousness?"

This was clever—an attempt to catch her out—and she regarded him thoughtfully. "It's hard for me to remember, of course, but—" Reaching for the most outrageous words that might close this line of inquiry she said, "I believe Mr. Forbes was shouting 'bloody bastard' at Peter Fox."

"The quarrel was about Mrs. Iris Damson?"

"Yes," said Mrs. Pollifax calmly. "Also about Peter being young, callow, exploitive, immoral, and taking advantage of a woman traveling alone."

Mr. Chang took this in stride. He said, "You fainted then, but not when you discovered Mr. Forbes dead and Mr. Fox missing?"

She said with equal politeness, "I suppose I fainted at that particular moment from the shock of falling off a horse and breaking my wrist."

"Ah yes, and thus missed everything that happened next," he murmured, and she thought that he looked amused again. "I think you may go now, Mrs. Pollifax, we shall continue our investigations." He bowed courteously. "Thank you."

Returned to the hotel Mrs. Pollifax found Iris looking drawn and tired. "Those damn raisins," Iris cried indignantly. "The ones Jenny bought at the bazaar in Turfan and so generously shared? I found some and soaked them for a few hours in my bathroom sink and you wouldn't *believe* the hay and dung that floated off them. No wonder everybody's sick!"

"Mercifully they didn't make you sick," said Mrs. Pollifax. "Have you had any sleep at all?"

Iris gestured this aside impatiently. "Nothing makes me sick, I have an iron stomach, and no I haven't slept, but never mind that. How did it go at security headquarters?"

Mrs. Pollifax said dryly, "Well, I'm still at liberty, as you can see."

Iris grinned. "Mr. Li told me that Peter and Joe had a fight over me." Their glances met and there was laughter in Iris' eyes. "That makes me quite a *femme fatale,* doesn't it?"

"Exactly what Mr. Pi said," she told her. "Now give me a report on everyone if you will. After all, I'm group leader and trying to get us out of here."

Iris nodded. "George is still pretty sick and he glares at me furiously and won't speak but he let me change his bed sheets and wash his face with a wet towel."

"Generous of him," said Mrs. Pollifax tartly.

Iris considered a moment and grinned. "Malcolm is making sketches between trips to the bathroom, but so far he's kept down two tablespoons of tea so it looks promising. He also tried to kiss me."

"Shocking," said Mrs. Pollifax, with a smile.

"But it's Jenny who's the problem," Iris said, sobering. "She's tuned out, I can't get through to her. It's been a ghastly shock for her, of course, but she's begun to act as if her own life's ended. I wish you'd go and talk to her. As group leader," she added with a faint smile.

Mrs. Pollifax nodded. "I'll go right now. Which room?"

"At the end of the hall, last door. No point in knocking, she doesn't want to see anyone, she'll just say 'go away.' "

"Yes," said Mrs. Pollifax and walked down the hall, opened the door and went in.

Jenny, sitting up in bed, looked at her stony-eyed. "I want to be left alone," she said angrily. "You didn't even knock, you have no right to be here, I want to be left *alone.*" Her voice trembled on the verge of hysteria.

Mrs. Pollifax said coldly, "As group leader I have every right to find out how you are, so let's have no more of that nonsense. Is your dysentery better now?" She walked to the window and pulled the curtains open, letting light and air into the room.

"Oh that," said Jenny. "Yes, that's gone."

Mrs. Pollifax moved to Jenny's bed and stood over it, looking down on her. "Then don't you think it's time you left your bed to help? Iris has had absolutely no sleep looking after you all and if you're feeling stronger—"

"Iris again," flung out Jenny. "God if I hear that woman's name once more I'll—I'll—"

"You'll what?" demanded Mrs. Pollifax.

"Kill her," said Jenny furiously.

Mrs. Pollifax shook her head and said gently, "More deaths, Jenny? *More* deaths?"

"She took George away from me, and then she took—took Peter—and—oh damn," she cried out, "everything ends. Everything! I can't bear it."

Mrs. Pollifax sat down on the bed and took Jenny into her arms. "Cry, Jenny, cry hard, get it all out. Try. It will help."

"I don't want to," stormed Jenny.

"Try," repeated Mrs. Pollifax, holding her close.

Jenny gave her one startled desperate glance and began to cry. Her whole body cried until she wrenched herself away from Mrs. Pollifax's embrace and threw herself across the bed to beat her fists soundlessly, furiously against the pillows, her sobs engulfing and shaking her. Presently her sobs grew less passionate, the fist ceased its relentless fury and Jenny glanced at Mrs. Pollifax, gave one last sob and sat up. "Why?" she asked like a child. "Why both of them, and in a fight over *her?*"

Mrs. Pollifax looked at her helplessly; she had been so involved in proving this to Mr. Chang and to Mr. Pi that she'd forgotten it was an assumption with which the others must always live as well. "But you're not crying for Peter or for Joe Forbes, are you?" she asked very gently. "Aren't you crying for Jenny?"

The girl flushed. "I don't see what's wrong with wanting to be happy," she said. "Peter liked me, I know he did. It could have had a happy ending, I know it could have. If he hadn't been killed."

Mrs. Pollifax thought of people passing each other like ships in the night, cherishing illusions, assumptions, and misunderstandings, so rarely *knowing,* and she sighed. She considered leaving Jenny to her illusion but quickly discarded the idea: ruthlessness, she decided, was sometimes the greater kindness. "Do you *really* believe that, Jenny?" she asked.

Jenny said mutinously, "I don't see why you ask. We were together a lot, you saw that. He liked me."

"Many men will like you," she pointed out.

"They don't seem to have," Jenny told her bitterly. "Everything ends for me. I was engaged to Bill for six months, we traveled together through Europe backpacking, we were going to be married and then he decided he was in love with someone else. And now Peter . . . You must know, being older . . . why doesn't *anything* end happily?"

"Because," said Mrs. Pollifax slowly, "there *are* no happy endings, Jenny, there are only happy people."

Jenny stared at her in astonishment. "Only happy—but without happy endings how—" She stopped, looking baffled.

"It has to happen inside," Mrs. Pollifax told her. "Inside of *you*, Jenny, not from outside. Not from others but in yourself. You may hate Iris for her persistent cheerfulness, even for her joy in living, but you could learn something from her. You'll find—if you talk to her—that she's had three husbands who seem to have treated her quite abominably, she decided late to go to college, against formidable odds, and earned her way as a go-go dancer."

"Iris?" Jenny looked appalled. "But then how can she—I don't get it."

"No you don't," said Mrs. Pollifax quietly, "and that's your problem. Stop feeling sorry for yourself; relationships aren't business transactions. Get out of bed and *do* something. Some people never grow up but it's worth a try, Jenny, and now if you'll excuse me my wrist hurts and I think I'll prop it up somewhere on a cushion for a while."

Jenny flushed. "Oh, I forgot—your *wrist!* Mrs. Pollifax, what happened, was it broken? Does it hurt a great deal?"

Mrs. Pollifax only gave her a brief smile as she opened the door. "See you later, Jenny," she said, and went out.

Malcolm, when she opened his door, looked up and said cheerfully, "The Sepos seem to have fallen in love with you, it seems forever since I've seen you. How's your broken wing?"

"Tiresome," she said.

He nodded. "Quite a change from that Heavenly Lake we

were supposed to be visiting today. If anyone asks, I'm ready to terminate the whole darn tour and fly home. After all," he added with a smile, "I've progressed to three teaspoons of tea now, I'm practically well."

George Westrum gave her a hostile glance when she stopped in to see him. "I'm ready to sue," he told her angrily. "Sue the whole damn tour company for allowing this to happen. I've missed Heavenly Lake today, and tomorrow we're off to Inner Mongolia, and if anyone suggests canceling the rest of this tour they'll have a real fight on their hands. I paid good money to see China, and I'm damn well going to see China!"

"Yes, George," said Mrs. Pollifax, and left him to his spleen and went back to endure two more interrogations that afternoon at security headquarters.

Chapter Sixteen

S he was awakened at five o'clock the next morning by an anxious-looking Mr. Li. "You are to be taken to security headquarters now," he told her. "The car is outside, they want you immediately. At once."

"Before breakfast?" she said in alarm. *"Now?"*

He nodded. "For this I am very sorry," he said, and from the sympathy in his voice she had a sinking feeling that the interrogations were to accelerate now and that she might not be returned this time to the hotel. *They must have found Peter,* she thought. *There must be something changed, something terribly wrong.*

"I'll be dressed in two minutes," she told him, and this time chose a jacket with pockets into which she placed her last chocolate bar, a handful of peanuts from yesterday's breakfast, and snapshots of Cyrus and her grandchildren. She walked alone through the silent hall to the lobby, out to the driveway, and climbed into the waiting gray limousine. It was a misty morning, the sun not warm yet; she was again in the car with the cigarette hole in the seat beside her and she tried to remember whether her previous trips in this car had been fortunate or unfortunate. Above all, she wondered if somehow they had discovered that Peter wasn't dead; it had been some forty hours now since she had said good-bye to him.

Once again she was escorted into the same spartan room at

headquarters, but this time she was shaken to find only Mr. Chang waiting for her. He sat behind the table that had previously been occupied by Mr. Pi. A few papers lay spread out before him but his elbows rested on them and his chin was in his hands; he was staring into space but he glanced up at her arrival and spoke sharply to the guard, dismissing him. He watched her cross the room and sit down on the same plain wooden chair. He said curtly, "Good morning," and shuffled the papers in front of him.

Mrs. Pollifax waited, practicing a calm that she didn't feel.

He said at last, looking at her, "You have maintained—with remarkable consistency—that you were unconscious—in a deep faint—during very important moments, Mrs. Pollifax." He paused, the very slightest hint of a smile passing across his face. "I would like to tell you now, Mrs. Pollifax, that I have been aware since the very first interrogation that you have been lying."

"I'm sorry to hear that," she told him politely, thinking *no holds barred now, off we go.* "I can't think why or how you've reached such a conclusion. Perhaps one might ask why?"

He smiled. "Certain nuances, shall we say? Certain techniques familiar to me?" He stopped, staring at her with an expression not at all unpleasant, and then he startled her by leaning forward and saying, "There are no tapes recording our conversation this morning; there is the utmost privacy at this hour."

"Oh?" she said, not believing him.

"Yes. You see," he went on, "I consider myself—if I may be forgiven such immodesty—a long-time student of character, and in you I have found many of the attributes of my first wife, long since dead."

She had not expected this diversion. Thoroughly startled she said, "Oh?"

"At the time of our Revolution," he continued, "she was a most fervent and conscientious soldier. She underwent several interrogations—yes, and some torture—by the Nationalists. Two of the interrogations I witnessed myself, having been captured with her. She was a small woman, and very feminine, and she cultivated an innocence that was most deceptive, so deceptive, in fact, that it saved her life. She was like a rock that could not be moved." He bowed slightly. "It has been uncanny for me to see in yourself this same quality, one might say technique? My wife sustained it even when tortured. I think you would, too."

Mrs. Pollifax sat very still and held her breath; she had been right to know this man was dangerous.

"There has been, you see, an autopsy on Mr. Forbes' body," he told her casually. "He was not killed by the knife after all, as one might suppose from appearances, but by a sharp blow of a hand to his temple, a blow so expertly aimed as to cause instant death." He said musingly, watching her, "A most vulnerable area . . . I would—myself—suspect that someone at that scene knew karate."

"I see," said Mrs. Pollifax, feeling a chill run up her spine.

"Which you, of course, could not have known or seen," he emphasized, "having fainted."

"No," she whispered.

He bowed politely. "Because you and I have been adversaries for these past two days, Mrs. Pollifax, and because you and I are of the same generation, I will tell you quite frankly of a small temptation that I have experienced."

"Yes?" she said, feeling her throat grow increasingly dry.

His smile was ironic. "To move suddenly toward you with a front choke or a middle knuckle punch and see if you would meet my action with a countering karate stance before you had time to think."

Yes, very definitely a dangerous man, she realized, and forced herself to say aloud, lightly, "How very interesting, except what is a counterstance, Mr. Chang?"

He chuckled. "I think you have cultivated an exquisite oriental inscrutability that I should not care to see damaged, Mrs. Pollifax, which is why I brought you here at this particularly early hour, for the sake of privacy for us both. You see," he added, "the facts of the autopsy bring a certain insoluble question to mind."

"Oh?" she said.

"One must ask," he said imperturbably, "how Mr. Forbes could have been killed by a strong karate blow when his opponent Peter Fox had already slipped over the edge of the canyon and dropped into the rapids below."

Oh God, thought Mrs. Pollifax, and caught off guard, against her will, she reacted with a start as she realized what had been overlooked during those frenzied moments. Her eyes widened and then dropped. Recovering quickly she forced herself to look at Mr. Chang.

He met her gaze serenely and said nothing.

She said, "Of course it's possible that—" She stopped, realizing that what he said was unanswerable; there had been no thought of autopsies when she'd arranged Forbes' body and there was no longer any possible explanation that could divert this man.

He said gently, sympathetically, "I am not a cat playing with a mouse, Mrs. Pollifax, but I think we understand each other better now."

She could only stare at him. "Maybe," she said cautiously, "but what—how—" She stopped.

"I said that I am not a cat playing with a mouse," he repeated, "which is why I brought you here at this hour, to say to you that you may go now."

Go, she thought wildly, *what does he mean by go*. "Back to the hotel?" she asked, scarcely daring to hope.

He said pleasantly, "Mr. Forbes' body is being flown to Beijing today, to your embassy there, on the late morning plane. You will also be on that plane, land briefly in Beijing, and then be flown at once to Tokyo. All of you."

She gaped at him in astonishment.

"I am in charge of these interrogations," he told her calmly, "and I am taking the responsibility of ending them." He looked at her and said harshly, "I do not know—I find that I do not *want* to know—what took place by the river. Two Americans are dead, and I am satisfied with my verdict of Causes Unknown. I feel—from my aforementioned study of character," he added with a faint smile, "that whatever happened was done out of grave necessity. I therefore have no interest in pursuing this investigation further—or even," he added, "the stomach for it."

She had prepared herself for imprisonment at the very least;

she had actually expected worse. She stammered, "I—I scarcely know what to say."

"I'm sure you don't," he said, standing up.

"Except to thank you," she told him, rising with him. "Thank you for the—the courtesies you've extended me, Mr. Chang. *Shown* me."

He chuckled and with a slight bow said, "You will be taken to the airport, all of you, within the hour. I would like to say in return that it has been a pleasure to know you, however briefly, and it must be hoped," he added with a twinkle, "that we do not meet again. Brown or black?"

She did not pretend to misunderstand him. "Brown."

He nodded. "I myself practice Tai Chi now, but once I too had a brown belt in the martial art of karate." He bowed again, graciously. "Good-bye, Mrs. Pollifax, and I wish you a safe return to your own country."

$E_{pilogue}$

For her wedding Mrs. Pollifax had found a dress that Cyrus pronounced stunning. And so it was, but it was several days before she realized that its colors were a beige and dusty jade-green so that when she looked at it now she saw the cliffs of Jiaohe, the desert of Taklamakan and the clay walls of Xian. And her heart ached for Peter. Not even Cyrus, huge and twinkly and affectionate, could quite dispell her awareness of the weeks passing by and her thoughts of Peter, Sheng, and X struggling to reach safety.

The news that she'd brought Carstairs and Bishop had shaken a number of departments at the CIA. When she had reached Tokyo she had placed phone calls to both Cyrus and Bishop and then had sat wearily on her bed waiting for one of them to come through.

It was Cyrus who reached her first. "Emily?" he shouted. "Damn it, Emily, where are you? My God, Emily, I've worried—"

"Oh Cyrus, how wonderful to hear your voice," she'd said, and had burst into tears. "I'm in Tokyo, how was your trip?"

"My trip be damned, Emily. Are you all right? All in one piece?"

"Only a broken wrist," she'd told him.

" 'Only!' "

"Cyrus, if you haven't changed your mind about us—"

He'd said gruffly, "Don't be ridiculous, m'dear. Nobody like you. Why?"

"I've missed you tremendously," she'd told him with a catch in her voice. "Russian roulette can be quite exhilarating when a person has nothing to lose, but oh Cyrus I discovered how much I could have lost—so easily—and almost did."

"When does your plane get in?" he asked, and his voice was thick with emotion.

"I don't know, I don't know, I've put in a call to Bishop—"

"I'll fly to San Francisco tonight," he told her, "and I'll meet every plane from Tokyo until you get there. Don't leave San Francisco without me," he said flatly, and hung up.

Almost at once the phone had rung a second time and the operator was saying, "Your call to Virginia has been put through . . . Go ahead, please . . ."

Abruptly Bishop came on the line saying, "Mrs. Pollifax, where are you?"

"Tokyo," she told him. "We're all in Tokyo but, Bishop— *two* people haven't returned from this tour."

"Two?" he'd said. "I don't understand, did you—"

"Have you a list of the people on the tour, Bishop?"

"Yes, but—"

"Please look, it's important, it's why I'm calling."

"Half a minute," he'd said, and she'd heard the rustling of paper and then Bishop's voice again. "I have the list but what do you mean, *two?* And Peter, what about—"

"You find the name Joseph Forbes there?"

"Let's see . . . yes, Forbes . . . history professor, Chicago."

"The important thing just now is to look into his background, Bishop. How much can I say on the phone?"

"As little as possible."

"There were complications, Bishop, and it very nearly ended badly. The problem has to have begun with the source who gave you the information that took us to China. Do you remember explaining to me how you learned about—er—X? Those boundaries?"

"Good God," he'd said.

"This person on the tour came from the other side of them, if I'm not being too abstract?"

"I'm following you," Bishop told her grimly. "Good Lord, you mean this Forbes—"

"Yes, he's the one."

"Where is he now?"

"Dead," she'd told him, and being nearly exhausted after countless hours without sleep her voice trembled. "It had to be done, Bishop—for the sake of the others. I had no choice."

"Steady there," he'd said softly. "You're telling me that *you . . .* ?"

"Yes."

"I see. All right," he said. "Are you feeling better now?"

"I will soon," she'd told him unsteadily. "I have a broken wrist but—but the purpose of the trip was salvaged, and somewhere out there, heading for the mountains—I'm sorry, Bishop," she'd said, her voice breaking again, "I'm just so *tired*. And those mountains—"

"It had to be the mountains?"

"He thought so, yes, but the most important message right now is Forbes, Bishop, and whoever—well, betrayed you."

There had been a long pause and then Bishop said, "We've got to get you home as quickly as possible. I'll immediately get in touch with the airlines and demand top priority passage for you. In the meantime, however, we'll start things rolling at once on Forbes, with all the repercussions *that* will bring, for which our eternal thanks, Mrs. Pollifax. Obviously our man in you-know-where is no longer ours."

"No," she said, and then, "Could you, when you learn on what plane I'll be returning, let Cyrus know in Connecticut?"

"Gladly," he said and he, too, rang off.

Several hours later she had been on her way to the airport, and she had been deeply touched by the fact that Iris and Malcolm insisted on accompanying her to the air terminal. They had parted warmly, with promises to write, and before moving through the electronic gate she had turned to watch them go—both so tall and slim, Iris still pushing back her tempestuous hair—and she had seen that they were holding hands.

It had occurred to her at that moment—suddenly and with sadness—that Jenny would now feel that Iris had captured the last man on the tour: first George, then seemingly Peter and seemingly Joe Forbes, and now Malcolm, and she would never know the truth.

As so few of us ever do, she thought, and walked through the gate to fly home to Cyrus.

It was a small and private wedding: Mrs. Pollifax's son, Roger, and her daughter, Jane; Miss Hartshorne; a few members of her Garden Club, and a few members of Cyrus' bird-watching club. Bishop had called to announce that wild horses and assassinations abroad wouldn't keep him away. "Besides," he'd added on the phone, "Carstairs is entrusting me with a wedding gift that he thinks you may like and it's too fragile to mail."

The day was very warm—it was late August, after all—but the chapel was cool. Cyrus, giving her an enormous hug, said, "It's a promise—wander off any time you please, Emily, but damn it, m'dear, never again without me."

"Never," she vowed fervently.

There was a slight delay while the organist searched frantically for a missing sheet of music; they waited patiently in the small room near the rear of the chapel until it became apparent that a mild commotion was taking place outside the door.

Cyrus opened it and Mrs. Pollifax heard Bishop's voice say, "Hello there, from the size of you I think you have to be Cyrus?"

Mrs. Pollifax spun around and cried, "Bishop! Oh do come in!"

He stuck his head inside the door. "It's me, bringing your wedding present. Everybody decent and ready?"

And he walked in, followed by a young man on crutches, wearing jeans, a T-shirt, and a broad grin.

"Peter!" cried Mrs. Pollifax.

"Yes," he said, beaming at her.

His face was burned from overexposure, there was a clown-like white paste daubed on his nose, his jaw was peeling, and there was that crutch that he leaned on as he moved toward her. But he was alive. He was well. He'd survived.

"Thank God," she whispered. "Oh Cyrus—Cyrus, this is—"

"No need to say," remarked Cyrus. "It's Peter, of course. Hello young man."

"Told her to marry you," Peter said, with a grin.

Cyrus nodded. "She'll be able to sleep nights now, young man . . . No more nightmares."

So Cyrus had guessed, Cyrus had known. Hugging Peter, her eyes filled with tears, she reached out and groped for Cyrus's hand and then with her other hand she reached for Bishop's, too. . . .